OBLOMOV

IVAN GONCHAROV

OBLOMOV

Ivan Goncharov

Translated from the Russian by Stephen Pearl

With an introduction by Galya Diment

Foreword by Tatyana Tolstaya

B&B

Bunim & Bannigan
New York Charlottetown

Translation and Translator's Note © 2006 Stephen Pearl
Introduction © 2006 Galya Diment
Foreword © 2006 Tatyana Tolstaya

Published by BUNIM & BANNIGAN, LTD.
PMB 157 111 East 14th Street New York, NY 10003-4103
BUNIM & BANNIGAN, LTD.
Box 636 Charlottetown
PEI C1A 7L3 Canada

www.bunimandbannigan.com

Manufactured in the United States of America

Design by Jean Carbain

Frontispiece and cover portrait of Ivan Goncharov (N. A. Maikov, 1860, oil on canvas) reproduced courtesy of the Goncharov Museum, Ulyanovsk, Russia

Cover illustration (Vasily Tropinin, portrait of K. G. Ravich. 1823, oil on canvas) reproduced courtesy of The Tretyakov Gallery, Moscow, Russia

This book is printed on acid-free paper.

Library of Congress Cataloging-in-Publication Data

Goncharov, Ivan Aleksandrovich, 1812-1891.
[Oblomov. English]
Oblomov / Ivan Goncharov ; translated from the Russian by Stephen Pearl ; with an introduction by Galya Diment ; foreword by Tatyana Tolstaya.—1st ed.
p. cm.
ISBN-13: 978-1-933480-08-4 (trade hardcover : acid-free paper)
ISBN-10: 1-933480-08-4 (trade hardcover : acid-free paper)
ISBN-13: 978-1-933480-09-1 (trade pbk. : acid-free paper)
ISBN-10: 1-933480-09-2 (trade pbk. : acid-free paper) 1. Russia—Social life and customs—1533-1917—Fiction. I. Pearl, Stephen, 1934- II. Title.

PG3337.G6O1213 2006
891.7'33--dc22

2006018219

Trade Hardcover
ISBN: 1-933480-08-4 ISBN-13: 978-1-933480-08-4

Trade paperback
ISBN: 1-933480-09-2 ISBN-13: 978-1-933480-09-1

135798642

First edition 2006

CONTENTS

FOREWORD

Even Russian critic Nikolai Dobroliubov (1836–1861) was struck by the fact that a novel about a recumbent character could prove so entertaining. The protagonist of the novel *Oblomov*, a good-natured, likeable, intelligent young man in his thirties, spends practically the whole book on his divan and almost always asleep. When he *is* awake, he spends his time fantasizing, eating, and drifting off again. He doesn't work, never has, and never will, because he is a member of the landed gentry for whom it is only natural that it should be others who do the work for him: "Do you see me rushing about, do you see me working? Am I short of food or something? ... Never in my life have I pulled on my own stockings, praise the Lord!"

This order of things seems entirely natural to Oblomov, as indeed it does to his manservant, a person just as lazy, just as sleepy, just as scatter-brained, and just as idle as his master. One would think that there are some things that even the idlest person would have to do, like, for example, reading, going out for a ride in his carriage, or writing an important letter if his income depended on it; but even this is too much for Oblomov. According to the Russian Symbolist critic Innokenty Annensky: "To a man who could be lying down, work smacks of greed and hustling, both equally repugnant to him."

So what *does* he actually do when he is not eating and squabbling list-lessly with his servant? When he is not sleeping, he is daydreaming. He begins with more practical accomplishments and sees himself as a doer: reforming, changing, building, and organizing. Later, his fantasies take a more private turn; now he is teaching mankind virtue and goodness; now he is a mighty leader of armies, or failing that, a great artist or philosopher:

> The moment he rose in the morning, he would drink his tea and imme-diately lie down on the divan with his head propped on his hand and start thinking hard and relentlessly until, exhausted from the intensity of the effort, his conscience would tell him that he had toiled enough for the common good for one day. Only then would he permit himself to rest from his labors and to switch from a posture of frowning con-centration, to a less businesslike and rigorous one, which gave a freer

rein to idle daydreaming and relaxation. Once he had freed himself from his workaday cares and responsibilities, Oblomov liked nothing better than to withdraw into himself and a world of his own creation.

Asleep, he dreams of his childhood, a blissful time when he was also cocooned in a drowsy lethargy. In their dilapidated home, his parents would be asleep, the servants would be stirring sleepily, and time itself would seem to have come to a standstill. Meals, somnolence, peace and quiet, life, in its even tenor, ticking away, punctuated only by the observance of the appropriate rites and ceremonies—weddings, births, name days and funerals—and all around nothing but kindness and love:

> There was nothing to disturb the sameness of this life, and the Oblomov household did not feel it as at all tedious or cloying since they were simply incapable of imagining anything different, and even if they could have, they would have recoiled from it in horror. As far as a different way of life was concerned, they simply did not want to know. They would have hated anything which forced them to change any detail of their existence....They spent decades dozing, half asleep, yawning and splitting their sides with good-natured laughter at incidents that tickled their rustic sense of humor, or huddling together to tell each other their dreams.

Oblomov remains to this day one of the most popular novels in Russia, successfully surviving the abolition of serfdom in 1861 and the radical social reforms which followed it, as well as wars, revolutions, the wholesale change of the social system, and both totalitarian and democratic eras. There is something deeply Russian in the character of Oblomov, something that strikes a chord in every Russian heart. This something lies in the seductive appeal of laziness and of good-natured idleness, the golden conservatism of a serene, untroubled childhood when everyone loves one another and when life with its anxieties and demands is still over the horizon. It is to be found in the tact and delicacy of "live and let live," in taking the path of least resistance, in unassertiveness, and an aversion to fuss and bother of any kind. It manifests itself in insouciance about money matters: all well and good, of course, if money somehow happens to appear from somewhere, provided, of course, that no effort or trouble is required. There is a lack of acquisitiveness: "Just take whatever you want, only don't bother me about it!" And there is trustfulness: "My dear fellow, please handle that business for me any way you want; I'll reimburse all expenses and sign anything you want."

The author's idea would seem to be that this kind of character is produced by social circumstances and the interplay or symbiosis between master and servant; and indeed nineteenth-century critics of *Oblomov* did view its hero through a social prism. They proclaimed the need for the emergence of a new breed, the man of action, alert and wide-awake. However, although Goncharov describes in detail the setting, the way of life, and the life cycle of the inhabitants of Oblomov's ancestral village, Oblomovka, he provides no social commentary and makes no suggestion of injustice. He neither chides nor scolds, but just uses gentle irony in his description of Oblomov's "home sweet home," a place so remote that it is practically in Asia. It is a paradise that has never known robbery, murder, or disasters of any kind; as a matter of fact, people practically never even die there. It's a place outside of time and space; it is a utopia; it is heaven itself.

Oblomovka is a place we never actually get to visit in the novel, but just see through the eyes of our slumbering hero, while he for his part sees in his dream others who are either asleep themselves or awake and recounting their dreams to one another. Doesn't this dream within a dream remind us of a Buddhist sutra? And is it no accident that our slumbering hero happens to be wearing a real oriental robe, which does not bear the slightest suggestion or trace of Europe? And with what is it that Oblomov is actually engaged in the following passage if not meditation?

> Oblomov meanwhile had sunk into a silent reverie, somewhere between sleeping and waking, just letting his thoughts wander at will, without focusing on anything in particular and listening calmly to the steady beat of his heart. Every now and then he blinked, his eyes as unfocused as his thoughts. He had lapsed into a mysterious, hallucinatory, trance-like state.

Lev Tolstoy once said: "The more difficult the situation, the less action one should take."

J. Krishnamurti in a lecture in 1970 said:

> The silence of the mind is beauty in itself. To listen to a bird, to the voice of a human being, to the politician, to the priest, to all the noise of propaganda that goes on, to listen completely silently, is to hear much more, to see much more. Such silence is not possible if your body is not also completely still. The organism, with all its nervous responses—the fidgeting, the ceaseless movement of fingers, the eyes—with all its general restlessness, must be completely

still. Have you ever tried sitting completely still without a single movement of the body, including the eyes? Do it for two minutes. In those two minutes the whole thing is revealed—if you know how to look.

The Russian pop singer Boris Grebenshchikov offered the following thought in an interview:

The Chinese have a concept they call "Wu Wei" or "non-action." This does not mean sitting with your arms folded and doing nothing. It simply means doing what is "you:" what flows spontaneously from your very nature. For a tree its nature is to grow. For a tree, to grow is not to act. It is just being itself. Growing is a sine qua non of its being. The same applies to people; it is always possible to act in a way prompted by your mind, but you can also act without being aware of what you are doing—because it is your very nature to do so.

There is virtually no Buddhist tradition in Russia. The first signs of interest were obliterated by the 1917 revolution, along with all religious belief and practice. The end of the twentieth century saw a reawakening of interest in Buddhism and the possibility of studying it. Russians began to understand that Buddhism was a profound teaching which warranted their close attention and study.

In Goncharov's time, few knew anything about Buddhism and this is what makes the Buddhist motifs in *Oblomov* (of which Goncharov was apparently quite unconscious) particularly interesting. This was Buddhism Russian-style—tentative, organic, barely out of its shell, unfledged, stranded halfway, inchoate, and not yet a fully coherent doctrine. Russia was a country hovering between Europe and Asia—neither one nor the other and yet at the same time, both—a country which had not found its way but was marking time; a country vacillating between moving towards the West with what many at the time thought were clear but tiresome (because of the effort and thought involved) principles of democracy, the Protestant ethic, secularism, productive labor, atheism, and bourgeois society on the one hand, or embracing the visionary East with what was perceived as its inertia, spirituality, tradition, mysticism, inaction, drug-induced trance, and its dreams where time stands still. Only God knows when Russians will finally make up their minds about their true nature. Maybe never.

Oblomov, the Russian landed gentleman, is one of nature's Buddhists, although he doesn't know it. Readers of the novel themselves would only come to realize this a hundred and fifty years later, and many are now beginning to say that it is not Dostoevsky, the neurotic, troubled genius, but the kindly, sleepy, more enigmatic Goncharov who is our true national writer, and anyone who wants to understand the inscrutable Russian soul should start by reading *Oblomov.*

In the novel the slumbering Oblomov is contrasted with his childhood friend, Stoltz, a man of action who gets things done, up-beat and mobile. He succeeds in whatever he turns his hand to....But what does this "success" amount to? He has multiplied his family fortune and become rich, he has traveled the world over...and what does he have to show for it? Well, nothing really...Stoltz is half German, a man of the West with a different scale of values, which suits him fine. And Oblomov is equally comfortable with *his* value system.

Which of them is right? Stoltz rescues Oblomov from destitution and ruin—good for him! Without him, Oblomov would not have eaten as well: instead of truffles and peaches he would have had to subsist on a dreary beggar's diet of fried eggs. But Oblomov is content even with fried eggs; it simply doesn't matter to him, just as he hardly even notices it when he is fleeced by some crooks and had it not been for Stoltz....So what difference does it make, and who comes off worse? It's the westerner Stoltz, not the Buddhist Oblomov.

At the end of the story, as Stoltz sees it, Oblomov dies a spiritual death: our hero marries a common woman. The landed gentleman marries a woman of the lowest class! Most probably, Goncharov's contemporaries, or at least some of them, were equally shocked. This is hard for us to understand today; after all, what's so wrong with this nice, loving, caring, and feminine woman, the kind he always dreamed of, and the peaceful refuge that he had always longed for and where he has found his peace of mind. It's a case of "Wu Wei," just doing what flows spontaneously from your nature.

Basically, Goncharov offers no clear explanation of why his hero would rather be asleep than awake. He presents us with the phenomenon and then simply refrains from offering an explanation—he probably doesn't even know the answer himself; and when all is said and done, it is the business of the true artist to depict, not to analyze.

"But I really would like to know...how come I'm like this?" His voice sank to a whisper again and his eyes were tightly shut. "Yes, why...it must be...because..." But no matter how hard he tried, he just could not get out the words.

So he never did figure out the reason and his lips and tongue stopped moving after uttering the last syllable, while his mouth remained half open. Instead of a word, there came a sigh followed by the even, stertorous breathing of someone peacefully sleeping.

In the last lines of the book the author introduces himself as the person who actually wrote the story of Oblomov: "…a writer. He was stout, with an inexpressive face and thoughtful, seemingly sleepy eyes."

It was with the same sleepy eyes that he saw through to the very essence of his fellow sleeper; and what he saw there won his heart, his understanding, and his pity. He gently covered him with a blanket and left him with us for all eternity.

Tatyana Tolstaya
Moscow, June 2006

Translated by Stephen Pearl

Tatyana Tolstaya is a Russian short-story writer, essayist, novelist, and great-grandniece of Leo Tolstoy. Her translated books include *On the Golden Porch* (1990), *Sleepwalker in a Fog* (1992), *Slynx: A Novel* (2002), and *Pushkin's Children: Writings on Russia and Russians* (2003).

ACKNOWLEDGMENTS

My thanks to Igor Korchilov and many other U.N. Russian interpreter colleagues who endured my relentless badgering of them with such good grace. Thanks also to Natasha Ward for granting me access—and badgering rights—to her "knitting circle." I am particularly grateful to two of its members, Anna and Misha Minevich for their encouragement and the erudition which they so freely shared with me. My appreciation to Nelli Tillib and Leonid Kutikov for their hospitality at their Bykovo dacha and for the light they were able to shed on some of the less fathomable Oblomovian locutions and allusions that were on my mind at the time.

My admiration and appreciation also goes to Sophia Lubensky for her masterly *Russian-English Dictionary of Idioms*, to which I so frequently had resort, and my gratitude for her generous personal help in mopping up the last remaining pockets of hard-core and arcane linguistic resistance still holding out in the text of *Oblomov*.

Stephen Pearl

INTRODUCTION

The name of Ivan Aleksandrovich Goncharov, the author of three novels in Russian, is today virtually synonymous with just one of them, *Oblomov*, an indisputable classic of enduring artistic stature and cultural significance. This achievement is even more remarkable when one remembers how many other "single masterpieces" were quickly obscured in the golden age of Russian prose which was the second half of the nineteenth century. Among Goncharov's most ardent fans were, in fact, two Russian literary giants, Leo Tolstoy and Anton Chekhov, the latter once stating that Goncharov was "10 heads above me in talent."

Goncharov is often referred to as one of the major Russian Realists. This formulation, however, tends to overlook the rich ambiguity of his works, the psychological complexity of his characters, and the surprising sophistication of some of his literary techniques which appear to anticipate twentieth-century Modernism. He was likewise precocious and refreshingly frank in probing both male and female sexuality and, above all, even to the modern readers accustomed to the ambiguity of twentieth-century literature, Goncharov still stands out as a great master of presenting ambivalent impulses and inextricable conflicts.

And, yet, Goncharov's fame was slow to penetrate every corner of the globe. In 1946 Peggy Guggenheim published her memoirs, *Out of This Century*, where, appalled by the apathy and lack of zest for life in one of her former lovers, she gave him a name which was both fictitious and fictional: "Oblomov." This thinly-disguised lover was Samuel Beckett who, in turn, gladly turned the nickname into a moniker, using it to sign many of his letters. It is sad but safe to assume that very few people in the United States reading Ms. Guggenheim's reminiscences at the time knew who the "real" Oblomov was. Sigmund Freud, alas, never discovered Goncharov, which some may consider a missed opportunity while others a blessing. Had he done so, Oblomov's complicated, angst-ridden, phobic, and dream-obsessed personality could have easily provided a great resource for Freud's pet theories. Among other things, Freud would have probably immediately seized on Oblomov as a classic example of the struggle between the ego-driven "reality principle" and the id-driven "pleasure principle."

Another reason why *Oblomov*'s reputation in the West remained unheralded was that the book was a latecomer: it took the novel fifty-five years to reach its first English-speaking readers. For reasons not entirely clear, Constance Garnett, who made many Russian masterpieces available to the English public at the turn of the twentieth century and who actually started her career in 1894 by translating Goncharov's earlier novel, *A Common Story*, passed over it. It was translated instead by C. J. Hogarth, and came out both in England and the United States in 1915.

It is a very different story in Russia, of course. There Oblomov is as well known and as widely read as Tolstoy's *Anna Karenina* or Dostoevsky's *Crime and Punishment*, while its protagonist has become an essential part of what many Russians consider their collective national psyche. As such, he is arguably the most recognized Russian literary archetype. Just as in English-speaking countries, even people who have never read Dickens know what it means to be a "Scrooge;" everyone in Russia, whether they have read Goncharov or not, knows what being "an Oblomov" is all about.

Since few countries are as addicted to politics as Russia, it should not come as a surprise that the fictional Oblomov, who is quite averse to politics and politicking of any kind, has become an integral part of Russian political discourse as well. Already in the 19th century, Oblomov was frequently used—and abused—as a tool of ridicule; but the apogee of his political infamy came with Lenin, who could hardly make a speech without conjuring his image. To Lenin, Oblomov was someone "who typified Russian life...always lolling on his bed and mentally drawing up schemes," and, therefore, a total antithesis to the very spirit of dialectical change for which Lenin and his cohorts stood. Before the Revolution Lenin would hurl Oblomov in the faces of his political opponents, claiming that they were "making ready to lay themselves down to sleep on the sofa graciously provided to all Russian Oblomovs...when suddenly the proletariat squared its shoulders and impolitely shook [them] off." After the Revolution, he lamented that despite a new regime, Russian Oblomovs still abounded, "for there were Oblomovs not only among the landowners but also among the peasants; not only among the peasants, but among the intellectuals too; and not only among the intellectuals, but also among the workers and Communists."

Lenin may have had a special soft spot for Oblomov also because he and Oblomov's creator shared—albeit almost sixty years apart—the same birthplace, the city of Simbirsk, where Ivan Aleksandrovich Goncharov was born on June 6, 1812. As the birthplace of both Goncharov and Lenin (as well as another famous Russian writer and historian, Nikolai Karamzin), this medium-sized Volga town may have a certain claim to fame, but there was little else that was dynamic about the place at the time Goncharov—or later Lenin—spent their childhoods there. It, in fact, struck many a visitor as one of the "quietest, sleepiest and most stagnant" towns in all of Russia, its legendary sloth rendered immortal in an 1836 poem by one of Russia's greatest poets, Mikhail Lermontov: "Sleep and laziness had overtaken Simbirsk. Even Volga rolled here slower and smoother." Goncharov, though fond of Simbirsk, described it in similarly somnolent terms. "The whole appearance of my home town," he said in 1887, "was a perfect picture of sleepiness and stagnation.... One wanted to fall asleep as well while looking at all this immobility, at sleepy windows with their curtains and blinds drawn, at sleepy faces one saw inside the houses or on streets. 'We have nothing to do!'—they seemed to be saying while yawning and lazily looking at you. 'We are in no hurry...'" Simbirsk, therefore, did not just beget Goncharov, it went a long way to beget his Oblomov as well.

Goncharov's father, Aleksandr Ivanovich Goncharov, was a wealthy grain merchant and the owner of a candle factory. As such he was much respected in Simbirsk, whose citizens stayed awake long enough to elect him several times to the post of mayor. He was fifty years old and a childless widower when he married the writer's mother, the nineteen-year-old daughter of another merchant. Aleksandr Goncharov's paternal ambitions still took a long time to come to fruition, though, for it was not till fully five years into the marriage that the couple's first child, Nikolai, was born. Five more children followed (of which only three, Ivan and his two sisters, survived infancy), and the still-young mother would have undoubtedly borne more had Aleksandr Goncharov not died in 1819, at the age of sixty-five. Avdotya Matveevna Goncharova was thus left with four small children, the youngest less than two years old. Ivan was seven. Understandably, in later years Goncharov could hardly remember his father. On the other hand, his attachment to and his memory of his mother remained profound for the rest of his life and was probably largely responsible for making the character of Oblomov, whom some critics see as "a classic example of a man suffering from a severe mother complex," so believable.

Avdotya Matveevna never remarried but soon after her husband's death, an old friend of the family, Nikolai Tregubov, a rich and well-educated retired Naval officer who was the godfather of all her children, joined the household as a "tenant" and quickly assumed the role of the surrogate father, guardian, and, in all probability, husband (which may explain why Avdotya Matveevna's name and patronymic appear to be echoed in "Agafya Matveevna," Oblomov's common-law wife). Tregubov was, according to Goncharov, honest, honorable and noble, but also quite an Oblomov-like figure who spent most of his days indoors, wearing a dressing gown and reclining after each rich meal. He was equally laid back about his young charges' education.

After several years of incompetent and often abusive local tutors, Ivan and his brother were sent to study in Moscow's School of Commerce. For sons of merchants it was of course a natural place to attend, but for Goncharov, an avid reader whose mind inhabited imaginary worlds, this was a very poor fit. The situation was made even more miserable by the fact that, unlike his brother, who was four years older, Ivan was not even the right age to be enrolled there—remaining in the same elementary grade for the first four years. The experience was so traumatic that Goncharov would try hard to forget those long eight years, marked as they were by the cruelty and stupidity of his alcoholic teachers and a general atmosphere of boredom and gloom. And this was supposed to be his joyful and carefree youth! "If only you knew how much dirt, indecency, pettiness…I had to go through since birth," he lamented to a friend later in life. "What to others is given by nature and by their surroundings . . .had all been ruined by the lack of early, careful education."

Finally unable to take it any more, Goncharov quit the School of Commerce and persuaded his mother and Tregubov to get a special dispensation so he could enter the Moscow University, which usually accepted only members of the Russian nobility. The request was granted, and the nineteen-year-old Goncharov was finally on his way to a career more worthy of his intellect and talents. Upon graduating in 1835, Goncharov moved to St. Petersburg and began working as a translator in the Department of Foreign Trade of the Ministry of Finances.

In addition to being famous for *Oblomov*, Ivan Goncharov is also legendary in Russia for the fact that all of his three novels start with the same two letters—an "o" followed by a "b." It all began with *Obyknovennaia istoriiia*, usually translated as *A Common Story* (1847), culminated in *Oblomov* (1859), and ended with *Obryv*, known to English-speaking readers as *The Precipice* (1869). It was probably at least somewhat intentional. Like Oblomov, Goncharov was just superstitious enough to think that since his first novel became successful beyond his wildest dreams, it behooved him to embody at least some of its lucky letters into the titles of the successive novels. And *A Common Story* was, indeed, a success of the magnitude that few literary novices ever experience.

Goncharov started working on it in 1843 with few hopes that it would even be published. As a novel of education, *A Common Story* is reminiscent of both Flaubert's *L'Éducation sentimentale*, which was to come later, and Balzac's *Illusions perdues*, which had preceded it by several years. The work was simultaneously intensely personal, insofar as much of its material came from Goncharov's own life in Simbirsk and St.

Petersburg, and pointedly universal, since, as the title suggests, Goncharov believed he was presenting "a common story" of his entire generation. Anticipating the dramatic pairing in *Oblomov* of Oblomov and his life-long friend, Stolz, *A Common Story* depicted a duo consisting of an idealistic nephew, Aleksandr Aduev, an aspiring writer both blessed and burdened with protected and indolent childhood, and his older and much more pragmatic uncle, Petr Aduev, a successful St. Petersburg bureaucrat.

Like any first novel, *A Common Story* had its share of shortcomings, among them too much reliance on dialogue, with excessively long exchanges occupying much of its fairly short bulk. Much to the bewilderment and delight of its insecure author, the book hit a collective nerve and was not just approved by people whose critical opinion he and his generation most respected, it was loved by them. Leo Tolstoy urged his friends to immediately read "the delightful *A Common Story*." "It teaches you how to live. You see different views expressed here on life, on love. You may not agree with a single one of them but, as a result, your own views become clearer and more intelligent."

Inspired by such an overwhelming critical welcome, Goncharov immediately busied himself with writing his next novel. Two years after *A Common Story* came out, he published a story, "Oblomov's Dream," which would later form Chapter 9 of Part I of *Oblomov*. It did not disappoint Goncharov's fans. If *A Common Story* lacked a certain degree of subtlety and complexity, the "Dream" had both in spades. It took its protagonist back to his childhood village, Oblomovka, with its simple pleasures and peaceful sloth. Goncharov effortlessly mixed judgment and nostalgia, comedy and pathos, idyll and unvarnished reality, without feeling compelled to resolve the simultaneous longing and revulsion that the world of Oblomovka produced in him or would produce in his readers. One of the more interesting aspects of the "Dream" is its complex treatment of maternal love. Far from being "selfless," maternal love, though genuine and warm, is shown to be at times very selfish, with overly-protective mothering becoming suffocating.

Goncharov's work on *Oblomov* continued for several years after the publication of "Oblomov's Dream" but was interrupted by several personal losses, including the death of his godfather and guardian, Nikolai Tregubov, in 1849. Torn by guilt that he had not been home for fifteen years, Goncharov spent the summer of that year visiting his family. He found most of them much changed—except his mother who, he wrote to a friend, "has aged much less than I expected." Less than two years later, however, she, too, was dead.

The blow was so harsh that Goncharov put aside his work on the novel and, stunning friends who always thought of him as a sedentary and unadventurous man, joined an around-the-world trip on *The Frigate Pallada*, a ship sponsored by the Russian government to explore commer-

cial possibilities in new markets. Goncharov considered it both a necessary distraction from his paralyzing grief and a tribute to Tregubov, a former naval officer, who had made his young godson dream of the magical
world of sea voyages. He may also have hoped that the glitter of a great
adventure in distant lands just might make him more interesting to the
eligible women he, still a bachelor at the age of forty, was now and then
pursuing. The frigate left from a port near St. Petersburg on October 7,
1852, and for the next two years Goncharov, often sea-sick, exhausted,
and in an Oblomov-like fashion longing for his own bed and home com-
forts, sailed around Europe, Asia, and Africa.

Like many real sea voyages, the trip contained much excitement as
well as long stretches of excruciating tedium—as when the ship would be
stuck for weeks in the doldrums. And not all excitement was good, either.
Around the Cape of Good Hope the ship encountered a very severe storm
that badly damaged it. Among the more positive highlights was the wit-
nessing, while anchored in London, of the funeral procession for Lord
Wellington.

Goncharov came back to St. Petersburg in February of 1855. While
at sea, he kept detailed journals which he later used for publishing travel
essays and then a two-volume book, appropriately entitled *Fregat Pallada*.
When the book was finally translated in its entirety into English in 1987,
the *New York Times* found just the right reviewer for it, Anne Tyler, the
author of *The Accidental Tourist*. The reception for *Fregat Pallada* was very
favorable and helped to cement Goncharov's excellent literary reputation.

Soon after his return, the forty-three-year old Goncharov found himself very much in love with Elizaveta Tolstaya. She was in her mid-twen-
ties at the time, and, according to many who knew her, strikingly beautiful and intelligent. The hard-earned sheen of distant exotic lands did not
appear to do the trick, though. Tolstaya was no doubt flattered by the
attention and courtship coming from a very famous writer and enjoyed
his company and ironic wit, but she was in love with another man, and
by December of 1855, much to Goncharov's desperation, she rather
abruptly stopped answering his letters. This brief but intense courtship
undoubtedly had its impact on *Oblomov* and the depiction of Oblomov's
relationship with Olga.

Distracted by these painful matters of the heart, as well by a new and
challenging job (to the consternation of many of his friends, he accepted a
position as a government censor), Goncharov did not get into the full
swing of writing *Oblomov* until the summer of 1857. He was in Marienbad
at the time, where he had gone to take the waters. It proved to be the best
experience of creative writing he ever had: "I wrote as though taking dicta-
tion. Really, a lot of it simply appeared, unconsciously; someone invisible
sat next to me and told me what to write." By the end of August the novel
was complete. Soon after, Leo Tolstoy, whose own greatest novels still lay

ahead, declared himself "in rapture over *Oblomov*." "*Oblomov* is a truly great work, the likes of which one has not seen for a long, long time....I...keep rereading it." The intensity of Tolstoy's feeling was all the more stunning because it was visited on a novel where the main protagonist hardly gets out of bed, and this element of the novel did, of course, get its share of detractors. One Russian critic pointedly compared *Oblomov* to George Eliot's *Adam Bede*, published the same year, in which, according to the critic, the heroine manages to live through the most traumatic stages of her life, like seduction, pregnancy, and incarceration, in a shorter span of time than it took Oblomov to go from one dream to the next. And yet Tolstoy's enthusiasm was shared by many major critics, among them Nikolai Dobroliubov, who in the late 1850s assumed the mantle as the most influential liberal critic of his generation. Dobroliubov's review, called "Chto takoe oblomovshchina?" ("What Is *oblomovshchina*?"), was the first to forcefully introduce the notion that Oblomov and "*oblomovshchina*" were true manifestations of the Russian national character. Goncharov was jubilant. In 1879, long after Dobroliubov's premature death, Goncharov performed a rare feat for any writer in crediting his critic for making him better understand his own novel.

But Goncharov, of course, did not have to be educated by Dobroliubov. He had been knowingly creating cultural archetypes ever since the publication of his first novel. The greater degree of subtlety was what made *Oblomov* a masterpiece: he was now crafting his characters through suggestive details rather than merely verbal pronouncements. Take, for example, the symbolic role that Oblomov's dressing gown plays not just in the life of its owner but that of the whole nation. This Asian-looking garment which, we are told, bears no hint of anything European, speaks directly to the origins of Oblomov's—and by extension, Russia's—passivity. Like Russia, which spans Asia and Europe, Oblomov and his countrymen, according to Goncharov, consist of two unequal and contradictory tendencies: a much stronger Eastern one (indolent, easy going, and dreamy), and a weaker Western one (industrious, practical, and socially useful). By the time Oblomov's close friend, Stolz, whose half-German heritage saves him from the peculiarly Russian malaise, attempts to separate Oblomov from his Asiatic gown by putting him in a European-looking suit, the gown has already become Oblomov's second skin. And by the 1850s, Goncharov is telling us, it may have already become Russia's collective skin as well....

Oblomov truly abounds in sumptuous, meaningful details, whether it is a twig of lilac that seems to reflect the stages in Oblomov and Olga's romance, or the landlady's fast-rotating elbows on which Oblomov fixes his sleepy gaze. While Freud missed his chance to mine this delicious "elbow fetish" for the good of his science, the reader can savor doing his or her own analysis on its meaning and the role it plays in the outcome of the novel. But Goncharov's interest in the female body went beyond the mechanisms of attraction it held for men. There is a strong hint in the novel, for example, that Olga's restlessness has a powerful sexual component to it, which makes itself quite visible during a walk she takes with Oblomov in the dark garden. Goncharov's lengthy and graphic description of Olga's bewildering sensations has made some critics identify the scene as a depiction of female sexual awakening unprecedented in Russian literature.

Yet the novel is, obviously, not all about details and sensations. As is appropriate for a book dealing with national trends and archetypes, *Oblomov* also tackles the big social and political issues of the day—such as serfdom. Serfdom would not be abolished in Russia until 1861, two years after the novel's publication, but it was already so unpopular during the ten years when Goncharov was writing *Oblomov* that even Nicholas I, otherwise not known for his liberal tendencies, had declared in the 1840s that there was "no doubt that serfdom, as it exists at present in our land, is an evil, palpable and obvious to all." Soviet critics used to go as far as to suggest that *Oblomov* "reflected the anti-serfdom longings of Russian society." And yet, as was the case with the village "Oblomovka," serfdom in Goncharov is never simply and straightforwardly "evil." Zakhar, Oblomov's manservant and the only serf we actually meet, takes for granted his position vis-a-vis his master. And when, through Stolz, Goncharov upbraids Oblomov for mistreating his peasants, he actually blames him not for being a serf owner but for being a bad one and therefore not taking appropriate care of those who live on his estate. This rather nuanced position betrayed two aspects of Goncharov's worldview in the 1850s: he was not as politically liberal as some of his friends wished him to be, and he was a realist who knew that freed peasants would have little in the way of a safety net in place to be able to fend for themselves. In addition, his sentiment underscored, once again, a personal response to the comfortably routine way of life that he had come to both despise and idealize. "Goncharov, of course, mentally rejected the '*oblomovshchina*,'" wrote a very perceptive contemporary, "but deep inside he loved it with profound love beyond his control."

The same can be said about the reactions of many generations of Russian readers to Oblomov. They have known better than to approve of his lethargy and gluttony, yet even strong propagandists like Lenin failed to make him merely a figure of ridicule. The attributes that endeared him to Stolz and Olga are indeed very powerful. There is simply too much charm, warmth, loyalty, and basic good nature in the character to ever render him as one-dimensional.

Goncharov started writing *The Precipice* during the same period he was working on *Oblomov* but it took him another ten years to finish it. It was a very ambitious attempt at a crowning achievement which would surpass *Oblomov*. It was also intended to surpass Ivan Turgenev's *Fathers and Sons* as a book portraying the rift between radicalism and more traditional ways of life, except that, in Goncharov's novel, "new men" were not to possess any of the admirable and attractive qualities of Turgenev's protagonist. Liberal critics objected to the message of the book and Goncharov was accused of turning into a reactionary. Sadly, he spent the rest of his life defending *The Precipice* from hostile attacks and trying to provide a more nuanced context for his positions.

When Goncharov retired from his post as a government censor early in 1868, his life started imitating art, which, earlier, had imitated life. In the late 1870s, upon the death of his German manservant, Goncharov assumed the responsibility for his widow and her young children. Just like Agafya Matveevna was in relation to Oblomov, the widow was of a much lower social rank; but unlike Oblomov, he never married her. He was fond of all three children but in particular of the oldest girl, Sanya (Alexandra) Treigut, whom he first sent to a good gymnasium and then to a teachers college. In September of 1891, several months after Sanya's marriage, which he blessed, Goncharov died among his adopted family, to whom he willed all his accumulated assets. He was seventy-nine. One of his friends left the following description of his final resting place: "When Ivan Aleksandrovich Goncharov passed away, when *a common story* inevitable to all of us, happened to him, his friends…chose a place for him at the edge of a stiff cliff, and there now rests the author of *Oblomov*…at the edge of *the precipice*."

Someone also apparently planted lilacs near his grave.…

Galya Diment
Seattle, Washington, March 2006

Galya Diment is Professor and Chair of the Department of Slavic Languages and Literatures at the University of Washington, Seattle. She edited *Goncharov's Oblomov: A Critical Companion* (Northwestern) and is the author of *The Autobiographical Novel of Co-Consciousness: Goncharov, Woolf, and Joyce* (University Press of Florida). Her other books include *Pniniad: Vladimir Nabokov and Marc Szeftel* (University of Washington), *Between Heaven and Hell: The Myth of Siberia in Russian Culture* (St. Martin's), and the forthcoming *Approaches to Teaching Lolita* (MLA).

To Brigitte—and all she stands for.

And to Ed "It's Doable" Lavitt—faithful friend who toiled so indefatigably in the vineyard, but, sadly, "left the picture," before the grapes ripened.

PART I

CHAPTER ONE

One morning in his apartment in one of those big houses on Gorokhovaya Street, which could have accommodated the whole population of a country town, Ilya Ilyich Oblomov lay in bed.

A man of thirty-two or -three years of age, of medium height and pleasant appearance, with dark-gray eyes, his features left absolutely no definite impression except that of vagueness itself. A thought would flit, bird-like, randomly across his face, glint briefly in his eyes, light on his gently parted lips, hide in the furrows of his brow, and suddenly vanish; then his whole face would radiate an even glow of unconcern. This unconcern would pass from his face into the lineaments of his body, into the very folds of his dressing gown.

Sometimes an expression of something like weariness or boredom would darken his brow; but neither the weariness nor the boredom could for a minute erase the mildness, which was not merely the dominant expression of his face, but the very essence of his whole being—an essence that glowed naked and clear in his eyes, in his smile, in the least movement of his head or his hand. A casual observer taking a cold detached glance at Oblomov might have said: "A good-natured, simple soul, no doubt of it." A more sympathetic observer taking a longer and closer look at his face would have come away with a good feeling and a contemplative smile on his lips.

Ilya Ilyich's complexion was neither rosy nor swarthy nor even positively pale, but rather, nothing in particular, or at least that was how it seemed, perhaps because Oblomov had grown flabby beyond his years, either through lack of exercise or lack of fresh air—or maybe both. His whole body, in fact, to judge by the lustreless, unnatural whiteness of the skin of his neck, his small pudgy hands, and soft shoulders, seemed altogether too delicate and pampered for a man. His movements, whenever he was in the least perturbed, were somehow subdued by the same mildness and a lethargy that was not without its own grace. If ever a dark cloud of concern—issuing from deep within him—drifted over his face, his eyes would dim, his brow would furrow, and his face would begin to show traces of doubt, gloom, or fear. Rarely, however, would such perturbation harden into an idea of any definite kind, much less an actual intention. The tremor of anxiety would resolve itself into a sigh and die away into a torpid doze. Oblomov's clothing was a perfect match for his tranquil features and his delicate, pampered body. He wore a dressing gown of Persian cloth, a real oriental robe without the slightest European touch. No tassels, no velvet, no waist, and so capacious that two Oblomovs could have wrapped themselves in it. The sleeves, in true Asiatic fashion, were much wider at the shoulder than at the wrist. Although the dressing gown had lost its pristine freshness and had in places shed its original lustre, which had been replaced by a shine born of honest wear and tear, it still preserved the brightness of its oriental colors and the cloth had worn well.

In Oblomov's eyes, the dressing gown possessed a multitude of priceless merits. It was so soft and supple that it could barely be felt, and yielded with slavish obedience to his slightest movement. At home, Oblomov never wore a tie or a waistcoat, because he loved to feel free and unconfined as he moved about. His slippers offered a target so wide, long, and soft, that even without his troubling to look, his feet were sure to find them every time he lowered them from the bed to the floor.

For an invalid or for someone trying to sleep, lying down is a sheer necessity, for someone who is tired, it is an occasional need, while, for the congenitally lazy, it is the sheer pleasure of the sensation; but for Ilya Ilyich, it was simply his normal state. When he was at home—and he was almost always at home—he was always lying down and always in the same room, the very one where we discovered him, a room that served at once as bedroom, study, and drawing room. He had three other rooms where he hardly ever even poked his head; in the morning, at a pinch, and not every day at that, and only when his servant was sweeping his study—by no means an everyday occurrence. In these other rooms, the furniture was covered with dustsheets and the blinds were lowered. The room where Ilya Ilyich lay seemed, at first glance, beautifully furnished. There was a mahogany desk, two couches upholstered in silk, and handsome screens embroidered with birds and fruits impossible to find in nature. There were silk curtains, carpets, pictures, bronzes, porcelain, and a great deal of pretty bric-a-brac.

A person of impeccable taste, running a practiced eye over the room and its contents would have seen in them only an attempt on the part of the owner somehow or other to preserve the decorum of the normal conventions, if only to be able to wash his hands of them—and this was indeed Oblomov's sole concern in furnishing the room. A more refined taste would not have been happy with those heavy cumbersome mahogany chairs, or the rickety bookshelves. The back of one couch had collapsed and the wood veneer had come unstuck in places. The pictures, vases, and bric-a-brac were in exactly the same state.

Whenever their owner absently cast an indifferent glance at these furnishings, his eyes seemed to be wondering: "who could have dumped all this stuff in here?" Because of this indifference of Oblomov towards his own property, and perhaps also because of the even greater indifference of his servant, Zakhar, the whole study, on closer inspection, created an overwhelming impression of neglect and disarray. The pictures on the walls were festooned with dust-covered cobwebs; the mirrors had ceased to reflect anything and could have been put to better use as writing tablets for scrawling messages in the dust. The carpets were covered with stains. A long forgotten towel lay on the couch, and it was a rare morning that did not find on the table a dirty plate with a saltcellar and a gnawed bone left over from the night before—not to mention a scattering of breadcrumbs. Had it not been for the plate and the still smoldering pipe by the bed and Oblomov himself lying on it, one might have thought that no one was living there, everything was so dusty, worn, and faded and the room simply bore no trace of human habitation. There were, it is true, two or three books open on the shelves and a discarded newspaper lying around, there was even an inkwell with pens on top of the desk; but the pages at which the books were open had yellowed, were covered in dust, and had clearly been discarded long ago; the newspaper was last year's and if you tried to dip a pen in the inkwell, only a startled fly would come buzzing out of it.

Ilya Ilyich had woken up at about eight o'clock, an unusually early hour for him. Something was really worrying him. His face showed alarm, distress, and annoyance by turns. Obviously, he was in the throes of an internal struggle, and his mind had not yet come to his rescue.

What had happened was that the evening before Oblomov had received a letter from the bailiff of his country estate containing unpleasant news. Everyone knows the kind of unpleasant news a bailiff is liable to send, a bad harvest, arrears, a drop in revenue, etc. Even though the year before and the year before that the bailiff had written identical letters to his master, this latest letter had still had just as strong an impact as any other unpleasant surprise. He was faced with the grim prospect of having to think of some way of doing something about it. However, it would be doing less than justice to the trouble taken by Ilya Ilyich in the management of his affairs not to mention that several years before, after receiving the first unpleasant letter from the bailiff, he had already begun, mentally, to draw up a plan for various changes and improvements in the management of his estate.

The plan provided for a number of new economic, judicial, and other measures. The plan, however, was still far from complete, and the bailiff's unpleasant letters kept on coming every year, rousing him to action and thus interfering with his peace and quiet. Oblomov realized that, pending completion of the plan, something decisive had to be done. The moment he woke up, he made up his mind to get up right away, wash, and after his cup of tea, get down to some serious thinking, come up with some ideas, put them down on paper, and really get to work on the problem. For fully half an hour he lay there, tormented by his decision, but then he began to reason that he would still have time for everything even after his cup of tea, and that he could just as well have his tea in bed, just as he always did, especially since there was nothing to say he couldn't think just as well lying down.

So that is exactly what he did. After his tea, he actually raised himself into a sitting position and was practically on the point of getting out of bed; he looked at his slippers and even began to lower one foot from the bed towards them, but immediately drew it back again. The clock struck half past nine; Ilya Ilyich started. "What am I thinking of?" he said aloud, with some irritation, "I've got to snap out of it and get right down to business! I just have to pull myself together and..."

"Zakhar!" he called.

From the room that was separated from Ilya Ilyich's study only by the distance of a small corridor, there first issued a growling like that of a roused watchdog, followed by the sound of feet hitting the floor. It was Zakhar jumping down from his place on top of the stove on which he spent most of his time slumped in a drowsy stupor.

An elderly man entered the room. He wore a gray tailcoat and his shirt was poking through a tear in the armpit. His waistcoat was of the same gray, with brass buttons and his pate was as bald as your kneecap. The color of burnt straw and streaked with gray, his sideburns grew so thick and luxuriant on either side of his face as to provide enough material for three beards each. Zakhar had made no attempt to alter either his God-given appearance or the clothes he was used to wearing in the country. His clothes were still made from a pattern he had brought with him from the country. He favored the gray tailcoat and waistcoat because he saw in these uniform-like garments a faint reminder of the livery he had sported in the old days when he escorted his long-dead master's family to church or on social calls; and in his mind the livery was the sole lingering emblem of the glory of the house of Oblomov.

Nothing more remained to remind the old man of those old spacious and tranquil days in his master's house in the depths of the country. The old master and mistress were dead now, and the family portraits had remained at home, probably gathering dust in some attic. Memories of the old ways and glories of the house of Oblomov were growing dim and lived on only in the minds of the few remaining old people in the village. This is why Zakhar was so attached to the gray tailcoat. It was the gray tailcoat together with one or two other things about the face and manner of his master that brought his parents to mind, as well as his master's whims, which although they made him grumble both aloud and privately to himself, at bottom actually commanded his respect as the right and proper exercise of a master's power and served Zakhar as reminders, however pale, of past glories. Without these whims he did not really feel he had a master over him, without them there was nothing to bring back his youth, the village they had left so long ago, or the stories about the old place that were the only records, kept alive by the old servants, nannies, and wet-nurses and passed on from generation to generation.

The house of Oblomov had at one time enjoyed wealth and distinction within the surrounding area; but later, for some reason, it fell into decline and impoverishment and by imperceptible degrees became indistinguishable from the newer noble houses. Only the aging servants preserved and shared with each other authentic memories of the past that they cherished and kept holy. That is why Zakhar was so fond of his gray tailcoat. He may even have prized his sideburns so highly because in his childhood he had seen so many old servants sporting these antique, aristocratic adornments.

Ilya Ilyich, wrapped in his thoughts, was oblivious to Zakhar standing silently before him. Finally Zakhar gave a little cough.

"What is it?" asked Ilya Ilyich.

"You called, didn't you?"

"Called? What on earth for? I really don't remember," he replied, stretching, "Anyway, go back to your room for now, while I try to remember."

Zakhar went, and Ilya Ilyich went on lying there, thinking about the damned letter.

A quarter of an hour went by.

"Well, that's enough lying down, it's really time to get up," he said, "still, what if I just read the bailiff's letter through carefully once more and then get up."

"Zakhar!"

Again, the same sound of feet slapping the floor and the growling—only this time louder. Zakhar came in to find Oblomov in the same trance-like state. Zakhar stood there for a couple of minutes surveying his master with some displeasure out of the corner of his eye and finally headed for the door.

"Where are you going?" asked Oblomov suddenly.

"You don't say anything, so what's the point of standing here?" Zakhar wheezed. According to him, it was the only voice he had left. He claimed to have lost his normal one while out one day riding to hounds with the old master because the high wind had given him a cold in his throat. He stood in the middle of the room at right angles to his master, swiveling his eyes to look at him.

"Have your legs withered away or something, so that a little standing is too much for you? You can see I've got something on my mind, so just wait! You've done plenty of lying around over there! Find the letter I got from the bailiff yesterday. Where did you put it?"

"What letter? I haven't seen any letter."

"But you took it from the postman, it was all dirty!"

"How should I know where it was put?" said Zakhar, patting the papers and various objects lying on the table.

"You never know anything; take a look in the waste paper basket there. Or maybe it's slipped down behind the couch—the back still needs mending by the way. Why can't you call the carpenter and get it repaired, you're the one who broke it. You never think of anything!"

"I didn't break it," replied Zakhar, "it just collapsed, you can't expect things to last forever—it had to go sometime!" Ilya Ilyich did not feel it necessary to contest the point and asked only: "Found it yet?"

"Here's some letters."

"They're not the ones."

"Well, that's all there are," said Zakhar.

"Alright, leave it then!" said Ilya Ilyich impatiently, "I'll get up and find them myself."

Zakhar had gone back to his room and had barely put his hands on the edge of the stove in order to lever himself up on to it, when once again there came the impatient shout: "Zakhar, Zakhar!"

"Lord in heaven," Zakhar grumbled as he made his way back to the study. "This is killing me, I'd sooner be dead!"

"What is it?" he said, with one hand on the study door and his head averted at such an angle—as a mark of his displeasure—that he could only see Oblomov out of the corner of his eye, thus presenting his master with a view of an immense thicket of whiskers out of which you wouldn't have been at all surprised to see a couple of birds come flying.

"My handkerchief, quick! You could see for yourself that I need it, you just don't look!" Ilya Ilyich snapped.

Zakhar saw nothing particularly surprising or unpleasant about his master's command or his reproach; indeed for his part he found both entirely natural.

"How should I know where it is?" he grumbled, going around the room, feeling for it on every chair, although anyone could see there was nothing on any of them.

"You're always losing things," he muttered, opening the door to the livingroom to see if it was there.

"Not there! Look in here! I haven't been in there since the day before yesterday! And hurry up!" said Ilya Ilyich.

"Where is it? I can't see any handkerchief!" said Zakhar, spreading his hands helplessly and peering into every corner. Suddenly he spotted it. "Look, there it is!" he croaked indignantly. "It's right underneath you! The end of it's sticking out, you're lying right on it and asking me where it is!" And without waiting for an answer, Zakhar made for the door.

Oblomov felt a little embarrassed at having been made to look so stupid, but soon found another pretext for putting Zakhar in the wrong.

"Is this what you call clean? Look at all this dust and dirt; good God! Just look in the corners; you don't do a thing!"

"You call it doing nothing." Zakhar was offended. "I practically work myself to death here; why, I dust—and almost every day, I sweep …!"

He pointed to the middle of the floor and the table at which Oblomov ate.

"Just look, it's all swept and tidy, you could hold a wedding here. What more could you want?"

"And what about this?" Ilya Ilyich broke in, pointing to the walls and ceiling. "And this? And this?" He pointed to a discarded towel from the day before and a plate with a piece of bread on it that had been left on the table.

"Yes, well that I'll clear away," Zakhar conceded, picking up the plate.

"What about the rest, the dust on the walls, the cobwebs?" said Oblomov, pointing to the walls.

"Well, that I do for Easter, cleaning the ikon and clearing away the cobwebs."

"And what about dusting the books and pictures?"

"The books and pictures I do for Christmas; Anisya helps me and we clear out all the cupboards. Now there's never any chance of clearing up, you're always sitting around at home."

"Sometimes I go to the theatre or I'm invited out, you could …"

"You expect me to clean up at night?"

Oblomov looked at him reproachfully, shook his head and sighed, but Zakhar just looked out of the window indifferently and also sighed. His master looked at him as if to say, "you know, you're even more of an Oblomov than I am myself," while Zakhar was thinking to himself something like: "Don't expect me to believe all that! Oh yes, you're very good at thinking up clever things to say—not that they add up to anything—but when it comes to things like dust and cobwebs, you couldn't care less."

"Don't you know," said Ilya Ilyich, "that dust breeds moths? I sometimes even see bugs on the walls."

"I even have fleas in my room," Zakhar responded, unruffled.

"Is that something to be proud of? It's disgusting," said Oblomov.

A grin spread all over Zakhar's face taking in even his eyebrows and whiskers that jutted out even further on either side; it was like a red stain covering his whole face right up to the hairline.

"Why is it my fault if there are bugs in the world?" he said with unfeigned surprise. "Was it me who invented them?"

"It's because of dirt," Oblomov broke in. "Why are you telling me all this rubbish?"

"I didn't invent dirt either!"

"You have mice running around your room all night, I know, I can hear them."

"I didn't invent mice either. There's a lot of creatures everywhere, mice, cats, bugs."

"How come other people don't have moths or bugs?" An expression of disbelief appeared on Zakhar's face, or, more accurately, of quiet conviction that such things simply don't happen.

"I always have a lot," he persisted. "You can't watch every single bug or crawl into their crannies after them." Privately, he was probably thinking: "who can sleep without bedbugs?"

"Just take a broom and sweep the dirt out of the corners and there won't be any at all!" Oblomov admonished him.

"Clear it away and the next day it all piles up again," said Zakhar.

"No, it doesn't, or at least it shouldn't," his master put in.

"Yes it does, I know," asserted the servant.

"Well, if it piles up, sweep it away again!"

"What do you mean? Clean out all the corners every day?" asked Zakhar. "What kind of life is that? I'd sooner the Good Lord took me to his bosom!"

"How come other people's places are clean?" Oblomov objected, "just take a look at the piano tuner's apartment opposite; it's a pleasure to see, and just one girl ..."

"How do you expect Germans to collect dirt?" Zakhar objected, "Just see how they live! One bone feeds the whole family for an entire week. A coat goes back and forth between the father and the son. The wife and daughters wear these short little dresses and sit with their legs tucked up under them like geese. So where is their dirt going to come from? They don't let their worn out old clothes pile up in cupboards for years the way we do, or throw bread crusts onto a heap in a corner for the winter. They don't waste even a single crust; they save them and use them as rusks to go with their beer!"

The thought of such a cheeseparing existence so disgusted Zakhar that he actually spat through his teeth.

"All this talk is getting us nowhere," Ilya Ilyich intervened, "you'd better start cleaning up!"

"What about the times I'm all ready to clean up and you don't let me!" said Zakhar.

"There you go again, it's always me who is in the way."

"Yes it is! How do you expect me to clean with you always sitting around at home? Go out for a whole day, then I'll clean up."

"Another one of your ideas, 'go out'. Why don't you just go back to your room?"

"No, I mean it!" Zakhar persisted, "just go out today and Anisya and me'll have the place cleaned up, though maybe the two of us won't be enough; we'll have to get in some women to scrub the place out."

"Get in some women! Where do you get these ideas?" said Ilya Ilyich. "Back to your room!" By now he was sorry he had provoked this whole conversation with Zakhar. He was always forgetting that the slightest reference to this delicate subject was liable to stir up a hornet's nest.

Oblomov would actually have liked to see everything clean, only he wanted it to happen somehow by itself, spontaneously and in a flash, but if you so much as raised the question of asking Zakhar to dust or sweep or anything like that, he would always give you this tremendous argument. He would make it clear that there was no way of avoiding major domestic upheaval, knowing full well how the very prospect of it would horrify his master.

Zakhar went out leaving Oblomov in a brown study. After a few minutes the half-hour struck again.

"Oh, no!" Ilya Ilyich exclaimed in dismay, "almost eleven and I haven't even got up, and still haven't washed!"

"Zakhar, Zakhar!"

"Oh God! There you go again! Well?" Zakhar's voice carried into the room from the hallway, the words followed by the familiar sound of feet hitting the floor.

"I want to wash, is everything ready?"

"Yes, and it has been for ages! And you're still lying there!"

"Well, why didn't you tell me, I would have been up long ago? You can go, and I'll be right with you. I have work to do. I'm going to sit down and write!"

Zakhar went out, but a minute later returned carrying some scraps of paper and a notebook all smudged and soiled and covered in writing.

"Here, as long as you're going to be writing, you might as well check the accounts; we have bills to pay."

"What accounts, what bills?" Ilya Ilyich asked unhappily.

"There's the butcher, the greengrocer, the laundress, the baker. They all want to be paid."

"That's the only thing they care about—money!" Ilya Ilyich grumbled. "And you, why don't you give me the bills a little at a time instead of all at once?"

"But you always throw me out, it's always 'come back tomorrow'."

"Alright, why don't I just tell you 'come back tomorrow' right now?"

"No, this time they really mean it—no more credit. It's already the first of the month."

"Another problem!" Oblomov said dejectedly. "Well, what are you standing there for? Put it on the table! I'm getting up right away. I'll wash and look at it. You're sure everything's ready?"

"It's ready!" replied Zakhar.

"Alright, here goes!"

Groaning, he was on the point of levering himself up into a sitting position when Zakhar broke in.

"Oh, yes, I forgot to tell you, just now while you were still sleeping, the manager sent the porter over with a message; he wants you to move out right away, they need the apartment."

"What of it? If they need it, we'll just move out. What's the problem? You don't have to nag, it's the third time you've told me!"

"Yes, but they're nagging me!"

"Tell them we're leaving!"

"Yes, but they say you've been promising to move for a month now but you don't do anything about it; they say they're going to call the police."

"Let them!" Oblomov said decisively, "We'll be leaving ourselves anyway in three weeks or so as soon as it begins to get a little warmer!"

"What three weeks? The manager says that in two weeks he's sending in the workmen; they're going to tear the place apart. He says you have to leave tomorrow—or the day after at the latest!"

"You see, now they're trying to rush me out! Why wait? Why not tell me to get out right now? I forbid you to mention the apartment to me. I told you the same thing last time, and now you come and mention it anyway!"

"What do you want me to do?" Zakhar responded.

"What do I want you to do?" Ilya Ilyich came back, "see how he tries to get out of it! He's asking me! It's not my business. Don't bother me! You work it out any way you want, just so long as we don't have to move. Try to help your master out a little!"

"But, Ilya Ilyich, how am I going to work it out?" Zakhar wheezed softly. "It's not as if it's my house; if you're in someone else's house and they want you out—that's it, you just have to leave! Now if it was my house, then with the greatest of pleasure …"

"I'm sure you can find some way of bringing them around. For instance, something like: 'we're old tenants and we pay the rent regularly'."

"I told them," said Zakhar.

"Well, what did they say?"

"The same old thing, what else? 'You have to move out. We need to do the whole apartment over completely'. They're going to make this one and the doctor's into one big apartment so that the landlord's son can move in after his wedding."

"Good God, to think that there are idiots around who want to get married!" said Oblomov in annoyance. He turned over onto his back.

"Maybe you yourself, begging your pardon, could write to the landlord, perhaps he would leave you alone and tell them to start work on the other apartment first." Zakhar gestured vaguely to his right.

"Alright, I'll get up and write. You can go now and I'll think about it. You can't do the slightest thing—even nonsense like this I have to be bothered with."

Zakhar went out and Oblomov began to think. The problem was that he did not know what to think about first. The letter to the bailiff? Moving to a new apartment? Do the accounts? He was overwhelmed by the rising tide of practical problems and just lay there twisting and turning from side to side. From time to time a disconnected exclamation would escape him, "God, how life reaches out and grabs you—nowhere to hide!"

There is no telling how long he would have lain there in a torment of indecision, if the doorbell had not rung.

"Oh no! Someone already here?" said Oblomov, wrapping his dressing gown around him, "and I'm not even up yet. It's a disgrace! Who could it be so early?"

He lay there looking at the door, wondering who it could be.

CHAPTER TWO

A young man of about twenty-five entered, aglow with health, his cheeks, lips and eyes smiling. It made one positively envious to see him. He was immaculately groomed and attired and there was a dazzling freshness about his face, linen, gloves and tailcoat. He wore a watch-chain on his waistcoat, festooned with tiny trinkets. He drew out a handkerchief of the finest cambric, perfumed with oriental fragrances, took a sniff, passed it nonchalantly over his face and glossy hat and dusted off his patent leather boots.

"Ah, Volkov, good morning!" said Ilya Ilyich.

"Good morning, Oblomov," said this dazzling personage, moving towards him.

"Stop! Stop! You're just in from the cold!" said Oblomov.

"How pampered you are! What self-indulgence!" said Volkov, looking for somewhere to put his hat, but seeing dust everywhere, kept it in his hand. Parting the tails of his coat he was about to sit down, but after taking a close look at the armchair, he decided to remain standing.

"Not up yet! What's that dressing gown you've got on? No one has been wearing that kind for years now," said Volkov to Oblomov's discomfiture.

"It's not a dressing-gown—it's more of a kimono," said Oblomov wrapping the voluminous folds of the gown lovingly about himself.

"Keeping well?" asked Volkov.

"Well!" said Oblomov, yawning, "Anything but; the blood pressure is killing me. How about you?"

"Me? Fine, absolutely on top of the world as a matter of fact," the young man added exuberantly.

"What are you doing up and about so early?" asked Oblomov.

"I've just come from the tailor's. How do you like my tailcoat?" he said, turning around for Oblomov to see.

"Perfect! Beautifully tailored," said Ilya Ilyich. "But why is it so wide at the back?"

"It's a riding habit."

"Oh! So that's it, do you ride then?"

"Of course, what do you mean? I ordered it especially for today. Today's the first of May; I'm riding out with Goryunov to Yekaterinhof. But maybe you didn't know, Misha Goryunov's been commissioned, so it's our big day!"

"It certainly is!" said Oblomov.

"He has a 'chestnut'," Volkov went on, "they all have chestnuts in his regiment; mine is a black. What about you? Are you walking or driving?"

"Well, neither really," said Oblomov.

"You mean you're not going to Yekaterinhof on the first of May? Really! Ilya Ilyich. Why, everyone will be there!"

"What do you mean 'everyone'? Don't exaggerate!" Oblomov observed lazily.

"My dear fellow, you really must come! Sofia Nikolayevna and Lydia will be the only two in their carriage and the little jump seat facing them will be empty, so you could…"

"No, I won't fit, I'm not sitting on any little jump seat. And what would I do there anyway?"

"Well, if you like, Misha will find another horse for you."

"God knows what he will come up with next!" said Oblomov in a kind of private aside.

"You seem to have the Goryunovs on the brain."

"Ah!" exclaimed Volkov excitedly," can I tell you?"

"Out with it!"

"But not a word to anyone—you promise?" said Volkov sitting beside Oblomov on the divan.

"Yes, alright."

"I'm…in love with Lydia," he whispered.

"Good for you! When did it happen? I hear she's very nice."

"Three weeks ago," Volkov answered with a deep sigh, "and Misha is in love with Dashenka."

"What Dashenka?"

"Where have you been Oblomov? You don't know Dashenka? The whole town is raving about her dancing. I'm going with him to the ballet today, he's going to throw a bouquet. He has to be encouraged; he's shy, still just a novice…oh! yes, we still have go for camellias."

"More rushing around? Why don't you come and have dinner with me, we could talk. I have these two big problems …"

"I can't, I'm dining with Prince Tyumenev; all the Goryunovs will be there and," his voice dropped to a whisper, "she will be there, my Lydia. Why have you dropped the Prince? There's never a dull moment in that house. They really live in style! And their country house—smothered in flowers! They've built on a Gothic style gallery. In the summer they say there are going to be tableaux and dancing. You will be going, won't you?"

"No, I don't think so."

"But there's so much going on in that house! On Wednesdays this winter there have never been fewer than fifty guests, sometimes as many as a hundred."

"Good God, the boredom must be deadly!"

"What do you mean, boredom! The more the merrier, Lydia…was

there all the time, but I never noticed her, and suddenly …" He broke into song:

"Tho' I strive with might and main, my efforts to forget her are in vain," and sat down unthinkingly in an armchair, but immediately sprang to his feet and began to brush the dust from his clothes.

"Everything is covered with dust here!" he said.

"It's Zakhar's doing," Oblomov complained.

"Well, time for me to be off," said Volkov, "have to get the camellias for Misha's bouquet. Au revoir!"

"Come and have some tea this evening after the ballet, you can tell me what went on!" said Oblomov.

"I can't, I promised the Mussinskys; they're 'at home' today. Why don't you come along, I'll introduce you if you like?"

"No thanks, what is there to do there?"

"At the Mussinskys'? My dear fellow, you'll find half the town there. You'll find people talking on every possible subject."

"That's the very subject that's so boring—every possible subject," said Oblomov.

"Well then, go to the Mezdrovs'," Volkov put in, "there's only one topic of conversation there, the arts; that's all you hear, the Venetian School, Beethoven and Bach, Leonardo…"

"Endless talk about the same thing—what a bore! Just a lot of pedants." Oblomov yawned.

"There's no pleasing you. But there are so many houses and now they all have their days for receptions. The Savinovs give a dinner on Thursdays, the Maklashins on Fridays, the Vyarnikovs on Sundays, Prince Tyumenev on Wednesdays. I'm busy every day!" Volkov concluded, his eyes shining.

"Don't you get tired of this endless social round?"

"Tired?" What tired? It's tremendous fun!" he said breezily.

"In the mornings there's the reading, to keep up with what's going on, to keep abreast of the latest. Thank God, with a job like mine, you don't have to go to any office! Just twice a week I go to the General's for dinner, and then go visiting where I haven't been for a long time. I might meet a new actress from the French or the Russian theatre. Soon it will be the opera season and I'm subscribing. Now I'm in love…the summer is beginning. Misha has been promised leave and we'll go to the country for a month for a change. There'll be hunting. The neighbors are first-class, they give 'bals châmpétres'. I'll take Lydia for walks in the woods. We'll go out in a boat, pick flowers, just imagine! He wheeled around in his elation.

"Time to go now. Good-bye," he said, attempting futilely to inspect himself, back and front, in the dust-covered mirror.

"Wait a minute," said Oblomov in an attempt to keep him from going. "I have some business to discuss with you."

"Sorry, no time," said Volkov in a rush, "next time; why don't you come with me to eat oysters, we can talk at the same time. Come on, it's Misha's treat."

"No, thanks just the same."

"Good-bye then!" He moved towards the door and then turned back. "Seen this?" he asked, extending his hand in a skin-tight glove.

"What is it?" asked Oblomov, puzzled.

"It's the new 'lacets', see how well it fastens; you don't have to fiddle with a button for hours, just pull the lace and there you are. Straight from Paris. I'll bring you a pair to try, if you like?"

"Fine, bring them!" said Oblomov.

"Take a look at this, really nice isn't it," said Volkov, picking out from a heap of little trinkets a visiting card with its corner turned up.

"I can't make out what's written on it."

"Pr. prince M. Mich," said Volkov, "there was no room for the sur-name 'Tyumenev'. He gave it to me at Easter instead of an egg. Well, good-bye now, au revoir! I still have a dozen calls to pay, God, never a dull moment!" The next moment he was gone.

"A dozen places to go in one day, poor thing!" thought Oblomov, "what a life!" Oblomov gave an emphatic shrug. "What's left of a person after frag-menting himself and dispersing himself in so many different directions? Nothing wrong, of course, with dropping in at the theatre or falling in love with a Lydia, she's nice. Picking flowers in the country, going out in a boat—all fine—but a dozen places in a day, poor fellow!" he concluded, turning over on to his back and relishing the thought that he at least was free of such vain desires and ideas, and instead of rushing around, just lay quietly at home preserving his human dignity intact.

The doorbell rang again, breaking into his ruminations. A new visi-tor entered. It was a gentleman in a dark-green tailcoat with crested but-tons. He was clean-shaven with whiskers evenly framing his face. His expression was troubled but with a quiet knowing air about his distinctly worn face and a thoughtful smile.

"How are you Sudbinsky?" Oblomov greeted him cheerfully, "so you finally found time to look in on your old colleague. Stop, don't come any closer, you're just in from the cold!"

"How are you, Ilya Ilyich, I've been meaning to call for a long time, but I don't have to tell you how much work there is in the office. I'm lug-ging this suitcase full of papers for the reports, and in case anyone needs me for anything, I've left orders to send a messenger here. There's not a minute to yourself."

"You're still on your way to work at this hour?" asked Oblomov, "why in the old days, at 10 o'clock ..."

"That was in the old days, now it's quite different; now I ride to the office at noon," he said with particular emphasis on the word 'ride'.

"Ah! I get it now, you've been made department head; how long ago?"

Sudbinsky nodded significantly. "Since Easter," he said, "but what a tremendous workload! From eight to twelve at home, twelve to five at the office. I even work at night. I've absolutely no time for people any more!"

"Well, well, department head, fancy that," said Oblomov, "congratulations, just imagine! To think that we worked together in the civil service. I should think you'll be a Counsellor of State by next year!"

"Good lord, no! This year I should be awarded my 'Order of the Crown'; I thought I would be getting a commendation but instead I got this new promotion. Two years in a row you can't …"

"Come for dinner and we'll drink to the promotion!" said Oblomov.

"I can't, I'm dining at the deputy director's. I have to have the report ready by Thursday. I'm going to have to work like a slave. Can't rely on the memos from the provinces, I'll have to check the lists myself. Foma Fomich is so obsessive, he insists on doing everything himself. Today, for example, we're going to work together after dinner."

"Not after dinner?" Oblomov asked incredulously.

"What did you think then? Why, I'll be lucky if I get away barely in time to get to Yekaterinhof. That's why I came by, to ask if you wanted to go to the festivities. I wouldn't mind going."

"I don't feel all that well, as a matter of fact. I don't think I can." Oblomov frowned, "anyway I have too much to do, no, I really can't!"

"Too bad!" said Sudbinsky, "it's such a fine day, I just thought I might take a break for today."

"Well, what's new with you?" asked Oblomov.

"Oh! all kind of things; in letters there's no more of 'your obedient servant', now it's 'accept my assurances'. Personnel files no longer have to be in duplicate. They've put in three more desks and two more people on special assignment; they've terminated our commission, and I don't know what else!"

"And what about our old colleagues?"

"Nothing much, Svinkin lost a file."

"Really! What about the director?" his voice trembled; his old fear still lingered.

"He's holding up the award until it's found. It's an important matter, a question of 'disciplinary action'. The director thinks," Sudbursky lowered his voice to a whisper, "that he lost the file on purpose."

"Can't be!" said Oblomov.

"No, no, of course not," Sudbinsky pronounced, loudly and patronisingly.

"Svinkin is a muddlehead. Sometimes he comes up with results you couldn't imagine, he gets everything mixed up. I'm at my wits end with him. But no, something like that wouldn't be like him at all, no, he would never…The file is just lost somewhere; it will turn up in due course."

"So it's nothing but work, work, work?" said Oblomov.

"Yes, it's terrible, although it's nice working for a man like Foma

Fomich, he always finds something to give you, even if you've done nothing to deserve it. When the time comes for a promotion he'll recommend you, and even if you don't have enough seniority for a promotion or a decoration, he'll manage to get you some kind of bonus ..."

"How much do you get?"

"Well, there's 1200 roubles salary, 750 food allowance, 600 lodging allowance, 900 roubles special allowance, 500 traveling expenses, and up to a thousand in bonuses."

"Good God!" said Oblomov springing up from the divan, "I didn't know your voice was that good; anyone would think you were an Italian singer!"

"That's nothing, there's Peresvetov who gets extra pay, does less than I do and understands nothing. Of course, he doesn't have my reputation. They think a lot of me," he said modestly, lowering his eyes. "Only recently the minister himself said something about my being 'a jewel in the ministry's crown'."

"Good for you!" said Oblomov, "and all you have to do is work from eight to twelve and then again from twelve to five, not to mention working at home. Good God!" He shook his head.

"But what would I do without my work in the ministry?" asked Sudbinsky.

"Hundreds of things! You could read, write ..." said Oblomov.

"But that's exactly what I do now—read and write."

"That's not what I mean, you could be published ..."

"We can't all be writers, you don't do any writing for one!" Sudbinsky objected.

"Yes, but I have my estate on my hands," sighed Oblomov, "I'm working on a new plan; I have all kinds of improvements in mind, I'm absolutely breaking my back. But you, you're doing other people's work, not your own."

"There's no way around it, if you get paid you have to work. In the summer I'll be taking it easy. Foma Fomich has promised to find a special assignment just for me, so I'll be getting a travel allowance for five horses, three roubles a day for expenses and then there'll be a decoration ..."

"They must have money to burn," said Oblomov enviously and then lapsed into a thoughtful silence.

"I need the money, I'm getting married in the autumn," Sudbinsky added.

"No! Are you really? Who to?" asked Oblomov, his interest piqued.

"No, really, to the Murashins' daughter. You remember, they live near my place in the country. I think you met her when you came to tea."

"No, I don't remember; is she pretty?" Oblomov asked.

"Yes, she's nice. Why don't we go there for dinner if you'd like?"

Oblomov was put out. "Well yes, but ..."

"Next week." said Sudbinsky.

"Yes, good! Next week," said Oblomov brightening up, "my suit's not ready yet. So is it a good match?"

"Oh, yes! The father is a Counsellor of State, still in service. He'll be giving 10,000 with her and he has an official apartment. We'll be getting the whole of one half of it; twelve rooms, fully furnished, heating and lighting included—quite tolerable…"

"I should think it is. Good going, Sudbinsky!" added Oblomov, not without a touch of envy.

"How would you like to be my best man, Ilya Ilyich?"

"Absolutely, of course!" said Oblomov. "But what about Kuznetsov, Vasilyev or Makhov?"

"Kuznetsov got married a long time ago, Makhov took over my job and Vasilyev's been transferred to Poland. Ivan Petrovich got the Order of St. Vladimir and Olyeshkin is now 'His Excellency'."

"A good fellow!" said Oblomov.

"He really is; he earned it."

"A really nice fellow, good-natured and even-tempered."

"So obliging," added Sudbinsky, "and not the kind of toady who will stab you in the back or try to trip you up; not at all pushy and always ready to help."

"A terrific fellow; if you make a blunder, miss something or put in the wrong opinion or quote the wrong precedent, you don't have to worry, he'll just tell someone else to do it over. A first-class fellow," Oblomov concluded.

"Old Semyon Semyonich is just the same as ever," said Sudbinsky, "always trying to create an impression. You'll never guess what he did just recently. A request came in from a field office for building dog kennels in some buildings belonging to our department to protect government property against theft. Now, our architect is a responsible, conscientious fellow and knows his job and he came up with a very reasonable estimate; but no, suddenly it's too high for Semyon Semyonich and he has to go into the matter to find out the cost of building a dog kennel and comes up with a tender all of thirty kopeks cheaper, so now there's a memorandum…."

The bell rang again.

"I have to go," said the man from the ministry, "I've been talking too long anyway, I'll be needed at the office."

"Stay a little longer," Oblomov urged him, "as a matter of fact I need your advice about two problems …"

"No, it's better if I come back in a day or two," he said on his way out.

"You're really in deep, my dear friend," mused Oblomov as he watched him go, "blind, deaf and dumb to everything else around you. Oh yes, you're sure to get on and climb the ladder and end up a big shot…and that's what we call success! How little of himself a person uses for this; the rest is just so much excess baggage, his mind, his will, his feelings—all wasted. To the end of his days so much of himself will be left untouched! And here he is, everyday in his office from twelve to five and working at home from eight to twelve, the poor booby!"

It was with a certain quiet smugness that he contemplated his freedom to lie around on his divan from nine to three and from eight to nine and congratulated himself on not having to submit any reports or draft any documents, thus freeing his energies for giving the widest possible play to his feelings and his imagination.

Preoccupied with these thoughts, Oblomov was oblivious to the figure standing by his bed; an exceedingly thin, swarthy, bewhiskered gentleman, sporting a moustache and an imperial. He was dressed with studied negligence.

"Good day! Ilya Ilyich."

"Good day! Penkin. Don't come too close, you're bringing the cold in with you!" said Oblomov.

"Just as cranky as ever," said the visitor, "the same old idle layabout without a care in the world!"

"No cares!" said Oblomov, "well, what do you call this letter from my bailiff? Here I am breaking my head and that's what you call carefree? Where have you just come from?"

"From the book shop. I went to find out if the papers had come out. Have you read my article?"

"No!"

"I'll send you a copy—read it!"

"What's it about?" asked Oblomov, yawning widely.

"Oh, about trade, the emancipation of women, the wonderful days we had in April and a new invention to stop fires. How can you possibly do without reading—you're missing life's passing show? But mainly I'm advocating more realism in literature."

"Are you very busy?" asked Oblomov.

"Yes, pretty busy. Two newspaper articles a week, then there's reviewing fiction and I've written a short story ..."

"What about?"

"About a town where the mayor beats up the townspeople."

"Well, now that's what I call realism alright." said Oblomov.

"Yes, it really is!" the literary gent confirmed gleefully.

"You see, this is my idea and I know it's a bold and novel one. A visitor who has witnessed these beatings goes and complains to the governor. The governor tells an official who has gone to the town on an investigation to make a point of checking into the story and to report on the mayor and his conduct. This official calls a meeting ostensibly to ask these tradesmen about the business situation and uses it as an opportunity to question them about this other matter. Well, believe it or not, these people do nothing but laugh a lot and positively fall over themselves to heap praise on the mayor. The official starts making inquiries on the side and finds out that these tradesmen are absolute crooks, dealing in the shoddiest goods, giving short weight and short measure and fiddling on their taxes, totally unscrupulous, so that when it came to beatings they were getting no more than they deserved."

"So the beatings from the mayor were the equivalent of nemesis in the ancient tragedies?" said Oblomov.

"Exactly," put in Penkin, "you have a wonderful feel for these things, Ilya Ilyich, you really should be a writer. At the same time I've succeeded in revealing the mayor as a bully as well as exposing the moral depravity of the lower classes, the inefficiency of low- grade officials and the need for stern but lawful measures, now that's a pretty novel idea, you must admit!"

"It certainly is for me," said Oblomov," since I hardly ever read ..."

"Well, there are certainly no books to be seen around here," said Penkin, "but please do me a favor and read one thing that's going to be published, it's a wonderful—well you'd have to call it a poem; it's called 'The Love of the Bribe Taker for the Fallen Woman.' I'm not at liberty to reveal the author's name, it's still secret."

"What is it about?"

"It reveals all the workings of our society, but all depicted with a poetic palette. All the wellsprings are tapped and every rung on the social ladder is explored. The author summons to his court, as it were, the weak but corrupt dignitary and his whole retinue of duplicitous officials. The ranks of prostitutes are all held up for inspection—Frenchwomen, Germans, the women from Finland—all breathtakingly true to life... I've heard parts of it—the author is brilliant, he makes you feel you're listening to Dante or Shakespeare."

"Aren't you laying it on a bit thick?" Oblomov almost rose to his feet in his amazement. Penkin was brought up short, realizing that his enthusiasm really was running away with him.

"Well just read it and you'll see for yourself!" he added, his ardour cooling.

"No, Penkin, I won't."

"But why not, it's all the rage, it's the talk of the town ..."

"Well, let the town talk, some people just haven't got anything better to do; chattering is what they live for."

"Aren't you even curious?"

"What is there for me to be curious about? You know why they write that stuff—it's just for self-gratification ..."

"What do you mean 'self-gratification'? It's absolutely true to life, practically truer! It's as if real life had posed for a portrait. Every character, a shopkeeper, a bureaucrat, an officer, a policeman, you name it, they're all captured in the raw."

"But why do they bother; just to amuse themselves by picking some character and catching a likeness? As a matter of fact there's no life in what they do, no understanding, no feeling, and what we call humanity is totally lacking. They're just feeding their own vanity and self-importance. When they depict thieves or prostitutes, it's just as if they were hauling them off the streets to prison. When you read their stories all you get is what you can see on the surface, the coarse laughter, the malice; you get none of the 'hidden tears'."

"What else do you want? You've said it yourself, they do a fine job of depicting sheer malice, the vindictive persecution of vice, the scorn and heartless mockery of the sinner, that's precisely the point."

"No, it's not!" said Oblomov heatedly. "Show us your thief, your prostitute, your pompous idiot! But where's the human being, where's the humanity in all this? You're just writing from the head," Oblomov was spluttering, "you don't understand, the idea is not complete without the heart, it's love that brings it to life! Stretch out your hand to the sinner to raise him up, or shed bitter tears over him if he is doomed, but don't gloat! Love him, try to see yourself in him and treat him as you would yourself; then I will read you and respect your work."

Oblomov subsided gently back onto the divan. "Oh, they can describe thieves and prostitutes alright, but when it comes to human beings they forget or don't know how to. What's artistic about that? What is this poetic palette of yours? Expose corruption or filth if you must, but please don't call it poetry!"

"So you want us to portray nature—roses, nightingales, frosty mornings, while everything is in ferment? What we need is to lay bare the anatomy of society, this is no time for lyric verse!"

"It is the human being I want to see. I want to see you loving the human being."

"Love the usurer, the hypocrite, the corrupt, narrow-minded official! Listen to yourself! It's unbelievable! You obviously know nothing about literature," said Penkin heatedly, "no, they have to be punished, driven out of civilized society!"

"Driven out of civilized society!" exclaimed Oblomov spiritedly, rising to his feet in front of Penkin. "In other words, forget that this unworthy vessel once contained a higher essence! Forget that this creature, for all his flaws, is no less of a human being than you! Drive him out? Just how are you going to cast someone out of human society, from nature's bosom, from God's mercy?" Oblomov was almost shouting, his eyes blazing.

"Well, look who is being carried away now!" said Penkin in amazement.

Oblomov, realizing that he too had allowed his feelings to get the better of him, stood for a moment before lowering himself back onto the divan with a yawn.

It was Penkin who broke the silence.

"So what do you read?"

"Well…it's mostly books on travel."

More silence.

"So, will you read the poem when it comes out? I could bring you a copy."

Oblomov shook his head.

"Well, shall I send you my story?"

Oblomov nodded.

"Anyway, I have to get to the printer's now," said Penkin. "You know why I came? To ask you to come to Yekaterinhof—I have a carriage. I have to cover the festivities. We could go and watch them together and any time you see something that I miss, you could fill me in, it would be more fun that way, so why don't you come?"

"No, I don't feel too well," Oblomov replied, wrinkling his brow and pulling the blanket over himself, "I can't take the damp and there's still some about. But what about coming to have dinner with me; we could talk, I have these two problems…?"

"Sorry, but all my colleagues on the magazine are at St. George's today and we are setting out from there for the festivities. Then I'll have to spend the night writing it up and send it off to the printer's at the crack of dawn. Good-bye!"

"Good-bye, Penkin!"

"Spend the night writing," thought Oblomov, "what about sleeping? I wouldn't be surprised if he makes as much as five thousand! Some living! But all that writing, wasting all that thought, squandering your very essence on trivia. Constantly chopping and changing your opinions, prostituting your intellect and imagination, doing violence to your true self; always in the grip of violent emotions, your feelings in turmoil, an endless hurly-burly; never any let-up, rushing here, there and everywhere. And writing, writing all the time, spinning like a wheel, a machine—tomorrow, writing, the day after, more writing. Come holidays, come summer, still writing. When does he ever stop and rest, the poor wretch?"

He turned his head towards the desk. It was quite uncluttered, no such thing as a pen to be seen and even the ink had dried up. How contented he was, lying there without a care in the world like a newborn infant, husbanding his energies, not selling anything…Suddenly the thought struck him. "But what about the bailiff's letter—and the apartment?"

He was just beginning to think about it all, when the doorbell rang again.

"It's a regular party here today!" said Oblomov and waited to see who it was.

A man of indeterminate years and nondescript appearance entered the room. He was at that time of life when it is difficult to put an age to a man; he was neither good, nor bad looking, neither tall nor short, neither fair nor dark. Nature had simply neglected to endow him with features that left the slightest distinctive impression one way or the other. He was known to many as Ivan Ivanych, to some as Ivan Vassilyich and to others again as Ivan Michailych. There was the same uncertainty about his family name; some said Ivanov, others called him Vassilyev or Andreyev, still others thought it was Alekseyev.

Anyone who was introduced to him for the first time would immediately forget his name, his face and anything he may have said. His company was neither noticed when he was present or missed when he was absent. He was devoid of wit or originality and his mind, like his body, bore absolutely no distinguishing features.

At a pinch, it is just possible that he might have been capable of holding his listeners' attention by recounting everything that he had seen and heard, except that he had never been anywhere—apart from St. Petersburg of course, where he had been born and that he had never left. So the only things he had ever seen or heard were the very same things that everybody else had.

Was he likable? Did he love, hate, suffer? Well it had to be assumed that he did, if only because that is the common lot of mankind. Somehow or other he contrived to like everyone he knew. There are people like this; no matter what you do to them, you will never provoke hostility or resentment. No matter how badly you treat them, they will still eat out of your hand. To be fair, they are capable of feeling love, but in terms of degree it never amounts to what you might call passion. Of course, such people are usually described as "nice" simply because they like everyone, but the truth is that they do not really "like" anyone and are "nice" simply because they are incapable of malice.

If this kind of person is with someone who gives something to a beggar then he too will throw in some small change; but if the people he is with abuse, deride, and chase the beggar away then he will be there abusing, deriding and chasing with the best of them. You could not call him rich, because he is not. As a matter of fact he is on the poor side, but you could not describe him positively as poor, if only because there are a lot of people poorer than he is.

He has a private income of sorts—three hundred or so roubles a year—and he also earns a modest salary in some insignificant post. He is not hard up and does not need to borrow, but the idea of borrowing from him would never remotely occur to anyone.

At work he has no clearly defined tasks because his colleagues and supervisors have never been able to detect in him any particular skills or competence. Whatever task he is given he performs in such a way that his supervisor is always hard put to it to say whether he has performed it well or badly. No matter how closely he looks or how carefully he reads, the best he can come up with is: "Leave it for now, I'll take a look at it later...yes, well it seems more or less alright..."

You would never catch in his expression any trace of regret or yearning to suggest that he ever spent a moment communing with himself, nor would you ever see his glance betray the slightest curiosity about some external object in which he might conceivably take an active interest. If an acquaintance chanced to meet him in the street and asked: "Where are you going?" he would reply: "I'm on my way to work" or "to the shops" or "to see someone." But the acquaintance would only have to say: "Why not come along with me to the post office, to the tailor's or just for a walk?" and there he would be on his way to the tailor's and the post office, not to mention a stroll in completely the opposite direction from his original destination!

Just as practically no one, apart from his mother, noticed his entry into the world, and practically no one notices his presence in it, the chances are that no one will notice his departure from it. No one will inquire, no one will miss him, and no one will even be relieved. He has no enemies, no friends; just a host of acquaintances. It may well be that the only thing about him ever to attract attention will be his funeral procession and for the first and only time some passer-by will vouchsafe this indeterminate figure a gesture of respect—a deep bow; perhaps there will be someone curious enough to run ahead of the procession to ask the name of the deceased, only to forget it instantly. When you get down to it, this Alekseyev, Vassilyev, Andreyev or what have you, amounts to nothing more than the merest insubstantial, impersonal suggestion of humanity in the mass, a dim echo, a fleeting glint.

Normally, Zakhar, foregathering with his cronies at the gate or gossiping at the shop would find some apt description of his master's visitors, but whenever it came to describing this...er what's his name...well, let's say Alekseyev, even Zakhar was at a loss. No matter how long or how hard he thought, there was absolutely nothing about this one's appearance, behavior or character that stuck out enough for him to get a grip on. In the end he would give up and spreading his hands helplessly would say: "There's just nothing about him you could cotton on to."

"Oh, it's you, Alekseyev!" said Oblomov by way of greeting. "How are you! Where are you coming from? Don't come too close; I won't shake hands, you're bringing the cold in with you."

"What do you mean 'cold!' I wasn't coming to see you today but I bumped into Ovchinin and he took me home with him, so I've come to fetch you."

"To go where?"

"To Ovchinin's of course, so let's go! Matvey Andreyich Alyanov, Kazimir Albertych Pkhailo, Vassily Sevastyanych Kolymyagin are all there waiting."

"What are they all doing there and what do they want from me?"

"Ovchinin wants you to come to dinner."

"Hmm, dinner." Oblomov repeated tonelessly.

"And then everyone is going to Yekaterinhof and they said to tell you to hire a carriage."

"What do they want to do there?"

"What do you mean? Surely you haven't forgotten, it's the May Day celebrations today"

"Sit a while and we'll think about it," said Oblomov.

"Come on, time to get up and dressed!"

"There's no hurry, it's still early."

"What do you mean 'early'! The invitation is for noon; we'll finish a little earlier, around two, and then leave for the festivities. So let's get a move on! Shall I have your clothes laid out so that you can dress?"

"Dress! I haven't even washed yet."

"Well, get washed then!"

Alekseyev started to pace to and fro, stopped in front of a picture he had seen a thousand times before, glanced out of the window, took something down from a shelf, turned it in his hands and examined it from all sides before returning it to its place and then started walking around once again—all to keep out of Oblomov's way while he washed and dressed. Ten minutes went by.

"Well?" Alekseyev broke in.

"Well what?"

"You're still lying there!"

"Why, am I supposed to get up?"

"Of course, they're waiting for us. You wanted to go..."

"Where to? I didn't want to go anywhere."

"But Ilya Ilyich you just agreed to go to dinner at Ovchinin's and then to Yekaterinhof!"

"You mean travel in this damp! Anyway, there's nothing to see I haven't seen before. Look, it's going to rain, see how dark it's getting outside!" Oblomov said languidly.

"But there isn't a cloud in the sky, you're just imagining the rain. The only reason it's looking dark is because your windows haven't been cleaned for ages. It's dirt, just dirt, that's why you can't see a damned thing and anyway one of the blinds is almost all the way down!"

"Yes, but if you so much as breathe a word about it to Zakhar, the next thing you know, he'll be bringing in cleaning women and throwing me out of the apartment for the whole day."

Oblomov fell back into his reverie, while Alekseyev drummed his fingers on the table at which he was sitting, his eyes running distractedly over the walls and ceiling.

"So, what's happening, what's it going to be? You going to get dressed or just stay like this?" he asked after a few minutes.

"What do you mean?"

"I'm talking about going to Yekaterinhof."

"You've really got Yekaterinhof on the brain, haven't you?" Oblomov rejoined irritably. "What's wrong with sitting here? Is it too cold for you or is there a bad smell, is that why you keep looking out?"

"No, I'm always pleased to be here, it's fine," said Alekseyev.

"Well, if it's fine here, why are you so anxious to go somewhere else?

Why not spend the day with me here? Stay for dinner and later in the evening you can please yourself. Anyway, I was forgetting, I can't go anywhere, Tarantyev is coming to dinner, today is Saturday."

"Well in that case…alright…whatever you…" said Alekseyev.

"Haven't I told you about my problems?" said Oblomov with some animation.

"What problems? I don't know," said Alekseyev looking at him wide-eyed.

"That's why I'm taking so long to get up. You see, all the time I've been lying here, I've been thinking about how to get out of my troubles."

"What's wrong?" asked Alekseyev, doing his best to look alarmed.

"Two kinds of trouble! I really don't know what to do."

"What are they?"

"I'm being thrown out of the apartment; can you imagine, having to move, all that turmoil and upheaval, just thinking about it makes me shudder! I've been here for eight years and now the landlord comes and pulls something like this on me. 'You have to leave,' he says 'and quick!'"

"And quick into the bargain! He's really in a hurry; he must need it. Moving—it's just unbearable—all that bother!" said Alekseyev. "Things get lost and broken—so tiresome! And you have such a great apartment! How much do you pay?"

"Where on earth am I going to find another one like it—and at such short notice? It's dry and warm and in a quiet building; only one burglary! Of course, the ceiling isn't all that solid and the plaster has all peeled off, but still it's not caving in."

"Well I never!" said Alekseyev, shaking his head.

"How can I manage it so that I don't have to move?" Oblomov was thinking aloud more to himself than his visitor.

"Do you have a lease?" asked Alekseyev, his glance taking in the whole room from ceiling to floor.

"Yes, but it expired; since then I've just been paying rent from month to month…I…I don't know for how long exactly."

"So what do you think?" asked Alekseyev, breaking the silence. "Will you move or stay?"

"I don't think anything, it's too painful to think. Let Zakhar think up something."

"There are some people who like nothing better than moving," observed Alekseyev. "They're never happier than when they are changing apartments"

"Fine, then let those 'some people' do the moving, I can't abide changes of any kind! Anyway, that's only the apartment; wait till you see what the bailiff has written to me—here, I'll show you the letter—if only I could find the damned thing! Zakhar, Zakhar!"

"God in heaven!" Zakhar wheezed as he scrambled down from the stove. "When will you take me to your bosom?"

Zakhar entered and regarded his master blankly.

"How come you haven't found the letter?"

"Where would I look for it? How I am I supposed to know what letter you're talking about, I can't even read!"

"Well, look for it anyway!" said Oblomov

"You were reading some letter yourself yesterday evening," said Zakhar, "and that was the last I ever saw of it."

"Where was it?" Oblomov responded irritably, "I didn't swallow it. I clearly remember you taking it from me and putting it somewhere around here; see where it is, look!" He shook the blanket and from its folds the letter fell to the floor.

"Yes, it's always my fault!"

"Alright, out with you, out!"

Oblomov and Zakhar were both shouting at each other at the same time. Zakhar left the room and Oblomov started to read the letter that looked as if it had been written in kvass instead of ink on gray paper and sealed with brown wax. Huge, pale letters followed each other in single file, without touching, in a stately procession from the top to the bottom of the page, interrupted now and then only by a large pale, inky blotch.

"Dear Sir," Oblomov began, "Your Honor, Our Father and Provider, Ilya Ilyich…"

Oblomov skipped various greetings and good wishes for his health and resumed somewhere in the middle: "I wish to report to Your Honor that everything is well, Your Beneficence, on your estate. There's been no rain for five weeks. The Good Lord must be angry at something not to send rain. The oldest people here don't remember such a drought. The spring crop is burnt to a cinder. Caterpillars and early frosts ruined the winter crop. We thought of ploughing under the spring crop, but there was no knowing if anything would grow. Maybe the Lord in his mercy will take pity on Your Honor; for ourselves we are not worried—even if we drop dead. On St. John's Eve three more peasants went off and Vaska, the blacksmith's son went off on his own. I sent the womenfolk after them, but they didn't come back either and we hear they are living in Chelki. Someone in my family went to Chelki from Verkhlyovo; the farm manager sent him. You see, they had got a plough from abroad and the manager sent him to have a look at it. I told him to find out about the runaway peasants. He paid his respects to the local police officer and he said: 'submit the necessary application and all appropriate measures will be investigated to return the peasants to their lawful domicile'. He didn't say anything else except that. I begged him on my bended knees with tears in my eyes, but he just bellowed at me: 'Get out of here, you've been told, the matter will be dealt with, just hand in the paper!'"

I didn't hand in any paper—and there's no one left to hire here. They've all left for the Volga to work on the barges. That's how stupid the people down here have become these days, Your Honor, Sir! This year we'll have no cloth to sell at the fair. I've had to lock the drying room and the bleachery and gave instructions to Sychug to keep watch on them day and night. He's not given to drink, but just to make sure he keeps his hands off the master's property, I keep watch on him around the clock. The others drink themselves silly and want to pay money instead of working off what they owe. But they're behind in their arrears. There will be a little something to send you this year in the way of income, but a thousand or two less than last year; but let's hope that the drought doesn't end up killing the crop; otherwise we'll be sending Your Honor what we said."

There followed various professions of loyalty and the signature: "Whereto your bailiff and most humble servant Prokofiy Vytyagushkin by his own hand has set his hand." In place of a signature he had put a cross because he could not read or write and this was followed by "the words of the bailiff taken down by his brother-in-law Dyomka Krivoy."

Oblomov glanced at the end of the letter: "there's no month or year," he said, "so the bailiff must have kept the letter lying around since last year, there's all that about St. John's Eve and drought, I wonder when he realized?"

Oblomov trailed off and was lost in thought.

"Oh, yes," he resumed, "what do you think? He writes: 'a thousand or two less', how much does that leave? How much was it I got last year?" he asked looking at Alekseyev, "didn't I tell you?"

Alekseyev looked up at the ceiling trying to think.

"Have to ask Stoltz when he comes," Oblomov went on, "it was something like seven or eight thousand…too bad I didn't make a note of it. Now he's trying to fob me off with six, I'll starve—no way to live on that!"

"No need to get upset! Ilya Ilyich," said Alekseyev." Never give way to despair, things will work out in the end."

"Did you hear what he wrote? He couldn't send a little money, give me some encouragement. Oh no! He just seems to enjoy making trouble for me. And it's the same thing every year! Right now I'm really not myself. 'A thousand or two less' indeed!"

"Yes, it's a big difference," said Alekseyev, "two thousand is no joke! They say Aleksei Loginych too is only getting twelve thousand this year instead of seventeen."

"Twelve thousand is still a long way from six," Oblomov put in, "that bailiff has really upset me! If things really are the way he says—the ruined crops and the drought—why give me all this grief before it's necessary?"

"Yes…well, of course, you're absolutely right, he shouldn't have, but you can't expect a peasant like that to be sensitive about people's feelings, their kind just doesn't understand these things."

"Well, what would you do in my place?" asked Oblomov, looking inquiringly at Alekseyev, squeezing whatever comfort he could out of the prospect, dim though it might be, that he might be able to suggest something helpful.

"Have to give it some thought, Ilya Ilyich, mustn't rush into anything." said Alekseyev.

"Write to the governor, maybe?" Oblomov mused aloud.

"Who is your governor?" Alekseyev asked.

Oblomov again lapsed into a reverie without replying. Alekseyev too ruminated in silence. Oblomov crumpled the letter into a ball and with his elbows on his knees and his head resting in his hands continued to sit, tormented by the unpleasant thoughts teeming in his brain.

"If only Stoltz would hurry up and come," he said, "he wrote to say that he'd be here soon, but God knows where he's fooling around. He would know what to do!"

His mood darkened again. They both sat in silence. It was Oblomov who finally broke it.

"Alright, I know what to do!" he said decisively, practically on the point of getting up from the divan. "And no more shilly-shallying! First…"

Just then the doorbell rang with an urgency that sent shivers down the spines of Oblomov and his visitor—and Zakhar sprang down from his spot on top of the stove.

CHAPTER THREE

"Anyone at home?" a voice bellowed in the hallway.

"Who's calling at this time of day?" Zakhar shouted back even louder.

The man who entered was about forty, powerfully built, massive in the shoulder and everywhere else. His head was big, with features to match; a bull neck, protruding eyeballs and thick lips. One's first impression was of a presence totally without polish or refinement—someone clearly not out to impress you with his dress or appearance. You would be lucky ever to catch him freshly shaved, not that this or indeed the state of his clothes seemed to bother him in the slightest. In this indifference to his appearance there was something defiantly unapologetic.

It was Mikhei Andreyevich Tarantyev who hailed from the same village as Oblomov. Tarantyev took a dark, almost contemptuous view of everything and everyone around him. A man clearly without a trace of benevolence, he was ready to lash out at anything or anyone, for all the world like a victim of some slight or injustice or someone embittered by the world's refusal to recognize his true merits. It was as if he were some kind of tragic hero relentlessly persecuted by fate but defiantly and irrepressibly refusing to bow to it. His movements were bold and uninhibited; he had a loud voice and a ready tongue and when he spoke it was almost always angrily. At a distance he sounded like three empty carts rumbling over a bridge. He was never inhibited by anyone's presence, never at a loss for words and always outspoken and abrasive even with friends. Even when he was a guest at your table he made you feel that he was doing you a great favor just by speaking to you.

Tarantyev's ready tongue was matched by his sharp mind. There was no topical matter or legal issue, no matter how tangled, for which he did not have the answer; in a flash he would come up with a plan of action for any situation and cleverly produce arguments in its favor, but almost always managing to give offense to the person who had brought the matter to his attention in the first place.

Once, twenty-five years before, he had found a job as a clerk in some office, and now, twenty-five years later, the aging Tarantyev was still sitting at the same desk. The idea of his moving upwards was something that had never entered his—or anyone else's—head for a moment. The fact of the matter was that Tarantyev was all talk; with his tongue there was no problem he could not dispose of just like that, especially when it was someone else's problem. Yet the moment it came to lifting a finger or bestirring himself in the slightest and actually doing something practical about his armchair theorizing and demonstrating any effectiveness or ability to get things done, he became a different person. Suddenly it was all too much for him; there were difficulties, he didn't feel up to it; or it was awkward or something else would come up that, of course, he wouldn't do anything about either, or, even if he did, there was not a chance of his seeing it through. Just like a child, he would rush into something without a moment's thought, brush aside the niggling details, leave things too late and end up leaving the job half done. Or he would start the whole thing the wrong way around and make such a thorough mess of it that it was impossible to put right and then he would be the one to curse and yell and blame everyone else.

His father was one of those old time provincial jobbers who had intended handing down to his son his skill and experience in the craft of running other people's errands so that he could follow in his father's nimble footsteps in the corridors of the law courts and other official institutions, but fate had decreed otherwise. The father, whose own parents had struggled to give him some elementary schooling, was anxious for his son to keep up with the times and wanted him to learn something other than the difficult craft of the jobber so he sent him to the priest to learn Latin.

The boy had natural gifts and in three years had learned Latin grammar and syntax and was ready to construe Cornelius Nepos, when his father decided that what he had already learned was enough to give him a tremendous edge over the older generation and that, when all was said and done, too much learning might prove an impediment to an office career.

The sixteen year old youth, not knowing what to do with his Latin, began to forget it under his parents' roof and, pending the honor of attending the district and provincial courts, attended all his father's get-togethers and it was in this school with its free and frank conversation that his youthful mind was so finely honed. With the absorbency of youth he drank in the talk of his father and his cronies about different civil and criminal cases and all the curious business that passed through the hands of those old-time courtroom jobbers and clerks. In the end it all came to nothing and all his father's efforts and strivings to make a courtroom jobber and facilitator out of him were to no avail, although they might have been successful if fate had not intervened to thwart the old man's designs. Mikhei had undoubtedly absorbed all the tradecraft that was to be learned from all the talk in his father's circle; it just remained to put it into practice. However, on his father's death, before he had had a chance to set foot in the law courts, he was taken to St. Petersburg by some benefactor who found him a post as a clerk in some government office and then promptly forgot all about him.

That is how Tarantyev came to remain nothing but a theorist for the rest of his life. His work in St. Petersburg gave him no opportunity to use his Latin or his finely honed judgment to rule on the rights and wrongs of various cases, but all the time he was aware of some slumbering power within himself locked in by adverse circumstances with no prospect of any outlet, in just the same way that in fairy tales, evil spirits were once kept chained to the walls of stifling dungeons by magic spells to keep them out of mischief. Perhaps it was this feeling of blocked potential within himself that made Tarantyev so rude and abrasive in company and so hostile, aggressive and quick to anger.

His attitude towards his actual duties, copying documents, filing papers and the like, was bitter and contemptuous. His last glimmer of hope, remote as it was, was the prospect of moving to an alcohol tax collection firm. He saw this as the only meaningful opportunity of making up for the aborted career intended for him by his father. In the meantime, robbed of his birthright of a provincial career that would have afforded him the right and proper scope for the application of the theories of life and work, of bribery and chicanery handed down to him by his father, he was left to apply them to the trivia of his meaningless existence in St. Petersburg where, for lack of any more formal outlet, they infiltrated his dealings with his friends and acquaintances.

He had a natural instinct for bribery and corruption, a vocation that was thwarted for lack of the proper kind of business and clientele, so he made it his business to exploit his colleagues, friends and acquaintances for the purpose and neglected no opportunity to trick or badger them into wining and dining him. In return for the favor he was granting them he demanded the unqualified respect—which he had done absolutely nothing to earn—of his hosts with whom he was quick to find fault.

His worn out clothing never caused him a moment's embarrassment, but he was a prey to anxiety at the prospect of a day without a free dinner, or rather a feast accompanied by copious amounts of wine and vodka.

As a consequence, among his acquaintances he had taken on the role of a great watchdog whose bark keeps everyone at bay while he catches in his teeth any scrap of meat that happens to come flying in his direction.

These were Oblomov's two most assiduous visitors. Now what brought these two members of the Russian proletariat to him? They knew very well why: to eat, drink and smoke good cigars. At Oblomov's they found a nice, snug and cosy refuge and were always sure of a willing if not warm reception.

But why was Oblomov willing to admit them? He could probably not have answered that question himself. Well, it was probably for the very same reason that in those days in a thousand Oblomovkas all over the country every household of a certain standing had its own similar throng of hangers-on of both sexes in attendance; people almost always with some official rank or title but without means or gainful employment, idle hands attached to empty bellies that needed filling.

There are still those idle rich who need to surround themselves with such hangers-on to relieve the tedium of their lives. Who would there be to hand you your snuffbox or to pick up a dropped handkerchief? Who would be there to complain to about your headache in the confident expectation of appropriate commiseration? To whom could you recount your bad dream of last night and be sure of an obliging interpretation. Who would there be to read you to sleep? And, of course, it was always useful to keep such representatives of the lower orders around you so that they could be sent into town on errands or help around the house—things, after all, you could hardly be expected to do for yourself!

Tarantyev made a lot of noise and forced Oblomov out of his apathy and immobility. He would rant and rave and put on a kind of one-man show, thus relieving Oblomov of the need to do or say anything himself. Into a room of cloistered calm and slumber Tarantyev brought life, movement and sometimes even news from the outside world. Oblomov could listen and watch without lifting a finger in the comfort of his own living room, something vital that actually moved and spoke. In his simplicity he even believed that Tarantyev was someone from whom he could get useful advice.

As for Alekseyev's visits, Oblomov tolerated them for a different but equally weighty reason. For someone who wished for nothing more than to be left undisturbed to drowse in total silence or walk around the room, Alekseyev's was the perfect presence, in fact, he might just as well not have been there at all. He too would remain totally silent and would just doze off, glance at a book or idly inspect the pictures and ornaments until his yawning brought tears to his eyes—and he could keep this up for days on end. But if ever Oblomov grew bored with his own company and felt the need to express himself, to speak, to read, to discuss something or to give vent to some feeling, there was always a willing and compliant audience and sounding board to hand, equally ready to share his silences, his conversation, his moods and his views, whatever they might happen to be.

Other visitors such as the first three came more rarely and stayed only for a minute, and live contact with them was becoming more and more rare. Sometimes Oblomov's interest would be piqued by some piece of news, but after a brief spurt of animation, he would lose interest and the conversation would peter out. His guests needed some reciprocity; some show of interest in what interested them. They were mixing with people all the time and each had his own view of life, a view Oblomov was not inclined to share. They were always trying to involve Oblomov in this life, something that rubbed him entirely the wrong way, which he instinctively resisted and from which he recoiled.

There was one person for whom he had genuine feeling and even he did not leave him in peace. He too had an appetite for news, for people, for the life of the mind and indeed for life itself, but in a deeper, more genuine way, and although Oblomov was nice to everyone, he only really liked and trusted this one person because he had been brought up with him, had been at the same school and lived under the same roof with him. This person was Andrei Ivanovich Stoltz.

He was away, but Oblomov expected him back at any moment.

CHAPTER FOUR

"Hello, old pal!" Tarantyev greeted Oblomov curtly and familiarly and held out his hairy hand. "What are you doing lying around at this hour of the day like a log?"

"Keep away, keep away, you're just in from the cold!" said Oblomov covering himself with a blanket.

"In from the cold, that's a new one," boomed Tarantyev, "you could at least shake a hand if it's offered. It's almost noon and here he is still lying around!"

He was about to lift him up but Oblomov just beat him to it by lowering his feet and finding his slippers at the first try.

"I was just getting up anyway," he yawned.

"Oh yes, I know all about you getting up; left to yourself you'd be sprawled here until dinner time. Hey, Zakhar! Where is the old fool? Get in here right this minute and get your master dressed!"

"Bring your own Zakhar and then you can start bellowing!" said Zakhar, coming into the room and giving Tarantyev a black look, "look at all these dirty footmarks," he went on, "like a peddler's been trampling over the floor!"

"Now he's talking back, the nerve of him!" said Tarantyev, raising his foot to give Zakhar a kick as he walked past, but Zakhar, bristling, stopped and turned.

"Just try touching me," he wheezed fiercely, "the very idea! I'm leaving," he said and headed back for the door.

"Alright, that's enough Mikhei Andreyich, don't you ever give up? Why don't you leave him alone?" said Oblomov, "and you, Zakhar, bring me my things!"

Zakhar turned around and, without taking his eyes off Tarantyev darted swiftly by him. Oblomov, leaning on Zakhar for support, grudgingly allowed himself to be levered up from the bed and, showing every sign of extreme exhaustion, just as grudgingly allowed himself to be helped over to the big armchair where he flopped down without moving a muscle.

Zakhar took the pomade, brushes, and comb from the small table applied the pomade to his master's scalp, made a part, and brushed his hair.

"You want to wash now?" he asked.

"Maybe later," replied Oblomov, "why don't you go back to your room!"

"Oh, so you're here too!" remarked Tarantyev, suddenly noticing Alekseyev while Zakhar was brushing Oblomov's hair, "I didn't see you; what are you doing here? I've been meaning to tell you, that relative of yours, what a bastard!"

"What relative, I don't have any relative?" Alekseyev replied meekly, his eyes bulging out of their sockets with alarm.

"You know, the one who still works in that government office, what's his name? That's it, Afanasyev! What do you mean 'no relative', of course he is!"

"Yes, but I'm Alekseyev, not Afanasyev and I have no relative."

"There he goes again, with his 'no relative'! He's no beauty, just like you, and the same name too, Vassily Nikolayevich."

"No, really, no relation, and my name is Ivan Alekseyevich."

"Well, anyway, he looks just like you, only he's a bastard and you be sure to tell him so when you see him!"

"But I don't know him; I've never seen him!" said Alekseyev, opening his snuffbox.

"Give me some snuff!" said Tarantyev. "Oh, yours is the cheap stuff, not the French? Yes, the cheap stuff," he said, taking a sniff, "why don't you use the French?" he demanded sternly.

"Yes, what a bastard he is, that relative of yours—never met one like him. I once borrowed fifty roubles from him; it must be a couple of years ago now. Fifty roubles, anyone would think it was a fortune or something; you wonder how someone could even remember it! But no, a month goes by and wherever he sees me it's, 'so how about that money you owe me?' He doesn't let up. To top it all, yesterday he comes to our office and says, 'well you must have just been paid, so you can pay up'. Give him my pay, not likely! I gave him hell, showed him up in front of the whole office; he couldn't find the door quickly enough. 'I'm a poor man, I need the money myself', he whined. As if I didn't need it; like I was some kind of millionaire to be going around handing out fifty roubles to the likes of him! Anyway, how about a cigar, old pal?"

"The cigars are over there in the box," Oblomov replied, pointing to a small table.

He was sitting abstractedly in his armchair in a gracefully relaxed posture, oblivious to what was going on around him and what was being said. He was lovingly inspecting and stroking his small white hands.

"But these are the same old cigars!" Tarantyev said accusingly, taking one out and looking at Oblomov.

"Yes, the same," replied Oblomov without thinking.

"But I told you to buy different ones, the imported kind! You never listen to what people tell you. Well, you'd better make sure that they're here by next Saturday, otherwise you won't be seeing me again for a long time! Good God, what rubbish!" he went on, lighting the cigar, puffing out a cloud of smoke, and then taking a deep drag on it—"unsmokable!"

"You're early today, Mikhei Andreyich," Oblomov said with a yawn.

"Oh, you mean you've had enough of me?"

"No, I was just remarking, you usually come just in time for dinner and it's not even one o'clock yet."

"I came early on purpose, to find out what's for dinner. You usually serve me such rubbish, so I want to know what you've ordered for today."

"Why don't you ask in the kitchen?"

Tarantyev left the room.

"For goodness sake!" he said, re-entering the room, "beef and veal! Come on Oblomov, is this any way to live? And you're supposed to be a landed gent. Some gentleman you are, more like a tradesman—no idea how to entertain a friend! Well, did you buy some Madeira at least?"

"I don't know, go and ask Zakhar," said Oblomov who had not really been listening, "I'm sure you'll find some wine there."

"But isn't that the same old stuff from the German? No, you'll be good enough to buy it from the English place!"

"Well, let's make do with that, otherwise it will mean sending out again."

"Look, just give me the money, I'll be passing the shop on my way and I'll bring it back, I still have a few calls to make."

Oblomov rummaged in a drawer and took out one of those old red ten rouble notes.

"Madeira costs seven roubles, and this is ten."

"Just give me the ten roubles, they'll give me change, don't worry!"

He snatched the note from Oblomov's hand and whipped it into his pocket.

"Well, I'm off," he said, putting on his hat. I'll be back by five; I have some calls to make. I've been promised a post in an alcohol tax collection agency and they asked me to call...by the way, Ilya Ilyich, how about hiring a carriage today to go to Yekaterinhof and you could take me with you?"

Oblomov shook his head.

"What is it, too lazy or worried about the money? What a stick in the mud! Well, I'll see you later…"

"Just a moment, Mikhei Andreyich!" Oblomov cut in, "I need to ask you about something."

"Well, what is it, make it snappy, I have no time?"

"Well, you see, two big problems have just landed on my plate. They're going to turn me out of the apartment…"

"Well, naturally, if you don't pay the rent, you've only yourself to blame," said Tarantyev turning to leave.

"What do you mean? I always pay the rent in advance. No, they want to decorate another apartment—no wait! Where are you going? Tell me what to do! They're in such a hurry, they want me out of here in a week."

"What, have I suddenly become your adviser? If you think…"

"I'm not thinking anything," said Oblomov, "so there's no need to shout and get excited. I just want you to think what to do, you're a practical man."

Tarantyev had already stopped listening and was following his own train of thought.

"Alright then, you can start thanking me," he said, taking off his hat and sitting down, "and you can order champagne for dinner, your problem is as good as solved."

"What do you mean?" said Oblomov.

"Is there going to be champagne?"

"Well yes, if the advice is any good."

"No, the trouble is, good advice is wasted on you. I shouldn't really be wasting my time giving it to you. Why don't you try asking him, or his relative?" he added, pointing to Alekseyev.

"Alright, alright, just tell me!" urged Oblomov.

"This is what you do; tomorrow you'll pack up and move to…"

"What, that's your brilliant idea! I could have thought of that myself!"

"Hold on, don't interrupt!" Tarantyev shouted. "Tomorrow you'll move into an apartment at the house of an old friend of mine on the Vyborg side."

"That's a new one, the Vyborg side! They say that wolves are on the prowl there in the winter."

"It's been known; they come over from the islands, but what difference does it make to you?"

"But it's a wasteland, there's nothing to do, there's not a soul there!"

"You don't know what you're talking about. This woman I know lives there; she has her own house with a big garden. She's a respectable woman, a widow with two children and lives with her bachelor brother. Now he's got a head on his shoulders, not like that one sitting in the corner over there," he said, pointing at Alekseyev, "he's smarter than both of us put together!"

"But what's all of this got to do with me," said Oblomov impatiently, "since I'm not moving there."

"We'll see if you don't; if you ask for advice, you should listen to it!"

"I'm not going!" Oblomov said with finality.

"Then to hell with you!" Tarantyev retorted, pulling his hat on and moving towards the door where he turned to face Oblomov. "You're such a crank; what's so wonderful about this place?"

"What do you mean, what's so wonderful? It's so near everything," said Oblomov, "shops, theatres, my friends; it's the center of town, it's got everything."

"What's this I'm hearing?" Tarantyev broke in, "tell me, just when was the last time you went out; when was the last time you went to the theatre? When do you ever go to see friends? What the hell good does it do you, living in the center, if I may ask?"

"How can you say that? Why, there's all kinds of reasons."

"See, you don't even know yourself! Now over there you'll be living in the house of this respectable woman I know in perfect peace and quiet; nobody to disturb you—no noise, no racket; everything clean, neat, and tidy. Just look how you live here—it's like a common lodging house, and you in your position—a gentleman! Over there everything is clean and quiet, and if you ever get tired of your own company there's always someone to talk to. No one else except me will even come to see you. There's two little kids—you can play with them as much as you like. So what is there to think about? And think how much you'll be saving! What are you paying here?"

"Fifteen hundred."

"Well, over there you'll be getting practically a whole house—and for just one thousand; and the rooms are nice and bright and cheerful. She's always wanted a quiet respectable lodger, so I'm recommending you." Oblomov just shook his head distractedly.

"No, no, you have to do it!" said Tarantyev, "just work it out; you'll see, you'll be paying half of what you're paying now. You'll be saving five hundred roubles a month on the apartment alone and the food will be twice as good and twice as clean and Zakhar and that cook won't be robbing you."

Growling sounds could be heard from the hallway.

"Everything will be kept in proper order," Tarantyev continued, "your table here is a disgrace, I can hardly bring myself to sit down at it. You reach for the pepper and it's not there; no one has remembered to buy vinegar, the knives are unwashed; you say yourself the linen keeps disappearing—dust everywhere, it's disgusting! Over there the woman really knows how to keep house and neither you, nor that idiot Zakhar..."

The growling from outside increased in volume.

"That old cur won't have to bother about anything, everything will be laid on. So what is there to think about, all you have to do is make the move, that's all there is to it!"

What are you talking about? Get up and go, just like that, over to the

Vyborg side, from one moment to the next?"

"Just listen to him!" said Tarantyev, mopping his brow, "it's summer now, so it's just as if you were going to your dacha. Why ever would you want to spend the summer stewing here on Gorokhovaya Street? Over there you have the Bezborodkin Gardens, Okhta is close by, the Neva within a stone's throw, plus your own garden, no dust, no stifling heat! Nothing to think about; I'll just dash over there and back before dinner and see her, just give me the fare for the cab, and you'll move tomorrow."

"You're wonderful!" said Oblomov, "what will you come up with next? The Vyborg side, of all things! That doesn't take too much ingenuity! No, if you want to come up with something clever, think of a way for me to stay here—a place where I've been living for eight years now and have no wish to leave…"

"Case closed; you're moving and that's all there is to it! Now I'm off to see the widow, I'll go and see about the job another time."

He was on the point of leaving when Oblomov stopped him.

"Hey, wait a minute, where are you going? I still have another more important matter to discuss. Here, look at this letter I got today from my bailiff; tell me what to do about it."

"What a pathetic creature you are," retorted Tarantyev, "you can't do a thing for yourself! Everything has to be me! You're absolutely useless; what are you, a man or a mouse?"

"Now, where's that letter? Zakhar, Zakhar! Where's he gone and hidden it now?"

"Here it is," said Alekseyev, picking up the crumpled letter.

"Yes, that's it," Oblomov agreed, and proceeded to read it aloud.

"So what do you think? What am I to do?" asked Oblomov after he had finished. "Drought, arrears…"

"You're a hopeless case—hopeless." Said Tarantyev.

"What do you mean 'hopeless'?"

"What do you mean, what do I mean?"

"Well, if I'm that hopeless, why don't you just tell me what to do?"

"And what do I get out of it?"

"I told you, there'll be champagne, what more do you want?"

"The champagne was for finding you an apartment. Here am I doing you a big favor, but do you notice? No, instead of thanking me you argue with me! So find your own damned apartment! But why are we talking about apartments? The important thing is your peace of mind; it will be just like living with your own sister. Two little children, an unmarried brother, and me coming to see you every day."

"Alright, alright," Oblomov interrupted him, "but right now what I want is you to tell me how to deal with the bailiff."

"Alright, make sure that there's good, strong beer on the table for dinner and I'll tell you."

"So now it's beer as well! You're never satisfied…"

"Goodbye then," said Tarantyev, putting his hat on again.

"You're impossible! Here the bailiff is writing to tell me that my income will be 2,000 less and he wants beer on top of it. Very well, buy your beer!"

"I need some more money!" said Tarantyev.

"But you'll have the change from the ten rouble note!"

"But what about the cab fare to the Vyborg side?" replied Tarantyev.

Oblomov took out another silver rouble and thrust it irritably in his direction.

"Your bailiff is a crook, I'll tell you that right away," Tarantyev put in as he pocketed the rouble, "and you trust him like some wide-eyed innocent. What a cock and bull story! Drought, failed harvest, arrears, runaway peasants—it's a pack of lies! I've heard that back home where we come from the Shumilov estate has paid off all its debts with the proceeds of the last harvest, but with you somehow there's nothing but drought and failed harvests and your place is just fifty versts* from the Shumilov's! How come the heat didn't destroy their crop? And then he comes up with these 'arrears'! Wasn't he supposed to be running things instead of letting everything go to the dogs? Why arrears? Isn't anything produced in those parts? Is there no market for the produce? It's highway robbery; I'd soon teach him! And those peasants running away, I'll bet you he let them go himself after extorting some money from them and didn't go anywhere near the police to report it."

"Couldn't be," said Oblomov, "he even included the police chief's reply in the letter, it's too authentic for him to have made up."

"That shows how much you know! All con men know how to make things sound convincing, take my word for it! Take him, for example," said Tarantyev, pointing at Alekseyev, "as honest as the day is long, meek as a lamb, but could he write anything and make it sound convincing, not on your life! But that swine, that villain of a relative of his wouldn't have the slightest trouble. Even you couldn't make it sound convincing. So this bailiff of yours has to be a crook, if only because he's cunning enough to write such a convincing letter. Look how carefully he chooses his words: '…to return the peasants to their lawful domicile'."

"So what should I do about him?"

"Get rid of him right away."

"But who can I put in his place? I mean, I don't know anything about the peasants on the estate, someone else might be even worse; I haven't been there for twelve years."

"You'll have to go there yourself, it's the only way. Spend the summer there and in the autumn you can move straight into the new apartment. I'll make sure that everything is ready for you."

* equivalent to about two-thirds of a mile

"New apartment! Go to the country! Myself! Why are you always coming up with these desperate measures?" Oblomov protested unhappily, "What's wrong with avoiding extremes and adopting some middle-of-the-road solution?"

"Ilya Ilyich, my friend, you're a lost cause. If I were in your shoes I would have mortgaged the estate long ago and bought another or a house here in a good location—it beats that country place of yours—and then I would have mortgaged that house and bought another. Just give me an estate like yours and I would soon make a name for myself!"

"Well, stop bragging and start thinking, and find a way for me to get everything settled, without having to leave my apartment, or go to the estate."

"You'll never get up off your backside, will you?" said Tarantyev. "Just look at you—good for nothing—what contribution do you make to society? Can't even take the trouble to visit your own estate!"

"But it's no good going before I've finished work on all the changes I'm planning for the place—there'd be no point now. You know what, Mikhei Andreyich?" Oblomov had a sudden thought, "what if you go? You know what it's all about, you know the place, and I wouldn't grudge the expense."

"What am I, your manager?" Tarantyev objected disdainfully, "anyway it's ages since I've had anything to do with those peasants."

"What then?" Oblomov inquired pensively, "I really don't know."

"Why don't you write to the police officer and ask if the bailiff has reported any farm hands on the loose, and ask him to go to the village and take a look; then write to the governor and ask him to order the police officer to report on the bailiff's conduct, something like: "Your excellency, may I beg your indulgence and ask for your benevolent attention to the terrible and imminent misfortune with which I am threatened because of the wanton and wayward conduct of my bailiff and the total ruin I am facing together with my wife and my twelve infant children doomed to the poor-house without a crust to their name..."

Oblomov chuckled, "And where am I going to find all those kids if I'm required to produce them?"

"Forget it, just put, 'twelve children,' no one's going to pay any attention, no one's going to investigate; the main thing is it will sound convincing. The governor will pass the letter on to his secretary, and you should also write to the secretary enclosing a copy, because he will be the one to issue the order. And ask around among your neighbors—who do you have there?"

"Well, Dobrynin's pretty close, I meet him here in town quite a lot, he's down there now."

"Then write to him and put it nicely, like: 'There is a great favor I have to ask of you as a Christian, a friend and a neighbor', and be sure to include some treat from St. Petersburg, like a cigar or something. What a dead loss you are! If a bailiff tried to pull that kind of stuff on me, I'd soon show him what's what! When does the mail go?"

"Day after tomorrow."

"Then you'd better start the letter right now."

"But why now? The mail doesn't go for two days. Tomorrow will be time enough. And listen Mikhei Andreich," Oblomov added, "while you're at it, there is one other little thing; of course, I'll see that there's something extra for dinner, some fish or poultry…"

"What is it?" Taryantev asked.

"Why don't you sit down and write the letters. Why, it wouldn't take you long to dash off three letters. You express yourself so 'convincingly'," Oblomov added, barely suppressing a grin. "And Ivan Alekseyev there could copy them."

"What an idea," Taryantev retorted, "now you want me to write the letters! For three days now I haven't written a thing even at the office. The moment I sit down I get tears in my left eye: I must have caught a draft and my head begins to swell when I bend over. You're such a slug! I tell you Ilya Ilyich you're a lost cause!"

"Ah! If only Andrei would hurry up and come," said Oblomov, "he'd soon settle everything."

"So that's your great benefactor," Taryantev cut in, "goddamned German, what a crooked con artist!"

Taryantev had an instinctive aversion to foreigners. In his eyes, the words "French," "English," "German," were synonyms for "swindler," "cheat," "con man" or "thief." Differences in nationality meant nothing to him; they were all tarred with the same brush.

"Listen, Mikhei Andreyich," Oblomov said sternly, "I asked you before to keep a civil tongue in your head, especially when you're talking about a close friend of mine."

"Close friend!" Taryantev interjected viciously, "what kind of family is he to you—he's a German, everyone knows that!"

"He's closer to me than family, I grew up with him, we were at school together and I won't permit offensive remarks."

Taryantev was livid with rage.

"Well if you prefer the German," he said, "then this is the last you'll be seeing of me!"

He put on his hat and moved towards the door. Oblomov momentarily relented. "All I'm asking is for you to curb your tongue a little, and at least show him some respect as a friend of mine. That's not too much to ask."

"Respect? For a German?" Taryantev was dripping with scorn. "Why on earth?"

"I've already told you, if only because he's someone I grew up with and went to school with."

"Big deal! Who cares who anyone went to school with?"

"If he'd been here, he'd have taken care of my problems long ago—and without asking for porter or champagne," said Oblomov.

"Oh, so now I'm the bad one! To hell with you—and your porter and your champagne! Here, take your money back. Now where did I put it? Damned if I can remember!" He drew out of his pocket a sheet of greasy paper with writing on it. "No that's not it, where did I…" He went on rummaging in his pockets.

"Don't bother looking!" said Oblomov, "I'm not criticizing you, I'm just asking you to be a little more civil about someone who is close to me and has done so much for me."

"Done so much!" Taryantev retorted angrily, "Wait and see how much more he's going to do for you; just do as he says!"

"Why are you telling me this?"

"Why? Well just wait until that German of yours has robbed you blind; then you'll find out why you don't choose some vagrant over someone from your own parts, a fellow Russian!"

"Look here, Mikhei Andreyich…" Oblomov started to say.

"There is nothing you can say, you've already said too much; You've already given me quite enough grief; God alone knows how many insults. Of course in Saxony his father didn't even have two pennies to rub together, but he comes here and acts superior."

"Can't you leave the dead in peace? What have you got against his father now?"

"It's the two of them, the son and the father," Taryantev said darkly, "my father really knew what he was talking about when he warned me to watch out for those Germans."

"Well, what have you got against the father, for example?"

"He comes to our country with barely the clothes he stands up in and the next thing you know he's leaving a fortune to his son! You know what that means."

"As a matter of fact he only left his son 40,000, and part of that came with his wife as a dowry, the rest he earned teaching children and running the estate, so he had a good income. You can't fault the father for that. So now tell me what's wrong with the son?"

"He's a fine one! His father leaves him 40,000 and the next thing you know he's turned it into 300,000. In his career he's already risen to the rank of Court Counsellor, apart from being a scholar; not to mention traveling all over the place. He's in on absolutely everything! Can you imagine an honest-to-God Russian doing anything like that? No, a proper Russian chooses one thing, but no hurry at all, mind you, just gently and little by little and somehow or other. . . but that one, just look at him! OK, if he'd gone into the tax farming business, at least you could understand how he'd made his money, but with him who knows, it just comes out of thin air! It's criminal! I'd have the lot of them arrested! Now he's traipsing around God knows where! And anyway," Tarantyev went on, "what does he do all this time in all these foreign countries?"

"He wants to learn, to see things, to find out things."

"Learn? What for? Hasn't he done enough learning? Don't believe a word of it, he's having you on; you're as gullible as a child! When did you ever hear of grown-ups 'learning'? Do you really believe for a moment that a Court Counsellor has to 'learn things'? You went to school, right, and are you doing any 'learning' now? Come on! And him?" he pointed to Alekseyev, "is he 'learning'? And even that relative of his, is he 'learning'? Whoever heard of normal, decent people, 'learning'? You really think he's sitting at a desk in some German school learning his lessons? Not on your life! I heard he went to look at some machine to see if he wants to buy it; it's probably to use as a press for forging Russian money. I'd clap him in jail….and then there's some shares; well those shares, they really give me a pain!"

Oblomov burst out laughing.

"What's the grin for? I'm telling you the truth," said Taryantev.

"Alright, let's get off the subject!" Oblomov put in. "Why don't you just go where you were going and I'll get Ivan Alekseyevich to help me with the letters, and while I'm at it I may as well jot down my plan at the same time."

Tarantyev was on his way out when he suddenly turned back. "I totally forgot! Something I meant to ask you when I came," he began in a suddenly much more civil tone. "I've been invited to a wedding tomorrow, how about lending me your tailcoat, old friend, mine's a bit worn, you see"

"No!" said Oblomov frowning at this new imposition, "it won't fit you."

"What do you mean 'won't fit!' Of course it will." Taryantev interrupted, "don't you remember, I tried on your frock coat, it could have been made for me! Hey, Zakhar, Zakhar! Get in here, you old donkey!" he shouted.

Zakhar gave a bearlike growl, but did not appear. "Call him, Ilya Ilyich, I don't know who he thinks he is!" Taryantev complained.

"Zakhar!" Oblomov shouted.

Zakhar could be heard cursing from outside as his feet hit the floor.

"Well, what do you want?" he asked Taryantev.

"Bring my black tailcoat," Ilya Ilyich told him, "so that Mikhei Andreyich can try it on to see if it fits, he needs it for a wedding tomorrow."

"I won't do it!" Zakhar said flatly.

"How dare you go against your master's orders?" Taryantev shouted. "I don't know why you don't send him to the workhouse Ilya Ilyich?"

"That's all I need, to put the old man in the workhouse," said Oblomov. "The tailcoat, Zakhar, don't be obstinate!"

"I won't," Zakhar replied coldly, "not until he brings back our waistcoat—and the shirt, it's been four months now. That time he borrowed it for a nameday—and that's the last we saw of them. It's a velvet waistcoat, and the shirt's a fine Dutch cloth, it cost twenty-five roubles. I'm not giving him any tailcoat!"

"Then to hell with you, I'm off!" Taryantev said heatedly, shaking his fist at Zakhar on his way out. "And remember, Ilya Ilyich, I'm renting the apartment for you, you hear?" he added.

"Alright, alright!" Oblomov said impatiently, anything to get rid of him.

"And make sure the letters are written properly!" Taryantev continued, "don't forget to tell the governor about your twelve children—each one younger than the next." And the soup is to be on the table at five o'clock! And why didn't you order a pie?"

But Oblomov remained silent; he had long since stopped listening, and was sitting with his eyes closed thinking about something entirely different.

After Taryantev's departure, an unbroken silence filled the room for about ten minutes. Oblomov was worrying about the bailiff's letter and the impending move to a new apartment and was also exhausted by Taryantev's chatter. Finally, he sighed.

"Why don't you start writing?" Alekseyev asked quietly, "I'll get a pen ready for you."

"Yes, why don't you do that and then find yourself somewhere to go," said Oblomov. "I'll get down to it by myself and then after dinner you can copy it out."

"Yes, of course, absolutely," replied Alekseyev, "I'll only be in the way here…I'll go and tell them not to expect us in Yekaterinhof. Goodbye, Ilya Ilyich."

But Ilya Ilyich was no longer listening; he had tucked his legs underneath himself and curled up in the armchair, so that he was practically lying down and had drifted dejectedly into something between a reverie and a doze.

CHAPTER FIVE

Oblomov, a member of the nobility by birth and a Collegiate Counsellor by rank had never once left St. Petersburg in the eleven years he had been living there.

At first, while his parents were alive, he lived in rather more cramped quarters, just two rooms, and made do with the services of one servant, Zakhar, whom he had brought with him from the country. But on the death of his parents he had become the sole proprietor of three hundred and fifty souls left to him in a province so remote that it was practically in Asia.

At that point his income rose from five, to seven, to ten thousand rubles; and he was thinking of acquiring a pair of horses.

At that time, he was still young, and although it could not be said that even then he was exactly bursting with life, at least there was more life in him then than now. Then he was still full of aspirations and yearnings, he still had hopes and expected much of life and himself. He was preparing for a career, a role in the imperial civil service, which was, of course, the reason for his coming to St. Petersburg in the first place. Later he would take his place in society and ultimately, sometime in the distant future, he would pass from youth to maturity and his imagination warmed to the enticing prospect of family happiness.

But the days passed and one year followed another and the down on his cheeks turned to stubble, his eyes lost their sparkle and dimmed into two dull spots, his waist thickened and his hair remorselessly thinned. He was approaching thirty and had not made the slightest progress in any career and stood precisely where he had ten years before—in the wings of his life's theatre without setting foot on the stage. Not, of course, that he was not preparing and getting himself ready for action; he was always sketching the blueprints of his future in his mind's eye. Each year, as it flashed by, brought with it some adjustment to the grand plan. Life, as he saw it, was divided into two parts; one was work and tedium, which were synonyms in his vocabulary, and the other leisure and enjoying himself—in moderation! Consequently, the initial prospect of spending the major part of his life going to work was painfully depressing.

Raised in the heartland of provincial Russia with its warm and sheltered habits and customs, coddled for twenty years in the warm affection of family, friends and acquaintances, he was so steeped in the notion of family that he imagined even his future work in a government department to be like some kind of family activity, something like what his father did from time to time, making leisurely entries of income and outgoings in his ledger. He imagined that office colleagues were just one close, happy family constantly putting themselves out for each other's comfort and pleasure and that attendance at the office could not possibly be a kind of compulsory custom that you simply had to observe every single day and that slush, heat, or mere disinclination would be adequate and legitimate grounds for non-attendance.

Imagine his dismay on realizing that nothing short of an earthquake could excuse a healthy civil servant's absence from his place of work and that, in any case, St. Petersburg never had the good fortune to have earthquakes. No doubt a flood would also be acceptable grounds, but floods hardly ever happened there either.

Oblomov's misgivings only increased when he saw packages flashing by marked "urgent" and "extremely urgent," when he was made to write out and copy all kinds of papers and documents, rummage in files and fill writing pads as thick as your arm whimsically referred to as "notes." Everything had to be done fast, everyone was always rushing somewhere non-stop. People barely had time to finish one job before furiously grabbing another as if the fate of the world depended on it, only to dispose of it and drop it without a second thought as they launched themselves into the next job—and so on ad infinitum.

A couple of times they even got him out of bed in the middle of the night to make him write out some "notes"; at other times they sent messengers to drag him away from some party or dinner just for the sake of the same wretched "notes." The dreariness of it filled him with dread; "it doesn't leave a moment for living!" he complained.

At home, he had heard that a boss or a supervisor was a father to his subordinates and had formed an image of such a personage, an image as beaming and benign and indulgent as a member of his own family. He saw him as a kind of second father who lived and breathed only to reward his subordinates and to cater, unceasingly and unremittingly, regardless of their merits, not only to their needs but even to their pleasures. Ilya Ilyich thought that a superior was so intimately bound up in the welfare of his subordinates that he would inquire anxiously whether he had had a good night's sleep, why his eyes were a little cloudy and whether he might not have a little headache.

His first day on the job was thus a rude awakening. The moment the supervisor appeared, everyone started hustling and bustling and bumping into each other from sheer agitation, some even nervously fingering their clothing in case he might deem them not sufficiently presentable. The reason for this, as Oblomov subsequently became aware, was that in the person of a subordinate scared out of his wits and rushing to pay his respects, a certain type of boss saw not only proper respect for his person, but a mark of zealousness and indeed at times even of competence.

There was really no need for Ilya Ilyich to be afraid of his supervisor, a benign and pleasant person. He never behaved badly and his subordinates could not have been more content or wished for anything better. He was never heard to utter a harsh word or even to raise his voice; he never demanded but always asked. If he wanted you to do something, he asked; if he invited you to his house, he asked; if he had you arrested, he asked. He never used the familiar form of the personal pronoun "you," but always the respectful plural, whether he was addressing an individual or the whole office staff.

But, somehow his subordinates were still intimidated in his presence; if he asked them a friendly question, they found themselves answering in an unnatural voice that did not really belong to them and that they never used with other people.

Ilya Ilyich, too, was immediately intimidated without really knowing why; whenever the boss entered the room and the moment the boss addressed him, he would find that his natural voice had been replaced by something nauseatingly insipid.

At work, Oblomov was tormented by fear and tedium even under a decent and indulgent boss. God knows what would have become of him if his boss had turned out to be a martinet and taskmaster.

Oblomov somehow served out a couple of years of office life and might just have stretched it out for a third until he became eligible for promotion, if a particular incident had not precipitated his early departure.

Once he sent an urgent document to Archangel instead of Astrakhan. The error came to light and an investigation was started to find the culprit. All the others awaited with curiosity Oblomov's inevitable summons to the boss's office and his cold and calm question: "Were you the one who sent this document to Archangel?" They could not wait to see how Oblomov would respond. Some were of the view that he would not be able to bring himself to say anything at all. The reaction of the others terrified Oblomov, even though he and they knew that the boss would do nothing more than reprimand him. In fact, his own conscience punished him much more severely.

Instead of waiting to face the music, Oblomov went home and sent in a medical certificate. It read as follows: "I, the undersigned, certify and hereto set my seal, that Collegiate Secretary, Ilya Oblomov, is suffering from enlargement of the heart accompanied by dilation of its left ventricle (hypertrophia cordis cum dilatatione ejus ventriculi sinistri) as well as chronic liver pain (hepatitis), which pose a serious threat to the health and life of the patient. It is my opinion that these symptoms are caused by the patient's daily attendance at his place of work and indeed from mental and physical exertion of any kind."

This, of course, would only put off the evil hour; he would have to recover eventually and face the prospect of going back to work—every day! This was something Oblomov could not face and he sent in his resignation. Thus ended once and for all Oblomov's career in governmental service—a career never to be resumed.

His social prospects seemed at first more promising. For his first few years in St. Petersburg when he was still in the first flush of youth, his placid features would light up more frequently and his eyes would sparkle with life, transmitting hope and energy. He experienced emotions, and like anyone else his hopes could be raised or dashed by the merest trifles and his mood would swing from elation to despair.

But all this was now well behind him and belonged to those tender years when a man looks on every other man he meets as a potential bosom friend and falls in love with almost every woman, ready to offer her his heart and hand at the drop of a hat. In some cases this offer is actually accepted, often to the lifelong bitter regret of the parties.

In those blissful days, Oblomov too enjoyed his share of tender, melting, even passionate glances darting out from a bevy of young beauties. He reaped a whole harvest of significant smiles and even two or three stolen kisses and even more friendly hand-clasps that moved him to tears.

It must be said that Oblomov never allowed himself to be captivated or enslaved by these beauties or even to become an assiduous admirer, if only because of the trouble involved in establishing such close relations. No, Oblomov preferred to worship from afar, at a respectable distance.

On rare occasions, his social rounds would bring him into contact with a woman close enough to arouse his ardour and imagine himself to be in love for a few days. But these romantic episodes never blossomed into full-fledged affairs; they never got beyond the first stages, because Oblomov's feelings were as pure and chaste as the romantic dreams of an innocent schoolgirl.

He was particularly careful to avoid the pale "damsel in distress" type, usually with dark eyes hinting glisteningly at "tormented days and harrowing nights." These tragic young ladies of unfathomable sorrows and joys always had something to confide and to unburden; but when the time came to unburden, they would shudder, tears would well up in their eyes and suddenly their arms were wrapped around their companion's neck. They would look deep and long into his eyes and then up into the heavens and tell him that their lives were cursed and doomed and sometimes even faint in his arms.

He avoided these young ladies like the plague. His heart was still pure and virginal, and had perhaps been awaiting its love, its moment, its stirring of passion, but now, with the passing of the years, may have stopped waiting and had given up hope.

Ilya Ilyich parted even more coldly with his host of friends. Immediately after he had received the first letter from his bailiff about the arrears and the failed harvest, he brought in a woman to cook for him, to replace his first friend, the cook; next he sold his horses and finally dropped the rest of his "friends."

He became virtually housebound and with every passing day became more and more firmly and irretrievably immured within the four walls of his apartment.

At the beginning, he started to feel uncomfortable spending the whole day fully dressed, then he could not be bothered to go out to dinner except to the homes of recent acquaintances, mostly bachelors, where he could take off his tie, unbutton his waistcoat and even lie down and take a little nap.

Soon, even these evenings out became too much for him because it meant having to dress for dinner and shave every day. He read somewhere that only the morning air was healthy and that the evening air harmful and he started worrying about the damp.

In spite of all these foibles, his friend Stoltz managed to get him out of the house to visit people, but Stoltz was often away in Moscow, Nizhny, the Crimea, and later even abroad. In his absence, Oblomov buried himself totally in this solitude and isolation and nothing could pry him out of it except some really out-of-the-way event that departed drastically from his daily routine; but nothing like this ever happened or even seemed ever likely to happen.

On top of all this, as the years passed, the timorousness of Oblomov's childhood gradually returned and he saw or suspected danger or something sinister in anything outside the narrow sphere of his daily life because he had lost contact with outside life in all its varied manifestations.

The crack in his bedroom ceiling, for example, held no terror for him because he was used to it; nor did it ever occur to him that his sedentary existence within the four walls of his stuffy room with its stagnant air was just as bad for his health as the damp night air outside or that stuffing his belly every day was a kind of slow suicide. No, these were things he was used to, so they did not worry him.

What he could not get used to were movement, life, large groups of people and agitation of any kind. In crowds he could not breathe; if he sat in a boat he was gripped by anxiety about reaching the other shore safely and if he rode in a carriage he half expected the horses to bolt and crash into something.

At other times he would suffer anxiety attacks. He would suddenly be afraid of the silence around him; or for no reason at all his flesh would creep. Sometimes he would glance fearfully at a dark corner out of the side of his eye, half expecting that his imagination would play tricks on him and conjure up some supernatural spectacle.

In this way he gradually exited from the social scene altogether. Lazily, he waved good-bye to the hopes of his youth that had remained unfulfilled—perhaps because he himself had failed to fulfill them—as well as all those bittersweet, glowing memories, which even in later years can still make the hearts of some beat faster.

CHAPTER SIX

What did he do all day at home? Read? Write? Study? Well, yes, if he chanced upon a book or a newspaper he would pick it up and take a look. If he heard about some remarkable book, he would get the urge to see it and would try to get it or ask around for it and if someone brought it to him soon enough, he would sit down with it and begin to get an idea of what it was about, and even come within an ace of finishing it; but the next thing you know, there he would be lying down, staring vacantly at the ceiling with the book lying beside him unfinished and undigested like a half-eaten meal. He began to find giving things up much easier than taking them up, and a book once discarded, stayed discarded.

Of course, he had gone to school like anyone else, that is to say he attended a private boarding school until he was fifteen; then Oblomov's parents decided after lengthy debate to send him to Moscow where he somehow actually managed to complete his studies.

His timorous and passive nature inhibited him from revealing to others the true extent of his laziness and self-indulgence in a school where no allowances were made for the pampered darlings of doting parents. So he simply had no choice but to sit up straight in class and pay attention to his teachers and reluctantly force himself, groaning and sighing, to learn his lessons. All of this he looked upon as a kind of punishment imposed by some heavenly power for the sins of the world. He stopped reading strictly at the point in the text where the teacher had scored a line with his thumbnail; he asked no questions and required no explanations. He confined himself strictly to what was written on the page and exhibited no tiresome curiosity whatsoever even when there was something he did not understand. If he ever managed to struggle through a book on statistics, history or political economy, the achievement was enough to leave him feeling thoroughly satisfied.

Whenever Stoltz brought him books whose contents went beyond what he had already learned, Oblomov would look at him silently and then sighing, "Et tu Brute!" would apply himself to the books. Such excessive reading struck him as cruel and unusual.

Why all these notebooks, which only use up a vast amount of paper, time and ink? Why all these textbooks? Why, indeed, seven or eight years confined like a hermit, why all that discipline, punishment and being forced to sit toiling over lessons—no running around, no playing about, no fun—while there was still time? "What about time for living?" he asked himself again and again. " When am I going to have a chance to use all that knowledge I've accumulated, most of which in any case is going to be useless for my purposes? What am I going to do with political economy, algebra or geometry, of all things, in Oblomovka?"

As for history, it just depresses you; you read and you learn about troubles and disasters; people are miserable, they struggle, they toil, there is a ferment of activity, terrible hardship is endured and people work and strive for better days. And when these days come, you would think, now, finally, history can take a rest; not at all, the dark clouds roll in, the whole structure collapses and once again the cycle of work and frenetic activity begins all over again…The good times never last, they flash by—and life passes leaving destruction in its wake.

Serious reading was too much for him. The deepest thinkers failed to stimulate in him any appetite for abstract truths.

Poetry, on the other hand, really touched a nerve in Oblomov. He was suddenly young again, like the rest of the world. He too was possessed by that moment in life when happiness never fails, when life smiles on you, when your powers are at their height, your hopes are high, you reach for the noble, the heroic; it is a time when your heart beats faster, your pulse races, your emotions surge, your rhetoric is passionate, and your tears are sweet. His mind and heart were bright and clear; he had cast off dull sloth and was athirst for action.

Stoltz did his best to keep those moments alive—to the extent consistent with the temperament of his friend. Catching Oblomov under the spell of poets, he managed to sustain his interest in the things of the mind and culture for well over a year.

Seizing on the soaring flights of Oblomov's youthful dreams, Stoltz showed him that poetry was not just to be enjoyed, but had other purposes, and he harnessed its momentum to drive Oblomov towards the distant goals of both their lives, and directed his imagination firmly towards the future. They were stirred, they wept, and solemnly promised each other to tread the path of reason and enlightenment. Oblomov was infected by Stoltz's youthful enthusiasm, and was seized by a burning desire to work and strive for a distant but beckoning goal.

But his youth withered on the vine without bearing fruit. Oblomov became jaded and only rarely—and only when prompted by Stoltz—read a book, and not all at once, but slowly and listlessly, and lazily skimming the pages. No matter how interesting the place he had reached, if it was time to eat or sleep, the book would immediately be abandoned, open at that page and face down, while he went to the table or put out the light and went to sleep.

If he was given the first volume of a work, after he had read it, he never bothered to ask for volume two; and if someone brought it, he would read it, but slowly.

As time went by, even getting through the first volume became too much for him and he spent most of his time with his elbow on the table and his head propped on his hand, although sometimes instead of his elbow he propped his head on the very book Stoltz wanted him to read.

Thus ended Oblomov's educational career, and the date on which he attended his last lecture became the Pillars of Hercules marking the outer limits of his erudition. The head of the institution at which he had studied, by affixing his signature to his diploma in the same way that his teacher at school had scored a line on the page with his thumbnail, had marked a boundary that our hero had no inclination to cross in a quest for further learning.

His brain was an archive, honeycombed with defunct events, persons, epochs, figures, religions, and totally irrelevant political, economic, mathematical and other axioms, problems and propositions. It was a kind of library with tomes on all the various branches of knowledge stacked randomly on its shelves.

All this knowledge had a strange effect on Oblomov. Between this academic baggage and real life there yawned a vast chasm that he made no attempt to bridge. Life was one thing and his academically acquired knowledge an entirely separate thing.

He had studied every existing system of law, as well as those which had long since ceased to exist, and had taken courses in legal practice and the administration of justice, but when it came to reporting a burglary to the police, he would sit pondering over a sheet of paper with his pen in his hand and end up sending for a professional scribe.

On his estate in the country it was the bailiff who kept the books. "What help is all this mathematics?" he wondered in his perplexity.

So he returned to his seclusion without the burden of knowledge that might have given some direction to his idle musings or the thoughts flitting randomly through his head.

So what *did* he do? Well, he continued to draft the blueprint of his life, and in it he found so much wisdom and poetry that there was absolutely no need of book learning. Having turned his back on a career and society, he began to take a different approach to the problem of existence. As he reflected on the meaning and purpose of his life he began to realize that the horizons of his day-to-day existence lay within himself. He realized that fate had assigned him two functions in life: family happiness and taking care of his estate. Hitherto he had not had much of a grip on his affairs; it was Stoltz who took care of things for him from time to time. He did not even have any real idea of his income or expenditures and had never tried to work out a budget.

Old Oblomov had passed on the estate to his son just as he had inherited it from his own father. Although he had lived his whole life in the country on the estate, he had never given it a second thought, never bothered about new schemes or plans the way people do nowadays. He never tried to devise new ways of generating income from his land or even of increasing the productivity of traditional agricultural methods. Whatever crops and farming practices, whatever methods of marketing his produce had been good enough for his grandfather, were good enough for him. And if a harvest was particularly good or there was a rise in prices that brought in a higher income than the year before, the old man was very happy and looked upon it as God's blessing; but the idea of actually planning or striving for extra income went against his grain.

"Our fathers and grandfathers were not stupid," he would say when people offered what he judged to be bad advice, "and they lived contented lives just as we will and, with God's help, keep our bellies full." Since the estate, without any tricks or contrivances, produced enough income to put more than enough food on the table every day at dinner and supper to feed his family as well as their various guests, he just thanked God and would have thought it sinful to strive for more.

If the bailiff brought him two thousand, and kept the other thousand in his own pocket, tearfully invoking hail, drought or a poor harvest to account for the shortfall, old Oblomov would just cross himself and say, "It's the will of God and we just have to accept it and be grateful to Him for what we have."

After the death of Oblomov's parents, the finances of the estate, far from improving, actually took a turn for the worse, as is clear from the bailiff's letter, and it was clear that Ilya Ilyich's presence was required to determine the reason for the persistent decline in income.

He kept on meaning to go, but kept on putting it off, because, among other reasons, the journey itself was such a vast and daunting enterprise, a virtually novel and unfamiliar adventure.

Only once in his life had he undertaken such a journey, going for long stretches at a time accompanied by bedding, chests, suitcases, ham-hocks, loaves of bread, roast and boiled meats, poultry of every description, and a retinue of servants.

This was the style in which he had traveled the one and only time up from the country to Moscow, and he regarded this as the norm for a journey of any kind, although he had heard that nowadays people did not travel like that any longer, but galloped at breakneck speed. There was also another reason for putting off his journey: he was not yet entirely prepared to deal properly with his affairs.

Unlike his father and grandfather, he had gone out into the world and received an education and therefore entertained ideas that would never have occurred to them. He understood that not only was acquisition no sin; but that it was the duty of every citizen to sustain the welfare of society as a whole by honest labor. Hence the blueprint of his life, which he had drafted in his seclusion, consisted principally of a new and original plan, in keeping with the requirements of the time, for the organization of the estate and the management of his workforce.

The broad outlines of the plan, the layout and main sections had long been ready—in his head; it remained only to fill in the details, estimates and figures.

He had been working tirelessly on the plan for years, thinking, pondering, whether walking around or lying down, and even while he was a guest in people's homes, adding a detail here, removing a detail there, trying to recall something he had thought of the day before and forgotten during the night. Sometimes such a thought would flash unbidden into his mind and the ferment in his head would trigger off a new bout of creative effort.

He was not just some petty functionary dutifully carrying out someone else's ready-made ideas, but the creator and executor of his own.

The moment he rose in the morning, he would drink his tea and immediately lie down on the divan with his head propped on his hand and start thinking hard and relentlessly until, exhausted from the intensity of the effort, his conscience would tell him that he had toiled enough for the common good for one day. Only then would he permit himself to rest from his labors and to switch from a posture of frowning concentration, to a less businesslike and rigorous one, which gave a freer rein to idle daydreaming and relaxation. Once he had freed himself from his workaday cares and responsibilities, Oblomov liked nothing better than to withdraw into himself and to a world of his own creation.

He gave himself up to the delights of his soaring fancies, although by no means oblivious to the universal woes of mankind. Deep in his soul he wept at times for the calamities afflicting his fellow men and felt the pangs of ineffable, nameless suffering and a longing and yearning for something out of reach in the great beyond, perhaps in that very world that Stoltz used to invite him to enter—and sweet tears would trickle down his cheeks.

At other times, he would be filled with contempt for the vices of man, for the lying, the malice, the evil that permeated the world, and he would conceive a burning desire to confront mankind with its sins. Suddenly thoughts would be sparked and seethe to and fro like waves in a boisterous sea, then they would harden into intentions, set his very blood aflame; his muscles would flex, and his veins stand out, and the intentions grow into fierce determination. In the grip of this powerful moral force, he would shift his position two or three times a minute and, with eyes blazing, would find himself actually sitting up with his arm outstretched, his eyes sweeping around, carried away by his enthusiasm; at that instant, what he had willed so vividly was on the very point of triumphant consummation—and then, by God, what marvels, what tremendous good would result from such heroic efforts!

But, in a flash, the morning has passed and the day is waning towards evening; Oblomov's energies too are on the wane until, exhausted, he subsides and rests from his labors. The turmoil and agitation of his thoughts die away, his fevered brain calms down and his blood slows in his veins. Oblomov turns quietly and reflectively onto his back and focussing his gaze sadly on the window and through it the sky, sorrowfully follows the sun as it sets majestically behind his neighbor's four-story house—just as he has done so many, many times before!

It is morning again, and time for his imagination to go to work and the day-dreaming to begin. In his dreams of glory he sometimes sees himself as a conquering hero, beside whom not only Napoleon but even Yeruslan Lazarevich pales into insignificance. He fantasizes wars and the causes of war; he sees whole peoples pouring into Europe from Africa; he is masterminding new Crusades. He is on the rampage, determining the fate of nations, destroying cities in his path, mercifully sparing lives here, ruthlessly putting others to the sword there, and scaling the heights of benevolence and magnanimity. Or perhaps he chooses the role of philosopher or artist; he sweeps all before him, laurels and honors are heaped upon him, crowds follow him exclaiming, "Look, look it's Oblomov himself, the one and only Ilya Ilyich!"

There are bad times when he is gripped by anxiety; he tosses and turns and lies face down until he can stand it no more and kneels on the bed and starts to pray hard and fervently to heaven to spare him from the gathering storm. Once he has placed his fate in the hands of the Almighty, he feels perfectly at ease and indifferent to the world and everything in it, no matter what havoc the storm chooses to wreak.

This then is the way Oblomov expended all his nervous energy, and spent whole days in a ferment of agitation and only ever surfaced with a deep sigh from his delightful reverie or the throes of his anxiety towards evening as the vast disk of the sun sank in all its glory behind the four-story house. Then with pensive gaze and a wistful smile he would follow its descent, and his tranquility would be restored after the turbulence of the day.

No one witnessed or knew of this inner life of Ilya Ilyich. Everyone thought that Oblomov just lay around eating whatever he wanted whenever he felt like it and that was all there was to him, and that he barely had two thoughts to rub together. And this was the impression shared by all who knew him.

Every detail of his abilities, of the volcanic workings of his fevered imagination and the kindness of his heart were well known to and could have been attested to by Stoltz, but Stoltz was hardly ever in St. Petersburg. Zakhar alone, having spent his whole life by his master's side, was more intimately acquainted than anyone with his inner life, but he was convinced that he and his master were simply going about their business and living their lives in the most normal way possible and that no other way of life was conceivable.

CHAPTER SEVEN

Zakhar was over fifty. He was not exactly your typical faithful retainer of the old Russian school, one of those legendary knights of the servants' hall, a "*chevalier sans peur et sans reproche*," impeccable in deportment and behavior and selflessly devoted to the service of his masters—the very paragon of all the virtues and entirely without flaw.

Zakhar's bearing and behavior were anything but impeccable and left much to be desired in both the "fear" and the "reproach" departments. He belonged to two traditions and both had left their marks on him. From the first tradition he had inherited a boundless devotion to the house of Oblomov and from the second, more recent tradition a certain sophistication and a loosening of moral standards.

Fiercely devoted to his master though he was, rarely a day went by without his lying to him about something or other. A servant of the old tradition would do his best to curb extravagance and excess on his master's part; Zakhar, on the other hand, enjoyed having a drink with his cronies at his master's expense. Your old-style servant was as chaste as a eunuch, while Zakhar was always running off to see a certain female acquaintance of doubtful reputation. Your old- style servant guarded his master's money more securely than a locked safe, while Zakhar, whenever he was sent on an errand, always contrived to pocket a few pennies for himself and never neglected an opportunity to appropriate any small change he saw lying around on the table. In the same way, if ever Oblomov forgot to ask Zakhar for the change, it would never find its way back into his possession.

He drew the line at more significant sums, perhaps because his needs could all be measured in pennies or simply to avoid attracting attention, but certainly not from an excess of scruples. Your old faithful retainer, like a well-trained hunting dog, would die sooner than so much as lay a finger on any foodstuff placed in his charge, while Zakhar was constantly on the lookout for a chance of wolfing down any food or guzzling any drink he could lay his hands on. The only thought of the one was to see that his master got as much as possible to eat and would feel badly if his master did not eat, while the other would feel badly if his master finished up every last scrap on his plate.

On top of it all, Zakhar was a blabbermouth. In the kitchen, in the village store, in the sessions at the gate with his cronies he would complain every day about his miserable existence; the world had never known such a bad master; capricious, stingy and bad-tempered, there was absolutely no pleasing him; in short, a dog's life and he'd be better off dead.

Zakhar did not do this out of malice, nor did he wish his master ill, but just from force of habit inherited from his father and grandfather—that of neglecting no suitable opportunity to revile their masters. Sometimes to revive a flagging conversation or when he ran out of material, or simply to entertain his audience, he would invent an entirely fictitious story about his master. "Mine keeps going around to see this widow," he would say, lowering his voice to a confidential wheeze, "yesterday he wrote to her." Or he would announce that his master was a gambler and a drunkard the like of which had never been known and stayed up till all hours at the card table—and drinking himself under it. But there was not a word of truth in all this: Ilya Ilyich never visited any widows and spent his nights sleeping peacefully and had never held a card in his hand.

Zakhar was scruffy and unkempt. He rarely shaved, although he did wash his hands and face, or at least went through the motions, and in any case the soap had not been invented with which you could wash them clean. Even when he went to the bathhouse and the dirt disappeared from his hands exposing the red skin beneath, they were black again within a couple of hours.

He was very clumsy; if he tried to open the gates or the double doors, one side would swing shut, while he was opening the other and while he ran to stop it the first side would swing back.

When a handkerchief or something fell on the floor he never managed to pick it up on the first try; he would stoop and miss it a few times and, if he was lucky, managed to grab it on the fourth attempt, and even then was as likely as not to drop it again.

If he carried dishes, crockery, or other objects across the room, the ones on top would begin to abandon ship, sliding off the tray the moment he took his first step. As the first one went over the side, he would make a belated and futile movement in an attempt to stop it and two more would go and fall off. He would watch the falling objects, his mouth agape with astonishment, instead of keeping his eyes on the ones that still remained on the tray that he was holding tilted, so that they too continued to slide off onto the floor. Sometimes he would reach the other side of the room with only one last glass or plate remaining and even that he would sometimes hurl to the floor to the accompaniment of oaths and curses. He could not cross the room without tripping over or bumping into a table or a chair, or even get through the open half of the double door without hitting the other with his shoulder, whereupon he would heap recriminations on both halves or the landlord or even the carpenter who built the door. Nearly everything in Oblomov's study, especially delicate objects that need to be handled with care, was broken or damaged, thanks to Zakhar's attentions.

Everything he touched received exactly the same treatment; he made no distinctions and exercised no discrimination. If he were told to snuff out a candle or pour a glass of water, he would use as much force as he would for pushing open the gates.

But God help us whenever Zakhar, fired up with zeal to please his master, would suddenly take it into his head to undertake a wholesale spring cleaning operation there and then and turn the whole apartment upside down. It was utter devastation—as if an invading army had stormed through the apartment and laid it waste. Furniture was broken, ornaments and other objects crashed to the floor, crockery was smashed, chairs were overturned and in the end Zakhar had to be driven from the room, that is if he had not already stormed out himself, leaving the room ringing with a string of curses and profanities. Happily, such attacks of zeal were few and far between.

The reason for all this was, of course, that he had been brought up and learned his ways, not in the stuffy, curtained atmosphere of luxuriously and exquisitely appointed drawing rooms and boudoirs crowded with expensive bric-à-brac, but in the country with its quiet, space, and open air.

It was there that he had served his apprenticeship, where everything was big and solid and there was no need to inhibit his movements. There he got used to working with solid, robust tools; spades, crowbars and the like; there the doors were mounted on cast iron brackets, and the chairs were too heavy to shift.

A candlestick, a lamp, a picture, or a paperweight would have been where it was for three or even four years and suddenly, if Zakhar so much as picked it up, there it was, smashed to smithereens.

Sometimes when this happened he would turn to Oblomov, in astonishment and say, "would you believe it, sir, all I did was pick the thing up and it just fell apart?" Or else, he would just say nothing and just put it quickly back in its place and then assure his master that it was he himself who had broken it; at other times he would argue, as we saw him do at the beginning of this story—that everything must come to an end sometime and that nothing lasts forever, even if it is made of iron.

Against his first and second line of defense you could at least put up an argument, but when he resorted to this third, ultimate, ironclad defense, recriminations were useless, his logic invincible.

At some time in the past Zakhar had laid down prescribed limits to the range of his activities, which in no circumstance would he exceed of his own free will.

In the morning he would put on the samovar, clean the boots and whatever other articles of clothing his master had specifically told him to clean, but in no circumstances would he touch anything not specifically requested, even if it had been gathering dust for ten years. Then he would sweep, but not every day, mind you, the center of the room, stopping short at the corners and, to save himself the trouble of actually removing things, would only dust a table with nothing on it. After that, he felt fully entitled to lie down on his bunk and doze off, or chat with Anisya in the kitchen or the gatekeeper out in the courtyard without a care in the world.

If he was ordered to do something over and above this, he would perform the task grudgingly and only after a big argument and protesting that the task was unnecessary and in any case impossible to carry out.

There was no way in the world anyone could force him to add any new permanent item whatsoever to his self-ordained work agenda. If he was told to clean or wash some item or other or fetch and carry something, he would usually do it, grumbling as he went, but if anyone tried to make the task part of his standing orders, there was no way of making it happen. The next day, and the day after, and the day after that, you would have to tell him over and over again to do the very same thing and each time go through the same tedious and acrimonious routine rigmarole.

For all this—Zakhar's drinking, his slanderous gossiping, his petty pilfering, the damage and breakages and his minimalist work habits—the fact remained that he was a servant deeply devoted to his master.

He would have gone through fire and water for his master without a second thought and it would never have occurred to him that there was anything heroic or amazing or even especially meritorious about it. If he had thought about it he would have regarded it as an entirely natural act, something that went without saying, but, of course, he did not think about it or "regard" it as anything; there were no "why's and wherefores," it was just something he did.

He was not given to theorizing on the subject and indeed the idea of analysing his feelings about or relations with Ilya Ilyich never entered his head; they were not of his own making, he had simply inherited them from his father, his grandfather, his brothers, and the household servants among whom he had been born and raised, and they had become second nature to him.

Zakhar would have given his life for his master, seeing it as a duty as inevitable as it was natural. He would simply not have given it a second thought, any more than a dog when it meets a wild beast in the woods and springs at it, would ponder the reasons why it should not be the master, rather than the dog, who does the springing.

However, when it came to sitting up all night at his master's bedside to keep watch over him, that was another matter entirely, even if his master's health or, for that matter, his very life depended on it, nothing could keep him from nodding off.

On the surface, Zakhar showed no sign of deference towards his master; in fact his manner was familiar and even abrasive. He would get angry with him over the slightest thing and was not afraid of showing it and, as we have seen, would complain bitterly about him to his cronies at the gate, but this would merely—and temporarily—overshadow, but in no way detract from the visceral feelings of devotion that ran in his blood, feelings not so much towards Ilya Ilyich as such, as towards anything that bore the name of Oblomov, a name that meant the world to him and that he cherished and held dear.

This feeling may have been hard to reconcile with Zakhar's actual opinion of Oblomov as a person and it may well have been that careful consideration of his master's character put quite different thoughts in Zakhar's mind. Probably, if someone had pointed out to Zakhar the depth of his attachment to Ilya Ilyich, his reaction would have been to deny it.

Zakhar loved Oblomovka the way a cat loves its box, a horse its stable, and a dog its kennel, the way any creature loves the place where it was born and raised; but within the framework of this attachment he had over time developed his own specific and personal preferences.

For example, he liked the Oblomovs' coachman better than the cook, and the dairy-maid, Varvara, better than either of them, and he liked Ilya Ilyich even less than any of them; but for all that, to him the Oblomovs' cook was the number one cook in the whole world and Ilya Ilyich the world's top member of the landed gentry. He could not stand Taraska, the footman, but would not exchange him for the best the world had to offer simply because Taraska was an Oblomov man. He treated Oblomov with familiarity and even rudeness in the same way that a witch doctor treats his juju. He dusts it, drops it, and sometimes even knocks it about when he is annoyed, but deep down he is always conscious that he is in the presence of a being of an entirely higher order.

It took very little to summon up this feeling from the depths of Zakhar's being, compelling him to regard his master with awe, and the strength of his emotion moving him at times to tears. God forbid that he should even think of any other gentleman as his master's equal, let alone his superior, and God forbid that such an idea should even enter anyone else's head. There was a hint of disdain in Zakhar's attitude to all the other gentlemen of Oblomov's acquaintance who called on him, and whenever he served them tea or anything, he did so with a certain condescension, as if to convey to them what a great honor it was for them to be received by his master. He would rebuff them unceremoniously. "The master is resting," he would say haughtily looking them up and down.

Sometimes, instead of the usual backbiting and malicious gossip, he would take to lauding his master to the skies in the shops and at the gatherings at the gate and at these times his praise knew no bounds. He would then proceed to enumerate his master's virtues; his intelligence, his good nature, his generosity, his kindness, and if his master should not happen to possess some of the virtues needed to complete the panegyric, he would borrow them from others and endow him with distinction, wealth, and extraordinary power and influence.

If he ever wanted to put the gatekeeper, the building superintendent, or even the owner himself in their places, he would threaten them with his master: "just you wait, I'm going to tell my master," he would warn them, "then you'll be in for it!" He could not conceive of any more powerful authority figure on God's earth.

Yet somehow there was always an edge of friction to the outward relations between Oblomov and Zakhar. Because of the intimacy in which they lived they got on each other's nerves. Intimate daily contact between people inevitably has its effect, and both parties need a great deal of maturity, good sense and good will if they are to make the most of each other virtues and to avoid needling—and being needled—by each other's faults.

If there was one pure and undiluted virtue of Zakhar's of which Oblomov had no doubt, it was his boundless devotion to himself; he was used to it and had come to take it utterly for granted, so much so, that he had long since ceased appreciating it as a plus or something to Zakhar's credit, so that in the context of his indifference to everything around him, he was unable to make the slightest allowance for, or put up with, Zakhar's innumerable petty faults or shortcomings.

Now, while Zakhar harboured deep in his heart the devotion to his master characteristic of an older generation of servants, he differed from them in sharing the faults of the current generation, Ilya Ilyich, for his part, although deep down he welcomed this devotion, was no longer capable of responding with that warmth and family feeling with which an earlier generation of masters had treated their servants, and sometimes really lost his temper with Zakhar.

Zakhar also found his master difficult to take. In his youth he had served his apprenticeship as a household servant and was then promoted to be Ilya Ilyich's personal attendant. From that time on, Zakhar had grown to regard himself not so much as a necessity, but exclusively as a luxury item, an aristocratic appurtenance whose sole purpose was to maintain and enhance the standing and glitter of the ancient house of Oblomov. Accordingly, apart from dressing the young master in the morning and undressing him in the evening, he did absolutely nothing the rest of the time.

Lazy by nature, his apprenticeship as a household servant made him even lazier. With the other servants he gave himself airs and did not trouble himself to set up the samovar or dust the shelves. He either dozed in the hallway or went to the servants' hall or the kitchen to chat; otherwise he would stand for hours at the gate with his arms folded, drowsily watching the world go by. So you can imagine what it was like for him after a regime like this suddenly to find himself saddled with the tremendous burden of taking care of a whole household, dancing attendance on his master, sweeping, cleaning, even running errands! It was this that had soured him, making him testy and bad-tempered and it was because of this that he started grumbling whenever the sound of his master's voice roused him from his resting place in the bunk over the stove.

The fact was, however, that under Zakhar's sullen and surly surface there beat a heart that was really quite soft and kind. He even liked to spend time with small children and at the gate or in the courtyard he could often be seen surrounded by a crowd of them. He would pacify them, tease them, play games or just sit with a child on each knee while another little rascal would throw his arms around his neck from behind or tousle his whiskers.

Oblomov constantly interfered with Zakhar's life by his incessant demands for his services and attentions when Zakhar's every instinct, his sociable temperament, his love of idleness and his constant, insatiable craving for chin-wagging were all tugging him in the direction of his lady friend, the kitchen, the shop, or the gate.

They had known each other and had lived together side by side for almost as long as they could remember. Zakhar had dandled the infant Oblomov on his knee, while Oblomov remembered Zakhar as a nimble, sly youth with a tremendous appetite. Time had forged indissoluble bonds between them. Just as Ilya Ilyich could not imagine getting up, going to bed, getting washed or dressed or getting fed without Zakhar's help, so Zakhar could not imagine serving any other master but Ilya Ilyich or any other way of life but that of dressing, feeding, abusing, cheating and lying to him—none of which affected his deep, underlying feelings of veneration towards him.

CHAPTER EIGHT

After closing the door behind Tarantyev and Alekseyev as they left, Zakhar did not go and sit on his bunk because he could hear his master getting ready to start writing and he expected to be summoned at any moment. In Oblomov's study, however, there was nothing but dead silence. Zakhar peered through a crack only to see Ilya Ilyich lying down on the divan with his head resting on his hand and the book lying in front of him.

Zakhar opened the door. "Lying down again?" he asked.

"Don't bother me, can't you see I'm reading?" said Oblomov curtly.

"It's time to get washed and start writing," Zakhar persisted.

"Yes, it really is," said Oblomov, snapping out of his reverie. "Leave me alone now, I need to think!"

"How did he manage to get lying down again so quickly," Zakhar muttered to himself, jumping up onto his bunk, "he can move fast when he wants to!"

Oblomov did actually manage to finish reading the age-yellowed page of the book where he had stopped reading a month ago, before putting the book down, yawning and giving himself over to his gnawing anxiety over his "twin misfortunes."

"It's so tiresome," he whispered, alternately stretching and bending his leg.

He started drifting off into a blissful reverie, lifting his eyes up to search the skies for his favorite celestial body, but it was at its zenith, bathing with its blinding rays the stone wall of the house behind which Oblomov liked to watch it go down in the evenings.

"No," he mentally reproached himself, "first I have work to do, perhaps later…"

In the country, the morning was long past and in St. Petersburg it was already ending. A medley of human voices and other sounds reach Oblomov's ears from outside in the courtyard; the singing of strolling entertainers mingled mostly with the barking of dogs. Some creature from the sea was being exhibited and all kinds of products and wares were being hawked in a chorus of discordant voices. He turned on to his back and placed both hands behind his head. Ilya Ilyich was at work on his plan for the estate. He swiftly reviewed in his mind some important and fundamental issues connected with the quit rent system and the ploughing; he devised new and stricter measures to combat idleness and vagrancy among the peasants and then started on planning his own lifestyle in the country. First, he concentrated on the building of his country house, dwelling with satisfaction for several minutes on the layout of the rooms and the dimensions of the dining room and the billiard room, then he considered the matter of the direction that the windows of his study should face and even took time to reflect on the question of furniture and carpets.

Then he turned his attention to the matter of an additional wing to the house, bearing in mind the number of guests he would be entertaining, taking care to provide space for the stables, barns, servants quarters, and various other facilities.

Finally, he took up the question of the garden; he decided to leave all the lime and oak trees as they were, cut down the apple and pear trees and plant acacia in their place. He thought for a moment of planning for a park, but after mentally estimating the cost, concluded that it would exceed his budget, decided to defer the matter and took up the matter of the flower gardens and greenhouses. At that moment, there flashed into his mind the captivating image of the fruit that would grow there, a picture so vivid that his mind leapt forward through time and he actually saw himself several years later living permanently in the country after all his plans for the estate had come to fruition.

He saw himself sitting out on the terrace of a summer's evening at the tea table under a canopy of trees that blotted out the sun, lazily puffing at a long pipe and, amid the cool and tranquility of the evening, quietly enjoying the view through the trees, while in the distance over the yellowing fields the sun was setting behind the old birch woods and spreading a rosy blush over the mirror-like surface of the pond; a haze was rising from the fields, a chill was in the air, dusk was beginning to fall and droves of peasants were wending their way homewards.

The servants were sitting by the gate taking their ease; there was the sound of light-hearted banter, the strumming of a balalaika, little girls were playing tag, his little ones were romping around him, climbing on his knee, clinging to his neck and, presiding at the samovar, the queen of this whole universe, his goddess…his woman, his wife! Meanwhile, in the dining room, decorated with elegant simplicity, the lights were glowing brightly and invitingly and the great round table was being set. Zakhar, now promoted to majordomo, his whiskers now completely gray, was preparing the table, setting the places with silverware, the wineglasses tinkling as he placed them, and tumblers and forks slipping constantly from his fingers to he floor.

Then they were sitting down to an abundant supper. Beside him sat his childhood friend and inseparable companion, Stoltz, and around the table a circle of familiar faces; then it was time for bed…Oblomov's face was suffused with a ruddy glow of happiness; his daydream was so real, so vivid, so lyrical that for a moment he pressed his face into the cushion. He was suddenly overcome by a wave of longing for love, for a tranquil happiness, a yearning for the fields and hillsides of his youth, for his home, for a wife and children…

He lay face down for five minutes and then slowly turned over onto his back again. His face glowed with gentle, tender feeling—it was happiness. He stretched his legs slowly and langorously causing his trouser legs to ride up his calves but he was oblivious to this minor sartorial embarrassment; his obliging fancy was wafting him clear and free, far into the future. Now he was absorbed in his favorite fantasy; he was seeing the little circle of friends who would settle in farms and hamlets within a radius of fifteen or twenty versts from his own village and would take it in turns to visit each other every day for dinner, for supper, for dancing; he saw nothing but sun-filled days, beaming faces, free of cares and wrinkles, round smiling faces, cheeks rosy with health, double chins, and healthy appetites; there would be endless summer, unflagging good humor and high spirits, and the food as delectable as the leisure to enjoy it.

"God, oh, God!" he exclaimed, overwhelmed with happiness, and woke up. Outside, five discordant voices were stridently crying their wares: "Potatoes! Sand! Get your sand here! Please donate for the building of a temple to the Lord, good people!" And from a house being built nearby came the shouts and banging of workmen.

"Oh, God," Ilya Ilyich groaned bitterly, "what kind of life is this! The din in this city is unbearable! When am I going to start living the blissful life I long for? When am I going to see the fields, the woods I grew up in," he thought. "If only I could be lying on the grass under a tree with the sun glinting through the branches. Some apple-cheeked servant girl would be bringing me breakfast or lunch, a girl with soft, round elbows and a sunburned neck. She would lower her gaze coquettishly and smile. When, oh when...?"

"But what about the plan, the bailiff, the apartment?" something stirred in his memory.

"Yes, yes, this instant!" Oblomov started saying.

Oblomov quickly raised himself to a sitting position, lowered his feet to the floor and inserted them straight into his slippers and sat there for a moment, and then he raised himself to his feet and stood there thoughtfully for a minute or two.

"Zakhar, Zakhar!" he shouted, looking at the table and the inkwell.

"Now, what is it?" Zakhar's feet could be heard slapping the floor, "I'm moving as fast as my legs can carry me," Zakhar wheezed.

"Zakhar!" Oblomov repeated absently, without taking his eyes off the table. "You see..." he began, motioning towards the inkwell, but he trailed off and lapsed once again into a trance. His arms began to reach up and his knees begin to bend and he began to yawn and stretch..."There was some," he began, taking his time as he stretched, "there was some cheese left, yes and bring some madeira, it's a long time until dinner so I'll have a little snack..."

"What do you mean 'left'?" said Zakhar, "nothing was left!"

"How can you say 'nothing left'," Oblomov cut in, "I remember clearly, it was a piece like this..."

"No, no, there wasn't any piece!" Zakhar persisted stubbornly.

"Yes, there was!" said Oblomov.

"No, there wasn't!" replied Zakhar.

"Well, go and buy some!"

"I'll need some money."

"There's some small change there, take it."

"There's only one rouble forty and I'll need a rouble sixty."

"There were some copper coins there too."

"I didn't see them," said Zakhar shifting from one foot to another. There was some silver, see, here it is, but no coppers!"

"Yes, there were, that peddler put them right into my hand yesterday."

"Yes, and I was right there and saw him give you some silver, but I never saw any coppers…""Could it have been Tarantyev who took them?" Ilya Ilyich started wondering, "no, he would have taken all the small change."

"Well, what else do we have left?" he asked.

"There was nothing. But maybe there's some of yesterday's ham, I'll have to ask Anisya," said Zakhar, "should I bring it?"

"Bring whatever there is! And anyway what do you mean, 'there was nothing'?"

"Well, there just wasn't!" said Zakhar, and left the room. Ilya Ilyich slowly paced his study pondering. "So much to do!" he said quietly, "just with the plan alone—an enormous amount of work left to do!…and there *was* some cheese left," he thought to himself, "it was that Zakhar who ate it up, and all the time he's saying there wasn't any. And where did those copper coins disappear to?" he muttered as he rummaged among the things on the table.

After a quarter of an hour Zakhar appeared at the door carrying a tray with both hands. As he entered the room he tried to kick the door closed with his foot, but his foot missed and connected only with empty space; the wine glass fell off and with it the stopper of the decanter and the bread.

"He can't take a step without dropping something!" said Ilya Ilyich, "can't you at least pick up what you've dropped, no, he just stands there admiring his handiwork!"

Zakhar, still with the tray in his hands, tried to bend down to pick up the bread, but it was not until he was down on his haunches that he realized he was still using both hands to clutch the tray and had no hand to spare to do the picking up.

"Well, pick it up then!" said Ilya Ilyich derisively, "what are you waiting for?"

"Oh, to hell with you, damn you!" Zakhar burst out heatedly, addressing the fallen objects, "whoever heard of a snack right before dinner?" He put down the tray and picked up the things he had dropped, then he took the bread, blew on it and placed it on the table.

Ilya Ilyich started eating while Zakhar stood at a certain distance from him looking at him out of the corner of his eye and clearly gearing up to say something. But Oblomov just went on eating, not paying him the slightest attention. Zakhar coughed once or twice. Still no reaction from Oblomov.

"The building manager just sent around to say," Zakhar finally began a little nervously, "that the contractor just came to see him and is wondering if he can come and take a look at our apartment? It's about the renovation…"Ilya Ilyich just went on eating without uttering a word. After a moment's silence Zakhar even more timidly ventured, "Ilya Ilyich!"

Ilya Ilyich pretended he had heard nothing.

"They want us to move out next week," Zakhar wheezed. Oblomov drank a glass of wine in total silence.

"But what are we going to do, Ilya Ilyich?" Zakhar's voice sank practically to a whisper.

"I forbade you to mention that subject to me," Ilya Ilyich said sternly, getting up and moving towards Zakhar. Zakhar retreated.

"What a poisonous creature you are Zakhar" Oblomov added with feeling. Zakhar took offense. "Oh, so now I'm poisonous, what do you mean 'poisonous', who have I killed?"

"If you're not poisonous, how come you're poisoning my life?"

"I'm not poisonous!" Zakhar persisted.

"Then why are you pestering me about the apartment?"

"But what do you want me to do?"

"And what am I supposed to do?"

"You were going to write to the landlord?"

"And so I will, but give me a little time, I can't write just like that on the spot!"

"You should be doing it right now."

"Right now, right now! Anyone would think I don't have more important business, you think it's just like chopping wood, just a snap of the fingers? Look!" said Oblomov twisting the dry pen in the inkwell, "there's not even any ink, how do you expect me to write?"

"Look, I'll go and dilute it with kvass," said Zakhar taking the inkwell quickly out of the room while Oblomov started looking for paper.

"Never any paper when you want it!" he grumbled to himself, rummaging in the drawer and running his hands over the table. "Can't find any wherever you look! That Zakhar will be the death of me!"

"You see what a poisonous creature you are!" said Ilya Ilyich to Zakhar as he entered the room, "you neglect everything, there's not even paper in the house.

"Why are you treating me like this Ilya Ilyich? I'm a Christian and you're calling me 'poisonous'? A fine thing to call someone, 'poisonous'! When I was growing up under the old master, he might call me a whelp or twist my ear, but he would never have dreamed of coming out with a word like that! God knows what things are coming to! Anyway here is your paper."

He handed Oblomov half a sheet of grayish paper he had taken from a bookshelf.

"You don't seriously think I can write on that?" said Oblomov throwing it aside, "it's the paper I used to use to cover my glass overnight in case anything fell in it…yes, poisonous!"

Zakhar turned away and faced the wall.

"Well, never mind; give it here anyway! I'll just use it for a rough draft and then Alekseyev can make a fair copy."

Ilya Ilyich sat down at the table and unhesitatingly wrote out: "Dear Sir…"

"What lousy ink!" said Oblomov, "next time, Zakhar, just look sharp and do your job properly!"

He thought for a while and began to write.

"The apartment on the second floor, which I rent and in which you are proposing to undertake some renovation is entirely suitable to my style of life and the routine I have developed over the many years I have lived here. On learning from my man, Zakhar Trofimov, that you had required him to convey to me that the apartment I rent…" Oblomov stopped writing and read what he had written.

"It reads awkwardly" he said, "I've written 'that' twice in a row and I've put 'which' twice too."

Whispering to himself, he tried rearranging the words, but it was no good because the first 'which' went with 'the floor', and not 'the apartment', it still did not hang together. He tried to improve it and racked this brains in an effort to avoid the doubling of 'that'. He tried crossing out one word and replacing it with another.

He put 'that' in three different places and only succeeded in either making nonsense of the sentence or ending up with the three 'that's' too close together again.

"Just can't get rid of this damned second 'that', he said in exasperation, "well to hell with it—and the damned letter too—breaking my head over such niggling details! I've just lost the knack of writing business letters—and it's almost three o'clock!"

"Are you satisfied now, Zakhar?" He tore the letter in four and flung the pieces on the floor.

"Did you see?" he asked.

"Yes, I saw," replied Zakhar, picking up the pieces.

"So stop bothering me with the apartment! And what's that you have there?"

"It's the accounts."

"You never stop, do you? Just keep on tormenting me! Alright, tell me right now how much!""Well you owe the butcher eighty- six roubles, fifty-four kopecks."

Ilya Ilyich threw up his hands. "Are you out of your mind? All that just for the butcher?"

"If you let it pile up for three months, you end up owing a pile! Look everything's itemized, no one's robbing you.""See, there you go, being poisonous again!" said Oblomov, "spending a fortune on beef. I just don't see what you get out of it; at least if it did you some good…"

"It wasn't me who ate it!" Zakhar retorted indignantly.

"Oh, no?"

"Well, forgive me for eating! Here, see for yourself!" He thrust the accounts at him.

"Who else then?" said Ilya Ilyich, pushing away the greasy account books in disgust.

"There's also a hundred and twenty-one roubles, eighteen kopecks owing to the baker and greengrocer."

"This is ruin! Just unbelievable!" said Oblomov, beside himself.

"What are you, a cow or something to chew up so much greenstuff?"

"Oh, no, not me, I'm a poisonous creature!" Zakhar, shot back bitterly, standing now at right angles to his master. "If you didn't keep letting in that Mikhei Andreyich, there wouldn't be so much money going out!" he added.

"Well, what is it altogether, add it up!" said Ilya Ilyich and began to calculate himself.

Zakhar began to count on his fingers.

"I can't make any damn sense of it, it comes to a different figure each time," said Oblomov, "what do you make it—two hundred?"

"Hold on, just give me a minute," said Zakhar grumbling and frowning with concentration. "Eight tens plus ten tens is eighteen and two tens…"

"You'll never finish that way," said Ilya Ilyich. "Go back to your room and give me the accounts tomorrow, and get some paper and ink while you're about it. All that money! I told him to pay it off a little at a time, but no, he has to try to get me to pay it all at once…Some people!"

Meanwhile Zakhar had worked it out and said, "It comes to two hundred and five roubles, and seventy-two kopecks, so if you could give me the money…?

"What, you mean right this minute! Just wait a little and I'll see tomorrow…"

"It's up to you Ilya Ilyich, but they're pressing…"

"Alright, alright, drop it! I said 'tomorrow' and tomorrow you'll get it. Now leave me, I have work to do—more important things to attend to."

Ilya Ilyich settled on to his chair with his legs tucked under him, but before he had time to start thinking, the doorbell rang. A short man with the beginnings of a paunch entered the room. He had a pale face with red cheeks and a bald patch at the back of his head around which thick, black tufts of hair formed a fringe. The patch was completely bald and round and gleamed as it if had been carved out of polished ivory. The new guest's face bore an expression of anxious attentiveness to everything around him.

His glance was restrained and his smile reserved, and his manner was marked by a certain self-effacing, official civility. He wore a comfortable tailcoat that opened wide and easily like a gate practically at a single touch. His linen was of such a shining whiteness that it seemed designed to match his gleaming pate. On the index finger of his right hand he wore a massive signet ring with a dark stone.

"Doctor, what brings you here?" Oblomov exclaimed extending one hand to his guest and moving up a chair with the other.

"You're so healthy these days and I miss hearing from you, so I just thought I'd drop in," was the doctor's jocular reply. "But, seriously, I happened to be upstairs visiting your neighbor so I thought I would look in."

"Thank you, and how is my neighbor?"

"Him? I give him three or four weeks, or until autumn at the most—it is the dropsy, you see, in the chest—nothing to be done. And what about you?"

Oblomov shook his head dolefully.

"I don't feel at all well, doctor, as a matter of fact I was thinking of consulting you myself. I don't know what to do. My digestion has practically stopped working, I have this heavy feeling in the pit of my stomach as well as terrible heartburn and I'm short of breath," said Oblomov, grimacing queasily.

"Give me your hand!" said the doctor taking his pulse and closing his eyes for a minute. "Any cough?" he asked.

"At night, especially when I've eaten late."

"Hmm, do you feel your heart beating, any headaches?" The doctor asked a few more such questions and then lowered his bald pate and thought deeply. After two minutes he suddenly raised his head and pronounced his verdict: "If you spend another two or three years in this climate, lounging around and eating heavy, fatty food, you'll die of a stroke."

Oblomov was alarmed. "What should I do, tell me for God's sake?"

"What everybody else does, go abroad!"

"Abroad," Oblomov repeated in dismay.

"Yes, what's the problem?"

"But, doctor, going abroad, it's out of the question!"

"What do you mean, 'out of the question'?"

Oblomov silently regarded himself and then looked around the room and repeated mechanically, "Abroad!"

"What's to stop you?"

"What's to stop me? Why everything…"

"Everything! Come on now, you don't mean you don't have the money?"

"Yes, that's it, that's exactly it, I don't have the money" Oblomov chimed in eagerly, delighted at being offered such a perfectly natural pretext to duck behind.

"Just take a look at what my bailiff has written me…now where did I put that letter? Zakhar!"

"Alright, alright, that's nothing to do with me," said the doctor, "it's my duty to tell you, you must change your lifestyle radically, the location, the air, your activities—everything!"

"Very well, I'll think about it," said Oblomov, "but where should I go and what should I do?"

"Go to Kissingen or Ems," began the doctor, "for June and July, and take the waters. Then to Switzerland or the Tyrol for the grape cure. Stay there until November…"

"The Tyrol! What next?" Ilya Ilyich muttered to himself.

"And then somewhere dry, like Egypt perhaps."

"Oh, great, wonderful!" Oblomov thought to himself.

"Leave your worries and your problems behind you…"

"It's all very well for you to say!" Oblomov pointed out, "but you're not the one getting these letters from your bailiff…"

"You've also got to stop brooding," the doctor continued.

"Brooding?"

"Yes, mental stress."

"But what about the plan for the estate? I mean, after all I'm not just a block of wood."

"Well, you must do as you please. My job is just to warn you. You should avoid all excitement—it interferes with the treatment. You should try to get some recreation in the form of horse-riding, dancing or some gentle exercise in the open air; light conversation, especially with ladies, to make your heart beat just a little faster, but only from pleasurable sensations."

Oblomov heard him out, his head bowed.

"What else?" he asked.

"Well, avoid reading or writing like the plague! Rent a villa with windows facing south, surround yourself with flowers, music, women!"

"What about food?"

"Avoid meat and all animal products as well as all farinaceous goods and gelatinous substances. Eat plenty of broth and greenstuff; but be careful, there is a lot of cholera around now, so take every precaution. Walk eight hours a day. Get a gun…"

"My God!" Oblomov groaned.

"Finally," the doctor wound up, "go to Paris for the winter season, plunge into the hurly burly and live it up without a second thought. Never a dull moment, non-stop entertainment, theatres, balls, fancy-dress parties, excursions, social life; fill your days with friends, noise, laughter…"

"You're not leaving anything out by any chance?" Oblomov asked with barely concealed irritation.

The doctor thought for a moment; "Well, a little sea air wouldn't hurt, catch a ship from England and take a trip to America…" He got up and started to leave. "If you follow all this advice carefully…" he said.

"Of course, of course, absolutely, to the letter!" replied Oblomov acidly as he showed him out.

The doctor left, leaving Oblomov in a state of despair. He closed his eyes, put his head in his hands and just sat there curled into a ball, seeing and feeling nothing.

He heard his name called timidly behind him.

"Ilya Ilyich!"

"Well?" he responded.

"What should I tell the manager?"

"What about?"

"About moving."

"I can't believe you're on about that again!" Oblomov burst out.

"But Ilya Ilyich, please, what do you want of my life? You've got to figure it out for yourself, my life is already a misery, the grave is staring me in the face!"

"No, it's you who are driving me to my grave with all your talk about moving!" said Oblomov, "You want to know what the doctor told me?"

Zakhar was at a loss for words, he just sighed, so deeply that the ends of his neckerchief fluttered on his chest.

"So you want to be the death of me, is that it?" Oblomov asked again, "You've had enough of me, I suppose? Well, answer me!"

"God bless you, live in good health! Who wishes you any harm?" Zakhar protested, utterly confounded by the tragic turn of the conversation.

"You do!" said Ilya Ilyich, "I forbade you to so much as mention moving in my presence, but a day doesn't go by without you throwing it in my face half a dozen times and yet you know how much it upsets me. And with my health in such a delicate state!"

"Well, I was wondering why...you know, why exactly, we, er, couldn't move, kind of thing." Zakhar stammered out in a voice trembling with trepidation.

"Why we can't move? Oh, yes! It's easy for you to say," said Oblomov, swiveling in his chair to face Zakhar, "do you really have any idea of what it means to move? Well, do you?"

"Alright, I don't," Zakhar conceded meekly, more than ready to agree with his master on any subject if only to avoid the kind of harrowing scene he dreaded more than anything in the world.

"Since you don't understand, I'll explain it and then you tell me whether you still think it's such a wonderful idea. What does it mean to move? Well, for one thing it means your master has to get out for the whole day—and wander about fully dressed at that, right from the morning..."

"Well, what's wrong with that?" Zakhar observed. "What's so terrible about leaving for the whole day? It's bad for you to lounge around at home. Look how unhealthy you've been looking lately! You used to look as fresh as a cucumber, and now you just sit around looking like, well

God knows what you look like! You should be out on the street looking at people or whatever…"

"Enough of that drivel! Why don't you listen?" said Oblomov. "Walk in the streets indeed!"

"No, I mean it," Zakhar continued heatedly, "for instance I heard, they put this weird monster on display, you could go and see it. Or there's the theatre or a fancy dress ball and we could move while you were out."

"Stop talking nonsense! You have a fine way of looking out for your master's welfare. If you had your way, I'd be out wandering around all day. God knows where I'd end up eating dinner or what I'd find to eat, not to mention finding somewhere to lie down for a nap afterwards, but it's all the same to you! Move while I'm out! Oh yes! If I'm not here to keep an eye on things, there will be nothing but bits and pieces left to move out. I know all about," Oblomov's voice carried growing conviction, "moving house! It means damage and commotion—everything piled on the floor in a heap; a suitcase, the back of a divan, pictures, assorted pipes, books, hour-glasses that you never see at normal times but appear out of nowhere when you're moving. You have to keep an eye on everything if you don't want to see it all lost or smashed…half the stuff is still here, the rest is on the cart or already in the new apartment. You feel like a smoke and take up your pipe only to find that the tobacco has already left…you want to sit down but there isn't a chair in the place. If you so much as touch some-thing you get dirty; everything is covered in dust. There is nothing to wash with and there you are walking around with hands as filthy as yours…"

"My hands are clean!" Zakhar protested, extending two hands that looked more like the soles of his feet.

"Just don't show them to me!" said Ilya Ilyich, hastily averting his eyes.

"And when you want something to drink," Oblomov continued his tirade, "you pick up the jug but there's no glass…"

"You could drink out of the jug," Zakhar suggested helpfully.

"That's just like you; you don't have to bother to sweep, dust or beat the carpets. And in the new apartment," Oblomov went on, warming to his theme as as he pictured the move vividly in his imagination, "every-thing is lying around just anywhere for days on end; pictures stacked against the walls or on the floor, galoshes on the bed, boots flung into a corner with the tea and the pomade. You look at an armchair—a leg is broken, or a framed picture—the glass is smashed, or the divan—it's all stained. It doesn't matter what you ask for, nobody knows where it is; either it's lost or it's been left behind and somebody has to run back to the old place to look for it.

"Yes, back and forth a dozen times," Zakhar put in.

"Well, there you are," Oblomov continued, " and when you get up in the morning in the new place, what a pain! No water, no coal, and in the winter you're frozen stiff, the rooms are freezing and there's no firewood, so someone has to run about looking for some."

"And what neighbors you get!" Zakhar chimed in again. "Some of them won't even let you have a cup of water, let alone a bundle of firewood."

"Exactly!" said Oblomov. "Anyway, you make the move and by the evening you would think that all your troubles would be over; not a bit of it! It drags on for weeks. Just when you think everything has been put in its place, there's always something you've overlooked; the blinds haven't been put up, pictures have to be hung—you're worn out as if the very life has been wrung out of you…and the expense, the expense!"

"Last time eight years ago, I remember as clearly as if it were yesterday, it was two hundred roubles," Zakhar volunteered in corroboration.

"That's no joke!" said Ilya Ilyich. "And what about getting used to a new apartment? It's murder at the beginning! It takes me a week before I can get to sleep in a new place; everything feels wrong. When I get up, instead of the sign over the carpenter's shop I'm used to seeing through the window, there's something different, or if I don't see that old woman with the cropped hair looking out of her window before dinnertime, life loses interest. Now do you understand what you've done to your master?" Ilya Ilyich said reproachfully.

"Yes, I do," Zakhar whispered, crestfallen.

"Then why are you pestering me about moving? It's more than a human being can bear."

"Well, I just thought if other people just like us can move, then why can't we?"

"What did you say?" Oblomov was so astounded by this pronouncement that he almost got up from his chair, "I want to hear you say that again!"

Zakhar was confounded; he had no idea what he could have said to provoke such an emotional outburst from his master. He could find nothing to say.

"Other people just like us!" Ilya Ilyich was horrified. "So you finally came out with it; it took me until now to find out that to you I'm just the same as 'others'!"

Oblomov bowed ironically in Zakhar's direction, looking for all the world like someone mortally offended.

"But Ilya Ilyich, what do you mean I'm saying you're the same as anyone…?"

"Get out of my sight!" Oblomov dismissed him peremptorily, pointing to the door. "I can't stand the sight of you; 'other people', thanks a lot!"

"Zakhar gave a deep sigh and went out. "What a life!" he growled as he settled onto his bunk.

"Oh God!" Oblomov was groaning at the same time, "here I was going to devote the whole morning to getting down to business and now the whole day is ruined. And who did it? Why, my very own devoted, tried and true personal servant—and what a thing to say! How could he?"

Oblomov was unable to calm down; he lay down, got up and paced the room by turns. He felt that his reduction by Zakhar to the ranks of 'others' had undermined his claim to Zakhar's unswerving loyalty to the person of his master to the exclusion of all others. He delved deeply into this comparison in an attempt to elucidate the precise essence of 'others' and himself and to determine exactly to what extent such a parallel was possible or fair and how deeply offended he should feel by what Zakhar had said.

He was also exercised by the question of whether Zakhar's insult was deliberate, that is, whether he had said that Ilya Ilyich was "just like others" out of genuine conviction or whether it was just something that had tripped off his tongue without passing through his brain. Oblomov's self-esteem was wounded and he decided that Zakhar had to be taught the difference between himself and those whom Zakhar meant by "others," and in this way to bring home to him the full enormity of his wickedness.

"Zakhar!" he called solemnly and portentously.

Zakhar, hearing his name called, instead of jumping down from his bunk in his usual manner and slapping his feet on the floor and growling, slid down slowly and made his way towards Oblomov quietly and reluctantly, bumping into everything in his path, like a dog who can tell from the sound of his master's voice that some naughtiness has been found out and that retribution is at hand.

Zakhar opened the door halfway but could not bring himself to enter the room.

"Come in!" said Ilya Ilyich.

Although the door swung freely on its hinges, Zakhar made it appear that it was resisting his attempts to open it, so that he was somehow stuck in the doorway and could not get into the room.

Oblomov was sitting on the edge of the bed. "Come over here!" he insisted.

Zakhar managed to extract himself from the doorway with an effort but immediately closed the door behind him with his back right up against it.

"Over here!" said Ilya Ilyich, pointing to a spot right in front of him. Zakhar took half a step forward and stopped four or five yards short of Oblomov.

"Closer!" said Oblomov.

Zakhar went through the motions of taking a step but just rocked back on his heels and stamped his foot back in precisely the same spot.

Ilya Ilyich, realizing that there was no way he was going to get Zakhar to come any closer, let him remain where he was standing and regarded him reproachfully for some time in silence. Zakhar, discomfited by this wordless scrutiny of his person, pretended not to notice and stood sideways at an angle even greater than his usual ninety degrees, this time not even glancing at Ilya Ilyich out of the corner of his eye in the usual way. He looked fixedly to his left in precisely the opposite direction, focusing on a long familiar object, a fringe of cobweb around one of the pictures and the spider itself—a living reproach to his negligence.

"Zakhar!" Ilya Ilyich intoned quietly and with dignity. Zakhar remained silent, obviously thinking to himself: "What's all this about? There's only one Zakhar here and he's standing right in front of you!" He continued to look around the room, carefully avoiding eye contact with his master, and found himself looking at the mirror, which served him as a further reminder of his shortcomings, covered as it was in a thin film of dust that could have been taken for a layer of muslin. Scowling back at him from the mirror as if through a fog he glimpsed his own sullen and unlovely visage.

Repelled by this only too familiar melancholy sight, he averted his eyes and focused for a moment on Ilya Ilyich. Their eyes met. Unable to stand the reproach written in the eyes of his master, Zakhar lowered his gaze to his feet, but there again in the stained and dust-engrained carpet he saw further sorry evidence of his less than zealous service to his master.

"Zakhar!" Ilya Ilyich repeated with feeling.

"Was there something?" Zakhar whispered barely audibly, trembling slightly as he sensed the onset of an emotional tirade.

"Get me some kvass!" said Ilya Ilyich.

It was as if a great weight had been lifted from him and Zakhar in his relief practically skipped to the sideboard like a small boy and returned with the kvass.

"Something bothering you?" Ilya Ilyich inquired mildly, drinking from the glass in his hands. "Feeling bad about something?"

The forbidding expression on Zakhar's face was softened by a momentary glimmer of remorse. He was feeling the first stirrings of that veneration towards his master that had filtered back into his heart and suddenly found himself able to look him straight in the eye.

"Are you feeling sorry for what you did?" asked Ilya Ilyich.

"What does he mean 'what I did'," Zakhar wondered, his heart sinking, "it has to be something heart-rending, something that's going to bring tears to my eyes; it always does when he starts in on me like this."

"But Ilya Ilyich," Zakhar began on the lowest note in his range, "all I said was, well…"

"No, hold it!" Oblomov interrupted, "do you understand what you did? Now just put that glass down on the table and answer me!"

Zakhar could find nothing to say in reply and had absolutely no idea what he had done, but that did not stop him regarding his master with veneration and even hanging his head a little as if in recognition of his guilt.

"So you see what a poisonous creature you are?" said Oblomov.

Zakhar still kept silent but blinked three or four times, opening his eyes very wide.

"You hurt your master!" Ilya Ilyich pronounced the words with particular emphasis and deliberation, staring Zakhar right in the face and relishing his discomfiture.

Zakhar felt so bad that he did not know which way to turn.

"You hurt me didn't you?" Ilya Ilyich asked.

"Yes, I did." Zakhar whispered, totally flustered by the use of this new "heart-rending" word. He did not know where to look and his eyes swivelled wildly in every direction, seeking some refuge; and once again the cobweb, the dust, his own reflection and his master's face flashed before him.

"If only the ground would swallow me up, if only I could be struck dead!" he thought, seeing no hope of avoiding an emotional scene whatever he did. In his desperation he began to blink faster and faster and felt he was on the very brink of tears. Finally he answered his master with the same old song only this time in prose.

"But how did I hurt you, Ilya Ilyich?" he said, practically in tears.

"How?" Oblomov repeated. "Have you thought about what 'others' means?" He stopped and kept on looking at Zakhar. "Shall I tell you what it means?"

Zakhar shuffled like a caged bear and gave a sigh that filled the whole room.

"These 'others' you talk about, they are your down-and-outers, coarse, unwashed, unschooled ruffians; they eke out their miserable, squalid existence in attics, they sleep in a bundle of rags on the street. They're beyond redemption. Nothing can help them. They gobble down a potato or a piece of herring. They are indigents, constantly on the move, tossed from pillar to post. They're the kind you'll find moving to new apartments. Take that Lyagayev, he would think nothing of jumping into a carriage with his two shirts wrapped in a handkerchief, his ruler tucked under his arm, and he's off! You ask him where he's going and it's 'Oh, just moving'. That's your 'others' for you! And that's what I am to you, 'others'? Well?"

Zakhar looked at his master, shuffling from one foot to the other and said nothing.

"You want to know who these 'others' are?" Oblomov continued. "They are the kind who clean their own boots and dress themselves. Sometimes they try to pass for gentlemen, but it's a sham; they have no notion of what a servant is. They have no one to fetch and carry for them and they run their own errands. They light their own stoves and even do their own dusting…"

"There are a lot of Germans like that." Zakhar said despondently.

"Exactly! And me? You still think I'm one of the 'others'?"

"No, you're in another class altogether!" said Zakhar plaintively, still having no idea of what his master was driving at. "God knows what started you off on this?"

"Oh, so I'm in 'another' class altogether? Just listen to yourself for a moment; there you go again with your 'another'! Have you ever stopped to consider how those 'others' live? These 'others' of yours have to work all the time, constantly busy and rushing here and there; if they don't work they don't eat. These 'others' bow and scrape, they beg, they humble themselves…so what about me? Make up your mind! What's your verdict? Am I one of these 'others' or not?"

"Please sir, haven't you tormented me enough with these heart-rending words?" Zakhar implored him. "God in heaven!"

"So I'm one of the 'others'! Do you see me rushing about, do you see me working? Am I short of food or something? Am I such a pitiful sight, all skin and bones? Do I lack for something? Do I have to fetch and carry and do things for myself? Not as far as I can see. Never in my life have I pulled on my own stockings, praise the Lord! Should I start to worry? What for? And look who I'm telling all this to! The very one who has been looking after me since I was a child. You know better than anyone, you've seen for yourself what a sheltered upbringing I've had, how carefully I've been protected; never exposed to cold or hunger, never wanted for anything, never had to work or even dirty my hands in any way. So how on earth did you ever take it into your head to compare me with 'others'? Do I really have the constitution to stand up to what 'others' have to do and put up with?"

Zakhar had by now lost any sense of what Oblomov was talking about, but his lips were trembling because of the agitation seething inside him. The storm clouds of the emotional scene he had been dreading were rumbling over his head. He remained silent

"Zakhar!" Ilya Ilyich repeated.

"Would you be wanting something?" Zakhar's whisper could hardly be heard.

"Bring me some more kvass!"

Zakhar brought the kvass and, after Oblomov had drained the glass and handed it back to him, was about to make a swift exit.

"Oh no, you just stay right where you are!" Oblomov stopped him in his tracks. "I'm asking you a question. I want to know how you could bring yourself to hurt your master's feelings so deeply, the master you carried in your arms when he was a baby, the master you've spent a lifetime serving, the master who has been so good to you?"

Zakhar broke down. It was the words "so good to you" that were the last straw. He began to blink faster and faster. The less he understood of Oblomov's emotional tirade, the more miserable he became.

"I'm sorry, Ilya Ilyich," he began, his voice husky with remorse," it was out of stupidity, yes, stupidity, that's what it was that made me…" And Zakhar, having no idea of what he was supposed to have done, did not know what verb to use to end his sentence.

"And all the time," Oblomov continued in the pained tone of one whose pride has been wounded and whose merits are unappreciated, "here I am worrying and laboring day and night—sometimes overheating my brain and weakening my heart. Sleepless nights, tossing and turning, racking my brain to do everything for the best. And who is this all for? It's all for you, the peasants—and that includes you! Perhaps when you look at me you get the impression that all I'm doing is putting my head under the covers and sleeping like a log. Well, you're wrong! What I'm really doing is thinking hard about making sure that the peasants have everything they need, that they don't have to envy others, so that they don't complain tearfully about me to God on the Day of Judgment but remember me gratefully in their prayers. What an ungrateful lot!" Oblomov ended on a note of bitter reproach.

These last "heart-rending" words finally broke Zakhar's resistance and he began to sob; the sound of his sobbing combined with his husky, throaty wheeze produced a tone beyond the range of any known musical instrument except perhaps some kind of Chinese gong or Indian tom-tom.

"Dear Ilya Ilyich," he implored him, "please don't go on! The Lord have mercy on you, what is it you're going on about? Holy Mother of God! What terrible catastrophe has suddenly struck out of a clear blue sky?"

Oblomov went on relentlessly without hearing a word. "You should be ashamed of yourself for saying such things! What a viper I've nurtured in my bosom!"

"Viper?" Zakhar exclaimed, throwing up his hands and his lamentations filled the room as if a swarm of buzzing insects had flown in, "when did I ever mention a viper?" he sobbed, "vile things like that don't even come into my dreams!"

Both of them had by now totally ceased to understand the other and even themselves.

"How could you even bring yourself to say such a thing?" Ilya Ilyich continued, "and in my plan here I was assigning him a house all to himself, a garden, a supply of food and wages! You're my manager, my majordomo, and my right-hand man! The other peasants defer to you, they touch their forelocks. It's 'Zakhar Trofimych, yes, Zakhar Trofimych, no, Zakhar Trofimych!' But there's no pleasing him, so he confers this title on me, 'others'. That's my reward! A fine way of showing respect for your master!"

Zakhar continued to sob and Ilya Ilyich himself was becoming emotional. In the course of admonishing Zakhar he was so moved by the generosity of the blessings he had conferred on his peasants that he delivered these last recriminations in a voice trembling with emotion and with tears in his eyes.

"It's alright, you can go now," he told Zakhar in a conciliatory tone, "but first just give me some more kvass; my throat is parched. I would have thought that you could have heard for yourself that your master was getting hoarse—and all because of you! I hope you understand now what you did wrong," said Oblomov when Zakhar brought him the kvass, "and that in future there'll be no more talk about your master being 'just like others'. To make amends, just arrange it somehow or other with the landlord for me not to have to move. And this is what you call protecting your master's peace and quiet? By thoroughly upsetting me and making it impossible for me to do any more useful thinking? And who is it you're hurting? Nobody but yourself!

"It's to your good that I've been devoting myself body and soul, it's for you that I gave up my career and live in such seclusion. Well, let's just leave it at that! Do you hear the clock striking three? Only two hours until dinner. Not enough time to do a thing—and so much to be done. Well, I'll just have to put off the letter until the next post and I'll start drafting the plan tomorrow. I might as well lie down for a little now. I'm absolutely wrung out. Lower the blinds and make sure that the doors are properly locked so that no one can disturb me; perhaps I'll even take a little nap, but wake me at four-thirty."

Zakhar began to cocoon his master in the study. First he tucked the blanket snugly around him, then he lowered the blinds, locked the doors and went back to his bunk.

"He's the very devil, he can drive you to your grave!" he grumbled, wiping the tears from his eyes and clambering onto his bunk, "that's the only word for him—all his talk about my own house, a garden and wages!" said Zakhar, repeating the only words he had actually understood. "He's an expert when it comes to finding words to pluck at your heartstrings, it's like he's twisting a knife in your heart! This here's my house and my garden, this is where I'll kick the bucket," he said, kicking his bunk furiously. "Wages? You scratch together a few pennies here and a few coppers there and you still don't have enough to buy a few shreds of tobacco or a little treat for your woman. To hell with you, I'd be better off dead!"

Ilya Ilyich turned over onto his back but did not fall asleep right away. He could not stop fretting and worrying.

"Two headaches at once," he said aloud, putting his head under the covers, "it's beyond endurance!"

In actual fact, however, these two "headaches," the ominous letter from the bailiff and having to move to a new apartment, were no longer causing him anxiety and had already faded into nothing more than bad memories.

"It's still a long time before the worst threatened by the bailiff can actually happen," he thought, "and a lot can change by then. Who knows? Maybe rain will save the harvest, or the bailiff will make up the arrears, or the runaway peasants will be returned 'to their domicile', as he put it."

"But where could they have gone?" he wondered, allowing his imagination to picture the circumstances creatively. "Well, it must have been at night in the damp without a scrap of food. Where would they sleep? Could it have been in the woods? Why can't they just stay put? It's true, their huts are not so comfortable, but at least they're warm—in spite of the bad smell. And why worry anyway?" he thought, "the plan will soon be ready, it's not worth getting all upset beforehand, I'll just…"

It was the thought of the move that troubled him most. It was this "headache" that was uppermost in his mind because it was the most recent. But Oblomov's mind was always receptive to mitigating circumstances and he was already constructing a comforting scenario. Although he had the vague notion that the move was inevitable, especially now that Tarantyev was in the picture, he had mentally projected this unpleasant reality into the future, if only for one week, so that he was already one more week of peace and quiet ahead of the game.

"And who knows? Maybe Zakhar will manage to arrange it so that we won't have to move at all—I mean it could be that they won't need to evict me. Conceivably something may come up and they won't need to do the renovation until next summer, or maybe even forget the whole thing—well something or other may turn up! No, moving? It's just not possible!"

Oblomov fluctuated in this way between between anxiety and relief and finally, in the comforting and encouraging formulae, "you never know" and "somehow or other," he found on this occasion, as he always managed to do, an ark of hope and consolation just as our forefathers did in the Ark of the Covenant, and out of this constructed a protective wall between himself and his two "headaches."

A gentle, pleasant drowsy numbness was beginning to suffuse his limbs and cloak his senses like the first mild frost blanketing the surface of the water; another minute and his mind would have drifted off into some different realm, when suddenly Ilya Ilyich awoke with a start and opened his eyes.

"But I haven't even washed! How can that be? And I haven't done anything," he whispered. "I was going to put the plan down on paper and I didn't; I didn't write to the police official—or the Governor. I began a letter to the landlord and didn't finish it. I didn't check the accounts and I didn't pay the money, and the whole morning is shot!"

He started thinking and the thought flashed through his mind: "maybe one of those 'others' would have done all those things. Who are these 'others'? What kind of people are they?"

He found himself engaged in a deep analysis of the comparison between himself and 'others'. He thought and thought and finally arrived at a definition of 'others' diametrically opposed to the one he had given Zakhar. He had to admit that 'others' would have finished all the letters, without the "which'es" and the "that's" getting in each other's way; 'others' would have moved into a new apartment by now and would have put the plan into effect and would have been to the estate and back by now.

"But I could have done all that myself," he thought, "it's not as if I don't know how to write; after all in my time I've written things a lot harder than letters. Where did all that go? And what's so special about moving, it's just a matter of making up your mind to it. 'Others' never put on dressing gowns," he thought, adding another item to the inventory of attributes of 'others'. 'Others'," here he yawned, practically asleep, " 'others' enjoy life, go everywhere, see everything, involve themselves in everything and I'm...well, I'm just not one of them!" he said, for the first time with a tinge of regret, and plunged into a deep reverie; he even poked his head out from under the covers.

He now experienced one of the most vivid flashes of insight in his whole life.

It was simply frightening how clearly and vividly he could suddenly picture the meaning of life and the destiny of man and was able to apprehend in a flash the contrast between that meaning and that destiny and his own life. One after another, like a flock of birds startled by a sudden ray of sunshine rising pellmell in a panic from a drowsy nook, thoughts about some of life's fundamental questions fluttered into his head. He suffered pangs of remorse and regret for the stunting and retarding of his moral development, for the obstruction that blocked his path. He was prey to a gnawing envy of others who could live life to the full and whose horizons were so broad, while the narrow and woefully constricted path of his own life was blocked by a kind of giant boulder.

In the depths of his timorous being there burgeoned a painful awareness that many aspects of his personality remained totally unawakened, while others had barely been tapped, and not a single one had been developed to the full. He was also painfully aware that entombed within himself there was this precious radiant essence, moribund perhaps by now, like a gold deposit lying buried deep in the rock that should long ago have been minted into coin and put into circulation.

This treasure was, however, buried deep under a great heap of sludge and silt. It was as if someone had stolen the gifts that life had handed to him on a plate and locked them away in his inmost recesses. Something was preventing him from throwing himself wholeheartedly and uninhibitedly into life's race and from letting the wind fill his sails. It was as if the dead hand of some unknown enemy had been laid on him at the starting line and hurled him far outside the course of his normal human destiny.

It now seemed far too late for him to return from the wilderness and the wasteland to which he had been banished and set his feet back on his true path. The thickets surrounding him and within him were becoming denser and darker and the path was disappearing under a heavy undergrowth. His momentary flashes of lucidity were becoming ever more rare and were capable of rousing him to action only in briefer and briefer spurts. His mind and will had long been in a coma from which they seemed unlikely ever to emerge.

The events of his life had been pared down to microscopic proportions, but even these proved too much for him. He did not so much proceed from one event to another as allow himself to be tossed from one to another like a cork bobbing on the waves. There were events he no longer had the resilience of will to resist and others he no longer had the strength of purpose to pursue.

This silent confession to himself was a painful thing. Futile regrets about the past and the bitter recriminations of his own conscience pricked him like sharp needles. He strove desperately to find some guilty party or other to whom he could shift the burden of these recriminations and the pain that went with them. But who was there?

"Yes, it's all Zakhar's fault," he whispered.

As he recalled the details of the scene with Zakhar his face flushed hot with the shame of it.

"What if someone had been listening?" His blood ran cold at the thought. "Thank God Zakhar won't be able to tell anyone—and even if he did, no one would believe him, thank God!"

He sighed, he heaped reproaches on himself and tossed and turned in unavailing attempts to find someone to blame. His sighing and groaning finally reached Zakhar's ears.

"The kvass must have gone to his head!" Zakhar muttered heatedly.

"But why am I like this?" Oblomov asked himself almost in tears and covered his head with the blanket, "really?"

Frustrated in his efforts to find some hostile element that was preventing him from leading the normal kind of life that 'others' led, he sighed and closed his eyes and in a few minutes a drowsy numbness began to invade his senses.

"I would like to...also..." he said, blinking, "...you know, like...am I really a victim of nature...? No, of course not...thank God, I can't complain..."

This was followed by a sigh of profound resignation, and his agitation passed as he returned to his normal state of placid apathy.

"Well, obviously it's fate...nothing I can do," he barely managed to whisper, already half asleep.

"But it looks like a couple of thousand less this year!" he suddenly said aloud, his mind wandering in his sleep, "wait, just a minute!" and almost woke up. "But I really would like to know...how come I'm like this?" His voice sank to a whisper again and his eyes were tightly shut. "Yes, why...it must be...because..." But no matter how hard he tried, he just could not get it out.

So he never did figure out the reason and his lips and tongue stopped moving after uttering the last syllable, while his mouth remained half open. Instead of a word, there came a sigh followed by the even, stertorous breathing of someone peacefully sleeping.

Sleep had cut off the slow, leisurely flow of his thoughts and carried him off in an instant to another time, to other people, and to another place to which we will follow him in the next chapter.

CHAPTER NINE

Oblomov's Dream

Where are we? What is this blessed plot to which we have been transported by Oblomov's dream? What wonderland? It is true that there is no sea, no high mountains, cliffs or precipices, no dense forests, nothing at all imposing, wild or menacing.

After all, what need is there for the imposing, the menacing? The sea for example, you can keep it! It only induces melancholy thoughts; just looking at it makes you want to cry. The heart shrinks at the sight of those boundless expanses of water. In vain does the eye seek relief from the aching monotony, from the spectacle of unending, unendurable sameness. The insensate roaring and thundering of the waves does not soothe our delicate hearing, it just keeps on pounding out that same old unfathomable threnody that it has been pounding out since time began, wailing and groaning like some monster doomed to endless torment—a chorus of doom-laden voices that cannot be muffled. There is no twittering of birds; only seagulls, in the silence of the damned, wheel and circle despairingly over the waters offshore.

Even the roar of the most powerful beast is drowned by the howl of nature itself, and the human voice obliterated; and man himself, so tiny, so feeble, shrinks to the merest pinpoint in this vast panorama. Perhaps this is why it is so hard for man to contemplate the sea. But who needs the sea? Its silence and motionlessness do nothing to gladden the heart. In the barely perceptible movement of that watery mass, man sees nothing but that same boundless, dormant power that, when unleashed, so humiliatingly crushes his proud will and lays so low his boldest designs, the most cherished fruits of his labor and ingenuity.

Nor do mountains and precipices exist to bring comfort or joy to man. They are menacing and fearsome like the unsheathed claws and bared fangs of some wild beast going for the throat; they remind us only too vividly of our fragility and keep us in fear and trembling for our lives.

And even the sky itself towering over the cliffs and crags seems so remote and out of reach, as if it had washed its hands of the human race.

The peaceful spot to which our hero had been transported in his dream could not have been more different. There, even the sky seemed to crouch closer to the earth, but not so as to hurl its darts with greater force, but rather so as to enfold it more snugly, more lovingly in its embrace. It seemed that it had spread itself so low over our heads in order to provide us with a parental shelter, proof against all the elements, and to protect this chosen spot from all possible harm. There the sun shines bright and warm for half the year and when it finally moves away it does so without haste and, reluctantly and looking regretfully over its shoulder once or twice as if it hated to leave the place, gives it an extra day or two of warm sunlight as a parting gift to relieve the dreariness of autumn.

There the hills are but scale models of those fearsome crags to be found in other parts, crags whose towering heights stagger the imagination. A series of gentle slopes that are fun to slide down on one's back, or where one can sit and watch the sun go down in a mood of quiet contemplation.

The river burbles merrily and playfully along, widening in spots into a pool and then narrowing into a swift thread of a current, pauses for reflection and just trickles over the rocks, branching into frisky rivulets whose babbling lulls the surrounding countryside into a sweet slumber.

The whole area for fifteen to twenty versts around presents a series of charming, attractive, picture-postcard landscapes. The sandy, gently sloping banks of the glittering stream, the small bushes running down the hillsides to the water's edge, the crooked gully with the brook flowing along its bed, and the thicket of birch all seemed part of a carefully arranged composition by a master landscape artist.

This spot that time had passed by invites the careworn and the carefree alike to come and hide themselves away there and lead a life of a happiness that no one dreams could exist. It holds out the promise of a long peaceful life where extreme old age lapses imperceptibly into a sleep-like death.

The seasons would succeed each other in a serene and orderly cycle. Spring would arrive like clockwork in March and the streams would run down dirty from the hills, the ground would thaw, and warm vapors would rise; peasants would cast off their winter coats and emerge in shirtsleeves from their homes and, shielding their eyes with their hands, look up long and gratefully at the sun, rolling their shoulders with the sheer pleasure of it. They would grasp their overturned carts by one shaft or the other to right them, or look around and idly kick a plough that happened to be lying nearby under a tarpaulin in preparation for a return to their labors.

In the spring no sudden blizzards return to blanket the fields or break the boughs of trees under the weight of the snow. Winter, like some cold unapproachable beauty, stays in character right through until the appointed time for the warmth to return; there is no taking by surprise with sudden thaws and no imposition of the harsh tyranny of cruel frosts. Everything proceeds in the orderly sequence ordained by nature.

November sees the beginning of snow and frost, which reach their peak by Epiphany, when peasants venturing forth from their huts never return without hoar frost on their beards; but in February a keen sense of smell can already detect the faintest scent of approaching spring in the air.

Ah, but summer is a particular delight in these parts! It is there that you must go to find fresh, dry air, heady, not with the scent of lemon or laurel, but rather with the fragrance of wormwood, pine and bird-cherry; that is where you will find fine days and the warm, but not scorching, rays of the sun and cloudless skies for almost three months of the year.

When the clear days come they last for three or four weeks; the evenings are warm and the nights close and the stars twinkle oh, so invitingly and benignly in the heavens. When the rain comes it is a friendly summer rain, gushing down freely and abundantly and splashing cheerfully like generous hot teardrops of sudden joy spurting from someone's eyes, stopping only when the sun comes out again to embrace and dry the fields and the hillsides with its bright, warm, loving smile so that the whole countryside beams with happiness in response. How joyfully the peasant welcomes the rain with that old saying: "The rain makes you nice and wet and the sun makes you nice and dry!" relishing the feel of the warm rain on his upturned face, back, and shoulders.

There, even the thunderstorms are harmless and well-meaning and occur only on the proper scheduled occasions, hardly ever missing a St. Ilya's Day, as if they were doing it in order to maintain a popular tradition. It even seemed that the number and strength of the lightning bolts were precisely the same every year, as if the central distributing authority had allocated a specific annual ration of electricity to the whole area. Violent destructive storms were unheard of in these parts. You would never find in your newspaper a reference to anything remotely like that happening in that blessed spot. As a matter of fact you would never have read or heard anything whatsoever about the place if Marina Kulkova, a peasant's widow of twenty-eight, had not happened to give birth to quadruplets—something that was bound to get out in any case!

It was a place that the Lord never visited with plagues of any description, let alone the Egyptian kind. No one who lived there recalled ever seeing any sinister celestial signs or omens such as balls of fire or darkness at noon. It is not a habitat for poisonous snakes, locusts keep away, the roar of the lion or tiger is never heard, nor even the howl of the bear or wolf because there is no forest. All you ever hear is the mooing of the cows, the bleating of the sheep, and the cackling of the chickens as they roam all over the fields and the countryside.

God knows whether a poet or a philosopher would be content with the simplicity of nature in this quiet spot. It is well known that such gentlemen like to gaze up at the moon and listen to the nightingale's song. They like to see a coquettish moon given to dressing up in the flimsy garments of pale yellow clouds and who glints mysteriously through the branches of trees and trains her beams of silvery light down onto the upturned eyes of her doting admirers. In these parts no one has ever heard of this poet's "moon"; as far as they are concerned it is just a disc or crescent-shaped object in the sky. It looks down benignly on the fields and villages, flooding them with its light and looking for the entire world like a polished copper bowl. A poet would be wasting his time gazing rapturously up at it; it would just stare back down at him simply and straightforwardly like a round-faced village maiden, returning the passionate and elegant glances of some slick seducer from the city.

Another thing you do not hear in these parts is the voice of the nightingale, perhaps because there are no shady nooks or rose bushes, but there are hosts of quail. In late summer at harvest time, small boys catch them by hand. Nor does anyone there ever get the idea of declaring the quail a gourmet delicacy; no, such an aberration could never become part of the code of conduct of the people who live there. To them the quail is just another bird, not an item on the inventory of comestibles. It's only function there is to delight the human ear with its song; that is why under almost every roof there hangs a latticed cage containing a quail.

Neither a poet nor a philosopher would have remained content for long even with the look of this modest and unassuming place. There they would never see the kind of evening you see in Scotland or Switzerland when the whole landscape—the woods, the water, the walls of the huts are all ablaze with a kind of crimson glow and, thrown into sharp relief against this crimson backdrop, you see a column of men winding its way along a twisting road, escorting some noble lady on an outing to view a grim ruin and hurrying towards a mighty fortress, where awaiting them are an episode from the Wars of the Roses recited by an ancient bard, a wild goat for their supper and a ballad sung by a young damsel to the accompaniment of a lute—all scenes so vividly etched in our imaginations by the pen of Sir Walter Scott. No, nothing of this kind ever happened in these parts.

How quiet, how sleepy was the life of the three or four villages making up this little corner! They stood not far apart, as if cast at random from a giant hand, and wherever it was they happened to land, that is where they have remained to this very day. One of the peasants' log cabins had been left teetering on the brink of a gully exactly where it seemed to have been dropped ages ago, one half poking out into the void and the other resting on three poles. Nevertheless, the same family has been living quietly and cheerfully in it for generations. You would think that even a chicken would be afraid to go inside it, but Onisim Suslov lives there with his wife, and he is a strapping fellow who cannot even stand up straight in his own house. Not everyone who comes to visit Onisim can even get into the cabin except perhaps by using the magic formula out of the Baba Yaga fairy tales and commanding the cabin to "turn on its chicken's legs so that its back faces the forest and its door faces front." The porch was on the side overhanging the gully and you had to hold on to the roof with one hand and grab a tuft of grass with the other in order to lever yourself onto it.

Another cabin clung to the side of the gully like a swallow's nest.

Three cabins were huddled together for no particular reason on the same slope and two stood at the very bottom of the gully.

Not a thing stirs in the village as it sleeps. The doors of the silent cabins stand wide open and there is not a soul to be seen—just swarms of flies buzzing around in the stuffy interiors. If you enter a cabin you can shout as loudly as you want, but dead silence is all you will get in response, although perhaps in the odd cabin you may possibly provoke a feeble groan or the dry cough of an old grandmother spending her last days bedridden on a stove-top bunk, or maybe from behind the partition a three-year-old child will emerge clad only in a tiny shirt and will silently observe the visitor before retreating to safety behind the partition.

The same profound peace and quiet envelops the fields; just here and there you might spot the odd ploughman straining at his plough, burrowing like an ant into the dark soil, scorched by the sun and dripping with sweat.

The ways of the people who live here are dominated by the same placid and unruffled calm. There are no robberies, murders, or other calamitous events; their tranquility is never broken by strong passions or ambitious enterprises. And, after all, what passions or ambitions could possibly have troubled them? The people in these parts know themselves very well and have always lived far apart from other people. The nearest villages and the county town were twenty-five or thirty versts away.

There was a time when the peasants would take their grain to the nearest river port on the Volga, the equivalent to them of Colchis and the Pillars of Hercules of classical Greek mythology—or once a year some of them traveled to a fair, and that was about the limit of their contact with the outside world. Their attention was focused on themselves and did not intersect or overlap with the concerns of others.

They know that eighty versts away there was something called the provincial capital but hardly anyone had actually been there, and they knew that even further away there was Saratov or Nizhny. They had heard of Moscow and St. Petersburg, and that beyond St. Petersburg there lived people called French or German, but for them, like the people of antiquity, beyond that there stretched a dark, obscure world, unknown lands inhabited by monsters, two-headed people and giants; then came the outer darkness and ultimately the fish that bore the world on its back.

Their little corner of the world was so far off the beaten track that news of the latest doings in the outside world simply had no way of reaching them. Even the caravan people, who traveled around selling their wooden kitchenware and lived only twenty versts away, were no better informed. They simply had no points of comparison against which to measure their own way of life; did they live well or not; were they rich or poor; were there things that other people had that they could have wished for? They lived happily in the belief that this was the way things were and had to be, convinced that everyone lived exactly the same way and that anything else could only be an aberration. They would never have believed you if you had tried to tell them that other people did their ploughing, sowing, reaping, or marketing in some different way. So what could there possibly be to excite or trouble them?

Of course, they had their problems and shortcomings like anyone else; paying their quit rent and taxes, laziness and idleness, but they never let their troubles get the better of them or allowed them to raise their blood pressure. Over the previous five years, out of a population of several hundred souls there had not been a single death even from natural causes, let alone violence.

And when, every now and then, someone did pass away from sheer old age or a chronic disease, it took a long time for people to get over such an extraordinary event. They did not find it in the least surprising, on the other hand, that Taras, the blacksmith, should have practically steamed himself to death in his dugout bath house before anyone thought of throwing cold water over him to revive him.

As far as crime was concerned, there was really only one that was at all commonplace and that was the theft of peas, carrots, and turnips from kitchen gardens, although once, it is true, two piglets and a chicken did disappear, an event that had the whole neighborhood up in arms and which was blamed by common consent on some caravan people who had passed through the village the day before with their wagonloads of wooden dishes on their way to market. In fact, however, incidents of this type were an exceedingly rare occurrence. Another time too, a man was found lying in a ditch on the outskirts of the village by the bridge. Apparently he had been a member of a traveling workmen's guild on its way to town. He was found by some small boys who ran back to the village in terror, telling of some fearsome serpent or werewolf that was lurking in the ditch and had chased them and had almost caught Kuzka and eaten him.

Some of the bolder spirits among the men armed themselves with pitchforks and axes and marched off in a group to the ditch. The old people urged caution: "Hey, what's the hurry, what are you, a bunch of hotheads? Are you sure you know what you're doing? Forget him! No one's doing you any harm." The men pressed on regardless, but when they were a hundred yards or so from the ditch they all started shouting at once at the monster. Getting no response, they stopped and then advanced again.

The man was lying in the ditch with his head propped on a mound; his bag and stick had been dropped on the ground and hanging on the stick were two pairs of bast shoes. The men could not nerve themselves to move any closer or to touch anything. They called out in turn, scratching the backs of their necks: "Hey, you there, what happened, what are you doing there?" The stranger made a motion as if to raise his head, but could not do it; clearly he was too sick or too tired. One of the men raised his fork as if about to prod but a lot of the others started yelling: "Hold it, don't! How do we know who he is? He hasn't said a word; who knows what he may be…don't touch him boys!"

"Let's go!" some of them urged, "seriously, let's go! He's nothing to do with us, he'll be nothing but trouble!"

So they all left and went back to the village and told the old men that it was some outsider lying there, not uttering a sound, and God knows what he was doing there.

"An outsider! You don't want to have anything to do with them," said the old men sitting on the earthen wall with their elbows resting on their knees, "leave him be, you should never have gone in the first place!"

Such was the spot to which Oblomov had been instantaneously transported in his dream.

Of the three or four villages dotted around, two of them, Sosnovka and Vavilovka were within one verst of each other. They were part of the Oblomov family estate and for this reason had become known collectively as Oblomovka. The family seat and residence was in Sosnovka. Five versts from Sosnovka lay the hamlet of Verkhlyovo, which had also once belonged to the Oblomovs but had long since passed into the hands of others along with a few scattered, outlying peasant cabins that went with the property.

The village belonged to a rich absentee landowner who had never set foot on the estate and was run by a manager of German extraction.

And that is about all there is to say about the geography of the area.

It was morning when Ilya Ilyich awoke in his little bed. He was seven years old again. He did not have a care in the world and was in high spirits. What a delightful, chubby, rosy-cheeked child! His cheeks were so plump that if someone else had deliberately tried to puff out his cheeks just for fun, he could not have matched them. His nanny is waiting for him to wake up. She begins to pull on his stockings but he is making it hard for her with all his wriggling and frolicking; she gets him to hold still and they both dissolve in a fit of giggling. She finally manages to get him onto his feet, washes him, combs his hair, and presents him to his mother.

Oblomov, seeing in his dream his long dead mother, started quivering with joy and his heart contracted with a fierce spasm of love for her as two warm tears slowly slid from beneath his eyelids and hung motionlessly on his lashes. His mother smothered him with passionate kisses and devoured him hungrily and anxiously with her eyes.

"Could his eyes be a little cloudy? Could he be sickening for something?" she questioned the nanny. "Did he sleep soundly? Did he wake up in the night? Did he toss and turn? Did he have any fever?"

Then she took him by the hand and led him to the ikon. She knelt and with one arm around him made him repeat after her the words of the prayer. As he recited the words his attention wandered to the window through which the morning chill and the scent of lilac wafted into the room.

"Are we going for a walk today, mummy?" he asked suddenly in the middle of the prayer. "Yes, we will, darling," she replied hurriedly, keeping her eyes fixed on the ikon and resuming her recital of the sacred words as quickly as possible. The boy continued half-heartedly to mumble the words while his mother was putting her heart and soul into them. After this the boy was taken to his father and then to the breakfast table for tea.

Seated at the table Oblomov found the aged aunt who lived with them. She was eighty years old and complained constantly to her maid who stood in attendance behind her chair, her head shaking from the effects of old age. Also at the table were three elderly spinsters, distant relatives of his father, his mother's slightly demented brother-in-law, Chekmenyev, the owner of seven peasants, who was staying with them, as well as a number of other elderly persons.

The whole of this company as well as the entire Oblomov household immediately started making a tremendous fuss of Ilya Ilyich, smothering him with caresses and compliments and he barely had time to wipe away the traces of all these unsought kisses. He was then regaled with rolls, rusks and cream. Next, his mother, after a further flurry of endearments and caresses, allowed him out to run around in the garden, the courtyard and the meadow, with the strictest instructions to the nanny not to leave the child alone, not to let him near the horses, the dogs or the goat, or to wander too far from the house and, above all, not to let him near the gully that was the most terrifying spot in the whole neighborhood and enjoyed a most unsavory reputation. It was there that a dog had once been found that was deemed mad simply on the grounds that it had run away from the people who had set upon it with pitchforks and axes and which had finally disappeared over the hill. It was in this gully that people dumped the rotting carcasses of dead animals, and it was here that desperados and wolves were rumored to lurk as well as a variety of other nameless creatures the like of which had never existed on God's earth, let alone in this particular corner of it.

The child, however, had dashed out into the courtyard long before his mother had completed her list of admonitions. His wonderment and delight as he ran around and surveyed the family home was as fresh as if it were the first time; its gates leaning crookedly at an angle, its wooden roof sagging in the middle with fresh green moss growing on top, its rickety porch, its various outhouses and annexes and the overgrown garden. He was longing to climb up to the gallery that ran around the outside of the whole house so that he could look at the brook from there, but it was in a dilapidated state and might collapse at any moment, so that the only people allowed up there were the servants and the laborers and it was out of bounds to the master's family and their guests.

Heedless of his mother's instructions, he was already on his way to the stairs that drew him like a magnet, when the nanny appeared on the porch and managed to intercept him. Freeing himself from her grasp, he darted off towards the hayloft, intending to climb the steep staircase, but no sooner had she managed to catch up with him, than there he was, scampering off again and, whether he was making for the pigeon loft or the cattle pen, or even, God help us! heading down towards the dreaded gully, it was as much as she could do to nip all these plans in the bud.

"My God, what a jack-in-the-box that child is! Could you possibly sit still for a minute, young sir? Now behave yourself!" said the nanny.

The nanny's days and nights were filled with bustle and turmoil; pangs of anxiety for his welfare alternated with bursts of delight at the sheer life of the child. One minute she would be afraid that he would fall and hurt himself and the next minute her heart would melt at his child-like, unfeigned affectionateness, or her heart would lurch at the thought of what the dim distant future held for him. For this alone did her heart continue to beat; it was these emotions alone that kept the old woman's blood warm and maintained her slackening grip on a life that would otherwise long since have petered out.

The child, however, was not constantly on the go; he would sometimes suddenly quiet down and, sitting beside his nanny, would watch everything around him very closely. His child's mind would absorb everything that was happening and the deep impressions that were left took root and ripened with the passing years.

It was a perfect morning; there was a chill in the air and the sun was still low in the sky; the house, the trees, the pigeon loft, and the gallery were still casting long shadows. In the garden and the courtyard, small oases of coolness still remained ideal for a spot of quiet contemplation or even a nap. It was only in the distance that a field of rye seemed to be ablaze, and under the sun's glare a stream sparkled and gleamed too brightly for the naked eye.

"Nanny, why is it all dark over here and so bright over there—is it going to get bright here too?" the youngster asked.

"You see, dear, the sun is looking for the moon and screws up his eyes as he searches, but as soon as he sees the moon in the distance he starts beaming."

The child continues to look around thoughtfully and sees Antip riding off to fetch water, but on the ground next to him there looms another Antip ten times bigger than the real Antip, and the barrel seems the size of the whole house, while the shadow of the horse covers the whole meadow and crosses it in two strides before it disappears behind the hill—and all this before Antip has even had time to leave the courtyard.

The child also took two steps; one more step and he would disappear behind the hill. He wanted to look behind the hill in order to see what had become of the horse, but as he was on his way to the gate his mother's voice could be heard calling from the window: "nanny, can't you see the boy has run out into the sun; get him back into the cool or his head will get baked and he'll get sick and start feeling bad and lose his appetite. If you're not careful he'll stray into the gully!"

"You're so naughty!" the nanny scolded him quietly, dragging him back onto the porch.

The child continues to keep his watchful and impressionable eyes trained on what the grown-ups are doing and exactly how they are spending the morning. No detail, however small, escapes his keen scrutiny. The picture of the daily routine of the household is indelibly etched on his tender mind, which busily absorbs all these vivid impressions of the life around him and stores them up to be drawn on unconsciously later on when he comes to chart the course of his own life.

It could not be said that the morning was not being put to good use in the Oblomov household. The rat-tat-tat of knives dicing meat and cutting vegetables in the kitchen carried right into the village itself. From the servants' quarters came the sound of the spindle whirring and the softly lifted voice of a woman, although it was hard to tell if she was crying or just improvising some melancholy song without words.

Outside, as soon as Antip had returned with the water, a crowd of women and coachmen with pails, tubs, and pitchers suddenly surrounded him.

An old woman is carrying a bowl of flour and a pile of eggs from the storehouse to the kitchen; the cook suddenly empties some water out of the window, drenching Arapka who has spent the whole morning with his eyes glued to the window and his tongue hanging out, wagging his tail ingratiatingly.

The master himself, the elder Oblomov, did not remain idle either, but sat the whole morning at the window keeping everything that was going on outside under the most intense observation.

"Hey, Ignashka! What are you carrying there, you idiot?" he asked one individual on his way across the courtyard.

"I'm taking some knives for sharpening to the servants' quarters," he replied without looking up at his master.

"Alright, carry on and make sure those knives are really sharp!"

Then he stops one of the women.

"Hey you, that woman there, where have you been?"

"To the cellar, sir," she replied, stopping, shading her eyes with her hand to look at the window, "getting some milk for dinner."

"Alright, carry on then, and make sure you don't spill any! And you, Zakharka, what do you think you're up to—all this dashing about?" he shouted. "You won't get away with it; don't think I don't know this is the third time you've run out. Now, get back to the hallway!" And Zakharka went back to the hallway to do some more dozing.

When the cows came in from the field it was Oblomov the elder who was the first to see that they were watered. If he saw through the window a dog chasing one of the chickens he would immediately take the firmest measures to restore order.

His wife too was extremely busy. She had spent three hours with

Averka, the tailor discussing the problem of how to make her husband's quilted jacket into a jacket for Ilyusha. She made the chalk marks herself and watched Averka to make sure that he did not steal any cloth. Then she went into the maids' room to issue instructions about how much lace each one was to make for the day. Next she summoned Nastasia Ivanovna or Stepanida Agapovna or one of her other personal maids to accompany her to the garden for a purely practical purpose—to see how the apples were ripening and whether any had already ripened and fallen the day before and to check what needed pruning, what needed grafting and so on.

However, the number one priority was, of course, preparing the dinner. The whole household was involved in consultations on the subject and even the aged aunt was included in the deliberations. Everyone proposed a favorite dish; it could be giblet or noodle soup, brawn, tripe, a white or a red sauce, or whatever. Every piece of advice was given due consideration, thoroughly discussed and either adopted or rejected depending on the final verdict handed down by the mistress of the house. Nastasia Petrovna or Stepanida Ivanovna shuttled constantly between their mistress and the kitchen with reminders to add one ingredient or eliminate another, to bring sugar, honey, or wine for the meal and to make sure that the cook used all the provisions that had been issued.

Food was far and away the number one priority. How many calves were fattened for the birthdays and anniversaries! How many fowl were plumped for the table! What pains were taken, what refinements, what skill, what effort invested in these endeavors! The turkeys and the chickens destined for the festive board on name days and other celebrations were fed on nuts, the geese were deprived of all exercise and were hung motionless in sacks for days before the feast so that they were swimming in fat. What an abundance of preserves, pickles and pastries! What varieties of honey, of kvass and what a selection of pies were baked in Oblomovka!

So, up to midday it was nothing but hustle and bustle; the whole household was a veritable hive of frantic and conspicuous activity. Even on Sundays and holidays there was no let up and the house was abuzz with activity. At these times, the clatter of knives in the kitchen was thicker and faster than ever; the kitchen maid had to make several journeys from the store room to the kitchen with a double load of flour and eggs and the barnyard was a bedlam of squawks and gushing blood. A pie was baked so gigantic that the family and guests were still eating it the next day, and on the third and fourth days the leftovers were sent to the maids' room, and even on Friday enough scraps survived for a by now stale crust with no filling to be offered to Antip as a special treat. Antip would then cross himself and, nothing daunted, would attack this curious fossil with noisy relish, more gratified by the knowledge that it had come from the master's table than by the actual taste of the pie; rather like an archaeologist drinking with every sign of enjoyment some putrid wine from a recently excavated thousand-year-old drinking vessel.

Nothing of all this escaped the keen child's eye or the absorbent mind of the young Oblomov and, after all the purposeful busyness of the morning, he watched as the afternoon approached, and with it dinnertime.

The midday heat was at its most oppressive—not a cloud in the sky. The sun stood motionless overhead and scorched the grass. The air hung still and heavy. Not a tree rustled; not a ripple on the water and an implacable silence lay over the village and the fields—it was as if life were extinct. In the emptiness the sound of a human voice carried clear and far. The drone of a flying bug could be heard in the far distance and from the thick grass there arose the sound of snoring as if someone had just subsided on the spot and fallen into a delicious sleep. In the house a deathly silence reigned. The time had come for one and all to take their after dinner nap.

As the child watched, the mother, the father, the aged aunt, and the whole company repaired to their favorite spots. For those who did not have one, there was the hayloft, the garden, or the cool of the vestibule. Others, overcome by the heat and the weight of the heavy meal, just dropped wherever they happened to be, covering their faces with handkerchiefs to keep off the flies. The gardener stretched out beside his spade under a bush and the coachman lay down in the stable.

Ilya Ilyich looked into the servants' hall where they were all lying in rows on benches, on the floor and in the entranceway. The small children, left to their own devices, were crawling around the courtyard and playing with the sand. Even the dogs hid as far inside their kennels as they could go, since there was no one left to bark at. You could wander right through the whole house without meeting a soul and it would have been the easiest thing in the world to strip the house bare and cart everything off in broad daylight without the slightest interference, except that in those parts no one went in for robbery.

Trying to wake any of them from this profound, all-conquering slumber would have been like trying to raise the dead. The silence was broken only by the ragged chorus of snoring in every sharp and flat that arose from every corner of the house. Once in a while someone would raise a sleepy head and stare, startled and uncomprehending, in both directions and flop back onto the other side or, with eyes still closed, spit in his sleep, and then, with a smacking of the lips and muttering something incomprehensible, drop right off again. Another sleeper would suddenly and without the slightest warning spring up onto his two feet from where he was lying, and as if in fear of wasting precious minutes, grab a mug of kvass, and blow the flies that were floating on the surface to the side of the mug. This sent the flies, which had been motionless up to that point, into a frenzy of activity in the hope of improving their situation. The sleeper, after wetting his throat would then collapse onto the bed as if pole-axed.

Meanwhile the child just watched and watched.

After dinner the nanny had taken him outside again, but even she, in spite of the stern admonitions of her mistress and her own best intentions, could not resist the blandishments of sleep and succumbed helplessly to the epidemic that had engulfed the entire Oblomov household.

To begin with she exercised her vigilance actively, not letting the child out of her sight and scolding him when he grew too boisterous, but with the onset of the symptoms of the infection she started pleading with him not to wander outside the gate, to leave the goat alone and not to climb up to the gallery or the pigeon loft. She started looking for places to sit out of the heat, on the porch, on the steps leading down to the cellar or right on the grass with the evident intention of knitting stockings and keeping an eye on the child, but soon her attention began to waver and her head started to nod.

"Before you know it, the little scamp will be climbing up to the gallery," she thought to herself as she drifted off, "or maybe…even down to the gully…"

The old woman's head slumped to her knees and the stocking fell from her grasp. She lost sight of the child and with her mouth half open began to snore gently.

Finally the moment came that he had been waiting for so impatiently, the moment that marked the beginning of his independence. It was as if he were alone in the world. He tiptoed away from the nanny and looked around to see who was sleeping where, watching carefully to see who was waking up or spitting and grunting in their sleep. Then, with his heart pounding, he scampered up the stairs to the gallery and ran all the way around it on its creaking boards. He climbed to the pigeon loft, burrowed into the garden where it grew thickest, listened to the humming of a beetle, following its flight with his eyes as it soared high into the air. He heard something chirping in the grass and started searching for the disturbers of the peace, finally catching a dragonfly. He would tear off its wings to see what it would do or skewer it with a straw to see how it would fly with this appendage. He watched with bated breath the absorbing spectacle of a spider sucking the blood of a trapped fly and the wretched victim struggling and buzzing in its captor's toils, finally administering the coup de grace to both the victim and its tormentor.

Next he scrambles down into the ditch and rummages around for some roots or other, scrapes off the outsides and bites into them greedily; they taste much better than the apples and jam given to him by his mummy. He runs out of the gate; he wants to go to the birch woods—it seems so near that he could get to it in five minutes—not going by way of the road, but straight through the ditch, the fence, and the holes in the ground; but he is afraid. He has heard about the goblins, the bandits, and the fearsome beasts that lurk there.

He even wants to run down into the gully; it is only about fifty yards from the garden. He has already got to the edge and screwed up his eyes to look down into what seems like the crater of a volcano…but suddenly all the talk and legends about the gully started flooding back and he is seized with terror. So he rushes back, more dead than alive, and, trembling with fear, flings himself into the arms of his nanny and wakes her up.

She woke with a start and adjusted her headscarf, tucking the clumps of gray hair underneath with her fingers. Trying to act as if she had never been asleep at all, she looked at Ilyusha suspiciously and then at the windows of the house and with trembling fingers began to click against each other the needles she was using to knit the stocking that lay in her lap.

The heat had now begun to abate a little and nature began to stir, while the sun moved towards the wood. Sounds of life began to break the silence of the house. Somewhere a door creaked; footsteps could be heard in the courtyard and someone sneezed in the hayloft.

Very soon a man hurried out of the kitchen, staggering under the weight of the huge samovar he was carrying. The household began to gather for tea. There were crumpled faces, watering eyes; red streaks lingered on cheeks and temples and voices were still thick with sleep. People were breathing heavily, sighing, and clearing their throats, yawning, running their hands through their hair, and stretching, not yet fully awake.

The heavy dinner and the sleeping had left everyone with a raging thirst, and throats were parched. Even after as many as twelve cups of tea people were still thirsty and there was much groaning and sighing as they tried cranberry juice, pear water, or even looked up remedies in the medical manual in their attempts to ease the dryness in their throats. Everyone was seeking rescue from thirst as if from some divine punishment and they milled around desperately with their tongues hanging out, like a caravan in the Arabian Desert hunting for an oasis.

The child was by his mother's side watching the strange faces around him, taking in their halting sleepy talk. It was fun to watch them and he was fascinated by whatever nonsense they happened to utter.

After tea they all went about their business. One would go down to the brook to stroll quietly along the bank, idly kicking stones into the water; another would sit by the window to catch the passing show—a cat running past, a jackdaw in flight—the spectator's head swiveling from left to right and back again as the eyes and the tip of the nose followed the trajectory of both creatures. This is exactly what dogs like to do, sometimes sitting the whole day long, sunning themselves on a window ledge and closely scrutinizing everyone who passes by.

Ilyusha's mother takes his head and puts it in her lap and slowly strokes his hair, inviting Nastasia Ivanovna and Stepanida Tikhonovna to share her delight in its softness and chatting with them about Ilyusha's future and making him the hero of some glorious epic of her own creation, while they in turn predict the most brilliant career imaginable.

Now dusk is beginning to fall. Once again a fire is crackling in the kitchen and again the drumbeat of the knives can be heard; supper is being prepared.

The servants have gathered at the gate; there is the strumming of a balalaika mixed with sounds of laughter. People are playing tag.

The sun had already dropped behind the trees and still cast a few tepid rays that cut a fiery swathe through the wood, setting the tops of the pines ablaze with gold. One by one the rays disappeared, the last lingering for an eternity and piercing the dense canopy of branches like a fine needle until it too was gone.

Objects were losing their outlines and began to merge, first into a gray and then into a dark formless mass. The bird chorus grew fainter and fainter, finally dying away altogether, except for one obstinate bird that defiantly breached the consensus of silence with its call monotonously reiterated at ever longer intervals until finally, giving one last almost soundless chirp, it fluttered its wings and fell silent, leaving, the faintest rustle in the leaves around it

Silence descended. Only the sound of the grasshoppers remained as they tried to out-chirp each other. White vapor rose from the earth and wafted across the meadow and the river. The river too quieted down; after a while there was one last splash and then all motion ceased.

There was a smell of damp. The darkness thickened. The trees merged into monstrous shapes. In the wood, now grown sinister, something creaked as if one of the monsters was on the move and a dry twig had snapped under its foot.

The first star appeared in the sky, twinkling brightly like a glistening eye and lights gleamed in the windows. It was the time when nature's majestic silence holds sway, a time when creative juices pump more strongly, when poetic impulses boil to the surface, when emotions surge, and nameless yearnings stab the heart, a time when the seeds of crime flower more boldly and resolutely in the malignant soul and when…in Oblomovka, people simply settle down quietly for a good night's sleep.

"Mummy, let's go for a walk!" says Ilyusha.

"What an idea! Going out at this time of night!" she replied. "It's dark out there, you'll catch a chill in your feet. And it's scary, the goblin comes out at night in the woods looking for small children to carry off."

"Where does he take them? What does he look like? Where does he live?" the child asks.

And his mother proceeded to give free rein to her unbridled fantasies. The child listened, opening and closing his eyes until finally overcome by sleep. The nanny came in and, taking him from his mother's lap, carried off the sleeping child with his head lolling over her shoulder and put him to bed.

"Well, that's another day over, praise God!" said the members of the Oblomov household as they got into bed, grunting and crossing themselves. "We got through that one safely, may God send us another just like it tomorrow, praise be to the Lord!"

Now Oblomov dreams of another time, an endless winter evening when nanny is whispering into his ear, as he snuggles close to her for protection, about a mysterious land where there is no cold, no night, where miracles happen and the rivers flow with milk and honey, where no one does a stroke of work all year long and where they know only that theirs is a world where handsome lads like Ilya Ilyich himself and maidens whose beauty defies description even in a fairy tale, live lives of ease and pleasure.

There is a good fairy who lives there who sometimes appears among us in the form of a pike and who chooses as her favorite someone quiet and harmless, that is to say some totally passive type whom everyone is always picking on, and, just like that, showers upon him all the things his heart desires. He eats to his heart's content and arrays himself in the finest clothes and finally marries some fabulous beauty, a veritable Militrisa Kirbityevna. The child, all eyes and ears, is enraptured by this tale.

The nanny, or the tales themselves that had been handed down, so skillfully contrived to avoid reality that to the end of his days, Oblomov remained in thrall to the legends and fantasies that had captured his imagination as a child. Nanny, in a spirit of simple good nature, told him the story of Yemelya the Fool, that sly and malicious satire that ridicules our ancestors, or maybe even ourselves.

The adult Ilya Ilyich, of course, eventually came to realize that there were no such things as rivers of milk and honey or good fairies, and cheerfully dismissed his nanny's tales with a smile, but the smile was not entirely genuine and was always accompanied by a wistful sigh. For him, real life and fairy tales were hopelessly intertwined and, in spite of himself, the thought that life was not a fairy tale and fairy tales were not life, depressed him at times. He could not help thinking about Militrisa Kirbityevna; he was drawn to that far off land where there was nothing but good times and where cares and worries were unknown. He never lost the urge to lie down on the stove-top bench, walk around in clothes that just appeared out of nowhere, and eat food conjured up by the good fairy.

Oblomov's father and grandfather had also spent their childhood listening to the same fairy tales that had been handed down unchanged through the ages, learned and repeated by rote, from one generation of nannies and child minders to another.

The nanny, however, also told tales of a different kind, which gripped the child's imagination. She recounted to him the exploits of our own Achilleses and Ulysseses, the derring-do of Ilya Muromets, Dobrynya Nikitich, Alyosha Popovich, of the Giant Polkan, and the Pilgrim Kalyechishche and how they roamed the length and breadth of Russia, smiting the numberless hordes of infidels and vying with each other to see who could quaff the goblet of vodka in a single gulp without flinching. She told of bloodthirsty bandits, sleeping princesses, of towns and people turned to stone. She told tales of our demons, the living dead, monsters and werewolves. With Homeric simplicity and directness she brought to life starkly and in vivid detail an Iliad of Russian life, leaving an indelible impression on the young Oblomov's mind and imagination.

It was an epic composed by our Homeric bards of those remote times when man had not yet mastered the dangers and secrets of nature and life and went in fear of werewolves and goblins and sought protection from the likes of Alyosha Popovich against the evils surrounding him, times when marvels and portents ruled the air, the waters, the woods and the fields. In those times the life of man was frightening and treacherous; it was dangerous to set foot outside his home; at any moment he might be savaged by a wild beast, cut down by a bandit, robbed of all his possessions by a marauding Tatar, or simply disappear without trace. Portents and omens would suddenly appear in the heavens, pillars and balls of fire; a light would flare over a grave and something would move around in the woods, carrying what seemed like a lamp and cackling terrifyingly, its eyes flashing in the darkness. Also, so many strange and incomprehensible things would happen to an individual who, after a long and good life, would suddenly and for no apparent reason say something inauspicious or would up and cry out in a strange voice or start sleepwalking, or would suddenly start pounding and beating the ground without rhyme or reason. Such events were always immediately preceded by a hen crowing like a cock or a raven cawing on the roof.

The puny mortal, in terror and bewilderment, would reach out for anything in his environment or his imagination that could provide him with the key to the mysteries of the nature around him and the nature within him.

Of course, it is possible that a life of unvarying, sleepy tranquility, a life dull and uneventful, and unmarked by real adversity, vicissitude, adventure, or danger, makes people invent another fantasy world amid the real one around them in a search for excitement and stimulation for the idle imagination, or for ways of explaining quite normal sets of circumstances, and inclines them to seek the causes of events outside the events themselves.

Our poor ancestors groped their way through life; neither curbing nor giving free rein to their wishes, and then naively greeted hardship and misfortune with surprise or dismay and sought the reasons in the mute, obscure hieroglyphs of nature. According to them death occurred because a dead body had previously been carried out of the house and through the gates head first instead of feet first; a fire broke out because a dog had been howling for three nights in a row under the window. So they saw to it that the dead were carried out feet first, but went on eating the same food in the same amounts and kept on sleeping on the bare grass. If they found a dog howling they would beat it or chase it away and still shook the sparks from a burning torch down through a crack in the rotting floor.

To this very day, Russians amid the grim, down-to-earth reality of their lives still succumb to the charms of these tales of yore and will no doubt go on clinging to these beliefs for a long time to come.

Listening to his nanny's tales of our Golden Fleece, the Firebird, of the traps and secret chambers of the wizard's castle, the boy would thrill to the exploits of the hero, imagining himself in the role; shivers would run up his spine and he would suffer the hero's reverses in his own flesh. The tales succeeded each other in an endless stream. The nanny narrated vividly, with feeling and with fervor. At times she was herself transported because she half believed her stories herself. The old woman's eyes sparkled, her head trembled with emotion, and her voice would rise to an incredibly shrill pitch. The child, filled with nameless terror, would cling tightly to her with tears in his eyes.

Whether it was the story of the dead rising from their graves at midnight, the monster's victims languishing in his dungeon, or the bear with the wooden leg stumping through the villages in search of his own leg that had been cut off, the child's scalp would tingle with horror and his child's imagination would run hot and cold and, his nerves strung tight, he would experience an exquisitely painful thrill. When his nanny dolefully repeated the words of the bear: "creak, creak, wooden leg! I have walked through villages, through the countryside and all the women are asleep except one, who is sitting on my hide, cooking my flesh and spinning my hair into yarn..." and when she told how the bear finally entered the hut and was about to pounce on the wretch who had robbed him of his leg, the child would panic and fling himself into her arms, his eyes welling with tears of fright, while at the same time chortling with gleeful relief at having escaped the claws of the bear and finding himself safe and sound on the stove bench nestling beside his nanny.

The child's imagination was haunted by strange phantoms; dread and foreboding had burrowed their way into his psyche and would long remain there, perhaps forever. He viewed life with misgiving and saw everything around him as sinister and menacing, and dreamed longingly of that magic land from which all evil, trouble and sorrow had been banished, the land of Militrisa Kirbityevna, where the finest food and clothing are provided without charge or effort. These tales exerted a powerful influence not only on the children, but held even the adults in their thrall to the end of their days.

From the master and his wife on down to Taras the brawny blacksmith, everyone in the village started getting nervous as darkness fell; every tree could turn into a giant, every bush into a bandit's lair. Grown men and women and children alike would turn pale at the creaking of the shutters and the howling of the wind in the chimney. At Epiphany no one would venture out beyond the gate alone after ten at night, and on the night before Easter no one dared to enter the stables for fear of coming across the house goblin there.

In Oblomovka people believed in everything from werewolves to the living dead. Tell them that a sheaf of hay has been seen running loose in the field and they will swallow the story without a second thought. If someone starts a rumor that a ram is not really a ram but some witch called Marfa or Stepanida they will be terrified of both the ram *and* Marfa. It would never occur to them to question why the ram is suddenly not a ram and Marfa is suddenly a witch and they would even set upon anyone who dared to entertain doubts on the subject—such was the strength of belief in the supernatural in Oblomovka.

Later Ilya Ilyich would come to see that the dead do not rise from their graves, that in real life any giant who turns up is immediately exhibited in a sideshow as a freak and bandits are thrown into jail; although even if people stop believing in ghosts there is still a lingering vestige of fear, an unaccountable feeling of uneasiness. Ilya Ilyich came to realize that it is not monsters which cause life's dangers—although he had hardly ever been exposed to any real danger—but he expected something terrible to happen at any moment and was full of apprehension. Even now, when he is alone in a dark room or sees a dead body, his blood runs cold from the nameless dread that had been instilled in him as a child. In the mornings he laughs at his own fears, but at night they would drain the blood from his face.

Now Ilya Ilyich suddenly saw himself as a boy of thirteen or fourteen. He was by then at school in the village of Verkhlyovo, about five versts from Oblomovka. It was a small boarding school run by the manager of the Verkhlyovo estate, a German by the name of Stoltz, for the children of the gentry in the area. One of the other pupils was Stoltz's own son, Andrei, a boy of about the same age as Oblomov. There was also another boy, who rarely attended classes since he suffered from scrofula and spent most of his boyhood with his eyes or his ears bandaged and snivelling to himself because he had been taken away from his grandmother and put in a strange house among tormentors where there was no one to show him affection or bake his favorite pies. These were the only boys in the school at that time.

There was no help for it, his parents had to send their little darling away to school for his education and in the end, in spite of all the tears, protestations and tantrums, that is where he was sent. Stoltz, like almost all Germans, was strict and efficient. Maybe Ilyusha might have ended up getting a decent education at his school if Oblomovka had been more like five hundred versts away, but in the circumstances what hope was there?

As it was, Verkhlyovo too was under the spell of Oblomovian attitudes, habits, and way of life; it had after all once been part of the Oblomov estate and with the exception of the Stoltz household, the whole place exuded the same old lethargy, simplicity of manner, quiet, and passivity.

The child's mind and heart were full of the pictures, scenes and values of that lifestyle long before he set eyes on his first book, and who is to say how early the seed of intellectual development takes root in a child's brain? Is it possible to trace the formation of the first ideas and impressions in the mind of a child? Maybe it all starts when the child is just beginning to utter his first words, or even before that when he has not yet even started to walk but is just watching everything with the mute, intent gaze of an infant that adults think of as vacuous; maybe it is then that the child is already seeing and guessing the meaning and relationships of the things around him, although neither he nor others are aware of it.

Perhaps Ilyusha had long been noticing and understanding what was being said and done around him; his father in his velveteen trousers and brown quilted jacket day in day out, doing nothing but pacing the room from one corner to another with his hands behind his back, taking pinches of snuff and blowing his nose; his mother shuttling from coffee to tea to dinner; his father never dreaming of checking the number of sheaves reported to have been cut and harvested and calling the culprit to account for any inaccuracy. But let there be the slightest delay in bringing him a handkerchief and he would cry blue murder and turn the whole household upside down.

Perhaps the child had already made up his mind that the one and only way to live was the way the adults around him lived. And what other conclusion would you have him draw? And how *did* the adults of Oblomovka actually live?

Did they ever ask themselves: "What's the purpose of life?" God knows. And what was their answer? Most probably, none at all; it all seemed so simple and obvious. The notion of a life of toil was something unknown to them. They had never heard of people constantly weighed down by the burden of worries and responsibilities, scurrying hither and thither over the face of the earth and giving themselves up to a life of unremitting and ceaseless labor.

The people of Oblomovka found it difficult to believe in painful emotions; to them the constant drive for movement and activity could not be described as life and overpowering emotion was something they avoided like the plague, and while in other places people's bodies were swiftly consumed in the furnace of the volcanic emotions surging within them, the souls of the inhabitants of Oblomovka languished gently and untroubled within their soft bodies. Life did not mark them, as it did others, with premature wrinkles or strike them with crippling psychological afflictions.

These good people saw life as nothing but an ideal of peace, quiet, and total inactivity interrupted from time to time by certain unpleasant events such as illness, loss, disputes, and, yes, even work. They put up with work as a punishment inflicted long ago on their remote ancestors and inherited by them, but they could never grow to like it and took every opportunity to avoid it, regarding such avoidance as right and proper.

They never bothered themselves with abstruse intellectual or moral questions and as a result enjoyed consistently good health, high spirits, and long lives. At forty the men looked youthful and the old people never had to wrestle with protracted, painful illness, but, after reaching an incredibly advanced age, would just slip quietly away, stiffening imperceptibly before finally and almost soundlessly breathing their last. This is why people are said to have been stronger in those days. And stronger they were. In those days people were in no hurry to explain the meaning of life to a child or to treat life as something complicated and solemn that a child had to be trained for. They did not break a child's head with books that just fill it with a host of questions, which in turn eat away at the mind and heart and shorten your life.

The rules of life were simply handed down just as they were, from father to son as they had been for countless generations, and with them the injunction to preserve them intact and inviolate like a sacred flame. Ilya Ilyich's father did things the way they had been done by his father and grandfather, and, for all we know, that is the way things are still being done in Oblomovka to this very day. After all what was there to think about, to get excited about, to find out about; what goals were there to strive for?

None of this was necessary; life like a stream flowed gently past them and they had only to sit on the bank of the river and watch the inevitable procession of events as they passed by of their own accord before their very eyes.

So, as he slept, Ilya Ilyich began to see in his imagination living tableaux of the three main acts in life's pageant, acts which were performed in his own family and those of his friends and relatives, birth, marriage, and death. A colorful procession of particular scenes, both joyful and sorrowful, from the pageant stretched out before him; christenings, namedays, family celebrations, fast and feast days, noisy dinners, gatherings of relatives, welcomes, congratulations, formal occasions of tears and smiles. All these occasions were meticulously and solemnly marked and observed.

He could even pick out the familiar faces and gestures of the guests at these various gatherings amid all the fuss and bustle. Confront them with the most delicate matchmaking introduction or the most formal wedding ceremony or nameday celebration and they will know exactly the right thing to do without the slightest deviation from the traditional forms. Who to seat where, what should be served and how, who should ride with whom to the ceremony and how to read the signs and omens. In all these matters no one in Oblomovka was ever known to put a foot wrong.

Perhaps you think they don't know how to raise children there? Well, just take a look at the chubby, rosy-cheeked little cherubs going around with their mothers. What matters to the mother is only that her child should be nice and plump with a white complexion and free from sickness.

They shun the spring and will have no truck with it until they have baked their first lark pastry. This is the kind of thing everyone knows and no one would dream of going against it. This is where their life is and this is the code they live by. Here are the only joys and sorrows they know. They banish the thought of any other care or sorrow and recognize no other joys. Their lives are filled with these elemental, ever recurring events that leave no room for other thoughts and engage their emotions to the full. They can hardly wait for the next rite of passage, feast, or ceremony, but once they have done with christening, marrying, or burying someone, they forget all about whoever it is and sink back into their habitual torpor from which they are aroused only by the next name-day, wedding or similar event.

As soon as a child is born the first concern of the parents is to see to it that all the required and appropriate customs, practices and rituals are scrupulously observed down to the last detail—especially the christening feast. Only then can the anxious and protective process of nurturing and caring for the child begin. The mother makes it her business as well as that of the nanny to raise a healthy child, protect it against colds, evil eyes and other hostile influences, and they take great pains to ensure that the child is always happy and well fed. As soon as the boy is able to stand on his own two feet and no longer needs the nanny, the mother instinctively starts looking around for a girl for him, and the rosier-cheeked and sturdier the better. Then the whole round of rituals and feasts culminating in a wedding gets under way all over again, and it is this that gives life its zest and meaning.

And so the cycle is repeated: births, celebrations, feasts, with only funerals calling for a change of setting, but not for long. New faces take the places of the old, baby boys grow into marriageable young men who duly marry and reproduce themselves. Such is the pattern according to which life weaves itself this seamless length of identical fabric to be snipped gently only at the grave itself.

Other problems, of course, presented themselves from time to time, but the people of Oblomovka confronted them for the most part with stolid passive resistance, and the problems, after hanging over their heads for a while, would just flutter away like birds, which, unable to find a comfortable perch on a smooth stone wall, flap their wings uselessly over it and then just give up and fly on.

For example, there was the time when part of the gallery on one side of the house collapsed and buried the brood hen and her chicks under the debris and would have hit Aksinya, Antip's wife, who was about to return to her seat under it with her spinning, if she had not had the good fortune to have chosen that very moment to fetch some flax. There was a great commotion. Everyone from the eldest to the youngest came running and were horrified at the thought that it might very well have been the mistress herself passing underneath at the time with Ilya Ilyich, instead of the hen with her chicks. Everyone was "oo"ing and "ah"ing and starting to blame one another for not thinking of it long before; this one should have said something about the problem, that one should have given orders to fix it and someone else should have gone and fixed it. They were all amazed that the gallery should have collapsed when, only the day before, they had been equally amazed that it was still standing after all this time.

There followed a noisy disquisition about how to remedy the situation and regrets were expressed about the unfortunate fate of the chicken and her brood. The crowd then slowly dispersed, after issuing a strict injunction against allowing Ilya Ilyich anywhere near the gallery. Three weeks later, Andryushka, Petrushka, and Vaska were instructed to remove the debris, planks, and railings and drag it all to the sheds to get it out of the way, and there it mouldered until the spring.

Whenever old Oblomov spotted the debris through the window he was reminded of the need to repair the gallery. So he would call the carpenter and begin consultations about the best way to proceed; whether to build an entirely new gallery or just to pull down what remained of the old one. Inevitably the discussion would end with old Oblomov dismissing the carpenter with the words: "You be off home now and I'll think about it!" This went on until one day Vaska or Motka came to the master to report that only that morning Motka had clambered up to the part of the gallery that was still standing and had found that the corners had come loose from the walls and that the whole thing was about to collapse at any moment. Thereupon, the carpenter was called in for a final consultation at which it was decided to prop up the surviving portion of the gallery with the timber from the debris, and, sure enough, the job was completed by the end of the month.

"Well, the gallery is as good as new!" old Oblomov said to his wife, "look how nicely Fyedot has spaced the beams, it's like the colonnade in front of the Governor's mansion! Now we won't have to worry about it for ages." Someone then pointed out to him that while they were about it, it might not be a bad idea to fix the gates and the porch, otherwise, never mind about cats, but even pigs would be getting through the gaps in the steps into the cellar.

"Yes, yes, you're right," Ilya Ivanovich conceded worriedly and immediately set off to inspect the porch.

"Look, it's really on its last legs," he said as he set the porch rocking like a cradle with his foot.

"But it was always rickety from the moment it was built," someone pointed out.

"So what if it was rickety," riposted Oblomov, "it never collapsed even though it has gone sixteen years without repairs. Luka did a terrific job! That's what I call a carpenter, a real carpenter…he's dead now, God rest his soul! Nowadays they're a bunch of slackers, there isn't the same pride in workmanship!"

At this point something else caught his attention, but they say that the porch still rocks just as much as ever if you step on it, although it hasn't collapsed yet, so it does seem as if Luka really was a first rate carpenter.

However, we must give the Oblomovs their due, sometimes when there was trouble or things went wrong they would get deeply involved, and even get heated and indignant. They would see something that needed fixing and say: "how could this possibly have been neglected and left like this for so long, something must be done right away!"

Then the topic on everyone's lips would be repairing the little bridge over the ditch or fencing in the garden to stop the cattle ruining the trees because part of the wattle fence had collapsed and was lying on the ground.

Just to give an example of how deeply Ilya Ivanovich could get involved, why, once when he was walking around the garden he stooped and, grunting and groaning with the effort, actually picked up a piece of the fence with his own hands and ordered the gardener to put in two stakes right away. Thanks to this display of efficiency on Oblomov's part the fence remained standing right through the summer and did not collapse again until the winter under the weight of the snow. Finally, the matter was pursued so vigorously that three new planks were actually laid on the little bridge—immediately that is—after Antip, attempting to cross it, had tumbled into the ditch along with his horse, barrel, and all. Indeed, Antip's bruises had hardly had time to heal before the bridge was repaired.

Nor did the cows and goats manage to do much scavenging after the garden fence had collapsed again; they had eaten the currant bushes and were just working on their tenth lime tree but had not yet gotten around to the apple trees, when the order came to hammer the fence more firmly into the ground and to dig a little moat around it. The two cows and the goat that were caught in the act got what was coming to them, in the form of a sound thrashing.

Now Ilya Ilyich saw in his dream the big dark living room in his parents house with the antique ash armchairs that were always kept under covers, a huge, clumsy, and uncomfortable divan upholstered in a stained and discolored blue fabric and one leather armchair. A long winter evening was drawing in. Oblomov's mother was sitting on the divan with her legs tucked under her idly knitting a child's stocking, yawning and scratching her head from time to time with a knitting needle. Nastasya Ivanovna and Pelageya Ignatyevna were sitting beside her with their heads bent intently over their sewing; they were working on something or other for Ilyusha or his father or for themselves for the holiday.

The father was pacing the room, his hands behind his back in a mood of perfect contentment. From time to time he would sit down in the armchair for a while and then get up and start pacing again, listening carefully to the sound of his own footsteps. Then he would take a pinch of snuff, blow his nose, and take another pinch.

The room was dimly lit by a single tallow candle, and even that was only a concession granted on autumn and winter evenings. During the summer everyone tried to go to bed and get up in daylight without the help of candles. This was partly because of habit but partly out of thrift. The Oblomov household was exceedingly sparing in its use of articles that had to be purchased and were not produced at home. They would happily slaughter the finest turkey or a dozen young chickens to entertain a guest but would never put one raisin too many in a dish, and would turn pale if they saw the same guest helping himself to another glass of wine. Of course, only on the rarest of occasions would anyone stoop to such a level of depravity. Only a total boor, a social pariah, would be capable of such behavior and such a guest would never be allowed anywhere near the house again.

No, this was not at all the accepted code of conduct. A guest would not dream of accepting anything before it had been offered at least three times, and was well aware that the initial offer of a dish or a glass of wine was much more likely to mean that he was supposed to decline it than actually to sample it. And it was not just any guest who warranted the lighting of two candles. Candles had to be purchased in town for good money, and the mistress herself kept all such purchased goods under lock and key. The candle ends were carefully counted and hidden away. They hated to spend money in any shape or form, and no matter how much they needed something it was only with the greatest misgivings that they could bring themselves to part with the actual cash even if only an insignificant sum was involved; but a major expenditure was accompanied by weeping, wailing, and gnashing of teeth. The Oblomovs would sooner have put up with the worst inconveniences or hardships, and indeed preferred not to think of them as inconveniences or hardships at all, than spend money.

This was why the divan in the drawing room had long been covered in stains; that was why Ilya Ivanovich's leather armchair was leather in name only. The leather itself had peeled away to reveal the stringy layer underneath. Only one patch of the original leather remained and that was on the back of the chair. Five years before, the leather had finally been reduced to shreds and tatters and had peeled off and disappeared. Perhaps this was also the reason why the gates were all crooked and the porch was so rickety, but the idea of spending two, three, or even five hundred roubles on the most vital necessity seemed to them nothing short of suicidal folly.

When he heard that one young landowner in the area had been to Moscow and spent three hundred roubles on a dozen shirts, twenty-five roubles on boots and four hundred roubles on a waistcoat for his wedding, old Oblomov crossed himself, grimaced with horror and snapped, "spendthrifts like that should be locked up!"

They were, of course, totally impervious to the economic principles of the need for the rapid and active turnover of capital, intensive productivity, and exchange of goods. In their simple way there was only one principle governing the use of capital that they understood and honored—keeping it locked in the trunk!

The members of the household and their regular visitors would sit around the living room in the armchairs half awake and lolling in a variety of postures. Conversation consisted for the most part in a profound silence. They saw each other every day and had long since exhausted their reserves of wit and wisdom, and they received very little news from the outside. This profound silence was broken only by the creak of the heavy homemade boots of Ilya Ivanovich, by the muffled tick of the pendulum of the wall clock inside its case, and by the occasional sound of thread being bitten off or snapped by Pelageya Ignatyevna or Nastasya Ivanovna.

Sometimes half an hour would go by before someone would give an audible yawn, cover his mouth and cross himself, muttering, "Lord, preserve me!" Then, one after the other, as if responding to some signal, everyone would start yawning with their mouths wide open; it was as if some respiratory epidemic had suddenly spread around the room, forcing them to suck air into their lungs and, in some cases, even bringing tears to their eyes. Or Ilya Ivanovich would go to the window, look out and remark with some surprise, "it's only five o'clock and already so dark outside!" And someone was sure to reply, "it always gets dark around now at this time of the year, the evenings are drawing in."

In the spring they would be just as surprised, only pleasantly, to find that the evenings were getting longer, but if you were to ask what difference did the longer evenings make to them, they would not be able to tell you.

More silence. Then someone would happen to snuff out a candle, causing a stir, and someone would be sure to say, "an unexpected visitor is coming!" and this would spark a whole conversation.

"Who could it be, this visitor?" the lady of the house would say. "It couldn't be Nastasya Faddeyevna? If only it were—but no, she wouldn't come before the holidays. How nice that would be though! What a time we'd have, hugging each other and crying together in each other's arms, going to matins and mass together...! But what am I talking about? I know I'm younger than her but I can't stand for nearly as long as she can!"

"Now when was it that she left?" asked Ilya Ivanovich. "Wasn't it after St Ilya's day?"

"Oh, come on, Ilya Ivanovich, you always get everything mixed up!" said his wife reprovingly, "she was gone by Whitsun!"

"No, she was still here for St. Peter's!" Ilya Ivanovich insisted.

"That's just like you!" his wife reproached him. "Whenever you argue you always end up making a fool of yourself!"

"But don't you remember, she must have been here for St. Peter's, we were still baking mushroom pies and you know how much she likes them...!"

"No, that must have been Marya Onisimovna, she's the one who likes the mushroom pies—don't you remember! And Marya Onisimovna stayed until St. Prokhor's and St. Nikanor's, not St. Ilya's!"

They kept track of time by the holidays on the church calendar, by the seasons, and by various family and domestic occasions, but never by dates and months. This may have been partly because it was not just Oblomov himself who always got the names of the months mixed up and the dates in the wrong order, everyone else did too.

Defeated, Ilya Ivanovich could find nothing to say and the company drifted back into its habitual torpor. Ilyusha dozed, huddled up against his mother's back, nodding off to sleep from time to time. After a while one of the guests would observe with a deep sigh, "that Vassily Fomich, Marya Onisimovna's husband, God rest his soul; such a picture of health, yet he died without even reaching sixty—you'd think someone like that would live to a hundred!"

"We all have to go when our time comes, it's God's will," Pelageya Ignatievna pointed out with a sigh, "here people are dying, yet the Khlopovs can't christen their babies fast enough, they say that Anna Andreyevna's just had another one, her sixth."

"It's not just Anna Andreyevna," said the lady of the house, "wait until her brother gets married and the children start coming, that will keep them good and busy! The mother can hardly wait for the young ones to grow up before they start eyeing them as prospects for their daughters; but where are they going to find matches for them around here? These days they're all demanding dowries—and in cash too!"

"What are you talking about?" asked Ilya Ivanovich, going over to join the conversation.

"We were saying…" they said and told him what they had been talking about.

"Well, that's life," Ilya Ivanovich pronounced weightily, "someone dies, someone is born and meanwhile we're all getting older. It's bad enough that every year is different from the one before, but even the days are different from one another. Why is that? Now, if every day were like the one before—and the one after—wouldn't that be something! It's really too bad when you think of it."

"The old get older and the young grow up," a sleepy voice chimed in from a corner of the room.

"It's best just to pray to God and put such things out of your mind," the lady of the house admonished them.

"You're right, you're right!" said Ilya Ivanovich, retreating hurriedly and in embarrassment from his attempts to pontificate and resumed his pacing of the room.

Another lengthy silence descended; the only sound was the clicking of the knitting needles. From time to time their hostess would break the silence. "It's really dark outside," she would remark, "soon it will be Christmas, please God! And the family will be here and we'll be having such a good time that we'll hardly notice how long the evenings are. Now, if Malanya Petrovna were to come there wouldn't be a dull moment. You never know what she'll be up to next. One minute it's telling fortunes with melted tin or wax, the next minute she's running outside the gate; my maids don't know whether they're coming or going when she's around. She's always dreaming up all kinds of games. What a character!"

"Yes, she's the life of the party," someone remarked. "Two years ago she organized tobogganing down the hill, that's how Luka Savich hurt his head."

At this, everyone began to liven up, looking over at Luka Savich and dissolving into giggles.

"So tell us about it, Luka Savich, what happened?" said Ilya Ivanovich, laughing fit to cry.

While everyone was laughing, Ilyusha woke up and joined in.

"But there's nothing to tell!" Luka Savich protested in embarrassment. "It was that Aleksei Naumich, he made it all up; it was absolutely nothing!"

This was met by a chorus of protest. "Come on, what do you mean it was nothing, what do you take us for? What about that scar on your forehead, it's still there?" And they went on laughing.

"What's so funny?" Luka Savich kept on protesting whenever the laughter died down for a moment.

"I didn't…it wasn't…it was all that blasted Vaska's fault. He palmed off some old sled on me and it fell to pieces under me so that…" But he just could not make himself heard above the laughter no matter how hard he tried to finish his tale of woe. The laughter was contagious and spread throughout the house until everyone, family, guests, servants, and all were caught up in it. The whole place rocked with laughter at the thought of the comical incident. They laughed long, unquenchably, and in unison like the Gods on Olympus. Whenever the laughter showed signs of slackening, someone would start up again, and they were off again. Finally, by degrees, the laughter died away as people struggled to catch their breath.

After a moment's silence Ilya Ivanovich asked: "thinking of taking your toboggan out again at Christmas, Luka Savich?" This sally set off another roar of laughter lasting a good ten minutes. "How about getting Antipka to build a toboggan run for…I mean, Luka Savich is such a great enthusiast, I'm sure he can hardly wait…" his last few words were drowned by the ensuing guffaws.

"I wonder if the toboggan escaped unharmed?" another wag in the company managed to gasp, weak with laughter. Another gust of laughter followed that went on and on, dying down only gradually as people wiped away their tears, blew their noses, coughed uncontrollably, spat, and weakly sputtered such remarks as: "Oh, God, he was absolutely soaked!" "It was hilarious!" "Unbelievable!" or " Upside down, with his coat-tails flying!"

This was greeted by one last prolonged outburst, which finally trailed away. Someone sighed, someone yawned, muttering something incoherent, then everyone lapsed into silence, a silence once again broken only by the sound of the clock ticking, the creaking of boots, and the occasional gentle snapping of thread. Suddenly Ilya Ivanovich stopped in the middle of the room and, with a look of alarm, touched the tip of his nose. "Oh, no, this is terrible," he said, "look, the tip of my nose is itching, there's going to be a death"

"There you go again!" his wife exclaimed, clasping her hands, "it's not the tip of your nose itching that means there's going to be a death, it's the bridge of your nose! Really, what a scatterbrain you are! What if you were to say something like that when we were visiting people or when we had guests—it would be so embarrassing!"

"Well, what *does* it mean then when the tip of your nose itches?" said Ilya Ivanovich, discountenanced.

"A death! Really, what can you be thinking of?"

"I'm always mixing things up," said Ilya Ivanovich. "How can a person be expected to know what it means when you itch in all these different places; the side of your nose, the tip, the eyebrows…?"

Pelageya Ivanovna was quick to supply the information. "The side means news, between the eyebrows means tears, the forehead means meeting someone, on the right a man, on the left a woman, the ears means rain, the lips, kissing, the whiskers, eating sweets, the elbow, sleeping in a new place, the soles of the feet, a journey"

"Well done, Pelageya Ivanovna!" said Ilya Ivanovich, "and isn't there something about the price of butter going down when the back of your head itches?"

At this the ladies began to laugh and whisper among themselves and some of the men were smiling, but the gathering burst of laughter was forestalled when the room was filled with a noise like the growling of dogs and the hissing of cats just at the moment when they are about to set on one another. It was the clock gearing up to chime.

"Good lord, nine o'clock already!" exclaimed Ilya Ivanovich like someone who had just heard some unexpected good news, "would you believe I hardly noticed the time passing! Hey, Vaska, Vanka, Motka! Three sleepy faces appeared.

"What about setting the table?" Oblomov said with annoyance and surprise. "How about giving the master and his guests a little service here? Well, don't just stand around, bring the vodka and quick about it!"

"Now you see why the tip of your nose was itching," Pelageya Ivanovna said triumphantly, "you'll be looking into a glass when you're drinking your vodka!"

Supper was followed by an exchange of smacking kisses and signs of the cross. Then they would all go off to bed and would soon be sleeping without a care in the world.

In his dream Ilya Ilich saw not one or even two such evenings, but whole weeks, months, even entire years of days and evenings spent in this unvarying fashion. There was nothing to disturb the sameness of this life and the Oblomov household did not feel it as at all tedious or cloying since they were simply incapable of imagining anything different—and even if they could have, they would have recoiled from it in horror.

As far as a different way of life was concerned, they simply did not want to know. They would have hated anything that forced them to change any detail of their existence and would have experienced a nagging uneasiness if the next day were not exactly like the day before and the one after. If other people wanted to go in for variety, change, the unexpected, they were welcome—but not the inhabitants of Oblomovka. If other people were interested in looking for trouble, let them, but the people of Oblomovka did not want any part of it. Other people could do whatever they wanted.

The unexpected, whatever its advantages, was simply unsettling; it meant trouble, bother, agitation; it meant keeping on the go, doing business, in other words busyness! No thank you!

They spent decades dozing, half asleep, splitting their sides with good-natured laughter at incidents that tickled their rustic sense of humor, or huddling together to tell each other their dreams. If it was a nightmare, everyone would worry and get seriously alarmed. If it was a prophetic dream, their delight or distress would be equally unfeigned, depending on whether the dream was good or bad. If the dream entailed some superstitious observance, prompt and effective action would be taken. Otherwise they would play card games like "fool" or "trumps," or, on holidays when there were guests, they would play "boston" or "grande patience" and tell fortunes with the king of hearts or the queen of clubs, which meant a marriage.

Sometimes Natalya Faddeyevna or someone would come to stay for a week or two. The old ladies would start by giving the whole neighborhood a thorough going over; who was doing what, etc. Not content with domestic trivia, they would pry into private lives, and infiltrate people's very souls. They would pick apart all the bad husbands, reserving particularly harsh criticism for those who had strayed. Then they would review the various events, name days, christenings, births, who had entertained whom, who had been invited–or not invited–where. Tiring of this, they turned to showing each other their new things: dresses, coats, even skirts and stockings. The hostess would proudly display various homemade linens, threads and lace. But after a time even that subject was exhausted. At this point they would fall back on tea, coffee and preserves, followed by silence.

And there they would sit for ages looking at one another, every now and then heaving a deep sigh, or one of them would burst into tears.

"What is it my dear?" one of the others would inquire anxiously.

"Oh, my dear, I feel so sad," the guest would reply with a deep sigh, "we have angered God, sinners that we are, nothing good can come of it."

"Oh, don't scare me like that, my dear!" replied the hostess.

But her guest continued, "The world is in its last days, nation shall rise up against nation and kingdom against kingdom, the Day of Judgment is at hand," Natalya Faddeyevna pronounced and they both started sobbing bitterly.

Natalya Faddeyevna had absolutely no grounds for such a conclusion, no one was rising up against anyone, and there were not even any comets that year, but old ladies sometimes have these gloomy premonitions.

Only rarely would this pattern be disrupted by anything unusual, such as, for example, the entire household from top to bottom being laid low by fumes from the stoves. Apart from this, other sicknesses were practically unknown in that house or, for that matter, in the whole village, except perhaps for someone stubbing a toe or banging a shin against something in the dark, tumbling from the hayloft or being hit on the head by a loose plank falling from the roof. Such occurrences, however, were exceedingly rare and were treated by tried and true domestic remedies. A bruise would be rubbed with a fresh- water sponge and angelica, and the victim would be given holy water to drink, incantations would be whispered over him and all would be well.

The smoke inhalation sickness was, however, relatively frequent. Then everyone would be sprawled on their beds and the house would be filled with moaning and groaning. Some would tie cucumbers around their heads with a towel; others would stuff their ears with cranberries and sniff horseradish. Yet others would go out into the frost clad in nothing but their nightshirts, and others again would just lie about helplessly on the floor, past feeling anything. This would happen regularly once or twice a month because they did not like heat to escape up the flue and they would shut off the stoves when flames flickered like those in the opera "Robert le Diable," and if you so much as touched a stove or the bench resting on top of it, you came away with a blister.

Only once was the unvarying pattern of their days broken by a genuinely unexpected event. It was when they had been resting after a heavy dinner and were gathering for tea. One of Oblomov's peasants suddenly returned from the town and after a great deal of rummaging and poking around, finally and with great effort succeeded in extracting from the folds of his garment a crumpled letter addressed to Ilya Ivanovich Oblomov. They were all dumbstruck and the mistress's face even turned pale. All eyes were focused on the letter and even their noses were trained on the target.

"How extraordinary, whom could it be from?" said the lady of the house, regaining her composure.

Oblomov took the letter and turned it slowly in his hands in his bafflement, not knowing what to do with it. "Where did you get it?" he asked his man, "who gave it to you?"

"Well, you see, where I was staying in the town, someone came twice from the post office to ask if there was anyone there from the Oblomov estate—something about a letter for the master."

"Well?"

"Well, at first I kept quiet and the soldier went back with the letter, but the sexton from Verkhlyovka saw me and said something; so someone came back from the post office and bawled me out and gave me the letter and even made me pay five kopecks! I asked what I was supposed to do with it, where to take it, and they said I was to bring it to your honor."

"You shouldn't have taken it!" the mistress snapped at him.

"Well, I wasn't going to; I told him we don't need no letters, what for? No one told me nothing about bringing letters, I mustn't do it; so why don't you take your letter back where it came from? Then the soldier starts giving me hell and threatens to report me, so I took it."

"You idiot!" said the mistress.

"But who could it be from?" Oblomov wondered aloud, inspecting the address, "the handwriting does look familiar."

The letter was passed around, there was a buzz of chatter and speculation: "who could it be from and what about?" But they got nowhere.

Ilya Ivanovich sent for his glasses. This took about an hour and a half, but finally he had put them on and was actually thinking of opening the letter when his wife became nervous and stopped him.

"Stop, don't open it, Ilya Ivanovich, who knows what's in it? Maybe there's some really bad news, something terrible. You know what people are like these days! Wait a day or two, it's not going anywhere!"

So the letter and the glasses were locked away and they turned their attention to their tea. The letter would have moldered for years if it had not been such an extraordinary event and touched off such excitement. Over tea and all the next day they could talk about nothing but the letter. Finally, after three days they could contain themselves no longer and they all gathered around while with great trepidation the letter was opened. Oblomov looked at the signature.

"Radishchev," he read, "ah, it's from Filipp Matveyich!"

"Oh, so that's who it's from!" came the response from every corner of the room. "To think that he's still alive after all this time, thank heavens! You'd think he'd be dead by now! What does he say?"

Oblomov began to read aloud. Apparently Filipp Matveyich was writing to ask for the recipe for a beer that was a speciality of Oblomovka.

"Send it, send it!" they chorused, "Write him a letter!"

Two weeks passed.

"I must write to him!" Ilya Ivanovich insisted to his wife. "Where's the recipe?"

"Yes, where is it? We'll have to look for it, but let's not be in a rush. We'll wait for the holidays, please God! And then when we're over the fast, then you can write—the letter will still be here!"

"Yes, you're right, why not wait for the holidays?" Ilya Ivanovich agreed.

The holidays came and went and the question of the letter arose again. Ilya Ivanovich prepared himself for the task in earnest. He shut himself in his study, put on his glasses and sat down at his desk. There was dead silence in the house; strict instructions had been issued to tread quietly and avoid making noise.

"The master is writing!" The word was passed around in the same hushed, respectful undertone that people use when there has just been a death in the house. He had just managed to spell out the words: "Dear Sir," laboriously, crookedly, with trembling hand, and with the exaggerated caution of one embarking on a dangerous mission, when his wife entered.

"I've looked everywhere, I just can't find the recipe," she said. "I still have to look in the wardrobe in the bedroom. Anyway, how are we going to send the letter?"

"By post," replied Ilya Ivanovich.

"How much will the postage be?"

Oblomov got out an old calendar. "Forty kopecks," he said.

"That's a real waste of forty kopecks!" she pointed out. "Better to wait until someone happens to be going back into town, tell your man to find out and let us know!"

"Yes, absolutely, much better to find someone who can take it," Ilya Ivanovich responded, tapping his pen on the desk before inserting it into the inkwell and taking off his glasses. "Yes, much better this way," he confirmed, "the letter will still be here, there's plenty of time!"

No one knows whether Fillip Matveyich lived to see the recipe.

Sometimes Ilya Ivanovich would pick up a book, it did not matter which. It was not that he thought in any way that reading books was a vital necessity, but rather a luxury, something you could take or leave in the same way that you could hang a picture on the wall or not, or go for a walk or not as you chose. So which particular book was a matter of total indifference to him; a book was just a diversion, a distraction, something to while away the time.

"I haven't read a book for ages," he would say or, putting it a different way, "why don't I read a book?" Or his eye would happen to fall on a small pile of books left by his brother and he would pick up one at random. Whether it was Golikov, The New Interpretation of Dreams, Heraskov's Russiad, a tragedy by Sumarkov or a two-year-old copy of The News, the pleasure he got from them was one and the same in all cases, and from time to time he would murmur, "where does he get such ideas, it's sheer wickedness, to hell with him!"

It was writers as a class that were the targets of his vituperation, their occupation was one that in his eyes was entirely undeserving of respect. He had assimilated the same disdain for writers that was typical of the previous generation. Like many people of his time he tended to regard practitioners of the craft as nothing but a bunch of frivolous wastrels and drunkards just out for a good time—no better than buskers. Sometimes he would read aloud from two-year-old papers or simply report the news items they contained.

"There's a report from The Hague," he would say, peering at his audience over his spectacles, "that His Majesty the King has returned safely to the Palace after a brief excursion." Or, "In Vienna such and such Ambassador has presented his credentials. And here they write," he told them, "that the works of Mme. Genlis have been translated into Russian."

"I bet they only translate that stuff," said one of the company who owned one of the smaller properties in the area, "in order to screw money out of landed gentry like ourselves."

Meanwhile, poor little Ilyusha was still going to Stoltz's school. As soon as he woke up on Monday mornings he was oppressed by the grim prospect. He would hear the harsh shout of Vaska calling from the porch: "Antipka, harness the piebald, it's time to take the young master to the German!" His heart would drop and, the very picture of misery, he would go to his mother. She did not need to ask why, and would do her best to cheer him up, while putting a brave face on her own distress at the prospect of parting from him for a whole week.

On those mornings, nothing was too good for him. They would bake him rolls and twists; they loaded him up with pickles, cookies, preserves, glazed fruits, and every kind of delicacy, as well as provisions to keep in reserve—with the idea that the fare at the German's was less than lavish.

"You won't have to worry about overeating there," they said, "for dinner you'll get soup and a roast with potatoes, there'll be butter with your tea, and as for supper, well the next morning your tongue will be hanging out!"

However, when Ilya Ilyich dreamed of Monday mornings it was usually not the ones when the first thing he heard was Vaska shouting for the piebald to be harnessed, but the ones when his mother greeted him at breakfast with a smile and the good news: "You won't be going off to school today, Thursday is an important holiday, it's really not worth traveling all that way and back just for three days." Or the times when she would greet him with the news: "It's Memorial week—not a time for lessons, we'll bake pancakes."

At other times his mother would examine him anxiously and say, "Your eyes look clouded today, aren't you feeling well?" and shake her head. And the boy, feeling perfectly well, knew better than to open his mouth. "You'd better stay at home this week," she would say, "and then we'll just have to see."

And so it became an article of faith in the Oblomov household that lessons and Memorial Saturday were incompatible, and that a holiday falling on a Thursday was an insurmountable obstacle to attending school for the whole week. Only rarely would a servant or a maid who had got into trouble because of the young master, complain, "You're so spoiled, the sooner you're off to your German the better!"

At other times Antipka would turn up at the German's on his piebald in the middle or even at the beginning of the week to fetch Ilya Ilyich and say that Marya Savishna or Natalya Faddeyevna or the Kuzovkovs with their children were visiting so he had to take him home.

So Ilya Ilyich would stay at home for a few weeks and by then, of course, it was already near Holy Week, and then there would be a holiday or someone in the family would decide that no one goes to school during St. Thomas's week after Easter; then it would only be a couple of weeks until the summer—hardly worth the journey—and in the summer even the German himself takes a vacation, so the best thing is to leave it until the autumn.

Alright, so Ilya Ilyich took six months off, but see how he has grown in that time, how he has filled out, how well he has been sleeping! Everyone in the house drools over the way he looks in contrast to the pale skinny child who comes home on Saturdays from the German.

"It's not so terrible," his father or mother would say, "the lessons will keep, but good health is beyond price, it's the most important thing there is! When he comes home from school you would think he has just come out of the hospital, no flesh on him at all, just skin and bones…and a real mischief, always up to something! "Yes," his father observed, "schooling is really not good for people, it can really take it out of you!"

So the doting parents kept on finding excuses to keep their boy at home, and when it came to excuses it was not just holidays. In winter it was too cold and in summer too hot, and if it was not too hot or cold then it was too wet or slushy for him to travel. Sometimes there was an unreliable look about Antipka, something strange, as if he might have been drinking, who knows, he might have an accident, get stuck or end up in a ditch or something. The Oblomovs were anxious to make their excuses as convincing as possible in their own eyes as well as in the eyes of Stoltz, who had no compunction in telling them to their faces what he thought of their mollycoddling.

The days of the benighted and ignorant Prostakovs and the Skotinins were long gone. The proverb "learning is light, ignorance is night" had already found its way into the villages along with the itinerant book peddlers.

The older generation understood the advantages of education, that is to say the superficial ones. They saw that these days the only way people were going to make their way in the world, that is to win promotions and decorations and make money, was through education, and that the old style self-taught pettifoggers who had learned on the job and clung to the habits they had acquired, had fallen on hard times.

There were ugly rumors going around that you not only had to know how to read and write but even study hitherto unknown subjects. The only way to bridge the yawning chasm between the rank of "titular counsellor" and "collegiate assessor" in the civil service was with some kind of diploma. The civil servants of the old school weaned on habit and nourished by corruption were on their way out. Many of those who had survived were dismissed for incompetence, others were arrested; the luckiest were those who saw the writing on the wall and got out while the going was good, scuttling to the boltholes they had been careful to prepare for themselves. The Oblomovs had got the message and understood the advantages of education, but only the obvious material advantages. About the inner need for learning they had only the foggiest and dimmest of notions, but enough to want to secure for little Ilyusha at least some of the glittering prizes it offered.

They imagined him in a braided uniform; they saw him as a counsellor in some grand office—his mother even as the Governor of a province. While they wanted all these things for him they wanted to get them on the cheap. They wanted to get around the hurdles and obstacles on the path to education and success by whatever devious means and shortcuts they could, rather than take the trouble of surmounting them. Their idea was for Ilyusha to go through the motions of schooling without undue wear and tear on his mind or body and without any loss of the treasured puppy fat of his childhood, so that by satisfying the very minimum requirements he could somehow acquire the piece of paper that would certify that Ilyusha "had completed his studies in all subjects."

This Oblomovian approach to education met with stiff resistance from the Stoltz camp. The battle was waged unremittingly on both sides. Stoltz attacked his adversaries openly, directly, and persistently while they defended themselves by various dodges and devices, including those already described.

The struggle went unresolved; perhaps in the end German persistence would have prevailed over the stubbornness and obstinacy of the Oblomovs if the German had not been handicapped by difficulties within his own camp, so that the conflict was ultimately bound to end in stalemate. The problem was that Stoltz's own son had taken the young Oblomov under his wing, helping him with his lessons and even doing his translations for him.

In his dream Ilya Ilyich clearly saw his own home life as well as the contrasting life style of the Stoltz household. In the morning, he would wake up to find already standing by his bed that very Zakharka who was later to become famous as his valet Zakhar Trofimovich. As the nanny had before him, it was now Zakhar who pulled on his stockings and put on his shoes, while Ilyusha, now a lad of fourteen, had nothing to do but to lie there and offer one leg and then the other, and if something displeased him he could just poke Zakharka in the nose with his foot. If the indignant Zakharka should take it into his head to complain, he would just get his ears boxed by the adults for his trouble. Then Zakharka would comb his hair, put on his jacket, carefully drawing Ilya Ilyich's arms through the sleeves so as to avoid causing him any discomfort, and remind him of the things he had to do once he was up in the morning such as washing etc. If there was anything Ilya Ilyich wanted he had only to blink and immediately three or four servants would come rushing to do his bidding; if he dropped something or needed to get something, or something needed to be fetched or carried, well, sometimes like a normal active youngster he would have liked nothing better than to run and get it himself, but any such impulse was immediately squelched by a chorus of two parents and three aunts: "But why, where are you going? What are Vaska, Vanka and Zakharka here for? Hey, Vaska, Vanka, Zakharka, what are you doing, just standing and watching, you dolts! I'll give you what for!"

So Ilya Ilyich never succeeded in doing anything for himself and gradually he himself came to realize that life was much easier this way; he learned to bark orders: "Hey, Vaska, Vanka, give me this, bring me that! No, not that, this! Run! Fetch!"

At times he found the loving solicitude of his parents cloying. If he so much as ran down the stairs into the courtyard he would be sure to hear a dozen voices raised in alarm behind him: "Oh dear, oh dear! What is he thinking of? Hold him! Stop him! He's sure to fall down and hurt himself. Stop, stop!" In the winter, if he made the slightest move towards the front door or to open the small pane in the window there would be the same chorus of protest: "Now where's he going, what is he thinking of? Don't run, don't walk, and don't open! You'll catch your death of cold!" So Ilya resigned himself sadly to staying inside, fussed over like some exotic hothouse plant, with the same slow and stunted growth. His natural energies were denied an outlet, turned inward, and wilted.

Sometimes he would wake up bursting with energy and high spirits and full of life. He felt as if he were possessed by some mischievous sprite urging him to climb on the roof or leap into the saddle and gallop into the meadows where the hay was being cut, or to sit astride the fence, or to tease the village dogs. Or he might just want to burst into a sprint through the village and into the field, down into the gullies, into the birchwood and race to the bottom of the ravine in three bounds or to get into a snowball fight with the other lads. The urge would grow so powerful that, unable to resist any further, suddenly in the middle of winter, without even stopping to put on his cap, he was off the porch into the courtyard in a flash and out of the gate; he would grab a snowball in each hand and hurl himself into the fray with the other boys. The raw wind would bite his face, the frost would nip his ears, his mouth, and throat; he would taste the cold and a fierce joy would grip his chest as he rushed about as fast as his legs could carry him, whooping and laughing. As he came upon the other boys he let fly with his snowball—and missed. He did not have the knack. He bent to scoop up some more snow and was smacked in the face by a big ball of packed snow. He fell down, smarting from the unaccustomed pain but his tears were also tears of laughter from the fun of it all.

Meanwhile back at the house consternation reigned. "Where's Ilyusha?" A commotion broke out. Zakharka rushed out of the house followed by Vaska, Mitka, and Vanka, and they raced around the courtyard in confusion with two dogs snapping at their heels, after all what dog can resist the sight of a man running. The men, yelling and screaming with their escort of yelping dogs careered through the village. They finally came upon the boys and set about dispensing justice, grabbing them by their hair, their ears, or the scruffs of their necks and even threatening their fathers. Then they caught the young master and wrapped him first in a sheepskin they had grabbed on their way, then in his father's fur coat, and finally in a couple of blankets and carried him home in triumph.

At home everyone had given up hope of ever seeing him alive again; so when his parents first set eyes on him alive and well their joy was indescribable. They gave thanks to God and poured mint tea down Ilyusha's throat followed by elderberry, and later that evening, by raspberry cordial. They kept him in bed for three days, but there was really only one thing that would have done him any good—to be out snowballing again…

CHAPTER TEN

As soon as the sound of snoring reached Zakhar's ears he jumped down carefully from his bench and, making as little noise as possible, tiptoed to the entrance, locked his master in and made his way to the gate where he was greeted by a motley chorus of coachmen, footmen, maids and small boys.

"Hey, good to see you Zakhar Trofimovich, it's been a long time!"

"Has he gone out or what—yours?" asked the gatekeeper.

"No, he's slumped in his bed," Zakhar replied morosely.

"A bit early for that isn't it, at this time of day; what is he, sick or something?" asked the coachman."Sick, not likely, he's sozzled!" Zakhar replied in a tone of such conviction that you would have thought he believed it himself. "Would you believe, all by himself he's put away one and a half bottles of madeira and two quarts of kvass, so now he's just slumped there dead to the world!"

"Wow!" the coachman said enviously.

"So, what made him take to the bottle this time?" asked one of the maids.

"No, Tatiana Ivanovna," said Zakhar, giving her his customary sideways glance, "it's not just this time, he's completely gone to pieces—it makes me sick to talk about it!"

"Just like mine," she sighed.

"By the way, is she likely to want to go anywhere today?" asked the coachman, "I need to go somewhere not too far away."

"Go somewhere? Not likely! She's sitting there with her one and only, they can't take their eyes off each other."

"Yes, he's always at your place," said the gatekeeper. "Makes a real pest of himself at night; everyone has come or gone except him—he's always the last. And then he gives me a hard time because the front door is locked. What am I supposed to do, man the porch all night long just for his convenience?"

"I don't know where you'd have to go to find such a fool!" said Tatiana, "you won't believe the stuff he gives her. She dolls herself up like a peacock, strutting about and putting on airs, but if you could see what petticoats and stockings she wears underneath all that finery you'd get a shock. She goes for weeks without washing her neck but paints her face…Sometimes I think, God forgive me, you're a disgrace, why don't you tie a scarf over your head and go to a monastery and pray to God!"

Everyone burst out laughing except Zakhar. There was a chorus of approval. "Yes, that Tatiana Ivanovna, she never misses!"

"But really," Tatiana went on, " how can respectable people have anything to do with the likes of her?"

"Are you on your way somewhere? What's in the bundle?" someone asked.

"I'm taking this dress to the seamstress for my oh, so fashionable mistress—it needs to be taken in, according to her! Why, when Dunyasha and me have been struggling to lace in her carcass we can't use our hands for days afterwards without breaking things. Anyway I have to go, 'bye!"

"'Bye, see you!" someone responded.

"'Bye, Tatiana Ivanovna!" said the coachman, "see you this evening."

"Well, I'm not sure, maybe…well, anyway, 'bye for now!"

"See you then!" they all said.

"'Bye then, take care!" she answered and left.

"'Bye, Tatiana Ivanovna!" the coachman called after her again.

"'Bye!" she called back over her shoulder.

It was as if Zakhar had been biding his time until she had left before having his say. He sat down on the iron post by the gate with his legs dangling, gloomily and distractedly watching the people walking and riding by.

"So what's yours up to today, Zakhar Trofimovich?" the gatekeeper asked him.

"Another one of his tantrums—and it's all because of you that I'm having all this trouble, thanks a lot! It's all about the damned apartment. He's giving me hell and absolutely refuses to leave."

"What have I got to do with it?" said the gatekeeper. "Stay as long as you like for all I care—I mean I just work here. I just do what I'm told. If I was the landlord that'd be another thing, but I'm not…"

"You mean he gives you hell?" asked one of the other coachmen.

"And how! Only God gives me the strength to put up with it."

"You don't know when you're well off, with a master who only curses you out," said one of the valets, slowly opening the creaking lid of a round snuffbox. Everyone except Zakhar stretched out their hands towards the snuff-box to take a pinch and they all began, sniffing, sneezing, hawking and spitting. The valet went on: "yes, the more they shout at you the better. When they're shouting and screaming at least they're not hitting. There's one I had once, before you knew what was happening he'd grab you by the hair—God knows what for!"

Zakhar waited scornfully until the man had finished his tirade before turning to the coachman and continuing. "Doesn't bother him in the least to insult and humiliate someone for no rhyme or reason."

"Yes, I know the type, impossible to please, right?" said the gatekeeper.

"And how!" Zakhar wheezed significantly, frowning. "He makes my life hell. Always going on at me, 'this is wrong; that's no good; you don't walk properly; you can't even hand me something; you break everything; you don't clean; you steal; you eat too much…'and I don't know what else! He really flew off the handle today—you wouldn't believe the language! And all over what? A moldy piece of cheese left over from last week, you wouldn't feed it to a dog! But let a human being touch it, oh no! So when he asked and I said, 'none left', he started in. 'Hanging's too good for you, you should be boiled in oil, torn apart with red-hot pincers, impaled on a stake!' Once he gets going, there's just no stopping him! What do you think of that? The other day I tipped some boiling water on his foot— God knows how—you should have heard him carry on! If I hadn't got out of his way pretty damn quick, he'd have punched me in the chest, yes, he was really trying to hit me, no mistake about it!"

The coachman shook his head and the gatekeeper said, "Can't put anything past that one, he don't give you an inch!"

"Well, so long as it's just calling you names and telling you off, that's what I call a pretty nice master," the same valet repeated phlegmatically. "The other kind is worse, they watch you and watch you and suddenly grab you by the hair and you've no idea what for!"

"Well it didn't do any good," Zakhar went on, not paying the slightest attention to the valet's interruption, "his foot still hasn't healed anyway; he keeps smearing it with ointment—well, let him if he wants to!"

"Sounds like a difficult customer, your master," said the gatekeeper.

"He's going to kill someone one of these days," Zakhar continued, "mark my words, he'll do someone in! For the slightest thing he'll start calling me, 'you bald…' well, I'll spare you the rest. And just today he came up with this new insult, 'poisonous', he's got a really rough edge to his tongue."

"What's so bad about that?" the same valet chimed in, "you should give thanks to God that he only calls you names, and pray for his health! But when you get one who keeps quiet and just watches you go past and then suddenly grabs you, like the one I had—I tell you, being yelled at is nothing!"

"It served you right," said Zakhar, needled by this unwelcome heckling, "you wouldn't have got off so lightly if it had been me!"

"He called you a 'bald' what then, Zakhar Trofimovich?" one of the teenage under-footmen asked him. "Wasn't it, 'bald devil'?"

Zakhar turned his head slowly and gave him a dirty look.

"I'd watch out if I was you, you're too young to be such a smart aleck. I don't give a damn if you do work for a general, you'll feel the weight of my hand. Get back to where you're supposed to be!"

The boy retreated a step or two, stopped and grinned at Zakhar.

"Wipe that grin off your face!" Zakhar wheezed ferociously. "If you want to wait and see, I'll give you one on the ear and that'll give you something to grin about!"

At that moment a huge footman ran out onto the porch with his braided livery tunic unbuttoned and wearing lace-up boots. He went up to the youth, slapped his face and called him a fool.

"What was that for Matvei Moseyich?" said the boy taken aback and chagrined. He held his cheek and blinked furiously.

"So here you are having a nice chat while I've been running all over the house looking for you!"

He took hold of the boy's hair with one hand, bent his head and slowly, rhythmically and methodically thumped him on the neck three times with the other.

"The master rang five times," he added by way of admonition, "so I get it in the neck because of you, you young pup. Let's go!" And he pointed imperiously to the stairs.

The boy stood there for a minute in some bewilderment, blinked once or twice, then looked at the footman and seeing that there was nothing to be expected from that quarter but more of the same, shook his head a couple of times and headed briskly for the stairs.

Zakhar was triumphantly vindicated. "That's the way, you give it to him, keep going, keep going, Matvei Moseyich!" he urged him on gleefully. "Don't stop now! Well, thanks; just what he needed, he was getting too big for his boots…That'll teach you with your 'bald devil'! Feel like grinning now?"

Everyone was laughing, siding unanimously with the footman who had administered the thrashing and with Zakhar who had so gleefully cheered him on. No one had any sympathy for the boy.

"That's my old master to a tee, exactly the way he used to act." The same valet who had kept on interrupting Zakhar chimed in yet again. "There you'd be, trying to think of something to cheer yourself up and he would pass by, and, as if he could read your mind, grab hold of you just like Matvei Moseyich just did. And all this fuss about being called names, 'bald devil', big deal!"

"Well in your case even his master," the coachman riposted, pointing to Zakhar, "would probably grab hold of you—with that thatch on your head. But with Zakhar Trofimovich there's nothing to grab hold of, he's as bald as a melon. Of course, he could always try grabbing him by those whiskers sprouting on both cheeks, I suppose. I mean they really give you something to grab hold of!"

They all burst out laughing, but Zakhar was simply stunned by the coachman turning on him like that; up to then the conversation between them had been entirely friendly."

"Well, when I tell my master," he wheezed furiously at the coachman, "he'll soon find something of yours to grab; oh yes, he'll soon iron out your beard for you alright! Look, it's covered in icicles!"

"You must have a pretty clever master if he's going to iron out other people's coachmens' beards for them! Why don't you get some coachmen of your own first and try it out on them? Right now, you're really jumping the gun."

"Oh yes, when we start recruiting, you're sure to be the first, you crook!" Zakhar wheezed. "Why, you're not even fit to be harnessed to my master's carriage!"

"Some master! Where on earth did you dig him up?" the coachman retorted maliciously.

At this the coachman himself, the gatekeeper, the barber, the footman and the valet who was such an ardent supporter of the tongue-lashing alternative, all burst into laughter.

"Laugh all you want, but wait 'till I tell my master!" Zakhar wheezed. "As for you," he said turning to the gatekeeper, "you should be making these hooligans behave themselves instead of joining in! That's why you're posted here, to keep order; it's your job! But instead…Just wait till I tell my master, then you'll be in for it!"

"Now, now, Zakhar Trofimovich!" the gatekeeper tried to pacify him, "what did he do?"

"Where does he get off saying such things about my master?" Zakhar argued heatedly, pointing at the coachman, "does he know who he's talking about?" he asked in a tone of deep reverence. "You," he said, addressing the coachman, "you'd be lucky to see such a master even in your wildest dreams; so nice, so clever, so handsome! Yours looks like some half-starved nag! It's painful to see the two of you driving out with that brown mare, looking like beggars. You live on kvass and radishes and your greatcoat has more holes in it than you can count!"

For the record it should be pointed out that there wasn't a single hole in the coachman's coat.

"How about this one then?" the coachman retorted as he grabbed a clump of shirt that was visible under Zakhar's arm and pulled it smartly through the hole in the armpit of his jacket.

"Alright, that's enough now!" declared the gatekeeper holding them apart with his arms.

"Tearing my clothes now!" Zakhar shouted, pulling even more of the shirt through the hole. "Wait till I tell my master! Look, all of you, take a good look at what he's done—torn my clothes!"

"What me?" said the coachman, beginning to get nervous, "it was your master giving you a thrashing, more likely."

"What? A thrashing, from a master like mine?" Zakhar objected, "why, he's got a heart of gold, you wouldn't take him for a master at all, God bless him! Working for him is sheer bliss, I have absolutely everything I could want. Never a harsh word. Why, he's kindness and mildness itself. I eat the same food and go wherever I want—what do you think of that! I have my own house on the estate in the country, my own garden, special rations, and the peasants show me every respect. I'm the foreman as well as the majordomo. And as for you and your..."

He was choking with rage and his voice failed him before he could finish off his adversary. He stopped for a moment to collect himself, but try as he might, he just could not come up with the final withering insult; his pent up fury was just too much for him.

"Well, just you wait, you'll pay for it, you'll learn to tear people's clothes!" was all he could finally come out with.

Any slight on his master cut Zakhar to the quick. Both his vanity and self-esteem were wounded. His latent devotion rose swiftly to the surface and exploded. He was ready to vent his spleen and spit his venom not only at his adversary, but his adversary's master and all of that master's kith and kin—whether he had any or not—as well as his friends and acquaintances. He was able to dredge up with remarkable accuracy all the malicious gossip and slanderous tittle-tattle about the coachman's master and his family that he had heard from the coachman himself in the past.

"You and your master are nothing but riff-raff, Jews, even lower than Germans! Don't think I don't know who your grandfather was—a peddler in the market! When your visitors left last night I thought to myself, just from the look of them, they must be a gang of cheap crooks who'd broken in! God, what a sight! Your mother, too, dealt in stolen and second-hand clothes from a stall in the market!"

"That's enough, that's enough!" the gatekeeper tried to break it up.

"At least my master is a true gentleman with a pedigree, thank God! His friends are all generals, counts and dukes. And it's not just any old count who's invited to dine with him, mind you! Some have to cool their heels in the hallway. Writers are constantly calling on him!"

"What do you mean exactly 'writers', my friend?" asked the gatekeeper, anxious to patch things up, "you mean civil service clerks?"

"No, these are gentlemen who think up things of their own to write—whatever they want," Zakhar explained.

"So what do they do at your place?" asked the gatekeeper.

"Well, you know, ask for a pipe to smoke or a glass of sherry." Zakhar began and then stopped when he noticed that nearly everyone was grinning derisively. "You're all as bad as each other, the whole rotten bunch of you!" he sputtered, eyeing them all sideways on. "You'll soon learn to tear people's clothes, I'm telling my master!" he added and quickly turned and left.

"Alright, alright, stop, come back!" the gatekeeper called after him. "Zakhar Trofimovich, let's go and have a drink, please, Zakhar Trofimovich!"

Zakhar stopped, turned briefly and, without looking back at the others, quickened his pace and stepped out onto the street. He kept going, looking neither left nor right, until he had reached the door of the tavern just opposite; then he turned around and gave the whole crowd a gloomy look and signaled them to follow him with an even more despondent wave of the hand before disappearing inside.

The crowd dispersed, some to the tavern, others heading home, leaving only the footman. "Well, what's so terrible if he does tell his master?" he said calmly and nonchalantly to himself, calmly and slowly opening his snuffbox, "his master's obviously a good-natured type; he only tells you off. So what if he does! Better than the others who watch and watch and then grab you by the hair..."

CHAPTER ELEVEN

Shortly after four o'clock Zakhar, making as little noise as possible, cautiously opened the door of the apartment and tip-toed through the hallway to his room. Once there, he went up to the door of his master's study and put his ear against it and then squatted in order to put his eye to the keyhole.

From the study there came only the sound of rhythmic snoring.

"He's sleeping," Zakhar whispered, "have to wake him up, it's almost half past four."

He coughed and entered the study. "Ilya Ilyich, Ilya Ilyich!" he began softly, standing at the head of the divan.

The snoring continued.

"He's dead to the world, sleeping like a log," he said, "Ilya Ilyich!" Zakhar gently plucked Oblomov's sleeve. "Time to get up, it's half past four!"

Ilya Ilyich just grunted in response, but kept on sleeping.

"Get up, Ilya Ilyich, it's a disgrace!" said Zakhar, raising his voice.

No answer.

"Ilya Ilyich!" Zakhar repeated more assertively, tugging at Oblomov's sleeve.

Oblomov turned his head a little and struggled to open one eye that stared blankly at Zakhar as if glazed.

"Who is it?" he croaked.

"It's me, get up!"

"Get out of here!" Ilya Ilyich snarled and went right back to sleep, but instead of snoring he started whistling through his nose. Zakhar tugged at the hem of his dressing gown.

"What do you want?" asked Oblomov irritably, suddenly opening both eyes.

"You told me to wake you."

"Alright, and now you've done it, so get out! What I do now is my own business."

"I won't go," said Zakhar, plucking at his sleeve again.

"Leave me alone!" Ilya Ilyich snapped and buried his head back in his pillow, but before the snoring could start up again Zakhar intervened.

"You mustn't, Ilya Ilyich, I'd be only too happy to let you sleep, but you simply mustn't!" he said, putting his hand on his master.

"Would you please mind leaving me alone!" Oblomov pleaded, opening his eyes.

"No, I wouldn't mind at all, but then you'll get mad at me for not waking you up."

"My God, what a nag you are!" said Oblomov, "just give me one minute for a little nap, that's all, just one little minute, it's nothing, yes, I know…"

Ilya Ilyich dropped off again suddenly in mid-sentence.

"Oh yes, if there's one thing you know, it's to lay in bed!" said Zakhar, confident that his master could not hear him. "Look at him, dead to the world, sleeping like a log; is this why you were put into this world? Why don't you get up when you're told…" Zakhar was about to raise the roof.

"What, what?" Oblomov snarled, raising his head from the pillow.

"Well, it's just that you're not getting up, sir." Zakhar responded mildly.

"No, what were you just saying? How dare you talk to me like that!"

"What do you mean?"

"So disrespectfully."

"You must have been dreaming, honestly!"

"You think I'm sleeping? No, I'm not, I hear everything…" Suddenly he was asleep again.

"My God, you can't just go on laying there like that," said Zakhar in despair. It makes me sick to look at you. My God, if people could see you!" He clicked his teeth with annoyance.

"Get up, get up!" he suddenly burst out nervously. "Ilya Ilyich, look! See what's happening all around you!"

Oblomov quickly raised his head, looked around and let it fall back again with a deep sigh.

"Leave me in peace!" he intoned solemnly, "I told you to wake me up and now I'm cancelling that order. You hear? And I'll wake up when I feel like it."

Sometimes Zakhar would just have given way and said, "fine, sleep away your life, who cares?" But at other times he stood his ground—as he did now.

"Get up, get up!" he shouted at the top of his voice and, using both hands, took hold of Oblomov by his sleeve and the hem of his dressing gown. Oblomov suddenly leapt to his feet, taking Zakhar by surprise, and lunged at him.

"I'll soon teach you to disturb your master when he's trying to rest, just you wait!" he said.

Zakhar was already beating a hasty retreat but after a couple of steps Oblomov had finally cleared his head and started stretching and yawning.

"Give me some kvass!" he said between yawns. Suddenly from behind Zakhar there came the sound of laughter. They both looked around.

"Stoltz, Stoltz!" Oblomov exclaimed delightedly as he rushed to greet his visitor.

"Andrei Ivanovich!" said Zakhar, grinning.

Stoltz was still roaring with laughter—he had witnessed the whole scene.

PART II

CHAPTER ONE

Stoltz was only half German—on his father's side. His mother was Russian and he had been brought up in the Orthodox faith. His mother tongue was Russian, which he had learned from his mother, from books, in the university lecture room, from playing with the village boys and conversations with their fathers as well as in the market places of Moscow. His knowledge of German came from his father and from books too.

Stoltz had grown up and gone to school in the village of Verkhlyovo where his father was the estate manager. From the age of eight he had pored with his father over maps, construed the works of Herder and Wieland and verses of the Bible. He had done the books of illiterate peasants, tradesmen and factory owners and with his mother he had studied the scriptures and Krylov's fables, and construed the French of Télémaque.

Whenever he could get away from his lessons he raided birds' nests with the other boys and quite often the sound of newly hatched jackdaws chirping could be heard from his pocket in class or during prayers. Sometimes his father would be sitting under a tree in the garden after dinner smoking his pipe while his mother was busy with her knitting or her needlework, when suddenly they would hear shouting and sounds of commotion from outside in the street and a crowd of people would burst into the house.

"What can it be?" his mother would ask anxiously.

"Probably bringing Andrei home again," replied his father, quite unruffled.

The doors would be flung open and a mob of men, women and boys from the village would pour into the garden, bringing Andrei with them as his father had so accurately predicted, but an Andrei in a state of utter dishevelment; barefoot and clothing all torn, with either Andrei or one of his companions sure to have a bloodied nose.

His mother was always worried when she saw Andrei disappear from the house for a day and, had it not been for the express orders of her husband not to interfere, she would have kept him at home. She would wash him, give him a clean change of clothing and for a few hours Andrei would remain a clean, tidy and well-behaved boy, but by the evening, or sometimes even before the morning was over, someone would be bringing him home unrecognizable, tattered and streaked with dirt. At other times he would be brought home by the field hands on a haywain or even by fishermen in a boat, asleep on one of their nets. His mother would be in tears, but to his father it was even good for a laugh. "A real little tough guy!" he would say approvingly.

"Now, come on, Ivan Bogdanovich," his wife would appeal to him, "can't you see how he comes home every day covered in bruises and just the other day with his nose bleeding!"

"What kind of boy would he be if he never got a bloody nose, or gave one to another boy?" he would say with a laugh.

His mother would cry and cry and then sit down at the piano and lose herself in the music of Herz as her tears splashed one by one onto the keys. But Andryusha would come, or be brought, home and would soon be recounting his adventures so vividly and zestfully that she too began to laugh—and also he was such a quick learner! In no time he learned to read Télémaque as well as herself and to play duets with her. Once he disappeared for a whole week. His mother cried her eyes out; his father just walked around the garden, smoking his pipe.

"Now if Oblomov's son had gone missing," he said when his wife proposed going to look for Andrei, "I would have roused the whole village and sent for the police. But Andrei will be back, he knows how to take care of himself, that one!"

The next day found Andrei sleeping as peacefully as you could wish in his bed, with someone's shotgun and a pound of powder and shot under it.

"Where on earth did you get to? Where did you get the gun?" His mother plied him with questions. "Why don't you say something?"

"No reason," was the only response she could get out of him.

His father asked him if he had done his German translation of Cornelius Nepos.

"No," he replied.

His father took him by the scruff of the neck and propelled him out of the gate, planted his cap on his head and helped him on his way with a foot in the backside that sent him sprawling.

"Get back to where you came from!" he responded and added, "don't show your face back here without that translation, two chapters instead of one! And learn the part from the French comedy that your mother set you!"

Andrei returned in a week with the translation completed and the part learned.

When he was older his father seated him by his side in the pony trap, handed him the reins and made him drive to the factory, the fields, the town, the markets and offices. He showed him some clay, which he stuck his finger in and sniffed and even licked. He would give it to his son to sniff and explain what it was and what it was used for. Or they would go to see potash, tar or tallow being produced.

At the age of fourteen or fifteen, the boy would often be sent off alone in the trap or on horseback with a saddlebag into the town on errands and he always carried out his instructions strictly, unerringly and to the letter.

"*Recht gut, mein lieber Junge!*"* his father would say after listening to his report and he would slap him on the shoulder with his broad palm and give him two or three roubles depending on the importance of the task.

Afterwards his mother would spend a long time washing off all the traces of the tar, grime, clay and grease that clung to Andryusha. She was not entirely happy about this kind of practical, hands-on education. She was afraid that her son would turn out to be a typical German "burgher" like his father's people. She looked upon all Germans as stereotypical boors and disliked the uninhibited, unabashed arrogance with which the Germans en masse flaunted the burghers' rights they were so proud of winning a thousand years before, like cattle with their horns which in any case they have nowhere to hide.

In her view the German race had never produced and could never produce a single "gentleman." She had never discerned in the German character any of the easy-goingness, delicacy, indulgence or any of the things that make life so agreeable in polite society and make it possible to get around the rules, defy convention and not to have to have slavishly to conform. No, those boors are so obstinately bent on doing what they are supposed to do, what they have made up their minds to do, that they would sooner butt their heads against a brick wall than deviate from the rules.

She had served as a governess in a wealthy family and had been abroad. She had traveled the length and breadth of Germany and lumped together all Germans as people who smoked short little pipes, spluttering shopkeepers, tradesmen, merchants, ramrod- stiff officers with parade ground faces, and functionaries with workaday faces, fit only for drudgery and interested only in making money by the sweat of their brow, petty order and discipline, dreary social correctness and the pedantic performance of their duties. In short, nothing but a race of "burghers" with their graceless manners, big clumsy hands, coarse, low class features and rough tongues.

"Dress a German up in any finery you can imagine," she thought, "the finest and whitest linen, gleaming polished boots and even yellow kid gloves, he will still look as if his clothes have been cut from shoe leather; his gleaming white cuffs cannot hide the calloused ruddy hands sticking out from under them, nor can the most fashionable suit disguise the counter hand, if not the baker, who happens to be wearing it. Roughened hands like that seem to cry out for a hammer

* "*Good boy, well done!*"

or chisel to hold or at the very best a fiddle-stick to wield in some dance-band."

Her dream was for her son to take his place among the Russian gentry for all his dubious origins as the upstart offspring of a common "burgher" since he was after all the son of a mother who was a member of the Russian gentry herself, and a gracefully proportioned boy with a pale face, small hands and feet, an unblemished complexion and clear, lively eyes of the kind that she had admired in wealthy Russian homes as well as abroad, although not, of course, among Germans. But here he would be practically turning the millstones with his own bare hands and coming back home from the factories and fields just like his father, covered in muck and grease with filthy, reddened, work-roughened hands and ready to eat a horse!

She would rush to cut his nails, curl his hair, to make him the most fashionable collars and shirtfronts and order him jackets from town. She taught him to listen to the elegiac melodies of Herz, sang to him of flowers and the poetry of life, inspired him with thoughts of a brilliant future as a warrior or a writer, and shared with him her dreams of the importance he was destined to achieve.

But the clicking of the abacus, the sorting of the greasy invoices of the peasants, and the rubbing of shoulders with factory owners doomed all these prospects. She even hated the cart on which Andrei rode into town, the oilskin cape given to him by his father, and his green suede gloves, all the vulgar accoutrements of common people who work for a living. What made it worse was that Andryusha was an excellent student and his father made him his assistant in his little school. And as if that were not bad enough, in typically German fashion he even paid him wages like a common workman; he paid him ten roubles a month, and even made him sign for it!

But take heart, good mother! Your son has been raised on Russian soil—not among the common herd of "burghers," those cattle, complete with horns, who turn millstones with their bare hands. Not far away was Oblomovka, the scene of unending festivities! There, work slips like a yoke from the shoulders. There the master does not rise with the dawn; he does not go around factories, brushing against axle grease and oily springs.

Now, in Verkhlyovka itself, there is a house that stands locked and empty most of the year and the resourceful youngster often finds his way in. There he sees long halls and galleries, dark portraits on the walls. He sees, not coarse, weathered complexions and big roughened hands, but languid blue eyes, powdered hair, white pampered faces, swelling bosoms, and delicate, blue-veined hands framed by frilly cuffs, resting proudly on the hilts of swords; he sees generation after generation of lives frittered away in genteel contentment, in brocades, velvets and lace. He reads in those faces the history of heroic times, battles and names; he reads in them tales of yore quite unlike the stories told to him by his father, spluttering through his pipe about life in Saxony among the turnips and potatoes, between the market and the vegetable garden.

About once every three years the great house would suddenly fill with people, pullulate with life, festivities and balls, with its long galleries ablaze with light in the evenings. The prince and the princess would arrive with their family; the prince old and gray with skin like parchment, drained of color, his eyes dim and protruding and his hair receding from his brow. He wore three stars and carried a gold snuffbox and a cane with a ruby knob, and his boots were of velvet. The princess was a woman of such majestic beauty, stature and carriage that, for all her five children, it was hard to imagine anyone ever approaching, embracing or kissing her, even the prince himself.

She seemed like a being from a higher plane who descended once every three years, spoke to no one, went nowhere, and spent all her time sitting in a green corner room attended by three old ladies, except when she proceeded on foot through the garden by the covered gallery to church where she sat on a chair behind a screen.

But apart from the prince and princess it was a gay and lively company that filled the house. It was as if three or four separate worlds had suddenly been opened up all at once to Andryusha's young green eyes. His sharp mind drank in greedily but unconsciously the kaleidoscope of colorful characters as if he were watching a fancy-dress ball. There were the princes Pierre and Michel. It was Pierre who taught Andryusha how they beat the tattoo in the cavalry and the infantry, which sabres and spurs belonged to the Hussars and which to the Dragoons, what breeds of horse were favored by which regiments, and which were the only decent, respectable ones to join after leaving school.

Michel, for his part, immediately after being introduced to Andryusha, positioned him carefully and proceeded to perform amazing feats with his fists, striking him on the nose and in the belly. He then told him that it was the English style of fighting. Four days later, purely by dint of his native, rustic spontaneity and muscular arms, Andrei gave him an English and a Russian style bloody nose, using no technique whatsoever, and immediately soared in the esteem of both princes.

There were also two little princesses aged eleven and twelve, tall, slim and elegantly dressed who kept to themselves and were frightened of the village men. Their governess, Mlle. Ernestine, was invited to coffee by Andryusha's mother and taught her to curl his hair. Sometimes she would take his head and place it in her lap and twist his hair around paper curlers until it hurt, and then she would take both his cheeks in her white hands and kiss him tenderly.

There was also the German who made snuffboxes and buttons on his lathe and the music teacher who drank non-stop from Sunday to

Sunday, as well as a gaggle of chambermaids and a pack of dogs with their puppies.

The uproar, the din, the banging, the shouting, and the music from all the festivities filled the house and the whole village.

The German elements in Andrei's make-up were countered both by the influence of Oblomovka and that of the princely house with its spacious, leisurely life of aristocratic ease and thus prevented his turning into the honest "burgher" or even the philistine he might otherwise have become.

Andrei's father was an agronomist and engineer and a teacher. From his own father, a farmer, he had learned practical agriculture; at factories in Saxony he had learned engineering and at the nearest university, which boasted some forty professors, he had acquired the taste for teaching to others whatever those forty sages had somehow managed to impart to him. Further than this he had not ventured and firmly made up his mind to turn back because it was time to get down to business. So he returned home to his father who gave him one hundred thalers and a new knapsack and sent him on his way.

Ivan Bogdanovich never saw his father or his homeland again. After spending six years roaming Switzerland and Austria he had been living in Russia for twenty years and had absolutely no regrets. He had been at a university and was determined that his son should follow in his footsteps. If it could not be a German university then it would have to be a Russian one, even if it meant that it would completely change the course of his son's life and that it would take a turn entirely different from the one that he had planned for him in his mind. It was all very simple; all he did was to draw a straight line from his grandfather and extend it right through to his grandson in total confidence, never suspecting for a moment that Herz's variations, a mother's stories and dreams, a gallery, and a boudoir in a princely mansion would divert this narrow German track into a broad avenue the like of which neither his grandfather nor his father nor even himself could ever have imagined. It was not that he was a stickler for tradition and was bent on having his own way; it was just that he would have been mentally incapable of charting any other course for his son. In any case he hardly gave the matter a second thought, and three months after his son had been living at home after returning from the university, his father told him that, since there was nothing left for him to do in Verkhlyovka, it was time for him to move on to St. Petersburg, for, after all, even Oblomov had been sent there.

But why was it necessary for him to go to St. Petersburg, why couldn't he have simply stayed in Verkhlyovka and helped his father to run the estate? This was a question that it never occurred to his father to ask himself. All he knew was that when he had completed his studies his own father had sent him away.

So what he did with his son was simply what they did in Germany. There was no mother around to suggest anything different.

On the day that Andryusha left, Ivan Bogdanovich gave his son a hundred roubles in banknotes.

"You'll ride to town," he said, "and get three hundred and fifty roubles from Kalinnikov and leave him the horse. If he's not there, sell the horse—the fair will be starting soon—it'll fetch four hundred roubles easily. It'll cost you forty roubles to get to Moscow and another seventy-five from there to St. Petersburg., so you'll have enough left. From then on it's up to you. You've been helping me with my business dealings so you know I have some savings, but don't count on seeing any of it before I die; and I'm probably good for another twenty years—unless I get hit on the head with a rock. There's still plenty of life left in the old dog, plenty of oil in the lamp! You've had a good education and you can take your pick of careers: government service, trade, writing, anything. I've no idea what you'll choose or what your inclinations are."

"Who knows, maybe I'll do all of them," said Andrei.

His father roared with laughter and started clapping him on the back hard enough to knock a horse down, but Andrei did not even flinch.

"If you can't make up your mind and decide what to do by yourself and you need some advice, go and see Rheinhold, he'll help you. He's..." he added, gesturing with his hand and shaking his head, "he's..." He wanted to say something to commend him to his son but could not find the words. "We came from Saxony together; he has this four-storey house. Let me give you the address..."

"Never mind, don't bother," said Andrei, "I'll go and see him when I have my own four-storey house; for now I'll get by without him."

Another slap on the back.

Andrei sprang onto the horse. Two bags had been strapped to the saddle, one containing the oilskin cape with a pair of stout hobnailed boots and some shirts made of the local coarse cloth sticking out—all things which had been purchased and packed at his father's insistence. The other contained an elegant morning coat of fine fabric, a shaggy overcoat, a dozen fine linen shirts, and a pair of shoes ordered from Moscow to honor his mother's wishes.

"So!" said the father.

"So!" said the son.

"That's it, then?" asked the father.

"Yes. That's it," the son replied.

They looked at one another in silence, searchingly and with deep intensity.

Meanwhile a throng of curious neighbors had gathered and watched open-mouthed as the manager of the estate sent his son off into the unknown.

Father and son shook hands and Andrei rode off at a good pace.

"The young pup! Not even a tear!" said the neighbors.

"Look at those two crows settling on the fence right at this very moment and cawing, they're trying to warn him."

"Crows don't mean a thing to him! Why he even goes into the woods on St. John's night—they're not even bothered; no Russian would have gotten away with it!"

"And that father, what kind of Christian is that?" one of the mothers exclaimed, "throwing him out into the street like that like he was a kitten, without a hug, without a sound."

"Stop, stop, Andrei!" the old man called after him.

Andrei reined in the horse.

"Ah, now his feelings have got the better of him!" the crowd murmured with approval.

"What is it?" asked Andrei.

"Your saddle girth is loose, better tighten it!"

"I'll do it when I get to Shamshevka, it's not worth taking the time now—have to get there before dark."

"Off you go, then!" said the father, waving his hand.

"I'm off then," responded the son and, crouching in the saddle, was on the point of spurring his horse.

"That's the way dogs behave, like complete strangers!" the neighbors grumbled.

But at that moment someone in the crowd burst into sobs, one of the women could hold it in no longer.

"You poor darling!" she exclaimed, wiping her eyes with a corner of her headscarf, "you poor orphan, no one to give you a mother's blessing—here let me make the sign of the cross over you, my love!"

Andrei rode up to her, dismounted, embraced the old woman and made to ride off, but he burst into tears as she gave him her blessing and kissed him. In her loving words he seemed to hear the voice of his mother and for a moment her tender features appeared to him. He hugged the woman tightly once again, swiftly wiped away his tears and leapt onto his horse, slapped its flanks and disappeared in a cloud of dust. Barking furiously, three mongrel dogs set off in headlong pursuit on either side of him.

CHAPTER TWO

Stoltz was the same age as Oblomov; and he was already past thirty. He had been in government service and after resigning had gone into business for himself. He had made money and bought the house he had promised himself. He was a partner in an export firm.

He was constantly on the move. If the firm needed to send someone to represent it in Britain or Belgium he was the one they sent. If someone was needed to draw up a project or put a new idea into effect, he was the one they turned to. At the same time he led an active social life and also read books, although God knows how he found the time.

He did not have an ounce of surplus flesh on his body, nothing but bone, muscle and sinew. He was built like an English thoroughbred. He was lean and his skin was drawn tightly over his cheeks and there was not a trace of fatty tissue to round out the skin and bone. His complexion was even and on the sallow side without a trace of pink, and his eyes were greenish but expressive.

His movements were economical. While he was sitting he was still and in action he expended the minimum energy. Just as his physique was lean and spare, so in his emotional life he strove to maintain a balance between the practical and the finer sensibilities. The two sides marched in tandem, criss-crossing one another, but never getting hopelessly entangled. He moved firmly and confidently through life, carefully balancing his accounts and, with unslackening vigilance, ensuring that he never wasted a moment of his time, an ounce of his energy, a scrap of emotion or a rouble of his fortune. He governed his joys and sorrows just as he controlled the movements of his arms and legs and took both good and bad weather in his stride.

When it rained he unfurled his umbrella and in the same way he limited his suffering to the duration of the pain. He reacted to suffering with annoyance and dignity rather than with meek submission, and bore up patiently because he would assign blame only to himself for his woes and never attempt to pin it on someone else.

He took his pleasures in the same way that he would enjoy a flower plucked from the side of the road, only until it lost its freshness, and would never drain his cup to the bitter dregs—the inevitable sour aftertaste of all pleasures.

He always made it his goal to look life straight in the face and see it unblinkingly for what it was, and as he slowly and surely learned to do this he came to understand how truly difficult a thing it was to do and took a quiet pride and pleasure in negotiating every deviation that lay in his path by stepping straight over it.

"How hard, how complicated it is to live life simply!" he would often say to himself, glancing rapidly around to see where his path twisted and turned and where the thread of life was beginning to get twisted into an impenetrable tangle.

More than anything he feared imagination, that two-faced companion, both friend and enemy! A friend when you trusted it the least, and an enemy when you trustingly allowed its seductive murmur to lull you to sleep. He shunned every kind of dreaming, and if ever he found himself within its range he would enter as you would a grotto with the words: *"ma solitude, mon hermitage, mon repos"** carved over the entrance, mind-

*"my solitude, my refuge, my retreat."

ful of the precise hour and minute when you will leave it. There was no room for the mystical, the mysterious, the illusory in his temperament. Anything that did not stand the test of practical experience or the scrutiny of analysis he rejected as an optical illusion, some kind of interplay of light and color on his retina, or else a phenomenon that still lay beyond the reach of experience.

There was in him nothing of the dilettante who loves to delve into the realm of the fanciful and indulge in idle speculation about the wonders and marvels that lie a thousand years into the future. He took a firm stand on this side of the threshold of the mysterious, free equally of a childlike credulity and the doubts of the over-sophisticated, and patiently reserved judgment until the evidence came in and provided a key to the mystery.

He kept as strict and careful watch over his heart as he did over his imagination. This was an area in which he had so often put a foot wrong that he was forced to recognize that the workings of the heart were still a closed book to him.

He was fervently grateful to providence if in this terra incognita he managed to distinguish a prettified lie from the plain truth before it was too late. He had no complaints when he was able to back away from artfully disguised and prettily decorated deception without actually losing his footing and escaped with nothing worse than a rapidly or even frantically beating heart and was immensely relieved if his heart was not actually drowning in blood, if cold sweat was not breaking out on his brow and if a pall was not cast on his life which it would take an eternity to throw off.

He counted himself fortunate if he could as much as keep on an even keel and, while mounted on the steed of feeling, could somehow avoid galloping over the fine line dividing the world of the emotions from the world of bogus sentimentality and the world of the genuine from the world of the ridiculous, but without retreating onto the sandy, barren soil of heartlessness, intellectualizing, mistrust, superficiality, and the encrustation of the heart.

Even in the pleasure of the moment he always liked to feel the ground under his feet and to feel sufficiently in control to be able to break free of the situation if it was getting out of hand. He was never dazzled by beauty and was able to maintain his vigilance and his male dignity by never prostrating himself slavishly at a beauty's feet, even though this meant that he never experienced the heights of ecstasy. He had no idols but preserved his intellectual and physical power as well as a chaste pride. He gave off a feeling of freshness and vigor that somehow baffled even the most forward of women. He knew the value of these rare and precious qualities and drew on them so sparingly that people called him selfish and unfeeling. His careful avoidance of excess, his restraint in staying within the bounds of the natural and spontaneous, provoked criticism and condemnation on the part of the very people who contrasted him unfavorably, sometimes with surprise and envy, with the example of others who hurled themselves headlong into the bog, ruining their own lives and the lives of others in the process.

"Passion justifies everything," people were always saying to him, "but you just selfishly protect and preserve yourself, but who you are saving yourself for? Well we'll just have to wait and see!"

"Yes, I suppose I must be saving myself for someone," he ruminated as if he were focusing on some distant object and he continued to distrust the poetry of passion and remained quite unimpressed by precipitate and headstrong action and their destructive effects and persisted in seeing in the strictest understanding of and control over one's life, the ultimate good of man's existence and strivings.

The more resistance his convictions met, the more deeply they became entrenched and, in his obduracy, at least in the course of argument, he would come across as a puritan fanatic. He would say that the proper role of a man was to live through the four seasons, that is to say the four ages of life, and to carry the cup of life to the last day without tripping and without spilling a single unnecessary drop along the way, and that the flame of life should burn slowly and steadily without ever bursting into a mighty blaze, no matter what poetry might be aglow within it. And he would conclude by saying that he would die happy if he could believe that his own life had been a vindication of these convictions, but that he did not expect to succeed in this because it was too hard a task.

Having chosen this path, he kept to it singlemindedly. He never gave the impression of agonizing over a decision. He never allowed regrets to gnaw at his soul and never lost heart. He never shrank from the challenge of new, forbidding or unfamiliar circumstances, but approached them unflinchingly as if they were old acquaintances and as if he were simply reliving former experiences. Whatever problems arose he immediately had the right solution ready to hand in, just the same way that a housekeeper knows instinctively which of the keys in the bunch hanging from her belt she needs to open a given door.

Above all he prized persistence; in his eyes it was the sign of true character and he could not help admiring persistence in anyone no matter how humble the objective.

"You have to hand it to them!" he would say.

Needless to say he pursued his own goals relentlessly, valiantly overcoming all obstacles and never giving up unless he ran into a brick wall or an absolutely unbridgeable chasm in his path. One thing he was incapable of was mustering the kind of blind courage necessary for leaping over the chasm or hurling himself against the wall regardless of the consequences. He would mentally calculate the height of the wall or the width of the chasm and if he concluded that there was no serious possibility of overcoming the obstacle, he would back off, regardless of what people might say.

Perhaps characters such as Stoltz can only be put together from that mixture of elements that had combined to produce Stoltz himself.

Our statesmen have traditionally come in five or six moulds. They have looked around lazily with half an eye, put their hands to the ship of state and steered it languidly along the same old course, following in the wake left by their predecessors. But now people are awakening from their coma and the sound of live voices and of marching feet taking long vigorous strides can be heard... How many Stoltzes are destined to emerge in the future bearing Russian names!

How could a man like this be close to an Oblomov, whose every feature, every move, whose very existence was in flagrant defiance of Stoltz's own life. Well, the mystery has now been explained; diametrical opposites, if they do not actively attract one another, as people used to think, are certainly no obstacle to mutual attraction. In any case there were the two powerful bonds of their shared childhood and schooling in addition to that Russian affectionateness, that warmth, those hugs, those kisses and embraces which had been lavished on the German boy by Oblomov's family; there was also the role of Oblomov's protector played by Stoltz, the physically stronger and also the stronger character of the two. Finally and most importantly, there was Oblomov's essentially good and generous nature, something pure, untarnished and radiant, which instinctively reached out to everything that was good and to everything that was sensitive and responsive to the appeal of that simple, ingenuous and eternally trusting heart.

Anyone, no matter how forbidding and malignant, who so much as happened to look into that innocent and childlike soul or made a point of doing so, could not help responding to it and, even if circumstances precluded any relationship, would at least carry away a heart-warming and lasting memory from the encounter.

Andrei would often break away from his business affairs or a social event, or leave a ball in the evening to go and sit on Oblomov's wide divan and, chatting idly with him, would unburden himself and forget the cares of the day. On these occasions he would always get the comforting feeling that comes when you leave palatial halls and come back under your own humble roof or return from the opulent beauty of the exotic south to the old familiar birch grove where you played as a child.

CHAPTER THREE

"Hello, Ilya, it's good to see you! How are things? Are you well?"

"No, not at all well, Andrei," Oblomov replied with a sigh. "I'm in really bad shape!"

"You mean you're sick?" Stoltz inquired anxiously.

"I've got styes breaking out all over; just last week I got rid of one on my right eye and now another one is starting."

Stoltz laughed. "Is that all? You're just sleeping too much."

"What do you mean, 'is that all?' I'm suffering from terrible heart-burn. If you'd heard what the doctor told me only this morning. 'You must go abroad!' he said, 'otherwise you're heading for trouble, even a stroke.'"

"So, what about it?"

"I'm not going."

"Why not?"

"Come on now, wait 'till you've heard all of it. I have to go and live somewhere in the mountains or go to Egypt or America..."

"So what," Stoltz said in a matter of fact tone. "You can be in Egypt in two weeks and in America in three."

"Not you too, Andrei! You were the only one I could rely on to talk sense and now you're talking crazy too! Who on earth goes to Egypt or America—except for the English, of course, and they can't help it, they're just made that way and in any case there isn't room for them all in their own country. But none of us would ever go—except maybe someone so desperate that life has lost all meaning."

"Well, you're absolutely right, after all it would require feats of hero-ic hardship and bravery, like getting into a carriage or getting on a ship, breathing fresh air, seeing foreign countries and customs and the wonders of the world. Ilya you're impossible! Well anyway, how are things going in Oblomovka?"

"Don't ask," said Oblomov with a wave of the hand.

"Why, what happened?"

"It's just that life won't leave you alone, that's what!"

"And a good thing too!" said Stoltz.

"What do you mean, 'a good thing'? If only life would be satisfied with giving you a gentle pat on the head, but no, it gets aggressive; just like in the old days in school when bullies would come up behind some mild-mannered boy and pinch him or come right up to him and throw sand in his face. I can't take it any more!"

"Your trouble is that you're only interested in a quiet life. What actu-ally happened?" Stoltz inquired.

"There's two problems."

"What problems?"

"I'm ruined."

"How do you mean?"

"Let me read you what the bailiff wrote… now where is that letter? Zakhar, Zakhar!"

Zakhar found the letter. Stoltz glanced through it and laughed, no doubt amused by the bailiff's style.

"What a crook he is, your bailiff!" he said. "He lets the peasants go and then he complains. Might as well give them their passports and kiss them goodbye."

"But just a minute, then they're all sure to want the same thing!" Oblomov objected.

"Then let them!"said Stoltz, quite unconcerned. "Those who are happy where they are and want to be there will stay, those who aren't are no use to you, so why keep them?"

"Where do you get such ideas?" said Ilya Ilyich. "The peasants on the estate aren't the adventurous type, they like to stay near home. Why would they want to take off?"

Stoltz cut him off. "But don't you know they're going to build a landing stage in Verkhlyovka and there's talk of building a road, so that even Oblomovka will be near a main road and they're going to have a fair in the town…"

"Oh, my God," said Oblomov, "that's all we need! Oblomovka was always such a quiet, out-of-the-way place—now suddenly a fair and a road! The peasants will start flocking into town and we'll be invaded by peddlers. It's the end, a disaster!"

Stoltz laughed.

"Of course it's a disaster, don't you see? The peasants were perfectly content, they never heard anything, good or bad, from the outside world and just went about their business; never aspired to anything else. The next thing you know, they'll be corrupted; tea parties, coffee parties, velvet trousers, accordions, polished boots—no good will come of it!"

"Well, of course, you're right, it *will* cause problems," Stoltz commented, "but what about setting up a school in the village?"

"Isn't it a bit early for that?" said Oblomov. "It's not a good thing to teach the peasants to read and write; the next thing you know, they won't want to do any more ploughing."

"Yes, and they will be able to read instructional information *about* ploughing. You really have some strange ideas! But, seriously, you really should go and spend some time in the village yourself this year."

"Yes, you're right, except that my plan isn't yet quite…" Oblomov objected feebly.

"Forget all that!" said Stoltz. "All you have to do is go there and see for yourself what needs to be done. You've been fussing about that plan of yours for ages—surely it must be ready by now? What on earth have you been doing?"

"Andrei, it's not as if the the only thing I have to worry about is the estate, what about my other problem?"

"Which one is that?"

"I'm being thrown out of my apartment."

"What do you mean, 'thrown out'?"

"Just like that, I've been told to get out—and that's it!"

"So what's the problem?"

"What's the trouble? I've been worrying myself to death and losing a lot of sleep over it all. I don't know which way to turn first. All these things coming up and I have to handle everything myself; accounts to be settled, bills to be paid, moving arrangements—you wouldn't believe the expense; I don't even know where the money goes! Before you know where you are you're down to your last kopeck."

"What a spoiled baby you are! Making such a fuss about moving out." said Stoltz in disbelief. "By the way, talking of money, if you have enough cash let me have five hundred roubles, I need to send it right away. I can get the money from the office tomorrow."

"Hold on, let me think! They've just sent me a thousand from the estate, let's see how much is left, wait a second!" Oblomov started rummaging through the drawers. "Look, here's ten, twenty, here's two hundred—another twenty, there were also some coins here…Zakhar, Zakhar!"

Zakhar jumped down from his bench in the usual fashion and entered the room.

"What happened to the twenty kopecks I left here on the table yesterday?"

"Why do you keep going on about the twenty kopecks, Ilya Ilyich, I've already told you, there was never any twenty kopecks on the table!"

"What are you talking about? It was the change from the oranges."

"You must have given the money to someone and forgotten," said Zakhar, turning towards the door.

Stoltz laughed. "You Oblomovs, never know how much money you've got in your pockets!" he said reprovingly.

"What about the money you gave to Mikhei Andreyich a while ago?" Zakhar reminded Oblomov.

"Right, Tarantyev *did* take another ten roubles," Oblomov said, turning quickly to Stoltz, "yes, I really did forget!"

"Why do you let that creature into your home?" Stoltz asked.

"No one lets him in!" Zakhar volunteered. "He just barges in here as if he owns the place or like it was some neighborhood bar. He even took Ilya Ilyich's shirt and waistcoat—and that was the last we saw of them. When he came before it was to borrow a tailcoat; 'let me put it on' he says. Oh, Andrei Ivanich, sir, if only you could put a stop to him…"

"It's none of your business, get out of here!" Oblomov reprimanded him.

"Give me a sheet of paper!" said Stoltz. "I want to write a note."

"Zakhar, bring some paper for Andrei Ivanich!" Oblomov commanded.

"But there isn't any paper, we just looked for some." Zakhar replied from the hall, without even bothering to come back into the room.

"Any scrap of paper will do." Stoltz insisted.

Oblomov looked on the table—not a shred of paper to be seen.

"Alright, what about a visiting card?"

"No, I haven't had any visiting cards for ages," said Oblomov.

"What's wrong with you?" Stoltz responded ironically. "How do you expect to be able to take care of your affairs? I thought you were supposed to be drafting a plan? So, tell me, have you been going out anywhere, who have you been seeing?"

"Where have I been going? Nowhere very much. I've just been staying at home, worrying about my plan—as well as the business about the apartment. Thankfully, Tarantyev offered to help look for a place."

"Who comes to see you?"

"Well, there's Tarantyev and Alekseyev. The doctor dropped in a while ago. Then there was Penkin, Sudbinsky, Volkov..."

"I don't see any books around," said Stoltz.

"Here's one." said Oblomov, pointing to a book lying on the table.

"What is it? asked Stoltz, taking a look at it. Voyage to Africa. The last page you read is starting to mildew. Not a newspaper in sight; don't you read the papers?"

"No, the print is too small; bad for the eyes. Anyway, there's no need; if there's any news it's on everyone's lips all day long—you can't help hearing about it."

"But, Ilya," said Stoltz, regarding Oblomov with astonishment, "what do you actually spend your time doing? Just lying around rolled up like a lump of dough, it looks like."

"Exactly, Andrei, just like a lump of dough." Oblomov conceded gloomily.

"But do you really think being aware of it makes it alright?"

"No, I'm not trying to justify it. I was just answering your question." Oblomov sighed.

"You've got to snap out of it!"

"I've tried before, but it didn't work, and now... what's the point. There's no real stimulus, no great urge, my mind is drowsing along nicely." He replied with the barest hint of bitterness. "Anyway, enough of that, let's talk about you; where have you just come from?"

"Kiev. I'm going abroad in a couple of weeks, why don't you come with me?"

"Yes, why not!" Oblomov said impulsively.

"Then sit down right now and write your application, you can hand it in tomorrow!"

"Here he goes with 'tomorrow'," Oblomov said, already beginning to regret his impulse. Some people are always in such a hurry—as if someone is behind them with a whip. Let's think about it, discuss it and then we'll see! Maybe I should really go to the estate first and go abroad. . . . afterwards sometime."

"Why afterwards? It's doctor's orders, after all. First, you need to shed that fat and lose weight and this listlessness of yours will just disappear. What you need is both mental and physical exercise."

"No, Andrei, all that will be too much for me. I'm in really poor health. It's better if you just forget about me and go by yourself."

Stoltz looked down at Oblomov and Oblomov looked back up at him from where he was lying. Stoltz shook his head and Oblomov sighed.

"It really seems that the effort of living is too much for you," said Stoltz.

"You're absolutely right, it is too much for me!"

Andrei tried to think of what stimulus could possibly goad his friend into action and how to find that stimulus, and as he silently contemplated him he suddenly burst into laughter.

"Do you realize you're wearing two odd stockings?" he said, pointing to Oblomov's feet. "And your shirt's on inside out!"

Oblomov took a look at his feet and then at his shirt. "You're right." He acknowledged in some embarrassment. "I tell you, that Zakhar has been sent to punish me! You can't imagine what trouble he gives me! He talks back, he has no respect, and as for his work, better not to ask!"

"Ilya, Ilya; no, I just can't leave you here like this! In a week you won't recognize yourself. I'll be back this evening with a detailed schedule of what I plan to do with you—and myself. Right now, just get dressed! You'll see, I'm going to give you a thorough shake-up. Zakhar!" he shouted, "see that Ilya Ilyich gets dressed!"

"You're not thinking of taking me out, surely? Tarantyev and Alekseyev are coming to dinner, and then we were going to..."

"Zakhar," said Stoltz, paying no attention to him, "get him dressed!"

"Of course, right away, Andrei Ivanich, but just let me clean his boots first!" said Zakhar, eager to please.

"You mean his boots aren't even cleaned yet and it's already five o'clock!"

"Oh yes, they're cleaned alright, they were done last week, but the master hasn't been out, so they've just lost their shine."

"Alright, bring them as they are; and bring my suitcase into the drawing room, I'll be staying here. Now I'm going to get dressed, and Ilya, see that you're ready! We'll be eating out and then we'll be calling at two or three houses and..."

"But hold it a minute, you can't just—I mean, suddenly like this—I have to think about it; and anyway I haven't even shaved..."

"There's nothing to think about, no need to start dithering. You can get a shave on the way, I'll take you."

'But whose houses are we going to call at?" Oblomov protested miserably, "people I don't know? What an idea! I should really go and see Ivan Gerasimovich, I haven't been there for three days."

"Who is this Ivan Gerasimovich?"

"We used to work in the same office."

"Oh, you mean that old head clerk. What can possibly interest you in him? What on earth makes you want to spend time with that dimwit?"

"You know, you're sometimes so hard on people, Andrei! God knows why? He's really a nice person even though he doesn't wear fancy Dutch shirts."

"But what *do* you do there, what do you talk about?" Stoltz asked.

"It's just that everything there is so cosy and nicely arranged. The rooms are small and the divans are so soft and thick that you can practically sink into them without trace. The windows are entirely covered in ivy and cactuses and there are more than a dozen canaries and three dogs—so good-natured! And always snacks and appetizers on the table. The pictures are all of family scenes. You feel so much at home you never feel like leaving.

You sit without a care in the world, not a thought in your head and you know that the person sitting opposite you—of course, he's no genius and you wouldn't even dream of exchanging ideas with him—but you know that he is an artless, straightforward, genial soul, totally unpretentious and quite incapable of backbiting."

"But what do you actually do there?"

"What do we do? Well, we sit facing one another on the divans with our feet up and he smokes…"

"What about you?"

"I smoke too and listen to the canaries chirping. Then Marfa brings in the samovar."

"Tarantyev, Ivan Gerasimovich!" Stoltz shrugged as he pronounced the names.

"Anyway, hurry up and get dressed!" he urged. Turning to Zakhar, he added: "when Tarantyev comes tell him that we are dining out and that Ilya Ilyich will not be dining at home at all this summer and that he is going to be very busy in the autumn and will have no time to see him."

"I'll tell him, I won't forget, I'll tell him everything just like you said," Zakhar responded, "but what am I to do about dinner?"

"Feel free to share it with anyone you want."

"Yes, sir!"

Ten minutes later Stoltz emerged, dressed, shaved, his hair brushed and combed while Oblomov was still sitting gloomily on his bed, mechanically trying to button up his shirt but unable to find the buttonholes. Zakhar was kneeling in front of him on one knee, holding up a single uncleaned boot like a dish waiting to be served once the master had finished buttoning his shirt.

"You haven't even got your boots on yet!" Stoltz exclaimed. "Come on Ilya, get a move on!"

"But where are we going, what's all this for?" Oblomov said despairingly. "I'm not going to get a thing out of it, I know; that's why I've given it all up. I'd really rather not!"

"Now, just get a move on and let's go," said Stoltz briskly.

CHAPTER FOUR

Even though it was already rather late they still managed to complete some business errands and then Stoltz brought the owner of a gold mine along to join them for dinner. Afterwards they went to his dacha for tea and found a lot of guests already gathered there and Oblomov, used as he was to the most total seclusion, suddenly found himself amidst a crowd of people. They returned home late at night.

The next day and the day after that were spent in the same fashion and suddenly the whole week had slipped past. Oblomov protested, complained and argued, but was swept along and followed his friend everywhere.

Once, after another late night out, he mounted a particularly vigorous protest against all this hustle and bustle.

"Going for whole days at a time without taking your boots off," Oblomov grumbled as he donned his dressing gown, "makes your feet itch unbearably. I don't like this St. Petersburg life of yours!" he added as he lay down on the divan.

"Then what kind of life do you like?"

"Not this kind!"

"But what exactly don't you like about it?"

"This whole endless rat race, the malicious impulses constantly at work, especially greed, people always trying to do one other down, the gossip-mongering, the backbiting, the sly digs, people always trying to size you up; if you listen to what people say, your head starts reeling and you come away befuddled. People seem intelligent and look so dignified, but when they open their mouths it's 'this one got that, that one was awarded a lease' and then you hear someone yell, 'but what on earth for?' And, 'this one lost money at the club yesterday and that one took home three hundred thousand.' God, it's all so boring. What has happened to human beings? To integrity? True values seem to have disappeared and been traded in for triviality of every kind."

"But people have to have something to hold their interest," said Stoltz, "and everyone has different interests—that's what life is about!"

"People. Society! It's as if you are deliberately making me go out to meet people and socialize in order to kill any possible inclination I may have had to do so. You call that life? Some life! Tell me, what's at the center of it all? Absolutely nothing! Nothing of any depth, nothing at all real. They are the living dead, they are even more asleep than I am—these society people of yours. What do they live for? Instead of lying down they spend their days flitting back and forth like flies—to accomplish what, I'd like to know? You go into one of these salons and what do you see? The guests could not be more symetrically arranged, couldn't look more dignified and thoughtful, and what are they doing? Playing cards! Well, you couldn't wish for a nobler goal in life than that! What finer kind of intellectual sustenance for the inquiring mind! There are your living dead. They are the ones who spend their whole lives asleep on their chairs. Is that so much better than what I do? At least I do my lying down in my own home without bothering my head with threes and jacks!"

"Yes, I've heard you say that a thousand times before," said Stoltz, "but isn't it about time you came up with something new?"

"And what about the best and brightest of our young people? Cruising up and down the Nevsky Prospekt, dancing away their time—is that any different from sleeping? Shuffling and reshuffling their days like the same old cards in a pack. And where do they get that insolent pride and the haughty disdain with which they look down on lesser beings who are dressed differently from them and who do not bear the same ranks and titles? And these poor things are deluded into believing that this somehow makes them a superior breed. 'Look at us,' they seem to be saying, 'look at the high level posts that only people like us occupy and our front row seats in the stalls, our exclusive invitations to Prince N's balls'. They are constantly in one another's company, getting drunk and pulling one another to pieces like savages. And you call these people awake and alive? And not just the young people; take a look at their elders!

"They meet, they feed one another without any real good will or sincere fellow feeling, without even taking any pleasure in one another's company. They meet for dinner or a party as if they were going to the office, grim and unsmiling, just to boast about their cooks or their decor and then they snigger at one another behind their hands and try to trip one another up. The other day I was at a dinner and was so embarrassed that I felt like crawling under the table when they started tearing down the reputations of their absent friends.

"This one is an idiot, that one is common, another one is a crook, and yet another is ridiculous.

"They were like bloodhounds in full cry. While they were talking they were looking at one another with that expression on their faces as if to say, 'the moment you step outside the door you'll be the next victim!' Why on earth do they bother to meet if that's all it's for? Why all these warm handshakes? No genuine laughter, not a spark of warmth. All they're interested in doing is hooking big names or people with impressive titles so that they can boast, 'oh yes, guess who came to dinner!' or 'you'll never guess where I was invited!' You call that a life! No thanks, not for me! I don't learn a thing from it and I can't think what I gain from it."

"You know, Ilya," said Stoltz, "you think just the way ancient writers used to, but at least that has its good side, it means you're exercising your brain instead of sleeping. Anyway, what else do you want to say, go on!"

"Why go on, just look for yourself, there isn't a single fresh, healthy looking face among the lot of them."

"It's just the climate," Stoltz retorted, "even your face has that crumpled look and you spend your time lying down instead of running about!"

"There isn't a single face that looks clear and unruffled," Oblomov continued, "it's like some kind of contagion, they all affect one another with this restless, tormented anxiety, as if they were all feverishly hunting for something. It wouldn't be so bad if it meant they were seeking truth or their own good or the good of their fellow men, but no, they shudder at the very thought of the good fortune of their friends.

"One of them has only one thing on his mind; to get to court first thing tomorrow. The case has been dragging on for five years and his adversary is getting the upper hand, and for five years he has been obsessed with a single idea, a single goal, to destroy his opponent and on his ruins to raise the edifice of his own good fortune. To spend five years running around, kicking your heels in waiting rooms—what an ideal! And to make that your life's purpose?

"Take another one; he finds it unbearable to be condemned to going to the office every day and watching the clock until it shows five p.m., while the next fellow is green with envy because he has not been blessed by such great good fortune."

"What a philosopher you are, Ilya!" said Stoltz. "Everyone else is hustling and only you are above the fray!"

"What about that yellowish fellow with glasses," Oblomov continued, "he came up to me, wanted to know if I'd read the speech of some deputy and his eyes popped out when I told him I never read the papers. Then he went on about Louis Philippe as if he were his own father. Then he insisted on knowing why I thought the French envoy had left Rome. Can you imagine spending your whole life loading up with a week's supply of world news and then going about filling everyone's ears with it until the supply runs out? Today Mehmet Ali sent a ship to Constantinople—and he's breaking his head trying to figure it out, what for? Tomorrow Don Carlos doesn't manage to do something or other—and he's in a panic. Somewhere they're digging a canal, somewhere else someone is sending troops to the East. My God, what agitation! He's petrified, running around, carrying on as if those troops were out to get him personally.

"Everyone has to have an opinion about everything, they argue right, left and centre, but underneath, they're bored stiff by it all and couldn't care less. Underneath this uproar they're all fast asleep. None of this concerns them in the least, they're just masquerading. They have no business of their own so they disperse their attention and energies in all directions, unable to focus on any one thing. Their interest in everything simply disguises their interest in nothing, it's just a way of filling a void.

"Just choosing some modest goal that requires some effort and moving steadily towards it, or making a small but perceptible mark on something—that doesn't appeal to them at all, it has no glamour, it doesn't make any impression. That way, all this information they've picked up would be wasted and wouldn't impress anyone."

"Well, you and I haven't allowed our energies to be dispersed, Ilya, but what about this 'modest goal requiring some effort etc.'?" asked Stoltz.

Oblomov was momentarily silenced.

"Well, you see I'm really putting the finishing touches to my plan," he said. "And to hell with them anyway!" he added irritably. "I'm not doing anything to them and I don't want anything from them. I just can't see that as a normal way to live. It's not what I call living—it's an aberration, a distortion of the proper way to live and the real purpose of life that nature has prescribed for us."

"And what is that exactly?"

Oblomov did not respond.

"Well, describe to me the kind of life you'd like to lead ideally!" Stoltz insisted.

"I already have."

"But what exactly—seriously, describe it to me?"

"What it would be like?" said Oblomov turning over on to his back and regarding the ceiling. "Yes well, I would go down to the estate in the country."

"But what's stopping you?"

"The plan isn't finished; and then I wouldn't be going alone, but with a wife."

"Ah, so that's it! Fine, but what are you waiting for? In another three or four years no one will have you."

"What can I do, it's fate," said Oblomov with a sigh, "I don't have enough to support a wife."

"Come off it! With Oblomovka—and three hundred peasants!"

"What about it, can't support a wife on that!"

"Just the two of you, come on!"

"But what about children?"

"You'll raise your children, and they'll fend for themselves—provided you give them the proper guidance."

"You want me to turn gentlemen into workmen?" Oblomov cut in drily. "Anyway, children aside, what's this 'two of you' you're talking about? In actual fact, the moment you get married, you suddenly find all kinds of women have somehow crowded into your home. Look at any family: relatives, total strangers, housekeepers, hangers-on, who knows? And even if they don't actually live in the house, they come for coffee, dinner or what have you every day. How can I be expected to support a houseful of boarders on just three hundred peasants?"

"Alright, let's suppose someone gave you another three hundred thousand, what would you do?" asked Stoltz whose curiosity was now well and truly aroused.

"Mortgage everything right away and live off the interest."

"The interest would be too low, why not invest it in some company, like ours for example?"

"No Andrei, I'd never fall for that."

"You mean you wouldn't even trust me?"

"Not on your life! I don't mean you personally, but you never know what might happen—a sudden collapse and there you are without a penny to your name. A bank is another matter."

"Alright, then what would you do?"

"Well, I would move into a new comfortably appointed house surrounded by nice neighbors—you, for example; but no, you could never stay in one place for long."

"Surely even you couldn't stay there forever; wouldn't you ever go anywhere?"

"Certainly not!"

"Then why on earth do people go to the trouble of building railways and ships if life is just about staying where you are? Maybe, Ilya, we should submit a proposal for them to stop, since we won't be traveling!"

"That still leaves a lot of people; think of all the businessmen, merchants, salesmen, officials, and people who just like to travel, and have no place of their own—let them travel all they want!"

"And who are you?"

Oblomov offered no reply.

"Which social category do you include yourself in?"

"Ask Zakhar!" said Oblomov.

Stoltz took him at his word.

"Zakhar!" he called.

Zakhar entered the room sleepy-eyed.

"Who is that lying there?" asked Stoltz.

Zakhar was suddenly wide-awake and regarded first Stoltz and then Oblomov suspiciously out of the corner of his eye.

"What do you mean 'who is it?' Can't you see for yourself?"

"No, I can't." said Stoltz

"Something funny's going on here! It's my master, Ilya Ilyich."

He chuckled. "Alright, you can go!"

"The master," Stoltz repeated and laughed out loud.

"No, 'gentleman'," Oblomov corrected him reprovingly.

"No, no, definitely 'master'," Stoltz was still laughing.

"What's the difference, 'gentleman' is the same thing."

"The difference is that a 'gentleman' is the kind of master who pulls on his own stockings and takes off his own boots," affirmed Stoltz.

"Yes, well, the English have to do these things themselves, because they don't have as many servants as we Russians."

"Anyway, please go on describing your ideal life. Here you are surrounded by all these nice, friendly neighbors—then what? How would you spend your time?"

"Well, in the morning I'd get up," Oblomov began, placing his hands behind his head, while his whole face radiated contentment. In his imagination he was already living in the country.

"The weather is beautiful; a clear blue sky, not a cloud in sight," he said. "The way I see it, in my plan one side of the house with the balcony is facing east, overlooking the gardens and the fields, the other side is facing the village. While I'm waiting for my wife to wake up I put on my dressing gown and take a walk in the garden to breathe the morning air. The gardener would already be there and I would help him water the flowers and trim the bushes and trees. I'd pick a posy of flowers for my wife, then I'd take a bath or bathe in the river. I'd come back and find the balcony opened. My wife would be there in a housecoat and a light summer headdress so flimsy that it looks as if it would blow off at any moment. She's waiting for me, 'tea is ready', she says. What a wonderful kiss! What wonderful tea! What a comfortable chair! I sit down at the table—on it there are rusks, cream, fresh butter..."

"Then?"

"Then I'd put on some roomy coat or jacket, take my wife by the waist and together we would plunge into the endless dark path between the trees. We would walk quietly, musing in silence or perhaps thinking aloud, daydreaming, counting the minutes of happiness like the beats of a pulse, listening to the rise and fall of our hearts beating. We would be moving along in tune with nature and find that we have emerged at the stream, the meadow. The river is lapping gently, the ears of corn ripple in the passing breeze. It's getting hot, we're gliding along in a boat; my wife is paddling and barely raising the paddle out of the water..."

"You're a real poet, Ilya," Stoltz broke in.

"Yes, a poet of life, for life is poetry—though, of course, you can't stop people distorting it! Then we might go into the greenhouse," Oblomov continued, intoxicated by the heady delights of the ideal life he was describing.

What he was doing was simply retrieving from his imagination scenes that he had created and stored there long ago, and that is why his imagination never flagged as he warmed to his theme without a moment's pause.

"We'd inspect the peaches, the grapes," he went on, "and discuss what to have served and then go back, eat a little breakfast and wait for our guests to arrive. There'll be a note for my wife from a Maria Petrovna with a book or some music, or someone would have sent a pineapple as a gift, or maybe a giant watermelon would have ripened in our greenhouse and we'd send it to a good friend for tomorrow's dinner that we'd been invited to.

"Meanwhile the kitchen is beginning to hum with activity; the chef in a snow-white apron and hat is getting busy. He takes off one pot and puts on another, stirs a little here, rolls some dough there and pours out some water over there. You can hear the clicking of knives chopping the greens and the ice cream being churned. I enjoy taking a look in the kitchen before dinner, taking the lid off a saucepan and sniffing, watching the pastry being wrapped for the pies and cream being whipped. Then I would lie down on the couch; my wife would read to me from a book—something new; and from time to time we would stop and argue about something she'd just read. Then the guests would begin arriving, maybe you and your wife."

"Now you've got *me* married!"

"Of course! Then two three more friends—all familiar faces. We'd continue the conversation where we'd left off the day before. Some good-humored banter or perhaps an eloquent silence, a pause for reflection— not because someone has lost a position, not because of some case before the Senate, but out of sheer contentment, a feeling of pleasurable anticipation. There'll be no vicious slandering of absent friends, none of those nasty looks that tell you that you'll be the next victim the moment the door closes behind you. If you feel that way about people you simply don't break bread with them! The eyes of your companions radiate goodwill; their laughter is an expression of genuine good humor not of malice. Everyone speaks and acts from the heart, and what is in the heart is what you see reflected in people's eyes and words. After dinner mocca is served and Havana cigars are lit on the terrace."

"This is the same scene you're always describing; what used to happen in our father's and grandfather's day."

"Not at all!" Oblomov riposted with some heat, "not the same at all. You wouldn't see my wife making jam or pickling mushrooms. You wouldn't find her counting lengths of yarn or sorting homespun cloth or slapping the faces of the servant girls. No, her time is spent with music, books, the piano, elegant furniture—don't you see?"

"Well, but what about you yourself?"

"Well, I wouldn't be reading last year's papers or traveling in one of those lumbering 'kolymaga' carriages or still be dining off noodle soup and goose but would have my chef trained at the English Club or at the embassy."

"And then?"

"Then, on hot days in the cool of the afternoon I'd send a cart with a samovar and refreshments to the birch grove or even to the meadow, and there, right on the newly mown grass I'd have rugs spread among the haystacks and have a wonderful time picnicking on everything, including the cold soup and beef. The peasants would be on their way back from the fields with their scythes on their shoulders, a haywain would pass us, dwarfing the horse and cart; poking out from the top of the heap of hay you would see a child's head under a peasant's hat with flowers on it. A crowd of barefoot peasant women carrying sickles would pass by, their voices raised in song. Catching sight of the master's family, they would lower their voices respectfully and bow deeply. One of them, with a sunburned neck and bare elbows, would coyly lower her mischievously twinkling eyes just for appearances sake to shield herself from her master's affectionate gesture, even though she is secretly delighted—and let's hope to God that the wife doesn't notice!"

At this, both Stoltz and Oblomov himself burst into laughter.

"There is a dampness in the air," Oblomov concluded, "darkness is beginning to fall and mist is starting to form over the rye like an inverted sea. The horses' shoulders are beginning to twitch and their hoofs are pawing the ground; it's time to go home.

"In the house the lamps have been lit and the knives are clattering furiously in the kitchen. Mushrooms are frying, there are chops and berries…There's music, 'Casta diva, casta diva,'" Oblomov broke into song with a snatch of the cavatina. "Every time I hear that 'Casta diva' I remember that woman crying her eyes out, and the poignancy of those notes—It does something to me! There she is all alone and everyone around her is oblivious. The weight of her secret is too heavy to bear, she can only share it with the moon."

"You like that aria? I'm glad; Olga Ilyinskaya sings it beautifully—I'll introduce you. What a voice, what a singer! And an altogether captivating child into the bargain! But maybe I'm not a fair judge; I have to confess I'm not altogether unaffected…But anyway, let's not get off the subject," Stoltz added, "please go on!"

"Well," said Oblomov, "that's really about *it*! The party breaks up, the guests go to their quarters and the next day they go about their various activities. Some go fishing, some go hunting, and others just sit around and take it easy."

"How do you mean 'just sit around'? You mean literally empty-handed?"

"What do you want? Well, maybe just a handkerchief. I suppose you wouldn't want to live like that—that wouldn't be living in your book?"

"You mean spending your whole life like that?"

"Yes, right into old age, to the grave in fact, that's what I call life!"

"No, that's not life!"

"How can you say that? What else do you need? Just imagine never having to see another haggard, anxiety-ridden face; no worries, never having to bother your head about some question before the Senate, prices on the stock exchange, reports, the minister's reception, promotions, extra allowances! All conversation would be from the heart. There'd be no need ever to move out of your apartment—and what a boon that alone would be! And that's not life?"

"Absolutely not!" Stoltz persisted.

"Well then, what is it according to you, if it's not life?"

"It's...." Stoltz paused, trying to find the right word to describe that version of life, "it's a kind of... *oblomovshchina*," he said finally.

"Ob-lo-mov-shchi-na,"* Oblomov repeated slowly, enunciating separately the syllables of this strange new word, "*ob-lo-mov-shchi-na!*"

He gave Stoltz a strange, searching look.

"Then what is the ideal life according to you, if you reject '*oblomovshchina*'?" he inquired mildly and without heat. "Isn't everybody looking for the same thing as me? After all," he continued more boldly, "surely the purpose of all this hustle and bustle of yours, all these passions, wars, trade and politics is to achieve precisely this very peace and quiet, to strive for this ideal of paradise lost?"

"Even your utopia has 'Oblomov' written all over it." Stoltz conceded nothing.

"Everyone wants peace and quiet," contended Oblomov.

"Not everyone, even you spent ten years looking for something else."

"Oh, what was it I was looking for?" Oblomov asked in some bewilderment as he tried to reach back in his memory to the past.

"Think back, try to remember. What happened to your books and your translations?"

"Zakhar must have put them somewhere," Oblomov replied, "They must be lying around in some corner."

"Yes, in some corner," Stoltz said reproachfully, "the same corner where your old aspirations are mouldering, as well as your plans to 'work as long as you have strength, because Russia needs hands and heads to develop and explore its inexhaustible reserves'—your very words—'so that your life outside your work can be richer, richer in the sense of living a different kind of life, a life of art, of aesthetic satisfaction, the life of the artist, the poet.' Has Zakhar taken these aspirations and dumped *them* in a corner too? You remember, after all the books, you were going to visit other lands so as to understand and love your own better? 'The whole of life is about thought and work,' you used to say in those days, 'never mind if your work is unknown and done in obscurity, as long as it is unremitting and you die with the satisfaction of knowing that you did your part.' Well, which corner is all that lying in?"

"Yes...yes..." said Oblomov, uneasily following every word uttered

---

* *Abstract noun coined by Stoltz, from the name Oblomov. See Translators Note.*

by Stoltz, "I do remember that…yes, indeed…well, of course," he said, as it all suddenly came back to him. "Yes, we were going to travel the length and breadth of Europe, cover the whole of Switzerland on foot, burn our feet on Vesuvius, walk down to Herculaneum. We must have been crazy—what foolishness!"

"Foolishness?" Stoltz objected. "Wasn't it you who said with tears in your eyes as you looked at reproductions of Raphael's Madonnas, Corregio's Night, and the Apollo Belvedere, 'my God, imagine never to be able to see the originals with your blood running cold at the thought that you are actually in the presence of the work of Michelangelo and Titian, and are treading the soil of Rome! Imagine spending your whole life seeing those myrtles, cypresses and wild orange trees in hothouses but never in their native habitat! Never to breathe the air of Italy, to delight in the azure of its skies!'—not to mention all the rest of the verbal pyrotechnics that exploded out of your head! Foolishness indeed!"

"Yes, yes, I remember," said Oblomov, searching his memory. "You even took me by the arm and made me pledge not to die without seeing these things."

"I remember," said Stoltz, "you once presented me with a translation of Say which you had inscribed for me for my nameday; I still have it. I remember the way you used to closet yourself with your mathematics tutor, determined to get to the bottom of the question of why it was so important to understand circles and squares, and then halfway through you just gave up. You began to learn English and then gave up and when I proposed traveling abroad and taking a look at the German universities, you jumped up and embraced me and sealed your solemn pledge with a handshake: 'I'm with you, Andrei, wherever you want to go!' Those were your very words! You always were a bit of an actor. So how do you explain it, Ilya? I've been abroad twice since we finished our studies and even after all that education I wasn't too proud to sit as a student in lecture halls in Bonn, Jena and Erlangen and then I got to know Europe as if it were my own backyard. Alright, let's say travel is a luxury, not everyone can afford it or feels it necessary to undertake it. But what about Russia itself. I've traveled the length and breadth of Russia and I work…"

"But you'll stop working some time," Oblomov observed.

"Never, why would I?"

"When you've doubled your capital," said Oblomov.

"Even when I've quadrupled it I won't stop."

"Then what's it all for?" he continued after a moment's silence. "Why knock yourself out, if it's not to make yourself financially secure for life so that you can then take it easy and live a life of leisure?"

"'*Oblomovshchina*' rustic style!" said Stoltz.

"Or even to make your mark in your career and achieve a position in society and then rest on your laurels and enjoy a well-earned rest."

"'*Oblomovshchina*' St. Petersburg style!" Stoltz retorted.

"Then when will there be time for living?" Oblomov shot back, stung by Stoltz's barbed remark. "Otherwise what's the point of all this endless striving?"

"For its own sake, and that's all there is to it! Work—both the idea and the substance—is the very point and essence of life, at least for me. Now that you've banished work from your life, what have you got left? I'm going to make one more effort—maybe the last—to help you. But if, after all that, you're still going to sit around with the likes of Tarantyev and Alekseyev, you're finished; you'll become a millstone around your own neck. It's now or never!"

Oblomov listened to him, his eyes betraying his alarm. It was as if his friend was holding up a mirror to him and he was horrified by his own reflection in it.

"Don't be hard on me, Andrei, I really need your help," he began with a sigh, "you can't imagine how painful it all is for me! If you could only have seen me and heard me today and watched me digging my own grave and mourning my own demise, you wouldn't have had the heart to reproach me. I see everything so clearly, I understand it all; I just don't have the will or the strength of character to do anything about it. You've got to inject me with your will, your strength of mind, and take me wherever you want. If you lead I might be able to follow, but, left to myself, I'm rooted to the spot. You're absolutely right, it's now or never—one more year and it will be too late!"

"I can't believe I'm hearing the same Ilya," said Andrei. "I remember the lively, clean-limbed boy you once were, how you would go to Kudrino every day from Prechistenki to that little garden... have you forgotten the two sisters? Have you forgotten how you would take them Rousseau, Schiller, Goethe and Byron and they would give you the novels of Cottin and Genlis to take away—to make a big impression on them and improve their taste?"

Oblomov jumped up from the bed.

"So you remember it too, Andrei? I could never forget it; how I would whisper my dreams and confide my hopes for the future to them, share my plans, my thoughts, even my feelings, feelings I kept from you, afraid you would make fun of me. All of that came to nothing and there was never another opportunity. What happened to it all, why did it all just vanish so irretrievably? It's not as if there have been any major upheavals or catastrophes in my life, any loss or any tremendous burden on my conscience—it's as clear as daylight. There's been no crushing blow to my self-esteem, but for some reason or other it all disappeared, God knows why!"

He sighed.

"You know, Andrei, in my whole life I've never been carried away by any passion, whether it would have meant my salvation or my ruin. My life has never been like a normal day, the way it is with other people, with a morning which gradually begins to glow with color and then turns into bright, incandescent daylight when the world is in motion, seething with activity, moving under the midday sun, and then things gradually quietening down and the color seeping out of the sky as the day gently and naturally declines towards evening. No, my life seems to have begun at twilight, strange as it may seem. As far back as I can remember, I've always had this feeling that I was on the wane, somehow fading.

"This feeling that life was slipping away began when I was copying documents in the office; it stayed with me all the time I was acquiring all that wisdom from books, wisdom that I didn't know how to use in real life. The feeling persisted when I was with friends, listening to all the chatter, the gossip, the derision, the heartless backbiting, the vacuousness. I saw friendships maintained by empty, mechanical socializing. I felt life slipping away and my energies draining when I was with Mina. I spent more than half my income on her and imagined that I was in love with her. The same feeling when I was walking idly and despondently up and down the Nevsky Prospekt among all those raccoon coats and beaver collars and when I was at parties and balls where I was accorded the hospitality due to a tolerably eligible prospect. I felt myself withering as I frittered away my life and my mind, as I moved from town to the dacha, from the dacha to Gorokhovaya Street and knew that spring had arrived by the appearance of oysters and lobsters, autumn and winter by the invitations to people's homes and summer by the outings, while life itself was distinguished by nothing more than an unruffled, mindless lethargy which we all shared.

"Even our ambition was frittered away—on what? Ordering clothes from fashionable tailors, getting invited to the right homes or having your hand shaken by Prince P. After all, ambition is an essential ingredient of life and look what happened to it!

"Maybe I just didn't understand that kind of life or it really was meaningless, but in any case that was all I knew and there was no one to show me any other kind. You would streak into and out of my life as briefly and brilliantly as a comet and I would forget everything and just decay..."

Stoltz was now beyond even dismissing Oblomov's words with his usual derision. He just listened in gloomy silence.

"You said before that my face had a crumpled and unhealthy look about it," Oblomov continued, "yes, I'm like a shabby, threadbare coat, worn out not because of exposure to the elements or hard work but because for twelve years a light has been burning inside me, unable to find an outlet and doing nothing but illuminating the walls of its own prison and, finding no opening to the outside world, has just been snuffed out for lack of oxygen.

"And that's how the last twelve years have passed, my dear Andrei, and I've lost any impulse to wake up from my coma."

"But why didn't you just break away and escape instead of just suffering in silence?" Stoltz asked impatiently.

"Where to?"

"Why not the same place as your runaway peasants, to the Volga. At least there is more going on there; things to get involved in, to give you a purpose in life, work to be done. I would have gone to Siberia, to Sitkha."

"You're always prescribing these drastic measures," said Oblomov dejectedly, "it's not as if I'm the only one. What about Mikhailov, Semyonov, Alekseyev, Stepanov—the list is endless, our name is legion!"

Stoltz was still reacting to Oblomov's confession and remained silent. Then he sighed.

"Yes, a lot of water has flowed under the bridge!" he said, "but I'm not going to leave you like this. I'm going to take you away from all this. First we'll go abroad, then to the estate; you'll lose a little weight and stop moping; and we'll find things for you to do."

"Yes, let's get away from here!" Oblomov said excitedly.

"Tomorrow we'll start getting you a passport to go abroad, then we'll start packing—and there'll be no backtracking, you hear, Ilya!"

"Everything is 'tomorrow' with you!" Oblomov grumbled, coming back down to earth.

"So you would really rather not 'put off till tomorrow what you can do today?' My word, you're really raring to go! Well, it's a little late today, but don't worry, in two weeks we'll be well away from here!" said Stoltz.

"What are you talking about, 'two weeks'? Up and go, just like that?" said Oblomov, "all this needs careful thought and thorough preparation. We'll need a large 'tarantass' carriage for one thing...maybe in about three months."

"So now a 'tarantass' is the problem! Forget it! We'll take a post-chaise to the frontier or a steamer to Lübeck, whatever is most convenient, and once there we'll have our choice of trains."

"And what about the apartment, and Zakhar, and Oblomovka? Something has to be done about them!" Oblomov contended.

"'Oblomovshchina, oblomovshchina'!" Stoltz said, laughing. Then he picked up a candle, said goodnight, and went off to bed.

"Now or never—remember!" he added, turning to address Oblomov as he left, closing the door behind him.

CHAPTER FIVE

"Now or never!" The words resounded ominously in Oblomov's head the moment he woke up the next morning. He got out of bed, paced back and forth several times and then looked into the drawing room; Stoltz was sitting and writing something.

"Zakhar!" he called, but no Zakhar appeared. Stoltz had sent him to the post office. Oblomov went and sat at his dust-covered desk, took up a pen and dipped it into the inkwell, but there was no ink; he looked for some paper, but there was no paper either. Without thinking, he started tracing something in the dust with his finger and when he looked he found that the word 'oblomovshchina' had appeared. He wiped it away smartly with his sleeve. During the night he had seen the word in a dream written in letters of fire like the writing on the wall at Belshazzar's feast.

Zakhar returned and stared dumbly at his master, so surprised was he to see him up and about instead of lying in bed. In this look of glazed incomprehension on Zakhar's face Oblomov read the word 'oblomovshchina'. "Just a single word," thought Oblomov, "but how painful!" Out of habit Zakhar took the comb, the brush and a towel and stepped towards Ilya Ilyich to do his hair. "Go to hell!" Oblomov shouted angrily and knocked the brush out of Zakhar's hands; Zakhar had already dropped the comb on the floor by himself in any case.

"Won't you be going back to bed then?" Zakhar asked, "I could get it ready."

"Bring me some paper and ink!" Oblomov replied.

Oblomov was brooding over the words: "now or never!" This desperate rallying cry of his mind and will rang in his ears, and after due consideration he concluded that he still had just enough determination in reserve and needed to think very carefully where to invest this meagre residue and what to apply it to.

After some agonizing, he grabbed the pen and pulled out a book from a corner, anxious to make up in one brief hour for all that he had failed to read, write or ponder in ten years of neglect. But what was he to do? Stay where he was or move on? This Oblomovian question was for him of even deeper significance than Hamlet's 'to be or not to be'. To move on would mean not only casting off his nice, loose dressing gown from his body but also stripping it from his heart and mind; it would mean not only wiping the dust and the cobwebs from the walls of his room, but from his eyes, and freeing his vision.

"But what would be the first step? How to begin? I don't know, I can't....no, I'm prevaricating—I do know; and anyway Stoltz is right here, he'll tell me right away. Only what will he tell me? He'll say: 'draft detailed instructions for your agent to take to the estate; take out a mortgage on Oblomovka, buy some more land, send a building plan, give up the apartment, get a passport and go abroad for six months, shed some fat, lose weight, let some fresh air into my soul, some of that air we used to dream about together, learn to live without my dressing gown, without Zakhar, without Tarantyev, pull on my own stockings, pull off my own boots, sleep only at night, travel the way everyone does, on trains and steamers, and then… then settle in Oblomovka, learn the difference between sowing and threshing, what makes peasants rich or poor, go into the fields, attend elections, visit factories, mills, docks—and all this within a week! Not to mention reading the papers, books and worrying about why the British are sending a warship to the East… Yes, that's what he'll say! In a word: 'get moving!'… and that's how it will be for life! It will mean goodbye to the poetic ideal of life—more like a life sentence in a blacksmith's shop than a life. Constantly surrounded by flames, smoke, heat, din… when would there be time for living? Maybe I'd be better off staying where I am?

"Staying—that means wearing my shirt inside out, the sound of Zakhar's feet slapping the floor, dinner with Tarantyev, not bothering about anything, not finishing 'Travels in Africa', growing old quietly in Tarantyev's friend's apartment… Now or never? To be or not to be?" Oblomov attempted to rise from the armchair but his foot missed his slipper on the first try and he sank back again.

Two weeks later Stoltz was already in England, having extracted a promise from Oblomov that he would go straight to Paris. Ilya Ilyich had made considerable progress. His passport was now ready and he had even ordered a traveling coat and bought a cap.

Zakhar had argued strenuously in favor of ordering only one pair of boots and having new soles put on the other pair. Oblomov had bought a traveling rug, a woollen sweater, a toilet bag and would have bought a bag for carrying food if so many people had not told him that one does not take one's own food abroad.

Zakhar rushed from one shop to another, dripping with sweat, and although he managed to pocket a lot of small change in the process, he cursed Andrei Ivanovich and whoever else had come up with this idea of traveling. "What on earth will he do there on his own?" he asked in the shop. "Over there the only servants are girls. How can a girl pull on the master's stockings over his bare legs?" He sniggered and one side of his mouth twisted upwards taking the whiskers with it. Nor was Oblomov idle; he busily wrote down what he was to take on the journey and what was to be left behind. Tarantyev was entrusted with the task of taking the furniture and the other things to the apartment at his friend's house on the Vyborg side to be locked in the three rooms and kept for his return from abroad.

Oblomov's acquaintances now began to comment, some in disbelief, others with derision, and others again with actual alarm: "Well, would you believe it? Oblomov's going on a trip, he's actually stirring!"

But a month passed—three months passed and still Oblomov had not left. The night before he was to leave his lip swelled up. "A fly must have bitten it, can't go to sea with a lip like this!" he said, and decided to wait for the next boat. August comes and Stoltz, who had arrived in Paris long before, writes him furious letters but gets no reply.

But why not? Could it be that the ink has dried up in the inkwell and there's no paper? Or perhaps there are just too many 'that's' and 'what's' jostling with one other in Oblomov's writing style, or maybe even because Ilya Ilyich, forced to choose between the stark alternatives of 'now' or ' never', had settled on the latter, placed his hands behind his head—and nothing Zakhar could do would rouse him.

The truth was that the inkwell was full of ink, the letters, as well as a supply of paper, were on his desk—crested writing paper for that matter—paper that was covered with his handwriting. He had filled several sheets and had not put two 'which's' together even once; his style was free flowing and even eloquent and expressive in places, as in the phrase 'days of yore' in reference to the time when he and Stoltz used to dream of a life of work and travel.

He would get up at seven, read, and carry books around. His face bore no trace of sleep, fatigue or boredom. There was even color in his cheeks and a glitter in his eye, a suggestion at least of self-confidence, if not actual boldness. The dressing gown was no longer to be seen. Tarantyev had taken it to his friend's house along with the other things.

Oblomov would sit with a book or write, wearing normal indoor dress, a coat with a light scarf around his neck and his snow-white shirt collar showing over his tie. When he went out he wore a finely tailored frock coat and a smart hat. He was cheerful, he hummed. What was going on?

There he is sitting at the window of his dacha (he is living in a dacha several versts out of town) with a bouquet of flowers at his side. He is hurrying to finish something he is writing and keeps on looking out through the shrubbery to the path beyond and then returning to his task. Suddenly he hears the gravel crunching under light footsteps. Oblomov throws down his pen, picks up the bouquet and hurries to the window.

"Is it you, Olga Sergeyevna? Just a moment!" he says and, snatching his cap and his cane, runs out to the gate, offers his arm to a certain beautiful woman and disappears with her into the woods, in the shade of the towering spruces.

Zakhar appeared from around a corner, watched his master disappear into the woods, locked the room and went into the kitchen.

"He's gone!" he said to Anisya.

"Will he be back for dinner?"

"Who knows?" Zakhar replied sleepily.

Zakhar had not changed; still the same enormous side whiskers, stubbly, unshaven chin, the same gray waistcoat and the same tear in his frock-coat, but he was now married to Anisya. Whether this was because he had broken up with his lady friend or simply out of the conviction that a man should be married, the fact remains that he was married and, in spite of the proverb, remained unchanged.

It was Stoltz who had introduced Oblomov to Olga and her aunt. When Stoltz had taken Oblomov to the home of Olga's aunt for the first time, there had been other guests and Oblomov had typically felt awkward and ill at ease. "I really feel like taking my gloves off," he thought, "it's so hot in this room. I'm not used to all this any more!"

Stoltz had taken a seat next to Olga who was sitting alone under a lamp away from the tea table, leaning back in her armchair and paying little attention to what was going on around her. She was very happy to see Stoltz, and although there was no sparkle in her eyes, nor any heightened color in her cheeks, her whole face radiated an even peaceful glow and she even produced a smile. She would have described him as a friend and liked him because he always amused her and she was never bored in his company, although she was a little intimidated by him because he made her feel like a child.

Whenever some question arose in her mind or she wanted something explained, she always hesitated to share it with him because she felt so dwarfed and outdistanced by him, and her self-esteem sometimes suffered from these feelings of immaturity and the gap in knowledge, experience and years between them.

For his part, Stoltz simply admired the fragrant freshness of mind and the spontaneity of feeling of this charming creature purely for their own sake. He saw her merely as a delightful child full of promise. However, Stoltz talked to her more readily and more often than to other women because she instinctively behaved in a simple natural way in harmony with her sunny temperament and, as a result of a healthy upbringing free of any spurious sophistication, gave spontaneous expression to all her thoughts, feelings and impulses right down to the slightest, barely perceptible movement of her eyes, lips and hands. Perhaps the reason why she strode so confidently along this path was because at times she heard the still more confident footsteps of her "friend," whom she trusted and whose stride she tried to match with her own.

The fact is that you will rarely meet a young girl of such simplicity and unfeigned naturalness of reaction, speech and behavior. You would never see in her eyes the look that tells you: "now I'm going to purse my lips a little and look thoughtful—don't you find it becomes me? Now I'll look over there, look a little frightened and give a little shriek and everyone will come running. Now I'm going to sit at the piano and just let the tip of my foot peep out..."

No affectations, no coquetry, no false attitudes, no play-acting, no striving for effect, but for all that, Stoltz was almost alone in appreciating her and she sat out more than one mazurka, unable to conceal her boredom, and even the most affable of the young men hesitated to approach her, not knowing what to say to her or how to say it.

Some thought her unsophisticated, shallow, and superficial because deep pronouncements on life and love did not come tripping off her tongue. There was no swift, original or bold repartee or weighty views on music or literature that had been picked up from reading or from conversation. Her words were few, but her own and unpretentious, and the cleverer and brighter of the eligible young escorts avoided her, while the not-so- bright young men, on the other hand, found her too complicated and rather forbidding. Stoltz alone talked to her without constraint and was able to amuse her.

She was fond of music, but sang mostly in private or just for Stoltz or one of her school friends; but she sang, as Stoltz put it, like no other singer. No sooner had Stoltz sat down beside her than the room resounded to her laughter, laughter that was so sonorous, so genuine and so infectious, that people within earshot would have to join in in spite of themselves, and without knowing what had provoked it.

But Stoltz did not confine himself to amusing her; after half an hour he succeeded in arousing her curiosity and it was with redoubled curiosity that she turned her eyes in Oblomov's direction. The effect on Oblomov was to make him wish that the floor would open up and swallow him.

"What can they be saying about me?" he wondered, darting an anxious glance in their direction. He had wanted to leave before, but Olga's aunt had invited him to the table and seated him beside her where he was caught in the crossfire of the looks being exchanged by his table companions. He turned nervously in Stoltz's direction, but he was no longer there; he looked at Olga and found that she was giving him that same curious look. "She's still looking at me." He thought and inspected his clothing with some embarrassment. He even wiped his face with his handkerchief in case there was something unsightly on his nose. He adjusted his tie, thinking that the knot may have come undone—it had been known to happen! No, he could find nothing wrong and yet she was still looking at him.

Meanwhile someone was serving him tea and biscuits on a tray. In his anxiety to quell his embarrassment and act relaxed, he got so relaxed that he grabbed such a pile of cakes and biscuits that the girl sitting next to him burst out laughing and everybody started to eye him and his pile curiously. "Oh, God, she's looking too!" Oblomov thought to himself, "what am I going to do with all this stuff?" Without even looking he could see that Olga had left her seat and moved to another corner—much to his relief. Meanwhile the girl was eyeing him expectantly, wondering what he would do with all the cakes and biscuits.

"I'd better swallow them quickly," he thought and began to dispose of them smartly; luckily they were the kind that melted in the mouth.

There were just two left; he sighed with relief and nerved himself to look at the corner of the room to which Olga had moved… "Oh, God, there she was standing by a bust, leaning against the pedestal and watching him." It looked as if she had left the corner where she had been sitting precisely so as to get a better look at him, and had witnessed the whole ignominious episode of the biscuits.

At supper, she sat at the other end of the table, so busy eating and talking that she appeared to be paying him no attention, but Oblomov had only to glance anxiously in her direction to reassure himself that she was not looking, to find that her eyes were trained on him, full of curiosity, but at the same time somehow conveying sympathy.

After supper Oblomov hurriedly took his leave of the aunt. She invited him to dinner on the following day and asked him to convey the invitation to Stoltz. Ilya Ilyich bowed and, keeping his eyes lowered made his way out across the room; only the piano stood between himself and the screen and the door. He took a look. Olga was sitting at the piano regarding him with intense curiosity. It seemed to him that she was smiling. "Andrei probably told her about the odd stockings I was wearing yesterday and how I had my shirt on inside out," he decided and went home in a troubled mood, partly because of this supposition, but even more because of the invitation to dinner to which his only response had been to bow—thus accepting it.

From that moment on Oblomov could not get Olga's insistent look out of his mind. He tried lying down on his back; he tried every possible relaxed and casual position, but nothing helped; he just could not sleep. But that was only half of it. Suddenly he could no longer stand the sight of his old dressing gown; he found Zakhar stupid and unbearable and the dust and cobwebs intolerable. Some patron of struggling artists had once foisted upon him some third-rate pictures; Oblomov had them thrown out. The blinds, which no one had been able to raise for years, he now fixed with his own hands. He got Anisya to clean the windows and brushed off the cobwebs. Then he lay on his side and spent a whole hour thinking—of Olga. First he concentrated on her appearance, reproducing a portrait of her from memory.

Strictly speaking Olga was not what you would call a beauty. She did not possess that pallor which is offset by the high color of the cheeks and lips and her eyes did not burn with that inner fire. Her lips were not of coral, nor her mouth of pearl, nor did she have the tiny hands of a five-year old child or fingers shaped like grapes. Yet if she were to be made into a statue it would be one of grace and harmony. She was on the tall side and her height was perfectly proportionate to the size of her head, which in turn was perfectly matched by the oval shape and dimensions of her face. All of this was in perfect harmony with her shoulders, and her shoulders with her waist. Anyone who met her, no matter how preoccupied, would stop for a moment at the sight of such an artistically crafted and carefully molded creation.

The line of her ever so slightly aquiline nose could not have been more graceful; her lips were slender and mostly compressed, a sign of concentrated thought. The light of this active intelligence shone also in the keen, lively look in her dark blue-gray eyes that missed nothing. Her eyebrows lent particular beauty to her eyes; they were not arched and did not rim the eyes with two slender, carefully plucked threads. No, they were a pair of reddish, bushy, almost perfectly straight lines, which were rarely arranged symetrically. One was slightly higher than the other and had left a little crease just above the brow that somehow gave the impression that a thought was lurking there.

Olga walked with her head bent slightly forward, a head so gracefully, so nobly poised on her proud, slender neck. Her whole body moved evenly with a step so light as to be barely detectable.

"Why was she watching me so intently yesterday?" Oblomov wondered, "Andrei swears that he never said anything about the stockings or the shirt, but just spoke about our friendship and how we grew up and went to school together—nothing at all negative! And also he told her how unhappy he (Oblomov) was and how his best qualities were atrophying from disuse and lack of involvement, and how his life force was draining away, and how..."

"But what was the smiling about?" Oblomov asked himself, "if she had a heart, it should have stood still, it should have swollen with pity, but instead....Oh well, what does it matter? I've got to stop dwelling on it! I'll just go this once today, eat and run, and never set foot in the place again."

But as the days passed, he found himself setting both feet in the place time and time again—not to mention his hands and his head!

One fine morning Tarantyev moved all Oblomov's possessions from his apartment into his friend's house in the little street on the Vyborg side and for the first time for years Oblomov spent three days with no bed and no divan, dining at the house of Olga's aunt. It so happened that there was a dacha to let right opposite theirs; Oblomov took it sight unseen and moved in. He was with Olga from morning to night; he read with her, he sent her flowers, he went for walks around the lake and in the hills with her—yes, Oblomov! Well, life is full of surprises, but how exactly did this happen? It was like this.

When he and Stoltz went to dinner that day at the aunt's house Oblomov suffered the same torment as he had the previous day. All the time he was chewing his food and talking he was conscious of that scrutiny scorching him like the sun, making him squirm, unnerving him and making his blood run faster. It was only for the briefest moment that he managed to escape this relentless, silent inspection and take refuge behind a screen of cigar smoke out on the balcony.

"What's going on?" he asked himself, twisting and turning in every direction, "this is murder! She seems to find me a figure of fun. I don't see her watching anyone else like that. She wouldn't dare! Just because I'm mild and inoffensive she thinks... I'm going to have it out with her," he resolved, "I'm going to tell her straight to her face whatever it is she's trying so hard to pry out from me with her eyes."

Just at that moment she appeared at the entrance to the balcony; he drew up a chair for her and she sat down next to him.

"Is it true that you're very bored?" she asked him.

"Yes," he replied, "although I wouldn't say 'very'. I do have some things to do."

"Andrei Ivanich says that you're working on some plan?"

"Yes, I want to go and live on my estate in the country so I have to make some preparations."

"And will you be going abroad?"

"Yes, certainly, as soon as Andrei Ivanich is ready."

"Do you really want to go?"

"Yes, very much so!"

He looked at her face and saw a smile begin to spread over her face, lighting up her eyes and creeping down her cheeks; only her lips were compressed as always. He did not have the heart to keep up the pretence.

"The truth is I'm a bit lazy," he said, "but..."

He could not help feeling annoyed that practically without saying a word she had managed to worm the confession of laziness out of him.

"What is she doing to me? Am I afraid of her or something?" he wondered.

"Lazy," she protested with evident insincerity, "impossible! A man who is lazy—I just don't understand."

"What is there not to understand?" he thought to himself, "what's the problem?"

"It's just that I'm staying at home more and more and that's why Andrei thinks that I..."

"But you're probably doing a lot of writing," she said, "and reading. Have you read—?"

She was studying him so carefully.

"No, no, I haven't!" he blurted out suddenly, afraid that she was about to test him.

"What is it you haven't read?" she asked, laughing, and Oblomov started laughing too.

"I thought you were going to ask me about some novel and I don't read novels."

"Well, you thought wrong. I was going to ask you about traveling."

He gave her a searching look; a smile covered her whole face except her lips.

"Oh yes, with her you really have to be careful," he thought.

"What *do* you read then?" she inquired curiously.

"Well, actually I do prefer travel books as it happens."

"African travel?" she asked quietly and mischievously.

He blushed, guessing, with good reason that she knew all about what he read—as well as his reading habits.

"Are you a musician?" she asked to ease his embarrassment.

At that moment Stoltz joined them.

"Ilya, yes I told Olga Sergeyevna how much you love music; I asked her to sing something... 'Casta diva'."

"Why do you make up these stories about me?" Oblomov replied, "I'm not that great an enthusiast."

"What's that, you're acting as if it's an insult. Here I am vouching for his respectability and he's telling you not to believe it!"

"No, it's just that I can't accept the title of 'music lover'. It's bogus and in any case I couldn't live up to it!"

"Well, what's your favorite kind of music?" Olga asked.

"That's a hard question to answer; all kinds really. Sometimes I'm entranced by the raucous sound of a barrel organ, if it reminds me of a familiar tune, but there are times when I leave the opera halfway through. Meyerbeer stirs my feelings—even a bargeman's song—it depends on my mood. Sometimes even Mozart makes me want to plug my ears."

"That shows you really love music."

"Sing something for us, Olga Sergeyevna!" Stoltz urged her.

"But what if Monsieur Oblomov is in the mood to plug his ears?" she said, turning to Oblomov.

"I suppose this is where I should pay you some compliment; well, I'm no good at compliments and even if I were I couldn't bring myself to do it..."

"Why is that?"

"Because what if you're no good?" Oblomov pointed out in all innocence, "I'd feel embarrassed afterwards."

"Like yesterday with the biscuits..." she blurted out—now it was her turn to blush and she would have given anything to be able to take back her remark. "I'm sorry, please forgive me!" she said.

For Oblomov this was totally unexpected and he was taken aback.

"That was really nasty and treacherous," he said under his breath.

"No, maybe just a little bit of revenge—and really unintentional at that—because you couldn't even come up with a compliment for me."

"Maybe I'll find one after I've heard you."

"But do you want to hear me sing?"

"No, he's the one who does," replied Oblomov, pointing to Stoltz.

"But what about you?"

Oblomov shook his head. "How can I possibly know before I've heard you?"

"You're a boor, Ilya!" said Stoltz. "That's what comes of lying around at home and wearing stockings that..."

"Look here, Andrei," said Oblomov, intervening forcefully before he could finish, "it would be no trouble at all to say something like: 'Oh, I would be delighted, so happy, you are such a talented singer'." Then, turning to Olga, he continued, "It would give me such pleasure etc. Is that what you really want?"

"No, but you could at least ask me to sing, if only out of curiosity."

"I couldn't," Oblomov replied, "you're not an actress..."

"Well, I'll sing for *you*," she said to Stoltz.

"Get your compliment ready, Ilya!"

Dusk was falling. A lamp was lit and shone through the ivy-covered trellis like the moon. The twilight softened the contours of Olga's face and figure and draped her in a gauzy veil. Her face was in shadow; only her voice could be heard, soft, but powerful and tremulous with feeling.

She sang many arias and romances of Stoltz's choice. Some expressed anguish with vague premonitions of happiness to come, others were joyful but tinged with sadness. The words, the notes, that pure, strong young girl's voice made the heart beat faster, plucked the heartstrings and made the eyes sparkle and brim with tears. At one and the same moment you felt like dying, to be lulled forever by the sound of the music and yet your heart thirsted for life. Oblomov was on fire, he swooned, barely able to hold back his tears and struggling fiercely to stifle his impulse to cry out for sheer joy. It had been so long since he had experienced such a lifting of the spirit, such a surge of strength which seemed to be welling up from somewhere deep within himself—he felt ready to take on the world!

At that moment, he would have gone abroad there and then if the carriage had been waiting and all he had had to do was to jump in.

To finish she sang "Casta diva." Oblomov was transported with delight, thoughts flashed like lightning through his head and his whole body tingled as if pricked by a thousand needles. He was overcome and exhausted by his emotions.

"Are you pleased with me today?" Olga asked Stoltz abruptly as soon as she had finished.

"Why don't you ask Oblomov what he thinks?" said Stoltz.

"I..." Oblomov was speechless. Impulsively he reached for Olga's hand but stopped himself and was left deeply embarrassed.

"Sorry!" he mumbled.

"You hear?" Stoltz said to her. "Tell me the truth, Ilya, how long has it been since anything like this happened to you?"

"It could have been this morning if a barrel organ had happened to be passing outside the window," Olga put in before Oblomov had a chance to reply. But she said it in such a benign and good-humored way that it took the sting out of the sarcasm.

He looked at her reproachfully.

"His winter windows haven't been removed yet, so he can't hear anything going on outside," Stoltz added.

Oblomov turned his reproachful look on Stoltz. Stoltz took Olga's hand. "I don't know what to put it down to, Olga Sergeyevna, but today you sang more beautifully than ever before; at least I can't remember when I've heard you in better voice. That's my compliment," he said, kissing every one of her fingers.

Stoltz had to leave. Oblomov also got up to go, but Stoltz and Olga stopped him.

"I have business to attend to," said Stoltz, "but you're only going to lie down—it's still early."

"Andrei, Andrei!" Oblomov implored him. "No, I can't stay today, I must go," said Stoltz and he left.

That night Oblomov could not sleep; he paced the room despondently, plunged in thought. At dawn he went out and walked along the Neva and through the streets, his thoughts and feelings in turmoil.

Three days later he returned and in the evening after the other guests had sat down at the card tables he found himself by the piano, alone with Olga. Her aunt was nursing a headache in the study and sniffing smelling salts.

"Would you like to see the drawings that Andrei Ivanich brought me from Odessa," Olga asked him, "if he hasn't already shown them to you?"

"I think you're just trying to be good hostess, aren't you?" Oblomov asked. "You needn't bother."

"What do you mean, 'don't bother'? I'm just trying to see that you're entertained, to make you feel at home, so that you feel at ease, relaxed and comfortable and so that you don't feel like going home and lying down."

"What a mischievous, sarcastic creature she is!" thought Oblomov, admiring her every movement in spite of himself. "Do you really want me to be entertained, to feel at ease, relaxed and comfortable?" he said, repeating her words.

"Yes," she said, giving him the same look as the day before, except that both the curiosity and the sympathy were now more intense.

"In that case, stop looking at me the way you are now—the same way you did the other day!"

Her look now expressed twice as much curiosity.

"That's exactly the look that makes me so uncomfortable—where's my hat?"

"But why more uncomfortable?" she asked softly, and the curiosity disappeared from her eyes, leaving just an expression of tenderness and sympathy.

"I don't know, it's just that that look of yours seems to be trying to siphon out of me all the things that I don't want other people to know—especially you."

"But why? You're Andrei Ivanich's friend and he's my friend so..."

"So, there's no reason for you to know everything that Andrei

Ivanich knows about me," he cut in, completing her sentence for her.

"There's no reason, but it's still possible…"

"Thanks to the willingness of my friend to share our confidences—not very nice of him!"

"You mean you have secrets?" she asked. "Maybe you've committed crimes?" she added, moving away from him.

"Perhaps," he sighed in response.

"Yes, that's a pretty serious crime," she said softly and timidly, "putting on odd stockings."

Oblomov picked up his hat. "I can't take it!" he said, "and you say that you want me to feel at ease! I'm finished with Andrei—he even told you that!"

"He had me in stitches today with that story," said Olga, "he's always so funny. I'm sorry; I'll stop, I promise, I'll try not to look at you like that any more." She put on a mock serious expression. "And that's just for a start," she went on, "look, I'm not giving you yesterday's look any more, so now you must be feeling at ease and relaxed. And now secondly, what can we do to entertain you?"

He looked straight into her tender blue-gray eyes.

"Now it's you giving me a strange kind of look!" she said.

He was indeed gazing at her, not so much with his eyes, but training his thoughts, his whole being upon her, as if attempting to mesmerize her, something he was powerless to stop in spite of himself.

"My God, how pretty she is! I didn't know such beings existed!" he thought, regarding her with something verging on fear in his eyes. "That dazzling whiteness, those eyes like deep wells where something is gleaming in the dark—it must be her soul! You can read her smile like a book, and behind the smile what teeth, what a head, balanced so delicately on her shoulders, bobbing like a flower exuding fragrance…! Yes, I am siphoning something out of her," he thought, "something is flowing from her to me; my heart is beginning to palpitate, to churn… right here I feel something new that wasn't there before… my God, what happiness just to look at her! I can hardly breathe…!"

His mind was in a whirl; he kept on looking and looking at her as if into an infinite distance, a bottomless chasm, in a state of blissful oblivion.

"Please, Monsieur Oblomov, you really must stop looking at me the way you are right now!" she said, shyly attempting to turn her head away, but her curiosity got the better of her and she could not take her eyes off his face.

Oblomov heard nothing. His gaze was riveted on her and he was deaf to her words. He was concentrating silently on what was happening within himself and found that his head too was awhirl and spinning out of control—his thoughts were whizzing around like a flock of birds, too quickly for him to catch, and there was a kind of pain in the left side of his chest.

"Stop looking at me in that strange way—it's making me uneasy too! I think you too are trying to draw something out of the very depths of my being."

"And what could that be?" he asked without thinking.

"I have 'plans' of my own too that I have started and never completed," she replied.

This allusion to his own uncompleted plan brought him back to his senses.

"It's funny," he observed, "you're so malicious and yet you have such a benevolent look in your eyes. No wonder they say that you should never trust a woman; she will lie to you deliberately with her tongue, and even unintentionally with her eyes, her smile and with the blush on her cheek—and even by fainting."

To avoid reinforcing this impression, she quietly took his hat from him and sat down on a chair.

"I won't do it again, I won't," she repeated earnestly, "I'm sorry, that awful tongue of mine! I wasn't trying to make fun of you, really!" She almost sang the words and her voice was tremulous with feeling.

Oblomov calmed down. "That Andrei!" he said reproachfully.

"Now, about the second item, what can we do to entertain you?" she asked.

"Sing something!" he said.

"Now there's the compliment I've been waiting for!" she exclaimed with delight. "You know," she went on animatedly, "if you hadn't reacted with that 'Ah!' the other day after I sang, I don't think I would have been able to sleep that night; I would probably have spent the whole night sobbing into my pillow."

"But why?" Oblomov was surprised.

She thought for a moment and then said, "I really don't know myself."

"It's because of your pride."

"Yes, that's it, of course," she said thoughtfully as she ran one hand over the piano keys, "there's a lot of it around, you find it everywhere. Andrei Ivanich says that it's practically the only thing that motivates us. Of course, you probably don't have any pride and that's why you always…"

Oblomov did not let her finish. "Always what?" he asked.

"No, never mind," she said and let the matter drop.

"I like Andrei Ivanich," she continued, "not just because he makes me laugh—sometimes when he is talking I end up crying—and not just because he likes me, but I think because he likes me better than others—so you see where my pride has tucked itself away."

"You like Andrei?" he asked, giving her a direct, intense, searching look.

"Yes, of course, if he likes me more than others, I like him all the more for that," she replied gravely.

Oblomov regarded her in silence and she responded with a straightforward, silent look.

"He likes Anna Vassilievna too and Zinaida Mikhailovna, but it's not the same," she continued. "He won't sit with them for two hours or make them laugh or tell them what's really on his mind. He just talks to them about business, the theatre or the latest news, but he talks to me like a brother—no, more like a father," she added quickly. "Sometimes he is even hard on me when I'm slow to grasp something or contradict him. But he never rebukes the others, and I do believe I like him all the more for that. Pride," she added pensively, "well I don't see how that's connected with my singing. I've always had a lot of praise for my singing, but you didn't even want to hear me sing, you practically had to be forced. And if you had left afterwards without a word, or if I hadn't noticed something in your expression, I really think my health would have suffered. Yes, it really is a matter of pride," she concluded firmly.

"And did you really notice something in my expression?" he asked.

"I noticed tears, although you were trying to hide them; that's always a bad sign in a man, it means he's ashamed of his feelings. That's a kind of pride too, but false pride. Men might be better off being ashamed of their thoughts; their thoughts betray them more often. Even Andrei Ivanich is ashamed of his feelings. I've told him so and he agrees with me. How about you?"

"Looking at you, it's impossible to disagree with anything you say," he said.

"Another compliment, but such a..." She had trouble finding the right word.

"Cheap one?" Oblomov suggested without taking his eyes off her.

Her smile indicated that he had found the right word.

"That's exactly what I was afraid of when I didn't want to ask you to sing. What can you say when you hear someone sing for the first time? Yet you have to say something. It's hard to come up with something that sounds intelligent and sincere at the same time, especially when you're in the grip of such powerful emotions as I was then."

"Yes, and I was singing in a way I've rarely ever sung before—if ever! But don't ask me to sing, I'll never sing like that again—but wait, there is one thing I want to sing," she said, and at that very moment her whole face glowed, her eyes sparkled and she sat down at the piano, struck two or three resounding chords and started singing. Her singing was so expressive; it encompassed the whole range of human emotion, hope, fear, menace, bursts of happiness, but it was not so much the song as the voice itself.

She sang for a long time, looking around at him occasionally like a child seeking his approval and as if to say, "wait till you hear this!" and then singing some more. Her ears and cheeks reddened with excitement. From time to time her face would light up with flashes of emotion and would radiate a mature passion as if in her heart she was feeling something from far in the future. Then just as suddenly that momentary radiance would ebb, leaving her voice as fresh and silvery as ever.

Oblomov was transported into this other life, this kaleidoscope of emotions, and felt as if he had lived a whole lifetime in those few moments. Although they were outwardly still, the same fire was raging in their breasts and they both trembled with the same excitement; their eyes brimmed with tears provoked by the same emotions. These were all symptoms of those passions which would one day surge in her young heart but which were now fleetingly aroused by the sparks escaping from the smouldering embers of life which would one day burst into flame.

She ended with a sustained ringing chord and her voice died away with it. She withdrew her hands abruptly from the keys and placed them on her knees. Her own feelings had been deeply stirred and she looked at Oblomov to see the effect on him. His face radiated the first glimmerings of a happiness that had been awakened and summoned up from the very depths of his being. His eyes, brimming with tears, were riveted on her. This time it was she who reached impulsively for his hand.

"What's the matter?" she asked, "you have such a strange expression on your face, what is it?"

She knew very well what it was and was inwardly quietly exultant at this evidence of her powers.

"Look in the mirror!" she said and with a smile showed him his own reflection in it. "Your eyes are shining. Good God, you even have tears in them! How profoundly you are affected by music!"

"No, it's not the music which is affecting me, it's love," Oblomov responded quietly.

She instantly let go of his hand and her whole expression changed. Her eyes met his insistent gaze, an unwavering, almost a demented gaze. They were not Oblomov's eyes, but the eyes of passion itself. Olga understood that the word had simply escaped him and he had been powerless to prevent it, and she knew it was the truth.

He came to his senses, picked up his hat and ran out of the room without looking back. She watched him go with an expression of curiosity on her face and stood motionless for a long time by the piano like a statue, her head rigidly bowed; the only movement was the heaving of her breast.

CHAPTER SIX

To Oblomov, as he had lazed around in his various recumbent postures or drifted into one of his stupors or even during his bursts of inspiration, the image of a woman that came to his mind first and foremost was that of a wife and only occasionally that of a lover.

The image that came to him in his dreams was that of a tall, slim woman with her arms gently folded across her breast, with a placid but proud look, sitting casually amidst the ivy in the shrubbery, treading lightly on a carpet, or strolling along a sandy path, swaying at the waist, her head rising gracefully from her shoulders and a pensive look on her face. This to him represented an ideal, the embodiment of the whole of life, a life of bliss, of consummate peacefulness, the very quintessence of peacefulness.

At the start of his dreams she would appear to him covered in flowers, standing at the altar in a long veil, then standing at the head of the conjugal bed with her eyes modestly lowered, and finally as a mother with her children gathered around her. He saw her with a smile on her lips, but not a smile that suggested passion, and with eyes not moist with desire, but rather with a smile of warmth towards himself, her husband, and of benevolence to all others, eyes that melted only for him but were cast modestly, even severely, on others.

The image he cherished was always free from agitation, from passionate yearnings, tearful outbursts, ineffable pinings and torments alternating with bursts of manic joyfulness—not for him delirious heights or depths of distress. She must not be one who suddenly pales, falls into a faint or is given to passionate outbursts... "Those are the kind of women who take lovers," he would say, "and provoke endless agitation, doctors, spas, a never ending series of whims and caprices—never a peaceful night's sleep!"

But beside the proud but modest, serene companion of his imagination a man could sleep untroubled. He would fall asleep secure in the knowledge that when he woke up he would be greeted by that same shy but warm look, and that for twenty or thirty years, until the grave itself, his own warm look would be met by her eyes radiating that very same glow of quiet, gentle tenderness.

"Isn't this everyone's secret wish—man or woman—to find in their mate this unfailing face of peacefulness, this constant even flow of feeling? Isn't this what love is all about, isn't this the paradigm? And doesn't the slightest deviation, change or falling short inevitably mean suffering? This ideal of mine must then be universal," he thought. "And surely this must be the best that human ingenuity can achieve in the realm of relations between the sexes? To give passion a lawful outlet, to give desire, like a river, a channel in which to flow, to the benefit of the whole surrounding area. This is a universal goal, the pinnacle of progress to which all those Georges Sands are constantly striving, for all that they may fall by the wayside. Once this goal is reached there will be no more betrayals, no cooling off, but just the steady beating of a heart content and at peace with itself, with life flowing in a full and steady stream, the sap of life steadily rising and moral health secure and stable.

"Examples of this blessed state do exist, but they are far and few between and are viewed as striking exceptions. People say that this is something you have to be born to, but isn't it possible that it could be taught so that we could learn to strive for it consciously? Passion! It's all very well in poetry and drama where actors stride about the stage with cloak and dagger and afterwards the murderers and their victims go out to supper together.... It would be nice if real life passions could be resolved in the same way, but the fact is that all that is left afterwards is the smoke, the stench and not a trace of happiness and, by way of memories, nothing but guilt and the tearing of hair. And if you should have the misfortune to be seized by passion, it is as if you were caught on a rocky, crumbling road where even horses cannot keep their feet and the horseman is on the brink of exhaustion; but his home is in sight and he must keep his eyes fastened on it and get clear of that dangerous terrain as soon as possible. Yes, passion must be contained, suppressed and domesticated in marriage..."

He would have fled in terror from a woman who suddenly scorched him with her eyes or collapsed on his shoulder with a groan and her eyes closed, and when she came to, wrapped her arms around his neck so tightly that he could not breathe. "But after all the fireworks and the exploding powder keg, what then? You are left blinded, deafened, and with your hair singed!"

But let us see what kind of woman Olga is.

For a long time after his involuntary declaration they were never alone together. He would hide like a schoolboy the moment he caught a glimpse of Olga. She now behaved differently with him. It was not that she avoided him or treated him coldly; it was just that she had become more contained. She regretted that because of what had happened she could no longer tease Oblomov by staring at him with curiosity or make good-natured fun of his fondness for lying down, his idleness and his awkwardness. Her sense of humor was at work, but it was the sense of humor of a mother who cannot suppress a smile when she sees how ridiculously her son is dressed. Stoltz had gone away and she was bored without anyone to sing to, and the piano lid was closed. In short, they both felt constrained, hobbled and ill at ease.

But how well everything had gone up to that point! How easily they had become acquainted and how freely they had communicated. Oblomov was not as complicated as Stoltz and was more good-natured, although he did not amuse her as much—or rather he himself was the source of her amusement and took her teasing in good part. In any case, before leaving, Stoltz had entrusted Oblomov to her care and had asked her to keep an eye on him and see that he did not just lie around at home.

In her clever, pretty little head she had already conceived a detailed plan for getting Oblomov out of the habit of sleeping after dinner, and not only that, but even for preventing him from lying down at all during the day; she even planned to extract a pledge from him!

She saw herself making him read the books left for him by Stoltz, and also read the papers every day and recount the news to her. She would make him write letters to the people on the estate, finish drafting the plan for reorganizing it and make preparations for going abroad. In a nutshell, there would be no drowsing under her supervision; she would set goals and renew his enthusiasm for all those things he had turned his back on so that when Stoltz returned he would no longer recognize the old Oblomov. And it would be she who would work this miracle, the shy, silent Olga whom no one had ever listened to before and who had barely experienced life herself—yes, she would bring about this transformation!

The process was already under way; all she had done was to sing and Oblomov was already a changed man. He would embrace life, he would act and he would bless life—and her. To restore a person's life—a doctor who saves the life of a mortally sick patient becomes a hero—so imagine what it would be to rescue a drowning mind and soul!

She quivered with pride and joy at the thought; it was as if she had been divinely appointed to this task. In her imagination she has already made him her secretary and librarian. And all this was to end so suddenly! She did not know what to do and this was why she was so silent whenever she met Oblomov.

Oblomov was tormented by the thought that he must have frightened her or offended her and apprehensively braced himself for her angry glances and icy hostility and kept out of her way whenever he saw her.

Meanwhile he had already moved to the dacha and spent three days wandering by himself over bumpy ground, through the marshland and into the woods. Or else he would go into the village and sit idly by some peasant's gate, watching the little children and the calves gambolling or the ducks splashing around in the pond. Near the dacha was a lake and a vast park but he was afraid to go there in case he should run into Olga by herself.

"What on earth possessed me to blurt it out like that?" he thought. It never even occurred to him to wonder whether what he had blurted out was the truth or whether it was the momentary effect of the music on his feelings. The feeling of embarrassment, shame or "disgrace" as he thought of it, which his outburst had induced, prevented him from analysing its significance or indeed the whole question of what Olga meant to him, and he was certainly not examining that extra something that was lodged in his heart, a kind of lump that had not been there before. Also his feelings had fused into a single clump—shame. When she *did* appear fleetingly in his imagination her image was the embodiment of the ideal of untroubled happiness. Everything about Olga matched this ideal to perfection and the two images merged into a single whole.

"What have I done?" he said to himself, "I've ruined everything. Thank God Stoltz left before she could tell him, otherwise I would be praying for the earth to open up and swallow me! Love, tears, is that really me? And no word from her aunt, no invitation—she must have told her; oh my God!"

Absorbed in these thoughts, he strayed further into the park and found himself on a path flanking it.

Olga was exercised by only one thought—what would she do when she met him and what would happen. Would she act as if nothing had happened and say nothing about it, or should she make some reference to it—and if so, what? Put on a stern expression and a haughty look, or not look at him at all, or remark drily and superciliously that she would never have dreamed that he was capable of such behavior and what did he take her for, and how dared he permit himself such a liberty? This was the line that Sonia had taken with a young subaltern at a ball during a mazurka even though she had been doing her level best to turn his head.

"But how could it be called 'taking a liberty'," she asked herself, "after all, if that's what he really felt what's wrong with saying so? Yet how was it possible, they hardly knew one another? No one else would have dreamed of saying such a thing after seeing a woman for only the second or third time; but then again, of course, no one but Oblomov would have been capable of falling in love so quickly…"

But she remembered that she had heard or read that love can strike from one moment to the next. "He couldn't stop himself, the impulse was overpowering and now he's too ashamed to show his face so it's obviously not a question of taking liberties. But then who is to blame?" she asked herself, "why Andrei Ivanich, of course, he was the one who had made her sing. In fact it was Oblomov who didn't want her to at first and it was she herself who had persisted out of pique," she blushed deeply at the memory, "yes, she had gone out of her way to stir up his feelings."

Stoltz had said that he was apathetic, that nothing interested him, that he was dead inside and she couldn't resist the challenge of proving that there was a spark of life there, so she sang—more powerfully than ever before.

"Dear God! It's all my fault, I have to apologize to him—but how?" she asked herself. "What can I say to him? 'Monsieur Oblomov, I'm very sorry for leading you on…' It's too embarrassing! Anyway, it's not true!" she exclaimed indignantly, stamping her foot. "The very idea! How could I know what it would lead to… but what if it hadn't happened and he hadn't burst out like that, what then? I just don't know," she thought.

From that day on a troubled feeling persisted; probably she was deeply offended. She even suffered hot flushes and her cheeks would burn and redden.

"It's just nerves, a slight fever," said the doctor.

"Look what that Oblomov has done! I'll teach him never to do anything like that again! I'll ask *ma tante* to stop inviting him to call. He must remember his manners....how dare he!" she thought as she walked in the park, her eyes blazing...

Suddenly she heard someone coming.

"Someone's coming!" thought Oblomov; and there they were, face to face.

"Olga Sergeyevna!" he said, trembling like a leaf.

"Ilya Ilyich!" she replied timidly. And they both stopped

"How are you?" he said

"How are you?" she said

"Where are you going?" he asked

"Oh, just..." she said, keeping her eyes lowered.

"Don't let me stop you."

"Oh, not at all!" she replied, glancing at him quickly with curiosity.

"May I join you?" he asked suddenly, giving her a searching look.

They walked along the path in silence. Never in his whole life had his heart beaten so violently as then, not even when his teacher had raised his ruler or his director his eyebrows. He wanted to say something and tried to force himself, but the words just wouldn't come and his heart just continued pounding wildly as if anticipating imminent disaster.

"Have you heard from Andrei Ivanich?" she asked.

"Yes, I got a letter." Oblomov replied.

"What does he say?"

"He wants me to join him in Paris."

"Will you go?"

"Yes."

"When?"

"Soon....well, tomorrow... .as soon as I can get ready."

"Why so soon?" she asked.

Oblomov remained silent.

"The dacha doesn't suit you....or....why is it you want to leave?"

"Now that *is* rudeness—now he wants to leave on top of everything!" she thought.

"I don't know what it is exactly, but something is bothering me, making me feel bad. I feel terribly uncomfortable," Oblomov whispered without looking at her.

She silently broke off a sprig of lilac, burying her nose and face in it to sniff.

"Smell this, it smells so good!" she said and put it to his nose.

"Here are some lilies of the valley—just a moment while I pick some," he said, bending down to the grass, "these smell better, they have the scent of nature about them—the fields and the woods. Lilac grows too near houses, the branches even come in through the windows; it has that sickly cloying smell. Look, these lillies of the valley still have dew-drops on them." He picked some for her.

"Do you like mignonettes?" she asked.

"No, the smell is too strong; I don't like them, or roses either. In fact, I don't really like flowers at all—they're alright when they're growing in the soil, but flowers in a room, no, too much trouble, too much mess!"

"Ah, so you like a room to be clean and tidy?" she asked, eyeing him slyly, "you can't stand a mess?"

"Yes, but you see, my servant is so…" he muttered, adding, "she's really wicked!" under his breath.

"Are you going straight to Paris?" she asked.

"Yes, Stoltz has been waiting for me for a long time now."

"Can you take him a letter from me if I write one?"

"Yes, but give it to me today because I'm moving back to town tomorrow."

"Tomorrow? Why such a hurry? It's as if you were running away from someone."

"Well, I am, as a matter of fact…"

"Who is it?"

"Shame…" he whispered.

"Shame!" she whispered mechanically. "This is where I tell him, 'Monsieur Oblomov, I hardly expected…'"

"Yes, Olga Sergeyevna"—he had regained control of himself—"you must be surprised, you're probably angry…"

"Now is the time… .this is exactly the right moment," her heart was also pounding furiously, "no, I just can't—oh, God!"

He tried to read her expression so as to understand what she was thinking, but her face was hidden in the lilies of the valley and the lilac as she smelled them, and she did not even know herself what to say or do.

"Oh, Sonia would come up with something, but I'm such a fool, I just can't….it's horrible!" she thought.

"I had completely forgotten…" she said.

"It wasn't intentional, you must believe me, I just couldn't help myself," he began, his confidence growing as he spoke, "even if a thunderstorm had started up at that moment and a stone had fallen on my head, I would still have said what I said—nothing in the world could have stopped me. For God's sake don't think that I meant to say it….the very next moment I myself would have given anything to be able to take back that reckless remark."

She continued walking, sniffing the flowers with her head lowered.

"Just forget that I said it; forget it, especially since it wasn't true..."

"Not true?" she echoed, suddenly straightening up and dropping the flowers. Her eyes opened wide with amazement. "What do you mean 'not true'?" she repeated.

"Now, please don't get angry and just forget it! I assure you I was just carried away for a moment... .by the music."

"Just the music?"

Her face suddenly turned pale, the color drained from her cheeks and her eyes dimmed.

"Oh, so it's nothing! He just takes back what he shouldn't have said and there's nothing to be upset about! That's wonderful—now everything is alright. Now we can just go back to polite conversation and banter..." she thought to herself and wrenched off a branch from a tree as she passed, tore a leaf from it with her mouth and hurled both the branch and the leaf to the ground.

"You're not angry? You've forgotten it?" said Oblomov, leaning towards her.

"But what is it, what are you talking about?" she responded heatedly, almost with exasperation, turning away from him. "I've forgotten the whole thing, I have such a bad memory!"

Oblomov was silent; he did not know what to do. He could see that she was annoyed but could not understand why.

"My God!" she thought, "now everything's back to normal; it's as if the whole thing had never happened, thank God! But why do I feel like this? Oh, Sonya, Sonya, how lucky you are!"

"I'm going home!" she said abruptly, walking faster and turning onto another path. She was choking back tears, she was afraid that she was going to cry.

"Not that way, it's quicker this way!" said Oblomov. "What a fool I am!" he said to himself in despair, "why did I have to go and explain? Now she's really upset—I shouldn't have brought it up and the whole thing would have been over and done with. Now all I can do is beg to be forgiven."

"If I'm feeling so upset it must be because I didn't get around to telling him: 'Monsieur Oblomov, I never dreamt that you would have permitted yourself...' but he preempted me... But it wasn't true! The nerve of him! So he was even lying then! How could he!"

"Have you really forgotten?" he asked quietly.

"Yes, I've forgotten the whole thing," she said quickly, hurrying to get home."

"Give me your hand then to show me you're not angry!"

Without looking at him, she extended just enough of her hand for him to brush her fingertips and immediately withdrew it.

"No, you are angry!" he said with a sigh. "How can I convince you that I just got carried away, otherwise I would never have dreamed of permitting myself such a liberty? And, of course, I will not listen to you sing again."

"You might as well save your breath, you'll never convince me because I've no intention of singing anyway!" she said with some vehemence.

"Very well, I won't say another thing," he said, "but please don't just walk away like that, you'll be leaving me with such a weight on my mind…"

She slowed down and started to listen to him intently.

"If it's true that you would have burst into tears if your singing hadn't made me gasp with delight, then if you just leave me like this without a smile, without a friendly touch of your hand, I'll…have pity on me, Olga Sergeyevna; I swear I'll get sick, look my knees are trembling, I can hardly stand up!"

"Why?" she asked suddenly, turning to face him.

"I don't know myself," he said, "I don't feel embarrassed any more, I'm not ashamed of what I said, but I think it was…"

Once again shivers ran up his spine and there were butterflies in his stomach; again there was this strange feeling in his heart and again her look, curious and tender, started to inflame him. She had turned to him so gracefully and waited for his response so anxiously.

"It was what?" she asked impatiently.

"No, I'm afraid to tell you, it will only upset you again."

"Say it!" she commanded him.

He said nothing.

"Well?"

"I feel like crying again, looking at you like this… .I've no pride, I'm not ashamed of my heart… ."

"But why would you cry?" she asked and her cheeks reddened.

"I can still hear your voice, I can still feel…"

"What?" she asked, the weight of tears lifting from her breast as she waited anxiously.

They had reached the porch of her house.

"I feel…"Oblomov was in a hurry to finish his sentence but stopped.

She mounted the stairs slowly as if it were an effort.

"The same music, the same excitement, the same feel—I'm sorry, I'm sorry; really, my feelings are too much for me!"

"Monsieur Oblomov…" she started to admonish him, but then suddenly her whole face lit up with a smile. "I'm not angry, I forgive you," she added gently, "but in future…"

Without turning around, she extended her hand behind her. He seized it and kissed her palm. She pressed it gently against his lips and vanished in a trice through the doorway, leaving him rooted to the spot.

CHAPTER SEVEN

With his eyes open wide and his mouth agape he continued to watch the spot where she had stood, long after she had disappeared, and he gazed blindly at the shrubbery.... People passed and a bird flew by. A woman passing asked him if he wanted berries, but he remained in a trance. He retraced his steps along the path and had slowly covered half the distance when he stumbled on the lilies of the valley that Olga had dropped and the sprig of lilac which she had broken off and thrown down in her annoyance.

"Why did she do that?" he started wondering, and recalled the scene. "What a fool I am," he exclaimed suddenly as he picked up the flowers and the lilac and practically sprinted down the path. "I apologized and she....No. it can't be! What an idea!"

Happy, beaming, "with the moon on his brow" as his nanny used to say, he arrived home, sat down on a corner of the divan and quickly wrote the word "Olga" in big letters in the dust on the table top.

"God, how dusty it is!" he remarked once he had simmered down. He kept on calling: "Zakhar! Zakhar!" But Zakhar couldn't hear him; he was sitting with the coachmen at the gate that faced the lane.

"You'd better come!" Anisya hissed at him urgently, plucking his sleeve, "the master has been calling you for ages!"

"Look, Zakhar, what is all this?" said Oblomov, but mildly and indulgently. He was in no mood for anger right then. "Are you trying to make the same kind of mess here too? Dust, cobwebs? No, I'm sorry, I won't have it! Olga Sergeyevna is giving me a hard enough time as it is. 'You like a mess,' she tells me."

"Yes, it's alright for them to talk, they've got five servants!" said Zakhar, turning towards the door.

"Where do you think you're going? Get a broom and start sweeping—there's nowhere to sit—or even lean; why it's sheer squalor, it's... *oblomovshchina!*"

Zakhar was offended and gave his master one of his sideways looks.

"There he goes again!" he thought to himself. "Now he's come up with another one of his 'heart-rending' words, only this time I recognize it."

"Well, don't just stand around, start sweeping!"

"Sweep what? I've already swept today." Zakhar answered stubbornly.

"Where's all this dust from then if you've already swept? Look at that, I want it removed, so get sweeping."

"I've swept it," Zakhar asserted, "you can't sweep ten times a day! The dust comes in from outside, this is a dacha, there are fields around, there's a lot of dust on the road."

"But, Zakhar Trofimovich, why do you sweep the floor first," Anisya said, looking in from the next room, "and then brush the dirt from the tables. It just goes on to the floor and stays there. You should first..."

"Who told you to come and give instructions?" Zakhar wheezed furiously, "go back where you belong!"

"Who ever heard of sweeping the floor first and then dusting the tables—no wonder the master is annoyed!"

"You watch it!" he growled, gesturing threateningly with his elbow in the direction of her chest.

She disappeared with a grin. Oblomov dismissed him too with a wave of the hand. He laid his head on an embroidered cushion, placed his hand on his heart and felt it beating.

"This is no good for me," he said to himself, "what am I going to do? If I ask the doctor he'll probably send me to Abyssinia!"

Before Zakhar and Anisya were married they each busied themselves with their own duties and kept them strictly separate so that Anisya was responsible for the shopping and the cooking and helped with the cleaning only once a year when she scrubbed the floors. After their marriage, however, her access to the master's quarters became freer. She would help Zakhar and the rooms became cleaner and tidier, and in effect she took over some of her husband's duties. This was partly of her own free will and partly because Zakhar tyrannically imposed them on her.

"Here, now go and beat the carpet!" he would command her hoarsely, or he would tell her, "why don't you clear out that stuff in the corner there and take everything that doesn't belong there into the kitchen!"

This blissful situation lasted about a month; the rooms were clean, his master made no complaints and uttered none of his "heart-rending" words while he, Zakhar, did absolutely nothing. Finally this blissful period came to an end—for the following reason.

From the very moment that the two of them assumed joint responsibility for looking after the master's quarters Zakhar could no longer do anything right. Every move he made was wrong or bad. He had lived for fifty-five years, secure in the conviction that every little thing he did could not possibly be done better or differently. And now it had taken only two weeks for Anisya to convince him that he was a dead loss, and the indulgent manner in which she conveyed this only rubbed it in. It was that undemonstrative and matter of fact manner in which one does things for children or total idiots and it did not help matters that she would grin whenever she saw him at work.

"Zakhar Trofimovich," she would say affectionately, "why do you close the flue before you open the small window, it just makes the rooms cold again?"

"Oh, and how would you do it?" he snapped at her in the way husbands do, "what's the *right* time to open the window?"

"When you've lit the stove, then the air circulates and it warms up again," she answered gently.

"What a fool you are! For twenty years I've been doing it this way, and now I'm going to change because of you?"

He used to keep tea, sugar, lemons, silver all together on the same shelf in the cupboard along with boot polish, brushes and soap. One day he came in and saw that the soap had been put on the washstand, the brushes and polish on the window ledge in the kitchen and the tea and sugar in a separate drawer of the dresser.

"So it's you who's been messing around with all my things and rearranging everything, uh?" he accused her. "I keep all the things in one place on purpose so that I know where to lay my hands on them, and you've gone and scattered them all over the place!"

"Just to stop the tea smelling of soap," she said meekly.

Another time she pointed out two or three holes made by moths in the master's clothes and told him that the clothes had to be shaken out and brushed once a week without fail. "Here, let me beat them with the birch brush!" she said gently.

He snatched the coat and the brush from her grasp and put them back where they had come from.

Another time when he had launched into his usual litany of complaints against his master for blaming him unfairly for the cockroaches because: "he wasn't the one who invented them," Anisya just quietly went and cleared the shelves of all the scraps of food and the crumbs of black bread that had been accumulating there from time immemorial, and then dusted and scrubbed the cupboards and the crockery so that the cockroaches all but disappeared.

But Zakhar still did not really understand what was happening and dismissed it all as just an excess of zeal on Anisya's part. But once, when he had been carrying a tray loaded with cups and glasses and two of the glasses had fallen off and broken, and he had launched into his usual ranting and raving and was about to hurl the whole tray to the floor, she had taken the tray out of his hands and replaced the broken glasses and even added a sugar bowl and some bread and arranged everything in such a way that not even a single cup moved. She had then shown him how to hold the tray with one hand and support it firmly with the other and carried the tray twice around the room, swivelling it in all directions, without even a spoon so much as quivering—and it was only then that it had dawned on Zakhar that Anisya was smarter than he was.

He had snatched the tray from her and the glasses had dropped off and smashed—something for which he never forgave her.

"Now do you see how to do it," she had commented softly. He gave her a look of stubborn, uncomprehending disdain while she just smiled.

"Who do you think you are, woman, a nobody like you, giving yourself airs, acting as if you know it all! Things were different in the house back in Oblomovka. Everything depended on me; I had at least fifteen servants under me—and that was just counting the men and boys! And as for you lot, the women, there were too many even to remember their names…and here you are… you just…!'"

"I was just trying to help…" she began.

"Just watch it!" he growled hoarsely and raised his elbow threateningly in the direction of her chest. "Get out of here, you've no business in the master's rooms, get back in the kitchen where a woman belongs!"

She left with a smile on her face as he watched her gloomily out of the corner of his eye.

He was suffering from wounded pride and this soured his attitude towards his wife. Whenever Ilya Ilyich happened to need something, or something had to be fetched or had been broken, or indeed when anything at all went wrong and trouble was looming for Zakhar and there was a threat of "heart-rending" words, Zakhar got into the habit of winking at Anisya and nodding and gesturing with his thumb in the direction of his master's study and issuing the curt, whispered command: "get in there and see what he wants!" Anisya would go in and the whole problem would be solved just like that. And even Zakhar himself, at the first sign of "heart-rending" words on the tip of Oblomov's tongue, would immediately suggest calling in Anisya.

So if it had not been for Anisya the Oblomov household would simply have slipped back into its old listless, stagnant torpor. She had already made herself part of the Oblomov household and had unconsciously harnessed herself to the indissoluble bonds which linked her husband to the life, household and person of Ilya Ilyich, and her womanly eye, and busy, efficient hands enlivened those forlorn, neglected premises.

Zakhar had only to turn his back and Anisya would be dusting the furniture, opening the windows, tidying the blinds, picking up the boots which had been dumped in the middle of the room and the trousers which had been draped over the best armchairs and putting them away. She would pick up everything that had been left lying around: clothes, papers, pencils, penknives and pens, and put them back where they belonged. She would shake out the crumpled bedclothes and plump up the pillows—and all in a trice. Then she would take a quick look around the room. Move up a chair here, push a drawer shut there, pick up a napkin from a table and slip quickly into the kitchen when she heard the creak of Zakhar's boots.

She was a lively, vigorous woman of forty-seven with a caring smile and quick eyes that took in everything at a glance, a strong neck, a firm bosom and capable and tireless, red hands. She had no face to speak of; the only thing you noticed was her nose. Not that it was big, it was just that it jutted out from her face at such an awkward angle and was so turned up at the tip that it distracted attention from the face behind it. The face itself, in fact, was so overshadowed that it faded into the background so that you would come away with a vivid, lasting impression of the nose, but without any image of the face it was attached to.

There are many husbands like Zakhar around. A diplomat, for instance, will listen off-handedly to some advice from his wife, shrug his shoulders and the next thing you know he will be using it in his next report. Or a high official will give a whistle and roll his eyes when he hears his wife prattling on about some important business of his, and the very next day will find him solemnly using that very same wifely prattle in his report to the minister.

The attitude of these gentlemen to their wives, whom they would barely deign to address, was just as sour and dismissive, for they regarded them if not, as Zakhar did Anisya, as just another common, working woman, at least as nothing more than decorative appurtenances to distract them from their weighty concerns and the serious business of life.

Meanwhile it was well past noon and the paths in the park were baking in the sun. Everyone had sought the shade and was sitting under awnings. Only groups of nursemaids and children were braving the midday sun and walking or sitting on the grass.

Oblomov still lay on the divan, endlessly interpreting and re-interpreting in his head that morning's conversation with Olga. "She loves me, she feels something for me. Can it be? I'm in her thoughts, it was for me that she sang so passionately and the music stirred the feelings of each of us for the other."

His pride was at work, life had flowered within him, beckoning to him from an enchanted future full of the light and color which had so long been absent from his life. He already saw himself traveling abroad with her to the Swiss lakes, to Italy, exploring the Roman ruins, riding in a gondola, mingling with the crowds in Paris and London…and finally…finally, in his earthly paradise, Oblomovka. She would be there, a goddess, charming everyone with her talk, her exquisite pale, dainty features and her slender graceful neck. The peasants would never have laid eyes on such a vision; they would prostrate themselves before this angel. Stepping lightly on the grass, she would walk with him in the shade of the birches, she would sing to him….

He feels the pulse of life, its gentle flow, its sweet eddies, the lapping of its waters; he is wrapped in thoughts of the consummation of his longings, his cup of happiness is overflowing. Suddenly his face clouded over.

"No, it's not possible!" he exclaimed, getting up and walking around the room. "Love me with my sleep-ridden eyes, my flabby cheeks—she must find me ridiculous!" He stopped in front of the mirror and examined himself at length, disapprovingly at first, but then brightening up and even smiling.

"I seem to look better, fresher than I did in town—my eyes are clearer. A stye was beginning but it just went away. It must be the air here; I'm walking a lot, not drinking any wine, no lying down. So no need to go to Egypt."

A servant came with a message from Marya Mikhailovna, Olga's aunt, inviting him to dinner. "Yes, yes, I'll come!" said Oblomov. The servant turned to go.

"Stop! Here!" Oblomov gave him some money.

He was bright and cheerful. The countryside was bright. People were good-hearted with happy faces and were all enjoying themselves. Zakhar alone was morose, watching his master out of the corner of his eye while Anisya smiled good-naturedly.

"I'll get a dog," Oblomov decided, "or a cat...yes, maybe a cat; cats are affectionate, they purr."

He rushed off to Olga's. On the way he thought: "but really, Olga loving someone like me! And she's so young and fresh! It's precisely now that her imagination must be fired by the most poetic elements of life. She must be dreaming of dashing youths with dark curly hair, tall and slender, full of quietly contained latent energies, with boldness and daring in their faces and wearing proud smiles, with that shimmering, melting gleam in the eye which goes straight to the heart and with a soft, fresh voice that resonates like a piano wire.

"Of course, it's not only the young with dashing good looks, nimble-footed in the mazurka, fearless horsemen who can win hearts; but even supposing that Olga is not just your run-of-the-mill young woman whose head can be turned by the sight of a moustache or the swish of a sabre, there must at least be something else, if only a powerful mind, for example, which can conquer and captivate a woman's heart and command the respect of others... .or a famous artist. But what am I? Oblomov, that's all.

"Now take Stoltz, what a contrast! Stoltz, intelligent, strong, self-controlled, knows how to stand up for himself against other people, even adversity itself. No matter what circumstances or people he confronts he is always master of the situation, like a virtuoso playing his instrument. And me—I can't even manage Zakhar, or myself, come to that! I'm just...Oblomov. Now Stoltz—by God, I do believe she loves him!" He was horrified by the thought. "She said herself: 'as a friend', her very words. But it can't be true; maybe she doesn't even know it herself....A man and a woman can't be 'friends'!"

He slowed down more and more, racked by doubts. "What if she is just flirting with me? If only..." he came to a complete halt, totally benumbed for a moment.

"What if it's all a cunning plot...? Anyway, how did I come away with the idea that she loves me—it wasn't from anything she said. It's just my own vanity whispering to me like the devil. Andrei? No, it can't be; she's so, so...well, like this!" he exclaimed delightedly as he caught sight of Olga coming towards him.

Olga held out her hand to him with a cheerful smile.

"No, that's not her at all, she's incapable of deceit," he decided, "no, women like that could never give you such a tender look or laugh so spontaneously; no, all they can do is twitter. No, but still, she didn't say she loved me!" He was alarmed at the thought; that was only something he himself had read into her words. "But then, why all that annoyance? Oh Lord, what a maelstrom I've fallen into!"

"What do you have there?" she asked

"A sprig."

"A sprig of what?"

"Lilac, as you can see."

"Where did you get it? There's no lilac around here. Where have you been?"

"It's the one you picked and threw away."

"What made you pick it up?"

"Well, I just liked the idea that you flung it down in annoyance."

"So you like it when people are annoyed, that's a new one! Why?"

"I can't tell you."

"Please, I want you to tell me!"

"Nothing could make me tell you!"

"I beg you!"

He shook his head.

"What if I sing something?"

"Well then, perhaps."

"So it's only music that works with you?" she said, frowning, "is that right?"

"Yes, music—performed by you."

"Well then, I'll sing...'Casta diva, casta di...'" she began Norma'a invocation and stopped. "There, now tell me!" she said.

He wrestled with himself for a while. "No, no!" he declared even more firmly than before, "not for the world, never! What if it's not true, what if it just seemed like that to me...? Never, never!"

"What are you talking about, it must be something terrible," she said, eyeing him curiously, while concentrating mentally on his question. Then understanding dawned and spread over her whole face; her every feature lit up with awareness, with a flash of insight, and her whole face positively shone with the realization—in the same way that the sun will sometimes emerge from behind a cloud and gradually illumine first one bush, then another, then a rooftop and finally flood the whole country-side with its light. Now she knew what was in Oblomov's mind.

"No, no, it's no use asking, I just can't bring myself to say it," Oblomov insisted.

"I'm not asking you," she answered with indifference.

"What do you mean? Just now you..."

"Let's go back!" she said in a serious tone, paying no attention to him, *ma tante* is waiting." She walked straight back to the house and, leaving him with her aunt, went immediately to her room.

CHAPTER EIGHT

That whole day was one of increasing frustration for Oblomov. He spent the whole time with Olga's aunt, a woman of considerable intelligence, eminently respectable and always the very picture of elegance, always in a new silk gown that fitted her perfectly, always in the finest lace collars. Her bonnet was always of a tasteful design with the ribbons artfully arranged to set off her fifty-year old, but still fresh, complexion to the best advantage. A gold lorgnette hung from a chain. She held herself with a dignity that was matched by her gestures and wore an elegant shawl skilfully draped around her. Her elbow would be propped on an embroidered cushion with the same studied elegance with which she reclined regally on the divan. You would never see her busying herself with any activity. Stooping, sewing or any such trivial pursuit would have seemed incongruous for one of such dignity of demeanor and bearing. Even her orders to her servants were issued in a crisp, dry and peremptory manner.

She did sometimes read, never wrote, but spoke well, mostly in French. However, she noticed right away that Oblomov was not entirely comfortable in French and switched to Russian after the second day.

Her conversation was free of fantasy and she did not try to be clever. It seemed that she had mentally drawn a firm line over which she never stepped. It was apparent that in her life, feelings, warmth, even love itself were on an equal footing with other matters, whereas with other women you can see right away that love, at least for conversational purposes, if not in practice, is all-pervasive and everything else is secondary and is allowed to occupy only what space is left over by love.

She was a woman who valued above all savoir vivre, poise, and striking the correct balance between the idea and the intention and between the intention and the act. She never allowed herself to be caught unprepared or off her guard, like a vigilant enemy who, no matter when you try to ambush him, always anticipates you and transfixes you with his ever watchful eye. Her natural element was polite society where tact and discretion in thought, word and deed were the paramount values.

She never divulged her private, innermost promptings or shared an intimate secret. You would never see her whispering together with some bosom friend of her own age over a cup of coffee. The only person she was often alone with was Baron von Langwagen. Some evenings he would stay as late as midnight, although almost always Olga would be present and even then they were mostly silent, but in a highly significant and pointed way, for all the world as if they knew something that nobody else did—but nothing more than that.

They obviously enjoyed one another's company—and that was absolutely the only conclusion you could draw when you saw them together. She treated him in exactly the same way that she treated everyone else; with friendliness and benevolence, but with the same serene blandness. Malicious tongues might have seized on this and hinted at some long-ago friendship, some trip abroad together, were it not for the fact that in her relations with him there was no hint or trace of any such suppressed special warmth—which would otherwise surely have manifested itself in some way.

The baron happened to be the trustee of Olga's small estate, which had been mortgaged as collateral and was still encumbered. The baron had gone to court or rather had gotten some clerk to draft the papers, read them with his lorgnette, signed them, and had dispatched them with the same functionary to the court and was using his social connections to arrange for a favorable outcome to the case. He had reason to expect a swift and successful conclusion to the proceedings. This put a stop to the malicious gossip and people got used to seeing the baron frequenting the house like a member of the family.

He was close to fifty but was very well preserved, although he dyed his moustache and had a slight limp in one leg. He was a man of exquisite courtesy, never smoked when ladies were present, never crossed his legs, and severely admonished young men who permitted themselves in company to sprawl in armchairs with their knees and boots raised level with their nose. Even indoors he never removed his gloves, except when sitting down to dinner.

He was always dressed at the height of fashion and sported numerous ribbons on his lapel. He rode everywhere in a carriage and was extremely careful with his horses. Before entering his carriage he would walk around it inspecting the harness and even the horses' hooves and sometimes would even produce a white handkerchief and pass it over a horse's shoulder or along its back to check whether it had been properly groomed.

Acquaintances he would greet with a polite, friendly smile; with strangers he was frosty at first, but after being introduced, his frosty expression would give way to the same smile which the new acquaintance could now be sure of receiving at every subsequent encounter.

He had views on every topic; on virtue, the cost of living, science, on the people who moved in the same circles, and on all these topics his views were clear-cut. He expressed them in lucid and completed sentences as if he were repeating by rote maxims copied from some textbook and were issuing them for the enlightenment of the company.

Olga's relations with her aunt had always been straightforward and harmonious and, although the warmth between them was never exactly excessive, their relations were never marred by the slightest hint of dissatisfaction. This was due partly to the character of the aunt, Marya Mikhailovna, and partly to the absence of the slightest reason for either of them to behave in any other way. It simply never entered her aunt's head to ask Olga to do anything that seriously conflicted with her wishes; just as Olga would never have dreamed of acting contrary to her aunt's wishes or failing to heed her advice.

And what kind of wishes are we talking about? The choice of clothes or hairstyle, or, say, whether to go to the French theatre or the opera.

Olga complied with her aunt's wishes and advice only to the extent that they were actually voiced. When they *were* voiced it was always in a low key and unemphatic manner and she never asserted any rights or authority beyond that to which her status as an aunt entitled her. Their relationship was so matter of fact that it was impossible to tell whether there was anything in her aunt's character that laid claim to Olga's obedience or any particular affection, or whether there was anything in Olga's character that disposed her to obedience to her aunt or any special affection for her. Still, the first time you saw them together you could tell right away that they were not mother and daughter but rather aunt and niece.

"I'm going to do some shopping, is there anything you need?" her aunt would ask.

"Yes, *ma tante*, I need a new dress to replace the lilac one," Olga would reply and they would go together. Or she would say: "No, *ma tante*, I went not long ago." Her aunt would touch her on the cheeks with two fingers and kiss her forehead and Olga would kiss her aunt's hand. Then her aunt would leave and she would stay.

"So we'll take the same dacha this year?" her aunt would say as if she were still debating the question with herself, so that there was no way of telling whether it was a question or a statement.

"Yes, it's very nice there," Olga would say.

So they would take the dacha.

And if Olga said, "Oh, *ma tante*, haven't you had enough of all those trees and that sand, couldn't we look somewhere else?" her aunt would say, "Yes, we'll look. Would you like to go to the theatre, Olga, my dear, people have been raving about that play?"

"I'd love to!" Olga would reply, but not because she was anxious to please and with no trace of submissiveness.

At times there were even mild disagreements. "*Ma chère*," her aunt would say, "do you really think those green ribbons suit you, why not take the pale yellow?"

"Oh, *ma tante*, I've already worn the pale yellow six times, it's really time for a change."

"Then take the violet."

"How about these then?"

Her aunt would look and slowly shake her head. "Well, it's up to you, *ma chère*, but if I were you I would take the pale yellow or the violet."

"No, *ma tante*, I really prefer these," Olga would say pleasantly and she would take the ones she wanted.

Olga would ask her aunt for advice, not as some authority figure whose word was law, but much in the same spirit as she would consult any other older, more experienced woman. "*Ma tante*, you've read this book—what's it like?" she would ask.

"It's disgusting!" her aunt would say, pushing the book aside, but making no attempt to hide it or doing anything to prevent Olga from reading it. After that Olga would not have dreamed of reading it.

If there was an issue they could not resolve between the two of them it was referred to Baron von Langwagen or Stoltz when he was available, and whether the book was read or not depended on their verdict.

"*Ma chère* Olga," her aunt would say when the occasion arose, "That young man who is always coming up to you at the Zavadskys', well, yesterday someone was telling some stupid story about him," and leave it at that. And then it was up to Olga to decide whether she spoke to him or not.

The appearance of Oblomov in the house raised no questions and no one, including the aunt, the baron or even Stoltz, paid it any particular attention. Stoltz had particularly wanted to bring Oblomov to the house because its atmosphere was rather formal and it was a house where guests, far from being encouraged to take a nap after dinner, did not even feel free to cross their legs, and where one had to be properly dressed and remember the subject of a conversation—a house, in short, where there was no dozing off and no taking it easy, and where the conversation was lively, topical and constant. Stoltz also believed that injecting into Oblomov's slumbrous existence the presence of a nice, clever, lively and somewhat ironic young woman would be like bringing a lamp into a dark and cheerless room where it would shine its light into all the dark corners, raise the temperature a few degrees, and generally liven the room up. This was the only kind of effect he was aiming at by introducing Oblomov to Olga, and if Stoltz himself could not have foreseen what sparks were to fly, Olga and Oblomov certainly could not have done.

Ilya Ilyich had sat stiffly through an uncomfortable couple of hours of polite conversation with the aunt without attempting even once to cross his legs. Twice he even deftly re-positioned the footstool on which his feet were resting.

Enter the baron, smiling politely and giving him a friendly hand-shake, whereupon Oblomov's demeanor became even more prim and proper and all three of them sat there looking immensely pleased with one another.

The aunt looked upon the huddled conversations between Olga and Oblomov and their walks together... or rather it would be truer to say that she didn't look at all. To go walking with some dashing young fellow would have been another matter, but even then she would not have actually said anything, although with her customary tact she would have contrived subtly to change the scenario. She would have accompanied them on their walks once or twice or would have arranged for someone else to do so and the walks would have ended of their own accord. But going for walks with "Monsieur Oblomov," sitting with him in a corner of the salon or on the balcony—that was a matter of no concern. After all he was past thirty and not a person likely to whisper sweet nothings or give her books to read—the idea never even entered anyone's head.

In any case her aunt had heard Stoltz telling Olga the day before he left never to let Oblomov doze off, to prevent him sleeping during the day, to bully him and boss him around, find him all kinds of things to do—in short to take him in hand. He had also asked her not to let Oblomov out of her sight, to invite him frequently to the house, take him on walks and trips and generally to goad him into action if he had not gone abroad by then.

Oblomov's conversation with the aunt seemed interminable to him, but Olga had still not put in an appearance. Once again Oblomov began to turn hot and cold by turns. The reason for the change in Olga had begun to dawn on him—a change that was somehow even harder to bear than the previous one.

His earlier gaffe had just alarmed him and made him feel ashamed, but now he felt dispirited, ill at ease, bleak, and depressed as one does on a dismal rainy day. He had intimated that he had inferred that she loved him, but maybe he had guessed wrong. That itself was bad enough—but even if he had guessed right, how could he have been so indiscreet and tactless. He was a complete nincompoop! He had probably frightened away the feeling that had been knocking timorously at the door of her young maidenly heart, the feeling that had been settling there so tentatively and gently like a tiny bird on a twig—the slightest noise or rustling and it was off!

It was with a sinking feeling that he waited for Olga to appear at dinner and he wondered what she would say, how she would sound and how she would look at him. When she finally came down and he saw her he could not get over the change in her. Her face and voice were so different that he hardly recognized her. The youthful, naïve almost childlike smile of amusement was gone from her lips; she never once gave him that old, open, wide-eyed look of interrogation, puzzlement or unabashed curiosity. It was as if she no longer had anything to ask him, anything she wanted to know; as if there was nothing about him that could possibly surprise her. She no longer watched him closely as she had before. When she did look at him it was as someone she had known for years and with whom she was utterly familiar, as someone who, like the baron, meant nothing in particular to her—in short it was as if he had not seen her for a year and she was suddenly a whole year older.

The annoyance and the grimness of the day before had disappeared and she joked and even laughed and gave complete answers to questions she would have ignored before. It was clear that she had made up her mind to behave in the same way as others, something she had never done before. No longer did she speak her mind with the old freedom and spontaneity—what had suddenly happened to all that?

After dinner he went up to her and asked her if she would like to take a walk. Instead of answering him she turned to her aunt and asked her: "shall *we* go for a walk?"

"If it's not too far," said her aunt, "and tell them to bring me a parasol!"

So they all went. They ambled along, looking into the distance in the direction of St. Petersburg, went as far as the woods and returned to the balcony.

"I get the impression you don't feel like singing today, I'm even afraid to ask," said Oblomov, wondering when all this constraint was going to end and when her cheerfulness would return and waiting for a spark of the old openness, blithe spontaneity and guileless innocence to be rekindled in a word, in a smile and, of course, in her singing.

"It's so hot!" the aunt remarked.

"I'll try anyway," said Olga and sang a romance. Oblomov could not believe his ears. This was not the Olga he knew; where was that passion that had been in her voice before? Her singing was pure and precise but at the same time so... so... well, it was exactly the way all young ladies sing for their guests when someone asks them—without real feeling. The singing had lost its heart and among the listeners not a single heartstring was plucked.

Was she putting on an act, just pretending; was she angry? Impossible to tell. Her look was friendly enough and she talked freely, but her talk was just like her singing, entirely conventional. What was going on? Without waiting for tea, Oblomov picked up his hat and took his leave.

"Do come more often!" said the aunt, "on weekdays we're always here alone, if that wouldn't be too dull for you, otherwise on Sundays there are always a few visitors so you won't be bored." The baron rose politely to say goodbye and bowed to him. Olga gave him a friendly nod as she would to any old acquaintance and when he had left, turned towards the window to watch him go, listening indifferently to the sound of his departing footsteps.

Those two hours and the next three or four days, a week at the outside, had a profound effect on her and in that short time she covered a lot of ground. It is only women who are capable of such rapid development of their powers and all-around emotional maturity. It was as if for her each hour counted as a day. In the course of a single hour, the slightest, even barely perceptible experience or event which flashed by like a bird and which would go unnoticed by a man even if it flew right under his nose, would be seized by a young girl with uncanny swiftness. She would follow its flight into the distance and its trajectory, however erratic, would be etched indelibly upon her memory as a marker, a point of reference, as a lesson learned. Where a man would need a clearly marked signpost, for her the slightest wisp of a breeze, a barely audible tremor in the air would be enough.

How could it happen so suddenly, what could possibly be the reasons why the face of a young girl, which only the week before had been so carefree, so hopelessly naïve, had suddenly come to betray such grim thoughtfulness? What was she thinking? What was the thought about? It was as if the thought was so all-embracing as to subsume the entire logic, the entire abstract and practical philosophy of a man, the whole of life's system!

A cousin who had not too long ago gone away to university and left behind a little girl, after graduating and putting on his epaulettes, returned, and, catching sight of her, ran up to her eagerly, intending as always to clap her on the shoulder, take her by the hands and whirl her around and clamber with her all over the furniture; but suddenly he stopped in his tracks and, after taking a long look at her face, would beat a hasty retreat in his embarrassment, realizing all at once that, while he was still a boy, she had become a woman.

What is it? What has happened? Something sensational? An astounding event? Some big news—something the whole city is buzzing with? No, nothing of the kind, nothing that *maman, mon oncle*, the nurse or the chambermaid know about. Nor had there been time for anything to happen; she had danced two mazurkas, a few quadrilles, had had a bit of a headache and spent a sleepless night. And then everything was back to normal, except that there was something new in her expression, a different look. She no longer burst into laughter, gobbled up a whole pear or told about "what happened in school." She too had graduated in her own way.

When Oblomov came the next day, he too, like the cousin, hardly recognized Olga. He looked at her timidly, while the expression with which she regarded him was entirely matter of fact and with no trace of the old curiosity or affectionateness. It was no different from the way others looked at him. What had happened to her? What was she thinking and feeling now? Questions gnawed at him. "I just don't understand anything!"

And how could he be expected to understand that what had happened to her was something that only happens to a man at the age of twenty-five with the help of twenty- five professors and libraries and after traveling about the world, and sometimes at the cost of a certain loss of moral sensibility, intellectual freshness and a certain amount of hair—in other words her eyes had been opened; and in her case how easily and cheaply had this breakthrough been achieved!

"No, it's too much, I've had enough!" he decided. "I'll move to the Vyborg side, I'll busy myself, I'll read, I'll go to Oblomovka—and alone!" he added in despair. "Yes, without her! Goodbye to my paradise, my glorious, quiet, ideal life!"

For the next two days he stayed away, did no reading and no writing and was on the point of going out for a walk and had actually set foot on the dusty road, but continuing would have meant going uphill. "Why should I drag myself out in this heat?" he said to himself, yawned, went back inside, lay down on the divan and fell fast asleep just as he was in the habit of doing back in Gorokhovaya Street, in that dusty room with the blinds drawn. His dreams were troubled and when he woke up he found his dinner had been served—there was cold soup and chopped meat. Zakhar was standing, looking sleepily out of the window and Anisya was rattling dishes in the next room.

Oblomov finished his dinner and sat at the window. "How depressing, how absurd, still alone! Nowhere I want to go, nothing I want to do!"

"Look sir, here's a kitten from the neighbors; would you like to keep it, you were asking about it yesterday?" said Anisya in an attempt to divert him and put the kitten in his lap. He started stroking it, but even that did nothing to relieve the tedium. "Zakhar!" he called.

"What would you be wanting, sir?" Zakhar responded listlessly.

"I may be moving back to town."

"Where to? You don't have anywhere to live."

"What about the Vyborg side?"

"What's the point of that? It'll just mean moving from one dacha to another. What's the big attraction? Mikhei Andreyich?"

"Well the problem with this place is..."

"That means all the stuff will have to be moved again, good God! We're all worn out as it is! Two cups are still missing, not to mention the broom, unless Mikhei Andreyich took them there—they plain disappeared just like that!"

Oblomov said nothing. Zakhar went out and came back lugging a suitcase and a traveling bag. "And what am I supposed to do with this?" he said, pushing the suitcase with his foot, "sell it or what?"

"Have you gone crazy or something? I'm going abroad in a few days and I'll be needing it!"

"Going abroad!" Zakhar sniggered. "Oh yes, you talked about it alright—but actually doing it...!"

"Oh yes, and what's so strange about that? I'm going, and that's that—I've even got my passport!" said Oblomov.

"And who's going to pull your boots off there," Zakhar asked ironically, "some chambermaid? You'll be lost without me there!" he grinned, pulling his whiskers and eyebrows further to the sides of his face in the process.

"What nonsense you talk! Just take it and get out!" Oblomov snapped at him.

The next day it was after nine when he woke up and Zakhar brought him his tea and said that when he had gone to the baker's he had met the young lady there.

"What young lady?" asked Oblomov.

"Why, the Ilyinskys' young lady, Olga Sergeyevna."

"So?" Oblomov asked impatiently.

"So she sent her greetings and asked how you were and if anything was wrong with you."

"And what did you tell her?"

"I said you were fine and what could possibly be wrong with you?"

"Why did you have to volunteer your own stupid ideas?" said Oblomov. " 'What could possibly be wrong...?' How would *you* know? So, what else?"

"She asked where you had dinner yesterday?"

"And..."

"I said you had dinner at home—and supper too. And the young lady said: 'you mean he has supper as well?' Yes," I said, "and he only ate two chickens."

"You idiot!" Oblomov barked.

"What do you mean 'idiot'? It's the truth! I can show you the bones if you like."

"That proves you're an idiot!" said Oblomov. "And what did she say?"

"The young lady just laughed and then said: "Is that all?""

"See what an idiot you are!" Oblomov declared, "You might as well have told her you put my shirt on inside out while you were about it!"

"Well, she didn't ask, so I didn't tell her."

"What else did she ask?"

"She wanted to know what you've been doing the last few days."

"And what did you say?"

"I told her you've been doing nothing—except lying down."

"Oh God!" Oblomov was really exasperated and raised his fists to his temples. "Get out of here!" he ordered Zakhar threateningly. "Don't you ever dare to say such stupidities about me again—or else. That man is pure poison!"

"You mean you want me to lie—at my age?" Zakhar said in his defense.

"Get out of here!" Oblomov repeated.

Mere abuse did not bother Zakhar at all, as long as his master did not use any "heart-rending" words.

"I said that you want to move to the Vyborg side."

"Out!" Oblomov commanded at the top of his voice. Zakhar left and could be heard sighing all the way down the hallway and Oblomov began to drink his tea.

He finished his tea, and from the great heap of rolls and biscuits he ate a single roll in fear of further indiscretion on Zakhar's part. Then he lit a cigar and sat at his desk, opened a book, read the first page, tried to turn to the next page and found that the pages were still uncut. He tore open the pages with his finger, leaving the edges all jagged, and the book was not even his own! It belonged to Stoltz who was fussy and meticulous about all his possessions, but none more than his books. Even such trivial items as paper and pencils had to be left exactly where they had been put, and God help anyone who disturbed them! He should have used a paper knife but he did not have one; he could, of course, always have called for a table knife, but Oblomov preferred to put the book back and headed for the divan. But scarcely had he placed his hand on the embroidered cushion in order to lever himself more comfortably into place for lying down when Zakhar entered the room.

"That young lady... she wanted you to come to... you know... what d'you call it?" he reported.

"Why didn't you tell me before, two hours ago?" Oblomov shot back.

"Well, you didn't let me finish, you told me to leave." Zakhar retorted.

"You'll be the death of me, Zakhar!" said Oblomov with feeling.

"He's at it again!" thought Zakhar, pointing the whiskers on the left side of his face at his master as he turned to face the wall, "just like he did before, he has to get his little dig in!"

"Where am I supposed to go?" Oblomov asked.

"You know... to that... what d'you call it... yes, a garden or something."

"The park?"

"Yes, that's it, the park, exactly! She said, to go for a walk if you'd like, she'd be there..."

"Get me dressed!"

Oblomov scoured the park, looking for Olga at the flower beds and the pavilions, but there was no sign of her. He went back to the path—the scene of that fateful conversation, and found her sitting on a bench not far from the place where she had broken off a sprig of lilac and thrown it to the ground.

"I'd given you up," she said in a friendly tone.

"I've been around the whole park, looking for you," he replied.

"I knew you'd be looking for me, so I made a point of sitting here on this path; I thought you'd be sure to come this way."

He was on the point of asking: "what made you think that?" but he looked at her and thought better of it.

Her face now wore a different expression from that time when they had walked along the path; it was more like the look on her face when he had seen her last, the look that had so disturbed him. The friendliness was somehow more restrained; her whole expression was more possessed, more controlled. He saw that their playful guessing games, hints and naïve questions were now out of place, and that that moment of carefree, childlike innocence was now a thing of the past.

Much that once had been left unsaid between them could be approached by way of some disingenuous question, and somehow or other could be tacitly and wordlessly settled and resolved. Now, however, there was no going back to that.

"It's been so long since we've seen you?" she said.

Oblomov did not reply. Once again he wanted to give her to understand indirectly that his old unspoken delight in their relationship had disappeared. He now felt oppressed by this new aura of controlled self-possession, which shrouded her like a cloud in which she had concealed herself so that he no longer knew how to behave in her presence. He felt that at the slightest hint of this she would react with a look of surprise followed by a cooling in her demeanor which might totally extinguish that spark of sympathy which he had so carelessly snuffed out at the very beginning. This spark had to be carefully nurtured and gradually fanned back into life—but how to do this was quite beyond him.

He dimly recognized that she had somehow outgrown him and that there was no going back to that childlike, trusting innocence of before. He knew that they were facing some kind of Rubicon and that their lost happiness lay on the far bank and that they had to find a way across. But how? And what if he crossed alone?

She understood more clearly than he did himself what was happening to him and thus had an advantage over him. She could see straight into his heart; she saw the birth of a feeling deep inside him and watched it work its way outwards and upwards; she saw that womanly wiles, guile, flirtatiousness—the weapons of a Sonia—would be wasted on him because there was simply no contest. She even saw that, in spite of her youth, hers was the dominant and leading role in their relationship, that nothing more could be expected of him than a deep impressionability, a passionate but passive submissiveness and a heart that would always beat in perfect accord with the rhythm and tempo of her own. She could expect no initiative, no stirrings of an independent will.

The magnitude of her power over him was apparent to her in a flash and she was attracted by the role of lodestar and guiding light, light that she would shed over the still waters of a lake and which would be reflected in it. She savored the varied delights of her victory in this duel.

In this comedy—or tragedy, depending on the circumstances—both of the protagonists have fixed roles, either as tormentor or victim. Olga, like any leading lady, that is, in the role of the tormentor, could not forego the pleasure of playing cat and mouse a little with her victim, although not as much as others might have done and, of course, quite unconsciously. Sometimes this would take the form of a sudden caprice, a change of mood which could strike like lightning out of the blue, and then, just as suddenly it would pass and she would withdraw back into her shell of watchful reserve; but mostly it was a case of her prodding him forward and onward, knowing as she did, that left to himself, he would never venture a step and would remain precisely on the spot where she had left him.

"Have you been busy?" she asked, continuing with her embroidery.

"I'd like to say 'yes', only Zakhar is sure to blab," he groaned inwardly. "Oh, I've been doing some reading," he replied casually.

"A novel?" she asked raising her eyes from her work to see what kind of expression would accompany his lie.

"No, I hardly ever read novels," he answered with total aplomb, "I've been reading A History of Inventions and Discoveries. Thank God I took a look at it today!" he thought to himself.

"Is it in Russian?" she asked.

"No, it's in English."

"So you read English?"

"Yes, although not without difficulty," replied, quickly adding so as to change the subject, "and have you been to town at all?"

"No, I've just been at home. I spend a lot of time in the park doing my needlework."

"Right here on the path?"

"Yes, I really like it here; I'm grateful to you for pointing it out to me, practically no one comes here..."

"It wasn't me who showed it to you," he broke in, "don't you remember, we just happened to meet here by chance."

"Yes, you're right."

They both fell silent.

"Has your stye completely cleared up?" she asked, looking at him straight in the right eye.

He blushed. "Yes, it's gone now, thank God!"

"If you moisten your eye with a little vodka when it begins to itch, it stops the stye developing," she continued, "my nanny told me."

"Why is she going on about styes?" Oblomov wondered.

"Also you must stop eating supper."

"That Zakhar!" he was barely able to bite back his bitterly indignant exclamation.

"If you're going to eat heavy suppers," she went on, without looking up from her needlework, "and then on top of it spend three days lying down, especially on your back, you must expect to get styes."

"You i-di-ot!" again Oblomov barely managed to suppress his roar of indignation.

"What is that work you're doing"? he asked, changing the subject.

"It's a bell ribbon for the baron," she said, unrolling the canvas to show him the design. "Do you like it?"

"Yes, it's very nice, isn't it a sprig of lilac?"

"Yes, I suppose it is as a matter of fact," she said casually. "I just chose a subject at random, whatever happened to pop up," and blushing slightly, she quickly rolled up the canvas.

"It's just pointless if we go on like this, if I can't get her to say anything," he thought. Someone like Stoltz, for instance, would have gotten it out of her, but not me!"

He frowned and looked around him apathetically. She looked at him and put away the needlework in her basket. "Let's go to the grove!" she said, giving him the basket to carry. She opened her parasol, smoothed her dress and set off.

"You don't look very cheerful?" she remarked.

"I don't know why, Olga Sergeyevna, and anyway why should I be? And how?"

"Find something to do, get a more active social life!"

"Something to do—that's all very well when you have a purpose. What purpose do I have—none!"

"Isn't living a purpose?"

"When you don't know what you're living for, you just live one day at a time; you're glad that the day has passed, that night has come so that you can bury in sleep the nagging question of why you lived the day before and why you're going to live the next one."

She listened in stern silence; there was a severity in her frown and a mixture of disdain and mistrust snaked across the line of her lips. "Why you lived the day?" she said, repeating his words. "Do you really think that anyone's existence is purposeless?"

"Possibly mine, for instance."

"And you still don't know the purpose of your life?" she asked. "I don't believe it," she continued after a pause, "you're just trying to make yourself look bad; otherwise you wouldn't deserve to be living…"

"I've already passed the point in life when you're supposed to find a purpose, so there's nothing left." He sighed and she smiled.

"Nothing left?" she asked rhetorically but animatedly, cheerfully and with a laugh as if she did not believe him in the least and knew for a fact that the opposite was true.

"Laugh if you want," he said, "but it's the truth."

She walked on quietly with her head bowed.

"Who or what do I have to live for?" he said, walking behind her. "What do I have to strive for, to plan for, to aspire to? The flowers of my life have fallen, leaving only the thorns."

They walked on slowly; she listened with her attention wandering and plucked a sprig of lilac in passing and handed it to him without looking at him.

"What's this?" he asked, dumbfounded.

"It's a sprig—you can see!"

"What of?" he asked, his eyes widening at her.

"Lilac."

"I know, but what does it mean?"

"The flower of life and…"

He stopped; she stopped too.

"And...? he questioned.

"My annoyance," she said, giving him a piercing look straight in the eye—her smile making it clear that she knew exactly what she was doing.

Suddenly the cloak of impenetrability dropped from her. The message in her eyes was eloquent and unmistakable. It was as if she had deliberately opened a book at a particular page so that he could read a specially reserved passage....

"That means that I can hope for..." he burst out exultantly.

"Everything! But..." she broke off.

It was an instant resurrection—Oblomov suddenly became unrecognizable to her. Gone were the blurred drowsy features of the old Oblomov. His face was transformed in a flash; the eyes opened, color flooded into the cheeks, the mind quickened into life, the eyes gleamed with will and aspiration. She too saw in that wordless drama of transformation being played out on his face, that Oblomov had suddenly discovered a purpose in life. "Life, life itself is opening up for me," he exclaimed ecstatically—"life, it is in your eyes, your smile, the sprig of lilac, in 'casta diva', it's all here!"

She shook her head, "no, not all—only half."

"The better half."

"Perhaps," she said.

"But this other half, where is it, what else can there be?"

"You'll have to find it..."

"Why?"

"...if you don't want to lose the first half," she completed her sentence, gave him her arm and they set off home.

Gripping the sprig of lilac, he stole delighted glances at her head, her figure, her curls. "All mine, mine!" he proclaimed to himself, but could not believe it.

"So you won't be moving to the Vyborg side?" she asked as he was leaving for home.

He laughed and it didn't even occur to him to call Zakhar an idiot.

CHAPTER NINE

Since then there had been no sudden changes in Olga. She conducted herself equably and normally with her aunt and in company but shared her real life and feelings only with Oblomov. She no longer asked for guidance about what to do or how to act nor did she now mentally model her behavior on that of Sonia. As life presented her with new situations, and she experienced new reactions, she observed keenly everything that was happening, heeding sensitively the voice of her own instincts and checking her responses loosely against whatever she had learned from previous experience. She proceeded cautiously, testing her footing before taking the next step.

In any case who was there to ask? Her aunt? She would only glide over such questions so deftly and elusively that Olga was never able to derive from her responses any clear-cut statement that she could pin down and fix in her memory. Stoltz was not around, and as for Oblomov, well, he was just the Galatea to her Pygmalion.

Her life had expanded, but so discreetly and imperceptibly that she had moved into her new dimension without attracting the attention of those around her and without any visible or dramatic swings of mood. As far as others were concerned her behavior was the same as it had always been—but with a difference. She went to the French theatre, but the plays now had a resonance for her own life; she would read a book and there were inevitably lines in it which struck a chord, which sparked something in her own feelings, which uncannily echoed words she had uttered only the day before, as if the author had overheard the beating of her own heart.

The trees in the wood were the same, but the rustling of the leaves took on a new significance that spoke of some active complicity between them and her. The birds no longer simply chirped or twittered but were talking to one another. Everything around her now spoke to her, everything responded to her mood; if a flower opened it was as if she heard its breathing.

Her dreams, too, took on a life of their own; they teemed with visions and images to which she sometimes spoke aloud; they were telling her something but too unintelligibly for her to understand; she would try to speak to them, to question them, but could not make them understand her either. In the morning Katya would tell her that she had been talking in her sleep.

She remembered what Stoltz had predicted. So often he had told her that she had barely begun to live, and she would sometimes demand indignantly to know how he could consider her a child when she was a woman of twenty. Now she understood that he had been right and that only now had she begun to live.

He had admonished her: "Just wait, when all your own faculties begin functioning then everything around you will come to life and you will see all those things to which your eyes are closed now; you will hear things you are still deaf to. You will hear the humming of your own nerves, the music of the spheres; you will be able to hear the grass growing. Just be patient, there's no hurry, it will just happen by itself!" And so it had.

"Yes, that's what it must be, my faculties are at work, my organism has awakened," she recalled his words as she registered this strange, new excitement, keenly and tremulously aware of each new sign of the powers surging within her. She did not allow herself to daydream, to fall prey to the sudden rustling of leaves, nocturnal visions or mysterious apparitions when it seems that a ghostly visitor is crouching by your ear and telling you strange unintelligible things.

"It's just nerves," she would say sometimes, smiling through her tears and struggling to prevent fear getting the upper hand in the battle raging within her between her delicate nervous system and her new burgeoning forces. She would get out of bed, drink a glass of water, open the window, fan her face with a handkerchief in an attempt to shake off the effects of her waking and sleeping dreams.

As for Oblomov, the moment he awoke he was confronted in his imagination with the vision of Olga standing tall with the sprig of lilac in her hand. Olga filled his thoughts as he fell asleep and when he was walking or reading—her image was everywhere. Day and night he conducted an unending dialogue with her in his head. Into the "Catalogue of Inventions and Discoveries" he was constantly entering new discoveries of his own about Olga's appearance or character and inventing situations where he would arrange a chance encounter with her or send her books or little surprises.

Whenever he left her company he would continue their conversation at home so that Zakhar would sometimes come in and however incongruously he would address him in the same soft, affectionate and tender tone of voice which he had just been using in his imaginary conversation with Olga: "You bald old devil, the boots you brought me before still hadn't been cleaned, you'd better watch out, I'm really going to settle your hash one of these days!"

His old apathy had left him from the very moment she had first sung to him. He no longer lived the old life where nothing mattered and it was a matter of indifference to him whether he was just lying on his back staring at the wall, whether Alekseyev had come to see him or he had gone to see Ivan Gerasimovich in those days when neither expected the day nor the night to bring anyone or anything. Now, night and day, and indeed every single hour had its own mood, ranging from sheer, glorious radiance to lustreless gloom, depending whether that hour had been filled with Olga's presence or had dragged by tediously and emptily without her. His whole being was affected; every minute of every day his head swam with new thoughts, new conundrums, anticipation, suspense, with the torment of uncertainty, a thousand questions. Would he see her or not? What would she say, what would she do? How would she look at him? What would she give him to do? What would she ask him? Would she be pleased with him or not? These became the vital issues of his existence.

"Oh, if only we could just enjoy the warmth of love without its troubles!" he wished. "Life catches you, there's no hiding from it, and then you feel its sting! All this extra activity it forces on you—all the things you have to do! Love—it really is life's hardest school!"

He had already read several books. Olga made him tell her what they were about and listened to him with incredible patience. He had written several letters to his estate, dismissed the bailiff, and had gotten in touch with one of his neighbors through Stoltz. He might even have gone to the estate himself if he had felt able to leave Olga. He had given up eating supper and for the last two weeks he had forgotten what it was like to lie down during the day.

During that time they had been everywhere in and around St. Petersburg. With Olga, her aunt and the baron, Oblomov had attended out-of- town concerts and festivities. There was talk of going to Imatra in Finland.

Left to himself, Oblomov would never have ventured further than the park, but Olga was constantly taking the initiative and the slightest hesitation on Oblomov's part about accepting an invitation to go somewhere made it a certainty that they would go—and Olga would be wreathed in smiles. There wasn't a hill for five versts around the dacha that Oblomov had not climbed several times.

Meanwhile the feeling between them grew stronger, and the relationship developed and responded to the inexorable laws that govern such things, and Olga evolved and flowered along with it. Her eyes took on an extra sparkle, her movements acquired an extra grace, her bosom, in its rhythmic rise and fall, swelled magnificently.

"You've been looking so pretty since we've been at the dacha, Olga,"her aunt would say, and the baron's smile conveyed the same compliment. Olga would blush and lean her head on the shoulder of her aunt, who would stroke her cheek affectionately.

Once at the bottom of a hill where they had arranged to meet to go for a walk Oblomov started calling Olga's name tentatively, almost under his voice. No answer. He pulled out his watch and looked at it. "Olga Sergeyevna!" he called, aloud this time. Silence. Olga was sitting at the top of the hill; she had heard him call but restrained her laughter and kept silent because she wanted to make him climb the hill. "Olga Sergeyevna!" he called again, clambering through the bushes halfway up the hill and looking upwards. "She said she would be here at five thirty," he said to himself.

She could not restrain herself any longer and burst out laughing.

"Olga, Olga, so you're up there!" he said and climbed to the top. "What's the idea—hiding at the top of the hill? Just to make me suffer, even though you had to drag yourself up here to do it?"

"Where did you come from, straight from home?" she asked

"No, I went to your place first and they told me you had left."

"So what have you done today?" she asked.

"Today..."

"Had a row with Zakhar?" she continued.

He laughed dismissively as if to suggest that such a thing was quite impossible.

"No, I was reading the "Revue," but listen, Olga..." He trailed off and just sat down next to her, lost in admiration of her head, her profile, the movements of her hands back and forth as she plied her needle and stitched her canvas. His gaze was as intense as a burning glass and he could not keep his eyes off her. He remained motionless; it was only his eyes that swivelled, left, right, up, down, as he followed the movement of her hand, but inside his whole organism was in ferment. His blood was surging through his veins, his pulse was going at twice its normal speed, his heart was racing and he was breathing slowly and deeply like a condemned man facing execution or a person in the grip of intense exaltation.

He had lost the power of speech and movement; the only signs of life were his eyes, moist with emotion and trained unblinkingly upon her.

From time to time she raised her eyes and gave him a searching look, observed the undisguised emotion etched upon his face and thought: "My God, he's so in love! What a darling he is—so doting!" And she could not help admiring and even taking pride in a person so deeply in her thrall and prostrate at her feet.

The time for suggestive hints, for significant smiles, for the symbolism of sprigs of lilac, was past. Love now came out boldly, demanding, exacting, transformed into a code of reciprocal rights and obligations. Less and less was held back between them and misunderstandings disappeared and gave way to increasingly clear-cut and unambiguous questions. She never stopped teasing him with her gentle sarcasm about his wasted years and pronounced harsher sentences on him and punished him more severely and more effectively even than Stoltz for his apathy. As they drew closer her sarcasm at the expense of Oblomov's sluggish and inert existence gave way to ruling him with a rod of iron, unabashedly reminding him of the purpose of life and his obligations and compelling him to action.

She worked tirelessly to stimulate his mental faculties, forcing him to rack his brains over subtle practical problems to which she knew the answers and confronting him with questions that were even baffling to her. He struggled, broke his head and turned himself inside out in order to avoid falling from grace or, if not actually to cut the Gordian knot with a single heroic stroke of his sword, at least to help her crack some difficult problem.

All her womanly wiles were infused with warmth and tenderness, while all his efforts to keep up with the workings of her mind bore the imprint of his passion. For the most part, however, he lay exhausted at her feet, pressing his hand to his heart to feel its beating, his eyes glued to her, unwavering in their wonderment and adulation.

"He's so in love with me!" she would say to herself at those moments in wonderment, and if at times she discerned lingering signs in him of the old Oblomov—and she was capable of seeing deeply into him—the slightest weariness, a barely perceptible retreat into the old torpor, she would heap reproaches upon him, reproaches tinged at times with an edge of remorse or a twinge of fear of misjudging him.

Sometimes he had only to sketch the beginnings of a yawn as his mouth opened and he would feel her look of dismay upon him and would immediately snap his mouth shut with an audible click of the teeth. She would pounce upon the faintest shadow of sleepiness that might appear on his face. She made him tell her not only what he was doing but also what he would be doing next.

It was not so much, however, her reproaches that recharged his energies as the fact that he noticed how his own weariness wearied her and had the effect of making her chilly and distant. At such times he would feel an upsurge of energy and vitality and the shadow would vanish and a strong, clear current of warmth would once again flow out of her towards him.

But all these actions and reactions were confined within the charmed circle of love; his activity was essentially negative. Instead of sleeping he read, thought about writing down his plan and spent a lot of time walking and going places. Going beyond that, however, finding a real purpose in life, finding something to do—all that remained within the realm of intentions.

"What more 'living' or activity could Andrei possibly ask of him?" Oblomov would ask after dinner, struggling to keep his eyes open to prevent himself falling asleep. "Isn't this living? Isn't love a full time occupation? Just let him try it some time! Walking as much as ten versts every day! Yesterday I even had to spend the night in town in some run-down inn, fully dressed with no one to take off my boots because Zakhar wasn't there, so I had to do it myself! And all because of the errands I had to run for her!"

The hardest thing of all for him was when Olga had a particular question for him to research for her and demanded as thorough an answer as she would have expected from some professor. This happened quite often, and not because of any pedantry on her part but simply out of a desire to get to the bottom of a matter; in fact, she often forgot the reason why she was making Oblomov do it in the first place, so intent did she become on finding out the answer.

"But why don't they teach us that?" she would sometimes say with barely suppressed annoyance as greedily, practically gulping it down, she drank in the information about something that is not normally considered necessary for a woman to know.

Once, for example, she started questioning him about double stars because he had made some incautious reference to Herschel, and he was dispatched to town for his pains and made to read the book and report back to her so as to satisfy her curiosity. Another time, talking to the baron in an unguarded moment, he happened to let slip something about the different schools of painting—a lapse which cost him a whole week's work of reading and book reports! And then nothing would do but actually going to the Hermitage with her so that she could see for herself what he had been telling her.

If he ever told her something off the top of his head she would immediately seize on it and start in on him. Then he would have to spend a week going around shops looking for prints of the best pictures. Poor Oblomov then had to brush up on the information he had gleaned, or rush around the bookstalls in search of new art books, and would sometimes sit up all night poring over them so that the next day he could casually produce the answers to her questions of the previous day as if he had known them all along but had just needed to jog his memory.

Olga's questions were not the product of mere casual curiosity, a fleeting feminine whim, but were posed with intensity and persistence and with an impatience that earned Oblomov, in the event of his silence on the subject, a prolonged and withering look—a look he learned to dread.

"Why are you just sitting there without saying anything?" she asked. "Anyone would think you were bored."

"Oh," he would say like someone coming out of a trance, "I love you so much!"

"Oh, really? Well, if I hadn't asked, it would have seemed hard to believe."

"Can't you see what's going on in me?" he began, "you know, it's even hard for me to say. Look... here, give me your hand... feel it, there's some strange congestion, like a stone, making it hard for me to breathe, as if I were in deep distress. Isn't it strange how joy and sorrow seem to produce the same symptoms? You feel troubled, it hurts to breathe and you feel like crying. If I could only cry! I know my tears would bring the same relief as if I were crying from grief."

She regarded him silently as if she were checking his words against what was written on his face; then she smiled, the results of the test were satisfactory. Her face radiated happiness, but a tranquil kind that you felt nothing could disturb. Her heart was like the morning itself, light and quiet with no dark shadows.

"What's the matter with me?" he wondered aloud.

"Do you want me to tell you?"

"Yes."

"You're in love."

"Well, of course I am," he declared lifting her hand from her embroidery frame and without kissing it, just pressed it firmly to his lips, looking for all the world as if he were ready to keep it there indefinitely. She tried gently to remove her hand but he gripped it firmly.

"Alright, it's time to let go now!" she said.

"But what about you? You're not...in love...?"

"In love, no; I don't like to put it that way. I love you," she said, giving him a searching look as if she were putting herself to the test to determine that she did really love him.

"Lo-ove!" Oblomov said emphatically, dragging out the single syllable. "But you can 'love' your mother, your father, your nanny, even your pet dog; it's such a comprehensive term that it covers that whole range like an old..."

"Dressing gown?" she suggested with a laugh. "*A propos*, where is your dressing gown?"

"What dressing gown, I've never had one?"

She gave him a reproachful smile.

"Why are you going on about that old dressing gown while here I am dying to hear about the emotions spurting from your heart and what name you give to those gusts of feeling? And you just... well... forget it Olga! I'm here to tell you that I am *in love* with you, and that's the only kind of love that counts; no one is *in love* with their father, mother or nanny, they just love them."

"I just don't know, "she said, as if pondering deeply and trying to detect what was happening deep within herself. "I don't know if I'm in love with you; if not, maybe it's because the time hasn't yet come, I can only tell you that I've never loved my father, mother or nanny like this."

"But what's the difference? Do you feel something special?" he probed.

"You really want to know?" she asked mischievously.

"Yes, of course I do; don't you feel any need to express your feelings?"

"But why do you want to know?"

"So as to live every moment with the knowledge; today, all night long, tomorrow—until our next meeting—that and that alone is what I'm living for."

"You see, that's the difference between being in love and loving; you need to recharge your feelings every day, while I..."

"You what?" The suspense was too much for him.

"My love is different," she said, leaning back on the bench and watching the clouds floating by. "I miss you when I'm not with you and I don't like to see you go even for a short time, and when it's for a long time it hurts. It was enough to hear you, see you tell me just once that you loved me, I believed it and I'm happy even if you never tell me again that you love me. I can't love any more or better than that."

"Those words could be Cordelia's!" Oblomov thought, giving Olga a passionate look.

"If you were...to die," she said hesitantly, " I would go into mourning for ever and would never smile again. If you should love someone else I wouldn't complain or make a scene, but would privately wish you happiness. That's my kind of love—it's just like life itself and life..." she tried to find the right words.

"And what is life according to you?" asked Oblomov.

"Life is duty, responsibilities, so love is also duty; it's as if it were sent to me by God," she added, raising her eyes to the heavens, "and he commanded me to love."

"Cordelia!" Oblomov said aloud, "and she's twenty-one too! So that's what love is, according to you!" he added reflectively.

"Yes, and I believe I'll have enough strength to live and love for a lifetime…"

"Who could she have gotten all this from?" thought Oblomov, looking at her with an expression little short of awe. "Certainly not on the basis of her own experience, and it's not through the fire and water of her own suffering that she has achieved such a clear and straightforward understanding of life and love."

"But aren't there keener delights—passions?" he put in.

"I don't know, I've never experienced them and I don't understand them."

"Ah, now I understand!"

"Maybe in time I'll come to understand them and I will experience the same impulses as you and find myself looking at you the same way you look at me and with the same expression of disbelief that it is really you before my very eyes…that must be very comical," she added in amusement, "sometimes you look at me with such moonstruck eyes that I think *ma tante* must notice."

"But what happiness do you get out of love," he asked, "if you don't feel the sheer thrill that I do?"

"What happiness—well, it's right here," she said, pointing at him and herself—at the very fact of their seclusion. "Isn't this happiness; could this be any more different from the life I knew before? Before I would never have spent even fifteen minutes here alone without a book, without music, among these trees. I never even enjoyed talking to a man except Andrei Ivanich; there was never anything to talk about and I wanted nothing more than to be left alone and now—just being here with you makes me happy, even when we're silent!"

She looked around at the trees and the grass and her eyes came to rest on him; she smiled and gave him her hand. "Don't you know how painful it will be for me to see you leave?" she went on. "Don't you know how anxious I'll be to get into bed and go to sleep so as to shorten the waiting time until tomorrow; and don't you know that I'll be sending a message to you first thing in the morning? Don't you know…?"

With each "don't you know" Oblomov's eyes lit up more brightly and his face positively glowed.

"Yes, yes," he echoed, "I'm the same, I can't wait for the morning to come so that I can send messages to you for no other reason than to be able to say and hear your name one more time, to glean the slightest detail about you from the messengers, and envy them for already having had the chance to see you. Yes, we're exactly alike in the way we think, wait, live and hope. Olga, I'm sorry for my doubts; I'm convinced you love me in a way you never loved your father, your aunt, your…"

"…my little dog," she finished the sentence for him and laughed. "You must believe me," she said earnestly, "just as I believe you, and stop these doubts; if you keep on nagging away at your happiness with this questioning, it will fly out of the window. Once I've claimed something as my own, nothing and no one can take it away from me, young as I am. I know this for a certainty, but you know," she stated with confidence, "in the month that I've known you I've done so much thinking, and I've felt so much, that it's as if I've been studying a thick book and learning a little more about myself every day. So don't have any doubts…"

"I can't help my doubts," he put in, "there's nothing you can do about that. Now, while I'm here with you, I'm sure about everything; your look, your voice convince me. You only have to look at me and it tells me everything, words are unnecessary. But when I'm alone doubts begin to torment me, I'm haunted by questions and I have to fly to your side so that I can look at you once again, otherwise I stop believing; why is that?"

"And yet I believe you, how do you explain that?" she asked.

"That doesn't need much explaining! When you see in front of you a moonstruck, lovelorn figure like this! When you look into my eyes it must be like looking into a mirror and seeing yourself. In any case, just look at yourself—just twenty years old. How could any man who meets you fail to betray—well, astonishment at the very least, if only with his eyes? But getting to know you, listening to you, seeing you for any length of time, loving you--that would drive any man mad! Yet you are so calm, so unruffled—but me, if so much as two days go by without my hearing you say, 'I love you', I begin to panic." He pointed to his heart.

"I love you, I love you, I love you—there now, you have three day's supply," she said, rising from the bench.

"Make a joke of it if you want, but what about me?" he sighed as they descended the hill.

Such was the theme that was played between them in its endless variations. They met, they talked—it was always the same song, the same sounds, the same light burning brightly, but a light which was refracted into rays of pink, green and yellow which rippled in the air around them and made it glow. Each day brought its own new sounds and new colors, but the colors were always from the same beam of light and the sounds were always the notes of the same melody. They both listened to the same sounds, picked them up and eagerly sang them back to one another, little suspecting that the next day the sounds and the colors would be different and, when the next day came, forgetting that the day before, the singing had been different. She arrayed the effusions of her heart in whatever hues her imagination happened to be colored at that moment and believed that they were true to life, and with unconscious and innocent coquetry was eager to display herself to her beloved in all her finery.

He believed even more deeply in these enchanted sounds and this magical light and hastened to show himself to her in the full panoply of his ardour and dazzle her with the incandescence of the fire which consumed his soul. They were not lying to themselves or to each other, they were just doing the bidding of their hearts, which spoke through their imaginations.

It did not really matter to Oblomov whether Olga was a Cordelia or whether she remained true to that image or whether she took another tack and was transformed into quite a different vision, as long as she was bathed in the same hues and tints with which she was colored in his heart and as long as it made him happy.

As for Olga, she was not worried about whether her fervent admirer would have put his hand in a lion's jaws to retrieve her glove if she had dropped it there, or whether he would have cast himself into the abyss for her sake; the only thing that mattered to her was to be able to see the outward signs of his passion, to see him remaining true to the ideal of a man, a man, moreover, who had awakened to life through her and to be assured that it was the power of her look, her smile, that fuelled the flame of his energy and that he never ceased to see in her the true purpose of his life.

And so the fleeting image of Cordelia, the flame of Oblomov's passion reflected only a single moment, one flickering breath of love, its brief morning, one fanciful simulacrum to be replaced as capriciously the very next day by another image, doubtlessly just as beautiful, but a different one for all that.

CHAPTER TEN

Oblomov's state of mind was that of someone who, glimpsing the setting sun, is so taken by its ruddy glow that he has no eyes for the night that is falling behind him and can think only of tomorrow's renewal of light and warmth. He lay on his back savoring the lingering memories of yesterday's meeting. His ears still vibrated to the sound of, "I love you, I love you, I love you," more responsively than to any of Olga's songs; the traces of her look in all its intensity still lingered within him. He was trying to decipher its meaning, to measure the depth of her love and was just on the point of nodding off into oblivion when suddenly...

The next morning Oblomov awoke pale and gloomy; his face bore traces of sleeplessness and his brow was all wrinkled; his eyes had lost their sparkle, their eagerness. His pride, his cheerful, buoyant look, the measured, deliberate purposeful movements of a man of action had all disappeared. He drank his tea listlessly; he did not so much as touch a book or sit down at his desk. Moodily he lit a cigar and sat down on the divan. Previously he would have lain down but he had gotten out of the habit and he was not even tempted to lay his head on the cushion. He did, however, rest his elbow on it—a gesture that conveyed an inkling of his former tendencies. He was plunged in gloom and every now and then gave a sigh or suddenly shrugged his shoulders and shook his head defeatedly. He was in the grip of some emotion but it was not love.

Olga's image was still there but was fading into the distance and becoming dim, blurred and disconnected. He contemplated the image with a troubled expression and sighed: "there's an old saying, 'live as God commands, not as you choose!' How true it is!" He started thinking.

"Yes, you cannot live as you choose, obviously," he heard a gloomy, hectoring voice saying, "otherwise you will end up in a chaos of contradictions which no single human mind, no matter how deep or how bold, can possibly resolve. Yesterday you made a wish, today you get your heart's desire but are worn out by the effort; the day after tomorrow you blush to think what it was you wished for and then you start cursing fate for giving you what you want. You see what you get for striking out on your own so boldly into life, for going around wishing for whatever you want. The thing is to feel your way, close your eyes to a lot, don't let happiness go to your head and don't start complaining when it slips from your grasp—that's what life is about! Who started the idea that it was about happiness or pleasure—the idiots! 'Life is life, duty', according to Olga, 'responsibilities', and responsibility is a burden, so let's do our duty'." He sighed.

"But to stop seeing Olga… my God! You opened my eyes and showed me my duty," he said, looking up at the sky, "where would I get the strength? To part! There's still time, no matter how painful—at least later on I won't be cursing myself for my weakness, for not making the break. But the messenger she was going to send will soon be back. She won't be expecting…"

What's the reason for all this? What wind had been blowing on Oblomov? What clouds has it brought? How has he come to be weighed down by such a crushing millstone? Only yesterday, it seems, he was still looking into Olga's soul and seeing there such a glorious destiny, such a bright future and reading both their horoscopes. What can have happened?

Most probably he had eaten late or slept on his back and his lyrical mood had given way to nightmares. It often happens that as you are falling asleep on a quiet, cloudless evening in the summer with the stars twinkling overhead, you think how beautiful the countryside is going to look the next day in all its bright morning colors. You look forward to plunging into the woods and hiding from the heat and the next thing you know is that you are awakened by the sound of rain pounding the shutters and the sky is dark with gray, lowering clouds and everything is cold and damp.

In the evenings Oblomov had gotten into the habit of listening to the beating of his heart and then palpating the area to check whether the callous had grown any larger. He would then immerse himself in a profound analysis of his happiness and inevitably dredged up some bitter dregs that would poison the whole cup. The effect of the poison was powerful and swift. He mentally reviewed his whole life and for the umpteenth time his heart would sicken with remorse and regrets over his past. He tried to imagine what he would be like now if he had stridden ahead boldly and confidently and lived a fuller and more varied life, a life of action. He contrasted this image with the person he had actually become and wondered how and why Olga could possibly have come to love him. "There must be some mistake," the thought flashed through his mind like a streak of lightning, lightning which jolted his heart with devastating effect. He groaned, "Yes, it's a mistake!" He could not get the thought out of his head.

Then suddenly he remembered, "I love you, I love you, I love you!" and his heart lightened, and then just as suddenly sank. After all, what did those three "I love you's of Olga's mean? Her eyes must have been deceiving her, it was the treacherous whisper of her still untenanted heart; it was not love, just the premonition of love. It was a voice that would one day make itself heard, but so powerfully that the whole world would be shaken by the thunderous chord. The sound of that voice would be heard by the aunt, the baron and for miles around. A feeling of that strength would not just dribble like a tiny rivulet through the grass, barely visible and with a barely audible gurgling.

The way she loved now was the same way she did her embroidery; she plied her needle quietly, without haste, and slowly and gradually a pattern appeared; she would turn it even more languidly this way and that, admiring it and would then set it aside and forget it. Yes, this was nothing but a training exercise for love, a rehearsal for the real thing and he was just a barely acceptable stand-in who happened to be at hand, someone to practice on.

It was only chance circumstances that had thrown them together—normally she would not have noticed him. It was Stoltz who had drawn him to her attention and it was the force of his own affection for Oblomov that had aroused the sympathies of her young impressionable heart. Then there was compassion for his situation as well as the challenge to her pride of shaking Oblomov's slumbering soul into full wakefulness—and then leaving it to fend for itself.

"Yes, that's it!" he said in dismay, getting up from the bed and lighting a candle with a trembling hand. "That's all there ever was to it! She was ready for love, eager to embrace it, the pores of her heart were open and then someone happened to come along—only the wrong one. The moment someone else comes along she will recoil in horror from her mistake and the very sight of him will become repugnant—it's awful, I'm a usurper, a thief! What am I doing, what am I thinking of? How could I have been so blind, my God!"

He looked in the mirror; his face was pale, yellow, his eyes dimmed. He thought of those fortunate young men with a slightly moist and thoughtful look, but a look at the same time strong and deep, with that same tremulous sparkle in their eyes that Olga herself had. They marched forward with a firm stride, with smiles and voices ringing with the certainty of victory. And here he was just waiting for one of them to arrive on the scene when she would come to her senses, take one look at him, Oblomov, and burst out laughing. He took another look in the mirror. "This is not a face that anyone's going to love!" he said.

He lay down with his face pressed into the cushion. "Goodbye Olga, be happy!" he murmured.

The next morning he called for Zakhar. "If anyone comes with a message from the Ilyinskys, say I'm not at home, that I've gone into town!"

"Yes, sir."

"No, maybe it's better if I write to her," he said to himself, "otherwise she'll think it's strange that I've suddenly disappeared; I have to explain."

He sat down at the desk and began to write quickly and with a feverish urgency, not at all the way he had written to the landlord at the beginning of May. Not once did he find himself putting two "who's" or two "what's" uncomfortably close together.

"You will find it strange, Olga Sergeyevna," he wrote, "to be receiving a letter instead of myself in person, considering how often we have been meeting, but if you read to the end you will see that there was nothing else I could have done. In fact, we should have begun with this letter and spared ourselves a great many subsequent pangs of conscience—but even now it's not too late. We fell in love with one another so suddenly, so fast that it was as if we had both been suddenly taken ill, and this is what made it so hard to come to my senses before this. In any case how could anyone who has spent hours looking at you and listening to you voluntarily take on the grim responsibility of breaking the spell? How could anyone be expected to have the self-discipline and strength of will to stop and ponder each and every time the slope gets steeper and not go full tilt downhill? Every day I've been thinking, 'I'm not going any further, this is where I get off—it's up to me,' but every time I did go further and now I'm in the throes of a conflict in which I need your help. It was only today—last night—that I realized that my feet were running away with me; it was only yesterday that I was able to look down deeper into the abyss—I'm standing on the brink and I have made up my mind to stop.

I am talking only about myself, but not out of selfishness, but because when I am lying at the bottom of that abyss you will still be flying high above it like an angel and I don't know whether you will even feel like glancing down into it. Look, let me say it simply and straight-forwardly, without mincing words, you do not and cannot love me. Take the word of someone with my experience and don't have the slightest doubt about it for my heart began beating long ago. Let's say it wasn't always beating true or for the right reasons but that itself helped me to learn how to tell whether it was beating true or false. There is no way you can tell, but I can and should know what is the truth and what is a mirage, so it's my responsibility to warn someone who is still too young to tell the difference. So this is my warning to you: 'Watch out, your deluding yourself!'

As long as love took the light-hearted, playful form of the strains of 'casta diva' and the scent of lilac, the unspoken sympathy, the shy glances, I didn't trust it and just took it for a trick of the imagination, the workings of my self-esteem. But that playfulness passed and I became sick with love and suffered all the symptoms of passion. You became serious and thoughtful and gave up your time to me. You start-ed living on your nerves and became moody and then, that is, only recently, I got frightened and began to feel responsible for stopping and saying what was happening.

I told you that I loved you and you told me the same thing. Don't you hear the dissonance? Well, if you don't hear it now you will hear it later when I'm lying at the bottom of the abyss. Just look at me, consid-er my existence. Can you love me, do you love me? 'I love you, I love you, I love you', you said yesterday. To that I answer resolutely, 'no, no, no!'

You do not love me, but it's not that you are lying—I hasten to add—and it's not that you are deceiving me, but you cannot say, 'yes' when everything inside you is saying 'no!'. I just want to make you understand that the 'I love you' that you are saying now is not about what is happening now but about some future love; it's just an uncon-scious need to love which, because it has nothing to feed on, no fuel to ignite it, is burning with a spurious flame which gives no heat, a love which women sometimes express in affection for a child or another woman or which sometimes even takes the form of tears and hysterics. I should have been firm with you from the very beginning and told you, 'the man you see before you is not the man of your dreams, the one you've been waiting for'. Be patient and he will come and then you will come to your senses; you will feel embarrassed and ashamed of your mis-take and that embarrassment and shame will hurt me.' Yes, this is what I should have told you if I had had it in me to be a little more perspica-cious and had had a little more spirit—and if, when all is said and done, I had been a little more honest. In fact I did tell you, but you remember how I did it? I was so afraid that you would believe me and that I would be proved right that I made a point of anticipating everything that other people might say later on so that you would be predisposed to disbelieve and ignore them. And I was always in a hurry to see you, knowing that someone else was sure to come along and yet thinking, 'well, I'm happy for now anyway.' That's the logic of infatuation and passion for you!

Now I see it all differently—what will happen when I've grown attached to her, when seeing her has ceased to be a luxury and become a necessity, when love has wormed its way into my heart (no wonder I feel a callous growing there!)? How will I be able to tear myself away then? How will I survive the pain? It will be terrible. Even now I shudder at the prospect. If you had only been more experienced, older, then I would have blessed my happiness and given you my hand forever but...

But why am I writing this instead of just coming to face you directly and saying that the urge to see you is growing stronger every day but that it is wrong to see you? Do I have the nerve to say this to your face? You can judge for yourself. Sometimes I'm on the verge of saying something of the kind but end up saying something totally different. Perhaps a look of distress would appear on your face (if you truly found some pleasure in my company) or you might fail to understand my good intentions and would be offended. Either way I wouldn't be able to bear it and once again I would end up saying something else instead and all my good intentions would go up in smoke and turn into one more attempt to arrange to see you the next day. Now, sitting here by myself without your gentle eyes, your kind, pretty little face in front of me it's quite different; the paper is patient and silent and I am writing calmly (not true!); we *will not see one another again* (true!).

Someone else might have added: 'tears are streaming down my face as I write,' but I am not trying to strike a pose or to dramatize my grief, because I don't want to increase the pain, to make the sorrow, the regret more poignant. All that kind of posturing usually masks the intention to dig the roots more firmly into the soil of feeling, while I am trying to dig up those roots in you and in myself. Crying is a favorite device of seducers who are trying to use words to catch a woman's self-esteem off guard or is the mark of wilting dreamers. I'm saying all this in the spirit of someone taking leave of a good friend whom one is seeing off on a long journey. In three or four weeks time it would be too late, too difficult; love makes incredibly rapid progress; it's a kind of gangrene of the soul. Already I'm going to pieces; I no longer count in hours or minutes, I don't go by sunsets or sunrises; I count time by, 'I've seen her, I haven't seen her, I'm going to see her, I'm not going to see her, she came, she didn't come, she's coming.'

All this is fine for the young, they can easily tolerate the agonies and the ecstasies, but at my time of life peace and quiet is the thing—it may be dull and soporific but it's familiar—I just can't take that kind of turbulence.

What I am doing would surprise a lot of people; 'what is he running away from?' they will say. Others will laugh at me; fine, I'm ready for that. After all, if I'm ready to give up seeing you I should be ready for anything.

In the depths of my despair I take some comfort from the fact that this brief episode in our lives will always leave me with this pure, fragrant memory which should be enough by itself to prevent me sinking back into my old spiritual torpor and that, while leaving you unharmed, it will serve you as a guide for that genuine love which awaits you in the future. Farewell, my angel, flutter away like a frightened little bird from the bough on which it has perched by mistake; take off as lightly, gaily and cheerfully as it does from the bough on which it has unwittingly settled!"

Oblomov wrote like a man inspired, his pen flying over the pages, his eyes and cheeks blazing. The letter was, of course, a long one like all love letters; people in love can never stop talking.

"How strange! I don't feel at all miserable or depressed," he thought, "I'm almost happy, I wonder why, what could it be? It must be that writing this letter has lifted a weight off my mind." He re-read the letter, folded and sealed it. "Zakhar!" he called, "when the man calls give him this letter for the young lady!"

"Yes, sir."

Oblomov was indeed in good spirits. He sat with his legs up on the divan and even asked what was for breakfast. He ate two eggs and lit a cigar. His heart and his head were both full, he was alive. He imagined her receiving the letter; her astonishment, the expression on her face when she read it and wondered what would happen then. He looked forward to the rest of the day, to the news it would bring. He listened anxiously for the knock at the door—wasn't anyone coming yet, wasn't Olga reading the letter yet? But no, the entrance was quiet. "What could it mean?" he began to worry, "no one is coming, how come?" He heard a little voice whispering in his ear: "what are you worried about? This is exactly what you wanted—nothing to happen so that the relationship would be broken off." But he refused to listen to the little voice.

About half an hour later he called out to Zakhar who was sitting outside with the coachman: "Has anyone come?" he asked, "No one?"

"Yes, someone came," Zakhar replied.

"And?"

"I said you weren't in, that you'd gone into town like."

Oblomov goggled at him. "Why on earth did you say that?" he asked, "what did I tell you to say when the man came?'

"But it wasn't a man, it was the maid," Zakhar responded, totally unruffled.

"But did you give her the letter?"

"Of course not, since you told me first of all to say you were out and then hand over the letter, so as soon as the man comes I'll give it to him."

"I don't believe it! You'll be the death of me! Where's the letter? Give it here!" said Oblomov.

Zakhar brought him the letter, already pretty badly soiled.

"Go and wash your hands quick!" Oblomov snapped angrily, pointing to the stain.

"My hands are clean!" Zakhar protested, looking off to the side.

"Anisya, Anisya!" Oblomov called. Anisya poked her head through the doorway.

"Look what Zakhar's been doing!" he complained to her.

"Take this letter and give it to the man or the maid, whoever comes from the Ilyinskys, to give to the young lady, you understand?"

"Yes, sir, of course, I will."

But as soon as she went back into the hallway Zakhar snatched the letter from her.

"Get out of here and attend to your woman's business!" he shouted.

Soon the chambermaid came running over again. As Zakhar was opening the door to her Anisya started moving towards her, but Zakhar stopped her in her tracks with a fierce look.

"What are you doing here?" he wheezed.

"I just came to hear what you…"

"Get back where you belong!" he bellowed, gesturing menacingly with his elbow.

She gave a grin and left but watched through a crack in the door from the next room to check whether Zakhar did what the master had told him.

Ilya Ilyich heard the noise and hurried out to see what was going on.

"What is it, Katya?" he asked

"The mistress sent to ask where you went, but you haven't gone anywhere, you're at home. I'll run back and tell her," she said and was about to run off.

"Yes, I'm at home, you can never believe what that Zakhar tells you," said Oblomov, "here, take this letter and give it to your mistress!"

"Yes, sir."

"Where is she right now?"

"She's gone out to the village and said to tell you that if you've finished the book, please to come to the garden after one o'clock." The maid left.

"No, I won't go… why stir up feelings when it's time to end it all?" Oblomov thought to himself as he started out towards the village. In the distance he saw Olga climbing the hill and Katya catching her up and giving her the letter. He saw Olga stop for a moment, look at the letter, nod to Katya and turn onto the path inside the park. Oblomov skirted the foot of the hill and entered the park at the other end of the path, walked halfway along it, sat on the grass behind the shrubbery and waited.

"She's bound to come this way," he thought, "I'll just take one last look at her from where I'm hidden and leave forever." He listened anxiously for the sound of her footsteps but there was nothing but silence.

Nature continued to go about its business; all around him was a ferment of unseen microscopic activity that gave the appearance of a majestic calm. The grass around him was bustling, rustling and crawling with movement. Ants were scurrying in all directions, busily and purposefully coming together and separating in constant, furious motion. It was as if you were looking down from a great height on a busy marketplace; people gathering knots, creating exactly the same hustle and bustle.

A bee was buzzing around the head of a flower and crawling into its pollen sac; flies were swarming around a drop of sap that had oozed through a crack in the bark of a lime tree and somewhere in the thicket a bird repeated the same sound over and over again—perhaps it was calling to another bird. Two butterflies were criss-crossing one another in an erratic waltz, weaving in and out of the tree trunks. The grass gave off a heavy scent, bristling and rustling incessantly.

"What a commotion!" thought Oblomov as he peered closely at all this turmoil and strained to catch the microscopic sounds of nature at work, "and yet on the surface it all seems so calm and quiet!" Still no sound of footsteps—but at last, suddenly, he heard something and quietly parted the branches. "It's her, it's her!" he murmured under his breath, "what? Oh no! She's crying, oh God!"

Olga was walking slowly and drying her tears with her handkerchief but she could not succeed in staunching them. In her embarrassment she tried in vain to choke back her tears and even to hide them from the trees.

Oblomov had never seen Olga in tears and had not expected to. The sight scorched him but left him warm rather than hot. He hurried after her. "Olga, Olga!" he called gently from behind. Trembling, she turned her head and gave him a look of surprise, then she turned away and continued walking. He drew level with her and said: "you're crying?" Her tears flowed faster; she could no longer hold them back and held the handkerchief to her face and then, sobbing uncontrollably, sat down on the nearest bench.

"What have I done!" he whispered in horror, taking her hand and trying to pull it away from her face.

"Leave me alone!" she said, "go away! What are you doing here? I know I shouldn't be crying; what for? You're right; yes, anything can happen."

"What can I do to stop these tears?" he asked on his knees, "tell me, I'll do whatever you order me to do!"

"It was you who caused these tears and it's not in your power to stop them, you don't have the strength. Let me go!" she said, flapping the handkerchief in her face.

He looked at her, cursing himself mentally. "That damned letter!" he said in a tone of bitter remorse.

She opened her workbasket, took out the letter and handed it to him. "Here, take it!" she said, "and take it away with you so that I don't have to cry my eyes out when I see it!" He pocketed it silently and sat down beside her, hanging his head.

"Can you at least give me credit for good intentions, Olga?" he said quietly. "It shows how much I value your happiness."

"Oh yes, you must really value it!" she sighed. "No, Ilya Ilyich, you must have been really envious of my quiet happiness to have been in such a hurry to ruin it."

"Ruin it? You couldn't have read my letter, let me tell you again..."

"No, I didn't finish reading it, my eyes were filling with tears; how stupid I must be! But I could guess the rest; so spare me a repetition, otherwise I'll start crying again."

The tears welled up again.

"Don't you see," he began, that I'm giving you up because I see that your happiness lies ahead and that's why I'm making this sacrifice? Do you really think it was so easy for me; that inside I'm not in tears—why else would I be doing this?"

"Why?" she repeated. She suddenly stopped crying and turned towards him. "Why? For the same reason you hid in the bushes just now, to see whether I would cry and to see me cry—that's why! If you had really meant what you wrote in the letter, if you had really made up your mind that we should part, you would have gone abroad without seeing me."

"What an idea!" he started to protest, but broke off, stunned by the realization that what she had said was the truth.

"Yes," she confirmed, "yesterday you needed to hear me say: 'I love you', today you needed my tears, perhaps tomorrow you'll want to see me die."

"Olga, how can you think so little of me? Can you possibly doubt that I would give half my life just to hear you laugh and banish your tears?"

"Yes, perhaps right at this moment, now that you've actually seen a woman crying over you . No, you have no heart. You say you didn't want my tears; but if you really hadn't wanted them you wouldn't have provoked them."

"But how could I have known?" he responded in a tone that was part question and part exclamation as he clutched his chest with his hands.

"A heart that loves knows these things," she countered, "it knows what it wants and knows what id going to happen. Yesterday I shouldn't really have come to meet you; we had unexpected visitors, but I knew how distressed you would be if you had waited for nothing, and you might have slept badly, so I came because I didn't want to make you suffer... but look how cheerful you are now that I'm in tears; look how you are enjoying it!" She burst into tears again.

"But I did sleep badly, Olga, I was in torment all night long..."

"And you couldn't stand the thought that I was sleeping soundly and peacefully—isn't that it?" she broke in. "If I hadn't been crying now you wouldn't have been able to sleep tonight either."

"Well, what should I do now? Say I'm sorry?" he asked meekly and gently.

"It's children who say they are sorry, or people in a crowd who've stepped on someone's foot, but apologies won't do any good in this situation," she said, flapping her handkerchief in her face again.

"But, Olga, what if it's true, what if I was right when I wrote that your love is all a mistake? What if you do fall in love with someone else and the sight of me makes you blush with embarrassment?"

"What of it?" she asked, giving him such a searching, penetrating look that he positively quailed.

"There's something she's trying to drag out of me," he thought, "keep your wits about you, Ilya Ilyich!"

"What do you mean, 'what of it'?" he repeated mechanically, giving her a worried look and unable to guess the thought that was taking shape in her mind, or how she was planning to justify her 'what of it?', when it was obviously impossible to justify the consequences of that love if it was all a mistake.

She looked at him so knowingly, with such certainty that it was clear that she had marshalled her argument. "You're afraid," she argued, "of falling into the depths of the abyss. You're worried about the blow to your pride if I stop loving you. 'I will feel terrible,' you wrote."

He still did not really understand.

"After all, I'll be fine if I fall in love with someone else; I'll be happy! But you say that you see that, 'my happiness lies ahead' and you are ready to make any sacrifice for me, even your life.'"

He was staring at her unblinkingly, his eyes widening. "So that's the logic behind it," he whispered, "I honestly didn't realize."

She looked him up and down venomously. "And this happiness you're out of your mind with," she went on, " and all those mornings and evenings, the park, my 'I love you's', all that is worth nothing, no sacrifice, no value whatsoever, not even the risk of the slightest pain?"

"Oh God, if only the earth would swallow me up!" he thought, his inner torment growing as the truth of what Olga had said dawned on him.

"And what if," she asked him heatedly, "you get tired of this love just as you got tired of your books, your work and meeting people; what if one day even without another woman, a rival for your affections, you fall asleep beside me the way you do when you're at home on your divan, and my voice doesn't wake you up; if that callous in your heart disappears and you even start preferring your dressing gown to me—let alone another woman?"

"Olga, that's impossible!" he protested, moving away from her.

"Why impossible?" she asked. "You say that I'm mistaken and that I'll fall in love with someone else, but I sometimes think that you will simply stop loving me—and what then? How will I justify to myself what I'm doing now? Never mind what people will say and the tongues that will be wagging, but what will I say to myself? I too sometimes lose sleep over it but I spare you these worries about the future because I have faith that things will be for the best. With me love is stronger than fear. To me it means something when I make your eyes light up, when you come and climb hills to look for me and forget your laziness and rush into town to fetch me a bouquet or a book, when I make you smile and embrace life... All I'm waiting for and looking for is happiness and I believe I've found it. If I've made a mistake, if it's true that one day I'll suffer for my mistake, at least I have the feeling here (she placed her hand on her heart) that it's not my fault but that it was just something that was never meant to be, it wasn't God's will. No, I'm not afraid of suffering in the future; my tears will not be for nothing, they will be the price of something of value, of a happiness... that I once had."

"Happiness that you will have again, yes, you must!" Oblomov implored her.

"But you see nothing but misery ahead," Olga went on, " happiness doesn't matter to you; that's not love, that's ingratitude, it's..."

"Selfishness." Oblomov finished the sentence for her, not daring to look at her, not daring to speak nor even to apologize.

"Why don't you go now to wherever you were going?' she said quietly.

He looked at her. Her eyes were now dry and she was looking down thoughtfully and tracing something in the sand with the tip of her parasol.

"Go and lie down on your back again!" she said finally, and you won't make any mistakes or end up 'at the bottom of the abyss.' "

"I've poisoned myself and you instead of being simply and straightforwardly happy," he mumbled remorsefully.

"Drink kvass and you won't get poisoned," she said acidly.

"Olga, that's mean!" he said, "after I've been punishing myself by trying to think things through!"

"Oh yes, you talk about punishing yourself, about throwing yourself into the abyss, about sacrificing half your life, and then there are your doubts, your sleepless nights! My, how solicitous you are becoming about yourself, how careful, how concerned—and how far-sighted!"

"It's all so true and so simple!" Oblomov thought but was ashamed to say so aloud. Why couldn't he have seen it for himself instead of having to hear it from a young woman just starting out in life? And how quick she was to see it when only a short time ago she was still seeing life through the eyes of a child.

"We have nothing more to discuss," she stated conclusively, standing up. "Goodbye, Ilya Ilyich, I wish you peace and quiet; that is, after all, what makes you happy."

"Olga, no, for the love of God, no! Now that everything is clear, don't drive me away!" he said, clutching her hand.

"What do you want from me, you're full of doubts about whether my love for you is all a mistake and I can't reassure you; maybe you're right, maybe it's a mistake—I don't know."

He let go of her hand; again he felt the knife poised over him. "What do you mean, 'you don't know'? Surely you can feel it?" he asked, doubt beginning to etch itself on his face, "do you mean you suspect... ?"

"I don't suspect anything; I told you yesterday what I felt, but what I'll feel in a year's time—I just don't know. Is one happiness followed by a second and then a third—all just the same?" she asked, looking him full in the face. "You tell me, you have more experience!"

But he did not want to encourage that line of thought and he said nothing, shaking a branch of acacia with one hand. "No, you only fall in love once in your life," he said like a schoolboy reciting a lesson.

"You see! And I believe it too. But if it's not true, perhaps I'll fall out of love with you, perhaps I'll bitterly regret my mistake—and you will too—maybe we'll part...! Fall in love two, three times, no, I just won't believe it!"

He sighed. That "maybe" depressed him and he trudged moodily after her. But with every step he began to feel better; the "mistake" that had been haunting him the night before was something in the far distant future. "Yes, it's not just love, it's true of everything in life," it suddenly occurred to him, "and if you reject every opportunity as a potential mistake, well, then everything becomes a mistake. What was I thinking of? I must have been struck blind or something... "

"Olga!" he said, just grazing her waist with two fingers. She stopped. "You're cleverer than me."

She shook her head, "No, just simpler and bolder. What are you afraid of? Do you seriously think that one can fall out of love?" she asked with proud confidence.

"Now I'm not afraid any more!" he announced cheerfully. "With you, fate has no terrors for me."

"Now where have I read those word recently? Oh yes, it was in something by Sue I think," she retorted ironically, turning towards him, "only there it was a woman talking to a man."

Oblomov flushed. "Olga, let's go back to the way everything was yesterday!" he begged, "I won't be afraid of 'mistakes' ."

Olga said nothing.

"Yes?" he inquired timidly. "Well if you don't want to speak, give me a sign... like a sprig of lilac."

"The lilac has gone, it's disappeared," she answered, "look, see what's left, it's all faded."

"Yes, it's gone, it's faded," he repeated, looking at the lilac, "like the letter," he said suddenly.

She shook her head. He walked behind her, mulling over the letter, yesterday's happiness and the faded lilac. "It's true, lilac does fade," he thought. "Why all that business about the letter? Why did I stay up all night and write the letter in the morning. Now that I have my peace of mind again," he yawned, "I'm terribly sleepy. If it hadn't been for that letter none of this would have happened; she wouldn't have been crying and everything would have been the way it was yesterday. We would have been sitting quietly in this very spot on this very path, looking at one another and talking about happiness--and the same today and tomorrow..." He opened his mouth as wide as it would go and yawned. Then the thought hit him; what if the letter had had the effect intended, if she had accepted his reasoning and had been frightened, like himself, by the thought of mistakes and the storms that might lay in store some time in the distant future, if she had trusted his supposed experience and good sense and had agreed to part and forget one another?

"God help me! Imagine saying goodbye, going back to town, moving to the new apartment. A long, endless night, followed by a dreary day, followed by another unendurable day and and endless succession of days, each one bleaker than the day before... Impossible, it would be a living death!" But that's the way it would have been; his health would have suffered. He did not even want to part from Olga, he could not have borne a separation; he would have come begging to see her. "Why did I ever write that letter?" he asked himself.

"Olga Sergeyevna!" he said.

"What is it?"

"There's something I have to add to my confessions."

"What?"

"That letter was entirely uncalled for... "

"On the contrary, it was necessary," she asserted.

She looked back and smiled when she saw the face he was making and how the sleep had gone from his eyes and how his eyes had widened in astonishment.

" Necessary?" he repeated slowly, his astonished eyes boring into her back. But all he could see there were the two tassels of her mantilla. "What was the meaning of those tears, those reproaches? Was she using her womanly wiles?" No, Olga was not that kind of person, he saw that clearly.

It is only women of somewhat limited intellect who resort to guile and live by it. It is because of these intellectual limitations that they feel it necessary to use guile and cunning to manipulate the minutiae of every day life and to weave the tissue of their household politics and they fail to register the broader patterns of life and notice what direction and shape they take.

When all is said and done guile, wiliness are just small change and do not buy you much. Just as small change will tide you over for an hour or two, so guile will help you here and there to hide something or in some petty deception or evasion. It does nothing to help you take the long view or to carry through any major, large-scale undertaking. Guile is shortsighted; it sees clearly what is under its nose but cannot see distant objects and for this reason often falls into the very traps it has set for others.

Olga was simply intelligent and the way she had so easily and decisively disposed of the immediate problem was the same way she disposed of all problems. She would immediately grasp the salient features of any situation and approach it by the shortest and straightest route. Guile is like a mouse; it scuttles around your feet and vanishes; but in any case this was not Olga's nature. So, what was it all about? What was the new twist?

"But why did you say the letter was necessary?" he asked.

"Why?" she repeated, turning to face him cheerfully, relishing her ability to keep him guessing at every turn. "Because," she began with great deliberation, "you were awake all night and wrote that whole letter for me; I'm selfish too! That's number one..."

"But why all those recriminations just before if you're agreeing with me now?" Oblomov cut in.

"Because you dreamed up all these sufferings of yours but I didn't have to imagine mine, I actually experienced them and now I'm relishing the fact that they're over. You, on the other hand, invented your own sufferings and enjoyed anticipating them. You're wicked and that's what I blamed you for. Also... your letter reflects thought and feeling... you spent the night and morning in a way that was quite untypical of you, the way that your friend and I wanted to see you living—that's number two, and thirdly..."

She moved so close to him that the blood rushed to his heart and his head and the surge of emotion made it difficult for him to breathe. She was looking him straight in the eye.

"Thirdly, because your letter reflects as clearly as a mirror your tenderness, your caution and your concern for me, your fears for my happiness, your clear conscience...all those things about you that Andrei Ivanich had reported to me and which appealed to me so much that I was prepared to overlook your laziness...your apathy. In your letter you couldn't help revealing yourself; you're not selfish, Ilya Ilyich, you didn't write what you did because you wanted to give me up—no, that wasn't what you wanted—but because you were afraid of misleading me...it was your honesty that was speaking, otherwise I would have been offended instead of bursting into tears the way I did—out of wounded pride. You see, I know why I love you and I'm not afraid of mistakes because I'm not mistaken in you."

As she spoke she seemed to be enveloped in a brilliant radiance. Her eyes were ablaze with the triumph of love, the awareness of her power; two bright pink spots reddened her cheeks—and he, he was the reason for it! It was the honorable promptings of his guileless heart that had infused her with this fire, this verve, this sparkle!

"Olga…you are the best, you are the queen among women!" he exclaimed ecstatically and, without thinking, spread his hands and bowed to her. "For the love of God, just one kiss as a token of inexpressible happiness," he whispered deliriously.

She recoiled for an instant; the triumphant radiance and the color disappeared from her cheeks and her gentle eyes glittered with menace.

"Never, never! Don't come any closer!" she exclaimed in fear, almost in horror, holding out the parasol in front of her with both hands as a barrier between them. She stood at an angle to him, rooted to the spot as if transfixed, unbreathing and with a threatening look.

He was cowed instantly; this was not the meek and mild Olga standing before him but an angry goddess, tight-lipped and eyes ablaze, whose dignity had been affronted.

"I'm sorry," he said, chastened and destroyed.

She turned slowly and left, glancing nervously at him over her shoulder to check, but he was just moving slowly away like a dog which has been stepped on, dragging his tail between his legs.

She was beginning to move at a brisker pace when, catching sight of his face, she slowed down, suppressing a smile. She was walking at a more measured pace now, only quivering slightly from time to time. The pink spots reappeared, first on one cheek and then on the other. As she walked on her face began to clear and her breathing became calmer and more regular and she resumed her even pace. She saw that for Oblomov her "never" was something sacrosanct and her initial outburst of anger began to abate, giving way to regret. Her pace grew slower and slower. She wanted to soften the effect of her outburst and searched for an excuse to say something.

"I've ruined everything, that was a real blunder! 'Never', my God! The lilac has faded," he thought, looking at the lilac hanging from the boughs, "now yesterday has faded and so has the letter along with the best moment of my whole life, the moment when a woman, like a voice from heaven, told me what good I have in me—now that moment is like a sprig of withered lilac."

He looked at Olga—she was standing and waiting, her eyes lowered.

"Give me the letter!" she said softly.

"It's withered, dead!" he replied bleakly as he handed it to her.

She moved close to him again with her head still lowered and her eyes practically closed. She was beginning to tremble. After he had handed her the letter she remained motionless, her head still lowered.

"You gave me a fright," she said softly,

"I'm sorry, Olga," he mumbled.

She said nothing.

"That terrible 'never'!" he said gloomily and sighed.

"That will fade too!" she whispered barely audibly and blushed. She gave him a bashful, tender look, took both his hands and grasping them firmly placed them against her heart. "You hear how it's beating!" she said, "you frightened me! Let me go!"

Without looking at him she turned and ran along the path, lifting the front of her dress to clear the ground.

"What's the hurry?" he called after her, "I'm tired, I can't keep up with you..."

"Leave me alone, I'm rushing off to sing, to sing, to sing...! she proclaimed, her face burning, "there's such a tightness in my chest, it's almost painful!"

He stood there for a long time watching her recede into the distance like an angel taking flight. "Can it be that even this moment will fade?" was his melancholy thought as he stood there, not knowing whether he was moving or standing still. "The lilac has gone, so has yesterday and last night with its ghosts and oppressiveness... yes, even this moment is sure to pass and wither like the lilac! But at the very time that last night was ending today was dawning..."

"I don't know what to make of it all," he said—he was speaking aloud without realizing it—"and what about love... love too? I always thought that love was like the midday sun, hovering eternally over the heads of lovers without anything ever moving or breathing within its range; but even love is never fully at rest, it is always moving onward, pressing forward in some direction or other 'like everything else in life' as Stoltz says; and the Joshua has yet to be born who could command it to stand still and not move."

"What will tomorrow bring?" he asked himself anxiously as he walked slowly homewards deep in thought.

As he passed Olga's windows he heard her relieving the tightness in her breast by singing Schubert; it was as if she was sobbing with happiness.

"My God, how wonderful it is to be alive!"

CHAPTER ELEVEN

At home Oblomov found another letter from Stoltz beginning and ending with the words, "now or never!" It was full of reproaches for Oblomov's total inaction and urged him to be sure to proceed at once to Switzerland where Stoltz himself was headed before going on to Italy. Failing that, he reminded Oblomov of the need for him to go down to his estate, take matters in hand, jerk the peasants out of the indolent, slack and inefficient ways into which they had fallen, check the books and work out the amount of the income and personally supervise the building of a new house. The letter ended with the words: "remember our agreement: 'now or never'!"

"Now, now, now!" Oblomov repeated, "Andrei doesn't know what a romantic drama my life has become. What more does he expect me to take on? How could I possibly be any busier than I am right now? I'd like to see him try! You read about the French or the English and how they supposedly do nothing but work, and that's all they have on their minds! Actually, they just take off when they feel like it and travel all over Europe; some even go to Asia or Africa for no particular reason except to sketch or dig for archaeological finds, shoot lions or catch snakes; either that or they just stay at home, enjoying a dignified leisure, lunching and dining with their friends and womenfolk—work of any kind couldn't be further from their minds! It's not as if I'm a convict who's been sentenced to hard labour! All that Andrei can think of is: 'work, work, work like a horse'! What for? I have food on my table, clothes on my back. But Olga has been asking again whether I intend to go to Oblomovka…"

He got down to the task of writing and planning and even went to see an architect and very soon plans for the house and garden lay on his desk, a nice, spacious family house with two balconies.

"This will be Olga's room, this will be mine, here's the bedroom, the nursery," he smiled as he contemplated the pleasurable prospect. Then his brow darkened and his smile faded, "But the peasants, the peasants. My neighbor goes into all sorts of details in his letter, ploughing, the grain yield, God, what a bore! He's even proposing to extend the road to the next big market town and to put up a bridge over the river at our joint expense. He's asking for three thousand roubles and wants me to mortgage Oblomovka. How am I supposed to know whether to do it, whether it makes sense? Maybe he's trying to put one over on me? Well, he is probably an honest man, after all Stoltz knows him—although, of course, even he might be misjudging him—and anyway I'm the one who will be throwing away the money. And where am I going to get a vast sum like three thousand roubles? No, it's too much for me! Then he also wants me to resettle some of the peasants on wasteland and demands a reply as soon as possible—everything 'as soon as possible'! He's willing to do all the paper work for the court for mortgaging the estate. All I have to do is to give him the power of attorney and go to the court to certify the document—what will he want next? I don't even know what a courthouse looks like, let alone which door to go in!"

So another week went by without a reply from Oblomov and even Olga was asking him if he had been to the courthouse. They had both received an earlier letter from Stoltz asking what Oblomov was doing.

As it was, Olga could not keep a very close watch on Oblomov's activities and only then in areas accessible to her. Was he looking cheerful, was he willing and eager to go on trips, did he turn up at the right time when they arranged to meet in the woods, did he maintain an interest in what was going on around town and hold his own in conversation? What she watched for most anxiously were signs of whether he was losing sight of life's main goal. If she did happen to ask him about the court proceedings it was only to have something with which to respond to Stoltz's enquiries about his friend's affairs.

The summer was at its height; July was passing; the weather was perfect. Oblomov practically never left Olga's side. In the heat of the day he would meet her in the park and they would disappear into the grove, and there among the pines he would sit at her feet and read to her while she worked away at a piece of embroidery—for him. They basked in the heat of high summer under a perfectly clear, blue sky, marred only by the occasional cloud that soon passed.

If he ever did have any bad dreams or gnawing doubts Olga was always standing guard like an angel of mercy, her bright eyes watching him as she extracted from him everything that was on his mind, and peace of mind was once again restored and feelings flowed smoothly and placidly once again like a river reflecting the ever-changing patterns of the skies above.

Olga's view of life, love and everything else grew ever more distinct and clear-cut. Undaunted by the future, she now regarded the world around her with greater confidence; both her mind and her character had developed in new ways. She displayed a wider and more varied range of mood and temperament and revealed greater depths, and all this evolved in a normal, natural, gradual and spontaneous manner. She possessed a certain quality of determination powerful enough to overcome any trouble or adversity and even Oblomov's apathy and laziness. Whenever she set her mind on something, action would follow, fast and furious, and that was all you would hear about; and even if you did not hear about it you could not miss her single-mindedness and determination as well as the concentration and unflagging efficiency with which she set about achieving the goal she had set herself.

Oblomov could not understand where this strength, this flair came from, how she know exactly what she wanted and precisely how to achieve it no matter what the circumstances. "It must be," he thought, "because one of her eyebrows was never level with the other but always cocked, with a very fine, barely perceptible fold or crease just above it... Yes, it was there, in that crease that her stubbornness resided." No matter how calm and serene the expression on her face, that crease was never smoothed away and the eyebrow was always cocked. But Olga showed no outward sign of forcefulness and her manner was free of any trace of sharp edges. Her purposefulness and strength of will did not for a moment cause her to stray outside the realm of the feminine; she had no wish to play the dragon, to discomfit a hapless admirer with the sharp edge of her tongue, to astound the company with the readiness of her wit or to elicit cries of admiration from her audience. There was even a timidity about her which is characteristic of so many women; she did not, it is true, tremble at the sight of a mouse, did not faint if a chair fell over but she did not like to stray far from home and would change direction if she saw a peasant who struck her as suspicious; she would also close her window at night in case of burglars—all very womanly.

She was very tenderhearted and easily moved to pity. Tears came easily to her and her feelings were easily affected. In love she was tenderness itself and in all her relationships she was gentle and affectionate to a fault—in a word, a real woman! In her conversation there were occasional flashes of sarcasm but delivered with such grace and so devoid of spite or malice that they were always taken smilingly and in good part.

On the other hand, she had no fear of drafts and would think nothing of going out of doors at dusk without any extra clothing. Everything about her smacked of good health—including her appetite; she had her favorite dishes and knew how to prepare them.

The same can be said, of course, about many people, but not many know what to do in a given situation, or if they do it is because they have been taught what to do or have heard it from others, but they could not tell you why they choose to do this rather than that except by appealing to the authority of an aunt or cousin. Many people do not even really know what it is they want, and if they do finally decide in favor of something they do so without conviction in a spirit of "maybe, maybe not" and the reason for this is probably that their eyebrows form perfectly symmetrical, carefully plucked curves and that little fold or crease is missing.

The relationship that had formed between Oblomov and Olga was invisible to and hidden from outsiders, every glance, every word, however trivial, uttered in their presence had a special significance for themselves. They saw in everything some secret intimation of or allusion to their love. Olga, with all her self-possession, would sometimes allow herself to be provoked when the dinner table conversation turned to some love affair or other reminiscent of her own situation; and since all love affairs have a lot in common she often found herself blushing. As for Oblomov, whenever the subject came up at the tea table he would grab such a huge pile of biscuits in his embarrassment that someone would always burst out laughing.

They became very sensitive and cautious. Sometimes Olga would not mention to her aunt that she had seen Oblomov, and when Oblomov was about to go out he would announce that he was going into town when he was actually going to the park. However, for all Olga's lucidity, awareness of what was happening around her and robust good health she began to develop new, disturbing symptoms. At times she found herself in the grip of an anxiety that she could not for the life of her explain. Sometimes walking arm in arm with Oblomov in the heat of the day she would allow her head to slump on his shoulder and, locked in silence, drag herself along in a kind of exhaustion. Her cheerfulness had disappeared, the life had gone from her eyes which had become listless and immobile, focusing unseeingly on some point in the distance as if it were too much of an effort to look at anything in particular. There was a weight on her mind, a feeling of constriction in her heart, she felt a nameless anxiety. She would take off her mantilla, remove her scarf from her shoulders—but nothing helped, the same constriction, the same pressure remained. She felt like lying down under a tree and staying there for hours without moving.

Oblomov was at a loss; he tried fanning her face with the leaves of a branch but she just dismissed his attentions with a gesture of impatience, her anguish unabated. Then suddenly she would give a sigh and look around her with restored consciousness; her gaze would fall on Oblomov and she would press his hand and smile and once again it was gaiety, laughter and she was back in control.

There was one evening in particular when she lapsed into this alarming state, a kind of love-induced trance, and was revealed to Oblomov in an entirely new light. It was hot and stifling, a warm wind from the woods stirred the air and heavy clouds were massing in the sky; it grew darker and darker. "It's going to rain," said the baron and left for home. The aunt went to her room. Olga sat at the piano for a long time, playing in a reverie and finally stopped.

"I can't play, " she said to Oblomov, "my fingers are trembling and I feel as if I'm stifling. Let's take a walk in the garden!" For a long time they walked in silence and hand in hand. Their hands were soft and clammy. They entered the park. The trees and bushes merged into a dark, indistinguishable mass, they could not see more than two paces ahead and could just make out the whitish strip of sandy pathway snaking ahead. Olga peered intently into the gloom and pressed closer to Oblomov. They wandered in silence.

"I'm frightened!" she said suddenly with a shudder as they groped their way blindly along the narrow path lined on both sides with dark, impenetrable walls of trees.

"What of?" he asked. "Don't be afraid, Olga, I'm here with you."

"I'm frightened of you too!" she whispered, "but it's a strangely pleasurable feeling! My heart is thumping. Here, give me your hand, now feel how it's beating!" She shuddered and looked around her. "Look, look!" she whispered, trembling and gripping his shoulder firmly with both hands, "can't you see, someone's moving there in the dark!"

She pressed even more closely to him.

"There's nobody there," he said, but he felt his flesh creeping.

"Quick, put your hand around my eyes—tighter!" she whispered. "Yes, that's better; It's just nerves..." she added anxiously, "look, there it is again...who is it? Let's find a bench and sit down!"

He groped around for a bench and helped her to sit down. "Olga, let's go back!" he urged, "you're not well!" She laid her head on his shoulder.

"No, the air is fresher here," she said, "I feel a tightness here around the heart." Her breath was hot on his cheek. He brought up his hand to feel her head and that was hot too. Her breast was heaving and she was breathing heavily, sighing frequently for relief.

"Wouldn't you feel better at home?" Oblomov persisted worriedly, "You should lie down…"

"No, no, leave me alone, don't touch me…!" she said faintly, almost inaudibly, "I'm burning here," she pointed to her breast.

"Really, let's go home," Oblomov broke in hurriedly.

"No, just wait a little and it will pass…" She squeezed his hand and from time to time gazed right into his eyes, saying nothing. Finally, she burst into tears, quietly at first, but was soon sobbing her heart out. Oblomov was frantic.

"Olga, for the love of God, we must get you home as soon as possible!" he urged her desperately.

"Never mind!" she sobbed, "forget about it, just let me have my cry, my tears will quench the fire and I'll feel better, it's just my nerves playing up."

He sat there in the dark, listening to her heavy breathing and felt her scalding tears dripping on to his hand as she clutched it convulsively. He sat motionless, hardly daring to breathe. Her head lay on his shoulder; her breath was hot on his cheek. He too was trembling but did not dare to graze her cheek with his lips. Gradually she grew quieter and her breathing became more regular. She became so still that he wondered whether she had fallen asleep and he was frightened to stir.

"Olga!" he called in a whisper.

"What is it?" she whispered back and sighed aloud. "There, it's over," she said wearily, "I'm better now—I'm breathing more easily."

"Let's go!" he said.

"Alright," she agreed reluctantly and then whispered blissfully, "darling!" squeezed his hand and, resting her head on his shoulder, set off for home still unsteady on her legs. In the hallway he took a look at her; she was still weak but there was a strange unconscious, dreamy smile on her face. He sat her on the divan, knelt beside her and kept on kissing her hand, moved by a profound tenderness. She let her hands hang loose and with the same smile watched him move towards the door. At the door he turned back; her eyes were still on him and her features still betrayed the same exhaustion but bore the same radiant smile over which she seemed to have no control.

He walked home deep in thought, "Where," he wondered, "had he seen that smile before?" He was reminded of some painting depicting a woman with that same smile…only it wasn't Cordelia…

The next day he sent someone to find out how she was. The message came back: "Thank God! Today she is asking for food and in the evening she wants to see the fireworks five versts away." He could not believe what he had heard and hurried over to see for himself. Olga was as fresh as a daisy, her eyes sparkling with vivacity, her cheeks flushed and her voice as resonant as ever! When she saw Oblomov approaching she was taken aback and almost cried out, answering in a flurry when Oblomov asked how she was feeling after yesterday: "Oh, it was just a little attack of nerves, *ma tante* says I should go to bed earlier. It's something quite recent that..." She stopped in mid-sentence and turned away as if pleading for mercy. As to why she was feeling such consternation—she simply had no idea. Why was it that the memory of the previous evening, of her attack of nerves, still nagged and smarted?

She felt a mixture of embarrassment about something and resentment at someone—Oblomov, herself, or maybe both. At other times she felt that he had become closer, dearer to her, a closeness that moved her to tears as if, since the evening before, she now shared a mysterious kinship with him. It took her a long time to fall asleep and in the morning she walked endlessly and restlessly back and forth between the house and the park, the same questions churning over and over in her mind. She frowned, flushed and smiled by turns but could find no answers. "Oh, Sonechka!" she thought in her exasperation, "how lucky you are, you would surely have thought it through by now!"

But what about Oblomov? How could he have been so mute and passive with her yesterday, in spite of her hot breath on his cheek, her tears scalding his hand and in spite of his practically carrying her home wrapped in his arms and hearing the indiscreet murmuring of her heart...while someone else in his place, well, other men would have had a bold and insolent look on their faces.

Although Oblomov had spent his youth among companions who knew everything, who had long since discovered the answers to all of life's questions, who believed in nothing and analyzed everything coldly and logically, he still nursed a faith in friendship, in love and honorable behavior, and no matter how often or how badly he had been mistaken in people or would be in the future and in spite of all the heartbreak he would suffer, he never wavered for a moment in his principles and belief in the good. Privately he venerated the purity of womanhood and acknowledged a woman's power and rights and he made sacrifices on the altar of this purity.

He did not, however, have the strength of character to acknowledge publicly his commitment to the doctrine of the good and his respect for innocence. Privately, the very aroma of innocence had a powerful effect on him, but outwardly he would often join the chorus of cynics who shuddered at the very thought that they might be suspected of chastity or respect for it and he would add his own flippant contributions to the raucous and boisterous hubbub. He never fully realized the weight and impact of words like "good," "truth," and "purity" when tossed into the current of human speech or what a deep channel they cut; it never occurred to him that these words, uttered loudly, squarely and without any tinge of false embarrassment but boldly and unabashedly, do not just disappear without trace amidst the cacophony of libertines but sink deeply like pearls into the silt of social intercourse and always end up finding a home in an oyster shell.

Many people hesitate to put in a good word for the good and redden with embarrassment at the thought, but think nothing of throwing in some casual, flippant remark, little suspecting that, unfortunately, such remarks, too, do not just disappear into thin air but leave behind their own long-lived, sometimes indelible trace of evil.

In terms of actual behavior Oblomov had absolutely nothing to reproach himself for, his conscience was clear and free from any blemish or hint of that cold, bloodless cynicism which is a stranger to strength of feeling and pangs of conscience alike. He could not stand casual talk of changing horses, furniture…or women; not to mention the costs entailed by such changes! How often he had grieved for a man's loss of his dignity and honor and wept for the disgrace and besmirched reputation of a woman who was a perfect stranger to him, but he kept his mouth shut for fear of what people would think. His true feelings could only be guessed at—and Olga had guessed.

To men such eccentrics are figures of fun, but women recognize them right away; pure chaste women love them—out of fellow feeling; women who have been corrupted try to get close to them—it makes them feel cleansed of the pollution.

The summer wore on and was drawing to a close. The mornings and evenings were getting darker and wetter. Not only the lilac bushes but even the lime trees had shed their blossoms and the last of the berries had gone. Oblomov and Olga met every day.

He was catching up on life—that is, he was once again keeping up with everything he had previously let go. He knew why the French Ambassador had left Rome, why the British were sending gunboats to the East, he took an interest in when a new road was to be built in Germany or France, but when it came to the road through Oblomovka to the market town he did not give the matter a thought; he did not swear out a power of attorney at the courthouse or send Stoltz a reply to his letter.

He limited the information he acquired to those topics which were likely to arise in the course of conversation in Olga's household and which were covered by the newspapers they took; he also applied himself to the task of keeping abreast of foreign literature with some diligence because of Olga's insistence. Outside of this, it was love itself that was the all-absorbing interest.

Although there were frequent variations in this rosy atmosphere, the one stable element was the cloudlessness of the horizon. Whenever Olga found herself meditating on Oblomov and her love for him, if that love ever left her an idle moment or a moment's respite, if her questions did not always receive a prompt and adequate response from him and her insistence was met by his silence; if ever her gaiety and liveliness provoked nothing more in him than a fervent but passive facial expression, she would fall into a depression and start to brood; something cold and snake-like would slither into her heart and jerk her back to sober reality and the fairy-tale world of love would be transformed into an autumn day when all objects appear in a dismal, gray light. She tried to trace the source of this feeling that her happiness was incomplete, that something was missing, a nagging dissatisfaction. What was it that was lacking? What more did she need? Surely it was her destiny, the bidding of fate, to love Oblomov? And her love was warranted by his meekness, his unsullied belief in the good and above all by his tenderness, a tenderness she had never seen in the eyes of other men. And what of it if he did not respond to her every glance with a look of understanding or if, at times, she failed to detect in his voice that sound which she seemed to remember once hearing in her dreams and fantasies—it was just her imagination, a case of nerves—why waste time listening to them and trying to interpret them.

And in any case, even if she did want to walk away from this love, how could she do it? The die was cast; her love was a fact and could not simply be cast off just like that, like an article of clothing. "One cannot love more than once in a lifetime," she thought, "that would be wrong, so people say." She was a student in the school of love, learning from each new lesson, meeting each new step with tears or smiles and applying herself in earnest to her studies. Later she began to wear that intense expression that masked her tears and smiles and which so alarmed Oblomov. However, she did not give Oblomov the slightest hint of any such soul-searching or conflict.

Oblomov was no student of love; he existed in the state of blissful somnolence, which he had once imagined aloud to Stoltz. At times he began to believe in the possibility of a life with never a cloud on the horizon and his old dream of Oblomovka returned, an Oblomovka peopled with benign, friendly and carefree faces, the lounging on the terrace, the contemplation of utter contentment.

Even now he sometimes succumbed to the mood of blissful contemplation and once or twice when Olga's back was turned actually dozed off in the woods when she was due any minute . . . then suddenly, unexpectedly a dark cloud appeared in the sky. The two of them were strolling silently back from somewhere and were just about to cross the main road when they were met by a cloud of dust stirred up by a carriage speeding by—in it were Sonechka, her husband, and another couple.

"Olga, Olga! Olga Sergeyevna!" they called. The carriage halted and all the ladies and gentlemen alighted and surrounded Olga, greeting her, kissing her, and all talking at once. It was a long time before anyone noticed Oblomov and then everyone turned to look at him and one of the gentlemen inspected him through his lorgnette. "Who is this?" Sonechka asked quietly. Olga introduced him: "Ilya Ilyich Oblomov." They all walked back to the house. Oblomov felt out of place and lagged behind and inserted a foot in the fence in an attempt to slip through it and sneak off home through the field of rye, but Olga stopped him with a glance. It would not have mattered except that all these ladies and gentlemen were giving him such strange looks; but even that might not have mattered, for in the past people always used to look at him like that because of his sleepy, apathetic expression and the sloppiness of his appearance. No,

what he found so chilling was that these ladies and gentlemen kept transferring the strange look from himself to Olga and that was what began to
gnaw at him and torment him—so painfully and unbearably that he left
and went home, brooding and despondent.

The next day, even Olga's playful and affectionate chatter could not
charm him out of his mood. His only response to her persistent questioning was to pretend he had a headache and patiently allowed seventy-five
kopecks worth of eau-de-cologne to be dabbed on his head. The day after
that they had returned home late. Olga's aunt gave them—and especially
him—a particularly knowing look and then lowered her large, slightly
swollen eyelids, but still contrived to continue looking through them and
sniffed her smelling salts thoughtfully for a moment. Oblomov was
squirming but kept quiet. He could not bring himself to confide his
doubts to Olga for fear of upsetting or frightening her and, if the truth be
told, for his own sake, for fear of disrupting the serene, cloudless tranquility of his life with such a profoundly unsettling question—a question no
longer merely of whether Olga had fallen in love with him, Oblomov, by
mistake, but whether their whole love affair, with its hole-and-corner
meetings in the woods, alone and often late in the evening, was itself a
mistake. When he thought how close he had come to kissing her he was
horrified—that was, after all, a criminal breach of the code of morality
and by no means the least or the mildest! There were all the steps leading
up to it, the pressing of hands, the declarations of love, the letter—they
had gone through all these stages. "But then," he thought, raising his sagging head, "my intentions are perfectly honorable, I..."

And at that moment the dark cloud disappeared from the horizon,
revealing Oblomovka, bright, shining and festive, glittering under the
sun's rays, its hills green and the stream flowing like silver. He was strolling
with Olga up that long avenue, his arm around her waist; they were sitting in the summer house on the terrace...Everyone is overawed by her
presence—just as he had reported to Stoltz.

"Exactly! And that's the way I should have begun!" Again he was horrified by the thought. The 'I love you' repeated three times, the sprig of
lilac, the confession—all that should be a lifelong gage of happiness not
to be repeated for a chaste and honorable woman. "Who am I? What am
I? What was I thinking of?" The question hammered away at him. "Some
kind of a seducer, a rake? The next thing you know, like that disgusting
old roué with his lecherous eyes and red nose, I'll be sporting in my but-
tonhole the rose I've filched from some woman and whispering to my
cronies about my latest conquest so that...so that...My God, how low I've
sunk! Yes, this is the abyss and I've dragged Olga down to the bottom of
it with me when she should be soaring way above it...why, oh why?"

He broke down and wept like a child because the rainbow of his life had
suddenly been drained of its bright colors and because it would be Olga who
would be the victim. All this love of his was a crime, a stain on his con-

science. And then for a moment his distress vanished and everything became clear when it occurred to him that there was a perfectly legitimate and honorable solution to the whole problem—to offer Olga his hand in marriage.

"Yes, yes!" he said in his excitement, "and she will respond with a bashful look of consent. She will not utter a word, but her elation will be obvious and a smile will well up from the depths of her being and then her eyes will brim with tears." Tears, a smile, the hand wordlessly extended, followed by a bubbling over of joyfulness and a ferment of excitement succeeded in turn by a long, long, intimate, whispered conversation between themselves, the murmured mutual commitment of two souls sealing a pact to merge two lives into one. Their most casual words and gestures, their everyday banalities would be charged with a love unseen to any but themselves and no one would dare to cast a contemptuous look...

Suddenly his face assumed a stern, solemn expression: "Yes," he said to himself, "that's where the world of straightforward, honorable and lasting happiness lies! I should be ashamed of the way I've been hiding these flowers, drifting along in the aroma of love and, like a boy, making assignations, walking in the moonlight, eavesdropping on the beating of a young, innocent girl's heart, catching the vibrations of her dreams—my God!" He blushed to the roots of his hair. "Olga will learn this very evening what strict obligations love imposes; today will be our last meeting alone, today..." He put his hand on his heart; it was beating fast but regularly, the way a heart is supposed to beat in an honorable breast. Again he was excited by the thought of how downcast Olga would be when she heard him say that they must stop seeing one another and how he would then timidly declare his intentions, but only after worming out of her the way she was thinking and thrilling to her confusion and then...

He went on to imagine her bashful consent, her smile, her tears as she wordlessly extended her hand and then that long, intimate, whispered conversation and the kiss in full view of everyone.

CHAPTER TWELVE

He ran to look for Olga. At the house they told him that she had gone out. He went straight to the village—no Olga! In the distance he spotted her walking up the hill like an angel ascending to heaven, her feet barely touching the ground, her body swaying. He started after her but she seemed to be barely skimming the grass, almost as if she were gliding. As he toiled after her up the hill he began to call her. She would stop to wait for him, but as soon as he drew to within a few yards of her she would move off again until she was way ahead of him and then she would stop, turn and start laughing. Finally, when he was certain that she would not go any further he stopped altogether and she ran towards him, took him by the hand and, still laughing, dragged him on after her. They entered the thicket; he took off his hat and she mopped his brow with her kerchief and started to wave her parasol in his face.

Olga was full of life, talkative and playful, or perhaps just yielding to an affectionate impulse, but then she lapsed into a mood of quiet reflection.

"Guess what I was doing yesterday?" she asked when they were seated in the shade.

"Reading?" She shook her head. "Writing?" "No." "Singing?"

"No, having my fortune told!" she said. "The countess's housekeeper came around yesterday evening—she can read cards and I asked her to tell my fortune."

"And?"

"Nothing much. She saw a road and a crowd of people and a man with blond hair who kept appearing, and I blushed all over when she suddenly said, while Katya was listening, that the king of diamonds was thinking of me. She was just about to say who I was thinking of when I mixed up all the cards and ran away. Do you think of me?" she asked suddenly.

"Think of you?' he said, "if only I could do less of it!"

"And what about me?" she said earnestly, "I can't even remember what life was like before! When you were sulking last week and stayed away two days in a row—do you remember—you were angry with me. I became a different person and turned nasty. I took it out on Katya—the way you do with Zakhar. I could see she was crying but I couldn't have cared less. I didn't answer *ma tante*, didn't pay attention to what she said, didn't do a thing and didn't want to go anywhere. But as soon as you came I became my old self again—I even gave Katya my mauve dress..."

"That's love!" he asserted with feeling.

"What, a mauve dress?"

"No, everything! I recognize myself in what you've been saying. For me too, without you there is no day, no life; at night I dream of nothing but valleys in bloom. When I'm with you I'm good-natured and active, without you I'm bored and listless, I just want to lie down and think of nothing... .the thing is to let yourself love boldly and fearlessly..." Suddenly he fell silent. "What am I saying, this is not what I came for!" he thought and began to clear his throat and furrow his brow.

"But what if I were to die?" she asked.

"What a thought!" he said dismissively.

"Yes," she persisted, "say I were to catch cold, run a fever; you come but I'm not here. You run to the house and they tell you I'm ill. The next day it's the same, my shutters are closed, the doctor is shaking his head, Katya comes tip-toeing out in tears and whispers, 'she's ill, she's dying...'"

"No!" Oblomov exclaimed. She laughed.

"What would happen to you then?" she asked, looking him in the face.

"What would happen? I'd go out of my mind, I'd shoot myself—and then you would suddenly recover!"

"No, stop it!" she said apprehensively, "look what we've ended up talking about! Just make sure you never come here dead, I'm afraid of the dead..." They both broke into laughter.

"My God, what children we are!" she said, serious again after all the prattle.

He cleared his throat again: "Listen, there's something I wanted to say..."

"What is it?" she asked, turning to him with interest.

He maintained a nervous silence.

"Out with it then!" she said, plucking his sleeve.

"Well, nothing really..." he stammered, losing his nerve.

"Are you sure? You obviously have something on your mind."

He remained silent.

"If it's something terrible, better not to say it!" she said, but immediately added: "No, say it!"

"No, it's really nothing, just a lot of nonsense!"

"No, no, there's something, tell me!" she insisted, grasping him firmly by the lapels and holding him so close that he was forced to swivel his face from side to side to avoid kissing her, although he only took this evasive action because her ominous "never!" was still ringing in his ears.

"Out with it now!" she pressed him.

"I can't, I really shouldn't..." he protested.

"Maybe you've forgotten your sermon about 'trust is the foundation of all happiness', and 'there must be no nook or cranny in the heart hidden from the eye of a friend', whose words were they?"

"All I meant was that I love you so much," he began slowly, "so much that if..." he tapered off.

"Well!" she said impatiently.

"...if you fell in love with someone else and it was someone who could make you happier....I would swallow my grief and yield to him."

She suddenly let go of his lapels. "But why?" she was surprised, "I don't understand that. I wouldn't give you up to anyone, I wouldn't want you to be happy with someone else—that 's too deep for me, I just don't understand it." She looked around at the trees for a moment as she thought. "In other words, you don't love me?" she asked finally.

"No, just the opposite, I love you so selflessly that I'm ready to sacrifice myself."

"But why, who's asking you to?"

"I'm just saying if you were to fall in love with someone else."

"Someone else! You must be crazy! Why would I if I love *you*? Would you fall in love with someone else?"

"I don't know why you're listening to me, I don't even know what I'm saying and here you are taking me seriously! This isn't what I wanted to say at all..."

"Well, what *did* you want to say?"

"I wanted to say that I've wronged you and I should have confessed it long ago..."

"What do you mean? How? You mean you don't love me? Maybe you've just been pretending, tell me right now!"

"No, no, it's not that at all!" he said in despair. "Look," he said hesitantly, we've been seeing one another... well, discreetly..."

"Discreetly? Why do you say 'discreetly'? Almost every time I've seen you I've told *ma tante*."

"Every time, really?" he said with alarm.

"What's wrong with that?"

"I'm really sorry, I should have told you long ago that it...it isn't done."

"You did," she said.

"I did? Well, I suppose I did hint at it, in that case I've done my duty." He cheered up at the thought that Olga had so easily lifted the burden of guilt from his shoulders.

"What else?" she asked.

"What else? Well, nothing really."

"That's not true," Olga asserted confidently, "you're keeping something from me."

"Well, I did think, "he began, trying to sound casual, that..." He broke off and she waited, "...that we shouldn't see one another so often." He gave her a nervous glance.

She thought for a moment before asking: "Why?"

"It's my conscience gnawing at me...We've been meeting alone for so long and it's worrying me, my heart sinks when I think of it; it's worrying you too..."

"I'm afraid..." he forced himself to add.

"What of?"

"You're young and you don't understand all the dangers, Olga. A man isn't always in control of himself, sometimes an evil force takes possession of him, darkness invades his heart, and his eyes flash with lightning. He stops thinking clearly and his respect for innocence, for chastity are swept away by a tornado; he forgets himself, he is in the grip of passion, he loses command of himself—that's when the abyss opens up under his feet!" He shuddered physically at the thought.

"What of it? What if it does open up?" she said, looking him full in the face.

He was silent; either there was nothing left to say or there was no need to say it. She scanned his face for some time as if trying to read the lines on his forehead like lines of print. She herself remembered his every word, every look and mentally reviewed the whole history of their love right up to that dark evening in the garden and found herself suddenly blushing.

"You're talking a lot of nonsense!" she blurted out, avoiding his glance. "I've never seen anything resembling lightning in your eyes; most of the time you look at me like...my nanny Kuzminichna!" she added and burst out laughing.

"Make fun of it if you like, Olga, but I'm serious—and I have more to say.

"And what's that," she asked, "about that abyss?"

He sighed. "It's about not going on seeing one another... alone."

"Why not?"

"It's not right..."

She thought for a moment. "Yes, people do say it's not right; I wonder why."

"What will people say when they find out, when it all comes out?"

"What people? I have no mother and she would be the only one who could ask me why I'm seeing you and only to her would I answer in tears that neither of us is doing anything wrong—and she would believe me. Who else is there?" she asked.

"Your aunt."

"My aunt?" Olga shook her head sadly. "She would never ask. Even if I went away for good she would never come to look for me or ask me anything—any more than I would come and tell her where I had been or what I had been doing. So who else?"

"Well, all the others...only the other day Sonechka was looking at you and then at me and smiling, and so were all those other ladies and gentlemen who were with her." He told her how worried he had been since then. "As long as she was only looking at me I wasn't bothered, but when she started giving you the same look I felt the blood running cold in my hands and feet..."

"And...?" she asked coldly.

"And...since then I haven't had a moment's peace, day or night. I've been racking my brains to think of a way of stopping the gossip; I didn't want to do anything to alarm you, but I've been wanting to say something to you for a long time..."

"Well, you've been worrying for nothing, I knew all about it anyway..."

"How could you have?" Oblomov was surprised.

"Sonechka talked to me and tried to worm it out of me; she was nasty and even tried to lecture me on how I should behave with you..."

"But you didn't breathe a word to me, Olga!" he said reproachfully.

"You didn't say anything to me either about what was worrying you."

"What did you say to her?" he asked.

"Nothing, what was there to say? I just blushed."

"My God, look what we've come to—you blushing!" he said, horrified, "We've been so reckless—God knows what will happen now!" He looked at her questioningly.

"Don't know," she said curtly.

Oblomov had thought that once he had shared his worries with Olga the flashing of her eyes and her crisp, clear response would dispel them but he was dismayed to find that this time there was no immediate and decisive response forthcoming. His face was the very picture of irresolution as his desolate glance traveled desperately around. His thoughts were in ferment; he had practically forgotten about Olga, he could see nothing but Sonechka, her husband and their guests milling around, chattering and laughing. Olga's normal resourcefulness had been replaced by silence; she simply regarded him coldly and had just as coldly uttered her "don't know," whose hidden meaning he was either unable or unwilling to penetrate.

He remained silent; it was like a ripe apple that could not fall from the tree of its own accord—someone had to pluck it; Oblomov simply could not formulate a thought or intention without being prompted.

Olga stood there watching him for several minutes then put on her mantilla, took her kerchief from the branch on which it had been hanging, tied it unhurriedly on her head and picked up her parasol.

"Are you leaving so soon?" he asked, suddenly snapping out of his trance.

"It's late. You were right," she said with quiet despondency, "we've gone too far and there's no way out except for us to part right away and wipe out all traces of the past. Goodbye!" she pronounced drily and bitterly and, lowering her head, started off along the path.

"Olga, please, come on now! Not see one another! Olga, I..."

She was not listening and quickened her pace, the sand crunching drily under her boots.

"Olga Sergeyevna!" he shouted. She continued on her way, unheeding.

"Come back for the love of God!" he pleaded in tears. "Even a criminal deserves a hearing...my God, doesn't she have a heart—that's a woman for you!" He sat down and buried his face in his hands; her footsteps could no longer be heard. "She's gone!" he said in dismay and raised his head. Olga was standing there in front of him. Overjoyed, he grasped her hand. "You didn't go, you're not going?" he said. "Don't go, remember, if you do I'm a dead man!"

"But if I don't, you and I are both criminals, remember that, Ilya!"

"No, no..."

"Of course we are! If Sonechka and her husband catch us together again, I'm finished!"

He shuddered. "Listen," he began hurriedly but with hesitation, "I didn't finish saying what I had to say..." He broke off. What had seemed so simple, natural and necessary at home, the prospect of his happiness, which had so warmed him, now yawned before him like a bottomless pit. The prospect of stepping over the edge took his breath away—a step that now loomed, bold and irretrievable.

"Someone's coming!" said Olga. Footsteps could be heard approaching.

"Can it be Sonechka?" Oblomov asked, his eyes frozen in horror. Two men and a lady passed by, strangers. A wave of relief swept over him. "Olga," he began hurriedly, taking her by the hand, "let's get away from here and sit over there on that empty bench where we can be by ourselves." He seated her on the bench and sat on the grass at her feet. "Olga, you lost patience and left before I'd finished what I wanted to say."

"And I'll leave again only this time for good if you go on toying with me. You enjoyed seeing me cry once before; perhaps you'd like to see me groveling at your feet and turn me little by little into your slave, at the mercy of your whims, first lecturing me and then bursting into tears, frightening yourself and me and then asking me what to do? Remember, Ilya Ilyich," she suddenly added with pride, getting to her feet, "I've grown up fast since the time I first met you and I know the name of the game you're playing—but you won't be seeing me cry again..."

"But, honestly, I'm not playing any game!" he said earnestly.

"So much the worse for you," she remarked drily, "to all your mis-givings, warnings and riddles I have just one thing to say. Until we met today I loved you and didn't know what to do about it; now I know!" she asserted confidently, getting ready to leave, "and I won't be asking your advice about it!"

"I know too," he said, without letting go of her hand and steering her back onto the bench. He was silent for a moment, trying to pluck up his courage. "Try to understand," he said, "there is only one wish in my heart and one thought in my head, but my will, my tongue won't obey; I try to speak but the words stick in my throat... and yet it's all so simple, so... help me Olga!"

"I don't know what's in your mind, Monsieur Oblomov..."

"Please, Olga, why are you suddenly so formal? You're killing me with that proud look, those chilling words..."

She burst out laughing. "You're crazy!" she said, putting a hand on his head.

"Now I've suddenly acquired the gift of thought and speech," he said, falling to his knees, "Olga, be my wife!" She turned away from him in silence and faced the opposite direction. "Olga, give me your hand!' he per-sisted. When she did not respond he seized her hand himself and pressed it to his lips. She let him keep it, it was warm, soft and slightly moist; the more he tried to look her in the face, the more she averted her head.

"Silence?" he said nervously and questioningly, kissing her hand.

"Means consent," she completed the phrase quietly but still without looking at him.

"What are you feeling now? What are you thinking?" he asked, remembering how he had dreamed about her bashful consent, her tears.

"Just the same as you,"she answered, continuing to stare into the woods. Only the heaving of her breast revealed the emotion she was sup-pressing.

"Are there tears in her eyes?" Oblomov wondered, but she kept her head obstinately lowered.

"Aren't you feeling anything, are you totally calm?" he asked, trying to pull her towards him by the hand.

"I do feel something but I'm quite calm."

"How can you be calm?"

"Because it's something I've been expecting for a long time and I've gotten used to the idea."

"Expecting for a long time!" he exclaimed in surprise.

"Yes, from the very moment when I handed you that sprig of lilac I've been thinking of you as..." she broke off.

"From that moment!" He was about to throw open his arms and draw her into his embrace.

"Watch out, the abyss is yawning, lightning is flashing!" she said mischievously, nimbly evading his embrace and fending off his outstretched arms with her parasol.

He remembered her ominous "never!" and restrained himself. "But you never said anything, you never even dropped a hint," he said.

"Well, we don't actually marry on our own initiative—men propose or fathers dispose."

"From that moment—I can hardly believe it!" he murmured wonderingly.

"Do you really think that if I hadn't known what was in your mind I would be here alone with you now or that I would have spent all those evenings in the summer house listening to you and confiding in you?" she said proudly.

"So that means..." he began. His expression changed and he let go of her hand. A strange thought flashed through his mind. She was regarding him with quiet pride and waiting confidently, but what he was looking for at that moment was not pride and confidence but tears, high emotion, ecstatic joy, if only for an instant; time enough after that for life to settle into its course of unruffled peace and quiet.

But there were no tears, no gasps of delight, no bashful consent. He did not know how to take it. In his heart a worm of doubt awoke and began to squirm. Was she in love or just accepting a proposal? "Of course, there is another path to happiness, "he said.

"What path?" she asked

"Sometimes love isn't patient, it can't wait, it rejects all reason and calculation; a woman is aflame, excited, in the grip of a kind of delicious torment..."

"I don't know anything about that kind of happiness."

"It's when a woman is ready to make any sacrifice, her peace of mind, her reputation, respect—all for the sake of love, her only recompense."

"Is that really the course we want to take?"

"No."

"Would you want to achieve that kind of happiness at the expense of my peace of mind, my reputation?"

"No, absolutely not! I swear to God!" he said hotly.

"Then why did you mention it?"

"Really, I don't even know myself..."

"Well, I do! You wanted to find out if I would be ready to sacrifice my peace of mind and whether I would be willing to take that path with you, isn't that right?"

"Yes, I think you've got it...and so?"

"Never, not for the world!" she asserted firmly.

He thought for a moment and then sighed. "Yes, it's a terrible course to take, and it takes a lot of love for a woman to follow a man down that path to certain ruin and yet to keep on loving." He gave her a questioning look, but her expression did not change except for a slight quiver of the crease in her brow.

"Imagine," he said, "Sonechka, who isn't worth your little finger, suddenly cutting you dead when you meet!" Olga smiled and her expression remained the same as ever, but Oblomov was still driven by the compulsion to feed his self-esteem by testing Olga's willingness to sacrifice herself for him. "Imagine men coming up to you and instead of lowering their eyes modestly and respectfully, giving you a bold and knowing grin..." He looked straight at her; she was studiously prodding a stone in the sand with the tip of her parasol, "...or you enter some salon and several of the lace caps start bobbing with indignation and one of them even pointedly changes her seat—would you be able to maintain your dignity and your awareness that you were their superior?"

"But why are you putting me through this horrible interrogation? I will never take that path."

"Never?" Oblomov asked dejectedly.

"Never!" she repeated.

"Yes," he said thoughtfully, "you wouldn't have the strength to look disgrace in the face. You'd probably rather face death or even execution than the preparations for it, the constant torment at the prospect; no, you wouldn't be able to take that, you would just waste away, isn't that right?" He was inspecting her closely through all this, watching for her reaction.

She maintained her good humor, unruffled by the horrors he was depicting, a faint smile hovering about her lips. "I have no wish to die or waste away!" she said. "You've gotten it wrong; one's love can be even stronger without taking that road..."

"If you're not afraid of it, then why wouldn't you take that road," he persisted with a touch of irritation.

"Because people who go down that road always end up parting and I'm not parting with you!" She stopped, placed a hand on his shoulder, gave him a long look and suddenly, dropping her parasol, quickly and warmly threw her arms around his neck and kissed him and then passionately pressed her face to his chest and added in a muffled voice: "Ever!"

A cry of joy burst from him and he fell to the grass at her feet.

PART III

CHAPTER ONE

Oblomov made his way home in a state of euphoria. His blood was on the boil, his eyes glittering; even his hair felt as if it were ablaze. It was in this mood that he entered his room where he was suddenly confronted with the disagreeable and unexpected sight of Tarantyev seated in his armchair; his elation turned to dismay on the spot.

"How can you keep people waiting around like this?" Tarantyev snarled, offering him a hairy paw, "and that old devil of yours was insufferable. I asked him for a bite—nothing! Wouldn't even offer me a drop of vodka!"

"I was just taking a stroll in the woods," Oblomov said casually, still stunned from the sudden appearance of his fellow Oblomovkan—and at the worst possible moment!

He had forgotten the dismal milieu he had for so long inhabited and had lost touch with its suffocating atmosphere. It was as if in a split second Tarantyev had plucked him down from the skies and dropped him right back into the swamp. Oblomov racked his brains. What was Tarantyev doing there? How long was he going to stay? He was nagged by the apprehension that Tarantyev would insist on staying for dinner and that he would be prevented from going to the Ilyinskys. Oblomov had only one thought in his head; how to get rid of Tarantyev—even if it was going to cost him something. He waited silently and gloomily for Tarantyev to speak.

"So, my old friend, what about taking a look at the apartment?"

"There's no need now," said Oblomov, avoiding Tarantyev's eye, "I'm...er...I won't be moving there."

"What's this? What do you mean you won't be moving?" Tarantyev growled menacingly. "Renting a place and then not moving in—what about the lease?"

"What lease?"

"You mean you've already forgotten? You signed a one-year lease. Then just give me eight hundred roubles in notes and go wherever you want. Four prospective tenants have already been to look at it and wanted to take it—they were all turned down; one even wanted to sign a three-year lease."

Only then did Oblomov recall that on the very day he was moving to the dacha Tarantyev had brought him a paper that he had signed in a hurry without reading it.

"Oh God, what have I done!" he thought. "No, I don't need the apartment," he said, "I'm going abroad…"

"Abroad!" Tarantyev cut in, "with that German? Who are you kidding? You'll never go!"

"Why not? I have my passport—I'll show you—and we've bought a suitcase."

"You'll never go!" Tarantyev repeated flatly, "you'd better give me the rent for six months in advance."

"I don't have the money."

"You'll find it somehow. The landlady's brother, Ivan Matveyich, doesn't play games. He'll take you to court at the drop of a hat if you don't pay up. Yes, and I paid with my own money and I want it back from you."

"Where did you get so much money?" Oblomov asked.

"What's it to you? Someone paid me back an old debt. So, let's have that money, that's what I came for!"

"Alright, I'll come in a few days and find someone else to take the apartment—I'm too busy right now…" He began to button his coat.

"But what kind of apartment are you looking for? You'll never find a better one in the whole city. I mean you haven't even seen it," said Tarantyev.

"And I don't want to either," replied Oblomov. "Why would I want to move over there—it's so far."

"Far from what?" Tarantyev demanded to know.

At first Oblomov could not think of a reply. Finally he came up with one: "From the center."

"The center of what? What difference does it make to you? All you ever do is lie down."

"No, I don't lie down any more."

"How do you mean?"

"Like today, for instance…" Oblomov began.

"What?" Tarantyev interrupted him.

"I'm not having dinner at home…"

"Then just hand over the money and to hell with you!"

"What money?" Oblomov asked in exasperation. "I told you, I'll come over in a few days and talk to the landlady."

"What landlady? She's just some woman I know, what does she know? No, it'll be her brother you'll be talking to—you'll see!"

"Alright, I'll go over and talk to him."

"That'll be the day! Just give me the money and to hell with you!"

"I don't have it; I'll have to borrow it."

"Well, at least give me the money to pay the coachman for the fare!" Tarantyev pressed him. "It'll be three roubles."

"Where is this coachman of yours? And why on earth three roubles?"

"I let him go; and what do you mean 'why three roubles?' Why he didn't even want to bring me in the first place—'not through all that sand', he said, and the fare back from here is three roubles too—that makes twenty-two roubles in banknotes."

"But the post-chaise from here only charges fifty kopecks!" Oblomov said, "Here you are!" He handed him four roubles in coins. Tarantyev pocketed the money. "That still leaves seven roubles in notes you owe me," he added, plus, "I need money for my dinner!"

"What dinner?"

"I won't get back to town in time now; I'll have to eat at some inn on the way; that's expensive, they'll charge a good five roubles."

Without speaking, Oblomov took out a rouble and tossed it to him. He was bursting with impatience to be rid of Tarantyev, but he would not go.

"Well, aren't you going to offer me a bite to eat?" he said.

"But you just said that you were going to stop for dinner at an inn on the way back!" Oblomov pointed out.

"Yes, for dinner, but it's not even two o'clock yet!"

Oblomov told Zakhar to bring something.

"There's nothing—nothing's ready yet," Zakhar observed off-handedly, giving Tarantyev a dark look, "and by the way, Mikhei Andreyich, when are you going to bring back the master's shirt and waistcoat?"

"What shirt and waistcoat are you talking about?" Tarantyev responded defiantly, "I brought them back ages ago!"

"When was that?" Zakhar inquired.

"I put them right in your hands when you were packing to move. You must have stuffed them into some bundle or other—and now you're questioning me…?"

Zakhar was dumbfounded: "God help us, what nerve!" he howled indignantly, appealing to Oblomov.

"Oh yes, a likely story!" Tarantyev shot back, "you probably sold them to buy booze, and now you're trying to put the blame on me!"

"No! Never in my life have I sold anything of the master's for drinking money," Zakhar wheezed, "why, you…!"

"Zakhar, stop it!" Oblomov snapped.

"Anyway, what about that floor brush and the two cups you took from us?" Zakhar continued his questioning.

"What brushes?" Tarantyev growled, "you old crook! Why don't you just bring me something to eat?"

"You hear how he snarls, Ilya Ilyich?" said Zakhar. "There isn't even a crust of bread in the house and Anisya's gone out," he added with finality and left the room.

"But where are you going for dinner?" Tarantyev asked. Wonders never cease! Imagine Oblomov walking in the woods, dining out…! "So when are you moving to the apartment? It's already autumn. Come and look at it!"

"Alright, alright, in a day or two…"

"And don't forget to bring the money with you!"

"Yes, yes, yes!" Oblomov replied impatiently.

"Do you need anything for the apartment? Just for you, Ilya, they've painted the floors, the ceilings, the window frames, the doors, everything; they've spent more than a hundred roubles."

"Yes, yes, good! But there was something I wanted to tell you," Oblomov suddenly remembered, "I want you to go to the court for me to sign a power of attorney as a witness…"

"Oh, so now I'm supposed to go to the court for you!" Tarantyev retorted.

"I'll give you extra money for dinner," Oblomov offered.

"It'll cost me more in shoe leather than the extra you'll give me!"

"Go for me, I'll make it worth your while!"

"I can't go to the court," Tarantyev announced dismally.

"Why not?"

"I have enemies; they've got it in for me, just waiting for me to walk into one of their traps so they can finish me off."

"Alright then, I'll go myself," Oblomov said and reached for his cap.

"Now when you come to the apartment Ivan Matveyich will really put himself out for you—you'll see, Ilya, he's a treasure—in a different class from some upstart of a German. No, he's one of your salt-of-the-earth, good old Russian types, loyal and reliable; why, he's been sitting at the same desk in the same office for thirty years now, runs the whole show. It's not that he doesn't have some money put by but he doesn't throw it away on coaches and carriages. His clothes are no fancier than mine, and so mild-mannered that butter wouldn't melt in his mouth; speaks so softly you can hardly hear him, and doesn't go rushing off to foreign countries—like some people I could name!"

"Tarantyev!" Oblomov shouted, banging his fist on the table, "Shut up! You've no idea what you're talking about!"

Tarantyev's eyes popped at this unprecedented outburst on Oblomov's part and he even forgot to be offended at being dismissed as Stoltz's inferior. "Well, well, look at him now," he muttered, picking up his hat, "a whole new, fire-breathing Oblomov!" He smoothed his hat with his sleeve and then looked over at Oblomov's hat on a shelf. "I see you're not using your hat—you're wearing that cap," he said, picking up the hat and trying it on. "How about letting me have it for the summer?"

Oblomov silently removed his hat from Tarantyev's head and put it back on the shelf and then stood there with his arms folded across his chest, waiting for Tarantyev to leave.

"Well, to hell with you!" said Tarantyev as he moved, discomfited, towards the door, "I don't know what's gotten into you today, Ilya. Anyway, you go and have a talk with Ivan Matveyich—and just try not bringing the money!"

CHAPTER TWO

Tarantyev left Oblomov in a bad mood. He sat in an armchair and it was a long time before he could shake off the unpleasant impression left by the abrasive interview. Finally he started to recall the events of the morning and the image of the ugly scene with Tarantyev receded; a smile appeared on his face.

He spent a long time in front of the mirror adjusting his tie, smiling and examining his cheek for traces of Olga's hot kiss. "Two 'nevers'!" he said in a voice of quiet exultation, "and what a difference between them; one has withered away but the other has burst into full bloom…" He started thinking, and the harder he thought, the more he began to feel that the sun-filled, cloudless holiday of love was over, that love had indeed become a duty, had woven itself into the very fabric of life and become one of its normal, everyday functions, that it had begun to lose its luster and that its radiant colors were fading.

Perhaps that morning had seen the very last of its rosy, glowing rays and henceforth it would no longer shine brightly but just imperceptibly lend its warmth to life and be absorbed by it; love would be life's powerful but hidden driving force. From now on the manifestations of love would be down to earth, humdrum.

The poem had ended and now began the prosaic narrative. The court, the journey to Oblomovka, building the house, getting the mortgage, laying the road, endless dealings with the peasants, organizing the work, the harvest, threshing, the clicking of the abacus, the worried face of the bailiff, the elections, the court sessions.

Only here and there, rarely, would he catch one of Olga's radiant glances, hear a snatch of "casta diva" or receive a hurried kiss—and then it would be back to work, going into town, the bailiff again, and once more the clicking of the abacus.

There would be visitors—he was not thrilled by the prospect. They would start talking about who was producing how much vodka at the distillery, who was delivering how many yards of cloth to the government. Was this really what he had been looking forward to? Is this what life was about? Well, people certainly act as if it is—even Andrei!

But what about marriage, the wedding itself? That after all is the poetry of life, a flower in full bloom. He imagined himself leading Olga to the altar—she with a crown of orange blossom and a long veil. A ripple of surprise runs through the congregation. Shyly, her breast heaving gently, her head gracefully and proudly inclined, she offers him her hand, unsure of how to meet the eyes of the guests. Smiles alternating with tears and now and then a thought fluttering in that crease on her brow.

Back at the house after the guests had left, still in her bridal finery, she would throw her arms around him and press her head against his chest, just as she had done this morning…

"No, I'll run back to Olga, all these feelings and thoughts are too much for me alone," he thought, "I'll tell everyone, the whole world...well no, first the aunt, then the baron, I'll write to Stoltz—won't he get a surprise! Then I'll tell Zakhar, he'll fall to his knees and howl with joy; I'll give him twenty-five roubles. Anisya will come in and cover my hand with kisses; I'll give her ten roubles. And then...then I'll shout out for all the world to hear and the world will respond: 'Oblomov is happy, Oblomov is getting married!' Now I'll run over to Olga, we'll have a long intimate, whispered talk and seal our private compact to merge our two lives into one."

He ran over to Olga's house and she listened with a smile as he poured out his hopes and dreams, but the moment he jumped up to rush and tell her aunt her frown stopped him in his tracks.

"No, not a word to anyone!" she said, putting a finger to her lips and warning him to keep his voice down so as not to be overheard by her aunt in the next room. "It's not the right time yet."

"Why not, if everything is settled between us? What should we be doing now? We have to begin somewhere," he said, "we can't just sit still doing nothing! It's time to face our responsibilities and start our new life in earnest."

"Yes, you're right!" she said, looking him squarely in the face.

"Well, that's why I wanted to take the first step and go to your aunt..."

"That's the last step."

"Then what's the first one?"

"The first step is to go to the court, you have some paper to sign, don't you?"

"Alright, tomorrow..."

"Why not today?"

"But today is special—I don't want to leave you today, Olga!"

"Alright, tomorrow—and then?"

"Then tell your aunt, write to Stoltz."

"No, next you go to Oblomovka, Andrei Ivanich has already written to tell you what needs to be done on the estate; I don't know exactly what business you have to attend to there, some building work, isn't it?" she asked, looking him full in the face. "My God!" said Oblomov, "if we listen to Stoltz it will be ages before we tell your aunt! According to him, first of all we have to build the house, then the road and also set up a school. It will take ages to do all of that. No, Olga, we'll go there together and then..."

"And when exactly will we go? Is there a house?"

"No, the old one's decrepit; I think the porch has simply collapsed..."

"Well then, where would we go?"

"We'll have to look for an apartment here."

"For that you'll have to go back to town," she pointed out, "that's step number two..."

"Then..." he began.

"But first you have to take these two steps and then we'll see..."

"What's going on here?" Oblomov wondered disconsolately, "What happened to that long, intimate, whispered talk and the sealing of the private compact to merge our two lives into one? It's all somehow so different from what I had imagined! What a strange thing Olga is! She never takes the time to dwell on anything, to savor or relish a moment of poetry; it's as if she takes no interest in dreaming or pleasure in rapt contemplation of happiness. It's 'go this minute to sign the papers, then see about the apartment'—just like Andrei! Anyone would think they're in a conspiracy to rush through life!"

The next day he went into town with a sheet of crested notepaper and headed first to the courthouse. He was not happy about making the journey, yawning and looking from side to side. He did not know exactly where to find the office and dropped in at Ivan Gerasimovich's to ask him which department he needed to get the document certified. Ivan Gerasimovich was pleased to see Oblomov and would not let him leave without eating something. Then he sent for another friend to find out from him what to do since he himself had long since lost touch with this kind of official business. The meal and the consultations went on until three o'clock by which time it was too late to go to the courthouse and the next day was Saturday when it would be closed. So the whole thing had to be put off until Monday.

Oblomov set off for the Vyborg side to the new apartment. It was a long journey through side streets with long fences on both sides. Finally he stopped to ask a constable the way. The constable told him that it was in a nearby street and pointed along one more street with no houses, just fences and grass, with ruts in the dried mud. Oblomov continued on his way, admiring the nettle beds along the fences and the rowan trees that could be glimpsed through them. Finally the constable pointed to an old house in a courtyard and said: "that's the one!" The sign on the gate read: "Widow of Collegiate Secretary, Pshenitsyn" and Oblomov told the coachman to drive into the courtyard. It was only about the width of a room so that the shaft of the carriage struck a corner on its way in causing a panic among a flock of chickens, scattering them in every direction with a frantic clucking and flapping of wings, some of them even taking briefly to the air, and provoking a big black dog to strain desperately at his chain, barking furiously in his attempts to charge the offending horses.

Oblomov was occupying a seat in the carriage right next to the windows of the house and had some difficulty in getting out. Through the mignonettes and marigolds on the window ledges he could see heads bobbing about inside the house. He finally managed to clamber down from the carriage, making the dog bark even more furiously.

He stepped up onto the porch and was confronted by a wrinkled old woman in a peasant smock with the hem of her skirt tucked under her belt.

"Who do you want?"

"The lady of the house, Mrs. Pshenitsyn."

The old woman lowered her head in bafflement. "Your sure you don't want Ivan Matveyich?" she asked, "he's out, he's not come back from the office yet."

"I want to see the lady who owns the house," said Oblomov.

Meanwhile, the whole house remained in turmoil. Heads were poking out from one window after another. Behind the old woman doors would open briefly and then close—just long enough for faces to peep out and take a look. Oblomov turned around; there were two children in the yard, a little girl and a little boy, watching him with curiosity. A sleepy looking peasant in a sheepskin coat appeared out of nowhere and, shielding his eyes from the sun with his hand, regarded Oblomov and the carriage lazily. The dog continued to bark in angry full--throated bursts; the slightest movement on Oblomov's part or the sound of a horse's hoof striking the ground was enough to trigger off a furious straining at the chain and a frenzy of barking.

Through the fence to the right Oblomov could see a vast plot sown with cabbage and through the fence to the left a few trees and a green wooden summer house.

"You want to see Agafya Matveyevna?" the old woman asked, "what about?"

"Tell the lady I want to see her about the apartment I've rented here…"

"Oh, you must be the new lodger, Mikhei Andreyich's friend; wait here a moment, I'll tell her." She opened the door behind her, revealing a number of heads that sprang back and beat a hasty retreat to the nearby rooms. He just caught a glimpse of a woman with a bare neck and elbows, bareheaded, white-skinned and full-figured who also rushed away from the door, giggling at being exposed to the view of a total stranger.

"Please come inside," said the old woman, turning and leading Oblomov through a small hallway into a fairly spacious room. She asked him to wait and said that the lady of the house would be with him shortly.

"The dog is still barking," thought Oblomov as he looked around the room. He suddenly realized that the objects he was looking at were familiar; the whole room was filled with his own things. Tables covered in dust, chairs piled in a heap on the bed, mattresses, crockery scattered all over the place, cupboards. "What is this? Everything just dumped anywhere, no attempt to put it in order! What a pigsty!"

Suddenly he heard the door creak behind him and into the room walked the same woman with the bare neck and elbows he had glimpsed before. She was about thirty, with very white skin and so full in the face that it seemed that the color could not make its way to her cheeks. She had practically no eyebrows and instead, in the place where they would normally be, there were two kind of fuzzy, shiny strips with just a few light--colored hairs here and there: her grayish eyes, like her whole face, projected an impression of simple good nature and her hands, which were white but roughened, were crisscrossed by a network of prominent blue veins. Her dress fitted tightly; it was clear that she resorted to no artifice in her appearance, not even an overskirt to emphasize her hips and minimize her waist, so that her bust, even covered as it was, but without a scarf around her neck, could have served as a model for a painting or a sculpture of a firm, healthy and substantial bosom without even a suggestion of immodesty. Her dress looked incongruously worn and shabby beside her elegant shawl and dressy, lace cap. She had not been expecting visitors and when Oblomov had asked to see her she had hastily thrown on her Sunday- best shawl and lace cap. She had entered the room timidly and stood looking shyly at Oblomov. He stood and bowed.

"I have the pleasure of meeting Mrs. Pshenitsyn, I presume?" he said.

"Yes, sir," she replied, "perhaps it's my brother you want to speak to?" she inquired uncertainly, "he's still at the office; he's never home before five."

"No, it's you I wanted to see," Oblomov began when she had sat down on the divan as far away from him as possible, eyeing the fringes of her shawl that enveloped her down to the floor like a horsecloth—even her hands were hidden beneath it.

"I had originally rented your apartment, but now due to unforeseen circumstances I need to find an apartment in another part of town, so I wanted to come and speak to you..."

She listened and paused for reflection with a vacant expression before coming out with: "my brother isn't here now."

"But this is your house, isn't it?"

"Yes," she answered simply.

"So that's why I thought you could settle the matter yourself..."

"But you see, my brother isn't here, he's the one who handles all this kind of thing," she said in an undertone, looking straight at Oblomov for the first time and then lowering her eyes once again to her shawl.

"She has a simple but nice face," was Oblomov's favorable verdict, "probably good-hearted!"

At that moment a small girl put her head around the door. Agafya Matveyevna gave her a silent, warning shake of the head and the child withdrew.

"And where does your brother work"

"In an office."

"Which one?"

"The one where they register peasants...I don't know exactly what it's called."

She smirked helplessly and at that moment her face resumed its normal expression.

"It's not just you and your brother who live here, is it?" Oblomov asked.

"No, there's my two children from my late husband, the boy's going on eight and the girl's going on six," the woman began, talking more responsively now and her face lighting up, "and then there's the old lady. She's ailing, can hardly walk, just enough to make it to church; she used to go to the market with Akulina but she's stopped going since St. Nicholas's Day, her feet get too swollen; even in church she mostly sits on the steps now. That's about it—except for a visit every now and then from my sister-in-law and Mikhei Andreyich."

"And Mikhei Andreyich, does he come often?"

"He sometimes stays for as long as a month, he's my brother's friend—they 're always together..." she broke off, having exhausted her conversational repertoire.

"It's so quiet here!" said Oblomov, "if it weren't for the dog barking you would think there wasn't a living soul around."

She smiled nervously by way of response.

"Do you get out much?"

"Sometimes in the summer. Just the other day on the Friday of St. Ilya's we went to the Gunpowder Works."

"Do you get a lot of people there?" Oblomov asked; her scarf had fallen open and his gaze rested on her high, ever placid bosom jutting out like a pillow on a couch.

"No, this year not many people came; it rained in the morning—only cleared up later—but usually there's a lot of people."

"Where else do you go?"

"Well, nowhere much. My brother and Mikhei Andreyich go to the fish ponds and make fish soup, but we just stay here."

"You mean you stay home all the time?"

"Yes, really, it's true. Last year we went to Kolpino and sometimes we go for a stroll in the woods nearby. My brother's name day is the twenty-fourth of June, so there's a big dinner and all his colleagues from the office come."

"Do you ever go visiting?"

"My brother does; me and the children go for dinner with my husband's family on Easter Day and Christmas."

All possible topics of conversation had now been exhausted.

"I see you have flowers, do you like them?" he asked.

She gave her nervous giggle. "No," she said, "no time to bother with flowers. It's just that Akulina took the children to the count's garden and the gardener gave them some, and the geraniums and aloes have always grown here even in my husband's day."

At that moment Akulina suddenly burst into the room, grasping in her hands a big rooster that was desperately beating its wings and cackling furiously. "This here rooster, Agafya Matveyevna, do I give him to the man from the shop?" she asked.

"What do you mean bursting in here like this?" Oblomov's hostess said in embarrassment, "out with you! Can't you see there's visitors?"

"I was just asking," said Akulina, lowering her head and grabbing the rooster by the legs, "he's offering seventy-five kopecks."

"Back into the kitchen with you!" said Agafya Matveyevna, "and it's the gray, speckled one, not this one," she added hurriedly and, in her embarrassment, hid her hands under her shawl and kept her eyes lowered.

"There's a lot to do, running a house!" observed Oblomov.

"Yes, we've got a lot of chickens; we sell the eggs and the chicks. People from the street and the dachas as well as the count's house—they all buy from us," she replied, looking at Oblomov much more boldly.

Her face took on a purposeful and capable expression; even the vacuous look disappeared as soon as she began to talk about familiar subjects, but to any subject that fell outside her range of familiar, specific concerns she could only respond with a nervous giggle and total silence.

"These things should have been put in their proper places," Oblomov said, pointing to the pile of his possessions dumped on the floor...

"We were going to, but my brother said not to," she intervened spiritedly, looking Oblomov in the face with no trace of her earlier shyness, " 'God knows what he's got on those tables and in those cupboards' he said, 'and if something gets lost we'll be blamed'..." she stopped and smirked.

"He's a very careful man, your brother!" Oblomov put in.

She gave a little giggle and then resumed her normal expression. Her giggle was more of a nervous tick that covered up her not knowing what to say or do in a given situation.

"Am I going to have to wait long?" asked Oblomov. "Perhaps you could tell him that something has come up and I won't be needing the apartment, so would he please let it to another tenant, and that I'll also be looking for someone to take the apartment."

She just listened with the same vacant expression, blinking at regular intervals.

"Now, about the lease, would you mind telling him...?"

"But you see, he's not home right now," she insisted, "it'll be better if you wouldn't mind coming back tomorrow; tomorrow's Saturday and he doesn't go to the office..."

"Well, you see, I'm terribly busy, I just don't have a moment," Oblomov countered, so please be good enough just to tell him that since you can keep the deposit and I'll be finding a tenant..."

"But my brother's not here," she repeated in a monotone, "I don't understand why he's not back yet," she looked out at the street. "Look, this is the way he usually comes, right past the windows, you can see him from here—but no sign of him yet!"

"Well, I must be off," said Oblomov.

"But when my brother comes, what shall I tell him about when you're coming back?" she asked, getting up from the divan.

"Just tell him what I told you," said Oblomov, "that something came up..."

"Maybe, if you wouldn't mind, you could come back tomorrow and speak to him..." she repeated.

"I can't tomorrow."

"Well then, the day after, on Sunday; after church we usually have vodka and some snacks and Mikhei Andreyich comes."

"You mean Mikhei Andreyich comes too?" Oblomov asked.

"Oh yes!"

"Well, I can't come on Sunday either," he asserted impatiently.

"Well then, next week sometime," she persisted, "and when will you be moving in, so that I can get the floors swept and the furniture dusted?" she asked.

"I won't be moving in," he said.

"But I don't understand; where will we put your things?"

"Just be good enough to tell your brother," Oblomov began, pronouncing his words with particular emphasis and focusing on her bosom, "that something has come up..."

"I really don't know why he's taking so long; he's nowhere in sight," she said in a monotone, watching the fence between the courtyard and the street, "I know the sound of his footsteps, you can easily hear who's coming along the boardwalk, not many people come by..."

"So you *will* tell him what I said?" Oblomov said, bowing and turning to leave.

"But he'll be here himself in half an hour..." she said with unusual anxiety in her voice in a desperate attempt to keep him from going.

"I simply can't wait any longer!" he pronounced conclusively and opened the door.

The moment the dog caught sight of him on the porch once again, he flew into a frenzy of barking and struggled to break free of the chain. The coachman, who had fallen asleep with his head propped on his hand, started to back the horses out, scattering the chickens squawking in a panic in every direction and causing heads to pop out of the windows.

"So I'll tell my brother that you came," said the lady of the house when Oblomov was seated in the carriage.

"Yes, and tell him that something came up so that I can't keep the apartment and that I'll find someone to take it or he should look for someone..."

"He's usually here about now," she said distractedly. "I'll tell him you wanted to see him."

"Yes, I'll come back in a day or two," said Oblomov.

The carriage left the courtyard to the accompaniment of the dog's desperate barking, shaking and rattling over the ridges formed by the hardened mud on the unpaved road. At the other end of the road a man came into sight. He was in his middle years, wearing a well-worn overcoat, with a large paper-wrapped package under his arm. He was carrying a thick stick and wearing rubber galoshes although it was a hot, dry day.

He was walking fast, looking from side to side and brought his feet down hard on the wooden boardwalk as if he were determined to smash it. Oblomov looked back at him as they passed and saw him turn in at the gate of Mrs. Pshenitsyn's house.

"It looks as if the famous brother has returned," he thought. "To hell with him!

It'll take an hour to explain and I'm hot and hungry! Anyway Olga's waiting for me—I'll leave it for another time! Get a move on!" he told the coachman.

"Maybe I should look at another apartment!" he reminded himself, looking at the fences on either side, "I'll have to go back to Morskaya or Konyushennaya Street... Another time!" he decided. "Hurry it up!" he told the coachman.

CHAPTER THREE

At the end of August it started to rain and smoke began to rise from the chimneys of those dachas that had stoves. The people whose dachas had no stove started wrapping themselves in mufflers and the dachas started to empty.

Oblomov had not even shown his face in town again when one morning he saw the Ilyinskys' furniture being carted past his windows. Although he was no longer daunted by the prospect of moving to a new apartment or dining out on the spur of the moment or spending a whole day without lying down he was at a loss about where to spend the night. To remain alone at the dacha now that the park and the woods were deserted and Olga's shutters were closed seemed to him quite out of the question. With a sinking heart he walked through the empty rooms of her dacha, around the park and down the hill. He told Zakhar and Anisya to go to the place on the Vyborg side where he had decided to stay until he could find a new apartment, while he himself left for town, snatched a bite of dinner at an inn and spent the evening at Olga's.

But the autumn evenings in town were quite different from those long days in the park and the woods when the light lingered late into the evening. Now he could no longer see her three times a day; Katya would not be running to him with messages and he would not be sending Zakhar five versts with messages for Olga. The whole of that summer's love poem seemed to have ended; it was as if it had lost momentum for lack of fuel. They sometimes sat for half an hour in silence. Olga would get absorbed in her work, using her needle to count out to herself the number of squares in the pattern, while his mind would be racing ahead, filled with disjointed imaginings about some distant future.

Only occasionally as he watched her would he feel a quiver of passion, or she would happen to glance up at him and smile as she caught a flash of tender devotion and inexpressible happiness in his eyes. On three successive days he drove into town to dine at Olga's on the pretext that he had not properly settled in yet and that he would be moving the very next week and that until then he could not treat the new apartment as his home. After three days, however, he felt it was becoming embarrassing to appear at the Ilyinskys' for dinner and on the fourth day he just prowled around the outside of the house without going in, sighed and drove back home. On the fifth day the Ilyinskys were invited out to dinner. On the sixth day Olga told him to meet her at a certain shop and then he could escort her home on foot with her carriage following them at a short distance.

This was all very awkward; they kept on running into acquaintances who would greet them, and some even stopped to talk. "Oh God, I can't take this!" he would say, breaking into a sweat out of fear and embarrassment.

Even Olga's aunt would run her big eyes languidly over him and take a thoughtful sniff at her smelling salts as if he were giving her a headache. And what a distance to travel! All the way over from the Vyborg side and then all the way back again in the evening—three whole hours!

"Let's tell your aunt!" Oblomov pressed Olga, "and then I can stay all day long without tongues wagging…"

"But have you been to the court yet?" Olga asked.

Oblomov had to fight an overwhelming urge to say: "Yes, I went and took care of everything," but he knew that Olga would give him such a penetrating look that his lie would show all over his face so, by way of reply, he just sighed. "If you only knew how difficult it is!" he said.

"And did you talk to the landlady's brother—and find an apartment?" she added, keeping her eyes lowered.

"He's never home on the morning and in the evening I'm always here," said Oblomov, delighted to have found a reasonable excuse. Now it was Olga's turn to sigh, but she said nothing.

"Tomorrow I'm definitely talking to the landlady's brother," Oblomov tried to mollify her, "it's Sunday and he doesn't go to the office."

"Well, until all this is settled," Olga said carefully, "we can't tell my aunt and we mustn't see each other so much…"

"Yes, yes, of course!" Oblomov anxiously hastened to agree.

"You'll come to dinner on Sundays when we have guests and maybe on Wednesdays by yourself," she announced. "And then we can also meet at the theatre; you'll find out when we're going and come at the same time!"

"Yes, you're right," he said, delighted that she had assumed responsibility for scheduling their meetings.

"And when the weather is good," she concluded, " I can go for a walk in the Summer Garden and meet you there; it'll be like our park...the park!" she repeated with feeling.

He kissed her hand silently and said goodbye until the Sunday. She watched him leave with a heavy heart and sat down at the piano and was soon wrapped up in the music. Something was making her heart weep within her and there were tears in the music she played. She wanted to sing, but could not bring herself to do it.

The next morning Oblomov got up and put on the outlandish jacket that he wore in the dacha. He had long since given up the dressing gown and banished it to a closet. Zakhar entered in his usual fashion with the coffee and rolls wobbling on his tray and made his precarious way to the table. Behind him, Anisya in *her* usual fashion poked her head and shoulders around the door to check whether Zakhar would make it successfully to the table with the coffee and then ducked noiselessly out of sight once Zakhar had laid the tray safely on the table; but if a single item threatened to slide off the tray she would rush to his side to prevent anything else falling. Zakhar would then start cursing the objects themselves before turning to his wife and poking his elbow menacingly at her chest.

"This is wonderful coffee! Who brews it?" asked Oblomov.

"It's the landlady herself," said Zakhar, "it's her who's been making it for the last five days. She told me I put too much chicory in it and I don't brew it long enough and why don't I let her do it!"

"It's wonderful!" Oblomov repeated, pouring himself a second cup, "thank her for me!"

"Look, she's in there now!" said Zakhar, pointing to the half-open door of the room on the side. "It's, like, their pantry. She does her work in there and that's where they keep their tea, sugar, coffee and crockery." Oblomov could only see the landlady's back, her head on its white neck and her bare elbows.

"What's she doing in there with her elbows moving so busily?" asked Oblomov.

"Who knows? Maybe she's ironing her lace."

Oblomov watched her elbows plying back and forth and her back bending and straightening. As she bent down he glimpsed her clean skirt and stockings and her full, round legs. "She's only a clerk's widow but she has elbows fit for a countess—and what dimples!" Oblomov thought to himself.

At midday Zakhar came in to inquire whether he would care to sample their pies—the landlady had sent him to ask. "It's Sunday and they're baking pies!"

"Yes, I can just imagine what kind of pie it is—with onions and carrots!" said Oblomov dismissively.

"No, they're just as good as our own pies in Oblomovka!" Zakhar observed, "with chicken and fresh mushrooms."

"My, that sounds good! Bring me some! Which one bakes them? Not that grimy old woman?"

"What are you talking about—*her?*" Zakhar said disparagingly. "If it weren't for her mistress she wouldn't even be able to make the dough by herself. The lady of the house does everything in the kitchen herself. But the pies—her and Anisya did them together."

Five minutes later a bare arm, left almost totally uncovered by the shawl he had seen before, poked out of the side room and extended a dish in Oblomov's direction; on the dish sat a huge piece of baking hot, steaming pie.

"Thank you very much!" he responded appreciatively, taking the dish and as he did so, catching a glimpse through the doorway of the high bosom and bare shoulders. The door closed hurriedly.

"A little vodka?" a voice inquired.

"Thanks very much! But I don't drink." said Oblomov even more appreciatively—"what kind do you have?"

"It's our own, home-made, currant-flavored vodka," the voice replied.

"I've never tasted currant-flavored, would you mind if I tried some?"

Once again the bare arm was thrust out, this time holding out a plate with a glass of vodka on it. Oblomov drained the glass; it was very good.

"Thank you very much," he said, trying to peer around the door, but the door banged shut. "Why don't you let yourself be seen—I just want to say 'good morning!'" Oblomov complained.

He heard the giggle from behind the door. "I'm still wearing my working clothes, I've been in the kitchen. I'll get dressed properly in a minute; my brother will be back from church soon," she replied.

"Incidentally, about your brother," Oblomov remarked, "I need to speak to him, please ask him to come and see me."

"Certainly, I'll tell him when he comes in."

"Who's that coughing in there; it's someone with a very dry cough?" Oblomov asked.

"It's granny, she's been coughing like that for seven years now." The door slammed shut again.

"She's such a simple soul," thought Oblomov, "and yet there's something about her...she keeps herself so clean!"

So far he had not succeeded in meeting the famous brother. Just occasionally from his bed early in the morning he caught a glimpse through the slats in the fence of a figure darting by with a big paper-wrapped package under its arm and disappearing into the side street. Then later in the day at five o'clock the same figure would flash by the windows with the same package and disappear into the porch. He could never be heard inside the house.

At the same time, however, there were signs that there were people living in it, especially in the mornings; there was the clattering of knives in the kitchen; through the window he could hear one of the women rinsing something in the corner, the gatekeeper chopping firewood, or wheeling a keg of water on two wheels. Through the wall Oblomov could hear children wailing or the persistent cough of the old woman.

Oblomov's quarters consisted of four rooms—in fact he occupied the whole of the front of the house. The landlady and her family lived in two of the back rooms, while the brother lived upstairs in what was called the attic. Oblomov's study and bedroom had windows facing the courtyard, his drawing room gave onto the small garden, and his living room faced the large kitchen garden with its cabbages and potatoes. The windows of the drawing room were curtained in faded chintz. The walls were lined with plain, imitation walnut chairs; a card table stood under the mirror, the window ledges were crowded with pots of geraniums and African marigolds, and four cages containing finches and canaries hung from the ceiling.

The brother tip-toed into the room and responded to Oblomov's greeting with a triple bow. His tunic was tightly buttoned from top to bottom so that it was impossible to tell whether he was wearing any linen underneath. His tie was knotted with a single knot and the ends were tucked inside the tunic. He was about forty with a tuft of hair sticking straight up from his brow and with two identical tufts sprouting, wild and untended, from each temple, resembling nothing so much as the ears of an average-sized dog. His gray eyes never settled on their target directly, but only after some stealthy reconnoitering in its vicinity.

It seemed as if he were ashamed of his hands and whenever he spoke to someone he did his best to keep them out of sight, either placing both hands behind his back or keeping one tucked inside his coat and holding the other behind his back. When handing a document requiring some explanation to a supervisor he would keep one hand behind his back and, with the middle finger of his other hand, making sure to keep the nail pointing downward, he would point to the line or word in question. Then, at the earliest possible moment he would tuck the hand out of sight, maybe because his fingers were on the thick side, reddish and trembling slightly, and he felt, not unreasonably, that it was somehow too indelicate to expose them too frequently to public scrutiny.

"I believe, sir, you left word," he began, his eyes first swiveling around and finally coming to rest on Oblomov, "that I was to come and see you."

"Yes, I would like to talk to you about the apartment, please take a seat!" Oblomov replied politely.

After being asked a second time, Ivan Matveyich consented to sit, leaning forward with his hands tucked into his sleeves.

"Owing to circumstances I have to look for another apartment, so I want to give up this one."

"That would be difficult now," Ivan Matveyich responded, coughing into his fingers and whipping them smartly back into his sleeve, "if you had been good enough to inform me before the end of the summer there would have been a lot of people coming to see it."

"I did come but you weren't here." Oblomov put in.

"Yes, my sister told me," said the clerk, "but don't worry about the apartment, you'll be very comfortable here; perhaps the birds are bothering you?"

"What birds?"

"The chickens, that is."

Although Oblomov had been hearing the incessant cackling of the brood hen and the chirping of her chicks since the early morning through his window, he had hardly noticed it. The image of Olga was constantly before him and he was practically oblivious to his surroundings.

"Oh no, that doesn't bother me at all," he said, "I thought you meant the canaries, they start chirping first thing in the morning."

"We'll take them away," replied Ivan Matveyich.

"No, that's not the problem, it's just that because of circumstances I can't stay here."

"Of course, sir, it's as you wish," Ivan Matveyich replied, "but if you don't find a tenant to replace you, then what about the lease? Will you be paying us compensation? If so you'll be out of pocket."

"So how much will it come to?" Oblomov asked.

"Just let me fetch the figures!" He brought in the lease and an abacus.

"You see, sir, it's eight hundred roubles in notes for the apartment, less a hundred roubles for the deposit; that leaves seven hundred roubles," he said.

"You mean you're going to charge me for a whole year when I haven't even stayed here two weeks?" Oblomov protested.

"But sir," Ivan Matveyich objected mildly and like someone only asking for what was right: "it wouldn't be right to leave my sister out of pocket. She's a poor widow and her only income is from the house, except for the little that she makes from the chicks and the eggs—and that's barely enough to clothe the children."

"Come now, be reasonable! I can't do that," said Oblomov, "after all, I haven't even been here two weeks, so how can you think of charging me for a whole year?"

"But if you'll be good enough to to look at what it says here in the lease, sir," said Ivan Matveyich, pointing to two lines in the document with his middle finger that he then promptly hid back inside his sleeve: "'...in the event that I, the undersigned, Oblomov, should leave the apartment before the expiration of the lease, I undertake to transfer the lease to a third party on the same terms and conditions, failing which I will compensate the owner, Pshenitsyna, in full for the rent for the entire term of the lease expiring on June 1, next year'. "

Oblomov read it and exclaimed: "But this just isn't fair!"

"But it's legally binding, sir," Ivan Matveyich pointed out, "you signed it your good self, sir—this is your signature!" The finger once again emerged briefly from the sleeve to point to the signature and then darted back into its hiding place in the sleeve.

"How much was that again?"

"Seven hundred roubles," Ivan Matveyich began to click the beads on the abacus with the same finger, swiftly clenching his hand into a fist after every click, "then there's the use of the stables and the shed; that's another hundred and fifty roubles." He did some more clicking.

"Excuse me, but there are no horses, I don't keep any, so why should you charge me for the stables and the shed?" Oblomov objected spiritedly.

"But it's there in the lease, sir!" Ivan Matveyich pointed out, indicating the clause in question with his finger. "Mikhei Andreyich said that you would have horses."

"Well, Mikhei Andreyich was wrong!" said Oblomov with some asperity. "Give me that lease!"

"Please take this copy, if you don't mind, the original belongs to my sister," Ivan Matveyich responded mildly, picking up the lease. "Then there's the kitchen garden produce; cabbage, turnip and other vegetables for one person," Ivan Matveyich continued reading from the lease, "that comes to about two hundred and fifty roubles…"

Before he could start clicking the beads again, Oblomov cut in: "What garden, what cabbage? I don't know what you're talking about—what's the idea!" Oblomov's tone was almost menacing.

"But sir, it's all in the lease; Mikhei Andreyich said that that was what you wanted in the lease."

"Where do you get off deciding what I eat without consulting me? I don't want any cabbage or turnips!" said Oblomov, rising to his feet, whereupon Ivan Matveyich promptly got up from his chair.

"Excuse me, sir, but what do you mean 'without consulting you', it's your own signature there!" he argued, and his stubby finger once again hovered tremblingly over the signature and the whole document quivered in his hand.

"So how much do you make it altogether?" Oblomov asked impatiently.

"Well, including the painting of the ceiling and the doors, replacing the kitchen windows, the new clamps for the door locks—that's a hundred and fifty-four roubles and twenty-eight kopecks in notes."

"What? You're charging me for that too?" Oblomov was dumbfounded. "That's always the landlord's responsibility, whoever heard of moving into an undecorated apartment?"

"But it's stated in the lease, sir, that it's at your expense," said Ivan Matveyich, pointing with his finger at a distance to the relevant clause in the lease, "the total comes to thirteen hundred and fifty-four roubles and twenty-eight kopecks in notes, sir," he pointed out humbly, hiding both hands and the lease behind his back.

"And where am I supposed to get this sum, I don't have any money?" Oblomov objected, pacing the room. "You can keep your cabbages and turnips!"

"As you wish, sir," Ivan Matveyich continued softly, "and don't worry, you'll be very comfortable here; and as for the money, my sister will wait."

"But don't you understand, I can't stay here, I can't stay here because of circumstances!"

"Of course, sir, whatever you want," Ivan Matveyich replied compliantly, taking a step back.

"Alright then I'll think about it and try to find someone for the apartment," said Oblomov, nodding to the clerk.

"It won't be easy, but of course it's up to you, sir!" Ivan Matveyich said before bowing three times and leaving the room.

Oblomov took out his wallet and counted his money; it came to just three hundred and five roubles—he was stupefied. "What have I done with it all?" he asked himself in astonishment, almost in horror.

"At the beginning of the summer they sent me twelve hundred roubles from the estate—and now there's only three hundred left!" He tried to recollect all his items of expenditure but could account for only two hundred and fifty roubles. "Where did the money go?" he said, "Zakhar, Zakhar!"

"Yes sir, what is it?"

"Where has all our money gone? There's nothing left!"

Zakhar began to rummage in his pockets and pulled out two coins, a fifty-kopeck and a ten-kopeck piece and put them on the table. "Here's some change I forgot to give you back from the moving," he said.

"I'm not interested in your kopecks. I want to know what happened to the eight hundred roubles!"

"How would I know? How am I expected to know how you spend your money? How much have you been paying for all those carriages you've been taking?"

"It's true, the carriage did cost a lot," Oblomov recalled, looking at Zakhar. "Do you remember how much we paid the coachman at the dacha?"

"How would I remember?" Zakhar replied, "I just remember once you told me to give him thirty roubles."

"Why can't you learn to write things down? It's no good not being able to read and write!"

"I've lived all these years without being able to read and write and I'm doing just as well as the next man, thank God!"

"Stoltz is right, there should be a school on the estate," Oblomov thought.

"People say that the Ilyinskys once had one of those educated house servants—and he ran off with the silver!"

"Did he indeed!" Oblomov mentally beat a hasty retreat. "Of course, it's those educated ones that are the worst—always hanging around taverns with their accordions, endlessly drinking tea! No, this is no time to be setting up schools!"

"So where else could the money have gone?" he asked.

"How should I know? What about the money you gave Mikhei Andreyich back at the dacha...?"

"You're right!" Oblomov brightened up as he remembered the money he had given Mikhei Andreyich, "yes, so that was thirty for the coachman, I think, twenty-five for Tarantyev...and what else?" He gave Zakhar a thoughtful and inquiring look. Zakhar responded with a gloomy look from the usual angle.

"Perhaps Anisya will remember?" Oblomov asked

"She's only a woman, the poor fool, how is she going to remember?" Zakhar observed disdainfully.

"I just can't remember!" Oblomov exclaimed in frustration, "perhaps we've had burglars?"

"If we'd had burglars, they'd have taken the lot!" said Zakhar as he left the room.

Oblomov sat down in the armchair and reflected: "But where am I going to get the money?" He kept on thinking, and broke into a cold sweat. "When are they going to send me some from the estate—and how much?" He looked at the clock; two o'clock, time to leave for Olga's. Today was the day he was supposed to go to dinner there. He began to cheer up, ordered a carriage to be brought around and was driven to Morskaya Street.

CHAPTER FOUR

He told Olga that he had talked to the landlady's brother and hastily interjected that that there was a chance of finding a tenant to replace him before the week was out.

Olga and her aunt were out visiting before dinner so he went to look at an apartment nearby. He saw two. The first had four rooms and the rent was four thousand in notes and the second was five rooms for which they were asking six thousand roubles.

"It's terrible, terrible!" he exclaimed as he ran past the astonished doormen with his hands clasped to his ears. On the way to Olga's he tried to add up how much rents like that plus the thousand or so that he owed to Pshenitsyna would come to, but he was too rattled to work it out and he just lengthened his stride so as to get to Olga's as fast as possible.

When he arrived he found that they had company. Olga was in high spirits, talking, singing and making a big impression. Oblomov could only listen distractedly, while Olga made a point of talking and singing for his benefit to prevent his just sitting there moping and barely able to keep his eyes open, in the hope that all the talking and singing would strike a responsive chord inside Oblomov himself and make him feel one of the party.

"Come to the theatre tomorrow, we have a box!" she said.

"All that way at night and through that mud!" Oblomov thought, but responded to her smile with a smile of consent.

"Why don't you reserve a seat for the season?" she continued. "The Mayevskys are coming next week; *ma tante* has invited them to our box."

"My God," he thought," and here I am with just three hundred roubles!"

"Yes, just ask the baron, he knows everyone there, and he'll send for the tickets tomorrow." She smiled again and he smiled back and, with a smile, asked the baron who—also with a smile—agreed to send for the tickets.

"So, for now you can sit in the stalls, but when you've settled all your business you can take your place with us in the box like one of the family." She gave him a dazzling smile, the one she gave him when her happiness was unalloyed.

What a wave of happiness surged over him whenever Olga lifted the curtain even slightly, affording him a glimpse of that distant but delightful vista garlanded with smiles! Oblomov even forgot about the money—at least until the next morning when he caught sight of the brother's bundle flashing past his window and remembered the power of attorney and asked Ivan Matveyich to have it registered at the court. Ivan Matveyich read the document and announced that there was one clause that was not quite clear and set about clarifying it. The document was redrafted, notarized and posted. Oblomov announced this triumphantly to Olga and this put his mind at rest for a long time. He was happy because until he received an answer there was no need for him to look for an apartment and the longer he stayed where he was, the more he would save by not having to pay a second rent.

"Living here wouldn't be at all bad really," he thought, "of course, it's a little far from everything, but it's a beautifully run household, so efficient!"

The household was indeed beautifully run. Although Oblomov kept a separate table, the landlady kept a watchful eye on the preparation of his meals. Once when Ilya Ilyich happened to enter the kitchen he found Agafya Matveyevna and Anisya practically in each other's arms. If there is such a thing as instinctive sympathy between two people, if there are truly kindred spirits that seek each other from afar, never was there such a clear-cut example as the affinity between Agafya Matveyevna and Anisya. From the very first look, word and gesture there was an immediate rapport and mutual appreciation between them.

Anisya's working habits, the way she rolled up her sleeves and, armed with a poker and a rag, got to work on the kitchen stove that had not been lit for six months and had it going again in five minutes, the way she cleared away the dust from the shelves, the walls and the table with a single stroke of her brush, the broad strokes of her broom on the floor and the benches, the brisk efficiency with which she raked the ashes from the stove—all of this won Agafya Matveyevna's immediate appreciation and respect and revealed what a great help and partner she was going to be for her in running the house. From that moment on Anisya won a place in her heart. Anisya, for her part, needed to take only one look at Agafya Matveyevna master-minding operations in the kitchen, to see her hawk-like, browless eyes taking in the least ineptitude on the part of the ill-coordinated Akulina, to watch her in the kitchen issuing a stream of commands to take out, to put down, to heat, to salt, and, in the market, to observe the unerring judgment with which, with a single glance and a great deal of fingering, she would pronounce on the precise age of a hen or exactly how long ago a fish had been plucked from the water or a lettuce or a bunch of parsley from their beds—after seeing all this Anisya eyed her with surprise and awed respect and realized that she, Anisya, had missed her true vocation. Her destiny did not lie in Oblomov's kitchen where her bustling haste and frenetic energies were harnessed exclusively to picking up after Zakhar whenever he dropped a plate or a glass and where her experience and quick thinking were suppressed by her husband's baleful jealousy and bullying high-handedness. The two women developed an instant rapport and became inseparable.

Whenever Oblomov dined out Anisya spent her time of her own free will in the landlady's kitchen, flying to and fro, fetching and carrying and opening the cupboard, taking out what she needed and closing the door in virtually a single movement before Akulina had had time even to realize what was going on—and all because she so much enjoyed the work for its own sake. By way of reward Anisya earned her dinner, endless cups of coffee in the morning as well as the evening and the pleasure of long heart-to- heart talks, sometimes conducted in a hushed, confidential whisper, with the lady of the house herself.

When Oblomov dined at home, Agafya Matveyevna would help Anisya by indicating with a word or a finger the right time to take the roast out of the oven, whether to add a little red wine or sour cream to the sauce, or the best way to cook the fish. You could not imagine the amount of domestic lore and housekeeping expertise they exchanged—and not just about culinary matters. No, they covered the whole spectrum, everything that an inquiring mind and the accumulated experience of the ages could contribute to that particular area of human knowledge; cloth, thread, sewing, laundering, dressmaking, how to clean gloves and lace—including the white silk variety—the removal of stains from different fabrics, the concoction of various domestic medicinal remedies and herbs.

Ilya Ilyich would get up at nine and sometimes, just before sitting down to his coffee, glimpse through the slats in the fence the rapid movement of the paper-wrapped bundle as it flashed by under the arm of the brother on his way to the office. The coffee was always just as delicious, the cream as thick and the rolls as rich and crumbly. Then he would light a cigar and listen intently to the loud cackling of the brood hen, the chirping of the chicks and the trilling of the finches and canaries. He had not ordered them to be removed. "They remind me of the country, of Oblomovka," he said. Then he would sit down to continue reading one of the books he had begun at the dacha, or sometimes he would be reading, sprawled on the divan. The quiet was idyllic; only every now and then would a soldier pass by, or perhaps a group of workmen with axes at their belts. Only on the rarest of occasions would a hawker stray into such an out-of-the-way place, station himself outside the fence and spend half an hour shouting his wares: "apples, Astrakhan water-melons!"—so that in spite of yourself you would end up buying something.

Sometimes the landlady's little daughter, Masha, would come to him with a message from her mother that someone was coming around selling this or that kind of mushroom and should she buy a basket or two for him; or he would call in Vanya, the son, and ask him about his lessons and make him read or write something to see how well he was doing. If the children forgot to shut the door behind them he would see the bare neck, busy elbows and back of Agafya Matveyevna that were in constant motion. She was always busy ironing, pounding or grinding something or other, and no longer troubled to cover herself with a shawl when she noticed him watching through the half open door; she would just give her little smirk and go on applying herself with the same diligence to her pounding, ironing and grinding on the big kitchen table.

Sometimes he would go to the door with his book in his hand, glancing at it while he struck up a conversation with her.

"You never stop working!" he said once.

She giggled and went on busily turning the handle of the coffee grinder, her elbow going around in such rapid circles that Oblomov grew dizzy watching her.

"You must get tired," he continued.

"Oh no, I'm used to it," she replied, still cranking the grinder.

"And what do you do when you're not working?"

"What do you mean 'when I'm not working'? There's always work to be done," she said. "In the morning there's dinner to be prepared, after dinner there's the sewing and then there's supper in the evening."

"You mean you eat supper?"

"Of course, why wouldn't we? On holidays we go to vespers."

"That's good," Oblomov observed approvingly. "What church do you go to?"

"The Church of the Nativity, it's our parish church."

"Do you ever read?"

She looked at him uncomprehendingly, unable to reply.

"Do you have any books?"

"My brother has, but he doesn't read them. We take newspapers from the inn and he sometimes reads aloud from them...and Vanechka has a lot of books."

"So you really never take any time off?"

"No, really!"

"Never go to the theatre?"

"My brother does at Christmas time."

"But what about you?"

"When would I have time? And who would make supper?" she asked, looking around at him.

"Well, your cook could without you…"

"That Akulina?" she exclaimed in astonishment, "impossible! Left to herself she wouldn't even have supper ready by the next day. I have all the keys."

Silence—which Oblomov filled by admiring her full, rounded elbows. "What nice arms you have!" Oblomov suddenly blurted out, "Someone should sit down and draw them this very moment."

She giggled in her embarrassment. "Well you see, the sleeves get in the way," she offered by way of explanation, "the kind of sleeves they make these days catch all the dirt."

Neither of them could think of anything else to say.

"I'll just finish grinding the coffee," Agafya Matveyevna muttered to herself, "then I'll chop the sugar—and I mustn't forget to send out for cinnamon."

"You should get married," said Oblomov, "you would make someone a wonderful home."

She giggled and started pouring the ground coffee into a big glass jar.

"Yes, I mean it, " added Oblomov.

"Who would take me with the children?" she replied and started to make some mental calculations. "Two dozen…" she murmured, thinking aloud, "surely she won't put them all in," and after putting the jar away in the cupboard ran into the kitchen. Oblomov went back to his room and resumed reading his book. "She still looks so young and healthy—and such a wonderful housekeeper on top of it! She'd really make someone a wonderful wife!" he said to himself and plunged into thought—about Olga.

When the weather was fine Oblomov would put on his cap and walk around the area; one time he would find himself treading in mud, another time he would have a disagreeable encounter with some dogs and return home. There he would find the table already laid, the meal delicious and cleanly and tidily served. Sometimes a bare arm would be stretched out through the doorway, holding a plate to offer him a taste of the pie that the landlady was serving to her family.

"It's so nice, so quiet over here, but dull!" Oblomov would say as he left for the opera. Once, returning late from the theatre, he spent almost an hour with the coachman knocking at the gate and the dog lost its voice from all the barking and struggling and straining at the chain. Oblomov was freezing and so angry that he swore he would move out the very next day. But the next day came and went and then the day after that—a whole week passed and he still had not left. On the days he was not supposed to see Olga, hear her voice or read in her eyes that familiar, unvarying tenderness, love and happiness, he just did not know what to do with himself. But on the appointed days he came to life and, as he had in the summer, listened to her singing and looked into her eyes. When there was company one glance from her was enough, a look that meant nothing to the others, but which to him was deeply significant. However, as winter drew closer they were alone together less and less frequently. The Ilyinskys began to receive more and more visitors and whole days would go by without Oblomov being able to get in a word with Olga. They had to be content with exchanging glances—and hers sometimes expressed weariness and impatience. Olga would glower at all the guests, and a couple of times Oblomov got so bored that once, after dinner, he was on the point of taking his hat and leaving.

"Where are you going?" Olga asked him in astonishment, appearing suddenly at his elbow and grasping his hat.

"I'm going home if you don't mind."

"Why?" she asked, raising one eyebrow, "what do you have to do?"

"It's just that..." he said, his eyes rolling sleepily.

"With whose permission? You're surely not thinking of going to bed?" she asked, looking him sternly in each eye in turn.

"Of course not!" Oblomov riposted with spirit. "Sleep while it's still daylight! I'm just bored," and he let go of the hat.

"We're going to the theatre today," she said.

"Yes, but we're not sitting together in your box," he said with a sigh.

"Is that so bad? Doesn't it mean anything to you that we can see each other, that you can drop in in the interval and after the performance you can come up and give me a hand into the carriage? Please be sure to come!" she added in a tone that brooked no dissent. "What will you think of next!"

There was no help for it; he appeared at the theatre, yawned wide enough to swallow the whole stage, rubbed the back of his head and kept crossing and uncrossing his legs. "It's time to stop this nonsense—I should be sitting next to her instead of having to drag myself all this way," he thought. "To think that after the summer we spent we should have to snatch a meeting here and there surreptitiously and to have to act like love-lorn adolescents...The truth is that if I were married I would not have come to the theatre tonight, it's the sixth time I've sat through this opera..."

In the interval he went to Olga's box and could hardly squeeze his way in because of two young men about town who were blocking the entrance. After five minutes he slipped out and joined the crowd at the entrance to the stalls. The next act had already started and everyone was hurrying to their seats. The two fashionable young men from Olga's box were also in the crowd but did not see Oblomov.

"Who was that character just now in the Ilyinskys' box?" one asked the other.

"Oh, just some Oblomov." came the dismissive reply.

"And who is this Oblomov?"

"Oh, some landowner, a friend of Stoltz."

"Ah!" said his companion significantly, "a friend of Stoltz. What's he doing here?"

"*Dieu sait!*" answered the other and everyone went to their seats, but Oblomov could not recover from the blow of that casual exchange. "Who was that character…some Oblomov…what's he doing here?…*Dieu sait!*" The phrases reverberated in his head. "…just some Oblomov.", "What am I doing here? What kind of question is that? I'm in love with Olga, I'm her…And yet everyone in St. Petersburg is asking what am I doing here. They've noticed….My God!…I have to do something!"

He no longer saw what was happening on stage—the cavaliers and their ladies making their entrances; the orchestra had struck up, but Oblomov heard nothing. He looked around the theatre, counting how many acquaintances there were in the audience. They were all over the place and all asking: "who was that fellow who went to Olga's box?" "Oh, just some Oblomov," they were all telling each other.

"Yes, I really am 'just some Oblomov'," he thought with despairing resignation, "I'm known only as a friend of Stoltz. What am I doing with Olga? '*Dieu sait*'. There they are, those young bloods, looking at me and then up at Olga's box." He looked up at the box; Olga had her opera glasses trained on him.

"Oh, my God!" he thought, "she never lets me out of her sight! What did she ever see in me? A real prize! Look, now she's nodding, pointing at the stage…yes, those smart young men seem to be laughing, probably looking at me…my God!"

In his discomfiture he feverishly resumed brushing the back of his head and the restless crossing and uncrossing of his legs.

She invited the young men back for tea after the theatre, promised to repeat the cavatina and told Oblomov to come back to the house.

"No, I'm not going back there today; I must clear up all this business quickly and then…why is it taking so long for them to send me an answer from the estate…I would have gone there long ago and I would have gotten engaged to Olga before leaving…oh no! she's still looking at me! It's an absolute disaster!"

He left the theatre and went home without waiting for the end of the opera. Little by little the effects of the episode wore off and he was once again able to feel that thrill of happiness when he saw Olga alone and, when they were in company, to listen to her singing with barely suppressed tears of delight. Returning home he would, unbeknownst to Olga, lie down on the divan, not in order to sleep or to lie there dead to the world, but to fantasize about her, imagining his future happiness and contemplating with excitement the prospect of tranquil domestic bliss with everything basking in the brilliance of Olga's radiant presence. As he lay there contemplating the future, his glance would stray sometimes by chance and sometimes by design through the half-open door into the kitchen and catch sight of the landlady's busy elbows.

There was one time when the peace and quiet inside and outside the house had attained absolute perfection; no crunching of carriage wheels, no banging of doors in the hall, only the even tick-tock of the clock's pendulum and the singing of the caged birds, far from disturbing the silence, actually added a touch of life. Ilya Ilyich lay sprawled on the divan, playing idly with his slipper, raising it from the floor with his toe, lifting it, twirling it until it fell and picking it up again with his foot. Meanwhile Zakhar had come in and stationed himself at the door.

"What is it?' Oblomov inquired idly.

Zakhar kept silent and for once almost looked straight at him instead of squinting at him sideways.

"Well?" Oblomov asked, looking at him with surprise. "Is it the pie, is it ready?"

"Have you found an apartment?" Zakhar asked in his turn.

"Not yet, why?"

"Well, I haven't sorted everything out yet; the crockery, the clothes, the trunks—everything's in a pile in the lumber room; you want me to sort it out?"

"You'd better wait," Oblomov said distractedly, "I'm waiting for a reply from the estate."

"So that means the wedding won't be until after Christmas then?" Zakhar responded.

"What wedding?" asked Oblomov, springing to his feet.

"You know what wedding, yours!" Zakhar replied with assurance, as if referring to a long established fact. "I mean you're getting married."

"I'm get...ting mar...ried! Who to?" Oblomov asked, horrified, his eyes devouring Zakhar with a look of utter dismay.

"The Ilyinskys' young la..." Before Zakhar had time to finish Oblomov was practically in his face.

"What gave you that idea, you miserable creature?" Oblomov exclaimed with barely restrained emotion, bearing down on Zakhar.

"What do you mean 'miserable'? Good Lord!" said Zakhar, backing towards the door. "Why it was the Ilyinskys' servants, they've been talking about it the whole summer."

"Ssh!" Oblomov hissed at him, wagging a finger menacingly at Zakhar, "not another word!"

"But I didn't make it up!"

"Not another word!" Oblomov repeated with a threatening look and pointing to the door. Zakhar left and gave a sigh that could be heard all over the house.

Oblomov was in a daze; he stood rooted to the spot, staring with horror at the space where Zakhar had been standing and then, clapping his hands to his head in despair, sat down in the armchair.

"Everyone knows!" the thought went around and around in his head. "It's a subject of gossip in the servants' halls and the kitchens—and to the point where Zakhar didn't even hesitate to ask when is the wedding! And Olga's aunt doesn't even suspect—or maybe she does suspect and suspects something even worse...Oh God, what might she be thinking! And where does that leave me—and Olga? I'm just hopeless, what have I done!" he exclaimed, throwing himself down on the divan and burying his face in the cushion.

"A wedding, a moment of poetry in the life of people in love, the crowning moment of happiness—and it's already the subject of tittle-tattle among the servants and the coachmen when nothing's even been decided and I haven't even received a reply from the estate, my wallet is empty and I haven't even found an apartment!"

He began to examine the moment of poetry that had been drained of all its splendor from the very moment when Zakhar had mentioned it. Oblomov began to see the other side of the coin and tossed and turned from side to side in his torment, lay for a moment on his back and suddenly leapt to his feet, took three paces along the floor and then flopped down again onto the divan.

"No good can come of this," Zakhar was thinking fearfully, huddled in his corner in the hall, "the devil must have gotten hold of my tongue!"

"How could they have found out?" Oblomov reasoned, "Olga didn't say anything, and I hardly even dared to think it aloud, but in the servants' hall it was all signed and sealed. This is what comes of all that meeting alone, all those poetic sunsets and sunrises, those passionate glances and enchanting singing! No, nothing good ever comes of all that poetry of love! The thing is first to kneel at the altar and then to float away in that rose-colored empyrean. Oh God, if only I could run to her aunt, take Olga by the hand and say: 'This is my bride!' But nothing is ready; no reply from the estate, no money, no apartment! No, first I have to drum that idea out of Zakhar's head, stamp out those rumors like flames before they spread so that there's no fire—or smoke—left...A wedding! What is a wedding?"

He almost smiled when he remembered his old poetic ideal of a wedding, the long veil, the bough of orange blossom, the hushed voices of the congregation...Now the colors were not the same, now the crowd contained the boorish, ill-kempt figure of Zakhar and the whole contingent of the Ilyinsky servants, a row of carriages, strangers with faces expressing only cold curiosity—and a whole procession of equally depressing and forbidding images crowded into his mind.

"I must drum that idea out of Zakhar's head, make him realize how absurd it is," he decided, alternating between fits of nervous agitation and tormenting imaginings. It took him an hour before he finally summoned Zakhar.

Zakhar tried to pretend that he hadn't heard and was trying to sneak into the kitchen unobserved. He had already succeeded in opening the door without making it creak, but in his anxiety to prevent his side bumping against one of the double doors he grazed the other with his shoulder so that both sides flew open with a bang.

"Zakhar!" Oblomov demanded summarily.

"What is it?" Zakhar called back from the hall.

"Get in here!" said Ilya Ilyich.

"You want me to bring you something? Tell me what and I'll bring it," he replied.

"Get—in–here!" Oblomov repeated; there was an edge to his words that he enunciated with particular emphasis.

"God, I'd be better off dead!" Zakhar wheezed, edging his way into the room. "Well, what is it?" he asked, stuck in the doorway.

"I want you right here!" Oblomov stated in a solemn and ominous tone, pointing to the exact spot where he wanted him to stand, a spot so close to his master that Zakhar would practically have had to sit on his knee in order to occupy it.

"How do you expect me to get so close, I can hear fine from here?" Zakhar argued, defiantly standing his ground near the door.

"I want you right here, didn't you hear me?" Oblomov insisted with menace in his voice.

Zakhar took one step forward and stood stock still, looking out of the window at the passing chickens, presenting a broadside of bristling whiskers to his master.

In the space of an hour Ilya Ilyich's whole appearance had changed from the shock; his face seemed to have become shrunken and pinched and his eyes were restless with worry.

"Now I'm in for it!" thought Zakhar, his mood darkening rapidly.

"How could you ask your master such a stupid question?" Oblomov demanded.

"He's off, now here it comes!" thought Zakhar, blinking rapidly in doom--laden expectation of words that would cut him to the quick.

"I'm asking you what could have put such a ridiculous notion into your head!" Oblomov repeated.

Zakhar was silent.

"Zakhar, do you hear me? How dare you think such a thing, let alone say it?"

"Please, Ilya Ilyich, let me call Anisya..." Zakhar replied and started backing towards the door.

"It's you I want to talk to, not Anisya!" Oblomov retorted, "Now why did you come up with this absurdity?"

"But I didn't come up with it...it's what the Ilyinskys' servants have been saying."

"And who told them?"

"How would I know? Katya told Semyon, Semyon told Nikita, Nikita Vasilisa, Vasilisa Anisya and Anisya told me..." Zakhar explained.

"Dear Lord! Absolutely everyone!" Oblomov exclaimed in horror. "Well, it's all a load of nonsense, idiocy, lies and slanderous gossip—you hear!" said Oblomov, banging the table with his fist. "It's out of the question!"

"Why, out of the question?" Zakhar put in evenly. "A wedding, what could be more normal! You're not the only one, everyone does it."

"Oh, so it's everyone again!" said Oblomov, "so you've become an expert—at putting me on the same level as everyone else! It's out of the question—and there never was any question! 'A wedding, nothing could be more normal'! You want to know what a wedding is, I'll tell you!"

Zakhar tried to look at Oblomov, but when he saw Oblomov glaring at him so fiercely he hastily averted his eyes and looked into the corner on his right.

"Alright, now I'll explain to you what we're talking about here! 'A wedding, a wedding', that's the kind of thing you hear from people who have nothing better to do, from women and children, around servants' halls, shops and markets. A man stops being called Ilya Ilyich or Pyotr Petrovich and becomes known as the 'bridegroom'. Only the day before no one gave him a second look, but the very next day everyone is goggling at him as if he'd just committed a crime or something. He can't go to the theatre or walk in the street without people turning and whispering to one another, 'there goes the groom!' People come up to him all the time, each one putting on a stupider expression than the one before—just like the one you're wearing right now!" (Zakhar again hastily averted his eyes and looked out of the window.) "And," Oblomov continued, "saying something even more idiotic than the one before. And that's just the beginning! There you are, every morning doomed to ride to your fiancée's house dressed to the nines, in your pale yellow gloves, and God forbid that you don't make the very best impression or that you should eat or drink normally or with a healthy appetite; oh no! You are supposed to live on a diet of thin air and orange blossom. And that goes on for three or even four months. You understand? So how do you expect me to go through that?"

Oblomov stopped to satisfy himself that his account of the drawbacks of getting married was having the desired effect on Zakhar's thinking.

"Can I go now then?" Zakhar asked, turning towards the door.

"No, stay right where you are! You're the great expert at spreading false rumors and now you're going to learn why they're false."

"What am I supposed to learn?" said Zakhar, his eyes sweeping the walls of the room.

"Maybe you've forgotten the endless fuss and running around involved for the bride and groom? And who do I have—except you, of course—to run all the errands—to the tailor, the shoemaker, the cabinet-maker? There's no way I can split myself up and do everything all at once.

Wait until people in town find out, it'll be: 'Oblomov's getting married, did you hear? No, really? Who to? Who's she? When's the wedding?' " Oblomov mimicked all the different voices. "Nothing but talk, talk, talk! I won't be able to take it; I'll probably have to take to my bed from that alone—and you had to dream up this whole wedding business!" He took another look at Zakhar.

"You want me to call Anisya now?" Zakhar asked.

"Why Anisya? It was you, not Anisya, who was responsible for all this reckless speculation."

"I don't know why the Lord is punishing me like this today!" Zakhar muttered, sighing so deeply that even his shoulders rose from the effort.

"And what about the expense?" Oblomov went on, "Where's the money coming from? You know how much money I've got?" The question came out almost as a threat. "And what about the apartment? I owe them a thousand roubles here alone, and renting another place will cost me another three thousand—and then there's the cost of decorating it! Then you have to add the coach, the cook and everyday expenses! Where am I going to get it all?"

"Then how do other people with three hundred serfs manage to get married?" Zakhar challenged him and immediately regretted his rashness when he saw his master practically leap out of his chair to pounce on him.

"There he goes again with his 'others'! Now look," he said, wagging a menacing finger, "'others' live in three rooms—some even have to make do with just two rooms, nothing but a dining room and a living room to be used for everything—even sleeping, yes, children and all. And there's only one girl to do all the work; the mistress even has to do her own shopping! Can you see Olga Sergeyevna going to the market?"

"The shopping, I could do," Zakhar pointed out.

"You know how much income we get from Oblomovka?" Oblomov asked. "Did you hear what the bailiff wrote; 'there will be about two thousand less this year'? And there's the road to be built, schools to be set up, and I have to go to Oblomovka; there's nowhere to live there—there's still no house! So much for this idea of a wedding you've dreamed up!" Oblomov stopped, dismayed by the idea of such a grim, forbidding prospect. The roses, the orange blossom, the splendor of the occasion, the whispers of surprise among the congregation—all this shriveled into nothing.

His face darkened and he was lost in thought for a while. Then he began to come around and caught sight of Zakhar standing there.

"What are you doing there?" he asked morosely.

"But it was you yourself told me to!" said Zakhar.

"Get out!" Oblomov waved him away impatiently.

Zakhar started moving towards the door.

"No, wait!" Oblomov suddenly stopped him.

"Well, what is it 'go' or 'stay'?" Zakhar growled, with his hand on the door.

"Where did you get the nerve to spread such mindless rumors about me?" asked Oblomov in an agitated whisper.

"But, Ilya Ilyich, when did I ever spread any rumors? It wasn't me, it was the Ilyinskys' servants who went around saying, like, your master's gotten engaged…"

"Shsh!!" Oblomov hissed, gesturing threateningly with his hand, "not another word! Ever! You hear?"

"Yes, I hear," Zakhar replied meekly.

"And you're going to stop spreading this nonsense?"

"Yes, I won't do it any more," Zakhar answered quietly, not understanding half of the words his master was saying, but simply recognizing that they were the kind 'that cut him to the quick'."

Oblomov continued in a whisper: "Now look, the moment you hear anyone start to say anything or ask anything like that, tell them it's rubbish; there's no such thing and there never was!"

"Yes, sir." Zakhar's whisper was almost inaudible.

Oblomov looked around and wagged his finger threateningly at Zakhar. Zakhar blinked in alarm and started to retreat towards the door on tiptoe, but Oblomov intercepted him and asked: "Who was the first to mention anything about all this?"

"Katya told Semyon, Semyon told Nikita," Zakhar whispered, "Nikita told Vasilisa…"

"And you went around blabbing to everyone! Just you wait!" Oblomov hissed at him angrily. "So you go around slandering your master, do you!"

"You're really hurting me with all these nasty words," said Zakhar, "I'll call Anisya, she knows the whole story…"

"What does she know? You tell me right now!"

Zakhar disappeared like a flash through the doorway and strode into the kitchen at an unusually brisk pace. "Put down that frying pan and come in, the master wants you!" he told Anisya, pointing to the door.

Anisya handed the frying pan to Akulina, untucked the hem of her dress from her belt and pulled it down, slapped her hips with the palm of her hand, wiped her nose with her forefinger and went in to her master.

In five minutes she had put his mind at rest. She told him that no one had said anything about a wedding, and was even prepared to take the icon down from the wall and swear on it; that this was the first she had ever heard about it, and as a matter of fact what people were saying was totally different, that is that the baron, of all people, had proposed to the young lady…

"What do you mean, the baron?" Ilya Ilyich leapt to his feet, his blood running cold throughout his body.

"But there's absolutely nothing to it!" Anisya hastened to amend, realizing that she had just fallen from the frying pan into the fire.

"It's just what Katya told Semyon, and Semyon told Marfa, and

Marfa got it all wrong and passed it on to Nikita who said: 'Too bad it wasn't your master, Ilya Ilyich who proposed to her!'"

"That Nikita's an idiot!" said Oblomov.

"Yes, he really is!" Anisya confirmed. "Anyone would think that he's asleep, the way he slumps when he's out on the carriage! Vasilisa didn't believe it either," Anisya rattled on, hardly stopping for breath, "she told her back on Assumption Day, and it was the nanny herself who told Vasilisa that the young lady has no intention of getting married, and that there's no way your master wouldn't have found himself a bride long ago if he'd wanted to get married, and that she had seen Samoila only the other day and she had even laughed at the idea: 'a wedding, you must be joking'; more like a funeral if you ask me, with her auntie and her eternal headaches and the young lady herself moping around and crying. In any case there's no sign of anyone preparing a trousseau, most of the young lady's stockings need darning and they're just being left like that, and only last week they even pawned the silver…"

"Pawned the silver? So they don't have any money either!" thought Oblomov in horror, his eyes traveling wildly around the room before alighting on Anisya's nose that seemed to be the only obvious resting place, since it was that organ rather than her mouth that seemed to have been doing all the talking. "Look here, you shouldn't be spreading all this idle gossip!" Oblomov wagged a threatening finger at her.

"What idle gossip? I wouldn't even think such thoughts, let alone speak them!" Anisya jabbered in a voice like splintering wood. "And there's nothing in it anyway, today's the first time I've heard any such thing, I swear to God and may the ground open up and swallow me if I'm lying! You could have knocked me down with a feather when the master mentioned it—I was that scared, all shook up! The very idea! A wedding indeed—no one would ever imagine such a thing in their wildest dreams! I never talk to anyone; spend all my time in the kitchen. I haven't seen any of those Ilyinsky servants for over a month; don't even remember their names. And who would I talk to here? With Agafya Matveyevna all the talk is about running the house; with the old woman, you can't even have a conversation what with her coughing and being hard of hearing. Akulina's a perfect idiot and the doorman drinks. That leaves only the kids; what on earth can you say to them? As a matter of fact, I've even forgotten what the young lady looks like…"

"Alright, alright!" Oblomov said, waving her away impatiently.

"Can't talk about what isn't there," Anisya added on her way out, "and as for what Nikita said, well fools rush in where angels fear to tread. Left to myself, the idea wouldn't even have entered my head; you work, you break your back day in and day out—who's got time for that kind of thing? God is my witness—look there's the icon on the wall…" With this the chattering nose disappeared through the doorway, but the chattering itself could still be heard for another minute or so from behind the door.

"There you are, even Anisya doesn't hesitate to say that the thing is impossible!" Oblomov whispered, clasping his hands together. "Oh, happiness, happiness, how brittle, how fleeting you are!" he intoned bitterly, "with your veil, your crown, your love! And where's the money to come from to live on? Even love has to be bought, one of the pure, honorable blessings of life!"

At that moment, Oblomov's peace of mind and dream of happiness left him for good. He slept badly, ate little, and grew distracted and melancholy.

He had wanted to give Zakhar a fright and ended up frightening himself even more; once he began to take a hard look at the practical side of a wedding he saw that while it was, of course, a moment of high poetry, it was at the same time a practical arrangement, an official step in the direction of a serious and substantive reality and the assumption of rigorous responsibilities. This was not at all the conversation he had imagined having with Zakhar. He remembered how solemnly he had intended to break the news to Zakhar, how Zakhar would whoop with delight and fall at his feet and how he would have given Zakhar twenty-five roubles and ten to Anisya…He remembered that thrill of happiness, Olga's hand, her passionate kiss—and his heart sank: "It's dead, it's over," the words reverberated inside him.

"What now?"

CHAPTER FIVE

After that evening in the theatre, Oblomov did not know what kind of figure he would now cut in Olga's eyes, what she would say or what he would say to her, and decided not to visit her the next Wednesday and to wait until the Sunday when there would be a lot of company and they would have no chance of being alone together. He did not want to tell her about all the stupid talk; there was no point in burdening her with that when the damage had already been done. But saying nothing was not that easy either; he simply could not pretend with her. No matter how hard he tried to bury something in his deepest recesses she would always manage to worm it out of him.

After taking this decision he felt a little better and wrote another letter to the neighbor who was handling his affairs, urgently requesting an early—and preferably positive—reply. Then he fell to considering how to use up the vast, intolerable expanse of time that would be left vacant in two days time, on Wednesday; a time which would normally be filled with Olga's presence, the unseen communing of their souls and her singing— if it had not been for Zakhar, suddenly and for no good reason, taking it into his head to upset him! He made up his mind to go and have dinner at Ivan Gerasimovich's so as to make that unendurable day pass as painlessly as possible. That way he would have time to get ready for Sunday, by which time he might even have received a reply from the country.

The day finally came. He was woken by the dog's furious barking and frenzied leaping on the chain. Someone had entered the courtyard and was asking for someone. The doorman called Zakhar and Zakhar brought Oblomov a letter that had arrived by post.

"It's from the Ilyinskys' young lady," said Zakhar.

"How would you know?" Oblomov snapped at him. "You don't know what you're talking about!"

"At the dacha they were always bringing letters like this from her." Zakhar stood his ground.

"Is there something wrong with her? What can it be?" Oblomov wondered as he unsealed the letter.

"I can't wait until Wednesday," Olga wrote, "I hate having to wait so long to see you, so you'll find me waiting for you at three o'clock tomorrow in the Summer Garden—I'll make a point of being there!" That was all.

The same surge of panic began to well up from deep within him and once again he began to pace the room restlessly in his anxiety about what to say to Olga and how to face her. "No, I just don't know how to handle it," he said, "if only I could ask Stoltz!" Still he comforted himself with the thought that she would almost certainly come with her aunt or some other lady like Marya Semyonovna, for example, who absolutely dotes on her. In their presence he felt he would somehow manage to cover up his confusion and embarrassment and prepared himself to act affably and agreeably. "And precisely at dinner time—her timing is perfect!" he thought as he set out, not with the greatest of alacrity, for the Summer Garden.

The moment he set foot on the long path, he saw a woman in a veil get up from a bench and walk towards him. At first he thought it must be someone else: she would never have come alone, she wouldn't dare, and in any case what pretext could she have given for going out? And yet...there was something about her walk; her feet moved so nimbly and rapidly that it was as if they were gliding rather than taking one step at a time, and there was the same forward tilt of the head and neck as if she were searching for something under her feet. Someone else might have gone by her hat or her clothes but he could spend the whole morning by Olga's side without being able to say afterwards what hat or clothes she had been wearing. There was practically no one else around, except for an elderly gentleman taking his constitutional and two ladies...well, not ladies exactly but women, and a nanny with two children blue in the face from the cold.

The trees were bare and there was no foliage to block the view, and crows in the trees filled the air with their ugly cawing, but it was a fine clear day and if you were well wrapped up you would not even feel cold. The woman in the veil moved closer and closer..."It's her!" said Oblomov and stopped in alarm, unable to believe his eyes. "What are you doing here? How did you manage...?" he asked, taking her by the hand.

"I'm so happy you came," she said, without answering his question, "I thought you weren't coming and I was beginning to worry!"

"But how did you get here? How did you manage...?" he asked in bewilderment.

"Stop it! Why all this interrogation? You're being tedious! I just wanted to see you, so I came—and that's all there is to it!" She squeezed his hand and gave him a cheerful, carefree look, so frankly and openly relishing the stolen moment snatched from the jaws of fate that he felt a stab of jealousy at not being able to share her playful mood.. For all his anxiety, he could not help forgetting himself for a moment when he saw her face unclouded by the usual tension lurking in her knitted brows and etched in that little furrow; at this moment her features displayed none of that amazing maturity which had so often daunted him in the past. For these few minutes her face radiated such a childlike faith in fate, in happiness, in him, that his heart melted.

"I'm so happy, so happy!" she burst out, smiling at him full in the face, "I thought I wouldn't get to see you today. Yesterday, I suddenly felt so depressed—I don't know why—so I sent you a note. Are you pleased?" She looked him straight in the face. "Why are you wearing such a frown today? Why don't you say something? You're not pleased? I thought you'd be delirious with joy—the man seems to be asleep! Wake up, my good sir! This is Olga here!" She pushed him away from her a little by way of reproach. "You're not feeling well? What·is it?" she persisted.

"No, I'm quite well and happy," he hastened to say, anxious to prevent the conversation taking the kind of turn where Olga would start dragging his secret thoughts out of him, "it's just that I was worried...you coming here alone and..."

"That's my problem," she interrupted impatiently. "Would you really have preferred seeing *ma tante* here with me?"

"Yes, I would, Olga..."

"If I'd known I would have asked her!" Olga cut in with annoyance and removed her hand from his. "I thought nothing could please you more than seeing me."

"No, nothing, nothing in the world!" Oblomov responded, "but coming here alone like this..."

"I really don't think that this is worth a long conversation; let's talk about something else!" she said, dismissing the subject airily. "Listen, there was something I wanted to mention, but now I've forgotten..."

"It couldn't have been about how you came here alone, could it?" he persisted, looking around anxiously.

"No, of course not, why do you keep harping on that? It's so boring! Now what was it I wanted to say? Well, it doesn't matter, I'm sure it will come back to me. How nice it is here! The leaves have all fallen. Do you remember *Feuilles d'Automne*—you know, Hugo. Look, the sun's out over there by the river; let's go to the river and take a boat out…!"

"Good God, what are you talking about, in this weather? All I have on is this quilted coat!"

"Yes, and all I have on is a quilted dress—and so what? Come on, let's go!" She ran off, dragging him along resisting and protesting, but nothing would do but getting into a boat and taking it out.

"Now, how *did* you get here alone?" Oblomov persisted anxiously.

"You want me to tell you?" she teased him mischievously when they had gone out as far as the middle of the river, "I suppose I can now that you can't get away, otherwise you would have run away…"

"Why?" he asked nervously.

Instead of answering him, she asked: "will you be coming tomorrow?"

"My God!" thought Oblomov, "it's as if she can read my thoughts and knows that I didn't intend to come!"

"Yes, I'm coming." he said aloud.

"In the morning—and stay all day?"

Words failed him.

"Then I'm not telling you!"

"Alright, all day."

"Well, you see…" she began seriously, "the reason I got you here today was to tell you…"

"What?" he broke in anxiously.

"To tell you….to come tomorrow…"

"Oh, for God's sake!" he burst out in exasperation, "would you mind just telling me how you got here!"

"Got here? Well I just came…I mean it's not worth talking about!" She scooped up a handful of water and splashed him in the face. He frowned and gave a shudder and she burst out laughing. "How cold the water is! My hand's all frozen! Isn't this great? It's such fun!" she said, taking in the view on both sides. "Let's come again tomorrow—only we'll come here straight from home…!"

"You mean you didn't come straight here today? Where did you come from then?" he asked quickly.

"From the shop," she replied.

"What shop?"

"What do you mean 'what shop'? I told you which one back in the Garden…"

"No, you didn't!" he responded impatiently.

"I didn't? How strange! I must have forgotten. I went straight from home to the jeweler's with one of the servants…"

"And?"

"Just that…what church is that?" she asked the boatman suddenly, pointing into the distance.

"Which one? You mean that one over there?" the boatman asked in turn.

"It's the Smolny!" Oblomov told her impatiently, "So once you were at the shop, what…?"

"Oh, they had some beautiful things, I saw a wonderful bracelet…"

"I'm not interested in bracelets," Oblomov cut in irritably. "What happened then?"

"Well, that was all," she replied absently, admiring the view with keen attention.

"But what happened to the servant?" Oblomov persisted.

"Oh him, he went home," she replied casually, concentrating on the buildings on the opposite bank.

"And you?"

"It looks so interesting over there, couldn't we go?" she asked, pointing at the opposite bank with her umbrella, "Isn't that where you live?"

"Yes."

"Show me which street!"

"But what about this servant?" Oblomov persisted.

"Oh, him," she replied casually, "I sent him for the bracelet. He went home and I came on here."

"How could you do such a thing?" said Oblomov, his eyes bulging with astonishment. He wore an expression of dismay that Olga mimicked.

"Be serious, Olga, this is no laughing matter!"

"I'm not joking, this is really the way it happened," she said evenly, "I left my bracelet at home on purpose and *ma tante* asked me to go to the shop. You would never have thought of doing that!" she added proudly as if she had brought off some extraordinary feat.

"But what if this servant comes back?"

"I told him to wait for me there and that I was going to another shop, and then I came here…"

"And what if Marya Mikhailovna asks which other shop you went to?"

"I'll tell her I went to the dressmaker's."

"And if she asks the dressmaker?"

"And if all the water in the Neva flows away into the sea and the boat capsizes, and if Morskaya Street collapses and our house with it, and if you suddenly fall out of love with me…" she said, splashing him in the face again.

"That servant has probably come back and is already waiting there," he said, wiping his face, "boatman, back to the boat station!"

"No, don't!" she ordered the boatman.

"We're going back, the servant must be back by now," Oblomov insisted.

"So what if he is? We're not going back!"

But Oblomov got his way and hurried Olga back through the Garden while she tried to hang back, clinging to his arm.

"What's the hurry?" she said, "slow down, I want to spend a little longer with you!"

She slowed her pace even more, pressing close to his shoulder and looking him closely in the face while he lectured her pompously and tediously about obligations and duty. She listened with half an ear, with her head lowered and a weary smile, glancing back and forth between his face and the ground at her feet, her mind on something quite different.

"Listen, Olga," he concluded solemnly, "at the risk of causing you annoyance and suffering your recriminations, I am nevertheless bound to say that we have overstepped the mark and it is my duty, my responsibility to tell you."

"Tell me what?" she said impatiently.

"That we are very wrong to be meeting secretly."

"You said that when we were still back at the dacha," she said pensively.

"Yes, but then I couldn't control my feelings; I pushed you away with one hand and pulled you back with the other. You were so trusting and I...well...wasn't being entirely honest with you—the feeling was so new and powerful then..."

"Oh, and now it's not new any more and it's beginning to pall!"

"No, Olga, that's not fair! It was new then, and it was impossible for me to come to my senses. Now I'm racked by guilt; you're young, you don't know much about the world or about people; and you're so innocent, your love is so pure that the idea doesn't even enter your head that what we are doing is going to earn us both a very bad reputation –especially me!"

"What do you mean 'what we are doing'?" she stopped to ask.

"You really don't know? You're lying to your aunt, you leave the house without telling anyone and you go and meet a man alone...try telling that to your guests on Sunday...!"

"Why wouldn't I tell them?" she said calmly, "I think I will..."

"And then you'll see what happens; your aunt will go into shock, the women will rush out of the room and the men will start giving you knowing and suggestive looks."

She pondered for a moment before protesting: "But we're an engaged couple!"

"Yes, my dear, dear Olga," he said, taking both her hands and squeezing them, "and that's precisely why we have to be all the more careful and watch our every step. I want to be able to take you by the hand and walk proudly along this very path for the entire world to see, instead of furtively and in secret. I want people to lower their eyes respectfully when they see you instead of giving you those knowing and insolent stares. I want to prevent anyone entertaining the slightest suspicion that a proud young woman like you could heedlessly throw aside concern for your reputation and upbringing and just forget yourself and your duty..."

"I haven't forgotten anything, myself, my upbringing, my reputation or my duty," she retorted, removing her hand from his.

"I know, I know, my pure innocent angel, but this is not what I think, it's what other people, the people who know us, say, and they would never forgive you. Please try to understand what it is I want; I want you to be as pure, innocent and irreproachable in the eyes of the world as you are in actual fact."

She continued walking thoughtfully.

"Please try to understand why I'm saying all this; you'll end up suffering for this and it will be all my fault. People will say that I led you astray and deliberately hid the disastrous consequences from you. I know that your behavior with me is proper and above reproach, but who are you going to convince of this, who will believe it?"

"It's true," she said with a shudder, "but listen," she added decisively, "we'll go to *ma tante* and tell her everything and then tomorrow she can give us her blessing."

Oblomov turned pale.

"What's wrong?" she asked.

"Wait, Olga! Why all the hurry?" he put in quickly. Meanwhile his lips were quivering.

"Wasn't it you two weeks ago who were trying to rush *me* into it?" she asked dryly, giving him a penetrating look.

"Yes, well then I wasn't thinking about all the preparations that would be necessary, there's so much to do," he said with a sigh, "let's wait at least until I get the letter from the estate."

"But why, surely it isn't going to make any difference to your intentions whatever answer you get?" she asked watching him even more intently.

"Of course not, what an idea? It's just that right now every scrap of information is important. After all, we're going to have to tell your aunt when the wedding is to be. We won't just be talking to her about our love but about matters I'm totally unprepared for right now."

"Then we won't raise those matters until you've got your letter, but at least everyone will know that we are engaged and we can see each other every day. I can't go on like this, it's so dreary and the days drag by so slowly. And people notice; they're always coming up to me and finding ways of bringing your name into the conversation suggestively—I'm sick of it!"

"Bringing my name into it?" Oblomov could hardly bring out the words.

"Yes, thanks to dear Sonechka!"

"You see, you see, you wouldn't listen to me then, you even got annoyed with me!"

"See what? I see nothing, only that you are a coward...I couldn't care less about their insinuations!"

"It's not cowardice, I'm just being careful. Let's get away from here, Olga, for God's sake—look, there's a carriage coming in this direc...! Oh God, it might be people we know! I'm breaking into a cold sweat—quick, let's go, let's move!" he said nervously.

His anxiety began to infect Olga. "Yes," the words tumbled out of her in a rush, "quick, let's get out of here!"

They practically ran along the path to where the Garden ended without uttering a word, Oblomov looking frantically in every direction, and Olga with her head lowered and wrapped in the veil.

"Tomorrow then!" she said when they had reached the shop where the servant was waiting for her.

"No, the day after is better…no, better still, Friday or Saturday," he answered.

"But why?"

"Well, you see Olga, I can't help thinking that the letter may have arrived by then."

"Maybe, but come tomorrow anyway for dinner, you hear?"

"Yes, alright, I will!" he replied hurriedly as she disappeared into the shop. "My God, to think that we've come to this! It's as if a boulder has fallen on top of me. What am I going to do now? Sonechka, Zakhar, those smart young men…!"

CHAPTER SIX

He did not notice that Zakhar had served him a cold dinner and had no notion of how he came to find himself in bed where he slept like a log. The next day he shuddered at the thought of going to Olga's; he just could not face the prospect of all those significant looks everyone would be giving him. As it was, the doorman already taken to greeting him in a particularly friendly way and if he so much as asked for a glass of water, Semyon would fall over himself to rush and fetch it, while Katya and the nanny would see him out with the warmest of smiles.

He could see the word "fiancé" written all over their faces and he hadn't even asked for her aunt's consent, hadn't a penny to his name, had no idea when he would have, or even how much income he could expect from his estate this year—not to mention that he didn't even have a house to live in on the estate—some fiancé!

He made up his mind that until he received some positive news from the estate he would see Olga only on Sundays with company present, so that on the morning of the next day he made no preparations for going to see Olga. He did not shave or get dressed and just idly leafed through the French newspapers he had borrowed that week from the Ilyinskys and did not keep glancing at the clock and frowning when he saw how slowly the hands were moving.

Zakhar and Anisya had assumed that he would be dining out as usual and had not thought to ask him what he wanted for dinner. Oblomov reprimanded them sharply and declared that the idea that he dined every Wednesday at the Ilyinskys' was far from the truth and "slanderous" into the bargain, and that as a matter of fact he had been dining at Ivan Gerasimovich's and that henceforth he would be dining at home except perhaps for Sundays—and not every Sunday at that!

Anisya instantly rushed to the market to buy giblets for Oblomov's favorite soup.

The landlady's children came in and he checked Vanya's addition and subtraction and found two mistakes. He ruled lines in Masha's exercise book and wrote out a row of capital 'A's. He listened to the chirping of the canaries and through the half-open door watched the landlady's elbows flashing back and forth.

Sometime after one o'clock she called through the door to ask him if he would like a snack; they had baked cheese tarts. She brought him some cheese tarts and a glass of currant-flavored vodka. Ilya Ilyich calmed down a little and lapsed into a mindless stupor that lasted almost until dinnertime.

After dinner he had stretched out on the divan and just as his head was beginning to loll from drowsiness the door was opened from the landlady's side and Agafya Matveyevna appeared with a pile of stockings in each hand. She put them down on two chairs and Oblomov jumped up and offered her a third chair but she would not sit down; she was always on her feet and on the move, there was always some job that needed doing. "I've just been sorting your stockings," she said, "fifty-five pairs and all in a bad way..."

"It's so kind of you!" said Oblomov going over to her and taking her gently and playfully by the elbows. She giggled. "You really shouldn't trouble yourself! I'm quite ashamed."

"Not at all, it's just part of the household chores; it's not as if you had someone to sort them for you, and anyway, I like doing it," she replied, "and there's twenty pairs that can't be worn again—not even worth darning."

"Please don't bother, just throw them all out! You shouldn't be wasting your time on such nonsense, I can easily buy new ones..."

"What do you mean 'throw them out', what for? Now these can all be repaired," and she proceeded busily to count them out.

"Why are you standing, do sit down please!" He offered her the chair again.

"No, really, thank you very much, I really have no time to sit," she replied, declining the offer of a chair again, "it's washing day and I have to get all the dirty laundry ready."

"You're a wonderful housekeeper!" he said, his eyes fixed on her throat and bosom.

She giggled. "So, should I repair the stockings then? I'll order some yarn and thread. There's an old woman who brings it from the country; the stuff you can get here isn't worth buying. It's rotten."

"It would be so kind of you—I would really appreciate it, but honestly, I feel so bad about putting you to all this trouble."

"No trouble at all! I mean, what are we here for? I'll do these myself and get granny to do the others. Tomorrow my sister-in-law is coming to stay; we'll have nothing to do in the evenings, so we can do them then.

My Masha is already learning to knit, only she keeps pulling out the needles—her hands are too small to hold them."

"You mean Masha is already learning, at her age?" Oblomov asked.

"Yes, she really is!"

"I don't know how to thank you," said Oblomov, eyeing her with the same

pleasure with which he had contemplated the steaming cheese tarts that morning. "I'm really so grateful, I must do something to repay you, especially for Masha; I'll buy her some silk dresses and dress her up like a doll."

"What are you thinking about? There's nothing to be grateful for! What's she going to do with silk dresses? She wears everything out so fast we even run out of plain cotton dresses—and as for shoes, we just can't buy them fast enough!" She gathered up the stockings and was about to leave.

"What's your hurry?" he said, "stay a little longer, I'm not doing anything."

"Maybe some other time—during the holidays; and you must come and have coffee with us. But now I really have to see to the washing—I must go and see if Akulina has started."

"Oh well, never mind, I don't want to keep you," said Oblomov, watching her back and elbows as she went out.

"Oh, and I got your dressing gown out of the box room," she added, "it can be cleaned and mended; the material is such good quality, it will last for ages!"

"No need! I don't wear it any more, I've given it up, I don't need it."

"Well anyway, it can still be washed; who knows, you might wear it again one day…for your wedding!" she added with a little giggle and shut the door behind her.

His drowsiness suddenly left him, his ears pricked up and his eyes popped. "So even she knows all about it!" he said, sinking onto the chair he had offered her, "oh, Zakhar, Zakhar!"

So once again Zakhar had to endure an avalanche of "words that cut him to the quick", once again Anisya's nose started wagging and protesting that no, it was the first time she had heard the landlady mention a wedding, that there had never been the slightest allusion to such a thing in their conversations and in any case there wasn't any wedding, it was out of the question. It must all be a malicious rumor, probably started by the devil himself, and may the ground open up and swallow her, and the landlady too was ready to take down the icon from the wall and swear on it that she had never heard of any Ilyinsky young lady and was thinking of someone else's fiancé altogether…Anisya went on and on so that Oblomov had to interrupt and wave her away, and when Zakhar tried to talk Oblomov into letting him go back to the old place in Gorokhovaya Street for a visit. Oblomov told him he would give him 'visits' alright!—

so that Zakhar was glad to get out of the room in one piece. "Oh, so there are still some people there who don't know, so you have to go and spread the malicious rumor around a little more—no you're staying right here!" Oblomov thundered.

Wednesday passed. On Thursday Oblomov received another letter by post from Olga asking him why he hadn't come, what did it mean and what had happened. She wrote that she had been in tears the whole evening and had hardly slept a wink the whole night.

"That angel crying, not sleeping, oh my God!" Oblomov exclaimed. "Why is she in love with me, why am I in love with her? Why did we ever meet? It was Andrei; he was the one who infected both of us with the germ. And what a life! Endless trouble, turbulence and consternation! When will I get some peace and quiet, some peace of mind?"

Sighing loudly, he lay down and got up again by turns and even went out into the street, all the time trying to imagine a pattern of life, an existence that would be full and yet would flow gently day by day, drop by drop, in silent contemplation of nature and those gentle stirrings and mild vicissitudes of family life. He was not inclined to see life the way Stoltz did, as a mighty, roaring torrent, surging forward with its foaming waves.

"It's a sickness, a fever—with its dangerous rapids, bursting dams and floods," said Oblomov.

He wrote to tell Olga that he had caught a chill in the Summer Garden and that he thought that he had better stay home for two days and dose himself with medicinal herb tea, but that now he was over it and looked forward to seeing her on Sunday.

She wrote back, commending him for taking good care of himself and advising him to stay home on Sunday too and added that the important thing was for him to take care of his health even if it meant her kicking her heels for a whole week without seeing him. This reply was brought by Nikita, the very one who, according to Anisya, had started the whole rumor. He also brought some new books sent by Olga with instructions to read them and report, when they next met, on whether she would find them worth reading herself. She asked him to report on his health.

Oblomov wrote his reply and personally handed it to Nikita, escorted him out to the courtyard and watched him leave by the gate to make sure that he did not duck into the kitchen and repeat his 'slanderous gossip' there and that Zakhar did not accompany him out into the street.

He was quite relieved at Olga's suggestion that he should take good care of himself and not come on Sunday, and wrote that in order to recover fully it was a good idea for him to stay at home for a few more days.

On Sunday he visited the landlady, drank coffee, ate hot pie, and sent Zakhar to the city to bring back ice cream and sweets for the children in time for dinner. Zakhar had trouble getting back across the river because the bridges had already been removed and the Neva was beginning to freeze over. The question of Oblomov's going to Olga's the next Wednesday did not even arise.

Of course, it was still possible to rush across right away and stay with Ivan Gerasimovich for a few days and to call at Olga's every day and even dine there, but he had an excellent excuse; he was stranded on the wrong side of the Neva and it was too late to get across.

Oblomov's first impulse was to act on this idea and he actually lowered his feet smartly to the floor, but after a moment's reflection his face took on an expression of worried concentration and he heaved a sigh and slowly lay back down again.

"No, it's best to let the talk die down and give all those visitors to Olga's house a chance to forget about Oblomov and only start seeing him there again every day after their engagement had been announced," he thought. "It's tedious just waiting with nothing to do," he sighed as he picked up the books Olga had sent. He had read about fifteen pages when Masha came into the room to ask him if he wanted to go down to the river—everyone was going to watch the Neva freeze over. He went and returned for tea.

The days passed. Time hung heavy on Oblomov's hands; he read a little, went outside to walk and kept glancing through the doorway at the landlady in order to relieve the boredom by exchanging a word or two. Once he even ground a few pounds of coffee for her with such enthusiasm that his forehead broke into a sweat. He tried to interest her in reading one of his books. After she had read the title to herself, slowly moving her lips, she handed the book back, saying that, come Christmas, she would ask for the book back and get Vanya to read it aloud so that granny could hear it too, but that she was too busy right now.

Meanwhile a footway had been laid across the ice and once the dog's frantic barking and leaping heralded the arrival of Nikita for the second time bringing a book and a note inquiring after his health. Oblomov, afraid that he too might have to cross the footway to the other side, hid from Nikita and replied in writing that there was a slight swelling in his throat and that he was therefore not quite ready to venture out and he deplored "the cruel fate that was depriving him for a few more days of the joy of seeing his beloved Olga." He issued strict orders to Zakhar on no account to exchange a word with Nikita and made a point of watching the latter until he had left by the wicket gate and shook a warning finger at Anisya when she was on the point of sticking her nose out of the kitchen in order to ask Nikita something.

CHAPTER SEVEN

A week went by. The moment he woke up in the morning Oblomov's first thought was to inquire anxiously whether the bridges had been put back. Once he had been reassured that they had not, he passed the days tranquilly, listening to the ticking of the grandfather clock, the grinding of the coffee mill and the chirping of the canaries. He no longer heard the chirping of the chicks as they had long since grown into mature hens and now hid in their coops. As for the books sent by Olga, he never finished reading them. One of them had been lying for days face down and open to page one hundred and five, just where Oblomov had gotten to when he had put it down for the last time.

He began to spend more time with the landlady's children. Vanya was such a quick learner that he was able to recite the names of Europe's major cities after only three attempts and Ilya Ilyich promised that as soon as he could get across the river he would bring him back a small globe. Little Masha hemmed him three handkerchiefs; they were crudely done, of course, but he had to smile when he watched her busy little hands at work and at the way she kept running to him every minute to show him her handiwork.

Whenever he caught a glimpse of her elbows through the opening in the doorway he would strike up a conversation with the landlady. He soon learned to tell from the movements of her elbows exactly what she was doing, sifting, grinding or ironing. He even tried making conversation with the grandmother, but she was quite incapable of conducting a proper conversation; she would stop suddenly in mid-sentence, support herself against the wall with her fist, bend down, cough away for all the world as if the enormous effort was too much for her and then start groaning—and that was the end of the conversation.

The brother he never saw at all except in the form of the bulky package flashing past his window and his presence in the house was so silent that he might just as well not have been there at all. Even when Oblomov happened to enter the room where they were having dinner, all huddled closely together around the table, the brother would hastily wipe his lips with his fingers and disappear into his attic.

One day Oblomov had just woken up and was reaching for his coffee without a care in the world, when Zakhar burst into the room with the news that the bridges had been put back. Oblomov's heart missed a beat. "And tomorrow is Sunday," he said, "and I have to go to Olga's and brave the significant and curious glances of the other guests and then tell her when I intend to talk to her aunt." And all this was at a time when he was still in the grip of total inertia. He could see only too vividly what would happen once his engagement was officially announced. The very next day would see the start of a procession of ladies and gentlemen coming to call; he would suddenly become an object of curiosity, there would be a formal dinner, his health would be drunk and then in accordance with tradition he would be obliged to bring a gift for his fiancée.

"A gift!" he said in dismay and broke into bitter laughter. "A gift, and here he was with two hundred roubles to his name! Even if they sent him any money, it wouldn't be before Christmas when they had sold the grain; but when it would be sold and how much there was and how much money it would fetch—all that was supposed to be detailed in the letter—and there was no letter. So now what? In any case it was goodbye to his two weeks away from it all!"

Amid of all these worries he saw clearly Olga's beautiful face, her fluffy, expressive eyebrows and those blue-gray eyes sparkling with intelligence: he saw her dear head, her hair falling low onto her neck, making the line of her back, head, shoulders and waist a graceful and harmonious contour. But the moment he began to melt with love his problems would weigh down on him and crush him like a stone—what action to take, what to do, how to handle the whole wedding business, where to get money, what were they going to live on...? "Maybe I'll wait a little longer—who knows, maybe the letter will come tomorrow or the day after," he thought, and tried to calculate how long it would have taken for his letter to reach the estate, how long his neighbor would take to reply and how long it would take for his answer to arrive. "It should arrive in three or, at the most, four days, so I'll put off going to Olga's," he decided, particularly since she was not likely to know that the bridges had been put back.

But unknown to Oblomov, the first thing that Olga had asked her maid that very morning on waking up was: "Katya, have they put the bridges back yet?" Moreover she repeated the question every day.

"I don't know, miss, I haven't seen the coachman or the doorman this morning and Nikita doesn't know."

"You can never tell me what I want to know!" Olga said irritably as she lay in bed examining the chain around her neck.

"I'll go and find out right away, miss. I didn't want to leave you before in case you woke up, otherwise I'd have gone to find out much earlier." And Katya dashed out of the room.

Olga opened the drawer of her bedside table and took out Oblomov's last note. "The poor thing isn't well," she worried, "he must be so lonely, all by himself like that. Oh dear, how much longer...?" At that moment Katya flew into the room, red in the face.

"They've been put back, they did it last night!" she announced jubilantly and held out her arms to her mistress as she bounced out of bed, threw a smock over her and brought her tiny slippers for her feet. Olga quickly opened the drawer, took something out and put it into Katya's hand. All of this—jumping out of bed, the coin pressed into Katya's palm and the kissing of the mistress's hand—happened within the space of a second.

"What a stroke of luck—it 's tomorrow, Sunday, that he's coming!" she thought to herself as she hurried into her clothes, snatched a cup of tea and went off to the shops with her aunt. "*Ma tante*, why don't we go to mass tomorrow at the Smolny?" she asked. Her aunt gave a little frown and after thinking for a moment replied: "Well, we could, but why on earth would it enter your head to go so far in the winter?"

The reason it had entered Olga's head was simply that Oblomov had pointed out the church to her from the river and she felt an urge to go and pray there…for him, for his health, for him to love her, to be happy with her…for a quick end to all the indecisiveness and uncertainty… Poor Olga!

Sunday arrived. Olga cleverly arranged for the dinner to consist of Oblomov's favorite dishes. She put on her white dress, wore the bracelet he had given her under her lace cuffs and arranged her hair the way he liked it. The evening before she had had the piano tuned, and in the morning had practiced "Casta diva". She was in better voice than she had ever been at the dacha. Then she started waiting.

The baron found her waiting and commented that she was once again looking as pretty as she had in the summer but was a little thinner. "It's the lack of country air and the slight disruption in your routine that has told on you," he said, "dear Olga Sergeyevna, you're someone who needs the country air." He kissed her hand repeatedly and the dye on his moustache left a tiny mark on her fingers.

"Oh yes, the country," she replied abstractedly, addressing the remark not so much to him as to some invisible presence.

"While we're on the subject," he added, "next month the legal proceedings will be completed and you will come into your inheritance, so you will be able to go to your estate in the country. It's not big, but a wonderful location! You'll like it. A wonderful house—and garden! There's a gazebo up on the hill. You'll love it. A river view…you probably don't remember it, you were only five when your father left the place and took you away."

"Oh yes, I'm so looking forward to it!" she said and started thinking: "Now that's settled, we'll go there, but he won't know about it until…Next month, baron, are you sure?" she asked excitedly.

"As sure as I am that you always look beautiful, of course, but especially today," he said and left to go and see her aunt.

Olga remained standing where she was, picturing the happiness that was soon to be hers, but she resolved to say nothing to Oblomov about this news or her plans for the future. She wanted to bide her time until at long last the force of love would triumph over his natural indolence and the weight of inertia finally slid from his shoulders, and he would reach out for the happiness within his grasp and, after receiving a favorable reply from his estate, would run, would fly to lay it jubilantly at her feet and they would race to her aunt and then…Only then would she reveal to him that she now had her own country estate complete with summer house, garden, river view and a house ready for them to move into, and she would tell him that they must go there first and then to Oblomovka.

"But no," she thought, "I don't want him to get a favorable reply, because then he'll feel proud and won't be so delighted to learn that I have my own estate with my own house and garden. No, it's better if he arrives distraught, with bad news from his estate that everything is in a mess and that he's going to have to go there alone. He'll rush off pell-mell to Oblomovka, and make some slapdash arrangements, forgetting a lot of things in his haste. He'll be unable to cope and will leave things any old how and will dash back to St. Petersburg only to discover that there was no need for all this rushing back and forth because all the time there was a house, a garden and a summer house with a view just waiting for him— a place to live even without Oblomovka...Yes, yes, I won't breathe a word until the very last moment; let him make the journey, let him make an effort, display some energy—for my sake, for the sake of our future happiness. But wait a minute! Why send him down to the country, why should we be apart?" No, when he came to say goodbye for a whole month, dressed in his traveling clothes, all pale and grim-faced, she would surprise him with the news that there was no need to go before the summer and then they would go together to..."

This was the scene she was picturing when she broke off to run to the baron and tactfully suggested to him that it would be better not to let anyone know about the news—with a special emphasis on "anyone." Of course, by "anyone" she meant only Oblomov.

"Yes, of course, there's no need to mention it," he agreed, "except to Monsieur Oblomov if the subject should come up..."

Olga forced herself to respond more casually than she felt and said: "No, better not tell him either."

"Whatever you say, you know that your wish is my command," he responded graciously.

Olga was not without her share of guile. If she felt a strong urge to look at Oblomov when there was company she would look at three other people in turn before allowing herself to look at him.

All this scheming and planning—just for Oblomov! How many times did the color mount to her cheeks! How many times did she strike one key or another to make sure that the piano was perfectly in tune, or shift the music from one position to another! And still no sign of him! What could it mean?

Three, four o'clock—still no Oblomov! By half-past four her glow, her radiance began to dim. She seemed to have shriveled as she sat down pale faced at the table. None of the others noticed a thing as they sat and ate the dishes prepared especially for him, chatting casually and light-heartedly with one another.

Dinner is over and it is evening, but still Oblomov has not come. Her feelings swung between hope and anxiety and at ten o'clock she went to her room.

Her first instinct was to vent on him mentally all the bile and bitterness that had been accumulating in her heart. In her mind she spared him no sarcasm, however biting, no recriminations, however bitter, and lashed him with the most scathing expressions in her vocabulary. One minute her whole being was ablaze with anger and the next minute it was in the throes of anxiety.

"He's sick, he's alone; he's too weak to write." This conviction took total possession of her and kept her awake all night. She dozed feverishly for a couple of hours, her mind racing deliriously, but when she rose, pale and wan, the next morning she was entirely calm, composed and resolute.

On the Monday morning the landlady put her head into Oblomov's study and said: "There's a girl asking for you."

"For me? Impossible," Oblomov replied, "where is she?"

"Right here, she must have come to our house by mistake; shall I show her in?"

Before Oblomov could make up his mind what to do Katya was standing in front of him. The landlady left.

"Katya!" Oblomov said in astonishment, "what are you doing here?"

"My mistress is here," she replied in a whisper, "she told me to ask..."

The color drained from Oblomov's cheeks. "Olga Sergeyevna!" he whispered in dismay, "It's not true, Katya, don't make such cruel jokes!"

"It's the truth, believe me! She hired a carriage and right now she's waiting in a tea shop and wants to come on here. She sent me to ask you to send Zakhar out on some errand and she'll be here in half an hour."

"I'd better go to her, she can't come here," said Oblomov.

"It's too late, she'll be here at any moment, she thinks you must be sick. Goodbye now, I must be off, she's alone and waiting for me..." She left.

Oblomov put on his tie, waistcoat and boots with unwonted speed and called Zakhar.

"Zakhar, you were telling me before that you wanted to go back to Gorokhovaya Street, over the other side, to pay a visit; well, now's your chance—you can go right now!" said Oblomov, seething with agitation.

"I don't want to," Zakhar replied categorically.

"No, you're going!" Oblomov insisted.

"No one goes visiting on weekdays! I'm not going!" Zakhar was obdurate.

"Now, just go, you'll have a good time. Don't be stubborn! If the master is good enough to let you go...go and see your friends!"

"Some friends they are!"

"You really don't want to see them?"

"They're villains, the lot of them! I don't care if I never set eyes on them again!"

"Just go, for God's sake!" Oblomov commanded him, the blood rushing to his head.

"No, I'm staying at home all day today, but I'll go on Sunday if you like," Zakhar coolly stood his ground.

"No, right now, this very minute!" said Oblomov in exasperation as he tried to hurry him out of the house, "you've got to..."

"But why should I go all that way for nothing?" Zakhar objected.

"Then go and take a walk for a couple of hours; look at your face, you're still half asleep, it'll do you good to get some fresh air in your lungs!"

"Nothing I can do about the face, it's pretty much the kind of face everyone like me has," said Zakhar, looking lazily out of the window.

"Dear God! She's going to be here any minute now!" thought Oblomov, wiping the sweat from his brow. "Alright, I'm asking you a favor, go and take a walk, please! Here's twenty kopecks, treat yourself and a friend to a beer!"

"It's better if I wait on the porch; that way I'll keep out of the cold— although I suppose I could sit by the gate..."

"No, I want you to go further than the gate!" Oblomov said with some vehemence. "Go into the next street, you know, on the left where it leads to the garden...over on the other side!"

"This is crazy!" thought Zakhar, "he's chasing me out of the house, the first time ever!"

"Ilya Ilyich, Sunday will be better..."

"Are you going or not?" said Oblomov through gritted teeth, bearing down on Zakhar.

Zakhar made himself scarce and Oblomov called Anisya. "Go to the market and do some shopping for dinner!" he told her.

"But sir, we've already bought everything we need; dinner will soon be ready," the nose started to say.

"Shut up and listen!" Oblomov shouted. Anisya was intimidated. "Go and buy....I don't know, asparagus," he added, desperately attempting to dredge up something, anything, to send her for.

"But sir, asparagus is out of season now—there's nowhere around here you'll find it."

"Out!" he shouted, and she took off. "Run as fast as your legs will carry you!" he shouted after her, "and don't look back, then come back as slowly as you can; I don't want to see your face back here for at least two hours!"

"What's all this craziness?" Zakhar said to Anisya, running into her outside the gate. "Go out for a walk!" he says and gives me twenty kopecks. "Where am I supposed to go for a walk?"

"The master knows his business," Anisya observed shrewdly, "so why don't you go around to Artemy, the count's coachman and treat him to some tea—he's always treating you, and I'll run to the market."

"It's crazy," Zakhar repeated to Artemy, "my master chased me out of the house and gave me money for beer…"

"Well, maybe he got the idea of getting drunk himself," said Artemy, making a shrewd guess, "and gave you the money so you wouldn't stay around and get envious, Let's go!" he gave Zakhar a wink and nodded in the direction of a certain street.

"Yes, let's go!" Zakhar echoed him, nodding in the same direction. "I can't get over it, it's so weird, sending me out for a walk!" he wheezed to himself with a grin.

They went on their way, while Anisya, who had run as far as the first crossroads, sat down in a ditch behind the fence and waited to see what would happen.

Meanwhile Oblomov was watching, listening and waiting. Soon he heard someone lifting the latch of the side gate, immediately setting off the furious barking and rattling of the chain.

"That damned dog!" Oblomov hissed through gritted teeth, picking up his cap and hurrying out to the gate. He opened it and practically carried Olga back to the porch. She was alone; Katya was waiting in the carriage not far from the gate.

"You're not ill? Not in bed? What's the matter?" she asked the moment they were inside his study, without taking off her cloak or hat and inspecting him from top to toe.

"I'm feeling better now, my throat's cleared up almost completely," he said, touching his throat and giving a little cough.

"Why didn't you come yesterday?" she asked, giving him such a penetrating look that he dared not utter a word.

"Olga, how could you do something so reckless?" he asked in horror, "Do you realize what you are doing?"

"We'll talk about that later!" she cut in impatiently. "I'm asking you what does it mean—your keeping away like this?"

He said nothing.

"Did your stye come back?"

More silence.

"You weren't ill, you didn't have a sore throat?" she said, frowning.

"No, I wasn't," Oblomov answered like a child to his teacher.

"You lied to me!" she looked at him in astonishment. "Why?"

"I'll explain everything, Olga," he said, attempting to exonerate himself, "there was a good reason why I didn't come to see you for two weeks…I was afraid…"

"What of?" she asked, sitting down and removing her hat and cloak. He took them and put them down on the divan.

"Talk, gossip…"

"But weren't you afraid that I wouldn't sleep at night, imagining all kinds of terrible things, and that I might be in a state of collapse?" she said, running a searching look over him.

"Olga, you can't imagine what I'm going through here!" he said, pointing to his head and heart; "I'm consumed with anxiety; you don't know what happened!"

"What else has happened?" she asked coldly.

"You've no idea how far these rumors about the two of us have traveled! I didn't want to alarm you and was afraid to show myself."

He recounted everything he had heard from Zakhar and Anisya, reported the conversation between the fashionable young men at the theatre and concluded by saying that since that time he had been unable to sleep and saw in every glance a question, a reproach or sly digs about their meetings.

"But we were going to tell *ma tante* last week," she objected, "and that would have put a stop to the talk."

"Yes, but I didn't want to talk to your aunt until this week after receiving the letter. I know it's not my feelings she's going to question me about, but about my estate—and in detail—and there's nothing I can tell her until I get an answer from my agent."

She sighed. "If I hadn't known you better," she mused, "God knows what things I would have been imagining. You were afraid to trouble me with servants' gossip, but thought nothing of worrying me to death! I just don't understand you."

"I just thought that all that talk would upset you. Katya, Marfa, Semyon and that idiot, Nikita, God knows what they've been going around saying?"

"I've known all along what they've been saying," she said with equanimity.

"What do you mean, you've known?"

"Just that Katya and nanny have been telling me all along, asking about you and congratulating me..."

"Actually congratulating you?" he asked, horrified, "And what about you?"

"Oh, I just thanked them and gave nanny a headscarf, and she promised to go on foot to pray at the shrine of St. Sergius. As for Katya, I promised I would try to arrange her marriage to the pastry cook she's been seeing—she 's been having her own little romance..."

He looked at her with his eyes wide with fear and astonishment.

"After all, you've been coming around every day; it's only natural that servants should talk—in fact they are the first! And the same with Sonechka; why does that bother you so much?"

"So that's where all these rumors come from?" he said slowly.

"But it's not as if there's nothing in them, it's all true!"

"True!" Oblomov repeated, neither questioning nor contesting the assertion and adding: "Yes, you're absolutely right, only I don't like the idea of people knowing about our meetings and that's why I'm afraid..."

"Yes, you are afraid, all aquiver like a small child—I don't understand; anyone would think that you were kidnapping me!"

He was embarrassed; she was watching him carefully. "Look," she said, "you're not telling me everything, there's something here that doesn't add up...come here and tell me what's really on your mind. Alright, maybe for a day or two, or even for a week, you could put it down to over-cautiousness, but even then you would have given me some warning, you would have written. I'm no longer a child, you know, and it's not so easy to fob me off with nonsense. Now what is all this really about?"

He thought for a moment and then kissed her hand and sighed. "Look, Olga, the way I see it, all this time I've been scaring myself by imagining the effect on you of all these terrible things; I've been worried sick; one minute I'm full of hope and the next minute those hopes are dashed and my heart can't take it—my whole system is affected and just seizes up, stops functioning and just needs a breathing space to recover..."

"Then how come my system doesn't seize up and continues functioning and the only respite I need is to be near you?"

"You're young and strong and your love is clear and untrammeled, while my love for you—well, you know the way it is...you know how much I love you..." he said, sinking to his knees and kissing her hands.

"Not yet, I don't really know—you act so strangely that I don't know what to think and my mind gives up and I lose hope...we'll soon stop understanding each other altogether and that will be really bad!"

They fell silent.

"So, what have you been doing with yourself all this time?" she asked, looking around the room for the first time. "It's not very nice here, such low ceilings, tiny windows, old wall-paper—where are your other rooms?"

He hastened to show her around the apartment, hoping to slur over the question of what he had been doing, but when she was seated on the divan again and he had settled on the carpet at her feet, she returned to the subject.

"So what have you been doing the last two weeks?"

"Oh, reading, writing, thinking about you."

"Have you read the books I sent? What were they like? I'll take them back with me. She picked up a book from the table and looked at the page it was open at—it was covered in dust. "You haven't been reading!" she said.

"No," he replied.

She looked at the rumpled embroidered cushions, the mess, the dust-covered windows, the desk, fingered some sheets of paper covered with dust, prodded the pen in the dry inkwell and eyed him with astonishment.

"What have you really been doing? Obviously not reading or writing."

"There's been so little time," he began hesitantly, "you get up and they start doing the room and get in your way; then they start asking you about dinner; then the landlady's children come in and ask you to check their homework, and before you know it, it's dinner time. And after dinner who has time to read?"

"You've been sleeping after dinner," she said with such certainty that after a moment's hesitation he simply answered: "Yes."

"But why?"

"Just to kill time; you weren't here, Olga, and life was dreary, unbearable without you..." He broke off under her withering gaze.

"Ilya," she began on a more serious note, "do you remember telling me in the park that life had been rekindled in you and assuring me that I was now your purpose in life, your ideal, and you took me by the hand and offered me your life—and I accepted it?"

"How could I forget? Something that turned my whole life upside down. Can't you see how happy I am?"

"No, I can't, you've been lying to me," she said coldly. "You're letting yourself go again..."

"Lying to you? How can you say such a thing? I swear to God I would throw myself into the abyss this very moment..."

"Oh yes," she cut him off, "if it were here now, right in front of you, you'd do it in a flash, but if you had to wait three days you would get scared and change your mind, especially if Zakhar or Anisya started prattling about it...that's not love!"

"You have doubts about my love?" he said heatedly, "You think all my delaying is because I'm frightened for myself and not for you? That I'm not trying to put a protective wall around your good name—that I'm not watching over you like an anxious mother to keep you safe from gossip...? Oh, Olga, you want proof? I tell you again, if I thought you could be happier with someone else I would give you up without a murmur; if I had to die for you I'd do so gladly!" There were tears in his eyes when he finished.

"There's no need for that, no one's asking you to die! What use would that be to me? Just do what is necessary! It's a clever tactic some people use, to offer to make sacrifices that are impossible or quite unnecessary as a way of avoiding making a sacrifice that is necessary. I know you're not like that, but still..."

"You have no idea how much harm all these emotions and all this worry have done to my health!" he said. "Ever since I met you it's been the only thought in my head. I tell you again, you are still my only purpose in life. I would die on the spot, I'd go mad, if I were to lose you! I only breathe, see, think and feel through you. Why should you be so surprised that I let go and fall asleep on the days I don't see you? Everything becomes distasteful, loses interest, I become a machine. I move about and act without noticing what I'm doing. It's you who are the fuel, the motor of that machine." He spoke on his knees with his body erect. His eyes sparkled the way they had in the park; once again they glowed with pride and strength of purpose.

"I'm ready to go right now wherever you say and do whatever you want. When you're looking at me, talking and singing, I feel that I'm alive."

Olga listened to these impassioned outbursts with grave attention.

"Listen, Ilya," she said, "I believe in your love and my power over you, but why do you frighten me with your indecisiveness, why do you put all these doubts in my mind? I'm your purpose in life, you say, but how is it that you pursue that purpose so feebly, so slowly? You're still so far from the goal; you should be outstripping me—I expect it of you! I've seen happy people; what they're like when they're in love," she went on with a sigh, "they're in a swirl of activity, and when they're at rest they're not like you with their heads drooping and their eyes shut; they hardly sleep, they're in constant motion! But you...no, you don't act like someone in love, like someone who had made me his purpose in life!" She shook her head doubtfully.

"Yes, you, you!" he burst out, kissing her hands again passionately at her feet, "Only you! Oh, my God, what happiness!" he exclaimed deliriously. "Do you really think I could disappoint you—that I could go back to sleep after such an awakening, be anything less than heroic? You'll see, both of you, you and Andrei!" he went on, his eyes wild with enthusiasm, "What heights a man can rise to when he is in love with a woman like you! Just look at me, can't you see how I've come to life again, how alive I am at this moment? Let's leave; let's get away from here! I can't stay here a moment longer, it's stifling, sickening!" he said with undisguised disgust as he looked around him. "I only hope this feeling lasts out the day...oh, if only the fire raging inside me today would burn as fiercely tomorrow and every day after that! Because when you're not here the fire goes out, the life drains from me! Right now I've come back to life—I'm living. I have the feeling that...Olga, Olga, you are the most beautiful thing in the world, no other woman comes close to you...you!" He buried his face in her hand and lay inert; words failed him. He pressed her hand to his heart to calm the furious beating, his moist, passionate eyes boring into her, his body motionless.

"How sweet, how sweet!" Olga said to herself, but with a sigh, not the way she had in the park, and for a while was lost in thought.

"Time to go!" she said affectionately when she came to.

Suddenly he sobered down. "My God, what are you doing here in my apartment?" he said, and his exultant expression gave way to a worried look as he glanced anxiously around; the passionate outbursts were over. He snatched up her hat and cloak and in his panic tried to put her cloak on her head. She burst into laughter.

"Don't worry about me," she tried to reassure him, "*ma tante* is out for the day and no one at home knows that I've gone out except nanny and Katya. Just see me out!"

She gave him her arm and calmly and quite unruffled crossed the courtyard to the accompaniment of the furious barking of the dog and the clanking of its chain, her head held high, secure in the conviction that she had nothing to be ashamed of. She entered the carriage and left.

Heads were poking out of the windows in the landlady's part of the house and Anisya's head could be seen around the corner, watching the house from behind the fence. When the carriage had turned into the next street, Anisya came back and said that she had scoured the market but there was no asparagus to be had. Zakhar returned three hours later and slept around the clock.

Oblomov spent hours pacing the room, oblivious to his own movements and deaf to the sound of his footsteps; he might have been walking on air.

The moment the creaking of the carriage wheels died away in the snow—never mind that it was carrying away his life, his happiness—his anxiety left him. His back straightened, his chin was up and his face once again glowed with that exalted expression and his eyes were moist with happiness and emotion. His whole being was suffused with a feeling of warmth and renewed vigor and vitality. He felt that same old impulse to rush off in any direction, to travel any distance, to do a thousand things all at once. To go to see Stoltz, with Olga, to the estate, to the country, the fields, the woods, to closet himself in his study and immerse himself in work, to travel in person to the Rybinskaya River port, to build the road, to read that book that had just come out and everyone was talking about, to go to the opera this very evening! Yes, in a single day she would have visited him, he would have been to see her and then they would go to the opera—what a full day it would be! How easy it was to breathe within the life, the atmosphere that Olga created around herself, to bask in the rays of her girlish radiance, her high spirits and energy and her youthful, yet subtle and profound intelligence. He moved around the room as if he were flying, as if unseen hands were carrying him.

"Onward and upward," Olga was saying, "onward and upward to that Rubicon where the powers of tenderness, grace and femininity yield sovereignty to the reign of the masculine!"

How clearly she sees life, how easily she can cut through the complexities of life's book and chart her course as well as instinctively discern the path *he* was to travel! Like two rivers, our two lives are destined to flow into each other to form one—and he was her pilot, her captain!

She sees his strengths, his abilities; she knows what he is capable of and is waiting humbly to accept him as her master. What a wonderful woman Olga is! Imperturbable, undaunted, unpretentious, but a woman who knows her own mind, as natural as life itself!

"It really is awful here!" he said, looking around the room. "And this angel has descended into this pit and graced it with her presence!" He cast a loving look at the chair on which she had sat and suddenly his eyes lit up as he caught sight of a tiny glove. "It's a token of her hand, it's a good omen! Ah!" A groan of passion escaped him as he pressed the glove to his lips.

At that moment the landlady put her head around the door to ask if he would like to look at some linen. A hawker had brought some to the door and maybe he needed something? He thanked her curtly, did not even give her elbows a glance and said he was sorry but he was too busy.

Then he fell to recalling the events of the summer, turning all the details over in his mind, dwelling on each and every leaf, shrub, bench, every single word that had been uttered and taking even more delight in everything in retrospect than he had at the actual time. He simply went overboard, singing, bantering affectionately with Anisya, teasing her about having no children and promising to be godfather as soon as she produced one. He played so rowdily with Masha that the landlady looked in and shooed Masha away to stop her interfering with the "gentleman's work."

Throughout the rest of the day his delirium continued to mount. Olga was in high spirits and sang. Then there was the opera—more singing—and afterwards he went back to the house for tea and the conversation among the four of them, the aunt, the baron, Olga and himself, was so warm and open that Oblomov really felt he was one of that small family. No more living by himself; now he had found his niche and had now gotten a firm grip on his life, he had warmth and light—and what a comfort that was!

That night he got little sleep; he spent it trying to catch up on his reading of Olga's books and got through one and a half of them.

"Tomorrow the letter from the estate is sure to come," he thought and his heart beat faster…and kept on beating. At last!

CHAPTER EIGHT

The next day as Zakhar was clearing up, he found the small glove on the desk, gave it a long look, chuckled and then handed it to Oblomov.

"It looks like the Ilyinsky young lady forgot it," he said.

"Damn you!" Ilya Ilyich thundered, snatching the glove from him. "Nothing of the sort! What Ilyinsky young lady? It was the seamstress from the shop who came to fit me for some shirts. How dare you invent such stories!"

"Why are you cursing me? What am I inventing? It's what they're saying over on the landlady's side…"

"Oh, and what are they saying?" Oblomov inquired.

"Well, just that the Ilyinsky young lady was here with her maid."

"Oh, my God!" Oblomov exclaimed in horror, "but how could they recognize her? You or Anisya must have been blabbing…"

Suddenly Anisya poked her head and shoulders through the doorway of the hall. "You should be ashamed of yourself, Zakhar Trofimovich, talking such nonsense! Pay no attention to him, sir! No one said a thing, no one even knows anything, I swear to God...!"

"That's enough!" Zakhar wheezed at her, waving his elbow at her chest, "don't poke your nose where it's not wanted!"

Anisya vanished. Oblomov waved both fists at Zakhar, then quickly opened the door to the landlady's quarters. Agafya Matveyevna was sitting on the floor, sorting odds and ends from an old trunk; she was surrounded by piles of old rags, wadding, old dresses, buttons and pieces of fur.

"Listen," he said in a friendly way but in an anxious tone, "my servants are going around talking all kinds of rubbish, for God's sake, don't listen to them!"

"I haven't heard anything," said the landlady, "what are they saying?"

"It's about the visit I had yesterday," Oblomov continued, "they're saying some young lady came to see me..."

"Well, it's none of our business who comes to see our gentlemen," said the landlady.

"Yes, but please don't believe it in any case, it's sheer malicious gossip! There was no young lady, it was just the seamstress about the shirts she's making for me—it was for a fitting..."

"Oh, and where did you order them from? Who's making them?" asked the landlady brightly.

"From the French shop..."

"Let me see them when they come; I have two girls, they do such fine work, such beautiful stitching; no Frenchwoman can compare with them. I've seen their work, they brought some things they were making for Count Metlinsky to show me. No one else does such fine work. Now take the ones you're wearing, for instance...not a patch on theirs!"

"Yes, fine, I'll remember that, only, for the love of God, please don't think it was a young lady..."

"It makes no difference to us who comes to see our gentleman, a young lady or whoever..."

"No, no!" Oblomov protested. "For goodness sake, the young lady that Zakhar was going on about is tremendously tall and has a really deep voice, but this one, the one who came, the seamstress, well, you probably heard what a delicate voice she has—it 's a wonderful voice, so please don't think..."

"It's nothing to do with us," the landlady said as he was leaving, "now don't forget, let me know the next time you need some shirts made; these girls I know do such beautiful work...they're called Lizaveta and Marya Nikolavna."

"Alright, fine, I won't forget, but please remember what I told you!"

He went back to his rooms, dressed and went to Olga's.

On his return that evening he found a letter waiting for him on his desk from his neighbor to whom he had entrusted the oversight of the estate. He carried it quickly to the lamp and read it—and his arms dropped helplessly to his sides.

"I am afraid that I must ask you to transfer the power-of-attorney to someone else," he read. "So much business of my own has been accumulating that I must confess that I cannot give the necessary attention to your estate. The best thing would be for you to come here yourself, or even better, for you to come and live here. Basically there is nothing wrong with the estate, except that it has been badly neglected. The first thing that needs doing is to sort out the question of exactly what is owed to you in work days and what is owed to you in quit-rent—it is impossible to determine this in the absence of the owner of the estate.

"The peasants are spoiled; they will not take orders from the new bailiff, and the old one is a bit of a crook and needs watching. It is impossible to estimate the income. With the state things are in right now the estate will yield barely three thousand, and that only if you are here yourself. I am just counting what the sale of your grain will bring in. As for the quit-rent you are owed, there is not much hope there. You will have to get a grip on those people and figure out exactly what they owe you; and all that will take a good three months. The harvest was good and so are prices, and you can expect the proceeds in March or April provided you supervise the sale yourself. Right now there isn't a penny available in cash.

"Now about the road through Verkhlyovo and the bridge, since I did not hear from you for so long I got together with Odintsov and Byelovodov and we decided that the road would run from my property as far as Nyelki so that Oblomovka will not be anywhere near the road.

"Finally, I can only urge you again to come yourself as soon as possible. In three months you should be able to figure out how much cash you can expect to raise next year. Incidentally, the elections are being held now. Do you want to be a candidate for Justice of the Peace? You must act quickly."

There was a PS: "Your house is in a very bad state and I have told the dairymaid, the old coachman and the two old maids to move out of there into a cottage; it has become too dangerous to live there any longer."

There was a note attached to the letter giving the figures for the amounts of grain harvested, threshed and stored in the granaries; how much was to be put up for sale and other such bookkeeping items.

Oblomov was haunted by the spectres of "not a penny in cash," "three months," "you have to come yourself," "getting a grip on the peasants," "figure out the income", "stand for election." He felt he was groping his way through a forest on a dark night with a bandit, a wild beast or a corpse lurking behind every tree and bush.

"It's outrageous, I won't give in!" he declared, trying to look these spectres in the face the way people do when they are scared and, with their eyes screwed up tight, they make a great effort to squint through them at the surrounding ghosts, but their blood runs cold and their hands and feet go numb.

But what had he been hoping for? Well, he had thought that the letter would spell out exactly what his income would be and, of course, that it would be on the high side, say six or seven thousand; that his house would still be in good condition and that, if necessary, it could be lived in while the new one was being built and that his agent would actually be sending him three or four thousand—in short, that in that letter he would be reading the same laughter, gaiety and love that he was used to reading in Olga's notes.

No longer did he feel that he was walking on air, no longer did he banter with Anisya or excite himself with the prospect of happiness; all that would have to be put off for three months! Except that in three months all that he would be able to do would be to sort out his affairs and learn his way about the estate, and as for the wedding... "That's not even worth thinking about for at least a year," he said fearfully, "yes, yes, a good year at least!" He still had his plan to complete, the architect to consult, and so on and so forth...he sighed.

"Borrow!" The idea flashed through his mind but he dismissed it. "How can I? What if I can't pay it back in time? What if things go badly? I'll be declared a debtor and my goods will be seized and the good name of Oblomov, never before tarnished...God forbid! Then it will be goodbye to peace of mind, to honor...no, no! Other people borrow and then they have to rush around, work, go without sleep, as if possessed. Yes, debt is a curse, a demon, a devil, and the only thing that can cast it out is money.

There are those types who think nothing of living off others their whole lives, scavenging, grabbing left and right, without turning a hair. God knows how they can sleep at night or sit down to dinner without a qualm. Debt! It can only mean one of two things, forced labor for life, or disgrace.

Take out a mortgage on the estate? But isn't that just the same as borrowing, only inexorable, remorseless, with no possibility of deferment. Payments have to be made every year—maybe not even leaving enough to live on.

Happiness would have to be postponed for yet another year! Oblomov groaned in pain and was about to flop down on the bed when he suddenly remembered what Olga had said to him and just stopped himself in time. She had challenged him to act like a man and had put her trust in his abilities. She was waiting for him to move ahead, onwards and upwards, to the point where he could reach out for her, take her by the hand, and lead her to their destination! Yes, yes, but where to start?

He thought and thought and then suddenly clapped a hand to his head and went through to see the landlady. "Is your brother at home?" he asked her.

"Yes, he's gone to bed."

"Then ask him to come and see me tomorrow, I need to speak to him."

CHAPTER NINE

The brother entered the room in precisely the same fashion as before, sat down carefully on a chair, tucked his hands into his sleeves and waited for Ilya Ilyich to speak.

"I've just received some very unpleasant news from my country estate in response to the power-of-attorney I sent—if you remember?" said Oblomov, "Here, take a look at the letter!"

Ivan Matveyich took the letter and scanned it with practiced eyes and slightly trembling fingers. When he had finished, he put it down on the table and hid his hands behind his back.

"So, what do you think I should do now?" Oblomov asked him.

"Well, they're advising you to go there," said Ivan Matveyich, "so why not go, it's not as if traveling twelve hundred versts is the end of the world! The road will be ready in a week and you can go then."

"I've gotten completely out of the habit of traveling, so what with that and the winter coming on too—I have to confess that I would find it very difficult. I really wouldn't feel up to it—and in any case it would be very dreary in the country all by myself."

"Do you have a lot of peasants who pay quit rent?"

"I don't really know, it's so long since I've been there."

"It's something you need to know, if I may say so, otherwise how are you going to work out what your income will be?"

"Yes, I'm sure you're right—and that's what my neighbor writes too. But now, with winter coming on…"

"But how much quit-rent do you estimate?"

"Quit rent? Wait a minute, I think I had it written down somewhere…Stoltz worked it out for me some time ago; I can't seem to find it. Zakhar must have dumped it somewhere. I'll show it to you when I find it—it 's something like thirty roubles per household."

"What are the conditions like for your peasants? How well are they doing?" Ivan Matveyich asked, "Are they prosperous, destitute, poor? What's the situation with the work-days, the labor they owe you?"

"Listen!" said Oblomov, going up to him, grasping him by the lapels and taking him into his confidence.

Ivan Matveyich rose smartly to his feet, but Oblomov sat him down again.

"Listen!" he repeated, articulating carefully, practically in a whisper, "I don't know anything about work-days or the work that is done on my land, I don't know the difference between a rich peasant and a poor one; I can't tell a bushel of rye from a bushel of barley and I have no idea what it's worth. I don't know what is sown, what is harvested, or when; I don't know how it's sold or when. I don't know if I'm rich or poor or whether my belly will be full or whether I'll be starving by this time next year—I don't know a damned thing!" he ended on a note of deep despondency, letting go of Ivan Matveyich's lapels and moving back, "So I'm simply asking you to tell me what to do as if I were a child…"

"But you have to know; otherwise it's impossible to work anything out," said Ivan Matveyich with an obsequious smirk, getting up and putting one hand behind his back and slipping the other into the front of his tunic. "A landowner must know what's going on his property and how to deal with it," he admonished him.

"Well, I don't know and I want you to tell me, if you can."

"It's not a subject I'm familiar with myself, I would have to consult people with experience in the matter. Now, here in the letter, if I may," Ivan Matveyich went on, pointing to the paragraph in question with his middle finger, nail down, "it says you should stand in the elections. That would be a great idea! You could live there, serve as a Justice of the Peace and learn how to run your estate at the same time."

"I have no idea what goes on in a district court or what a Justice of the Peace does!" Oblomov repeated with feeling but in a low voice, putting his face right up against Ivan Matveyich's.

"With respect, I believe you'll get used to it. After all you have seen service in a government department and it's just the same everywhere—except for slight differences in the details of the paperwork. Always the same old directives, memoranda, records…All you need is an efficient clerk and you have nothing to worry about—and you just have to sign. If you know how things work in government departments…"

"I don't know how things work in government departments," Oblomov stated in a monotone.

Ivan Matveyich gave Oblomov one of his two-stage looks and said nothing. "But of course you must have spent a lot of time reading books," he finally observed with the same obsequious smirk.

"Books!" Oblomov exclaimed bitterly and stopped. He could not bring himself to bare his soul to this lowly functionary for no good reason. It was on the tip of his tongue to say, "I don't know anything about books either," but he checked his impulse and contented himself with a mournful sigh.

"But I'm sure you've been engaged in some activity," Ivan Matveyich continued inoffensively, as if he had been able to read Oblomov's mind and was quite aware of his unspoken answer about the books, it's impossible for…"

"It's quite possible, Ivan Matveyich, I'll give you living proof. Take me—who am I, what am I? Go and ask Zakhar and he'll tell you, 'a landed gentleman'. And that's exactly what I am, a member of the landed gentry and incapable of doing anything! So I want you to act for me and help me if you can and take whatever you want for your trouble—knowledge deserves its reward!"

He started pacing the room, and as he moved around, Ivan Matveyich, without moving from the spot, slowly rotated his body so as to sit facing him. Neither of them spoke for some time.

"Where did you go to school?" asked Oblomov, stopping in front of him.

"I started high school, but my father took me out of school and found me a job in a government office, so my education didn't really go beyond reading, writing, grammar and arithmetic—and that was about it, you see. Of course, I learned on the job and I learned enough to get by. Your own situation is different, of course, you've had a proper education."

"Yes," Oblomov concurred with a sigh, "it's true, I did advanced algebra, political economy and law, but none of that helped me when it came to work. Look, even with my advanced algebra I still don't know what my income is. I went to live in the country, on the estate, I listened and watched, trying to learn how things were done at home, on the estate and all around us—none of it had anything to do with the law I had been taught. I came here and somehow thought that I would find my feet with the help of all that political economy but I was told that maybe that kind of thing would be useful to me later on in life when I was old, but first I would have to make a career in the civil service and for that you had to know only one thing—how to draft official documents. Anyway I never managed to get the hang of it and ended up just being a landed gentleman; but obviously you did get the hang of it, so tell me, how do I get out of this situation?"

"There is a way, it's no problem," Ivan Matveyich said after a pause.

Oblomov stood facing him, waiting to hear what he had to say.

"What you could do is put the matter in the hands of an expert in the field and transfer the power-of-attorney to him."

"And where do you find someone like that?" Oblomov asked.

"There's someone I work with, Isai Fomich Zatyorty; he's got a bit of a stammer but he really knows his business. He managed a large estate for three years but the owner dismissed him precisely because of his stammer and so he came to work in our office."

"But can he be relied on?"

"He's the very soul of honesty, you need have no worries on that score, Mr. Oblomov. He would spend his last penny just to please anyone he was working for. He's been with us for eleven years now."

"But how can he travel if he's working?"

"No problem, Mr. Oblomov, he can take leave for four months. You've only to say the word and I'll bring him here. Of course, if he goes he'll have to be paid."

"Of course!" Oblomov agreed.

"If you don't mind, you'll have to pay his travel and living expenses—some kind of daily allowance—and when the business is concluded there'll be whatever remuneration you've agreed on. He'll go, don't you worry!"

"I'm very grateful to you, you've taken a great weight off my mind," said Oblomov, extending his hand, "what's his name again?"

"Isai Fomich Zatyorty," Ivan Matveyich repeated hurriedly, wiping his hand on his other cuff. He grasped Oblomov's hand briefly, then swiftly withdrew his own and hid it at once in his sleeve. "I'll talk to him tomorrow, Mr. Oblomov, and bring him to see you."

"Why don't you bring him to dinner so that we can talk? I'm extremely grateful to you!" said Oblomov as he showed Ivan Matveyich to the door.

CHAPTER TEN

That same evening found Ivan Matveyich and Tarantyev seated together in one of the upstairs rooms of a two-story house one side of which overlooked the street where Oblomov was living; the other side gave on to the embankment.

It was what was known as a "public house" where there were always two or three empty carriages waiting outside, with their drivers sitting downstairs sipping tea from saucers. The upper floor was reserved for the Vyborg side "gentry." Ivan Matveyich and Tarantyev were drinking tea accompanied by a bottle of rum.

"It's genuine Jamaican," said Ivan Matveyich, pouring himself a tumblerful with a trembling hand, "so don't turn your nose up at what I'm offering you, old pal!"

"You have to admit, I have it coming to me," Tarantyev responded, "your house could have rotted before you could have got yourself a tenant like that."

"It's true," Ivan Matveyich cut in, "and if our plan works out and Zatyorty goes to the estate, we'll really have something to celebrate!"

"You're too tight-fisted, old pal, always haggling—fifty roubles for a tenant like that!"

"What worries me, he's threatening to go himself," said Ivan Matveyich.

"Huh, a lot you know! He's not going anywhere! You couldn't get him out of the house if you tried!"

"But what about his wedding? They say he's getting married."

Tarantyev chortled. "Him? Get married? Want to bet? Why, he can't even go to bed without Zakhar's help, and you want him to get married? It's me who's always done everything for him; if it weren't for me, my friend, he'd have died of starvation by now or landed in jail. If some official called or the landlord wanted to know something, he didn't know which way was—I had to help him out every time! He's completely out of it..."

"Yes, totally; he says so himself. 'I have no idea what goes on in a district court—or a government office either'. He doesn't even know what kind of peasants he has on his estate. What a dolt! I could hardly stop myself laughing out loud..."

"And that lease, can you imagine him signing a lease like that?" Tarantyev said triumphantly. "I swear there's no one to touch you when it comes to drafting a legal document, Ivan Matveyich, you're the champion! You remind me of my father when he was alive. I was pretty good myself once but now I'm out of practice, I've lost the knack, I swear! I sit down to write and my eyes start watering. He just scrawled his signature without even reading it—and with all that stuff about vegetable gardens, stables and barns!"

"Yes, old pal, and as long as there is a dummy left in Russia who will sign a document without reading it, people like us won't starve. Otherwise God knows what would have become of us, things have gotten so bad! To hear old timers tell it, things were different then. After twenty-five years of work how much have I managed to put by? Of course, you can always live on the Vyborg side and never poke your nose out of doors; plenty to eat, yes; I can't complain about that. But as for apartments on Liteiny Prospekt, carpets on the floor, marrying a rich wife and producing children with a chance of rising in the world, well those times are past! And with a mug like mine and these raw, red fingers—and you ask why I drink vodka; wouldn't you in my shoes? There's an expression, 'worse off than a flunkey'; well, these days even a flunkey doesn't have to wear boots like these and changes his shirt every day! No, there wasn't the right education. All these whipper-snappers are getting ahead, walking about with their noses in the air just because they can read French—and speak it..."

"Yes, but when it comes to practical matters, they're no good," Tarantyev put in.

"No, my friend, they are; it's just that the work itself has changed. Now everyone wants to simplify things—they 're ruining things for us! 'Write it like this, not like that!' 'Cut this out—it 's unnecessary, a waste of time!' 'It's quicker like this!' They're ruining everything, I tell you!"

"Well, at least the lease is signed, they haven't managed to ruin that!" said Tarantyev.

"Oh no, that had to be kept safe at all costs, so drink up, old pal! He'll be sending Zatyorty to Oblomovka and he'll siphon off what he can, and good luck to the heirs...!"

"Right!" said Tarantyev, "and who are these heirs anyway? Distant cousins, practically no relations at all."

"But there's still the wedding, that's the only thing that I'm worried about."

"You have nothing to worry about, I'm telling you; just mark my words!"

"Oh, you think so?" Ivan Matveyich remarked gleefully, "and what would you say if I told you that he's making eyes at my sister...?" he went on, dropping his voice to a whisper.

"What are you talking about?" said Tarantyev in astonishment.

"Just keep quiet about it! It's true, I tell you!"

"What a thought!" exclaimed Tarantyev, barely recovering from his astonishment; never in my wildest dreams...and what about her?"

"What about her? You know her, you know what she's like," he banged his fist on the table, "she'd never think of protecting her own interests. She's no different from a cow; you hit her or stroke her, either way you get the same stupid grin, just like a horse with a nose-bag of oats. Now, another woman in her place—well, I don't have to tell you. Anyway, I'm going to be keeping an eye on them—you can see which way the wind is blowing!"

CHAPTER ELEVEN

"Four more months, four months of constraint, snatched meetings, suspicious faces, false smiles," thought Oblomov as he mounted the stairs to the Ilyinskys. "God, when will it all end? And Olga is going to put pressure on me to leave as soon as possible; today, tomorrow! She's so persistent, so determined! You just can't argue with her..."

Oblomov had gotten almost as far as Olga's room without meeting anyone. She was sitting in her small drawing room next to her bedroom, immersed in a book. Oblomov's appearance was so sudden that she was startled but, recovering quickly, she extended her hand to him with a warm smile, although her eyes still seemed to be concentrating on the book and she had a distracted look.

"You alone?" he asked her.

"Yes, *ma tante* has gone to Tsarskoye Syelo; she asked me to go with her. We'll be practically alone at dinner—except for Marya Semyonova, otherwise I couldn't have let you come. So today you won't be able to have that talk with *ma tante*. How tiresome it is! But tomorrow..." she added with a smile, "and what if I had gone to Tsarskoye Syelo today?" she asked teasingly.

He said nothing.

"You're worried?" she asked.

"I got the letter from the estate," he said in a flat voice.

"Did you bring it?"

He handed her the letter.

"I can't make head or tail of it," she said, after taking a look.

He took the letter back and read it aloud. There was silence as she thought for a while and then she asked: "so what now?"

"I discussed it earlier today with the landlady's brother," Oblomov replied, "and he recommended that I give a power-of-attorney to a certain Isai Fomich Zatyorty, so I'll let him take care of everything..."

"You mean, a total stranger!" Olga protested in surprise; "to collect the quit-rent, decide which peasants owe you what, supervise the sale of grain?"

"He says this person is the soul of honesty and has been working with him for more than eleven years...he just has a bit of a stammer."

"And what about this brother of your landlady himself? How well do you know him?"

"Not very well, but he seems like a competent, practical type of person. Anyway I'm living under the same roof as him, so he's hardly likely to feel comfortable about cheating me."

Olga sat in silence with lowered eyes.

"The alternative would be for me to go myself," said Oblomov, "and I have to confess I really don't feel like it. I'm just not used to traveling on the roads, especially in winter...as a matter of fact I've never done it."

Olga kept her head lowered, making little circles with the tip of her shoe.

"And even if I went," Oblomov went on, "I'd get absolutely nowhere, I don't have the slightest grasp of such matters; the peasants will lie to me, and the bailiff can make up any story he wants—and I'll have no choice but to believe him and just accept whatever money he chooses to give me. It's just too bad Andrei isn't here, he would soon take care of everything!" he said grimly.

Olga gave a little smile, or at least her lips were smiling, but inside, in her heart, she felt only pain. She looked out of the window, crinkling one eye as she watched the carriages going by on the road.

"Oh yes, this Zatyorty used to manage a big estate," he continued, "but the owner got rid of him just because he stammers. I'll give him the power-of-attorney, and with the plans I'll give him he can arrange the purchase of the building materials for the house, collect the quit-rent, sell the grain and bring back the money and then...How happy I am, dear Olga," he said, kissing her hand, "that I won't have to leave you. I couldn't have stood being separated from you, all by myself, alone in the country—what an awful prospect! But now, of course, we'll have to be extra careful."

She looked at him, wide-eyed and waited.

"Yes," he said, speaking so slowly and deliberately that he was almost stammering, "not see each other so often; only yesterday they started talking about it again over on the landlady's side—and I don't want that! Then as soon as all the business is settled and my agent has taken care of building the house and comes back with the money—it shouldn't take more than a year or so—then there'll be no more separations and we'll tell your aunt and..." He looked at Olga. She showed no emotion. Her head leaned to one side and her lips had turned blue and parted, revealing her teeth.

Absorbed in his own relief and delight at his vision of the future, he failed to notice how, at the words: "when all the business is settled and the agent has taken care..." Olga had gone pale and stopped listening.

"Olga, my God, she's feeling faint!" he said, and rang the bell.

"Your mistress is feeling faint," he said to Katya, who had hurried into the room, "fetch some water, some smelling salts, quick!"

"Oh Lord, and the mistress was in such good spirits the whole morning! Whatever can be the matter with her?" Katya whispered, hurrying in with the smelling salts from the aunt's dressing table and a glass of water.

Olga came to, and with the help of Katya and Oblomov rose from the armchair and made her way falteringly to her bedroom. "It will pass," she insisted feebly, "it's just nerves; I didn't sleep much last night." She told Katya to close the door and asked Oblomov to wait until she felt better and came out again.

Left alone, Oblomov put his ear to the door and peered through the keyhole but could see and hear nothing.

After half an hour he went along the passage to the maids' quarters and asked Katya: "How is your mistress?"

"She's alright," said Katya, "she laid down on the bed and sent me away; when I went in later she was sitting in the armchair."

Oblomov went back into the drawing room and put his ear to the keyhole again but still could not hear anything. He tapped on the door very lightly with his finger—no response.

He sat down and in the next hour and a half he did a lot of thinking. He began to see a lot of things in a different light and came to a lot of new conclusions. He decided that he should go to the estate himself together with his agent, but only after he had obtained the consent of Olga's aunt to the marriage and had become officially engaged to Olga. He would ask Ivan Gerasimovich to find him an apartment and would even borrow some money…just a little to tide him over for the wedding. The debt could be repaid from the proceeds from the sale of the grain. Why on earth had he been so downhearted? Good Lord, how different things could look from one minute to the next! And once he was there on the spot, and with the help of the agent, he would collect the quit-rent; and then he would write to Stoltz who would send him money and come to Oblomovka himself and do a wonderful job of reorganizing the estate. He would build roads, put up bridges, and start schools! And he would be there with Olga! God, how happy they would be…! But why hadn't any of this occurred to him before?

Suddenly all his worries left him, he felt nothing but relief and his heart was light. He started to pace the room, clicking his fingers softly to curb his excitement and to stop himself crying out with joy. He went up to Olga's door and called out to her cheerfully: "Olga, Olga, you'll never guess what I have to tell you!" he said, with his mouth pressed against the door. He had even decided not to leave the house that day until the aunt had returned home. "We'll tell her the news this very day and I'll leave this house officially engaged to Olga."

The door opened slowly and Olga appeared. He took one look at her and his heart fell, his euphoria sank without trace. It was as if Olga had suddenly aged. She was pale, although her eyes were bright. Her tight lips and drawn features betrayed her inner tension as if her spirit were ice-bound and forcibly locked into a frozen immobility. It was apparent to him from her expression that she had taken a decision of some sort, although he did not know what, and his heart pounded in his chest as never before. Never before in his life had he experienced anything like this.

"Olga, please don't look at me like that, you're frightening me!" he said. "I've thought it all over, it all needs to be done differently," he went on, his excitement ebbing away as he stopped and tried to penetrate the meaning of that new expression in her eyes, lips and eloquent eyebrows, "I've decided to go to the estate myself together with my agent so that..." the sentence petered out in a whisper. She stared at him wordlessly as if she were seeing a ghost.

He was beginning to get a dim sense of the verdict that awaited him and picked up his hat but hesitated to put the actual question, fearful as he was of a decision which was likely to be irrevocable and which spelled his doom. Finally he steeled himself. "Am I understanding you correctly?" he asked in a faltering voice. She lowered her head slowly and gently in a sign of assent. Although it was the response he had anticipated he paled as he stood facing her.

There was weariness about her, but she stood there, still, motionless as if carved out of stone. It was the supernatural calm of those who are focused single-mindedly on the pursuit of a single goal or who have received a violent shock and who, for that fleeting moment, can summon up the strength to contain their feelings. She was like a wounded man who, squeezing the wound tightly with his hands, musters just enough strength to get out his last words before dying.

"Do you hate me now?" he asked.

"For what?" she said faintly.

"For what I've done to you."

"What have you done?"

"Loving you—it's an insult!"

She responded with a pitying smile.

"For being responsible for your mistake," he said, hanging his head, "perhaps you can find it in yourself to forgive me if you remember that I warned you that you would be ashamed and remorseful..."

"I feel no remorse; I feel only pain, terrible pain," she said, and stopped to get her breath.

"My pain is even greater," Oblomov responded, "but I deserve it; but why should you be suffering so much?"

"It's my pride," she said, "I'm being punished. I thought I was stronger than I am—*that* was my mistake, it wasn't what you were afraid of. My dream was not about the first flush of youth and beauty, no, it was about bringing you to life and making you live for me, but you've been long dead. I couldn't foresee my mistake; I kept on waiting and hoping, and now...Words failed her and she ended with a sigh. She stood in silence for a moment before sitting down. "I can't stand, my legs are giving way. With all the effort I've put in I could have brought a stone to life," she said with weary resignation, "there's nothing I can do now, it's not worth lifting a finger—I won't even—I won't even take a single step, not even to go to the Summer Garden—there's no point in trying any more—you 're dead! Don't you agree, Ilya?" she added after a pause. "I hope you'll never reproach me for leaving you out of pride or caprice?"

He shook his head.

"And you're as certain as I am that there's nothing left for us, no future, no hope?"

"Yes," he said, "it's true…but perhaps," he added hesitantly after a pause, "in a year…" He still lacked the courage to administer the *coup de grâce* to his happiness.

"Do you really think that in a year you'll succeed in putting your affairs and your life in order?" she asked, "Just think for a moment!"

He gave a sigh and tried to sort out his thoughts, and she could read on his face the signs of inner conflict.

"Listen," she said, "I've just spent a long time looking at my mother's portrait and I feel she has lent me some extra wisdom and strength. If, right now and in all honesty—and remember, Ilya, we're not children and this is not a game; we're talking about our whole lives here!— you search you conscience mercilessly and tell me—and I'll believe you because I know you—will you be there for me for the whole of our lives; will you be the person I need you to be? You know me, so you know exactly what I mean. If, after careful consideration, you give me a clear, unequivocal 'yes', I'll go back on my decision—here is my hand and we'll go wherever you want, abroad, to your estate, even to the Vyborg side!"

Oblomov was silent. "If you knew how much I love…"

She cut him off almost curtly: "It's not protestations of love I'm waiting for, but a 'yes or no' answer!"

"Don't torment me, Olga!" he implored in despair.

"Well, Ilya, am I right or wrong?"

"Yes," he replied clearly and categorically, "you're right!"

"Then we'd better part now," she said with finality, "before anyone finds you here or sees how upset I am!"

He still did not leave.

"What if you had actually married me?" she asked.

He said nothing.

"You would have sunk deeper and deeper into your lethargy every day—isn't that right? And what about me—you know what I'm like? I have no intention of ever getting old or tired of living. But with you our days would just go by one after another while we waited for Christmas and then for Shrovetide, or went visiting and dancing without a thought in our heads. We'd go to bed at night and thank God for making the day pass so quickly, and in the morning we'd wake up hoping that that day would be just like the day before…and that would be our future—right?

Is that living? I would just pine away and die—and for what? Would you be happy like that, Ilya?"

He raised his agonized eyes to the ceiling, desperate to leave, to escape, but his legs would not carry him. He tried to say something but his mouth was too dry, his tongue was tied, his voice was stuck in his chest. He held out his hand to her.

"Then it's…" he began, but his voice gave way and he added the last word with his eyes: 'goodbye!'"

She tried to say something but it would not come; she stretched out her hand but it fell to her side without touching his. She too wanted to say: "goodbye," but her voice failed and broke halfway through the word and a shudder convulsed her features. She rested her head and her hand on his shoulders and broke into sobs. It was as if she had suddenly been disarmed. All her intelligence was useless to her now; she had become just a woman, helpless against her grief.

"Goodbye, goodbye!" she sobbed.

He listened in silent horror as her tears flowed, not daring to staunch them. He felt no pity for her or himself, he was himself an object of pity.

She sank into the armchair, burying her head in a handkerchief and, with her elbows propped on the table, wept bitterly. Her tears did not gush out of her in a hot impetuous rush in immediate reaction to some sharp sudden pain, the way they had that time in the park, but flowed in a bleak, cold and steady stream like rain in autumn, remorselessly drenching the fields.

"Olga," he said finally, "why are you torturing yourself like this? You love me; you won't be able to bear it if we part! Take me as I am and love what is good in me!"

She shook her head without raising it. "No, no," she finally managed to get out, "don't worry about me or my pain. I know myself, I'll cry myself out until my tears dry up and won't come any more—and now just leave and let me cry….oh no, don't go! God is punishing me! Oh, how it hurts, it hurts so much…right here in my heart." The sobbing broke out again.

"But if the pain doesn't go away," he said, "and your health suffers? This crying is bad for you. Olga, my angel, don't cry, forget every-thing…!"

"No, let me cry; I'm not crying for the future but for the past," she managed to gasp between sobs, "it has faded away, vanished. It's not me crying, it's those memories!"

"The summer, the park, do you remember? I'm mourning for our path, the lilac…it has all grown into my heart; it's painful to cut it out!"

She shook her head in despair and continued sobbing, repeating over and over again, "it hurts so much, so much!"

"Don't Olga, don't, you could kill yourself like this!" he said in horror.

"No," she stopped him, raising her head and trying to look at him through the tears, "I've only recently understood that what I loved in you was what I wanted you to be, what Stoltz had put in my mind, what the two of us together had created. What I loved was the Oblomov to be! Ilya, you're a timorous, honest, gentle creature like a dove; you keep your head hidden under your wing and you're happy that way; you're ready to spend the rest of your life billing and cooing under the eaves. But that's not me, that's not enough, I need more than that; although what exactly I'm not sure. Can you help me, tell me what it is I'm looking for, give it to me so that…gentleness, that's easy to find!"

Oblomov's legs gave way; he collapsed into an armchair and mopped his brow and his hands with a handkerchief.

Oblomov was cut to the quick by this cruel remark; inside he was burning, while on the outside it was as if cold water had been thrown in his face. His only response was a pitiful smile, half pained, half ashamed, like some beggar who has been reprimanded for being in rags. He just sat there with this helpless smile on his face, all the wind knocked out of him by the shock of this insult, his downcast expression clearly conceding: "Yes, I am a worthless, pitiful, abject creature…go on and hit me!"

Olga suddenly realized how hurtful her remark had been and flew to his side.

"Forgive me , my dear!" she said gently on the verge of tears, "I didn't know what I was saying, I must have been mad! Please forget everything we've said, we'll start all over again—just the way it was before!"

"No, "he said, rising suddenly to his feet and dismissing her outburst with a decisive gesture, "we won't go back to the way it was! Don't be upset about telling the truth, I deserve it," he added in utter dejection.

"I'm too much of a dreamer, my imagination is too busy," she said, "I have this unfortunate temperament. How come other people like Sonechka can be so happy?" She burst into tears. "Please go!" she ordered him, twisting her tear-drenched handkerchief in her fingers. "I won't be able to bear it, the past is still too precious to me." She buried her face in her handkerchief again and tried to stifle her sobs.

"Who killed it all?" she asked, suddenly raising her head, "who laid this curse on you, Ilya? What have you done to deserve it? You're good-hearted, intelligent, gentle and decent…and yet you're moribund! What is it that's doomed you? There's no name for this affliction…"

"Yes, there is!" his voice was barely audible.

She looked at him inquiringly, her eyes brimming with tears.

"*Oblomovshchina*!" he whispered and took her hand, intending to kiss it but could not, and succeeded only in pressing it tightly to his lips and scalding her fingers with his tears. Without raising his head or facing her, he turned and left the room.

CHAPTER TWELVE

God knows where he roamed or what he did for the rest of the day, but he did not get home until late that night. The landlady was the first to hear the knocking at the gate and the barking of the dog and she shook Anisya and Zakhar awake to tell them that their master had returned.

Ilya Ilyich hardly noticed Zakhar taking his clothes off, removing his boots and wrapping him in, of all things, the dressing gown!

"What's this?" he asked simply when his eyes fell on the dressing gown.

"The landlady brought it back after she washed and mended it." said Zakhar.

Oblomov remained seated in the armchair into which he had flopped. The house was dark and everyone was asleep, and in the midst of it all he sat, his head propped on his hand, noticing neither the darkness around him nor the chimes of the clock. His mind was awhirl with a chaos of ugly, formless thoughts and images; they scudded through his mind like clouds in the sky in no particular sequence or direction and he was unable to latch onto any of them.

His heart had died within him; life itself had been temporarily snuffed out. His return to life, to normality, the restoration of his gradually recharging life forces to their former channels was a slow process—and a painful one. Oblomov did not feel his body, he was oblivious to fatigue and all his bodily needs. He would lie like a stone for days on end, and for days on end he would move about and go through the motions of living like an automaton.

Little by little, however painfully, a man learns to accept or resign himself to his fate, and then his organism slowly and gradually resumes its normal functions, or his grief will crush him and he will never recover, depending, of course, on the kind of grief and the kind of man.

Oblomov had no recollection of where he was sitting or even that he was sitting at all; he watched the day dawning with unseeing eyes; he heard the sound of the old woman's dry cough, the sound of the doorman splitting logs outside his window and the noises of the house coming to life, but without registering them; he saw the landlady and Akulina leave for the market and the parcel flashing past his window, but he had no awareness of seeing them.

Neither the crowing of the cocks, nor the barking of the dog, nor the creaking of the gate could rouse him from his stupor. Somewhere teacups rattled and the samovar began to hiss. Finally, some time before ten o'clock Zakhar pushed open the door to the study with his tray, attempting to kick it shut behind him and missing as usual. He managed, however, to avoid upsetting the tray, a skill he had acquired from long practice—he also knew that Anisya was watching him from behind the door and that if he so much as dropped a single cup she would come rushing out and embarrass him. He reached the side of the bed without mishap, hugging the tray so close that his beard was resting on it, and he was just about to place the cups on the bedside table and rouse his master when he noticed that the bed had not been slept in and his master was missing! He was so startled that a cup fell to the floor followed by the sugar bowl. He tried to catch the falling objects, tilting the tray in the process so that everything else slid off; the only thing he managed to save was a teaspoon.

"What the hell's going on here?" he said, watching Anisya picking up the sugar, the broken pieces of the cup and the bread from the floor, "where's the master?"

The master was sitting in the armchair, looking as if he had seen a ghost. Zakhar gawked at him, open-mouthed.

"Ilya Ilyich, why have you been sitting up all night in that chair instead of going to bed?" he asked.

Oblomov slowly turned his head towards him, giving Zakhar, the spilt coffee and the sugar scattered on the carpet, a befuddled look. "And why did you break the cup?" he said and walked over to the window. Snowflakes were falling thickly and covering the ground. "Snow, snow, snow," he repeated mindlessly, watching the snow pile up on the fences and the furrows in the vegetable beds. "Everything's covered," he whispered despairingly and lay down on the bed where he fell at once into a leaden, comfortless sleep. It was not until after noon that he was woken by the creaking of the door to the kitchen; a bare arm was thrust out with a plate clutched in the hand. On the plate was a steaming pie.

"It's Sunday today," a warm and friendly voice could be heard saying, "won't you try a nice piece of pie—we've just been baking?"

Oblomov did not reply; he was in the grip of a fever.

PART IV

CHAPTER ONE

A year had passed since Ilya Ilyich's illness, a year that had wrought many changes throughout the world. Turmoil here and calm there, one luminary in the ascendant here and another world figure on the wane there; a major new breakthrough in scientific discovery here and a whole civilization reduced to dust and ashes there. Old life disappearing and its place being taken by the green sprouts of new life.

Meanwhile, on the Vyborg side in the home of the widow Pshenitsyn, although the days and nights passed uneventfully, causing no sudden or abrupt disruptions in the unchanging patterns of life, even there life did not simply stand still. Everything was in the process of change, but change of the same imperceptible gradualness as the geological transformations of our planet, where a mountain will ever so slowly crumble away over the centuries or the sea will build up a whole island of silt or retreat from the coastline and create new outcroppings of soil.

Ilya Ilyich recovered. His agent, Zatyorty, made the journey to the estate and sent back the proceeds from the sale of the grain in full, content to deduct only the travel expenses, daily living allowances and remuneration for his work that had been agreed upon. As for the quit-rent, Zatyorty had written that it was impossible to collect because some of the peasants were ruined and some had moved away—no one knew where to—and that he was actively investigating the matter on the spot.

About the road and the bridges, he wrote that the matter was not urgent since the peasants much preferred the trouble of climbing the hill and negotiating the gully to get to the market town, to the trouble of building the road and bridges.

In short, Ilya Ilyich was quite satisfied with both the information and the money and saw no pressing need to make the journey himself, and on this score had nothing to worry about for another year.

The agent also had the construction of the house well in hand. Together with the provincial architect he had made estimates of the building materials required and had left instructions for the bailiff to start bringing in the timber at the beginning of spring and to build a shed to house the bricks, so that it remained for Oblomov only to go there in the spring and, after asking God's blessing, to stay and supervise the actual building of the house. By that time it was hoped that the quit-rent would have been collected, and there was also the prospect of taking out a mortgage on the estate so that there would be some funds to cover the expenses.

After his illness Ilya Ilyich remained depressed for a long time. He would spend hours on end wrapped up in his troubled thoughts, often failing to respond to Zakhar's questions or even to notice his dropping cups on the floor or neglecting to dust the table. Sometimes the landlady would appear at holidays to offer him a pie and would find him in tears.

Little by little the sharp pangs of grief gave way to a mute indifference. For hours on end Ilya Ilyich would just watch the snow falling and piling up in snowdrifts in the courtyard and the street outside until the heaps of firewood, the chicken coops, the kennel, the garden, the vegetable beds were enveloped in a blanket of snow and the fence posts were transformed into white pyramids, and everything around lay still and lifeless, wrapped in a snowy shroud.

He would listen for hours to the sound of the coffee being ground, the dog barking and clanking its chain, Zakhar brushing his boots and the steady ticking of the grandfather clock.

The landlady continued to come in to offer him something to eat or to do some shopping for him, and her children would run in to see him. With the landlady herself he was friendly in a distracted kind of way and he helped the children with their lessons, listening to them read and responding with a weak and effortful smile to their childish prattle.

Little by little the mountain began to crumble and the tide began to ebb and flow and Oblomov gradually began to resume his normal pattern of life. The autumn, summer and winter dragged by drearily, but Oblomov looked forward to the spring and traveling to the estate in the country. In March the traditional lark cakes were baked and in April the double windows were removed and it was announced that the ice was breaking in the Neva and spring had arrived.

He walked in the garden. Then the vegetable beds were sown. The holidays came and went, Whitsuntide, Commemoration Thursday, May Day, marked by the ceremonial birch boughs and garlands; tea was taken under the trees.

At the beginning of summer the talk was of the two forthcoming celebrations, St. Ivan's Day, the nameday of the landlady's brother and St. Ilya's Day, Oblomov's nameday —these were the two red-letter days on the calendar. So whenever the landlady bought or happened to see a particularly good side of veal at the market or produced a particularly successful pie she would inevitably come out with: "Oh, if only I could get some veal as good as this or bake a pie like this for St. Ivan's or St. Ilya's Day!"

The talk was of St. Ilya's Friday and the annual outing on foot to the Gunpowder Works and of the festivities at the Smolensk cemetery in Kolpino.

Outside the windows Oblomov could hear again the noisy clucking of the brood hen and the chirping of the new born chicks; chicken and fresh mushroom pies along with freshly salted cucumbers began to appear on the table followed soon after by berries.

"Giblets are not much good now," said the landlady to Oblomov, "yesterday they were asking seventy kopecks for two small pairs, but there's fresh salmon—you could have cold fish soup every day."

The cuisine at the Pshenitsyn house was excellent not only because Agafya Matveyevna was so gifted in that department, but also because Ivan Matveyich Mukhoyarov himself was a great gourmet. His attitude to dress, however, was distinctly slovenly. He wore the same clothes for years and the idea of buying new ones was actively repugnant and upsetting to him. Instead of carefully hanging up his clothes, he just flung them into a heap in a corner and he changed his underwear only once a week—on Saturdays like a common laborer. When it came to food, however, he did not stint himself. In this he was guided partly by a personal philosophy he had conceived right at the start of his career in the civil service: "No one sees what's in your belly, so there's nothing to start tongues wagging, but if you appear with a heavy watch chain, a new tailcoat or boots in a light shade, that will set off a lot of idle talk."

That is why the Pshenitsyn table was graced by the best cuts of veal, amber sturgeon and white hazel-grouse. Sometimes he would go to the market or the Milyutin delicatessen, sniff around like a bloodhound and bring back a plump capon under his coat, or even lash out four roubles on a turkey. He bought his wine wholesale, hid it away and kept it for his own use, so that the only alcoholic beverage that was ever seen on his table was a carafe of currant-flavored vodka, while the wine was consumed in the privacy of his attic room.

When he went fishing with Tarantyev there was always a bottle of the best Madeira tucked away in his coat and when they drank tea together in the "public house" he would bring his own rum.

All these geological processes—the sedimentation or the silting up of the sea bed, the erosion of the mountain—had their effect on everyone, not least on Anisya. The mutual attraction between her and the landlady was transformed into an indissoluble bond and they lived and breathed as one being.

Oblomov, seeing the landlady's active interest in his affairs, once suggested jokingly that she should take complete charge of feeding him and relieve him of all that trouble. Her whole face lit up with joy and her smile this time was one of genuine pleasure, not the usual nervous tic. Her little empire was growing—instead of just one household there were now two, or rather one big one, plus she now had Anisya! The landlady spoke to her brother and the next day everything was transferred from Oblomov's kitchen to the Pshenitsyn kitchen; his silverware and crockery went into her sideboard and Akulina was demoted from cook to poultry maid and kitchen gardener.

Everything was now done on a grand scale; the purchase of groceries, sugar, tea, the pickling of cucumbers, the bottling of apples and cherries, jam making, all this now assumed vast proportions. Agafya Matveyevna had come into her own and Anisya was like an eagle that had spread its wings, and the house seethed with life and bubbled with activity.

Oblomov dined with the family at three o'clock while the brother would eat alone later, mostly in the kitchen because he came home so late from work. It was now the landlady, instead of Zakhar, who brought Oblomov his tea and coffee.

If he felt like it, Zakhar would still sweep and dust, but if not, Anisya would burst in like a whirlwind and, in a blur of apron, bare hands and maybe even her nose, would have every trace of dust and dirt whisked away and everything tidied up in a flash and vanish as suddenly as she had appeared. Otherwise the landlady herself, when Oblomov went into the garden, would glance into the room and, if she found anything out of place, would shake her head, mutter something to herself and plump up the cushions; then her glance would fall on the pillow cases and, whispering to herself again that it was about time they were changed, would pull them off, give the windows a wipe, look down behind the divan and leave.

The gradual sedimentation of the sea bed, the erosion of the mountain, the build up of silt and even the occasional mild volcanic eruption were leaving even more of a mark on the life of Agafya Matveyevna, but she herself was the last person to notice it. The effect became noticeable only because of the far-reaching, unexpected and lasting consequences.

In what way was she now no longer her old self? Before, if the roast was burned or the fish for the soup was overcooked or the soup greens had not been put in, she would rebuke Akulina quietly but firmly and without losing her composure, and that would be the end of it. But why now, if something like that happened, did she jump up from the table, rush into the kitchen and let loose a torrent of the most bitter recriminations upon Akulina and even take it out on Anisya and, the next day, personally see to it that the soup greens were in the saucepan and that the fish was not overcooked?

Now you might say that perhaps she was simply embarrassed to appear to a guest in her house at all deficient in the matter of housekeeping, an accomplishment in which she had invested all her pride and self-esteem! Yes, but then how do you explain this? Before, come eight o'clock in the evening, her eyelids would begin to droop and at nine, after putting the children to bed and making sure that the fire was out in the kitchen stove, that the flues were closed and everything had been cleared away, she would go to bed—and not even the sound of a cannon being fired could wake her until six o'clock the next morning.

But now, if Oblomov went to the theatre or stayed late at Ivan Gerasimovich's, she could not sleep but tossed and turned restlessly, crossed herself, sighed and, even if she closed her eyes, sleep simply would not come no matter what! The moment she heard a knock from outside in the street she would raise her head and sometimes leap out of bed and open the window in case it was him. And if she heard a knock at the gate she would throw on a skirt, run into the kitchen and rouse Zakhar and Anisya and send them to open the gate.

Alright, you will say that maybe even this was just a matter of a woman's being house-proud and conscientious and anxious to avoid the unseemly spectacle of her gentleman locked out in the street at night and having to wait until the drunken doorman heard him knocking and opened up—not to mention the fact that prolonged knocking might wake up the children. Fine, but then explain this! Why, when Oblomov fell ill, would she let no one else into his room and lay down carpet and strips of felt, curtain the windows and fly into a rage—she who was normally so placid and good-natured—if Vanya or Masha so much as raised their voices or even laughed too loud?

Why, while he lay ill, night after night, instead of Zakhar or Anisya, did she herself keep watch over him at his bedside, never taking her eyes off him for a moment until she left for early mass? Before hurrying off to church she would throw on a coat and write "ILYA" in block capitals on a piece of paper. She would lay the paper on an altar so that a prayer could be offered for his health and then go into a corner, drop to her knees and prostrate herself. After spending a long time in this position she would get up and hurry to the market and, returning home, would look in at the door and whisper anxiously to Anisya: "How is he?"

"Nothing special about that!" you may say, "it's merely the normal, instinctive female compassion and caring impulse at work."

Fine, but how about this? Why, when Oblomov was recovering and spending the whole morning moping and brooding morosely, hardly speaking to her, never putting his head around her door, taking no interest in what she was doing, never bantering or joking with her—why then her sudden loss of weight, of zest, of interest in what was going on around her? She would grind coffee mechanically with no idea of what she was doing, or would heap so much chicory into the coffee that it was undrinkable—except that her own feelings were so numb that she was unable to taste the difference.

If Akulina had undercooked the fish and the brother grumbled and left the table, she heard nothing, as if she had been turned to stone.

Before, no one had ever seen her just sitting and brooding—it would have been totally out of character; she never sat still and was in constant motion and her sharp eyes never missed a thing, but now suddenly you would find her sitting motionless as if in a trance with the mortar in her lap, and then abruptly she would start pounding with her pestle so violently that the dog would start barking, mistaking the sound for someone knocking at the gate.

But as soon as Oblomov started showing signs of life, as soon as his old good-natured smile returned and he began to look at her again in the same old affectionate way and put his head around the door and joke with her, she began to fill out again and the house came to life again, bustling with the old cheerful activity, but now with a subtle, novel difference. Before, she would be on the move all day long like a well-oiled machine, working nimbly, efficiently at an even rhythm and speaking neither too loud nor too softly; she would grind coffee, chop up the sugar loaves, sift and strain, and sit down to her sewing, plying her needle as rhythmically as the hand on a clock.

Then she would get up calmly and without fuss, stop on her way to the kitchen, open a cupboard, take something out and carry it in—all with machine-like efficiency. But now that Oblomov had become a member of the family there was something different about the way she pounded and sifted. Her lace work was practically forgotten. She would settle down comfortably to her work and then Oblomov would suddenly call for Zakhar to bring him some coffee, whereupon she would spring up and appear in the kitchen in a trice, take everything in with a single glance and then home in on her target, snatch up a spoon, hold up two or three spoonfuls to the light to check whether it was properly steeped and the grounds had settled so that none would find their way into Oblomov's cup, and made sure that there was no skin on the cream.

If his favorite dish was being prepared she watched the saucepan, lifted the lid, sniffed, tasted, and then gripped the handle and held it over the flame herself. If she was grinding almonds or crushing something for him she would put so much effort and passion into it that she would break into a sweat.

Everything she did around the house, the grinding, the ironing, the sifting, and straining etc. took on a new meaning—the ease and comfort of Ilya Ilyich! Before, all of these things were chores; they had now become a pleasure. She was now living what was, by her lights, a full and varied life.

However, she had no idea what was happening to her and never questioned herself, just surrendering herself to this welcome yoke unconditionally, unresistingly, without over-reacting, quietly, matter-of-factly, without foreboding, ungrudgingly, without affectation or false attitudes. It was as if she had adopted a new religion and had gone about practicing it without examining its tenets or dogmas, but blindly following its dictates. It was as if a cloud had simply descended on her that she had neither sought nor attempted to avoid, and had come to love Oblomov in the same way that she would have caught a cold or come down with an incurable fever.

She herself suspected nothing, and if you had told her, it would have been news to her and she would have given her little smirk of embarrassment.

Taking care of Oblomov was just something she quietly accepted and she learned to recognize each and every one of his shirts and knew exactly how many of his stockings had worn out heels. She knew which foot he lowered to the floor first when he got out of bed and exactly when he was about to get a stye. She knew exactly what he liked to eat and how much, whether he was in a good mood or bad, whether he had slept a lot or a little, all as if she had been doing it her whole life and never asking herself why, or what was Oblomov to her, or why she should be taking such trouble.

If anyone had asked her whether she loved him she would have given her little smirk and an affirmative answer, but then she would have given exactly the same answer after Oblomov had only been living under her roof for one week.

Why and how had she chosen him to love in particular, why had she gotten married without being in love and why, after waiting for thirty years without being in love, should it suddenly have come upon her out of the blue?

Although love is often described as a capricious, unaccountable emotion, which develops like a disease it, nevertheless, like anything else, has its own laws and reasons. If it is true that these laws have not been the object of much study or research, it is because a love struck person is hardly likely to be inclined to engage in clinical observation of how the feeling worms its way into the heart, how the senses are benumbed as if by sleep, how the eyes stop seeing, the precise moment when the pulse, followed swiftly by the heart, begins to race, the process by which undying devotion and the self-sacrificing impulse are generated, the way in which the "I" gradually disappears and becomes the "him" or the "her," how the mind becomes extraordinarily dull or extraordinarily sharp, how one's will surrenders to the will of another, how the head, the knees tremble, the tears well up, the fever mounts...

Agafya Matveyevna had rarely seen people like Oblomov before, and when she had, it was from a distance; and even if she had felt an attraction, they inhabited a totally different universe from hers and there was no natural contact with them.

Ilya Ilyich even walked differently from her late husband, Collegiate Secretary Pshenitsyn, who took such short, busy steps. He did not spend all his time copying documents, did not tremble with fear in case he was late for work, did not look at people as if he were inviting them to saddle him up and ride him. No, he looked at people boldly and freely, in the confident expectation of their deference.

His features were not coarse, his face was not reddened, but white and delicate, his hands were not like the brother's, all red and trembling, but small and white. When he sat down, crossed his legs or propped his head on his hand, it was all done so naturally and gracefully and with such dignity. When he talked it was not like the brother, Tarantyev or her late husband. There was much that she did not even understand but she felt instinctively that there was something intelligent, beautiful and unusual about it—and what she did understand was expressed in a way that was somehow different.

He wore fine linen and changed it every day. He used scented soap, he cleaned his nails—just everything about him was so clean and wholesome. It was true that he did not have to do anything, nor did he; but then he had others to do things for him—he had Zakhar and three hundred more Zakhars for that matter.

He was a gentleman, he shone, he glittered! Also, he was so nice; his walk, all his movements were so gentle; the touch of his hand was like velvet, while the touch of her late husband's hand was like a blow! And the way he looked at her and spoke to her was just as gentle and kind.

These were not things that she thought consciously, but if anyone had made it his business to investigate and explain the effect on her being of Oblomov's appearance in her life his findings would have been exactly the same.

Ilya Ilyich understood the effect he was having on everyone in this little place, from the brother to the watchdog, which now enjoyed three times as many bones as before, but he did not realize how deeply rooted it had become or how unexpected a conquest he had made of the landlady's heart.

All the care she lavished on his meals, his laundry and his comfort, he saw as nothing more than the manifestation of a driving impulse, something he had noticed the first time he had come to the house when Akulina had suddenly brought the struggling rooster into the room and the landlady, in spite of her embarrassment, had kept enough composure to tell her not to give that one to the butcher, but to give him the gray one instead.

Agafya Matveyevna herself, far from being capable of flirtatiousness with Oblomov or betraying the least sign of what was going on inside her, was, as we know, entirely oblivious to it and had no comprehension of it; she had even forgotten that only a short time ago nothing of the sort had been happening to her. Her love was expressed only in her boundless, undying devotion.

Oblomov's eyes were closed to the true nature of her feelings towards him and he continued to believe that it was all just a matter of her natural inclinations. So Pshenitsyna's true feelings, normal, natural and unselfish as they were remained a secret to Oblomov, to everyone else in the house and to herself. That her feelings were truly unselfish was clear from the fact that when she had lit the candle in church and asked for a prayer for Oblomov's health it was purely and simply that she wanted him to recover and she never mentioned it to him. In the same way, she had spent nights sitting at his bedside, stealing away at daybreak and never saying a word about it.

His feelings towards her were much simpler; for him Agafya Matveyevna, with her elbows constantly in motion, her watchful eyes that missed nothing, her endless to-ing and fro-ing between cupboard and kitchen, cupboard and storeroom, storeroom and kitchen, her mastery of every detail of housework and home-making, was the very personification of that life of boundless and unruffled peace whose image had been indelibly imprinted on his psyche since his infancy under his father's roof.

There, his father, grandfather, the children, the grandchildren and guests would lounge or lie around idly, secure in the knowledge that somewhere in the house eyes and hands were hovering nearby and constantly at work to clothe them, to provide food and drink, get them dressed and shod, put them to bed, and close their eyes in death. In just the same way here, Oblomov could loll on his divan and, without lifting a finger, see all the bustle and activity going on around him for his exclusive benefit and know for sure that if the sun failed to rise tomorrow, if tornadoes filled the sky, if a tempest swept the entire length and breadth of the universe, soup and roast meat would still appear upon his table, his linen would be kept fresh and clean, and the cobwebs brushed from his walls: how it was done he never knew and did not even trouble to wonder. Anything he happened to want would somehow be divined and brought directly to him, and not boorishly by Zakhar's dragging feet and filthy hands, but with a cheerful and deferential expression, with a smile of deep devotion, with clean, white hands and those bare elbows.

Each day he became more and more companionable with the landlady but the idea of love never entered his head, at least not the kind of love from which he had so recently suffered, which was more like a kind of disease such as smallpox, measles or fever, and which made him shudder when he thought of it. He was drawing closer to Agafya Matveyevna in the same way that he might move closer to a fire that would make him warmer and warmer, but which he could never actually love.

After dinner he was happy to stay and smoke his pipe in her sitting room, watch her put the silver and dishes back in the sideboard, take out the cups, pour the coffee, and then carefully wash and dry one particular cup, fill it before any of the others and serve him, watching anxiously to see if he was satisfied. He took pleasure in letting his eyes dwell on her plump neck and round elbows whenever her door happened to be open, and even when it had remained closed for a long time he would casually maneuver it open himself with his foot so that he could joke with her and play with the children. But if the morning went by without his seeing her he was not bored; after dinner, instead of lingering in her company he would often take a nap for a couple of hours, but he knew that whenever he woke up his tea would be there waiting for him—and at the precise moment that he woke up!

What was most important was that all this happened calmly and peacefully, there was no swelling in his heart and he never had a moment of anxiety about whether he would see the landlady or not, what she would think, what he would say to her, how he would answer her questions, how she would look at him, or about anything whatever. Yearnings, sleepless nights, sweet and bitter tears—all these were things of the past.

He sat and smoked and watched her sewing, saying something every now and then or saying nothing, contented and tranquil, needing nothing and without the slightest urge to go anywhere, as if everything he could possibly want was right where he happened to be.

Agafya Matveyevna did not subject him to the slightest pressure or make any demands on him. He felt no need to do anything to bolster his self-esteem, no stirrings, impulses or ambitions to achieve anything; he did not agonize over the thought that time was ebbing away, that his energies were being wasted, that he had done absolutely nothing for good or ill, or that he was idle and was not even living, just vegetating.

It was as if an unseen hand had planted him, like some rare and delicate species, in the shade to protect him from the heat and under cover to protect him from the rain and was carefully tending and pampering him.

"Agafya Matveyevna, your needle whizzes past your nose so fast as you finish your stitch," said Oblomov, "that I'm really afraid that you'll end up sewing your nose to your skirt."

She gave her little giggle. "I'll just finish this seam," she murmured almost to herself, "and then we'll have supper."

"What are we having?" he asked.

"Pickled cabbage and salmon," she said, "there's no sturgeon to be found anywhere; I've been around all the shops and my brother keeps on asking—but there just isn't any. And if a live sturgeon does turn up, it's always reserved for some rich merchant from Carriage Row—but they've promised to keep a couple of slices for me. Then we're having veal and fried buckwheat…"

"Wonderful, it's so nice of you to remember, Agafya Matveyevna! Let's just hope that Anisya doesn't forget!"

"Don't you think I've got everything under control? Listen!" she said, opening the kitchen door a little, "can't you hear it sizzling, it's already cooking." She finished her sewing, bit off the thread, bundled up her things and took them into her bedroom.

And so he grew close to her - to the warmth of the fire - and once he got so close that he almost got burned, or at least felt the heat of the blaze. He was walking around his room and, turning towards the landlady's door and caught sight of her elbows working away unusually busily. "Always so busy!" he said, walking up to her, "what's that?"

"I'm grinding cinnamon," she replied, looking down into the mortar as if it were a deep pit, pounding away relentlessly with the pestle.

"And what if I don't let you?" he asked, seizing her elbows and stopping her.

"Let go! I still have to grind the sugar and pour out the wine for the pudding."

He kept hold of her elbows and brought his face up close to the nape of her neck. "What would you say if I fell in love with you?"

She giggled.

"Would you love me back?" he persisted.

"Why wouldn't I, God tells us to love everyone."

"And what if I kissed you?" he whispered, lowering his head so that she could feel his hot breath on her cheek.

"This isn't Holy Week," she said with another giggle.

"Come on, give me a kiss!"

"Let's wait for Easter, then, please God, we can kiss," she said without surprise, without embarrassment, unabashed, and standing up straight and still like a horse having its collar put on.

He brushed her neck with his lips.

"Don't make me spill the cinnamon or there'll be none to put in the pie!" she responded.

"Who cares!" he said.

"Where did you get that new stain on your dressing gown?" she asked solicitously, taking the hem of his dressing gown into her hand, "it looks like oil," she sniffed the stain, "where did you get it? Could it have dripped on you from the lamp?"

"I don't know how I got it."

"I bet you got it brushing against the door, "she said, suddenly realizing what must have happened, "yesterday we greased the hinges—they were creaking. Take it off and give it to me right away, I'll take it and wash it and tomorrow the stain will be gone."

"You're so good to me, Agafya Matveyevna!" said Oblomov, lazily shrugging the dressing gown off his shoulders, "you know what, why don't we go and live in the country, on my estate; that would really be the place for you to keep house, it has everything; its own mushrooms, berries, preserves, poultry, cattle..."

"But why?" she said with a sigh, "this is where we were born and lived all our lives and this is where we should die."

He looked at her with just a tingle of emotion but his eyes did not shine, did not brim with tears, his spirits did not soar and he felt no urge to go forth and perform mighty deeds. All he felt like doing was sitting on the divan and just watching her elbows.

CHAPTER TWO

St. Ivan's Day came and was celebrated in the proper fashion. The day before, instead of going to the office Ivan Matveyich dashed around town like a man possessed, returning from each foray with a new package or basket. Agafya Matveyevna lived for three days on nothing but coffee and a three-course meal was served only to Ilya Ilyich, the rest of the household making do with snacks here and there.

Anisya did not go to bed at all the night before and it was left to Zakhar to do the sleeping for both of them, viewing all these preparations, as he did, with a mixture of indifference and mild contempt.

"Back in Oblomovka every holiday was celebrated like this," he told the two cooks who had been borrowed from the count's kitchen for the occasion, "we used to have five kinds of cake and so many sauces you couldn't count them! The master's family and guests would spend the whole day eating - and the next day too! It would take us five days to finish the leftovers, and while we were still at it a whole new lot of guests would suddenly be arriving, and the whole thing would start all over again—and here it's once a year!"

At dinner he served Oblomov first and nothing in the world could induce him to serve even a gentleman wearing a big cross around his neck. "Our master is one of the old nobility," he would announce proudly, "not some Johnny-come-lately like these guests!"

Tarantyev, sitting at the very end of the table, he would either not serve at all or might just deign to dump whatever food he felt like on his plate.

Ivan Matveyich had invited all his office colleagues—some thirty in all.

This annual celebration was marked by a repast worthy of the occasion: a huge trout, stuffed chickens, quail, ice cream and excellent wine. At the end the guests embraced, praised the host to the skies for his excellent taste and then sat down at the card tables. Mukhoyarov bowed, expressed his gratitude, and allowed as how he was only too happy to spend as much as a third of his salary for the pleasure of entertaining his guests.

Towards morning the party broke up and the guests barely managed to stagger into their carriages or make their way on foot, and calm once again descended on the house until St. Ilya's Day.

On that day Oblomov had invited only two guests apart from the members of the household: Ivan Gerasimovich and the silent and unobtrusive Alekseyev, who at the beginning of this story had invited Ilya Ilyich out for the First of May. Not only did Oblomov not want to be outdone by Ivan Matveyich, but he even tried to impress his guests by wining and dining them with an elegance of refinement unknown in such quarters. Instead of the usual greasy meat or cabbage pies, there were puff pastries as light as air; before the soup, oysters were served and there were chickens *en papillote* with truffles, choice cuts of meat, the most delicate of salad greens and English trifle. The centerpiece was a huge pineapple surrounded by peaches, cherries and apricots and there were vases of fresh flowers.

They were just starting on their soup and Tarantyev was in the middle of complaining about the pies and the cook's stupid idea of putting no filling in them, when they were interrupted by the furious barking of the dog and the frantic jerking of its chain. A carriage rumbled into the courtyard and someone could be heard asking for Oblomov; everyone sat there open-mouthed.

"It must be someone I met last year who remembered my nameday," said Oblomov, "say I'm not at home, say I'm out!" he hissed at Zakhar.

They were eating in the summerhouse out in the garden, and just as Zakhar was on his way out to turn the visitor away he bumped into Stoltz who was on his way in.

"Andrei Ivanich!" he wheezed delightedly.

"Andrei!" Oblomov called out loudly and ran to embrace him.

"Well, well, just in time for dinner!" said Stoltz, "give me something to eat, I'm starving, I've been looking for you everywhere!"

"Sit down, sit down!" said Oblomov, fussing over him and showing him to a seat right next to himself.

At Stoltz's appearance, Tarantyev was the first to make a swift exit, slipping over the fence into the kitchen garden, quickly followed by Ivan Matveyich who disappeared behind the summer house and up to his attic. The landlady also rose from her seat.

"I'm sorry, I'm disturbing you!" said Stoltz, jumping up.

"Ivan Matveyich, Mikhei Andreyich!" Oblomov shouted, "what's the matter, why are you leaving?" He made the landlady sit down again but did not succeed in calling the others back.

Oblomov peppered him with questions: "Where have you just come from? How did you get here? How long are you here for?"

Stoltz had come for two weeks on business and was on his way to the country and then on to Kiev and God knows where after that. Stoltz was busy eating and said little; it was obvious that he was really hungry and the others felt constrained to continue eating in silence.

After dinner when the table had been cleared Oblomov kept the champagne and the soda water on the table and was left alone with Stoltz. They sat in silence for a time while Stoltz scrutinized him carefully.

Finally he came out with: "Well now Ilya!" so sternly and incisively that Oblomov hung his head and said nothing.

"So, it's 'never'?"

"What do you mean 'never'?" asked Oblomov, feigning innocence.

"So you've forgotten, 'now or never'?"

"Things are different now, Andrei," he said after a time, "I'm different; my affairs are in order, thank God! I don't just lie around any more, the plan is almost finished, I take two newspapers and I've almost finished reading the books you left."

"So what stopped you from coming to join me abroad?"

"Well, what stopped me traveling abroad was..." he broke off in embarrassment.

"Olga?" said Stoltz, giving him an eloquent look.

Oblomov flared up: "You mean you know; how did... where is she now?" he asked quickly, looking at Stoltz.

Stoltz, without answering him, continued to look at him as if he were trying to peer deep into his soul.

"I heard that she had gone abroad with her aunt," said Oblomov, "soon after..."

"Soon after she realized her mistake, Stoltz finished the sentence for him.

"So you know," said Oblomov, squirming with embarrassment.

"Everything, right down to the sprig of lilac. Aren't you ashamed, don't you feel any pain, Ilya, aren't you eaten up with remorse, regret...?"

"Stop! Don't remind me!" Oblomov intervened hastily. "As it was, I came down with a fever when I saw what an abyss stretched between the two of us and realized that I was not worthy of her. Ah, Andrei, if you love me, don't torment me, don't mention her! I told her she was making a mistake a long time before, but she didn't want to believe me...really, it's not all my fault..."

"I'm not blaming you, Ilya," Stoltz responded in a friendly, indulgent manner, "I read your letter. It's I who am the most to blame, then her, and you least of all."

"How is she?" Oblomov inquired timidly.

"How is she? She's moping inconsolably—and cursing you..."

Oblomov's face expressed alarm, compassion, horror, and remorse by turns as he listened to Stoltz's words. "What are you saying, Andrei?" he said, rising from his seat, "for God's sake, let's go there right now and I'll throw myself at her feet and beg for forgiveness..."

"Just stay where you are and take it easy!" Stoltz interrupted him, laughing, "she's cheerful, even happy; she sends you her greetings and even wanted to write but I told her not to because it would only upset you."

"Well, thank God for that!" said Oblomov, almost in tears, "that makes me very happy, Andrei, let me kiss you and we'll drink to her health!"

They each drank a glass of champagne.

"Where is she now?"

"Right now she's in Switzerland. She's going with her aunt to their country place for the autumn. That's why I'm here now; there are still some loose ends to be tied up at the court. The baron did not finish the job, he had taken it into his head to propose to her..."

"Do you mean it, are you sure?" Oblomov asked, "and how did she react?"

"She refused, of course, and he took offense and left, so it was left to me to wind up that business—it should all be settled next week. So, what about you, why have you buried yourself out here in this backwater?"

"It's quiet here, Andrei, no one bothers me..."

"In what way?"

"So that I can get on with my work..."

"Please! It's just Oblomovka all over again here, only more squalid," said Stoltz, looking around, "let's go to your place in the country, Ilya!"

"The country... alright, why not; work will soon be starting on the house, but not right away, Andrei, I have to think about it..."

"There you go again, 'think about it'! I know all about your 'thinking about it'. You'll 'think about it' just the same way you 'thought about' going abroad two years ago. Let's go next week!"

"You mean just like that, next week!" Oblomov protested, "you're just on your way through and I have to make preparations; all my possessions are here; how am I going to move everything—I don't have a thing down there that I need!"

"But there's nothing you need! Like what, for example?"

Oblomov said nothing.

"My health is not good, Andrei," he said, "I get short of breath. And my styes are coming back, first in one eye and then the other and my legs have started swelling. And sometimes at night when I'm sleeping I get this feeling that something is pounding at my head or my back and I have to jump out of bed."

"Listen, Ilya, and I mean this seriously, if you don't change the way you live you're risking a stroke or dropsy. As far as any future is concerned, you're a lost cause; if even an angel like Olga couldn't lift you out of your bog on her wings, what hope do I have? But the very least you can and must do is to mark out a limited range of activity for yourself, organize your village, busy yourself with the peasants, get involved in their affairs, build, plant crops—I'm not going to let up on you! And now it's not just my own wishes that I'm acting on, but Olga's too. What she wants—are you paying attention?—she doesn't want you to give up the ghost entirely, to be buried alive, and I promised to dig you out of your tomb..."

"So she still hasn't forgotten me! It's more than I deserve," said Oblomov with feeling.

"No, she hasn't and it doesn't look as if she ever will; that's the kind of woman she is. Also, you should go and visit her in the country."

"Yes, but not now, for the love of God, not now, Andrei; give me time to forget! You know, right here I still feel..." he pointed to his heart.

"What do you still feel? Is it love?" Stoltz asked.

"No, guilt and pain," Oblomov said with a sigh.

"Very well then, we'll go to your place, after all it's there that you need to see to the work on the house, it's the summer and valuable time is being lost..."

"No, I've given someone the power-of-attorney and he's there right now; I can go later when I'm ready and have thought things out."

He started boasting to Stoltz about how splendidly he had organized his affairs without moving from the spot, how his agent was tracking down the runaway peasants, selling the grain at a good price and had sent him fifteen hundred roubles and would probably collect the quit-rent and send it to him by the end of the year.

Stoltz threw up his hands when he heard this tale: "You've been robbed blind!" he said, "fifteen hundred from your three hundred peasants! Who is this agent? What do you know about him?"

"Well, actually it's more than fifteen hundred," Oblomov corrected him, "because you have to deduct his remuneration from the proceeds of the sale of the grain."

"How much was that?"

"I can't really remember, but I can show you, I have the accounts somewhere."

"Well, Ilya, you really are dead and buried!" Stoltz stated conclusively. "Get dressed, you're coming to my place!"

Oblomov started to protest, but Stoltz practically dragged him off by force to his place, drafted a document giving himself the power-of-attorney and made Oblomov sign it and told him that he was taking over the lease of Oblomovka until Oblomov himself came and learned how to run things.

"You'll be getting three times as much," he said, "but remember, I'll only be taking over for you for a time, I have my own affairs to attend to. Let's go to Oblomovka right away—or you can come soon after me! I'll be at Olga's estate—it's only three hundred versts away—and I'll go to your place from there, get rid of your agent and take charge of the situation until you come yourself—and don't think I'm going to let up on you!"

Oblomov sighed. "God, life!" he groaned.

"What about life?"

"It just won't let you alone, won't leave you in peace! If I could just lie down and sleep—forever!"

"You mean put out the light and hide in the dark! Some life! Ilya, you really should try and look at life a little more philosophically! Life comes and goes in a flash and you just want to lie down and go to sleep. Oh, if only life could be an eternal flame, if we could only live two hundred, three hundred years, what things we could accomplish!"

"Yes, well, it's different for you, Andrei," Oblomov argued, "you have wings; you don't live so much as fly, you have talents, you have pride, you haven't run to fat, you're not plagued by styes, the back of your head doesn't itch, you're out of a different mold…"

"That's enough of that! Man is born to mold himself and even change his nature; you've grown your own paunch and you blame nature for inflicting it on you. You had wings once but you cut them off yourself."

"What are they then, these wings?" said Oblomov despondently, "I'm capable of nothing…"

"You mean you don't want to be capable of anything," Stoltz interrupted him, "there isn't a man alive who isn't capable of something—and that's the truth!"

"Well, I'm not!" said Oblomov.

"To hear you talk, you couldn't even send in a form to the town council or write a letter to the landlord—and what about the letter you wrote to Olga? You didn't mix up 'whom' and 'what' then! And you managed to find satin quality paper and ink from the English shop—and no trouble at all with your handwriting!"

Oblomov flushed.

"And when you needed to you had no trouble at all finding the words and the language; why, it was worthy of a work of literature! But when you don't absolutely have to, suddenly you're not capable, you can't see; your hands are too weak! You stopped being able to do anything when you were a child back in Oblomovka surrounded by uncles, aunts and nannies. It started with you being incapable of pulling on your own stockings and ended up with you being incapable of living!"

"Everything you say may be true, Andrei, but there's nothing to be done about it, there's no remedy!" said Oblomov with finality, sighing.

"What do you mean 'no remedy'?" Stoltz objected angrily, "just do what I tell you, there's your remedy!"

But Stoltz left for the country alone and Oblomov stayed behind, promising to join him by the autumn.

"What do you want me to say to Olga?" Stoltz asked Oblomov before leaving.

Oblomov lowered his head and after a few moments of mournful silence said: "Don't mention me at all, just say that you haven't seen me and have heard nothing."

"She won't believe me," Stoltz objected.

"Then, say I'm dead and gone, a lost soul."

"She'll burst into tears and will be inconsolable; why upset her like that?"

Oblomov grappled with his emotions and his eyes grew moist.

"Alright then, I'll lie to her, I'll say you're living on her memory," Stoltz pronounced, "and that you're seeking a serious and demanding purpose in life. Remember, it's life itself and work that are the purpose of life, not a woman—you both made that mistake. How pleased she will be!"

They said goodbye.

CHAPTER THREE

The evening after Oblomov's nameday celebration Tarantyev and Ivan Matveyich met again at the same "establishment."

"Tea!" Ivan Matveyich ordered dejectedly, and when the waiter had brought the tea and the rum he shoved the bottle back at him testily and said: "That's not rum, it tastes like rusty nails!" and took his own bottle out of the pocket of his overcoat, pulling out the cork and offering it to the waiter to sniff.

"We don't need you pushing your own stuff in here!" he responded and turned away.

"Well, old pal, this is really bad news!" said Ivan Matveyich when the waiter had left.

"Yes, what the hell brought him here?" Tarantyev exclaimed furiously, "what a crook he is, that German! He's canceled the power-of-attorney and taken over the lease of the estate himself! Did you ever hear of such a thing? And now he's going to fleece our sheep!"

"If he knows his business, old pal; I'm afraid this isn't going to turn out too well for us. Once he finds out that the quit-rent has been collected and it's us who've gotten hold of it, he's probably going to take us to court..."

"Take us to court; is that what you're worried about? You're losing your nerve, old pal. This isn't the first time Zatyorty has helped himself to some landowner's money, he knows how to cover his tracks! You don't think he gives those peasants receipts, do you? And he makes damn sure there's no witnesses around! That German will get all excited and kick up a fuss and that's the last we'll hear from him; so, as for taking us to court, forget it!"

"You really think so?" said Mukhoyarov, brightening up, "let's have a drink then!" He filled their glasses with rum. "Whenever things look their worst a little drink always helps!" he said to raise his spirits.

"Now in the meantime this is what you have to do, old pal!" Tarantyev went on, "just produce some bills for firewood, for cabbage or whatever, since Oblomov has arranged for your sister to keep house for him—and make sure they show the expenses; and when Zatyorty gets back we'll say he brought back the quit-rent but it just covered the expenses."

"But when he gets the bills he's bound to show them to the German and when that one starts calculating he's sure to..."

"Come on! All he'll do is stuff them away somewhere and clean forget where he's put them, and by the time the German shows up next the whole thing will be forgotten..."

"Well, if you think so, let's have another drink, old pal!" said Ivan Matveyich, replenishing their glasses. "It's a crime to mix rum of this quality with tea—here take a sniff—three roubles! How about some stew to go with it?"

"Alright."

"Waiter!"

"But what a crook! 'Let me take over the lease' he says," Tarantyev flared up again, "the idea would never even occur to good Russians like you and me! This whole scheme has a German smell about it; that's the kind of thing they go in for there—farms and leases. Next thing you know, he'll be talking him into some share swindle!"

"What's that mean, shares—I don't quite get the idea?" Ivan Matveyich asked.

"It's one of those German ideas!" Tarantyev spat out viciously. "It's like when some swindler gets an idea like fireproof houses and decides to build a whole town of them. So he needs to raise capital and starts selling paper certificates for, say, five hundred roubles apiece, and fools start rushing in and buying them up and then reselling them to one another. Then word gets around that the business is doing well and the certificates go up in value, and if business is bad then the whole thing collapses and all you're left with is the paper, which is worth absolutely nothing. So what happened to the town, you ask; it burned down and they tell you, or they never finished building it, and meanwhile the inventor has run off with your money. That's shares for you! And that German is sure to drag him into it. It's a wonder he hasn't already! Of course, I did my best to prevent it, just to help out someone from my old village!"

"Well one thing is sure, we won't be collecting any more quit-rent from Oblomovka, that game is over, it's history!" Mukhoyarov said tipsily.

"To hell with him, old pal! Anyway, you're rolling in it," Tarantyev declared, more than a little befuddled himself, "it's a regular goldmine, it's just a matter of keeping on digging it out. Drink up!"

"Some gold-mine, old pal! You can waste a whole lifetime picking up one rouble here, three roubles there…"

"But you've been at it for twenty years, bite your tongue!"

"What twenty years?" Ivan Matveyich retorted in a blurred voice, you've forgotten I've only been a clerk in that office for nine or ten years. Before that I had nothing but small change in my pocket. Sometimes, I'm ashamed to say, I had to be content with a few coppers. What a life! No, my old pal, imagine—there are people in the world who've got it made; all they have to do is whisper one word in someone's ear, or dictate one line, or simply write their name, and the next thing you know, their pockets start swelling up; you'd think they had pillows in there you could sleep on! It would be great to be able to do that," he fantasized more and more drunkenly, "people who want favors from you can hardly get in to see you and, when they do, they don't dare come near you. You get into your carriage and shout, 'to the club!' At the club, people wearing the highest decorations shake your hand; you gamble, but not for peanuts! And then dinner—and what dinners! The fish stew we're having—you 'd be ashamed to mention the word, it would make you wrinkle up your nose in disgust and spit! In the winter those people make a point of ordering spring chicken for dinner, and serving up wild strawberries in April! At home there's a wife all dressed up in the finest silk lace, there's a governess for the children who are beautifully dressed and with every hair in place. Yes, old pal, there is a paradise—and we're kept out of it for our sins. Drink up! Here comes our stew."

"Bite you tongue, old pal, and count your blessings; you've got a pretty nice nest egg," said Tarantyev drunkenly, his eyes all bloodshot, "thirty-five thousand in silver isn't chicken-feed!"

"Not so loud, old pal, keep it down!" said Ivan Matveyich, cutting him off. "What's thirty-five thousand? When am I going to build it up to fifty? Even fifty won't get you into paradise. If you get married on that you'll spend your whole life counting every penny—and you can forget Jamaican rum, don't even think of it! Some kind of life that would be!"

"But it's nice and easy, old pal, a rouble here, a couple of roubles there, it soon adds up and there you are salting away seven roubles a day! No complaints, no one giving you any trouble, your hands are clean and no one can pin a thing on you! But if you ever put your name to anything really big, you spend the rest of your life trying to wriggle free. No, my friend, you really shouldn't complain!"

But Ivan Matveyich was not listening, he had been thinking.

"Listen," he broke in abruptly, his eyes bulging out of their sockets and looking so relaxed that the effects of the alcohol seemed to have evaporated, "never mind, I'd better not say anything, better not let this little bird out of my skull; I've just had a brain-wave! Let's drink to it, right away!"

"Not until you tell me," said Tarantyev, pushing his glass away.

"It's something really big," Mukhoyarov whispered, keeping his eye on the door.

"Well?" Tarantyev inquired impatiently.

"Well, I've really struck oil this time. It's like putting my name to something really big, believe me, my friend!"

"What is it then, are you going to tell me?"

"Well, are we going to drink to it then, if I do?"

"Well? Go on!" Tarantyev prompted him.

"Just a moment, give me a moment to think. Yes, there's really nothing to get in the way and it's within the law. Alright then, old pal, I'll tell you, but only because I need you, it would be awkward without you. Otherwise, as God is my witness, I wouldn't tell you; it's not the kind of thing to tell to another living soul."

"So that's what I am to you, just 'another living soul'? After all that I've done for you, acted as witness... and those copies, remember? What a bastard you are!"

"Now listen, my friend, you must keep mum about this! You know what you're like, a loose cannon, liable to go off at any moment!"

"Who the hell is going to be listening around here? Are you saying I can't control myself?" Tarantyev retorted with irritation. "Just put me out of my misery and tell me!"

"Now listen we both know that Oblomov scares easily and doesn't know what's what. Remember how he lost his head over the lease and when the power-of-attorney was sent back to him he had no idea what to do? He didn't even remember how much quit-rent he was getting; he said himself: 'I don't know anything'."

"Well?" Tarantyev inquired impatiently.

"Well, he's gotten into the habit of spending an awful lot of time with my sister. The other day he was sitting there until past midnight; I bumped into him in the hallway and he pretended not to see me. So let's see what develops and... Anyway, you take him aside and tell him it's wrong to bring the house into disrepute; that she's a widow; tell him everyone knows about it and that she'll never find a husband now; say that there was this rich merchant who was courting her but he's changed his mind now that he's heard about Oblomov spending the evenings with her."

"What good will that do? He'll just collapse onto his bed and wallow like some great pig and lie there sighing—and that will be it," said Tarantyev, "what do we get out of it? What's the big deal?"

"God, you're so…well anyway, you tell him that I'm planning to lodge a formal complaint, that people have seen him, that there are witnesses."

"And?"

"And, when you've got him good and scared, you tell him there's a way out—just a matter of sacrificing a little capital."

"But where's he going to get the money?" asked Tarantyev. "He'll promise anything if he's scared—even ten thousand if he's scared enough…"

"That's just when you give me the nod and I come in with the promissory note already prepared and made out to my sister, something like: 'I, the undersigned, Oblomov, received a loan of ten thousand roubles from the widow so and so, on such and such a date to be repaid by such and such a date etc.'"

"But what's the point of it, my friend? I don't get it; the money will go to your sister and her kids. What good is that to us?"

"But my sister will give *me* a promissory note for precisely the same amount—I'll just give it to her to sign."

"But what if she won't sign and digs in her heels?"

"You talking about my sister?" Ivan Matveyich cackled. "She'll sign, old pal, she'll sign; she'd even sign her own death warrant without asking why and just give her little giggle. She'll just scrawl 'Agafya Pshenitsyna' any old how on the paper and never know what she's signing. See, you and me, we'll be in the clear; my sister will have a claim against Collegiate Secretary Oblomov, and I'll have a claim against Collegiate Secretary Pshenitsyn's widow. The German can get as furious as he wants—it's all perfectly legal!" he said, throwing up his trembling hands triumphantly. "Let's drink to it, old pal!"

"All perfectly legal!" said Tarantyev delightedly, "I'll drink to that!"

"And if it comes off, we can have another go in a year or two—it's perfectly legal!"

"Perfectly legal," Tarantyev repeated, nodding in approval, "so let's have another go at the rum!"

"Right, another go!"

And they drained their glasses.

"The only problem might be is if this Oblomov of yours digs in his heels and decides to write to his German first," said Mukhoyarov worriedly, "then we'd be done for! We'd have no case; it's not as if she's an innocent young girl, she's a widow after all."

"Oh yes, he'll write alright, no doubt about that, only it'll be in a couple of years time," said Tarantyev, "and if he tries to stand up to us, I'll show him the rough side of my tongue!"

"No, no, not on your life! You'll ruin everything if you do that; then he'll be able to say he was coerced—he might even allege violence—a criminal offense! This is the way we'll do it. You'll go and have a drink and a bite with him first—he's very partial to currant-flavored vodka. And when the drink starts going to his head, you give me a sign and I'll come in with the promissory note. He won't even notice how much it's for and he'll just sign, the same way he did the lease. Then let him try and talk himself out of that once it's been notarized. A gentleman like him will be ashamed to admit that he was not entirely sober when he signed it—it 's perfectly legal!"

"Perfectly legal!" Tarantyev repeated.

"Then Oblomovka can go to his heirs."

"Yes, let them have it! Another drink, old pal!"

"To the dumbbells!" said Ivan Matveyich, raising his glass.

They drained their glasses.

CHAPTER FOUR

We now have to retrace our steps somewhat to a point in time before Stoltz's appearance at Oblomov's nameday celebration and to another place far away from the Vyborg side. There the reader will meet some people already known to him but on whom Stoltz has not reported fully to Oblomov, either for certain particular reasons or perhaps because Oblomov did not ask all the right questions—again, no doubt, for *his* own particular reasons.

One day while in Paris Stoltz was strolling along one of the boulevards, glancing idly at the people passing by and the shop signs, without taking notice of anything in particular. It had been a long time since he had received any letters from Russia, whether from Odessa, Kiev or St. Petersburg. He was bored. He had just gone to post three more letters and was on his way home. Suddenly his eyes lighted on something, lingered for a moment with astonishment, and then resumed their normal expression. Two ladies were entering a shop. "No, it can't be!" he thought to himself, "what am I thinking of? I would have known; it can't be them!" However, he went right up to the shop window and peered through the glass at the ladies, but it was no good, they were standing with their backs to the window. Stoltz entered the shop and pretended to be interested in buying something. One of the ladies turned around to the light and he recognized Olga Ilyinskaya—and yet he didn't! He was tempted to rush over to her but restrained himself and just stood there, taking a good look at her.

"My God," he thought, "how she's changed! It's her and yet it's not her." The features were hers but she was pale, her eyes somewhat sunken and that childlike smile was no longer playing on her lips; the old carefree innocence was gone. Some thought, serious and tinged with sorrow lurked in the furrow of her brow and her eyes betrayed a knowledge of many things they had never known or expressed before. Before, her look had been open, serene and sparkling; now her whole face was overcast and clouded with a film of sadness.

He went over to her. Her eyebrows rose slightly and she looked at him for a moment in bafflement. Then she recognized him and her eyebrows parted and, just for a moment, arched symmetrically; her eyes shone with a quiet, subdued, but profound delight—the kind of delight any brother would have been happy to see in a beloved sister's eyes.

"My God, is it really you?" she said in a voice quivering with a joy that welled up from the very depths of her being. Her aunt quickly turned around and all three started to speak at once. He reproached them for not having written and they tried to explain. They had arrived only two days before and had been looking for him everywhere. At one place they had been told that he had left for Lyon, so that they did not know what else to do.

"But what made you decide to come here—and without a word to me?" he scolded them.

"It was all done so quickly that we didn't want to write—Olga wanted to surprise you," said the aunt.

He glanced at Olga but her expression did not confirm what her aunt was saying. He took another, longer look at her but she remained inscrutable and he was unable to read her expression.

"What's happened to her?" Stoltz wondered. "In the old days I could read her at a glance, but now—what a change!"

"How grown up you've become, Olga Sergeyevna, how mature, you've changed so much I hardly recognize you! And it's only a year or so since I last saw you; what have you been doing, what's been happening to you? I can't wait to hear!"

"Oh, nothing in particular," she said, examining some material.

"What about your singing?" Stoltz said, continuing to study this new Olga and trying to interpret the unfamiliar expression flickering across her face; but it flashed by and was gone in an instant.

"It's months since I did any singing," she replied casually.

"And Oblomov?" The question caught her off guard. "Is he alive and kicking? Doesn't he write?"

At this point Olga might have given away her secret in spite of herself if her aunt had not hurried to the rescue.

"Just imagine," she said, walking out of the shop, "he was at our house every day and then suddenly disappeared. When we were getting ready to go abroad I sent him a message, but we were told he wasn't well and wasn't receiving visitors, so we never saw him."

"And you don't know anything either?" Stoltz asked Olga with some concern.

Olga was busily scanning a passing carriage through her lorgnette.

"Yes, he really was ill," she said, watching the passing carriage with exaggerated attention, "Look, *ma tante*, those people in the carriage, aren't they our traveling companions?"

"No, I demand a report on my Ilya!" Stoltz insisted, "What have you done with him? Why didn't you bring him with you?"

"*Mais ma tante vient de dire*,"* she said.

"He's dreadfully lazy," her aunt added, "and so unsociable; whenever we have more than two or three people in he just leaves. And would you believe, he took out a subscription to the opera and gave up going before the season was half over!"

"He didn't even come to hear Rubini," Olga added.

Stoltz shook his head and sighed. "So, what made you decide to come? How long are you going to be away? What gave you the idea so suddenly?" he asked

"The doctor recommended it for her," said her aunt, pointing to Olga, "St. Petersburg was obviously beginning to have a bad effect on her, so we left for the winter, but we haven't yet decided where—Nice or Switzerland."

"Yes, you've changed a lot," said Stoltz pensively, his eyes boring into Olga as he looked her straight in the eye and scrutinized every filament.

The Ilyinskys spent six months in Paris and Stoltz was their constant and sole companion and guide. Olga was visibly recovering; she did not spend so much time brooding and grew more tranquil and equable, at least on the surface. What was going on inside her, God alone knew, but little by little she was turning back into the old companion Stoltz had known, although her laugh no longer had that old, loud, childlike, tinkling quality and Stoltz's attempts to amuse her were rewarded only by a guarded smile. Sometimes it even seemed that she resented not being able to help laughing.

He soon realized that there was no point in trying to amuse her. She would often hear out his sallies, looking at him with the crease on her brow and her eyebrows tilted asymmetrically, one higher than the other and, instead of laughing, would just continue looking at him in silence as if reproaching him for his levity, or simply with impatience. Or sometimes, instead of responding to his attempts at humor, would suddenly pose some deep question accompanied by such a penetrating look that he felt ashamed of his frivolity and the vacuousness of his conversation.

Sometimes Stoltz detected within her such a deep weariness at all the idle chatter and mindless to-ing and fro-ing going on around her that he felt he needed to switch over to a different wavelength, one into which he only rarely and reluctantly strayed with women. How much thought, how much ingenuity went into his efforts to chase that tense, questioning look from her face and replace it with a more relaxed expression—one which was not constantly straining and searching for something somewhere beyond his reach.

*"But my aunt has just told you"

How alarmed he was whenever, in response to some casual explanation, her face would assume a severe, arid expression, her brow would furrow and the shadow of some ineffable but profound dissatisfaction would pass across it. It would take him two or three full days of the most delicate and subtle intellectual maneuvering, outright play-acting, inspiration, and all his experience in dealing with women before he could, with luck and oh so gradually, tease the tiniest glimmer of tranquility out of her heart and a trace of acceptance and acquiescence into her eyes and smile. Sometimes he would return home at the end of the day exhausted by the struggle, happy only when he had emerged victorious.

"My God, how that girl has grown up, how quickly she has matured! Who was her teacher? Where did she learn these lessons in life? The baron? No, for all the glibness, there is nothing you could learn from his beautifully manicured sentences. Certainly not Ilya…!"

But he just could not succeed in understanding Olga, and he would hurry back to her again the next day and, now with particular care, would anxiously try to read her face, but for all his efforts he could prevail only by drawing upon all his intellectual resources and his knowledge of life, as he grappled with all the questions, doubts and demands that swirled across Olga's countenance.

Carrying the torch of his experience in his hands, he descended into the labyrinth of her mind and every day discovered new facets and new phenomena to study, but still without seeing the light. He could only observe with surprise and trepidation how her mind demanded its daily sustenance and how restlessly her soul craved the enlightenment that only life and experience could bring.

Every day, Stoltz's life and work, full as it was, was becoming increasingly intertwined with the life and daily routine of another. He would surround Olga with flowers, books, music and albums and reassure himself with the thought that he had left his companion with plenty to occupy her. Then he would go about his business or go and inspect some mine or model estate, move among his circle of acquaintances, meet new and remarkable people and would return to Olga exhausted, sit by the piano, and relax to the sound of her singing. Suddenly he would become aware from the expression in her eyes that there were new questions waiting to be asked and reports on his activities that he would be required to deliver. And little by little he found himself slipping into the habit of recounting and explaining everything he had seen that day. Sometimes she would express the wish to see for herself and experience for herself what he had been seeing and experiencing. So he would go over the same ground again and take her to see a building, a place, a machine, to read some ancient inscriptions on a wall or a stone. Gradually he slipped into the habit of thinking aloud and expressing his feelings in her presence and at a certain point, after subjecting himself to some rigorous self-examination, he suddenly realized that he was no longer living by himself but was sharing life with someone and had been doing so since the day Olga arrived.

Almost without realizing it—and to the surprise of both of them—he found himself giving voice in her presence to his delight in the treasure he had found as if he were just talking to himself. He would then check carefully to make sure whether her face revealed a glimmering of a mind at rest and an acknowledgment that he was leaving the field victorious on that occasion. If he was satisfied that this was the case he would return home proudly and long into the night would prepare himself anxiously for the next day's challenge.

The most tedious tasks no longer seemed to him mere chores, but simply necessary; they operated at a deeper level and became part of the very fabric of life. Thoughts, observations, phenomena of any kind were no longer merely filed away quietly and unconsciously in the archives of his memory but invested each day with its own bright coloring.

How fiercely Olga's pale face would glow when, without waiting for that hungry, questioning look to appear in her eyes, he would enthusiastically and vigorously ply her with an abundance of new material! How complete was his happiness when her mind, with the same eagerness, tempered with a charming humility, would anxiously scrutinize his every glance, his every word and they would both be on the lookout, he to detect the hint of an unanswered question in her eyes, and she to detect the slightest thing that he might have left unsaid or even have forgotten altogether or, heaven forbid, unforgivably, that he might have neglected to illuminate for her some dark, obscure, still inaccessible corner of his thinking and explain it to her.

The more important and difficult the question and the more carefully he expounded it, the longer and more attentively would her grateful eyes rest on him and the warmer, deeper and more intense would be her expression.

"That child, Olga," he would think in amazement, "she's outgrowing me!"

He thought about Olga longer and harder than he had thought about anything else in his whole life.

In the spring they all left for Switzerland. While in Paris Stoltz had already decided that he could not live the rest of his life without Olga. Having settled that, he then tried to work out whether Olga could live the rest of her life without him—a much more difficult question!

He approached the task unhurriedly and with great caution and circumspection, sometimes just feeling his way and, at other times, moving boldly forward, confident that he was on the point of success and that at any moment the final piece of the puzzle would fall into place—in the form of a look, a word, a gesture of boredom or delight. He was just waiting for some slight final touch, a barely perceptible movement of her eyebrows, a sigh, and the next day the picture would be complete—he was loved!

On her face he read a trust in him that was as implicit as a child's. She sometimes looked at him in a way in which she looked at no on else, except perhaps her mother—if she had had a mother. His visits, the time spent together, days on end going out of his way to please her—all this she simply regarded as her due, not as an offering of love or the goodness of his heart. It was no more than would be owed to her by a brother, a father or even a husband, and to that there were no limits. For her part, her slightest action, her every word to him was as free and frank as if he were in total and undisputed authority over her.

He knew very well that he enjoyed such authority; not a minute went by without her confirming it and telling him that she trusted him alone and that she could rely implicitly and for everything only on him in the whole wide world.

He was, of course, proud of this, but he was also aware that any other intelligent and experienced older man like an uncle, or even the baron, would have been equally proud if he were clear-headed and a man of character. The question was whether it was the authority conferred by love. Did this authority include an element of that delightful delusion, that flattering blind infatuation in which a woman is ready to be so cruelly—and so happily—mistaken. No, her submissiveness was too deliberate. It was true that her eyes glowed when he expounded some idea or bared his soul to her. He would bask in the rays of her look, but the reason was always apparent; sometimes she even told him the reason herself. But in love approval does not have to be earned, does not have to be accounted for; it is bestowed blindly and it is in that unaccountability and blindness that happiness lies. As it was, when she did not like something he said, the reason for that was also apparent.

No matter how closely he watched her he never caught any sudden coloring, any transport of delight, any languishing or flame-edged flash of her eyes; the nearest he ever came to it, it seemed to him, was when her face twisted into a grimace of pain when he announced that he would be leaving for Italy in a few days time.

At those rare and precious moments, just as his heart would practically stand still and the blood drain from his face, a veil would suddenly be drawn over everything as she would say simply and straightforwardly: "What a pity I can't go with you, I would so much like to! You'll have to tell me everything and make me feel as if I'd been there myself!" And the spell would be broken by that innocent and undisguised wish so openly expressed in everyone's presence and by that polite formal praise of his narrative skills.

He would collect and store every last, tiny detail until he had crocheted every one of them into the most delicate lace—and all that would remain would be to add that finishing stitch and then at any moment... And suddenly there she would be, as tranquil, equable, simple, and sometimes, even as cold as ever. She would be sitting at her needlework, listening to him in silence, raising her head from time to time, and giving him such interrogative, questioning and attentive looks that more than once he would irritably throw down his book or break off his explanation, jump up and move away. When he turned around he would be greeted by a look of surprise and would return to his seat in embarrassment and improvise some plausible explanation. She would simply listen to him and take him at his word. She did not entertain the slightest doubt or permit herself even a knowing smile.

"Does she love me or doesn't she?" The questions played leapfrog inside his head. If she did, why was she being so cautious, so unrevealing? If she didn't, why was she being so accommodating, so submissive?

When he was about to leave Paris for London for a week he came and told her on the very day of his departure without having mentioned it to her before. If she had shown any sign of dismay or panic, that would have been it, the secret would be out and he would have been happy. But she merely shook his hand firmly and looked a little downcast; he was in despair.

"I'm going to be terribly bored," she said, "I could cry, I'll be an orphan. *Ma tante*, look, Andrei Ivanich is leaving!" she protested tearfully. She had pole-axed him.

"Now she's brought her aunt into it," he thought, "that's all I needed! I can see that she doesn't want me to go, maybe even loves me—but that kind of love can be traded on the exchange, purchased in exchange for so much time, so much attention, so much trouble. No, I won't come back!" he thought miserably. "Who would believe it? Olga, a little girl like that; she used to be so docile and obedient, and now...what's happened to her?" He was lost in the deepest thought.

What *had* happened to her? Well, there was just one little thing he did not know; that she had once been in love, that she had been through it all already—to the extent she was capable of it—that time in a young girl's life when she cannot control her feelings, cannot conceal her blushes, the pain in her heart, those tell-tale signs of excitement, that first passion. If he had known that, he would have known, if not the secret of whether she loved him or not, then at least the reason why it was so hard to divine what was happening to her.

In Switzerland they went everywhere that visitors go, but more often preferred to stop at places off the beaten track. Each of them, but particularly Stoltz, was so preoccupied by "their own problems" that they grew tired of the actual traveling, which had now become purely incidental. He followed her up mountains, looked down over cliffs and gazed at waterfalls, but in all the scenes it was she who was in the foreground. He would follow her along some narrow path, leaving her aunt sitting in the carriage down below. He would observe keenly but discreetly how she would stop to catch her breath on the way up and would turn and look at him and only him—that he was sure of. That would have been fine and would have gladdened his heart and left him with a warm feeling, except that she would suddenly take her eyes off him to admire the scenery and would stand rooted to the spot, lost in contemplation. Then, if he made the slightest movement, uttered the slightest sound, or did anything to remind her of his presence she would be startled or at times even cry out in alarm, so utterly had she forgotten whether he was nearby, far away— or indeed his very existence.

Yet later, back home, by the window, on the balcony she would talk only to him. She would talk and talk, unburdening herself of every last one of her impressions and thoughts. She would talk eagerly, intensely, stopping now and then to choose a word or to seize on an expression he had used, and for a moment a glint of gratitude for his help would show in her eyes. Or she would sit, pale and tired in a big armchair while her restless, hungry eyes would signal to him that he should talk to her.

She would listen without moving, without uttering a word and missing nothing. When he fell silent she would still be listening, her eyes would still be questioning and the silent challenge would stimulate him to greater efforts and recharge his enthusiasm.

This would have been fine, all was light and warmth, his heart was beating—at that moment she was alive and fulfilled, holding nothing back—her spirit, her fire, her intelligence given free rein. But the next moment she would get up, all her energies drained, and those same questioning eyes would be asking him to leave, or she would suddenly feel hungry and would start eating with such appetite...

And this too would have been fine; he was no dreamer and was not looking for giddy emotional heights any more than Oblomov himself, although for different reasons. What he would have liked, however, would be to see an even flow of emotion, boiling furiously at its source to begin with, so that he could steep himself in it and intoxicate himself so that he could then be secure in the knowledge for the rest of his life that his happiness was flowing in a steady stream from those wellsprings.

"Does she love me or not?" This was the question with which he tormented himself until he was practically sweating blood, almost in tears. The question burned more and more fiercely within him, it consumed him in its flames and paralyzed his will, it was now the key question not just of love but of his whole life. There was no longer room for anything else anywhere in his being.

It seemed that in the space of those six months he was prey to each and every one of those torments and tortures of love from which he had been at such pains to protect himself in his dealings with women. He felt that if these months of mental, nervous and psychic stress were to continue, even *his* healthy organism would not be able to stand it. He began to understand—something he had never given a thought to in the past— how one's strength is sapped by these internal struggles with passion that are hidden from view, how these untreatable wounds scar the heart, wounds that do not bleed yet make you cry out in pain and how life ebbs away. He began to lose his invincible confidence in his powers; he no longer reacted flippantly to stories about other people who lose their senses or pine away for a host of reasons one of which happened to be... love. It all began to frighten him.

"No, it's time to put a stop to this!" he said, "I'll take one more look into her heart and tomorrow I'll either be a happy man or I'll leave! I'm at the end of my tether," he told himself, looking into the mirror, "I look terrible... this has to stop!"

He went straight to the source—that is, to Olga.

But what was happening with Olga? Didn't she notice the state he was in or was she just indifferent to it? It was something she could not fail to notice. Even less sensitive women than she are able to tell the difference between a devoted friend and the attentions of someone prompted by a more tender emotion. Coquettishness on her part can be ruled out on the basis of a true understanding of her genuine, sincere and straightforward moral character that was constitutionally incapable of hypocrisy. That kind of cheap self-indulgence was beneath her. The only conclusion that remains is that she simply enjoyed—apart from any practical considerations—these constant, thoughtful and devoted attentions of a man like Stoltz. And why wouldn't she? These attentions restored her wounded self-esteem and little by little lifted her back onto the pedestal from which she had fallen; gradually she was recovering her lost pride. But what was she thinking? How did she imagine all this devoted attention would resolve itself? After all, the duel between Stoltz's relentless attempts to open her up and her mute resistance could not go on forever. Surely she must have had an inkling that all this effort on his part was not for nothing and that he would not have invested so much of his will and character in a losing cause. Was he just going to waste all this zest, this sparkle? Would these dazzling rays obliterate the image of Oblomov and their love?

She understood none of this; it was all too confusing. She wrestled desperately with these questions in her mind but could not see her way out of the labyrinth.

What was she to do? The situation could not be allowed to remain unresolved; at some point all this silent interplay of suppressed feelings would have to be put into words and then what would she say about the past? How would she describe what had happened and how would she describe what she felt for Stoltz? If she did love Stoltz, then what did this make that other love? Coquetry, a mere flirtation—or worse? Her face burned and flushed with shame at the thought. No, she could not saddle herself with such a burden of guilt. But if it had been a case of innocent first love, then what were her feelings for Stoltz? Was she play-acting again, toying with him and subtly manipulating him into an offer of marriage to camouflage the frivolity of her own conduct. The very thought drained the blood from her face and struck a chill to her heart.

But if it was not a game or an act or sheer calculation—then could it be love again? She was totally flustered by this supposition; a second love only seven or eight months after the first? Who would believe her? How could she ever breathe a word of it without provoking astonishment— or perhaps contempt! How dared she even think such a thing, she had no right!

She delved deeply into her own experience, but there was no information about second loves to be found there. She recalled the pronouncements of such authorities as her aunt, other older, wiser women and even what had been written by "philosophers of love," but the verdict from all these quarters was the same, inexorable: "a woman can be truly in love only once in her life." Oblomov too had handed down the same verdict. She wondered how Sonechka would have reacted to the idea of a second love, but travelers from Russia had reported that her friend was already on her third...

"No, no, she couldn't be in love with Stoltz," she decided, "it was out of the question." She had been in love with Oblomov and that love was dead and the flower of her life had withered forever. What she had with Stoltz was nothing but friendship, a friendship based on his splendid qualities as well as his friendship for her, expressed in his attentiveness and his trust. She rejected the idea, even the possibility of love towards her old friend.

This was the reason why Stoltz could not discern on her face or in her words the slightest trace of even positive indifference or a momentary flash of lightning, even a spark of feeling which strayed even by a hair's breadth beyond the bounds of warm, heartfelt, but perfectly normal friendship. To put an end to it once and for all there was only one thing she should have done. Once she began to notice the first signs of love on Stoltz's part she should have stopped feeding it and left at once. But by now she had let too much time go by. The first signs had appeared long before and in any case she should have foreseen that his feelings would grow into passion; after all this was no Oblomov, there was no getting away from him.

And even granting that it had been physically possible, leaving was morally impossible for her. To begin with she had simply resumed the old friendship she had enjoyed with Stoltz and had found in him the same old playful, witty and amusing companion she had known before, the same keen and penetrating observer of life—and of everything that happened to them or went on around them and seized their interest.

But the more they saw of each other, the deeper the psychic bonds they forged and the more active his role became. Where he had once been an observer he now imperceptibly became an interpreter of life and its manifestations, her guide and mentor, somehow ending up as her brain and conscience. He acquired new rights and new invisible ties began to bind him ever more closely to every aspect of Olga's life, every aspect, that is, save one tiny private corner that she carefully kept hidden from his scrutiny and judgment.

She accepted this moral tutelage of her mind and heart and saw that she in turn was acquiring her share of influence over him. An exchange of rights had taken place that she had somehow tacitly and unconsciously approved.

How could all that suddenly be uprooted; all that time spent together, all that she was learning from him, the pleasure of his company, the diversity... the life? What would she do if it all suddenly disappeared? And when it did occur to her to break away it was too late, she no longer had the power to do so.

Every day spent without him, every thought left unshared with him was devoid of color, of meaning. "God, if only I could have been his sister!" she thought. "What happiness to possess a lifelong claim on such a man, not just a claim on his mind but also his heart, to be able to enjoy his company legitimately, openly, without having to pay such a high price in heartache—and the revelation of my shameful secret. What role is left to me now? He's going away and not only have I no right to stop him but I should want him to go. If I try to stop him what can I say to him. What right do I have to see and hear him every minute of the day. Because I'm bored without him, because I would miss learning from him, being amused by him, because he fills a need and makes life agreeable? Of course that is a reason, but not a right. And what do I have to offer him in return? The right to admire me unselfishly with no thought of reward when so many women would be only too happy to..."

For all her agonizing over the situation she could see no way out. All she could see that lay ahead was frightening; his disappointment and the final parting of their ways. At times it occurred to her to reveal everything to him and to put both of them out of their misery, but the very thought of it took her breath away so deep was her shame and humiliation.

The strangest thing was that she had lost respect for her past and had actually started to feel ashamed of it from the time when Stoltz had become her inseparable companion and had taken over her life. If it had been a matter of the baron, for example, or anyone else finding out she would have felt embarrassed and uncomfortable but she would never have been nearly as mortified as she was at the thought of Stoltz finding out. She recoiled in horror when she imagined the expression that would appear on Stoltz's face, the look he would give her, what he would say and what he would go away thinking. He would suddenly see her as an utterly worthless, weak and contemptible creature. No, no, not for the world! She began to examine her own feelings and discovered to her horror that she was ashamed not only of that whole romantic drama but also of its leading man and she burned with remorse at her ingratitude for the deep devotion of her former friend.

Perhaps she would have gotten used to her shame and could have learned to live with it—people can get used to anything, after all—if her friendship with Stoltz had been entirely free from selfish considerations and interests. But even if she had suppressed all the insidious and insinuating whisperings of her heart, the shining image which, in spite of herself, so often stirred her imagination was just too powerful for her to resist; it was the image of that other love, an image that conjured up a dream of abundant happiness that grew more and more compelling and seductive. But this was not a happiness shared with Oblomov dozing away his life in idleness by her side, but a happiness in the vast arena of life in all its facets and dimensions, with all its joys and sorrows—happiness with Stoltz. At such moments she would dissolve in tears over her past and nothing could wipe them away. She would come back to reality and take refuge even more securely behind the impenetrable wall of silence and that bland friendliness that so frustrated Stoltz. Then, for a while, she would forget herself and innocently and simply allow herself to enjoy the company of her friend and become charming, outgoing and spontaneous until she was reminded once again by that dream to which she had forfeited her rights, that she had no future to look forward to and that rosy dreams were a thing of the past and that the blossom of her life had withered on the vine.

No doubt in time she would have come to resign herself to the situation and have learned to live without hopes for the future like all old maids, and would have sunk into a frozen apathy or busied herself with good works. But all at once her forbidden dream took on a more threatening aspect when, from a few words that Stoltz had inadvertently let drop, it became clear to her that she had lost him as a friend and gained him as an ardent suitor. Friendship had drowned in love.

On the morning that she made this discovery she went pale and stayed indoors all day in a state of consternation and inner turmoil; what should she do now, what was her duty? She could come to no conclusion. She could only curse herself for not overcoming her shame right at the start and confessing to Stoltz what had happened; now it was nothing less than horror that she would have to conquer.

There were times when the pain in her breast was so great and the tears were welling up so irresistibly that she felt a powerful impulse to rush to him and wordlessly but, by means of sobs, shudders and fainting spells, reveal the story of her love, so that he would see her suffering as a token of redemption. She had heard how others behave in such circumstances. Sonechka, for example, had told her husband-to-be about her young lieutenant, how she had toyed with him, that he was just a boy and how she had deliberately made him wait outside in the frost until she came out and got into the carriage and so on.

Sonechka would not have thought twice about telling the same story about Oblomov, about how she had just strung him along for amusement, that he was so ridiculous, and how could anyone be in love with such a fool and that nobody could possibly believe such a thing. This kind of behavior, however, could only be condoned by Sonia's husband and others like him, but not by Stoltz.

Olga could have presented the matter in a more favorable light; she could have said that she was just trying to reach down to pull Oblomov up from his abyss and that was why she had resorted to a kind of friendly flirtation—just to rescue a drowning man, as it were—and then leave him once he was out of the water; but that would have sounded much too far-fetched and strained, and in any case it wasn't true.

But no, that was no way out. Olga continued to agonize: "what a straight-jacket I'm in; tell him everything? No, not that! He mustn't ever find out! But if I don't tell him it's like being a thief; it's like cheating or playing up to someone. God help me!" But there was no help from that quarter. For all the pleasure she took in Stoltz's company, there were times when she would have preferred never to see him again, to flit through his life like the faintest of shadows and not to becloud the clear and lucid horizon of his existence with this forbidden passion.

She would have mourned her still-born love, shed tears for the past and buried the memory of it in her heart, then… then, perhaps, she would have found a "suitable match'—there was no lack of them—and have become a good, intelligent and dutiful wife and mother, dismissing the past as a maiden's folly and would have gone on, not so much to live but rather to put up with life—the way everyone does! But she was not in this alone, there was another party involved, and that party had invested his ultimate and dearest hopes in her.

"What made me think I was in love?" In a torment of regret she recalled that morning in the park when Oblomov had wanted to break away and she had thought that the book of her life would snap shut forever if he left. How confidently and casually she had decided the whole question of life and love, how clear everything had seemed—and how tangled and muddled everything had become! She had been too clever for her own good and had thought that you only had to look life straight in the eye and march boldly ahead and life, like a tablecloth at a picnic, would spread itself obediently under your feet—and hey, presto! No, there was no one else she could possibly blame; it was entirely her own fault.

Olga, not suspecting why Stoltz had come, got up from the divan with no cause for concern, put down her book and went to greet him.

"I'm not disturbing you?" he asked, taking a seat by the window that looked out onto the lake. "You were reading?"

"No, I'd already stopped, it was getting dark. I was waiting for you!" she said in a soft, friendly and unsuspecting tone.

"Good, because I have to talk to you," he said with a serious expression as he moved another armchair near the window for her.

She trembled and stood rooted to the spot, then sank into the armchair without thinking and just sat there, her eyes lowered, feeling acutely uncomfortable and wishing she were a million miles away. At that moment her past flooded back into her mind and she seemed to hear a voice saying: "Judgment is at hand, you cannot play with life as if you were playing with dolls! If you do, you'll pay for it!"

They sat in silence for a few minutes. He was clearly collecting his thoughts. Olga was fearfully eyeing his sunken cheeks, his furrowed brow, his tight-lipped expression of determination.

"Nemesis!" she thought, suppressing a shudder. It was as if they were both preparing for a duel.

"I'm sure you've guessed what I have come to say, Olga Sergeyevna?" he said with a questioning look.

He was sitting in an alcove with his face hidden, while the light from the window fell directly on her and he was able to read what was in her mind.

"How could I guess?" she answered softly. Faced with such a formidable adversary, she could not summon up the same strength of will and character, perspicacity and self-control that she had always displayed to Oblomov. She realized that the only reason why she had so far been able to elude Stoltz's sharp eyes and wage her campaign so successfully had nothing whatsoever to do with her own powers—as had been the case in her struggle with Oblomov—but rather Stoltz's stubborn silence and his unwillingness to come out into the open. Now that the forces were arrayed on the field of battle the odds were clearly not in her favor and her 'how could I guess?' was simply an attempt to give herself a little breathing space, to play for a little time in the hope ·that her adversary would show more of his hand.

"You can't guess?" he said simply. "Very well, I'll tell you."

"No don't!" she blurted out. She grasped his hand and looked at him as if pleading for mercy.

"You see, I was right, you *did* know!" he said. "Why did you deny it?" he added sadly.

She did not reply.

"If you already knew that I was going to declare myself at some point, you must have had an answer ready."

"Yes, I did know and that was what was tormenting me," she said, leaning back as far as she could against the back of her chair, turning away from the light and mentally sending out a distress signal for the dusk to come and rescue her and stop him from reading the conflict between embarrassment and regret registered on her face.

"You were being tormented! What a terrible word!" he said almost in a whisper. "It's Dante's 'abandon all hope'. That's all I have to say, that's it! But I thank you for one thing," he said with a deep sigh, "I've finally emerged from the chaos, from the darkness and now at least I know what I must do. My only hope is to get away as soon as possible!" He rose to his feet.

"No, don't, for the love of God!" She rushed towards him and seized his hand again, imploring him with fear in her voice. "Have pity on me! What will become of me?"

He sat down; Olga sat down too.

"I must tell you that I love you, Olga Sergeyevna!" he said almost sternly. "You see what these last six months have done to me? What more do you need—unconditional surrender? Would you like me to pine away, to lose my mind? My humble thanks!"

Her face dropped. "Leave then!" she said on a note of wounded pride mixed with a deep sadness that she was unable to conceal.

"Forgive me, I'm sorry," he apologized, "you see we're still in the dark and yet we're already quarrelling. I know you can't mean what you said, but you can't put yourself in my shoes either and you can't understand my impulse to run. People sometimes act selfishly in spite of themselves."

She shifted in her chair as if sitting made her feel ill at ease.

"But even supposing I were to stay, what then?" he said. "Of course you will offer me your friendship, but I already have that in any case. Even if I leave and a year, or even two years go by, your friendship will still be there. Friendship is a good thing, Olga Sergeyevna, when it is part of love between a young man and a woman or the memory of love between old people, but God help us if it is friendship on one side and love on the other. I know that you enjoy my company, but what does *your* company mean to me?"

"In that case, maybe it's better if you leave," she whispered almost inaudibly.

"To stay," he was thinking aloud, "would mean walking the razor's edge, yes, friendship's a wonderful thing!"

"Do you think it's any easier for me then?" she retorted unexpectedly.

"But why?" he asked with alacrity, "I mean you're not...you don't love...?"

"I don't know, I swear to God, I just don't know! But if you... if my life changes from the way it is now, what will become of me?" she said despondently, virtually to herself.

"How am I supposed to take that—give me some idea, for God's sake?" he said, moving his chair closer to her, perplexed by what she had said and the tone, spontaneous and stripped of all pretense in which she had said it. He scrutinized her features. She remained silent, but she was burning to reassure him, to take back the word "torment' or at least to give it a different meaning from the one he had understood; but she herself did not know what meaning to give it. It was just that she was dimly aware that they were both laboring under the same fateful misunderstanding and had both been placed in a false position that was hurting both of them, and only he, or she, with his help, could make sense of what was happening then and what had happened before. But for that she would have to cross the divide and reveal to him what had happened; how she longed for—and feared—his judgment!

"I myself don't understand any more than you do; I'm more confused, more in the dark than you are!" she said.

"Listen, do you trust me?" he asked, taking her hand.

"Totally, as if you were my mother, you know that," she replied faintly.

"Then tell me what has happened to you since the last time we met. You've become inscrutable to me now; before I could read your face like a book. I think now is our only chance to understand each other, you agree?"

"Oh yes, it's the only thing—we have to resolve things one way or another," she said unhappily, dreading the inevitable confession. "Nemesis, nemesis!" she thought, lowering her head. She stayed silent, her head buried in her chest.

A wave of dread surged over him at these simple words, and still more because of her silence.

"She's really suffering; my God, what could have happened to her?" His brow broke into a cold sweat and he felt his hands and feet beginning to tremble. He was invaded by the most fearful imaginings. She still could not bring herself to speak and was visibly in throes of an internal struggle.

"Well, Olga Sergeyevna?" he urged her anxiously. She still did not speak but just shifted nervously in her seat. It was by now too dark to see and he could hear only the rustling of her silk dress.

"I'm just trying to nerve myself," she said finally. "If you only knew how hard it is!" she added, turning away from him in an effort to gain control of her feelings. She wished that Stoltz could somehow hear the whole story in some miraculous fashion without her having to open her mouth. Fortunately night was falling and her face could not be seen in the dark; it was only her voice that could give her away. But the words would not come, as if she could not decide on what note to begin.

"My God, how guilty I must be if I feel this much shame, this much anguish." Her inner torment continued unabated.

And to think it was only recently that she had so confidently taken charge of her own destiny and that of another and had been so lucid, so strong! Now it was her turn to tremble like a child! She was being tortured all at once by shame for the past, the battering of her self-esteem at this very moment and by her false position. It was unbearable!

"Let me help you... you've... been in love?" Stoltz offered falteringly—so painful was it to bring out that word. Her silence was confirmation and another wave of dread swept over him.

"Who was it? It's not a secret, is it?" he asked, trying to speak in a firm voice, but felt his lips trembling. The situation was becoming more and more painful to her. If only she could have uttered a different name, told a different story! She hesitated for a moment, but it was no use. Like someone in the face of overwhelming danger who hurls himself off a cliff-top or plunges headlong into a fire, she blurted out the name "Oblomov!" He was dumbfounded and there was silence for a minute or two.

"Oblomov!" he repeated, astounded, "I don't believe it!" he added with assurance, lowering his voice.

"It's true!" she said calmly.

"Oblomov," he repeated again, "impossible!" he asserted with equal assurance. "No, something is wrong, you must have misunderstood yourself or Oblomov, or maybe even love itself!"

She said nothing.

"It wasn't love, it was something else, I'm telling you!" he insisted.

"Oh yes, I flirted with him, strung him along, made him unhappy… and now, according to you, I'm giving you the same treatment!" Her voice was restrained but simmering with tears of resentment.

"Dear Olga Sergeyevna! Don't feel bitter, don't talk like that—it' s not like you! You know I think nothing of the kind, but I just can't take it in, I can't understand how Ob…"

"Yet he's worthy of your friendship, you can't praise him too highly, so why shouldn't he be worthy of love?" she argued.

"I know that love is less demanding than friendship," he said, "in fact, it's often blind; it's not for their virtues that people are loved. For love, there has to be another ingredient, sometimes something quite trivial, something you can't put your finger on or define, but something which is totally lacking in my incomparable but hopeless Ilya. That's why I'm so surprised. Listen," he continued animatedly, "we won't get anywhere like this, it won't help us to understand each other. You'll have to tell the story in detail, so try to overcome your embarrassment for half an hour. Tell me everything and then I'll tell you what it was that was happening—and perhaps even what is going to happen. I can't help thinking that there is something that doesn't quite make sense here—if only it were true," he exclaimed eagerly, "if it was Oblomov and Oblomov alone, no one but Oblomov! Then that would mean that you're not a prisoner of the past, of love, but that you are free… out with it quick!" he ended on a calm, almost cheerful note.

"Oh yes, thank God!" she replied, casting off all reserve and delighted to have been freed from some of her chains, "I was going out of my mind from the strain of keeping it all to myself. If you only knew how pitiful I've been. I don't know whether I should feel guilty or not, whether I should feel ashamed of what happened or regretful, whether there is still hope for the future or whether I should give up hoping. You talked about your torment, but didn't suspect that I was suffering from torment of my own. I want you to hear me out, but not with your mind—I'm afraid of your mind—but with your heart instead. Perhaps your heart will understand that I had no mother, that I was somehow lost in the woods." These last words she uttered in a quiet dejected voice. "But no," she added, quickly regaining command of herself, "don't pity me. If it *was* love... you must leave!" she paused for a minute, "and come back later when only the call of friendship brings you back. But if it was just a matter of my being frivolous and flirtatious then punish me, get away from me and forget me, you hear!"

By way of reply, he squeezed both her hands.

Olga began her confession; it was long and detailed. Clearly and distinctly, omitting no detail, she unburdened herself of everything that had been preying on her mind for so long, everything that it made her blush to think of, everything that had once moved her and made her happy but had later left her with a burden of doubt and distress.

She told him about their walks, the park, their hopes, Oblomov's new lease of life and his backsliding, the sprig of lilac, even about the kiss. The only thing she left out was that sultry evening in the garden—no doubt because even now she had not made up her mind about what exactly had gotten into her at the time.

To begin with she spoke in a low muffled murmur of embarrassment, but as she gained confidence she began to articulate with greater clarity and freedom. What had started *pianissimo* became a *mezzo piano* that then swelled into a full-throated *forte*. At the end she was speaking as calmly as if it had been someone else's story that she was telling.

It was as if a curtain had been raised, revealing to her a past that up to that moment she had been afraid to confront and there was much to which her eyes were opened, and if it had not been dark she would have looked her listener boldly in the eye.

When she had finished she waited for the verdict; but the only response was a sepulchral silence. What was he doing? There was not a sound, not a movement, he did not even seem to be breathing; it was as if there was no one there with her.

This wordlessness began to stir up her doubts again. The silence continued. What did it mean? What verdict was being deliberated by what was for her the most perspicacious and lenient judge in the whole world? Anyone else would condemn her mercilessly, only he could be the counsel for her defense, he was the one she would have chosen... he would understand everything, weigh all the evidence and hand down a verdict even more favorable to her than she would have been capable of herself! Yet he was silent; could it be that she had lost her case? Her worst fears returned.

Suddenly the door opened and two candles brought in by the chambermaid lit up the corner where they were sitting. She gave him a timid, but hungry and questioning look. His arms were folded and he was looking at her with such a gentle wide-eyed expression and relishing her discomfiture. Her heart leapt and warmed into life and she heaved a sigh of relief, almost bursting into tears. In that instant she was once again able to judge herself less severely and to put her trust in him. She was as happy as a naughty child who has been forgiven, comforted and hugged.

"That's it?" he asked quietly.

"That's it!" she replied

"And his letter?"

She took out the letter from a document case and handed it to him. He went over to a candle, read it, and put it down on the table. He looked at her with that old expression that she had not seen on his face for so long. Once again there stood before her that old, familiar friend, self-assured and slightly ironic, whose benevolence and indulgence towards her knew no bounds. There was no trace of suffering or doubt in his expression. He took her hands, kissed each in turn and was soon lost in thought. She too fell silent and watched unblinkingly as his thoughts flickered over his face. Suddenly he stood up.

"My God, if only I had known that this was all about Oblomov I would never have gotten into such a state," he said, looking at her with such affection and trust that it was as if her dreadful past was simply something that had never happened. Her spirits soared, she was over-joyed, relieved. She now saw that it was only his judgment that she had feared, and that he was neither condemning nor shunning her. As to what the rest of the world might think of her, she could not care less!

He was his old self once again and in good spirits; but for her that was not the point. She saw that she had been acquitted but, as the defendant, she was anxious to hear the verdict—and he had picked up his hat.

"Where are you going?' she asked.

"You're overwrought right now, why don't you take a rest and we'll talk tomorrow?"

"You want me to spend a sleepless night?" she broke in, putting a restraining hand on his arm and pulling him down into a chair. "Do you really think you can just go without telling me what it was... that happened, what's happening to me now and what's... going to happen to me? Please, Andrei Ivanich, who else will tell me? Who is going to punish me, if that is what I deserve, or... pardon me?" She looked at him with such candid affection that he threw down his hat and had to restrain himself from dropping to his knees in front of her.

"You angel—or my angel, if I can call you that!" he said, "there's no reason for you to torment yourself, there's no question of punishing or pardoning you. I have absolutely nothing to add to your story. How can you possibly have any doubts? You really want to know what happened— give it a name? You've known yourself for a long time... where's Oblomov's letter?" He picked it up from the table and started reading: "The 'I love you' that you are saying is not about what is happening now, but about some future love. It's just an unconscious need to love that, because it has nothing else to feed on, a woman sometimes expresses in affection for a child or another woman or that sometimes takes the form of tears and hysterics...! You are mistaken"—Stoltz read out the word with particular emphasis—"the man you see before you is not the man of your dreams, the one you have been waiting for. Be patient and he will come and then you will come to your senses, you will feel embarrassed and ashamed of your mistake…"

"You see, it's all here!" he said. "You *have* been feeling ashamed and you *have* been kicking yourself for…your mistake. There's nothing else to be said. He was right but you wouldn't believe him, and that's all you were to blame for. That's when the two of you should have ended it, but he couldn't resist your beauty… and you were touched by his dove-like gentleness!" he added with a touch of mockery.

"I didn't believe him, I thought the heart couldn't be mistaken."

"No, it can be mistaken—and sometimes fatally; but it never got as far as your heart," he added, "it was just wishful thinking and pride mixed with weakness. You were afraid that that would be your only chance of happiness in your whole life and that that faint glow would light up your life and the rest would be darkness."

"But what about the tears?" she said. "Surely they were from the heart; when I cried I wasn't pretending, it was genuine…"

"Good God, a woman will cry about anything; you say yourself that you couldn't think about the sprig of lilac or your favorite bench without a pang of regret. Add to that hurt pride, your failure to rescue Oblomov, and a dose of habit—there are so many reasons for tears!"

"And our meetings, our walks—all that was a mistake too? Remember that I went to his place," she added with embarrassment, and it seemed that she was trying to muffle her own words. She was trying to put herself in the wrong so that he would then come even more fiercely to her defense and she would appear even more blameless in his eyes.

"It's clear that in your last few meetings there was nothing left for you to talk about. Your so-called love was simply lacking in substance and could not grow. Even before you actually went your separate ways you had really ended the relationship and your allegiance was not to love but a pale simulacrum of it, which the two of you had invented yourselves—and that's the whole mystery!"

"And the kiss?" she whispered so softly that he did not so much hear it as guess it.

"Oh yes, that's extremely important," he responded with mock severity; "You should really have been punished… by being docked one course at dinner!" He was now giving her a look of even greater tenderness and love.

"I'm afraid joking doesn't justify a 'mistake' like that!" she objected severely, offended by his casual and dismissive tone. "I would be happier if you had given me a serious dressing down and called what I did wrong by its proper name."

"I wouldn't have thought it a joking matter if it had been anyone else but Ilya," he countered, "then it could really have ended badly, but I know my Oblomov."

"Someone else, never!" she said, flaring up, "I knew him better than you…"

"There, you see!" he declared.

"But what if he had… changed, come to life, listened to me—wouldn't I have come to love him then. Was it really all false, a mistake even then?" she said in order to make sure that all the angles were covered, and that not the slightest shadow of doubt remained.

"In other words, if it had been someone else instead of Oblomov," Stoltz interjected, "then unquestionably your relationship would have solidified and developed into love and then…but that's another story with a different protagonist and has no bearing on us."

She gave a sigh as if she were shedding the last fragment of her burden. They both lapsed into silence.

"Ah, what a joy it is…to be restored to health," she uttered the words with particular care and distinctness, radiant as a flower in bloom, and shot him a look of such deep gratitude, such unprecedented warmth that he seemed to detect in it that spark he had been watching for so unavailingly for almost a year. A shudder of joy ran through him.

"No, I am the one who has been restored to health," he said, thinking to himself, "oh, if only I had known that, of all people, it was Ilya who was the leading man in that drama! So much time wasted, so much pointless worrying—and all for nothing, for no reason at all! Why?" he questioned himself in exasperation.

Suddenly he shook off his exasperation and snapped out of his dark, brooding mood. The furrows disappeared from his brow and his eyes brightened.

"Well, of course, it was inevitable—but I must say I'm relieved now… and so happy!" he added fervently.

"It's like a dream—as if it never happened at all," she mused almost audibly, astonished at the suddenness of her recovery. "You've taken away not only the shame and the remorse but even the pain and the grief. How did you do it?" she asked quietly. "And according to you it will all be forgotten…this 'mistake'?"

"Yes, as a matter of fact I think it's already forgotten!" he said, for the first time giving her a look of passion and making no attempt to conceal it, "and I mean all of it!"

"And what *will* happen…that won't be a mistake… but the truth…?" she did not complete her question.

"It's all written here," he stated with assurance, picking up the letter again: 'The man you see before you is not the man of your dreams, the one you were waiting for; he will come and you will come to your senses.' And, I want to add on my own account, you will find love and it will be a love so powerful that a whole lifetime will not be long enough for its expression, let alone a single year! Only I don't know… who it will be," he concluded, his eyes boring into her as he spoke.

She lowered her eyes and her lips but her eyelids could not conceal the gleam in her eyes and her tightened lips could not contain her smile. She looked at him and burst into laughter that welled up from so deep inside her that it brought tears with it.

"I've told you what happened to you and even what is going to happen to you, Olga Sergeyevna," he said, "but you're not giving me an answer to my question—which you didn't even let me finish."

"But what can I say?" she said in embarrassment, "And even if I could, would I have the right to say what you want to hear and... what you so richly deserve," she added in a whisper, giving him a bashful look.

Again he thought he detected sparks of such warmth of feeling that he felt a spasm of joy once again. "There's no hurry," he said, "you can tell me later what I deserve, after a decent interval of mourning for your dead love. In any case, I have picked up one or two clues over this past year. Now there's only one question that needs settling, shall I go...or stay?"

"See, now you're playing the tease with me," she replied high-spiritedly.

"Not at all!" he responded gravely, "now that old question has taken on a new significance: if I stay... it will be on what basis?"

She was taken aback.

"So you see, I'm not playing games!" He laughed, pleased to see that he had caught her out. "After this conversation we can't go on as before; today we're no longer what we were to each other yesterday."

"I don't know," she whispered, more confused than ever.

"Can I give you some advice?"

"Please do, I'll do whatever you say!" she said, almost passionate in her submissiveness.

"Marry me in the meantime, until Mr. Right comes along!"

"I don't dare, I'm not ready..." she whispered, hiding her face in her hands, overcome by her feelings—but feelings of happiness.

"Why not?" he whispered back, bringing her face close to his.

"And what about all that happened?" she whispered again, leaning her head against him as though against a mother's breast.

He gently pried her fingers from her face, kissed her on the head, relishing her confusion for a long moment and enjoying the sight of tears welling up in her eyes and receding back inside them.

"It will wither away like the sprig of lilac!" he assured her. "Now that you've learned the lesson, it's time to put it to use. Life is starting; just put your future in my hands and don't worry about a thing—I'll take care of everything, you have my assurance! Now let's go and see your aunt!"

Stoltz returned home late that night. "At last I've found what I've been looking for!" he thought, gazing with love struck eyes at the trees, the sky, the lake, even the mist rising from the water. "Finally, after all the years of yearning, of patience, of rationing my emotions; all that waiting—finally rewarded by the ultimate in human happiness!"

In his mind everything was now enveloped in a film of happiness, his father's office, his cart, his kid gloves, the greasy ledgers—the whole of that workaday life. Memories flooded back—his mother's fragrant room, the Herz variations, the prince's gallery, the blue eyes, the powdered brown hair—and over everything there rose Olga's gentle voice, he could hear her singing…"Olga, my wife" he whispered ecstatically, "no more searching, no more wondering! I've reached my goal, my journey is over!"

He walked home in a cloud of euphoria, oblivious to everything around him.

Olga watched him go until he was out of sight and then opened the window. For several minutes she breathed the chill night air: her excitement slowly abated and her breathing became even. Her gaze traveled over the lake into the far distance and she abandoned herself so quietly, so profoundly to her thoughts that she gave the impression of having fallen asleep. She wanted to register what she was thinking, what she was feeling, but she could not. Her thoughts rippled by smoothly and evenly like waves, her blood coursed placidly through her veins. She felt happiness but could not tell where it began or ended—or even exactly what it was. She wondered why she felt such quiet, such calm, such invulnerable well being, such tranquility… and yet.

"I am his bride…" she whispered.

"I am a bride!" a young girl thinks with a tremor of pride when that moment, so eagerly awaited, finally arrives and infuses the whole of her life with its light and warmth. She soars to a great height from which she surveys that dim, dark path along which she had been plodding only the day before, alone and unnoticed. Why then did Olga not feel this heady excitement? She too had been trudging that path, alone and unnoticed; yes, she too had met the man of her life at a crossroads and he had taken her by the hand and led her not into the glare of dazzling rays, but, as it were, into the flood plains of a wide river, to broad fields and welcoming hills. She did not have to screw up her eyes against the glare, her heart did not miss a beat and her imagination was not aflame.

It was with joyous serenity that she contemplated the broad expanses of life, its vast fields and green hills. There was no chill shiver between her shoulder blades, her eyes did not flash with pride. It was only when she turned her eyes away from the fields and hills and towards the one who had taken her hand that she felt a tear slowly trickling down her cheek.

And still she sat as if asleep, so tranquil was her dream of happiness; she sat without stirring, scarcely breathing. In her deep oblivion she projected her mind's eye onto a kind of blue-hued night bathed in a gentle, warm, aromatic glow. Her dream of happiness spread its broad wings and sailed slowly like a cloud in the sky over her own head.

In this vision she did not see herself decked out for a brief hour or two in delicate gauzes and lace and then reduced to dreary workaday garb for the rest of her life. She did not see a tremendous feast, lights, voices raised in celebration; rather she saw happiness, but a happiness so plain and unembellished that again, without a thrill of pride but with the proudest emotion, she whispered: "I am his bride!"

CHAPTER FIVE

Good God! How dreary and depressing everything looked in Oblomov's apartment a year and a half after that name day celebration when Stoltz had turned up so unexpectedly. Ilya Ilyich himself had grown flabbier and the boredom that had eaten its way into his system was reflected in his eyes like a kind of sickness.

He would pace the room again and again, then lie down and stare at the ceiling. He would take a book from the shelves, scan a few lines, yawn, and start drumming on the table with his fingers. Zakhar was now even more clumsy and unkempt. He wore patches on his elbows and had a destitute and hungry look like someone short of food and sleep and doing the work of three men.

Oblomov's dressing gown was in tatters; no matter how carefully the holes had been darned it kept on splitting all over the place, not just along the seams. It should have been thrown out and replaced long before. The blanket on the bed was also threadbare and patched in a number of places. The window curtains were badly faded and in spite of frequent washing were now little more than rags.

Zakhar brought in the old tablecloth and spread it over the half of the table nearest Oblomov and then, with his tongue between his teeth, carefully brought in the tray with the eating utensils and a carafe of vodka, set it down with some bread, and left.

The door to the landlady's side opened and in came Agafya Matveyevna expertly wielding a still sputtering pan of fried eggs. She had changed dramatically - and not for the better. She was emaciated. She had lost her white, round cheeks that had never been too pale or too florid; her sparse eyebrows had lost their gloss and her eyes were sunken. She wore an old cotton dress and her hands had coarsened and reddened either from work, from the heat of the cooking, or from the water—or from everything combined.

Akulina was no longer in the house. It was Anisya who worked in the kitchen and the vegetable garden, looked after the chickens, scrubbed the floors and did the laundry. It was too much for one pair of hands and Agafya Matveyevna had to help out in the kitchen; there was little grinding, sifting and grating for her to do because they could not afford much coffee, cinnamon or almonds, and she had given up any thought of lace. Now she would be more often chopping onion or grating horseradish by way of spices. Her face wore an expression of deep despondency. But it was not for herself, it was not for her own coffee that she sighed; she did not grieve because she could no longer keep house on a lavish scale, pounding cinnamon, putting vanilla in sauces or making thick cream, but because Ilya Ilyich would have to go for yet another year without tasting any of those things, because coffee was no longer delivered to him in bulk from the finest stores but was bought by the pennyworth from the local shop, because cream was no longer delivered by the Finnish dairywoman but came from the same little shop, because instead of a juicy chop she could only serve him fried eggs for lunch, garnished with some stale ham that had been lying around for too long in that same shop.

Now what was the explanation for this? Well it was the fact that this year again the income from Oblomovka, duly and promptly sent by Stoltz was going to pay off the promissory note given by Oblomov to the landlady.

The "entirely legal" scheme cooked up by the landlady's brother was working better than expected. At the first hint of scandal from Tarantyev, Ilya Ilyich simply went to pieces, and in his anxiety to placate the two of them they ended up settling the matter over a drink, with Oblomov signing the promissory note that would only be paid off after four years. Within a month Agafya Matveyevna had signed the note over to her brother without the slightest idea of what it was that she was signing. Her brother told her that he needed the document for the house and that she should write: "This promissory note was signed by [name and title] in her own hand." The only thing that bothered her was all the writing she was having to do and she even asked her brother to let Vanyusha do it instead "because he's really good at writing now" and she would probably make a mess of it. However, the brother insisted and she signed her name in big, crooked and lopsided letters, and that was the last that was ever heard of the matter.

When he was signing, Oblomov consoled himself, partly at least, with the thought that the money was going to the orphans and the next day when his head had cleared he was ashamed to think of what he had done and did his best to forget it by keeping out of the brother's way, and whenever Tarantyev tried to bring the matter up he threatened to leave the apartment immediately and go to his estate.

Later, when he received the money from the estate the brother came to him and told him that it would be easier for him, Ilya Ilyich, to begin the payments immediately out of the income and that in that way the claim would be paid off in three years, whereas if he waited until the deadline legal action would have to be taken for the recovery of the debt and the estate would have to be put up for auction since Oblomov did not have enough cash to cover the debt, nor was there any prospect of his acquiring it.

Oblomov realized what a trap he had fallen into when all the money that Stoltz sent him went to pay off the debt and he was left with only a small sum to live on.

The brother was in a hurry to conclude this "voluntary arrangement" with his debtor within a couple of years in case some snag or other arose, and that is why Oblomov found himself in such a difficult situation so suddenly.

At first, he hardly noticed what was happening because of his habit of never knowing how much money he had in his pocket, but then Ivan

Matveyich started courting the daughter of a grain merchant and moved out into a rented apartment. The scale of Agafya Matveyevna's housekeeping declined abruptly; sturgeon, the whitest cuts of veal and turkey now appeared in that other kitchen in Mukhoyarov's new apartment.

That is where the lights now burned of an evening and that is where company now gathered, including the brother's future in-laws, his colleagues from the office and Tarantyev. Agafya Matveyevna and Anisya were suddenly left open-mouthed and with idle hands contemplating their empty pots and pans.

For the first time Agafya Matveyevna realized that she possessed nothing but the house, the chickens and the kitchen garden and that neither cinnamon nor vanilla grew there, and she saw the vendors in the market gradually ceasing to welcome her with deep bows and ingratiating smiles and instead begin to lavish these attentions on her brother's stout and smartly dressed new cook.

Oblomov handed over to the landlady all the money the brother left him with for living expenses and for three or four months she went on heedlessly grinding coffee by the sackful, pounding cinnamon and roasting veal and turkey right up to the very day when she had spent her last ten kopecks and came to tell him that the money had run out. On hearing this news, he turned over three times on the divan and then looked into his drawer; but there was nothing there. He tried to remember what he had done with the money but could not recall; he combed the table-top, looking for loose change and asked Zakhar, who hadn't a clue. She went to her brother and in all naiveté told him there was no money in the house.

"And what have you and His Lordship done with the thousand roubles I gave him to live on?" he asked, "Where do you expect me to get the money from. You know that I'm about to become a respectable married man and I can't support two families, so you and your landed gent had better learn to cut your coats according to your cloth!"

"Why are you throwing my gentleman in my face?" she said, "What has he done to you? He doesn't bother anyone, just minds his own business. It wasn't me who lured him into renting the apartment, it was you and Mikhei Andreyich!"

He gave her ten roubles and told her that that was all she was getting. But later, after discussing the matter with his old crony at the "establishment" he decided he had better not just leave his sister and Oblomov to fend for themselves, otherwise it might come to Stoltz's ears and he would turn up in person and start asking questions and somehow or other upset the whole apple cart and there would be no way of collecting the debt, for all that it was "entirely legal." Oh yes, that German was a crafty one!

So he started giving Oblomov an extra fifty roubles a month with the idea of reclaiming it as part of the debt from Oblomov's income in the third year. At the same time he made it clear, and even swore to his sister, that that was his absolute limit and calculated down to the last kopeck exactly what she could afford to put on the table and how to reduce expenses to the bare minimum, even planning the fine details of her menu. He even worked out the prices she could expect for her chickens and cabbage and concluded that on that basis they would be living in clover.

For the first time in her life Agafya Matveyevna actually spared a thought for something outside the details of household management and, for the first time ever, shed tears over something other than irritation with Akulina for breaking a dish or a tongue-lashing from the brother for under-cooking the fish; for the first time she came face to face with the threat of destitution—not her own, but Ilya Ilyich's.

"How can a gentleman like him start eating buttered turnips instead of asparagus," she reasoned, "mutton instead of grouse, and instead of brook trout and amber sturgeon, salt-cod or even brawn from the local shop. Unthinkable!" She interrupted her brooding and hurriedly got ready to go out. She had herself driven to her husband's family and this time not for Easter or Christmas or a family dinner, but early in the morning with a problem and, most unusually, to ask their advice and to borrow money.

They had plenty and once they heard that it was for Ilya Ilyich they wouldn't hesitate for a moment. If it had been a matter of asking for money for her own tea or coffee or for clothes for the children, or for shoes or other such whims she wouldn't have dreamed of asking. But for a dire emergency like having to buy asparagus for Ilya Ilyich or grouse for his main course, and he was partial to French peas…!

To her surprise they gave her no money and instead advised her that if Ilya Ilyich had anything made of gold or maybe silver, or even fur, it could be pawned because there are some people so charitably disposed that they would give her one third of what she asked for until he next received money from his estate.

At any other time such practical advice would have sailed completely over her head and would have been totally beyond the grasp of our talented housekeeper, but now her heart made sense of it and instinctively understood, and her thoughts turned to the pearls that had come with her dowry.

The next day, Ilya Ilyich, suspecting nothing, was already drinking currant vodka, savoring the finest smoked salmon and dining off his favorite giblets and fresh white grouse. Agafya Matveyevna and the children shared the servants' fare of cabbage soup and buckwheat gruel and she herself drank two cups of coffee just to keep Ilya Ilyich company.

After the pearls, the next thing to go from the trunk where she kept her most treasured possessions was her diamond clasp, swiftly followed by her silver and her fur coat. The next time Oblomov received a payment from the estate he handed it all over to her. She redeemed the pearls and paid the interest on the clasp, silver and fur and once again served him asparagus and grouse and kept him company with the coffee just for appearances' sake—and the pearls went back to their usual place.

And so it went on; from week to week, from day to day she struggled and turned herself inside out to keep things going, selling her shawl, her Sunday best dress and wore her everyday cotton dress all the time, leaving her elbows bare, and on Sundays covered her neck with a threadbare old scarf.

So this is why she had grown so thin, why her eyes were sunken and why she served Ilya Ilyich his breakfast with her own hands.

She even managed to put a brave face on it when Oblomov announced that Tarantyev, Alekseyev or Ivan Gerasimovich was coming to join him for dinner, and the dinner would duly appear, tasty and served in style and always a credit to the host. But all this striving took a tremendous toll on her of worry, agitation, running around, bargaining furiously in the market, sleepless nights, and even tears.

How deeply she was now plunged into the hurly-burly of life with its good days and its bad days! But it was a life she loved; in spite of all the anxieties, tears and frustrations, she would not have traded it for the even and placid tenor of her old life before she knew Oblomov when she presided with such dignity over her array of brimming pots and pans, sizzling and bubbling away on the stove and had Akulina and the gatekeeper under her command. She even shuddered at the thought of dying, even though death would mean the end of unquenchable tears, her turbulent days and sleepless nights.

Ilya Ilyich ate his breakfast, listened to Masha reading her French lesson, sat in Agafya Matveyevna's room and watched her mending Vanya's jacket over and over again, alternating constantly between the inside and the outside of it and breaking off to run into the kitchen to check the mutton roast for dinner and to see whether it was time to start the fish soup.

"You're always busy with something or other, why don't you relax?" said Oblomov.

"And who will do the work then?" she answered. "As soon as I've sewn on a couple of patches here, it'll be time to start the fish soup. He's such a bad boy, that Vanya! Last week I'd just finished mending his jacket when he went and tore it again. It's no laughing matter!" she rebuked Vanya who was sitting at the table in his shirt and trousers, which were held up by just one strap of his suspenders. "I'm not going to mend it until tomorrow morning so you won't be able to run outside the gate. It's those other boys who must have torn it, you got into a fight—admit it!"

"No, mommy, it tore by itself!" said Vanya.

"Oh yes, by itself! You'd be better off staying in, studying your lesson, than running around the streets! The next time Ilya Ilyich says that you're not doing well in French I'll take off your boots myself and then you'll have to stay in and study!"

"I don't like French!"

"Why not?" Oblomov asked.

"There's a lot of bad words in French!" Agafya Matveyevna flushed and Oblomov burst out laughing, obviously it was not the first time that the subject of bad words had come up.

"Quiet, you bad boy!" she said, "wipe your nose, can't you see it needs wiping?"

Vanyusha sniffed but did not wipe his nose.

"Wait until I get my money from the estate, I'll have two pairs made for him," Oblomov put in, "a blue jacket and a uniform for next year when he starts at the high school."

"He can go in his old tunic," said Agafya Matveyevna; "we'll need the money for housekeeping. We'll stock up with salt beef and I'll make preserves. Have to go and see if Anisya has brought the sour cream..." She got up.

"What are we having now?" asked Oblomov.

"Fish soup, roast mutton and curd dumplings."

Oblomov made no response.

Suddenly a carriage pulled up outside; there was a knocking at the gate and the dog began jumping on his chain and barking. Oblomov went back to his room, thinking it must be someone for the landlady; the butcher, the greengrocer or some tradesman or other. Such visits were usually accompanied by demands for money and refusals from the landlady, followed by threats from the tradesmen and then by appeals for more time to pay from the landlady and ending with abuse, the slamming of doors and gates, and a furious outburst of barking and chain rattling from the dog—an altogether unpleasant scene. But this time it was a carriage that had drawn up, and butchers and greengrocers do not travel in carriages. Suddenly the landlady ran into his room in a panic.

"You have a visitor!" she said.

"Who is it? Tarantyev or Alekseyev?"

"No, the one who came to dinner on St. Ilya's Day."

"Stoltz?" Oblomov said in alarm, looking around for a way to escape. "God, what will he say when he sees...! Tell him I've gone out!" he added hurriedly and slipped into the landlady's room.

Agafya Matveyevna managed to convey Oblomov's instructions to Anisya in time for her to greet the visitor. Stoltz believed what he was told, although he did express surprise at not finding Oblomov at home.

"Well tell him I'll be back in two hours and will be staying for dinner," he said and went for a walk in the public garden nearby.

"He's staying for dinner!" Anisya reported in a panic.

"He's staying for dinner," Agafya Matveyevna reported to Oblomov in consternation.

"You'll have to change the menu!" he decided after a moment's reflection.

She looked at him in horror; she had only fifty kopecks left and there were still ten days to go before the first of the month when she got money from her brother. There was no hope of borrowing any.

"There isn't time, Ilya Ilyich," she pointed out timidly, "he'll have to eat what there is."

"He can't, Agafya Matveyevna, he can't stand fish soup—even if it's made from sturgeon—and he won't touch mutton either."

"I could get some tongue from the sausage shop," she said with sudden inspiration, "It's right near here!"

"Yes, that's a good idea, do that and order some vegetables, fresh beans..."

"Beans are eighty kopecks a pound..." she was about to say but the words stuck in her throat.

"Alright, I'll get some," she said suddenly, resolving to trade some cabbage for the beans.

"And order a pound of Swiss cheese!" he instructed, oblivious to Agafya Matveyevna's straitened circumstances, "and that'll be it. I'll explain that we weren't expecting him... although if you could find some bouillon?"

She was on her way out when he suddenly remembered: "What about wine?"

She gave him another horrified look.

"You'll have to send for some Lafitte!" he instructed her in a perfectly matter-of-fact tone.

CHAPTER SIX

Two hours later Stoltz reappeared.

"What's happened to you? How you've changed! You're all flabby and pale; are you ill?" Stoltz inquired.

"I'm not at all well, Andrei," said Oblomov, embracing him, "my left leg keeps going numb."

"Everything's so squalid here!" said Stoltz, looking around. "Why don't you throw out that dressing gown? Look, it's covered in patches!"

"I'm just used to it, Andrei, I can't bring myself to part with it."

"And the blanket and the curtains," Stoltz began, "I suppose you're used to them too? Too sentimental to get rid of those rags? Don't tell me you can really sleep on that bed! What's the matter with you?" Stoltz took a long look at Oblomov and then again at the curtains and the bedding.

"It's nothing," said Oblomov in embarrassment, "you know I've never paid much attention to my surroundings... why don't we sit down to dinner? Hey, Zakhar get a move on and set the table! So, are you here for long? Where have you just come from?"

"You really don't know?" asked Stoltz. "Doesn't any news from the outside world reach you here?"

Oblomov regarded him with curiosity, waiting to hear what he would say. "And Olga?" he asked.

"Ah, you still remember, I thought you'd forget!" said Stoltz.

"Oh no, Andrei, how could I forget her; it would be like forgetting that I was once alive, that I was in heaven... and now this!" he sighed. "But where is she?"

"She's on her country estate, running the house."

"With her aunt?" asked Oblomov.

"And her husband."

"She's married?" Oblomov exclaimed, his eyes popping.

"Why are you so alarmed—is it the memories?" Stoltz added quietly, almost gently.

"No, of course not, good Lord no!" Oblomov protested, regaining his composure, "I wasn't alarmed in the least, just surprised—for some reason I didn't expect it. When did it happen? Is she happy? Tell me everything, please! I feel that you've relieved me of a tremendous burden; although you did assure me that she had forgiven me—but you know, I still wasn't easy in my mind, something was still gnawing at me. Dear Andrei, I'm so grateful to you."

His joy was so genuine that he bounced up and down on the divan and became so animated that Stoltz was delighted and even touched.

"You're so good-hearted, Ilya!" he said, "Your heart was really worthy of her. I'm going to tell her."

"No, don't!" Oblomov protested, "She'll think I must have no feelings—to be so pleased to hear that she's married!"

"But isn't your pleasure a real feeling?—and such an unselfish feeling too—to feel such pure joy at her happiness?"

"Yes, it's true!" Oblomov put in, "I'm just babbling. So who is the lucky fellow, I didn't even think of asking?"

"Who?" said Stoltz. "How slow you are, Ilya?"

Oblomov looked fixedly at his friend and his face froze for a moment and the blood drained from his cheeks. "It's not...you?" he asked suddenly.

"You're looking alarmed again—why?" Stoltz asked with a laugh.

"Stop kidding, Andrei, tell me the truth!" said Oblomov in a state of agitation.

"I swear to God I'm not joking, I've been married to Olga for more than a year."

Gradually the alarm disappeared from Oblomov's face, giving way to a placid thoughtfulness. His eyes were still lowered, but within a minute his expression became one of quiet and heartfelt joy, and when he slowly raised his eyes to look at Stoltz they were moist with emotion. "My dear Andrei!" said Oblomov, embracing him; "Dear Olga!" he said and then added, "Sergeyevna" in order to curb his own impetuosity, "God has blessed you both! My God, I'm so happy! Tell her..."

"I'll tell her there's only one Oblomov!" Stoltz cut him off, deeply moved.

"No, tell her—remind her that fate threw us together just in order to steer her onto the right path and that I bless that encounter and bless the new path she has chosen. Tell her that if it had been someone else," he was horrified at the thought, "but now," he added cheerfully, "I'm not ashamed of the part I played, I have no regrets; a great burden has been lifted from me, my conscience is clear and I'm happy—thank you God!" Again he was practically dancing on the divan in his excitement, half crying, half laughing.

"Zakhar, let's have some champagne with our dinner!" he shouted, forgetting that he did not have a penny to his name.

"I'm going to tell Olga everything, everything!" said Stoltz. "No wonder she can't forget you. No, you were worthy of her, your heart is infinitely generous!"

Zakhar poked his head around the door. "Could you come over here please!" he said, giving his master a wink.

"What is it?" Oblomov asked impatiently, "why don't you get out!"

"I need some money, please," Zakhar whispered.

Oblomov abruptly fell silent. "Stop saying that!" he whispered to him through the doorway. "Say you forgot to bring any, you were in too much of a hurry! Now get along...! No, wait, come back here!" he said aloud, "There's some news, Zakhar! Congratulate Andrei Ivanich, he's married!"

"Oh sir, thank God for allowing me to live to see this great day! Congratulations, Andrei Ivanich, sir! May you live to a ripe old age and be blessed with children! Oh Lord, what happiness!" Zakhar bowed, smiled, wheezed and croaked.

Stoltz took out a banknote and handed it to him: "Here, buy yourself a new coat!" he said. "Look at yourself, you look like a beggar!"

"Who is the lady, sir?" asked Zakhar, clutching Stoltz's arm.

"Olga Sergeyevna—you remember her?" said Oblomov.

"The Ilyinsky young lady! My God, such a lovely young lady! Ilya Ilyich was right to tell me off then, called me an old cur! It was really wrong of me, I should have known better; I told everyone it was you—I even told the Ilyinsky servants, it wasn't Nikita! And it all turned out to be wrong—just tittle-tattle. Oh my God..." he continued his litany as he made his way out of the room.

"Olga wants to invite you to stay with us in the country; you're no longer in love, there's no danger, you won't feel any jealousy—so let's go!"

Oblomov sighed. "No Andrei, it's not love or jealousy that I'm afraid of, but I still won't come."

"What is it you're afraid of?"

"Envy; your happiness will be like a mirror to me in which I will see my whole poisoned, ruined existence; and now it's the only life I'm capable of living, it's all that's left."

"My dear Ilya, that's enough of that! Whether you like it or not, you'll live like the people around you. You'll keep your books, run your estate, read, and listen to music. Her voice has matured wonderfully now. You remember 'Casta Diva'?"

Oblomov gave a wave of the hand to show that he didn't want to be reminded.

"So let's go!" Stoltz insisted. "It's what she wants and she won't give up. I might but she won't. There's so much fire, so much vitality that at times it's too much for me. Your past will bubble up again, you'll remember the park, the lilac, and you'll start stirring…"

"No, Andrei, don't remind me, don't try to get me moving, for the love of God!" Oblomov cut in earnestly. "All that is painful, it's not a pleasure. Memories are the height of poetry, when they are the memories of the keenest happiness or excruciating pain, when they re-open old wounds… let's change the subject."

"Yes, I never thanked you for taking care of my business down on the estate. My dear friend, I'm just not capable of thanking you, it's beyond me; look for gratitude in your own heart, in your happiness, in Olga…Sergeyevna, but not in me! Forgive me for still burdening you with my problems. But it will soon be spring and I'll definitely go to Oblomovka then."

"Do you know what's happening in Oblomovka? You won't recognize the place!" said Stoltz, "I didn't write to you because you never answer letters. The bridge has been built; the house is ready for you, roof and all. All that's left is for you to decorate and furnish it to your taste—I wouldn't undertake that! There's a new manager in charge, chosen by me. You've seen the balance sheets, the expenses…"

Oblomov was silent.

"You haven't looked at them?" Stoltz asked him, "Where are they?"

"Just wait, I'll look for them after dinner! I'll have to ask Zakhar."

"Oh Ilya, Ilya! I don't know whether to laugh or cry!"

"After dinner, let's eat now!"

Stoltz frowned and sat down at the table. He remembered the St. Ilya's Day dinner party; the oysters, the pineapples, the snipe. What he saw now was a thick tablecloth, containers for vinegar and oil plugged with paper instead of corks, a chunk of coarse black bread on each of their plates, and forks with chipped handles. Oblomov was served fish soup and he was served barley soup and boiled chicken, followed by chewy tongue and then mutton. Red wine appeared on the table. Stoltz poured half a glass, tasted it, put the glass down and left it untouched. Ilya Ilyich drank two glass of currant vodka one after the other and then hungrily attacked the mutton.

"This wine is no good!" said Stoltz.

"I'm sorry, they didn't have time to go over the river," said Oblomov, "how about some currant vodka, it's excellent, try some, Andrei!" He poured himself another glass and drank it. Stoltz looked at him in surprise but said nothing.

"Agafya Matveyevna makes it herself—a wonderful woman!" said Oblomov, beginning to feel the effects of the drink. "I must admit, I don't know how I'll get along in the country without her; you'll never find anyone who can keep house like her!"

Stoltz frowned slightly as he listened to him.

"Who do you think cooks all this, Anisya? No," Oblomov continued, "Anisya looks after the chickens, waters the cabbages and scrubs the floors, but it's Agafya Matveyevna who does all this."

Stoltz did not touch the mutton or the curd dumplings and just put down his fork and observed the gusto with which Oblomov was attacking his food.

"Now you will never see me with my shirt on inside out," Oblomov went on, gnawing a bone with relish, "she keeps an eye on everything, doesn't miss a thing; she keeps all my stockings darned—and she does it all herself! And you should taste her coffee! I'll serve you some after dinner."

Stoltz continued to listen in silence with an expression of concern on his face.

"Her brother has moved out, he's getting married, so now the housekeeping is on a smaller scale. But before she really had her hands full! On her feet from morning till night, running to the market, to Gostiniy Dvor. I tell you," said Oblomov, his tongue beginning to run away with him, "let me have two or three thousand and I wouldn't be serving you tongue and mutton; no, there'd be a whole sturgeon, trout, filet mignon! And Agafya Matveyevna—without a cook—would be performing miracles—oh yes!" He swallowed another glass of vodka.

"Drink up, Andrei, yes, drink up—it's wonderful vodka! Olga Sergeyevna won't make you stuff like this!" he said thickly. "She may sing 'Casta diva', but vodka like this never!" She'll never make you such chicken and mushroom pies! Only back in Oblomovka in the old days could you get pies like that—and now I get them here! And I'll tell you another thing—you know what's so good about it? It's not just some cook who does the pie fillings—God knows where their hands have been!—no it's Agafya Matveyevna herself, the last word in cleanliness and tidiness!"

Stoltz took in all this information with the closest attention.

"She used to have such white hands," Oblomov continued, considerably the worse for wear, "you could even kiss them! Now they've roughened because she does everything herself—she even starches my shirts with her own hands!" Oblomov was moved to tears by his own words, "I swear to you, I've seen her myself. Even a wife doesn't take such good care of a husband! A wonderful woman, that Agafya Matveyevna! Andrei, why don't you move here with Olga Sergeyevna, rent a dacha—what a time we'd have! We'd drink tea under the trees and on St. Ilya's Friday we'd visit the Gunpowder Works with a cart loaded with provisions and a samovar following us. Once there, we'd spread a rug and lie on the grass. Agafya Matveyevna would teach Olga Sergeyevna how to be a really good housekeeper. It's just that, right now, things aren't going too well; her brother's moved out and if only we were the ones getting three or four thousand, I'd be serving you such turkeys…!"

"But you're getting five thousand from me!" Stoltz said suddenly, "What have you been doing with the money?"

"Well, it's the debt, isn't it?" Oblomov blurted out.

Stoltz leapt to his feet. "Debt? What debt?" He gave Oblomov an intimidating look, like a teacher at a cowering child.

Oblomov said nothing and Stoltz went and sat down next to him on the divan.

"Who do you owe the money to?" he asked.

Oblomov had sobered up a little and was coming to his senses. "No one, it wasn't true what I said."

"No, it's now that you're lying—and not very well. What's going on—what's wrong, Ilya? Yes, that would explain the mutton, the sour wine! You have no money! What have you been doing with it?"

"Well, I do owe some money actually… to the landlady for groceries," said Oblomov.

"For mutton and tongue! Ilya, I want to know what's going on. What's this story you're telling me? The brother moved out, so the housekeeping is suffering…? Something doesn't make sense here. How much do you owe?"

"Ten thousand on a promissory note…"Oblomov whispered.

Stoltz leapt to his feet and then sat down again. "Ten thousand—to the landlady? For groceries?" he repeated, horrified.

"Yes, they used to buy in a lot of things, I was living on a lavish scale… .you remember the pineapples and peaches… that's how I ran up the debt…"Oblomov mumbled, "anyway, what of it?"

Stoltz did not reply; he was thinking: "The brother moved out and they're living on a shoestring—and that's certainly the way it looks—everything has a threadbare, dilapidated, neglected look! What kind of a woman is this landlady? Oblomov sings her praises, talks about her so enthusiastically…" Stoltz's expression changed abruptly, suddenly everything had become clear and the revelation was chilling.

"This woman, what is she to you?" But Oblomov's head was on the table—he had nodded off. "She's obviously robbing him blind—it's the old story and yet it took me all this time to figure it out!" he thought. Stoltz got up and quickly opened the door to the landlady's side, so startling her that she dropped the spoon that she had been using to stir the coffee.

"I would like to speak to you," he said politely.

"If you'll give me a minute, I'll come into the living room," she replied timidly. She threw a scarf around her neck and followed him into the living room and sat on the edge of the divan. She no longer possessed a shawl and she tried to hide her hands under the scarf.

"Ilya Ilyich has given you a promissory note, I believe?" he asked her.

"No," she replied uncomprehendingly with a look of surprise, "Mr. Oblomov hasn't given me any promissory note."

"What do you mean?"

"I mean, I haven't seen any note," she insisted with the same startled and uncomprehending expression.

"It was a promissory note," Stoltz repeated.

She thought for a moment. "You should really speak to my brother," she said, "I've never seen any note."

"Is she crafty or just obtuse?" Stoltz wondered.

"But he does owe you money?" he asked.

She gave him the same vapid look but suddenly realization dawned and a look of alarm appeared on her face. She remembered the pearls, the silver and the fur coat she had pawned and thought that that must be the debt to which Stoltz was alluding, although for the life of her she could not imagine how he had found out; not only had she not whispered a word about her secret to Oblomov, but not even to Anisya to whom she normally accounted for every kopeck.

"How much does he owe you?" Stoltz asked her anxiously.

"Nothing, not a penny!"

"She's covering up, she's afraid to tell me, she's greedy and scheming and she's bleeding him white!" he thought, "but I'll drag it out of her!"

"Would it be ten thousand?" he said.

"What ten thousand?" she asked in dismay.

"Ilya Ilyich owes you ten thousand on a promissory note, yes or no?" he asked her.

"No, Mr. Oblomov doesn't owe me a thing. At Lent he did owe the butcher twelve roubles, fifty kopecks but we paid that two weeks ago, and we've also paid the dairywoman for the cream—so he doesn't owe anyone anything."

"So you really don't have any paper from him promising to pay you any money?"

Again she gave him that same uncomprehending look. "You really should speak to my brother," she replied, "he lives across the street in Zamykalov's house, look just here, it's the one with the drinking shop downstairs."

"No, I'd prefer to speak to you if you don't mind," he insisted. "Ilya Ilyich considers he's in debt to you, not your brother..."

"But he doesn't owe me anything," she protested, "and that silver, the pearls and the fur coat I pawned was for myself. I needed to buy shoes for Masha and myself; and then there was Vanyusha's shirts and paying the greengrocer, but not a penny went on Ilya Ilyich."

He was watching her, listening carefully and beginning to make sense of her story. It was the closest anyone had come to discovering her secret and the look of scorn, almost contempt, he had been giving her as they talked, gave way spontaneously to one of curiosity, almost sympathy. From the story of the pawning of the pearls and the silver he got a glimmering of the sacrifices she had been making, but he could not quite make up his mind whether it was all done out of sheer devotion or in the hope of some future reward. He did not know whether to be pleased or sorry for Ilya. It was now clear that Ilya did not owe her anything and that the debt was simply a scam engineered by the brother—and quite a lot of other things were also becoming clear... After all, how to explain that business of pawning her jewelry?

"So you don't have any claims against Ilya Ilyich?" he asked.

"Please be good enough to talk to my brother!" she persisted monotonously. "He should be at home now."

"So Ilya Ilyich doesn't owe you anything then, you say?"

"Not a penny, honestly, it's the truth!" she said, crossing herself with a glance at the icon.

"And you would swear to that in the presence of witnesses?"

"Yes, anyone, even the priest at confession! And as for the pearls and the silver, I only pawned them because I needed the money for myself!"

"Good!" Stoltz interrupted her. "Tomorrow I'll come back with two friends and you'll tell them what you've just told me, alright?"

"It will be better if you talk to my brother," she repeated, "I'm really not dressed properly....always in and out of the kitchen... I'd be ashamed for people to see me like this, I can't imagine what they'd think!"

"Never mind, don't worry; I'll talk to your brother tomorrow, right after you've signed the document..."

"Oh no, I've gotten right out of the habit of writing!"

"But there's hardly anything to write, just a couple of lines at the most!"

"Please don't make me do it; better to get Vanyusha to do it, he writes so much nicer...!"

"I'm sorry, it's really necessary for you to do it," he insisted. "If you don't sign the document Ilya Ilyich will still owe you ten thousand."

"No, he doesn't owe me anything, not a single kopeck," she protested, "honestly!"

"Then you'll just have to sign the document. Goodbye then, until tomorrow!"

"It would really be better if you went to see my brother tomorrow," she said as she showed him out. "Look, it's just on the corner, right across the street!"

"No, I'm sorry, and please don't say anything to your brother before I come, otherwise it will be very bad for Ilya Ilyich..."

"Then I won't say anything to him," she said compliantly.

CHAPTER SEVEN

The next day Agafya Matveyevna signed an affidavit for Stoltz testifying that she had no financial claims against Oblomov. Armed with this document, Stoltz suddenly appeared on the brother's doorstep. This was a real bolt from the blue for Ivan Matveyich. He took out the promissory note and with the trembling middle finger of his right hand, keeping the nail facing down and out of sight, he pointed to Oblomov's signature and the notary's seal.

"It's quite legal, sir," he said, "I'm not personally involved, I'm just protecting my sister's interests and I've no idea how much money Ilya Ilyich has borrowed."

"You haven't heard the last of this!" Stoltz threatened him as he turned to leave.

"But it's perfectly legal and I'm not involved, sir," Ivan Matveyich argued, hiding his hands in his sleeves.

The next day, the moment he stepped into his office a message arrived from the Director General requiring his immediate presence.

"The Director General!" the whole office chorused in consternation. "What can it be, what can he want? It must be some file, which one? Quick, quick, put the files in order, bring the records up to date! What's going on?"

That evening it was a severely rattled Ivan Matveyich who turned up at the "establishment." Tarantyev had arrived much earlier and had been waiting for him.

"What is it, old pal?" he asked impatiently.

"What?" responded Ivan Matveyich in a flat voice, "you're asking me 'what'? What do you think?"

"Did you get chewed out or what?"

"Chewed out!" Ivan Matveyich repeated, mimicking Tarantyev, "I'd rather have been laid out! And you're a fine one" he complained bitterly, "not telling me who this German was we were taking on!"

"But I did tell you he was a crafty one!"

"Oh yes, he's crafty alright—we've seen plenty of them; what you *didn't* tell me was what powerful connections he has! He's on first name terms with the Director General, just like you and me. I wouldn't have dreamed of taking on someone like that if I'd known!"

"But it was all above board and legal!" Tarantyev argued.

"Oh yes, 'all above board and legal'," Mukhoyarov mimicked him again, "I'd like to see you go in there and tell them; 'the tongue cleaveth to the throat' like it says in the Bible. You know what the Director General asked me?"

"What?" Tarantyev asked him, intrigued.

"Is it true that you and some crook got together, got the landowner Oblomov drunk and made him sign a promissory note in favor of your sister?"

"You mean he actually used the word 'crook'?" asked Tarantyev.

"Yes, that was the actual word!"

"Who would it be then, this crook?" Tarantyev asked again.

His companion looked at him. "Oh, and I suppose you don't have the slightest idea?" he replied acidly. "It couldn't be you, could it?"

"How was my name brought into it?"

"You can thank your old pal from your village and that German. It was him who started asking questions and ferreted it all out…"

"But listen, you could have said it was someone else and that I had nothing to do with it!"

"Oh great! You some kind of saint or something?"

"But what did you answer when the Director General asked you 'is it true that you got together with some crook'…? That was your chance to talk your way out of it."

"Talk my way out of it! I'd like to have seen you try! With those green eyes glued on me? I really tried as hard as I could to say 'No, it's not true, it's all a lot of slander, Your Excellency, I don't know anyone called Oblomov—it was all Tarantyev's doing,' but I just couldn't get the words out and just fell at his feet."

"So are they going to start proceedings?" Tarantyev asked tonelessly, "I'm not involved, of course, but you, old pal…"

"Not involved! You're not involved? Oh no, my friend, if anyone's head is going on the block, yours will be the first! Who was the one who got Oblomov drinking, who started all that talk of scandal and threatened him?"

"But it was you who put me up to it!" said Tarantyev.

"Oh, so you're a juvenile—is that the idea? No, *I* don't know the first thing about the matter."

"Don't you have any conscience at all? After all the profit you've made through me—and all I got out of it was three hundred roubles!"

"So, your idea is for me to carry the can by myself—you must think you're very smart! Well, I don't know a thing about it," he said, "it was my sister who asked me to get the letter notarized because women know nothing about such things—and that's all there was to it. You and Zatyorty were witnesses, so you two are going to have a bit of explaining to do too."

"You should make your sister toe the line—give her hell for going against her brother!" said Tarantyev.

"My sister's a fool, you can't make her see sense!"

"What does she say?"

"She just keeps crying and won't budge—just keeps on saying Ilya Ilyich doesn't owe her anything and that's that, and that she never gave him any money."

"But you still have her promissory note," said Tarantyev, "so you can still collect on that."

Mukhoyarov took his sister's promissory note out of his pocket, tore it into pieces and handed the pieces to Tarantyev.

"Here, this is for you, don't you want it," he said, adding, "What can I get from her? The house with the kitchen garden? It wouldn't fetch a thousand, it's falling apart. Anyway, I'm not a complete barbarian, you know—I'm not just going to throw her and the children out with nowhere to go!"

"So there'll be an inquiry then?" Tarantyev asked timorously. "The thing is to get off as lightly as possible, you'll have to get us off the hook!"

"What inquiry? There won't be any inquiry! The Director General was threatening to expel me from St. Petersburg, but the German interceded to spare Oblomov the scandal."

"Well then, old pal, that's a weight off our shoulders, let's drink to that!" said Tarantyev.

"Drink, who's going to pay? You?"

"What about you, you must have collected your seven roubles today?"

"Are you kidding, I can kiss that money goodbye; I didn't finish telling you what the Director General said."

"What did he say?" said Tarantyev, panicking once more.

"He said I had to resign."

"I don't believe it!" exclaimed Tarantyev, his eyes popping. "Well," he announced, "now I'm really going to let my good friend Oblomov have it!"

"Oh yes, you're really good at that, letting people have it!"

"I don't care what you say, I'm still going to let him have it. But maybe you're right, perhaps I'd better let that wait—I've just thought of something, listen!"

"What now?" Ivan Matveyich asked abstractedly.

"There's a real opportunity for you here! It's just too bad you've moved out of the house…"

"What opportunity?"

"What opportunity!" Tarantyev said, looking at Ivan Matveyich, "To keep an eye on Oblomov and your sister and see what they're getting up to—yes, and with witnesses! The German won't be able to do a thing about it; so then you'll have an entirely free hand—you can start proceedings, and you'll have the law on your side! Who knows, maybe the German will get cold feet and be willing to settle out of court."

"You know, you may have an idea there!" Mukhoyarov said thoughtfully, "you get some good ideas, but you're not much good when it comes to following up on them—and the same goes for Zatyorty; but I'll find a way if you'll just give me a minute!" he said, his spirits rising. "I'll show them! I'll send my cook around to help my sister in the kitchen and she'll get friendly with Anisya and pump her for information and then… .yes, let's drink to that, old pal!"

"Right! And when you've done that I'll go and give my good friend Oblomov a piece of my mind!"

Stoltz tried to get Oblomov to come away with him, but he pleaded so hard to be allowed to stay for just one month that Stoltz did not have the heart to insist. According to Oblomov, he needed the month to sort out his finances, find someone to take over the lease of the apartment, and tie up all his loose ends in St. Petersburg so that he would never have to return. He also needed to buy all the necessary furniture and fittings for his country house and finally he wanted to look for a good housekeeper, someone like Agafya Matveyevna, and indeed had not given up hope of persuading her to sell her house and move to the country to follow her true vocation—running a busy and large-scale household.

"While we're on the subject," Stoltz put in at this point, "I've been meaning to ask you, Ilya, what exactly is your relationship with her?"

Oblomov flushed. "What do you mean?" he asked hurriedly.

"I'm sure you know what I mean," said Stoltz, "otherwise you wouldn't have blushed. Listen, Ilya, I don't know if a little advice would help now, but I beg you in the name of our long friendship, please be careful!"

"About what? I mean, come on…!" Oblomov protested in his embarrassment.

"Well, it's just that you talk about her with such enthusiasm that I was beginning to think that you were…"

"In love with her, is that what you mean? Come on!" Oblomov cut in with a forced laugh.

"Actually, it would be even worse if there were absolutely no redeeming moral basis, if it were just…"

"Andrei! You surely can't be suggesting that I'm that kind of man?"

"The why did you blush?"

"At the very idea that you could have entertained such a thought."

Stoltz shook his head doubtfully. "Look, Ilya, please try to avoid that pitfall; she's a simple, unsophisticated woman and the lifestyle is squalid, your mind will decay in this intellectually stifling atmosphere, this coarseness, this vulgarity," Stoltz snorted contemptuously.

Oblomov was silent.

"Well, goodbye then," Stoltz said decisively, "and I'll tell Olga that we'll be seeing you in the summer, if not at our place then in Oblomovka. Remember, she won't give up!"

"Definitely, definitely!" Oblomov assured him emphatically, "and you can even tell her that if she has no objection I'll spend the winter with you."

"Now that would make us really happy!"

Stoltz left that day and in the evening Tarantyev called on Oblomov. He just could not wait to show him the rough side of his tongue on behalf of his pal. However, there was one thing he had failed to reckon with; that Oblomov, after spending so much time at the Ilyinskys, was no longer used to the company of such specimens as Tarantyev and that his insensitivity to and tolerance of such vulgarity and insolence had given way to revulsion. This was something that had happened long before and had already manifested itself to some degree at the time Oblomov had been living at the dacha. Since then, Tarantyev's visits had become very infrequent and these rare meetings were always in the presence of others so that there had been no unpleasant exchanges.

"How's it going, my old friend?" Tarantyev greeted him acidly, without offering him his hand.

"How are you?" Oblomov responded coldly, looking out of the window.

"So you've said goodbye to your protector then?"

"Yes, what of it?"

"Some protector!" Tarantyev continued venomously.

"Oh, you have something against him?"

"I'd string him up if I had the chance!" said Tarantyev, his voice hoarse with hatred.

"Oh, you would, would you?"

"Yes, and I'd string you up next to him."

"Oh, and why is that?"

"Do the honest thing! When you owe someone something, pay up, don't try to wriggle out of it! See what you've done now?"

"Listen, Mikhei Andreyich, spare me your fairy tales; for a long time I put up with you out of sheer laziness - and indifference; I thought you must have a spark of conscience in you somewhere, but I was wrong. You and that crook of a friend tried to swindle me—I don't know which of you is worse but you both disgust me. My friend rescued me from that stupid business..."

"Some friend!" said Tarantyev, "I heard that this great benefactor of yours helped himself to the girl you were engaged to! You're a complete fool, my dear old friend..."

"That's enough of your compliments, if you don't mind!" Oblomov cut him short.

"Oh no, there's plenty more where they came from! You didn't want to know me; not the slightest gratitude—after I fixed you up here and found you this treasure of a woman! After I supplied you with peace and quiet and every comfort! I did everything for you and protected your interests and then you snub me. You found yourself a benefactor, a German of all things! He's taken over the lease of your estate—well just you wait, he'll rob you blind and throw your money away on these shares of his and you'll end up on the streets, you mark my words! You're a fool I tell you—no worse than a fool, an ungrateful swine into the bargain!"

"Tarantyev!" Oblomov's voice rose menacingly.

"Don't you raise your voice to me! I'm the one who'll do the shouting, I want all the world to hear what a swine you are!" roared Tarantyev. "It was Ivan Matveyich and me who looked after you, protected your interests, waited on you like serfs, tiptoed around you, anticipating your every wish and then you go and slander him to his bosses! Now he's lost his job and everything! That was a low-down dirty trick! Now you're going to give him half of everything you possess—and I want a paper from you signing over the money to him; this time you're not drunk and you're in your right mind. Hand it over, I'm telling you; I'm not leaving until you do!"

"What's all this shouting, Mikhei Andreyich?" said the landlady and Anisya, looking in through the doorway, "two people passing by just stopped when they heard the commotion, wondering what was going on."

"I'll shout if I want to!" Tarantyev bellowed, "Let everyone know what a disgrace he is, what a dumb-bell! I hope that swindling German of yours strips the shirt off your back now that he's teamed up with your mistress!"

The room echoed to the sound of a resounding thwack. Tarantyev was momentarily silenced by the slap in the face from Oblomov and he subsided onto a chair, his eyes swiveling in dazed stupefaction.

"What? What did you do? What?" Tarantyev sat there, pale, breathing heavily and holding his hand to his cheek. "You've offended my honor and you're going to pay for it; I'm making a complaint to the Governor-General—you saw that?"

"We didn't see anything!" the two women chorused.

"Oh, so this is a conspiracy, a den of thieves, a gang of robbers and murderers...!"

"Get out of here, you scum!" Oblomov shouted, pale and shaking with rage—"if I don't see the back of you in one second I'll kill you like a dog!" He looked around for a stick.

"God in heaven! Murder! Help!" Tarantyev shouted.

"Zakhar, throw this crook out on his neck and make sure he never shows his face in here again!" Oblomov shouted.

"Alright then, here's the image of God, and there's the door!" said Zakhar, pointing first to the icon and then to the door.

"It wasn't you I came to see anyway, it was my friend's sister!" Tarantyev yelled.

"Oh no, you're nothing to me, Mikhei Andreyich!" said Agafya Matveyevna. "It's my brother you come to see, not me. You disgust me! You come here to guzzle and gorge yourself and then you call us names!"

"Oh, so it's like that is it, my dear friend! Fine, you'll be hearing from your brother! And you'll pay for this humiliation! Where's my hat? To hell with the lot of you—you're a bunch of thieves and murderers!" he shouted as he left through the courtyard, "Oh yes, you'll pay for the insult!"

The dog leapt on the chain and started barking and that was the last that Tarantyev and Oblomov ever saw of each other.

CHAPTER EIGHT

Stoltz did not return to St. Petersburg for several years and only once did he look in for a short time at Olga's estate and Oblomovka. Ilya Ilyich received letters from him in which Andrei urged him to go to Oblomovka and personally take charge of his now re-organized estate. He himself was leaving with Olga Sergeyevna for the southern coast of the Crimea for two reasons: he had business to attend to in Odessa and for the sake of Olga's health, which had been impaired by childbirth.

They settled in a quiet spot on the seashore in a small, modest house. Both the architecture and the interior had a style of their own and the decor and furnishings bore the imprint of the outlook and the taste of the owners. They had brought a great many things with them and the rest was shipped to them from Russia and abroad in bales, packing cases and cartloads.

A connoisseur of interior decoration might perhaps have shrugged his shoulders at the spectacle of such an eclectic collection of furniture; antiquated paintings, statues with broken limbs, and some prints and other "objets" that were worthless except for their sentimental value. Only a true connoisseur's eyes would have lit up greedily at the sight of one or two of the paintings, the odd yellowing book, a piece of old porcelain, a gemstone or a coin.

But this motley collection of furniture and paintings of different periods, all the bric-a-brac of no interest to the outsider but full of memories of happy times and moments for both of them, the piles of books and music, all gave off a warm breath of life that somehow stimulated the mind and pleased the senses. Like the perpetual beauty of nature that bathed its surroundings, the interior of the house was constantly abuzz with ideas and vibrated with the beauty of human activity. Room had been found for the tall writing desk inherited from Andrei's father as well as his suede gloves. In one corner there hung the oilskin cape next to an étagère displaying minerals, shells, stuffed birds, miniature clay sculptures and other items. Dominating all this was an Erard grand piano glittering with its gold filigree and inlay.

Outside, the house was covered from top to bottom with a tracery of climbing vines, ivy and myrtle. From the gallery there was a view of the sea on one side and a road into town from the other. It was from there that Olga would watch Andrei leaving the house on business and catch sight of him on his return when she would run down the stairs, out of the door, past the flower garden in all its glory, along the long avenue of poplars, and throw herself into her husband's arms, her cheeks blazing with joy, her eyes sparkling, always with the same eager, impetuous impatience of sheer happiness even after several years of marriage.

Stoltz looked at love and marriage from an original standpoint that may have been exaggerated, but was at least unique and independent. In this, as in all things, he pursued a free and—so it seemed to him—simple course, but what a hard apprenticeship of observation, patience and effort he had to serve before finally learning to take these "simple steps." From his father he had learned to consider everything in life, no matter how insignificant, with appropriate seriousness; he may also have inherited from him some of that pedantic rigor with which Germans tend to approach every step in life, including marriage.

The life of the elder Stoltz was an open book, or rather an open tablet of stone, and what was inscribed there left absolutely nothing to the imagination. But his mother, with her songs and her tender whisperings and, later, the diversity of life in the prince's house and, later still, the university, his books and his active social life had all conspired to divert Andrei from the straight and narrow course charted by his father; exposure to Russian life had engraved its invisible patterns on the original gray stone tablet and turned it into a rich and colorful mosaic.

Andrei did not impose pedantic restrictions on his feelings and even gave a reasonably free rein to his musings and daydreams, while being careful to keep his feet on the ground; although afterwards, true to the German side of his nature or for some other reason, he could not refrain from evaluating and trying to draw some practical conclusions from them.

He was physically energetic because of his lively mind. As a boy he had been mischievous and playful, but, when he was not up to his pranks, he knuckled down to work under his father's watchful eye and had no time to indulge in daydreaming. His imagination never became overheated and his heart remained unspoiled; under his mother's watchful eye the innocence and purity of both were preserved intact.

As a youth he had instinctively preserved the freshness of his powers and learned early on that it was this freshness that generated buoyancy and high spirits and shaped the manliness that in turn forged a character undaunted by life, whatever its challenges, a character which would look life straight in the eye, take on its challenges as a matter of duty and give as good as it got, and never see it as a burdensome yoke or a cross to be borne.

He devoted a lot of thought to the intricate workings of the heart. He observed consciously and unconsciously the effects of beauty on the imagination, how impressions grew into feelings and the effect they had in their turn and how they played themselves out. As he entered life he looked around him and arrived at the conviction that love, like the lever of Archimedes, was powerful enough to move the world and that love, properly understood and used, was as much a force for universal, absolute truth and good as, perverted and misused, it was a force for falsehood and evil. But where was good and where was evil and where was the line between them?

In response to the question: "what is falsehood?" he conjured up in his imagination a line of colorful masks stretching from the past into the present. With a smile and with blushes alternating with frowns, he watched the endless procession of love's heroes and heroines file past: he saw Don Quixotes in steel gauntlets and the ladies of their imaginations remaining true to each other through fifty years of separation; he saw ruddy-cheeked shepherd boys with their bulging, innocent eyes and their Chloës, minding their lambs. Powdered marquises with their knowing glances and lewd smirks paraded past him in their frills and furbelows; behind them came the Werthers who had shot, hanged and strangled themselves; there were the faded spinsters in their convents shedding the endless tears of the lovelorn; there were the mustachioed latter day heroes with their flashing eyes, the witting and unwitting Don Juans, the sophisticates who tremble at the very suspicion of love but secretly adore their housekeepers—the procession went on and on.

At the question: "what is truth?" he searched far and wide in his imagination and in real life for examples of simple but deep and abiding commitment to a woman by a man, but could find none. When he thought he had found one, the example turned out to be more apparent than real and he ended up disillusioned and pessimistic—and even gave up hope.

"Clearly, love is only ever partial," he thought, "or perhaps those hearts that are bathed in its light are shy; they hang back, unwilling to reveal themselves and have no interest in proving the cynics wrong; possibly they even pity them and forgive them, with the magnanimity born of their own happiness, for trampling that flower in the dirt for lack of the soil where it could put down roots and grow into the tall tree that would give them shade and shelter all the days of their life." He observed the marriages and husbands around him, and when it came to understanding their attitudes to their wives he was always faced with a riddle of the Sphinx; everything was somehow cryptic and unspoken. And yet the husbands themselves hardly spared a thought for these baffling questions and just trod the path to marriage with a deliberate, even stride as if there were absolutely no problem, nothing even to wonder about.

"Well, maybe they're right; maybe nothing more is necessary," he thought to himself without much conviction, observing how quickly some assimilate the code of love like some ABC of marriage, or a manual of etiquette that teaches you how to bow when you enter a salon—and then down to business! How impatiently they shrug off the springtime of their lives; many spend the rest of their days looking reproachfully at their wives as if the wives were to blame for the fact that their husbands were once foolish enough to fall in love with them. There were others whom love did not desert for years, sometimes until well into old age, although they never lost their satyr's grin...

Most men, however, entered marriage as if they were acquiring an estate and enjoying the advantages it had to offer: a wife who would run the house efficiently—she would be a housekeeper and a mother who would bring up the children; and as for love, they viewed it as a practical owner views the location of his property—he gets used to it quickly and then ceases to notice it.

"So which is it?" he asked himself, "an inherent, congenital disability, or simply a lack of training or education? Where is that closeness, that natural and unfailing source of such deep satisfaction that never dresses itself up in a jester's costume, that closeness which assumes a variety of forms but never fades? What is the natural color and hue of this omnipresent, all pervading force, this sap of life?"

He tried to peer into the crystal ball and glimpsed a blurred vision of the feeling and a woman dressed in its color and bathed in its hues, a vision so simple, but at the same time pure and bright.

"I'm dreaming, I'm just dreaming," he would say, emerging from his reverie, and he would smile at this futile mental aberration; but in spite of himself he could not shake off the sketchy memory of his vision. At first the vision came to him in the form of some universal idea of the woman in his future, but when, later on, he saw in the mature and fully grown Olga not only the opulence of her beauty in full bloom but also that force so eager to embrace life, avid for understanding and anxious to grapple with life, all the elements, in fact, of his vision, there rose before him that long forgotten image of love now embodied in the person of Olga, and he felt that some time in the far distant future the truth would be seen to lie in the closeness between them—without artifice and in total sincerity.

Leaving aside the question of love and marriage as such and without bringing in such issues as money, connections or position, Stoltz did nonetheless ponder the problem of reconciling his outer and hitherto ceaseless activity with an inner family life, and his role as a traveler and businessman with that of a homebound family man. If he were to give up the life of restless movement and activity, what kind of fulfillment would he find in a purely domestic existence? Of course, raising and educating children, guiding them through life was no easy task, but a worthwhile one; but that was far in the future, so what would he do in the meantime?

These questions had long and frequently troubled him and in any case he did not find bachelorhood irksome. It never entered his head that the moment his heart missed a beat when he felt the presence of beauty he should don the straightjacket of marriage. That was the reason for his virtual indifference to the young Olga, except that he admired her as a charming child with a lot of promise. Light-heartedly and in passing he would throw out scraps of bold new ideas or pithy comments about life that would be snapped up hungrily by her impressionable young mind. In this way, without the least suspecting it, he was cultivating within her a lively and true understanding of what went on in the world around her. Later he forgot all about Olga and the casual, off-the-cuff education he had given her.

At times, when he had noticed flashes of this unusual cast of mind and her somewhat original ideas and saw that she was free of false attitudes and was not trying to make an impression, that her feelings came and went quite freely and spontaneously, that there was nothing copied or borrowed in her reactions and that they were entirely her own and that they were always bold, fresh and firm, he failed to realize where all this had come from and did not recognize in them the product of his own casual, incidental instruction and observations. If he had paid more attention to her at the time he would have seen that she was striking out virtually alone on her own path, protected against going too far in one direction by the superficial tutelage of her aunt, but free from the oppressive burden of the supervision of a multitude of authority figures—nannies, grandmothers and aunts with their inherited traditions of clan, family and caste, their antiquated rules, customs and maxims. There was no one to force her along the beaten track and she was free to take a new path along which she had to make her own way solely on the strength of her own intelligence, ideas and feelings.

Nature had been generous to her in this regard: her aunt did not dictate to her or tyrannize her and Olga worked things out for herself or used her intuition through careful observation and listening attentively to, among other things, the words of wisdom of her friend…

He was oblivious to all this and simply expected her to come into her own some time in the future and never thought of her for a moment as a potential mate. For her part, she maintained her reserve as a matter of pride and it was a long time before she revealed herself for what she was. It was only during his travels abroad after his chance encounter with the promising child whom he had quite forgotten, and after much agonizing, that he finally came to recognize what a model of simplicity, strength and naturalness she had grown into. It was only there and only gradually that the hidden depths of her personality were revealed to him, depths that could contain more than he could ever give.

In the beginning it took him a lot of time and effort to master her mettlesome temperament, to quell her youthful exuberance, to keep her impulsiveness within bounds, and to keep their life on an even keel—if only for a time. For he had only to relax his vigilance for a moment and there would be new alarms and excursions, excitement would mount, and new questions would come bubbling up in that questing mind, that restless heart and once again he would have to calm her overwrought imagination, soothe or awaken her pride. Whenever she started wrestling with a problem he hastened to provide her with a solution. She lost the habit of seeing life as arbitrary and capricious and seeing things through a fog of illusion. She learned to look into the distance and see it bright and free as if she were looking into perfectly clear water where she could see every pebble and every fissure right down to the seabed itself.

"I'm happy!" she would whisper, looking back in gratitude over her past life and, peering into the future, she recalled her girlish dream of happiness that had come to her that time in Switzerland on that still, blue night and saw that the dream had trailed her life like a shadow. "What have I done to deserve this happiness?" she wondered in humility. She would worry and sometimes even panic at the thought that something might happen to destroy her happiness.

The years passed and they did not tire of life. It was a time of tranquility and the excitement and turbulence abated. They learned to take life's little reverses and vagaries in their stride and bear them patiently and cheerfully. Life lost nothing of its interest for them. Olga had now learned to understand life as it really was; two existences, her own and Andrei's, had merged into one, there was no longer any room for unbridled passions; harmony and tranquility ruled their lives.

Burying themselves in this well-earned peace and quiet might have seemed like a kind of hibernation—an existence of unalloyed bliss enjoyed by all those who live in out-of-the-way places, who come together three times a day, yawn at the same old conversation, lapse into a mindless stupor, eking out a dreary existence where everything has already been thought, said or done over and over again and there is nothing left to do or say because "that's the way life is."

On the surface they behaved just like other people. They got up early, if not at the crack of dawn. They liked to linger over their morning tea, sometimes saying nothing as if the effort were too much, and then busying themselves in different parts of the house or working together. They dined, rode in the countryside, played music just like anyone else and just as Oblomov had imagined...The difference was that the stupor, the dejection was missing; they spent their days free from boredom and apathy; there was never a listless look or word between them and they never ran out of conversation, which was often heated. The house rang with their voices, which could also be heard out in the garden, or they would communicate with each other as if sketching the bare outline of their dreams, by the merest flicker of the tongue suggesting the wisp of a thought, a barely audible whisper of the soul...

And their silences? Sometimes they were the moments of contemplative happiness of which Oblomov had once dreamed and, at other times, they were moments of individual mulling over problems and questions that they were constantly posing to each other.

There were moments of shared silent wonder at the ever-renewed beauties of nature. Their sensitivity to this beauty—the earth, the sky, the sea—was never dulled or eroded by habit, their feelings were always stirred and they would sit silently side by side as if with a single pair of eyes and experiencing with but a single soul in wordless harmony the splendor of creation. They did not greet the morning with passive indifference nor remain mindlessly oblivious to the velvety darkness of the warm, starlit, southern night. The restless activity of their minds, the constant ferment of their spirits, and their need to share their thinking and their feelings with each other, and to communicate, kept them perpetually stimulated.

But what was the actual subject of those heated arguments and conversations, what did they read and what did they discuss on all those long walks? Well, it was everything. While they were still abroad Stoltz had gotten out of the habit of reading and working alone; here in this close intimacy with Olga he even did his thinking with her and he had great trouble keeping up with the breathtaking pace of her mind and will. The question of what he would do within the confines of a purely domestic existence had long been laid to rest and had solved itself. He found himself having to include her in his working life because to her, life without activity was suffocating; it left her gasping for air.

A construction project, the affairs of his own or Oblomov's estate, company dealings—none of this was done without her knowledge and participation. No letter would leave the house without having been read by her; there was no idea, still less any action taken on it that passed her by. She knew about everything and everything was her business because it was his business.

To begin with he did this because there was simply no way of keeping it from her; every letter was written in her presence, every conversation with an agent or a contractor took place in her hearing and with her looking on. He continued the practice out of habit and ultimately it became a necessity for him as well as her. Her comments, her advice, her approval or disapproval became for him the acid test because he saw that her grasp of the subjects, her powers of reasoning and argument were equal to his own. Zakhar was put out by these abilities in his own wife and there are many who take exception to the same phenomenon, but Stoltz was only too happy with it!

And the reading, the learning, the constant stimulation and stretching of the mind! Any book or newspaper article that was not shared with her aroused Olga's jealousy and she seriously resented it when Andrei did not see fit to show her something that he felt was too serious, boring or difficult for her, and she would call him a pedant, a boor, a stick-in-the-mud, and an old German stuffed shirt. This was a source of some heated and acrimonious arguments between them. She would get angry, he would laugh, and that would make her even angrier, and she would be mollified only when he stopped treating it as a joke and agreed to share with her the thought, the information or the book or article in question. It was finally accepted that she needed to know everything and read everything that he did himself.

He did not want to saddle her with technical knowledge or expertise so that he could then brag idiotically about his "educated wife." If in the course of conversation she let slip a single word or conveyed the slightest suggestion of anything so pretentious he would be even more embarrassed than if she had responded with a look of sheer, dumb incomprehension to a question which would be common knowledge among experts in the field, but still beyond the grasp of a woman educated according to the prevailing standards of the day. All he wanted, and she doubly so, was for her to be capable of understanding anything that might come up, without necessarily being able to deal with it.

He did not actually draw her diagrams or go over tables with her, but he talked to her about everything. He shared with her a wide range of reading without fastidiously avoiding references to some new economic theory or social or philosophical issues and spoke with enthusiasm and passion and sketched for her a vivid picture of the state of contemporary knowledge. Later she would forget the details, but the overall picture, together with the colors with which he had so vividly illuminated the universe he had created for her, never faded from her receptive mind. He would burst with pride and pleasure whenever he saw the spark he had ignited flash in her eyes, when he caught an echo of some thought he had shared with her in something she said, and saw how her consciousness had absorbed and reprocessed the thought, so that when she came to utter it, the dry, severe original was invested with a new sparkle of feminine charm. He was especially gratified when the tiny grit she had absorbed from all his talk, his reading and his descriptions crystallized into a pearl that was deposited on the glittering sea bed of her life.

Like a philosopher or an artist he tenderly molded her intellectual development and never in his life had he found himself so deeply absorbed; not when he was a student, not in the difficult days of his early struggles when he had fought to free himself from life's entanglements, toughening himself and tempering his steel in the crucible of life's adversities. In all this there had been no task so challenging as that of nurturing the restless, volcanic intellect of his life's companion.

"How happy I am!" Stoltz said to himself, projecting himself, as was his tendency, far into the future and looking beyond the early raptures of married life. From a distance a new image smiled at him, not of a self-centered Olga, an adoring wife, the nurturing mother who fades into a drab, meaningless existence, but something different, something lofty, something practically never known before... He visualized her as a nurturing mother figure, shaping the mores and conduct of a whole fortunate generation. He worried about whether she would have sufficient strength of will and fortitude and tried to help her master life as quickly as possible and to acquire the necessary reserves of courage to stand up to life—and to do so without delay while they were both still young and strong enough, while life was still sparing them the worst and while the blows it did deliver did not feel so painful, while love was still strong enough to drown grief.

They saw some dark days but the gloom quickly passed. Business setbacks, major financial loss hardly affected them at all; it just caused them some extra trouble and traveling and was quickly forgotten. The death of her aunt caused Olga genuine pain and sorrow and overshadowed her life for half a year or so. Their keenest apprehensions were about the health of their children, which was a constant worry, but when the apprehensions passed, happiness was restored. Stoltz's greatest concern was Olga's health; she took a long time to recover from childbirth, and even when she did, he continued to worry—he could imagine no more terrible tragedy.

"How happy I am!" Olga too would say quietly to herself, contemplating her life with gratification, and at such moments she would fall to brooding, especially after some three or four years of marriage.

How strange people are! The greater her happiness, the more she brooded—and indeed the more apprehensive she became. She began to observe herself more closely and perceived that it was her life's moments of stillness, the moments of self-conscious contemplation of her happiness that disturbed her. She strove with might and main to shake off this tendency to brood and stepped up the pace and rhythm of her life, feverishly seeking noise, action and busyness, and she got her husband to take her with him into town and tried to venture forth into social life and meet people, but this stage did not last long.

The social whirl did not do much for her and she swiftly retreated to the familiar territory of her home to rid herself of a certain unaccustomed, oppressive feeling and plunged back into the world of petty domestic concerns and chores. She would spend days on end in the nursery, mothering her children and attending to all their needs, or she would be taken up with her reading with Andrei and discussing those "serious and boring" topics, or they would read poetry and talk about traveling to Italy.

What she feared was drifting into an Oblomov-like stupor; but no matter how hard she tried to fight against those moments of periodic apathy and spiritual torpor she would find that at first, before she knew it, daydreams of happiness would start creeping up on her and she would be enveloped in the blueness of a perfect night and the numbing drowsiness it brought, and soon that familiar state of brooding contemplation would steal over her as if she were taking a kind of break from life. She would then start to feel nervous, apprehensive and oppressed by some ineffable sadness, and troubling, unformed questions would start their whispering in her restless mind. Olga examined herself carefully, searching herself for signs and clues but was unable to fathom what it was that her soul was seeking at times, what it craved—she only knew that there was something it craved. It was even as if—and this was a terrible thing to say—that it was pining, as if happiness itself was not enough, as if it had palled and her soul was thirsting for new, unknown experiences and projecting ever further into the future.

"But this is terrible!" she thought. "How can I possibly be wanting something more, what more is there to want? Where is there to go? Nowhere! The road doesn't go any farther…No, it can't be, it can't be that I've reached the end of life's journey! Can this really be all there is, can this be it?" An inner voice was speaking, but its message was broken off. Olga looked around in alarm in case someone may have recognized or overheard the whispering of that inner voice. With her eyes she appealed to the sky, the sea, the woods—but no answer came, there was nothing out there but distance, nothingness and darkness.

Nature kept repeating one and the same thing over and over again, and in nature she saw the uninterrupted but unvarying cycle of life without a beginning, without end.

Of course, she knew whom to ask about what was troubling her and she would have gotten an answer—but what answer? What if it was the rumbling of a barren intelligence or, worse still, the craving of an unwomanly heart, a heart not made for closeness. Oh God! That she, his idol, should be without a heart—only a calloused, eternally questing intellect that could never find satisfaction! What would she turn into? Not a bluestocking! What would he think of her when these new, unlikely, but no doubt familiar, agonizings were revealed to him?

She kept out of his way or feigned illness whenever her eyes, in spite of herself, lost their velvety softness and took on a dry and hot look and her brow was darkened by a heavy cloud and she just could not bring herself to smile or to speak, no matter how hard she tried, and she just listened to him with indifference as he passed on to her the most sensational political gossip or the most intriguing account of some new scientific advance or the latest thing in the arts. At the same time she had no impulse to break into tears, there was no sudden agitation as there had been back in the days when her nerves would play up and her girlish feelings would erupt and flare up with full force. No, this was different! "But then what is it?" she would ask herself in despair when she suddenly found herself bored and listless, indifferent to everything on a fine languorous summer evening or sitting at the cradle even in the midst of the conversation of her loving husband.

She would suddenly freeze up and fall silent and then feign lively activity and an interest that she did not feel in order to hide her strange malaise, or she would plead a migraine and go and lie down.

But it was very hard for her to elude Stoltz's sharp eyes and she knew it, so she began to steel herself inwardly for the inevitable conversation with the same apprehension as she had once before when she was bringing herself to confess her past. And, sure enough, the time came.

One evening they happened to be strolling along the avenue of poplars. She was clinging closely and wordlessly to his shoulder. She was in the painful grip of another bout of her mysterious malady and, no matter what subject he raised, gave him only the briefest of responses.

"The nanny said that Olenka was coughing during the night. Do you think we should send for the doctor tomorrow?" he asked.

"I gave her a hot drink and I'll keep her inside tomorrow and then we'll see," she replied in a flat monotone.

They continued their walk in silence.

"How come you didn't answer your friend Sonechka's letter?" he asked, "I waited until the last moment and almost missed the post, it's the third letter from her you haven't answered."

"Well, the sooner I forget her the better!" she said and lapsed into silence.

"I gave your regards to Bichurin, you know he's in love with you; I thought perhaps it would be a little consolation for his wheat arriving late."

She gave a restrained smile. "Yes, you told me," she responded indifferently.

"Are you sleepy or something?" he asked.

Her heart gave a lurch, and not for the first time, whenever his questions started probing the sensitive area.

"Not yet," she said with feigned cheerfulness, "why do you ask?"

"You're not feeling well?" he asked again.

"No, what makes you think that?"

"Well, you look so listless!"

She squeezed his shoulder tightly with both hands. "Not at all!" she protested, doing her best to sound casual, although there was something in her voice that somehow suggested the listlessness she felt.

He led her off the path and made her stand facing the moonlight.

"Look at me!" he said, giving her a long searching look. "Anyone might think you were…unhappy! There's such a strange expression in your eyes today—and not just today, for that matter. What's the matter, Olga?"

He took her by the waist and led her back onto the path.

"You know what it is, I'm…hungry!" she said, forcing a laugh.

"No lies now, no lies!" he said, adding with mock severity, "I don't like that!"

"Unhappy!" she repeated the word in a reproachful tone, stopping him on the path. "If I'm unhappy, it can only be because I'm too happy!" she ended her sentence on such a gentle, loving note that he kissed her. She became bolder. The suggestion, however casual and joking, that she might be unhappy unexpectedly stimulated her to frankness.

"It's not that I'm bored, and I couldn't be, you know that and you don't even believe it yourself; I'm not ill… it's just a kind of sadness… sometimes I feel—oh, you're impossible, I can't hide anything from you! Yes, I feel sad, and I don't know why!" She laid her head on his shoulder.

"So that's it; but why?" he asked quietly, leaning towards her.

"I don't know," she repeated.

"But there has to be a reason, and if it's not me or anything that's happening around you, it must be something in you. Sometimes that kind of sadness just means you are sickening for something; are you sure you feel alright?"

"Yes, maybe that's it, something like that," she said seriously, "although I don't feel anything. You can see how well I'm eating, walking, sleeping and doing my work. It's as if something suddenly comes over me, a kind of melancholy… and life suddenly seems…well, as if there's something missing. No, don't listen to me, I'm talking nonsense!"

"No, don't stop!" he urged her eagerly. "So something is missing in your life, go on!"

"Sometimes it's as if I'm afraid," she went on, "that it will all change, that it will end....I don't know myself! What is this happiness...the whole of life...?" She was speaking more and more softly, ashamed of her own questions: "All the joys, all the sorrows...nature..." she whispered, "I'm being drawn to some place beyond all this; I get dissatisfied with everything...my God! I'm even ashamed of this nonsense...it's just my imagination. Don't take any notice of me, don't even look at me!" she said imploringly and lovingly, "this sadness will soon pass and I'll become my old bright, cheerful self again—like right now!"

She pressed close to him so timorously and lovingly, truly ashamed, as if asking forgiveness for her nonsense.

Her husband questioned her at length and she described to him in detail, like a patient to a doctor, the symptoms of her sadness and articulated all her vague, unformulated questions, depicted for him her inner turmoil—and then how this mirage had vanished—everything in fact that she could recall and bring to mind.

Stoltz continued along the path, his chin resting on his chest, ruminating deeply, apprehensive and baffled, over his wife's puzzling confession. She watched his eyes but could read nothing in them and when they reached the end of the path for the third time she would not let him turn back, and this time it was she who led him into the moonlight and regarded him questioningly.

"What are you doing?" she asked shyly, "laughing at my nonsense, yes? It's pretty stupid, this sadness, isn't it?" He said nothing.

"Why don't you say something?" she asked impatiently.

"You went for a long time without saying anything even though you certainly knew that I had long since noticed something in you, so now let me think for a while without saying anything; you've set me a difficult problem."

"See, now you're going to think while I worry about what's going on in your head and wonder what you're thinking to yourself—I should never have told you!" she added, "so I'd prefer you to say something..."

"What do you want me to say?" he said thoughtfully. "Perhaps these symptoms of yours are connected with that old trouble with your nerves, in which case it's for the doctor to diagnose you, not me. We'd better send for him tomorrow... unless it's..." he began and stopped to think.

"Unless it's what? Tell me!" she urged him impatiently.

He continued thinking as he walked.

"Well, come on!" she said, jerking his arm.

"Perhaps it's your imagination working too hard; your mind is too active... .or perhaps you've matured to the point..." he finished his point muttering to himself in an undertone.

"Speak so that I can hear you, Andrei, please! I can't bear it when you mumble to yourself," she complained, "I told him all that nonsense and now he goes and looks at the ground in front of him and mutters into his beard; I tell you I'm getting frightened of being alone with you here in the dark..."

"What to tell you—I don't know... 'sadness overwhelms you and you are troubled by unanswered questions', but what does it all mean? We'll talk about it later and we'll see—perhaps bathing in sea water again would help...?"

"You said something to yourself just then, something about 'unless... perhaps... you've matured', what was it you were thinking?" she asked.

"What was I thinking..." he said, lingering over his words as if he himself did not really believe what he was saying and was reluctant to say it, "Well, you see there are moments... what I mean is, if it's not a sign of some health problem and there's really nothing wrong with you, then perhaps you've reached that point in life when growth has ended and... and there are no mysteries left and life is an open book..."

"In other words, I've grown old, is that what you mean?" she interjected with some heat. "What nerve!" She even shook her fist at him, "I'm still young and strong," she added, straightening her shoulders.

He laughed. "Don't worry!" he said, "it's clear you have no intention of growing old. No, that's not it—when people are old they lose their fight, they give up. No, this melancholy of yours, this brooding—that is if it's what I think it is—is really a sign of strength. Sometimes an active questing mind tries to probe beyond normal limits and, of course, finds no answers, and that's when the melancholy sets in... .a temporary dissatisfaction with life... a deep-seated frustration with life for not yielding up its secrets. Maybe this is what's happened to you, and if it's true, there's nothing stupid or nonsensical about it."

She sighed, more, apparently, from relief that her worries were at an end and because she had not sunk in her husband's esteem but if anything, had actually risen.

"But I really am happy; my mind is occupied, my head is not in the clouds, my life is varied—what else do I want? Why all these questions?" she said, "It's a sickness, a burden."

"Yes, for a weak, clouded mind not equipped to deal with it. This kind of melancholy, this questioning has probably unhinged many minds; in some it takes the form of terrifying hallucinations, delirium."

"Here I am, brimming with happiness, I'm full of zest for life and suddenly it's all soured by this anguish."

"Yes, well that's the price we pay for Prometheus's fire, but don't think of it as a burden or a curse; no, this kind of sadness is something to be welcomed; all these doubts and questionings should be appreciated, they are the privilege of a rich and full life and tend to surface when happiness is at its peak and when we are not being driven by our baser appetites.

People leading commonplace, everyday lives are not prey to this kind of angst; it does not arise where there is material need and hardship. The vast mass of people come and go and are strangers to this fog of doubt and these gnawing questions, but for those who experience these things at the right time, they are not so much a millstone as welcome guests."

"Yes, but how do you deal with it? It leaves you brooding and indifferent," she said, adding hesitantly, "to practically everything."

"Yes, but for how long? In the long run all this adds zest to life," he said, "it leads you to the abyss from which there are no answers to be had and forces you to cherish life even more warmly. It challenges your battle-hardened forces to combat as if to deny them any respite and keep them on their toes."

"But to be tormented by this fog, by these ghosts!" she protested. "Everything is bright and clear and then life is suddenly overcast by some ominous shadow; surely there must be some remedy?"

"Of course there is, life itself provides the defense; the alternative would be a life without questioning, which would be stifling."

"So, what's the answer? Just give up and give way to this brooding melancholy?"

"Not at all!" he said. "We have to summon up all our resolution and keep going with perseverance and patience. You and I, we're no Titans," he went on, putting his arms around her, "we are no Manfreds or Fausts with the audacity to take up arms against these mutinous, questioning forces, we will not accept their challenge but, rather, bow our heads and wait out those difficult moments unresisting, until life and happiness smile on us once again."

"But if these questions don't go away, the melancholy will never leave you alone, will it?"

"Then we'll have to accept it as a new fact of life…but that doesn't happen, it's not possible! It's not your private melancholy, it's a malaise of mankind and you've been splashed with just a single drop. When a victim gives up on life, when he has nothing to fall back on, its effects can be terrible. But as for us, let's hope to God that this angst of yours is what I think it is and not the symptom of some disease—now that would be worse, that would be a grief against which I would be defenseless, helpless. But, as it is, this angst, this fog, these doubts, can they really rob us of what is precious to us, of what is…?"

Before he could finish she threw herself into his arms in a frenzy and with passionate abandon, the strength of her emotions blinding her to everything for a moment as she wound her arms around his neck. "Not fog, not melancholy, not sickness, not even death!" she whispered rapturously, happy, tranquil and cheerful once again. It seemed to her that she had never loved him so passionately as at that moment.

"Don't let providence overhear your complaining," his loving concern prompted him to express this superstitious admonition, "or it might take it as evidence of ingratitude! Providence doesn't like it when its blessings are not appreciated. Up to now you haven't really known what life can be like, but you will one day—and you'll see what trouble and hardship life can bring when it turns turbulent—there'll be no room for questionings then," he said, adding quietly, almost to himself, in response to her passionate outburst, "don't waste your energies!" There was a ring of sorrow to his words as if he were actually seeing the "sorrow and hardship" in the distance.

She was momentarily reduced to silence by the mournful tone of his voice. Her trust in him—and his voice—was boundless. The effect of his tone was contagious and she too was soon wrapped in thought and withdrew into an inner space of quiet meditation. Leaning against him for support she walked slowly and mechanically along the path in deep impenetrable silence. Like her husband before her, she too was peering apprehensively deep into the future, where, according to him, there loomed a period of "trials and tribulations" and where "sorrow and hardship" lay in wait.

She began to see a different vision; instead of the blueness of that idyllic night there was a view of life from another angle. It was not that festive, untroubled existence, tucked away with the man of her life in their peaceful retreat amidst boundless abundance; no, what she was seeing was an endless series of privations, inevitable losses and the tears they bring, a life of austerity and hardship where the whims born of a life of ease could no longer be indulged, she saw weeping and wailing from new and unfamiliar pain and hurt, she saw sickness, business reverses, her husband's death…

She shuddered and recoiled but forced herself with bold curiosity to look this new aspect of life squarely in the face, gazing in horror yet gauging her power to meet the challenge. In this vision love alone did not betray her and remained a loyal and steadfast ally in that new life—but it was now a different kind of love. Gone were the fever, the breathlessness, the bright rays, and the blueness of the idyllic night. Over time, all this came to be seen as mere childishness beside that love, a love fit for that far-off grimmer and deeper life. Gone were the kisses and the laughter, the thrillingly intimate talk in the copse, among the flowers, amidst life and nature in all its glory… all that had "faded and passed." It was an imperishable and undying love etched indelibly and powerfully in their features—in time of shared sorrow it glowed in the slow and silent look of pain that they exchanged, it was audible in the common fortitude with which they bore their sufferings, in the tears held back and the muffled sobs.

New visions, though from afar yet clear and distinct and frightening, quietly insinuated themselves into Olga's ineffable sadness and questionings… .In the comforting and confident words of her husband and in her boundless faith in him Olga found respite both from her strange and rare melancholy and from her sinister and ominous forebodings, and strode confidently ahead.

The night of "fog" passed, giving way to a bright, clear morning bringing with it only the cares of a wife and mother. Outside the flower beds and the countryside beckoned to her, inside there was the welcome of her husband's study. However, it was not a life of mindless self-indulgence that she led but rather one of tempered but buoyant optimism as she faced the future and waited.

She kept on growing in stature... Andrei saw that his old ideal of a woman and a wife was unattainable, but he was happy even with the pale reflection of himself in Olga—and this was something too that he had never expected. At the same time he too was faced with the never ending, almost lifelong challenge of maintaining his male dignity at the same high level in order to remain worthy of the esteem of the proud and demanding Olga, not just for the unworthy purpose of proving his superiority, but rather to prevent the slightest crack or blemish appearing in the crystalline texture of their life; and this could happen if her faith in him were to waver even slightly.

For many women this would not have been necessary. Once married, they passively accept their husbands' qualities, good and bad alike, acquiesce without a murmur in whatever position, circle or status they bring to the marriage or, just as passively, yield to the first temptation that happens to come their way, without finding it possible or necessary to offer the slightest resistance—"after all, it's fate; a woman is a creature of passion; a woman is a frail vessel" and all that kind if thing.

Even if the husband is conspicuous for his intelligence—such an attractive quality in a man—such women prize this asset in just the same way they would a precious necklace, and even then only if this intelligence remains blind to their pitiful feminine wiles. If he should venture to notice the petty comedy of their banal and sometimes downright decadent existence, then that intelligence can even become an imposition, a liability to them

Olga was a stranger to this logic of blind subservience to fate and knew nothing of these little feminine fads and fancies. Once she had recognized the worth of the man of her choice and his claims on her she simply believed in him and for that reason loved him. To have stopped believing in him would have meant stopping loving him—as had happened with Oblomov. Back then, however, she was, as it were, still unsteady on her feet and not entirely resolute. She had only just begun to look at life and examine it; she was still assembling the components of her intelligence and character and collecting material—the process of construction had not yet begun and life's possibilities had barely been glimpsed.

Now, however, her belief in Andrei was not blind but pondered and conscious and he was for her the embodiment of everything a man should be. The greater and the more conscious her belief in him, the harder it became for him to live up to that belief and to be for her the hero that not only her heart and mind, but also her imagination, demanded. Her belief in him was such that she recognized no authority, no mediator between them short of God himself. Consequently she could not have borne even his tiniest failure to measure up to all the qualities with which she had credited him; the slightest false note in his character or intellect would have had for her the impact of a clashing discord and the edifice of her happiness would have come crashing down, burying her under its rubble or, if she had survived, she would have used the very last ounce of her strength to look for....But no, women like that do not make the same mistake twice. When faith of that intensity is shattered, the love that goes with it cannot be regenerated.

Stoltz was profoundly happy with his full and busy life where it was always glorious spring and he cultivated, protected and cherished it zealously, actively and vigilantly. He shuddered with horror to the very depths of his being only when he remembered how Olga had come within a hair's breadth of ruin and how that junction in the road where their two lives were destined to converge could so easily have been missed, and that a simple failure to read life's road map might have permitted that fatal error, that Oblomov...

He shuddered to think of the life Oblomov was preparing to offer her. To imagine Olga as nothing more than the mistress of a country house, a nanny to her children, a housekeeper, her days crawling by in sluggish procession! All her questionings, doubts, her rage to live reduced to a preoccupation with household chores, with nothing to look forward to but holidays, visitors, family gatherings, childbirth, christenings, and the apathy and drowsy stupor of her husband! That marriage would have provided only the framework but not the content, the means but not the end; it would have served as nothing more than a broad and unvarying setting for visits, entertaining, dinners, social gatherings and idle gossip.

How could she have borne such a life? At first she would have struggled, attempting to probe and penetrate life's mysteries; there would have been tears, frustration and anguish. Then she would have grown used to it, put on weight, eaten, slept, and lapsed into mental torpor... No, that could never have happened to her! She would have wept, suffered, wasted away and died in the arms of her loving, good-hearted but helpless husband—poor Olga!

But if her flame had burned bright, if her life force had not waned, if her powers had remained undiminished, if she had spread her wings and, like a powerful, sharp-eyed eagle caught for a brief moment in a feeble grasp, had torn free and soared to the summit of a lofty crag where she had spied a mate, another eagle even stronger and keener-eyed than herself? Poor Ilya!

"Poor Ilya!" Once Andrei actually uttered these words aloud when he was thinking about the past. When she heard the name Olga suddenly let her hands with the needlework she was doing fall into her lap, threw her head back. The memories flooded back, evoked by the mention of that name.

"What's become of him?" she asked after a while. "Couldn't we find out?"

Andrei shrugged. "You know, it's not as if we're living in the times when there was no postal service, when people who moved away from each other really disappeared without trace and might as well have died."

"You could at least write to some friend or other and they could find out something…"

"They wouldn't find out anything except what we already know; he's alive and well and still living in the same apartment—I know that much without asking any friends. And as for how he is doing, how he is bearing up, whether he is dead inside or whether there is still a spark of life in him, those are things no outsider is going to find out."

"Please don't talk like that, Andrei—it frightens me and hurts me! I want to know and I'm frightened to find out…" She was on the point of tears.

"We'll be in St. Petersburg in the spring—we'll find out ourselves."

"Finding out is one thing, but what about all that needs to be done?"

"And what do you think I've been doing? Haven't I pleaded with him, urged him, gone out of my way to help him, taken charge of his affairs—you'd think he might show some sign of acknowledgment! When I'm there with him he's ready for anything, but the moment I'm out of his sight then you can forget it—he's back in his coma. It's like dealing with a drunk!"

"Then why let him out of your sight?" Olga cut in impatiently. "With him you have take charge, put him in a carriage and take him away with you. Now we're moving to the estate and he'll be near us—we'll take him with us!"

"That's quite a responsibility we'd be taking on!" Andrei argued as he paced back and forth. "It would be never-ending!"

"Are you saying you'd find it too much trouble?" said Olga, "that's something new! I've never heard you complain that Oblomov was too much trouble."

"I'm not complaining, I'm just explaining!"

"So now suddenly it's explaining! The truth is you've admitted to yourself that it's become a drag, a bother—isn't that it?" She gave him a challenging look.

He shook his head. "No, it's not that it's a bother, it's just that it's use-less—that's what I sometimes think."

"Stop, stop, I don't want to hear any more! Now I'm going to spend the whole day thinking about it and moping—just like last week! If you no longer feel you owe it to him to help him out of friendship, then do it out of sheer humanity. If you give up I'll go myself and I won't come back without him; my pleas are sure to move him. I'm sure I'll break down and burst into tears if I see him dead, a lifeless corpse! Perhaps tears…"

"Will bring him back to life, is that what you think?" Andrei broke in.

"No, they won't revive him, but they'll at least make him take a look around him and do something to improve his life. At least he won't be rolling in the dirt but will be near us, his own kind. Last time, the moment I appeared he saw himself in an instant and was ashamed…"

"It couldn't be that you're still in love with him?" Andrei asked teasingly.

"No!" Olga replied in all seriousness, as if carefully reviewing the past, "not the way I did then, but there is something in him that I still love, something to which I still feel an allegiance and which hasn't changed—not like other people…"

"What other people? Well, spit it out, you poisonous snake, strike, bite, it's me you mean, is it? You're wrong! If you want to know the truth, I was the one who taught you to love him; and it almost worked. If it hadn't been for me you would have passed by without even noticing him. I was the one who showed you that he was as intelligent as the next man, but his intelligence is buried, crushed under the weight of all the garbage and is just slumbering, just ticking over. If you want I'll tell you exactly why he's still dear to you, why you still love him."

She nodded her head in assent.

"It's because he possesses something more valuable than any intelligence, a pure, true heart! That's his priceless natural asset and he has kept it safe and intact throughout his life. He may have succumbed to life's adversities, become numbed, lapsed into a slumber and finally, defeated and disappointed, has lost the will to live, but he has never lost his honor and has stayed true to himself. His heart has never sounded a single false note, not a speck of dirt has clung to him. No lie has ever seduced him, no matter how elegantly dressed up, never once has he been tempted to set his foot on the path of insincerity. A whole ocean of dirt and sewage can be surging at his feet, the whole world can be polluted and turned inside out but Oblomov would never kneel before the idol of insincerity; inside he will always remain pure, clean and true. His is a transparent, incorruptible soul such as few people possess; he is one in a million, a pearl among men. His loyalty is unswerving and absolute and cannot be bought.

"That is why you have remained true to him and why helping him will never be too much trouble for me. I've known many people with remarkable qualities, but I've never met anyone with so pure, noble and honest a heart. I've felt love for many people, but never such a strong and lasting love as for Oblomov. To know him is to love him forever; right? Now you understand?"

Olga listened in silence, her head bowed, her eyes on her work.

After a moment's thought Andrei added: "Yes, that explains everything, there's nothing else to say. Oh yes," he corrected himself, "I totally forgot his 'dove-like gentleness'."

Olga laughed, quickly put down her sewing, ran to Andrei, threw her arms about his neck, her own radiant eyes looking straight into his for the longest time and then rested her head reflectively on his shoulder. She was remembering the gentle, soulful face of Oblomov, his tender glances, his submissiveness and, finally, the heart wrenching, embarrassed smile with which he had responded to her reproaches when they had parted. Her heart gave a painful lurch of pity for him.

"You won't abandon him?" she said, still clasping her husband's neck.

"Never; an abyss would have to open up between us, a wall would have to rise…"

She kissed him. "When we're in St. Petersburg you'll take me to see him?"

He hesitated before replying.

"Yes? Yes?" She was determined to get an answer.

"Listen, Olga," he said, trying to prise her arms from around his neck, "first of all we have to…"

"No, you must promise—I won't let up on you!"

"Well, I suppose so," he replied, "but I won't take you the first time, only the second time. I know how you will react if he…"

"Stop. Stop!" she interjected, "you must take me, and between us we'll succeed. You won't be able to by yourself, you'll give up!"

"Well, alright, but it's going to upset you—and it may take you a long time to get over it," he said, not too happy that Olga had succeeded in wringing grudging consent out of him.

"And remember," she pointed out as she sat down, "that you'll give up only when 'an abyss opens up or a wall rises between you'—I won't forget those words!"

CHAPTER NINE

A blanket of peace and quiet lay over the Vyborg side, its unpaved streets, its wooden boardwalks, its bedraggled gardens, its ditches overgrown with nettles where you would see a goat with a tattered rope around its neck drowsing, dead to the world, or busily nibbling away at the grass by a fence and where, at midday, a clerk would pass, his fashionable high heels clicking on the boardwalk and a prim lace curtain in a window would twitch and the functionary's wife would peep out through the geraniums. You would see a young girl's face bob up above the fence at that precise instant and promptly vanish, only to pop up again and immediately be replaced by another, and from the other side of the fence you would hear the sounds of the girls squealing and giggling on their swings.

In the Pshenitsyn house quiet reigned. As you entered the little court-yard you would be greeted by a perfectly idyllic scene; chickens would be milling around and rushing to hide in the corners; the dog would start jumping and pulling on his chain and barking frantically; Akulina would stop milking the cow and the gatekeeper would pause from his wood-chopping as they both regarded the newcomer with curiosity.

"Who do you want?" the gatekeeper would ask and, hearing the name, Ilya Ilyich, or the landlady's name would point silently at the porch and resume his wood-chopping. The visitor would then proceed along the clean, sandy path to the porch, up the steps covered with a strip of plain carpet, and tug at the handle of the brightly polished bell, and the door would be opened by Anisya, the children, sometimes by the landlady herself or even, exceptionally, by Zakhar.

Throughout there reigned an atmosphere of abundance and plenty that the house had not known even in the days when Agafya Matveyevna had shared the house with her brother.

The kitchen, the larders, the pantry, all contained sideboards equipped with a full range of crockery, dishes of every description, large and small, round and oval, sauce boats, plates by the dozen and pots of iron, copper and earthenware. There were cupboards full of silverware, the landlady's, purchased long ago and no longer used for pawning, as well as what Oblomov had brought with him. There were rows and rows of huge, big-bellied teapots side by side with miniatures and also several rows of china cups, plain, hand-painted and gilded, some decorated with mottoes, flaming hearts or Chinese figures. There were big glass jars of coffee, cinnamon, vanilla, cut-glass tea-caddies and cruets for oil and vinegar.

Then there was shelf after shelf loaded with packages, vials and boxes of domestic remedies, herbs, lotions, plasters, smelling salts, camphor, powders and fumigants. There were soaps and powders for cleaning lace, removing stains and what have you; everything, in a word, that you would expect to find in the home of any house-proud provincial housewife.

Whenever Agafya Matveyevna came to open the door of the cupboard crammed with all these articles, the smell of this heady mixture of drugs and herbs was so overpowering that at first she had to turn her head away for a minute.

To keep them out of the way of the mice, the ceiling of the pantry was hung with ham hocks as well as cheeses, loaves of sugar, dried fish, sacks of dried mushrooms, and walnuts bought from the Finnish peddler. On the floor stood tubs of butter, big covered pots of sour cream, baskets of eggs and—you name it! You would have to be a second Homer to be able to describe fully and in detail all that was stored in every corner and on every shelf of that temple of domesticity.

The kitchen was a virtual shrine to the presiding Goddess and her high priestess, Anisya. Everything you could possibly need was in the house, within easy reach and in its proper place. You could have said that the whole house was a triumph of cleanliness and order, if it had not been for one single spot that never saw the light of day, which never felt a breath of fresh air, on which the eye of the mistress of the house never fell and which had never known the benefit of the busy, all-cleansing hand of Anisya. This was Zakhar's den.

The eternal darkness of his windowless cubbyhole completed the transformation of a human habitation into a burrow. Whenever Zakhar caught the mistress of the house showing any sign of entertaining cleaning or tidying plans, he would firmly declare that it was not a woman's business to decide where his brushes, polish and boots belonged and it was absolutely no business of anyone's why his clothes lay in a heap on the floor and his bedding was stowed in a corner behind the stove in the dust, and that *he* was the one who wore the clothes and slept in the bedding and not her. And as for the broom, the planks, the two bricks, the barrel bottom, and the two logs that he kept in his room, well, they were essential items of equipment for his work—although he never explained why. As for the dust and the spiders, well, they never got in his way and, in any case, he never poked his nose into what they did in the kitchen so he didn't want them interfering with him.

Once he caught Anisya in there and gave her a look of such withering contempt and threatened her chest so convincingly with his elbow that she was too frightened to put her head in the place ever again. When the matter was referred to higher authority, to the judgment and discretion of Ilya Ilyich, the master went to see for himself with the intention of issuing a ruling which would impose some discipline, but the sight that met his eyes when he poked his head for a moment through the doorway reduced him to silence and his only reaction was to spit in disgust.

"So, did you get your way?" Zakhar asked Agafya Matveyevna and Anisya who had accompanied Ilya Ilyich in the hope that his intervention would lead to some change. He then gave them his special brand of grin, so broad that it stretched his eyebrows and side-whiskers far apart in opposite directions.

All the rooms were light, clean and airy. The old faded curtains had gone and the doors and windows of the living room and study were covered with blue and green drapery and muslin curtains with red ruffles—all hand made by Agafya Matveyevna. The cushions were white as snow and piled high almost to the ceiling, and the blankets were quilted and of silk. For weeks at a time the landlady's room would be crammed with rows of folding card tables where the blankets and Ilya Ilyich's dressing gown were spread out to dry.

Agafya Matveyevna herself did the work of cutting, stuffing and quilting them, leaning over them with her swelling bosom, and bringing them up close to her eyes and even her mouth when she needed to bite off a thread. She toiled lovingly and with tireless dedication with only the modest gratification of the thought that the dressing gown and the blankets would be wrapping, pampering, warming and comforting the exalted person of Ilya Ilyich.

He spent days on end lying on his divan, doing nothing but admire the way her bare elbows moved to and fro as she plied her needle and thread. It was not unknown for him to drop off to the gentle rustle of the thread and the click as it was bitten off - just the way it had been in Oblomovka.

"That's enough work—it's time to stop!" he would say in an attempt to slow her down, but she would reply: "God loves to see us work!" and keep her eyes down and her hands moving.

His coffee was prepared and served with the same painstaking care and was as pure and aromatic as it had been when he had first moved into the apartment several years before. Giblet soup, macaroni parmesan, meat and vegetable pie, fish soup, homebred chicken were all served in strict rotation, providing welcome relief from the sameness of the days in that small household.

The sun's gladdening rays shone through the windows of the house from dawn to dusk, half the day on one side and half the day on the other. Their path was totally unobstructed, thanks to the vegetable gardens on both sides of the house. The canaries chirped merrily in the small room, and geraniums and sometimes hyacinths brought by the children from the count's garden gave off their powerful scent, which combined pleasantly with the aroma of the fine Havana cigar and the hint of vanilla or cinnamon being ground so energetically by the mistress of the house with her busy elbows.

Ilya Ilyich lived his life within a kind of golden frame in which, like a magic lantern show, the only variations were the times of day and the seasons of the year. Apart from that there were no other changes, no major upheavals of the kind that turn life upside down and bring trouble and distress in their train.

Since the time that Stoltz had rescued Oblomov from the thieving clutches of the brother, both he and Tarantyev had totally disappeared from the scene and their disappearance had removed the last threat to Ilya Ilyich's tranquility and peace of mind. He was now surrounded exclusively by a circle of good-hearted, simple, loving people, unanimous in devoting their existence to supporting his and insulating him against noticing or feeling anything.

Agafya Matveyevna was in her prime; she lived and felt that the life she was living was a full one, fuller than ever before, but she was no more able now than she had ever been to give expression to such a thought, or rather even to entertain it. She prayed to God only to grant Ilya Ilyich a long life and to spare him any kind of sorrow, anger or need and pledged herself, her children and her whole household to do God's will. For all that, her face shone perpetually with an unvarying happiness, a happiness that was total, fulfilled and complete, a happiness, therefore, of a rare kind, a happiness impossible for those of a different temperament.

She had filled out, her shoulders and bosom gave off a rare glow of contentment, her eyes sparkled gently, untroubled by any but purely domestic concerns. She had recovered that old, tranquil dignity with which she had previously ruled the household with Anisya, Akulina and the gatekeeper as her subjects. When she moved now, she did not so much walk as glide in her old way, from the cupboard to the kitchen, from the kitchen to the storeroom and issued her orders with the serene self-possession of someone fully in command of the situation.

Anisya was now more active than ever because there was more to do; she was constantly on the go, bustling, running to and fro, putting her hand to any task at the bidding of the mistress of the house. Her eyes sparkled more brightly than ever and that eloquent organ, her nose, which jutted out so prominently ahead of the rest of her, that nose which glowed like a beacon which illuminated her actions, thoughts and intentions, and heralded them to the world, without her having even to open her mouth.

They both dressed in a fashion appropriate to their rank and station in life. The mistress of the house had acquired a wardrobe of silk dresses, shawls and coats. Her lace caps were ordered in the city from shops not too far from Liteiny Prospekt itself and her shoes were not from Apraksin but from Gostinny Dvor and she possessed a hat that actually came from Morskaya, no less! Anisya too, after she had finished her kitchen chores, and especially on Sundays, would put on a woolen dress.

Only Akulina went about with her skirts tucked up under her belt and the gatekeeper could not part with his sheepskin jacket even at the height of summer.

As for Zakhar, well, what can one say? He had made himself a kind of jacket out of that old tailcoat, and it would be hard to say exactly what color were his trousers or what his tie was made of. He would polish the boots, sleep, sit by the gate, staring vacantly at the few passers-by or would end up sitting in the nearby corner shop, doing essentially exactly what he had always done back in Oblomovka and later in Gorokhovaya Street.

And what about Oblomov himself? Oblomov himself was now the very embodiment, the true and perfect personification of peace, quiet, contentment and tranquility. As he examined and contemplated his existence, as he settled ever deeper into it, he had finally concluded that he had nowhere further to go, nothing further to seek, that he had achieved his ideal, although without the poetry, without the grace and distinction with which his imagination had sometimes invested it when he used to dream of a seigneurial, spacious style of life on his ancestral country estate amidst his peasants and retainers. He regarded the present course of his existence as an extension of that same Oblomovka style of life, only in a different setting and a somewhat different time frame. Here too, as in Oblomovka, he was able to extract a good bargain from life, distance himself from it and cheaply insure himself against the slightest impediment to his tranquility.

He was inwardly triumphant at having so successfully retreated from life's vexations, demands and dangers, at having put as much distance as possible between himself and that horizon, which flashed with the lightning of great joys and resounded with the thunder of great sorrows, where the sky is streaked with false hopes and the alluring mirage of great happiness beckons, where a man's own imagination gnaws and consumes him and kills passion, where his mind knows victory and defeat by turns, where he is constantly embattled and retires from the field bruised and battered and as frustrated and unfulfilled as ever. Oblomov, never having tasted the delights of battle, had mentally renounced them and could experience peace of mind only in some bolthole well away from the firing line, from the threat of activity and from life itself.

There were times when his imagination was over-active and long buried memories and unfulfilled dreams would surface, when his conscience would be pricked by feelings of remorse for the life he had chosen to lead and the other possible lives he had rejected. At those times he had trouble sleeping; he would wake up, jump out of bed, and sometimes find himself shedding cold tears of helpless regret for that once bright ideal of life, now extinguished beyond hope of rekindling, just as people mourn the death of a loved one with the bitter awareness of having failed him during his lifetime.

But then he would look at the world around him, savoring whatever pleasures came his way, and take comfort in contemplating the evening sun as it sank slowly and quietly in a fiery blaze and concluded that his life had not just happened to take a certain course, but had actually been created, indeed predestined, solely and simply to realize the ultimate potential for tranquility in human existence.

It was the lot of others, he thought, to express the turbulent side of life and to realize the human potential for creation and destruction; each man had his own destiny. It was this philosophy developed by our latter day Plato, Oblomov, which consoled and comforted him amidst the questions and rigorous demands of duty and destiny. He was not born and raised to fight like a gladiator in the arena but rather to be a passive spectator at the fight; it was not *his* timorous and sluggish soul that was meant to stand up to the turbulence of happiness or life's adversities. Consequently he exemplified one of life's extremes and there was no point in striving to change or to regret anything in his life.

With the passing years, occasions for strong emotion or regret became rarer and rarer, and he settled quietly and gradually into the simple, capacious tomb of his remaining existence, a tomb fashioned with his own hands, in the same way that a hermit who has taken refuge from life in the wilderness digs his own grave. He had by now given up all thought of organizing his estate or traveling there with his whole household. The manager appointed by Stoltz faithfully and regularly sent him a tidy sum every Christmas, the peasants brought him grain and poultry and his household flourished in plenty and high spirits.

Ilya Ilyich even kept a pair of horses but, with his characteristic caution saw to it that they were the kind that would only begin to move away from the porch after the third crack of the whip, while at the first crack one of the horses would stagger a little and move sideways and at the second the other horse would follow suit, and only then, with neck, back and tail tensed in protest, would they move off together and break into a trot with their heads wagging. They took Vanya across the Neva to his high school on the city side and Agafya Matveyevna to the shops.

At Shrovetide and Holy Week Ilya Ilyich and the whole family would go out for a ride or to the fair and, as a rare treat, he would take a box at the theatre—again, for the whole family.

In the summer they would go out into the country and on St. Ilya's Friday go on an outing to the Gunpowder Factory and life was marked by the usual recurrent events but, one might have said, without any devastating upheavals were it not for the fact that life's adversities do not spare even the smallest and most tranquil backwaters. The fact is, unfortunately, that the thunderbolt that rocks the very mountains and vast expanses of territory to their foundations, causes ripples that, although feeble and insignificant, still make themselves felt even in the tiniest mouse-hole.

Ilya Ilyich's appetite was just as keen as ever and he consumed just as much food as he had in Oblomovka, while exerting himself and exercising just as little. In spite of his advancing years he continued to drink wine and currant vodka in immoderate amounts and slept even more immoderately and longer after dinner.

Suddenly all this changed. Once, after a day spent drowsing, he was unable to get up from the divan when he tried, and when he tried to speak the words would not come. All he could do in his panic was to wave his hand in order to summon help. If it had been left to Zakhar alone he could have spent all night waving for help, and would have been dead by the time he was found the next day, but he was saved by the ever watchful and providential eye of the landlady, whose heart alone told her that something was wrong with Ilya Ilyich without needing the evidence of her senses. Relying only on the prompting of her heart, she sent Anisya off with the driver to fetch the doctor as fast as she could while she herself applied ice to his head and emptied her private medicine cabinet of all the remedies and nostrums that tradition and folklore had taught her to use in such cases. Even Zakhar had managed to put on one boot by this time and with one foot bare rushed to join the doctor, the landlady and Anisya who were attending to his master.

They brought Ilya Ilyich around, bled him and announced that he had suffered an apoplectic stroke and that henceforth he would have to change his habits. He was forbidden beer, wine and coffee except on the rarest of occasions, as well as all fat, meat products and spices. Instead, daily exercise was prescribed and he was ordered to confine his sleeping to the night hours.

Without the watchful eye of Agafya Mateveyevna none of this would have been possible, but she established a system whereby she controlled everything that went on in the house and, by a combination of cunning and cajolery, weaned Oblomov from the temptations of wine, post-prandial siestas and rich pies. The moment he began to doze off, if it was not one of his chairs falling over just like that, by itself, or an old discarded piece of crockery clattering to the floor and smashing in the next room, it would be the children raising such a din that you would have to rush out of the room. If that did not work, it would be the sound of Agafya Matveyevna's innocent voice calling him or asking him something.

The garden path was extended into the vegetable plot and Ilya Ilyich would walk there for two hours every morning and evening accompanied by Agafya Matveyevna, and if she was not available it would be Masha or Vanya or his old friend, the silent, docile and ever compliant Alekseyev.

Once Ilya Ilyich was walking slowly along the path, leaning on Vanya's shoulder for support. Vanya, in his high school tunic, was now almost a young man, barely able to restrain his natural, exuberant pace in order to keep in step with Ilya Ilyich, who now walked with a slight limp in one leg as a result of the stroke.

"Vanyusha, how about going back to my room!" he said, and just as they were about to enter the house Agafya Matveyevna met them.

"Back so soon?" she said, barring their way.

"What do you mean 'soon'? We've been back and forth twenty times and it's fifty sazhens* from here to the fence, that makes two versts!"

"How many times was it?" she asked Vanyusha. He did not want to say.

"Look at me and tell me the truth!" she said threateningly, looking him straight in the eye, "I'll know right away if you're lying! Otherwise there'll be no going to see your friends on Sunday, remember!"

"No, mommy, really, it was...twelve times."

"Hey, that's not playing fair!" Oblomov protested. "You were too busy picking leaves off the acacia to notice—I was doing the counting..."

"No, you'll have to do a few more turns—and anyway, I haven't finished making the soup yet!" She delivered her verdict and slammed the door on them. So Oblomov was forced to count off eight more turns before he could finally go back to his room where the soup was already steaming on the big round table. Oblomov took his seat alone on the divan; next to him on a chair to his right sat Agafya Matveyevna and on his left in a child's high chair sat a three-year-old child. Next to this child sat Masha who was now thirteen and next to her, Vanya. On this particular day they were joined by Alekseyev who sat opposite Oblomov.

"Wait a second, give me your plate and let me serve you some of the fish—it's a nice fat one today!" she said, putting some on Oblomov's plate.

"A piece of pie would go nicely with this," said Oblomov.

"I forgot, I clean forgot; I was going to make one yesterday but it simply slipped my mind," said Agafya Matveyevna with every appearance of sincerity and I forgot to make cabbage and rissoles for you too, Ivan Alekseyevich," she added, turning to Alekseyev, in order to make the pretence more convincing, "you'll have to forgive me!"

"It doesn't matter, I can eat anything," said Alekseyev.

"But really, what's the idea of not giving him the dishes he likes, ham with peas or steak?" asked Oblomov.

*a sazhen is equal to seven feet

"I went to look myself, Ilya Ilyich, but there wasn't any decent beef; but I've made some cherry jelly for you, I know how much you like it," she said to Alekseyev.

Of course, jelly was safe for Ilya Ilyich and that was the reason why the ever-compliant Alekseyev was obliged to like it and eat it.

After dinner there was nothing and no one that could prevent Oblomov from lying down. Usually he would lie down on his back right where he was sitting but was never allowed more than an hour. To prevent him from sleeping, Agafya Matveyevna would serve coffee right there on the divan and the children would be playing on the carpet right next to it and Ilya Ilyich had no choice but to join in.

"Stop teasing Andryusha now, otherwise you'll make him cry!" he would scold Vanyechka.

"Mashenka, watch out, Andryusha's going to hurt himself against the chair!" he would caution her anxiously when Andryusha crawled under the chair. And Masha would quickly grab her "little brother" as she called him.

The noise died down for a moment and Agafya Matveyevna went into the kitchen to see if the coffee was ready. The children had quieted down. Softly at first, as if muted, the sound of snoring could be heard, gradually growing louder, and when Agafya Matveyevna returned with the steaming coffee pot, her ears were assailed by snoring of a volume only to be heard in a cabmen's roadside shelter. She shook her head reproachfully at Alekseyev.

"I tried to wake Ilya Ilyich but he just wouldn't listen!" he said in his defense.

She quickly put the coffee pot down on the table, snatched up Andryusha from the floor and deposited him on the divan right next to Ilya Ilyich. The child crawled over him and grabbed him by the nose.

"Hey! What is it? Who's this?" said Ilya Ilyich, alarmed at being so rudely awakened.

"You dropped off, and Andryusha climbed on you and woke you up," Agafya Matveyevna explained gently.

"What do you mean 'dropped off', when ?" said Oblomov, attempting to deny the charge and embracing Andryusha, "you think I didn't hear him pulling himself up to me with his little hands. I hear everything! You little rascal, pulling my nose! You'll be sorry! Now, let go!" he said caressing him affectionately. Then he put him down on the floor and his sigh filled the room.

"So, what do you have to tell us, Ivan Alekseyich?' he said.

"Nothing, Ilya Ilyich, I've already told you everything," he replied.

"What do you mean nothing? I mean, you go out and about, you must have some news, I'm sure you must read things?"

"Well, I do sometimes, or other people do and talk about it and I listen. Just yesterday at Aleksei Spiridonovich's, his son, a student, was reading aloud..."

"What was he reading?"

"About the British, they've been sending rifles and powder to someone or other. Aleksei Spiridonovich said there's going to be a war."

"Who did they send them to?"

"To Spain or India or somewhere, I don't remember exactly, only that the ambassador was furious."

"Which ambassador?"

"I seem to have forgotten," Alekseyev said, pointing his nose at the ceiling in an effort to recall.

"Who is the war against?"

"The Turkish Pasha, I think."

"So, what else is happening in politics?" Ilya Ilyich asked after a few moments' silence.

"Well, it's been reported that the earth is cooling down and is going to be totally frozen eventually."

"Come on, you don't call that politics, do you?" said Oblomov.

This left Alekseyev momentarily tongue-tied. "Dmitry Alekseyich started off mentioning politics," he said in his own defense, "and then he kept reading out one thing after another without saying when the politics was finished; and then the next thing I knew he was onto literature."

"So what did he read out about literature?" asked Oblomov.

"Well, he read out that the best writers were Dmitriev, Karamzin, Batyushkov and Zhukovsky..."

"What about Pushkin?"

"He didn't mention Pushkin—I was thinking myself 'why not Pushkin?', I mean he's a khenius," he said, mispronouncing the word with a 'kh'.

A silence followed. Agafya Matveyevna brought in her sewing and started plying her needle back and forth, glancing up at Ilya Ilyich and Alekseyev from time to time and at the same time keeping an ear out for any tell-tale sounds of trouble from the kitchen, such as Zakhar bawling out Anisya, or to check whether Akulina was washing the dishes or whether the gate in the fence was creaking—which would have told her that the gatekeeper was sneaking out for a visit to certain premises.

Oblomov meanwhile had sunk into a silent reverie, somewhere between sleeping and waking, just letting his thoughts wander at will, without focusing on anything in particular and listening calmly to the steady beat of his heart. Every now and then he blinked, his eyes as unfocused as his thoughts. He had lapsed into a mysterious, hallucinatory, trance-like state.

In a lifetime there will be rare and brief moments when people feel they are re-living actual past experiences. This feeling of *déja vu* is of an actual or dreamed experience, but whatever it is, this feeling is seen very clearly and vividly. You see exactly the same faces seated around you, you hear exactly the same words uttered now as then; but somehow the imagination is powerless to take you back, the memory cannot reconstitute the past and you are left just with the feeling of *déja vu*.

This is what was happening to Oblomov at that moment. he was enveloped in a quiet he had previously experienced somewhere and sometime in the past. There was the same swinging pendulum of a grandfather clock, the click of teeth biting off thread, the sound of familiar voices whispering familiar words and phrases: "I can't seem to thread this needle, come and help me Masha, you have young eyes!"

As he looked lazily, dreamily and mechanically at the landlady's face, there welled up from the distant past the memory of a long forgotten but familiar image and he struggled to recall where and when he had experienced it all.

He could see the big drawing room in his parents' home lit with a tallow candle, his dear departed mother seated at the round table with her guests. All the ladies were sewing silently; his father was silently pacing the room. The present merged and intertwined with the past.

In his imagination he had reached that Promised Land where the rivers run with milk and honey, where people eat manna from heaven and are clothed in gold and silver.

He could hear the old stories of dreams and omens, the tinkling of plates and the clinking of knives, he was snuggling up to his nanny, drinking in that brittle, elderly voice uttering the words "Militrisa Kirbitievna"—but the face she was pointing at was that of Agafya Matveyevna.

He seems to see the same little cloud scudding across the blue sky and the same breeze as then blowing through the open window and riffling his hair; he sees the Oblomovs' turkey cock strutting and gobbling under the window.

Outside a dog started barking; a visitor must have arrived. Could it be Andrei and his father from Verkhlyovo? A real red-letter day! Yes, it must be him; the footsteps drew nearer and nearer, the door opens— "It's Andrei!" he says. Sure enough, there is Andrei standing in front of him, but Andrei, the grown man, not Andrei, the boy

Oblomov was suddenly fully awake, it was the real Stoltz in the flesh, standing right there, large as life and not a figment of his imagination. The landlady swiftly snatched up the child, scooped her needlework from the table and took the children out of the room. Alekseyev too disappeared. Stoltz and Oblomov remained alone, looking at each other, silent and motionless. Stoltz's gaze was nonetheless penetrating.

"Is it really you, Andrei?" Oblomov asked, his voice reduced to a whisper by his excitement, the whisper of a lover seeing his loved one after a long separation.

"Yes, it's me," said Andrei quietly, "are you alive and well?"

Oblomov embraced him, hugging him tightly. He answered with a long drawn out "Ah!", an "ah!" into which he poured all the pent up joy and sadness that had been stored up for so long within him, joy and sadness which he had perhaps been totally unable to express to anyone in any circumstances since he had last seen his friend.

They sat down and went on staring at each other.

"Are you well?" asked Andrei.

"Now, thank God!"

"You've been ill?"

"Yes, Andrei, it was a stroke..."

"I can't believe it; my God!" said Stoltz, alarmed and concerned, "but no after effects?"

"No, except for a little trouble with my left leg," Oblomov replied.

"Ilya, Ilya! What's happened to you? You've let yourself go completely! What have you been doing all this time. I can hardly believe it's really been five years since we've seen each other."

Oblomov sighed.

"Why haven't you been to Oblomovka? Why haven't you written?"

"What can I say, Andrei? You know me, there's no point in going on asking." Oblomov replied despondently.

"And all your things are here in this apartment?" Stoltz asked, looking around the room, "and you never left?"

"Yes, it's all here... I'll never leave now."

"Never? You really mean it?"

"Yes, Andrei, I really do."

Stoltz regarded him closely and started pacing the room, deep in thought.

"And Olga Sergeyevna, is she well? Where is she? Does she remember...?" he left the question unfinished.

"She's well and she remembers you as if it were only yesterday. I'll tell you where she is in a moment."

"And the children?"

"They're fine, but tell me the truth, Ilya, are you serious about staying here? I came specially to fetch you, to take you back with me to our place in the country..."

"No, no!" said Oblomov, lowering his voice and looking at the door with obvious anxiety, "please stop talking like that, please don't go on!"

"Why not? What's the matter with you?" Stoltz began. "You know me, I made up my mind to do this long ago and I intend to do it. Up to now I've been too busy with other things, but now I have the time. You must come and live with us, nearby; Olga and I have both made up our minds and that's the way it's going to be. Thank God I've caught you before you were in even worse shape than you are now. I didn't expect...Anyway, let's go! I'm ready to use force if necessary! You can't go on living like this, you must see..."

Oblomov was listening to this tirade with impatience. "Keep your voice down please, not so loud," he implored, "in there..."

"What's in there?"

"We can be heard, I don't want her to think I really intend to leave…"

"So what, let her think what she wants!"

"No, you don't understand!" Oblomov interrupted him. "Listen, Andrei!" he added in an unusually decisive tone. "You're just wasting your time trying to get me to leave, I'm staying here!"

Stoltz regarded his friend with astonishment. Oblomov looked back at him, calm and determined. "You're finished, Ilya!" he said, "this house, this woman… the life you're leading… I won't allow it; we're going!" He grabbed Oblomov by the sleeve and started pulling him towards the door.

"Why are you trying to take me away, where to?" he said, resisting.

"Away from this hole, this bog, into the wide world of a wholesome, normal existence!" Stoltz admonished him sternly in a tone that brooked no opposition. "Look where you are, look what you've become, come to your senses. Is this what you've spent your life preparing for, to hibernate like a mole in a burrow? Think back…"

"Don't remind me, don't dredge up the past—you can't bring it back!" said Oblomov, his expression reflecting total awareness of what he was saying and total commitment to it. "What do you expect to do with me in that world you want to drag me into? I'm irretrievably broken! There's no way you can put the pieces back together again or re-attach the two separate halves of me. I'm grafted to this pit, this hole by my vital parts and if you try to detach me, I'll bleed to death."

"But just look where you are and who you're with!"

"I know—and I feel it… my God, Andrei, don't you think I feel it all, understand everything? Why do you think I've been ashamed to show my face in the outside world for so long? Even if I wanted to, I couldn't go and live with you and live your kind of life. Maybe it would still have been possible last time, but now," he lowered his eyes and stopped talking for a moment, "now, it's too late. Just leave and stop wasting your time on me. I'm worthy of your friendship—God knows that—but I'm not worth your trouble."

"No, Ilya, you're talking, but you're not making complete sense. I'm going to take you with me anyway precisely because of what I suspect. Listen," he said, "put on your coat and we'll go to my place and spend the evening—I've so much to tell you. Don't you know what's been happening, haven't you heard?"

Oblomov looked at him inquiringly.

"I forgot, you don't see anyone; come with me and I'll tell you everything. You know who's waiting for me at the gate in the carriage—I'll call her in!"

"Olga!" Oblomov blurted in a panic, his face turning white. "For God's sake, don't bring her in here, please go, just leave, for the love of God!" He was practically pushing him out of the door, but Stoltz stood his ground.

"I cannot go to her without you, I gave my word, you understand, Ilya? It's no good trying to get rid of me—if not today I'll be back tomorrow, or if not tomorrow, the next day; sooner or later we'll meet again!"

Oblomov was silent, his head bowed, not daring to look at Stoltz.

"So…when? Olga is going to ask me."

"Andrei Andrei," he appealed to him in a gentle, imploring tone, embracing him and laying his head on his shoulder, "please, just give up, forget about me completely!"

"You mean, for good?" Stoltz released himself from his embrace and stood looking at him with astonishment.

"Yes," whispered Oblomov.

Stoltz took a step backward. "I can't believe it!" he said reproachfully, "you rejecting me—and for that woman! My God!" His voice had risen almost to a shout as if he had felt a sudden, sharp pain. "That child I just saw…Ilya, Ilya, get out of here, come with me now! What's become of you? How low you've sunk! That woman, what is she to you?"

"My wife," Oblomov said quietly.

Stoltz was dumbfounded.

"And that child is my son, his name is Andrei, in memory of you," Oblomov added and sighed with relief at finally having unburdened himself.

At this Stoltz turned pale and his eyes rolled helplessly in total dismay. It was as if that "chasm" was yawning before him, as if that "stone wall" had risen, hiding Oblomov from view, as if he had been swallowed up and had vanished from his sight, and he felt only the poignant anguish of someone who has rushed with eager anticipation to see a dear friend again after a long separation only to find that he had died long ago.

"Dead!" he whispered, without thinking. "What will I tell Olga?"

Oblomov caught these last words and tried to say something but the words would not come. He stretched out both hands to Andrei and they embraced silently and tightly the way comrades in arms do before battle, facing death. Words, tears, feelings were all smothered in that embrace…

"Don't forget my Andrei!" were Oblomov's last words, spoken in a failing voice.

Andrei turned and left slowly and silently, crossed the courtyard lost in his thoughts and climbed into the carriage.

Oblomov sat down on the divan and rested his elbows on the table, burying his face in his hands.

"No, I won't forget your Andrei," Stoltz thought sadly to himself as he crossed the courtyard, "you're dead and gone, Ilya; no point in telling you that your Oblomovka is now on the map, that it has now found a place in the sun. I won't be telling you that within four years the train will be stopping at Oblomovka's own station, that your peasants will be working on building the embankment, and then your grain will be hauled to the river port by rail… that there are now schools, education and soon…

No, the glare of the bright new future would only hurt your tender, unprotected eyes and frighten you. But I will take your Andrei where you could not go and it will be with him that I will live our youthful dreams. Goodbye to the old Oblomovka!" he said, taking one last look at the windows of the little house, "you've outlived your time!"

"What happened?" Olga asked, her heart beating faster.

"Nothing!" replied Andrei curtly.

"Is he alive and well?"

"Yes," Andrei responded grudgingly.

"How come you came back so quickly? Why didn't you call me in or bring him out to see me? Let me go in!"

"No!"

"But what's going on in there?" Olga asked in alarm. "Did that chasm open up? Are you going to tell me?"

He gave no reply.

"But what is it that's happening in there?"

"*Oblomovshchina!*" Andrei replied disconsolately and remained deaf to all further inquiries on Olga's part, preserving a gloomy silence for the whole journey home.

CHAPTER TEN

Five years went by. There were many changes on the Vyborg side: the empty street leading to Pshenitsyna's house was now lined with newly built dachas dominated by a long, tall, stone public building that blocked out the sun whose rays once played on the windows of that peaceful refuge of ease and tranquility.

The house was now looking somewhat run-down, neglected and shabby, like a man who needed a wash and a shave. The paint was peeling, the drainpipes leaked, leaving the ground covered with muddy puddles over which the same old narrow plank had been thrown. Whenever anyone entered by the gate in the fence the old dog no longer leapt about excitedly on its chain, but just emitted a hoarse and feeble bark without even bothering to leave its kennel.

And inside the house, what changes! An entirely different woman now ruled the roost and it was a different set of children romping. From time to time, the red, blotchy face of the boisterous Tarantyev would still make an appearance, but there was no longer any sign of the self-effacing inarticulate Alekseyev—nor for that matter, of Zakhar or Anisya. A stout new cook held sway in the kitchen, carrying out Agafya Matveyevna's quiet orders in a grudging, rough and ready manner. Akulina was still there with her skirts tucked up under her belt, still scrubbing the tubs and pots. The same dozy gatekeeper in the same old sheepskin coat was idly living out his days in his old hovel.

Early in the morning at the appointed time and again at dinner time, the figure of the brother could once again be seen flashing by through the slats in the fence with a big parcel under his arm, wearing the same galoshes summer and winter.

But what has become of Oblomov? Where is he now? Where indeed? His body lies in an obscure grave marked by a modest burial urn in the local cemetery. Sprigs of lilac placed there by a friendly hand lie dozing on the grave that gives off the gentle aroma of wormwood. It is as if the angel of tranquility is standing guard over his eternal rest.

For all the vigilance with which the loving eye of his wife watched over him every moment of his life, the eternal peace and everlasting quiet, the slow, uneventful passage from one day to the next eventually took their toll and brought the engine of his life to a gradual standstill. Ilya Ilyich's life ended seemingly without pain, without suffering, just like a clock winding down because no one had remembered to wind it up.

No one was there to witness his last moments or to hear his death rattle. Ilya Ilyich had suffered another stroke a year after the first one and had survived it, too, although he was left pale and weak. He ate little, rarely walked in the garden and grew ever more silent and withdrawn, at times even bursting into tears. He felt that death was near and it frightened him.

He was taken bad a few times but recovered on each occasion, but one morning Agafya Matveyevna took him his coffee as usual and found him stretched out as usual on his bed—only this time it was his death bed. The only difference was that his head had rolled slightly off his pillow and his hand had clutched convulsively at his heart where his blood must have clogged and stopped flowing.

Agafya Matveyevna had been widowed for three years and in that time things had returned to the way they had been before. The brother had gone into the contracting business but it had been a failure and, somehow or other by means of various ruses and through ingratiation, he had managed to get back his old job as a clerk in the government office where "peasants came to be registered." Once again he walked to his office and back, bringing home the same collection of small change which he stuffed into an old trunk hidden somewhere far away. The house was run on the same plain and simple lines as it had been before Oblomov's arrival, but with the same rich and plentiful fare.

The leading role in the household was now taken by Irina Panteleyevna, the brother's wife, which is to say that she reserved her right to get up late, drink coffee, and change her clothes three times a day and assumed responsibility for only one household task, namely seeing to it that her skirts were starched as stiffly as possible. She did not trouble herself about anything beyond that and Agafya Matveyevna remained the driving force in the house. She still presided over the kitchen and the table, supplied everyone with tea and coffee, did everyone's sewing and supervised the laundry, the children, Akulina and the gatekeeper.

Now why did she do all this? After all she was Madame Oblomova, a landowner's widow; she could have lived separately, independently, beholden to no one and lacking nothing. What could have persuaded her to take on the burden of running someone else's household, looking after someone else's children, and attending to all those details to which a woman commits herself either out of love, the sacred duty of family obligations or simply as a way of earning her daily crust of bread? And where were Zakhar and Anisya, whose services were owed to her by right? And where indeed was that living legacy left to her by her husband, the young Andryusha, and where were her children from her first marriage?

Her children were now leading their own lives; Vanyusha had now finished his studies and had gone into government service, Masha had married the superintendent of a government building and Andryusha had gone to live with Stoltz and his wife at their request, to be brought up as a member of their household. Agafya Matveyevna had never consciously placed Andryusha on the same level as the children of her first marriage or linked his destiny with theirs, although perhaps deep down they occupied an equal place in her heart. For her, Andryusha's upbringing, his manner of life and his future was a universe apart from that of Vanyusha and Mashenka. After all, they were nothing but urchins from the same stock as herself, she would say casually, the same humble origins; but this one, she would add, almost with a touch of deference, on the subject of Andryusha, as she caressed him, if not timidly at least with a certain reserve: "This one is a little gentleman! Look how white his complexion is, like the inside of a ripe apple, look at his tiny hands and feet, his hair like silk—the image of his father!"

It was therefore without protest, almost eagerly, that she agreed to Stoltz's proposal to take the boy and raise him as his own, believing as she did that that was his proper place, not in her own house among "the dregs of society," mixing with the likes of his cousins, the grubby offspring of the brother.

For six months after the death of Oblomov she continued to live in the house with Anisya and Zakhar, prostrate with grief. She wore a path to her husband's grave and cried her heart out, eating and drinking practically nothing except tea and often unable to get a wink of sleep at night; she was at the brink of exhaustion. She shared her pain with no one and it seemed that the further the loss of her husband receded into the past, the more she withdrew into herself and into her grief and locked herself away from those around her. No one knew what was in her heart.

"Your mistress is still crying over her husband," the stallholder in the market who supplied their groceries remarked to the cook.

"Still grieving for her husband," said the churchwarden, pointing her out to the woman who baked the communion bread in the cemetery church where the inconsolable widow went every week to pray and weep.

"She's still grief stricken!" they said in the brother's house.

One day the whole of the brother's family, children and all, accompanied by Tarantyev, descended on her in a body unannounced on the pretext of offering their sympathies. They lavished upon her their banal words of condolence and advice: "Don't punish yourself, you must save your strength for your children"—all the things that they had told her fifteen years before on the death of her first husband. At that time this had had the desired effect, but now she found it all somehow sickening and repugnant.

She found it much easier to take when they changed the subject and told her that now they could all live together again and that she would feel better "sharing her suffering with her nearest and dearest," and that they would benefit too because no one could keep house as efficiently as she could.

She asked them to let her think it over and grieved on for another couple of months before finally agreeing to their proposal. It was during this time that Stoltz had taken Andryusha to live with him and Olga, and she had been left alone.

So there she was in her dark dress with a black, woolen scarf around her neck, flitting from room to room like a shadow, still opening and closing cupboards, sewing, ironing lace, but listlessly, without energy, speaking rarely and in a low voice, and no longer casually inspecting everything around her with a sweeping glance, but with an intense expression and a look of deep inner significance in her eyes. It was a look that seemed to have settled imperceptibly on her face at the very moment she had looked so long and searchingly into the lifeless face of her husband, a look which had never left her since then.

She moved around the house, putting her hand to any task that needed doing, but her mind was elsewhere. The contemplation of her husband's corpse, the loss of him, seemed to have shocked her into introspection and for the first time she found herself taking stock of her life, and this inner preoccupation lay always like a shadow on her face.

Having wept away the keen edge of her grief, she focused on the awareness of her loss; nothing had any meaning for her any longer except little Andryusha. It was only when she saw him that signs of life seemed to stir within her, her face would light up, her eyes would radiate joy and brim with the tears brought on by memories of the past.

She was oblivious and indifferent to everything around her. When her brother blew up over a missed chance of gaining or saving a rouble, a burnt roast or fish that was not fresh, or when her sister-in-law made a fuss about some under-starched skirts or tea that she found weak and cold, or when the cook was insolent, Agafya Matveyevna simply did not notice, as if none of it had anything to do with her. She was even deaf to the whispered taunts of "her ladyship," or "aren't we high and mighty!" Her only response was the dignity of her grief and a submissive silence.

However, at Christmas, on Easter Sunday, during the merry-making at Shrovetide when everyone around her was celebrating, singing, eating and drinking, she would suddenly burst into tears in the midst of all the hilarity and go and hide in a corner. Then she would pull herself together and even watch her brother and his wife with something like pride and fellow feeling.

She understood that life had favored and smiled on her for a while, that God had put a light into her life and then snuffed it out, that the sun had shone within her for a time but now darkness had descended forever... Yes, forever—but at the same time it was forever that her life had been given meaning and she knew now why she had lived and that she had not lived in vain.

She had loved so completely and intensely; she had loved Oblomov as a lover and a husband and as someone of superior breeding, but there was no one else she could tell and there never had been. And no one around her would have understood in any case. What language could she have used? The lexicon of her brother, of Tarantyev, of her sister-in-law, did not contain such words because the very concepts were alien to them. Only Oblomov would have understood her but she had never tried to tell him, because even she herself did not understand at the time and was thus unable to.

As the years passed her understanding of her past became greater and clearer, and she kept it hidden deeper and deeper within herself and grew increasingly taciturn and intense. The rest of her life was infused with the lingering glow of those seven years that had passed in a flash, and there was nothing left for her to wish for, no further goal to attain.

It was only when Stoltz returned from the country to St. Petersburg for the winter that she would run to his house to feast her eyes on Andryusha and fondle him lovingly but with restraint. She would then be moved to say something to Andrei Ivanovich to thank him and indeed to unburden herself to him of everything that had been buried and yet lived on in her heart, but she could not bring herself to do it. All she could do was to rush to Olga and press her lips to her hands and dissolve in such a flood of burning tears that Olga too, in spite of herself, could not hold back her own tears. Andrei's emotions too were so stirred that he would have to leave the room in a hurry. They were all united by a single common bond—their memory of the pure, crystal clear soul of the departed. They urged her to come and live with them in the country to be near Andryusha but her answer was always the same: "Where you were born and lived out your days, that's where you should die."

No matter how hard Stoltz tried to account to her for the management of the estate or to send her the next installment of her income from it she would always send it back and tell him to save it for Andryusha. "It belongs to him, not me," she would stubbornly insist, "He'll need it, he was born a gentleman and I'll manage the way I am."

CHAPTER ELEVEN

One day around noon, two gentlemen were walking along the boardwalk on the Vyborg side; they were followed slowly by a carriage. One of them was Stoltz; his companion was a writer. He was stout, with an inexpressive face and thoughtful, seemingly sleepy eyes. They drew level with a church just as a service was ending and the congregation was spilling out onto the street and at the front of the crowd were a large and motley group of beggars.

"I'm curious about where all these beggars come from," said the literary gentleman as he regarded them.

"What do you mean 'where from?'? They crawl out of every nook and cranny..."

"No, that's not what I'm asking," the literary gentleman interjected. "What I want to know is how people become beggars, how they get into that situation. Does it happen gradually or suddenly? Is it genuine or are they putting on an act?"

"But why? Do you want to write a sequel to *Mystères de Paris* called *Mystères de Pétersbourg?*"

"Maybe..." said the literary gentleman, yawning lazily.

"Well, here's your chance, just ask any of these; for a silver rouble any of them will sell you his whole life story and all you have to do is to write it down and resell it at a profit. Look at that old man, your absolutely typical, common or garden beggar. Hey you, old man, come here!"

The old man turned around to see who was calling, took off his cap and went up to them. "God bless you, gentlemen!" he wheezed, "help out an old veteran down on his luck, wounded and crippled in thirty battles..."

"Zakhar!" exclaimed Stoltz in astonishment, "is it you?"

Zakhar suddenly stopped talking and shading his eyes from the sun with his hand, took a long look at Stoltz.

"I'm sorry, your Excellency, I don't recognize you...my eyes are so bad!"

"Have you forgotten your master's friend, Stoltz?" Stoltz reproached him.

"Oh my God! It's yourself, Andrei Ivanich! God, I must be going blind! Oh sir, you were always so good to me!" He was so agitated that he reached for Stoltz's hand but missed and kissed the hem of his garment instead. "Thank the Lord for letting this miserable cur live long enough to see this moment! What a pleasure it is!" he cried out, not knowing whether to laugh or cry.

His whole face had been burned crimson from forehead to chin and to cap it all his nose was tinged with blue. His head was completely bald, his side-whiskers were just as bushy as ever and in a crumpled, tangled mess like an old piece of matting—it looked as if he had a snowball sticking to each side of his face. He was wearing a tattered, discolored old overcoat which had one panel completely missing and on his feet were a pair of old, worn-down galoshes. In his hand he held an old, frayed, fur cap.

"Merciful Lord, what a miracle you've sent me today for the holiday...!"

"What on earth are you doing in this miserable state? What happened? Aren't you ashamed?" Stoltz questioned him sternly.

"Oh, Andrei Ivanich, sir! What can I do?" Zakhar began, sighing deeply. "I've nothing to live on! When Anisya was still alive, I didn't roam around like this—there was a crust of bread at least. But when she died of the cholera—God rest her soul!—the master's brother-in-law sent me packing, called me a parasite. And Mikhei Andreyich Tarantyev was always trying to kick me in the backside whenever I passed him— it was a dog's life! The insults I had to put up with. Believe me, sir, I couldn't even swallow a scrap of bread. If it hadn't been for the master's wife, God bless her!" Zakhar added, crossing himself, "I would've froze to death by now in the frost. She would give me something to wear for the winter, as much bread as I can eat and a bunk on the stove—all out of the goodness of her heart. She even got into trouble because of it and I just had to clear out with nowhere to go. It's been over a year now that I've been down and out like this..."

"Why didn't you find yourself another job?" Stoltz asked him.

"But where can you find another job these days, Andrei Ivanich, sir?" I went to two places, but I just didn't suit them. It's not the way it used to be; it's gotten worse. Servants have to be able to read and write these days. Even important gentlemen don't have, you know, like a hall full of servants. It's just one or two footmen at the most. They even take off their own boots—there's this new device!" Zakhar went on bitterly. "It's a disgrace, a crying shame; what's happened to the gentry—there's no standards any more?" He gave a sigh.

"I got this job with a merchant, a German, to sit in his hall and watch the door; it was going fine until he wanted me to serve in the dining room—well, that's not what I was trained for! So there I was carrying some crockery—Bohemian or something—and those floors are so smooth and slippery, God damn them! Suddenly my legs are sliding from under me and the whole thing—the tray and everything on it— crashes to the floor. Well, of course, they threw me out! Another time I went to work for an old countess, she took a liking to me. "You have the right look," she said, "and took me on as a doorman. A good job, like in the old days. You sit on the chair, trying to look dignified, one leg draped over the other, swinging a little, when someone comes you don't answer right away but growl a little and only then do you let them in— or throw them out on their necks as the case may be. With the right visitors, no problem, you give them a salute with the mace like this." Zakhar demonstrated, using his hand. "Not a bad job at all! But this mistress, there was just no pleasing her. Well anyway, she looked into my cubbyhole once and saw a bedbug; she stamped her foot and started screaming—anyone would think it was me who invented bedbugs! Whoever heard of a house without bedbugs? Another time she passed by and somehow got the idea that I smelled of vodka—can you believe it? Honestly! Anyway she kicked me out."

"But you really do reek of vodka, I can smell it from here!" said Stoltz.

"It's to drown my troubles, Andrei Ivanich, sir, honestly, that's the reason," Zakhar wheezed, his face wrinkling with distress. "I even tried driving a coach; I went to work for the owner. Froze my feet off, didn't have the strength—I'm too old. I had this vicious horse; once it ran into a carriage and almost crippled me. Another time I ran over an old woman—they took me to the police station…"

"Alright now, no more begging or getting drunk, you'll come to me and I'll find you a place to sleep and I'll take you to the country with us—you hear?"

"Yes, Andrei Ivanich…" He sighed. "But I really wouldn't like to leave, sir, here's where he's buried—you know, the master, Ilya Ilyich who was so good to us," he wailed. "God rest his soul! What a master the Lord took from us! He was the light of everyone's life—he should have lived a hundred years!" Zakhar pronounced hoarsely, his face crumpling.

"I was at his grave today; whenever I'm over the other side I visit it. I sit down and while I'm sitting there the tears are pouring down my cheeks; and sometimes it's so quiet that I get to thinking and I seem to hear him calling me: 'Zakhar, Zakhar!'; it sends shivers down my spine. A master in a million! And how he loved you, sir! May God rest his dear soul in heaven!"

"Well anyway, come to the house and take a look at Andryusha. I'll see that you're fed and clothed and then you do what you want," said Stoltz, giving him some money.

"Of course, I'll come—I wouldn't miss seeing Andrei Ilyich! He must have grown so big by now! Thank the Lord for letting me live to see him—what a joy it'll be! I'll come for sure, sir! May God grant you good health and long life…!" Zakhar growled as the carriage moved away.

"Well, did you hear that beggar's story?" Stoltz asked his companion.

"Who was that Ilya Ilyich he mentioned?" asked the writer.

"Oblomov, I've mentioned him to you many times."

"Yes, I seem to recall the name, he was your friend and schoolmate. What happened to him?"

"He died, just expired without leaving a trace—what a waste." Stoltz sighed and thought for a moment. "He was as intelligent as the next man—and with a heart as pure and clear as crystal; honorable and gentle. And now he's gone!"

"But why? What happened?"

"Why? What happened? Why, *oblomovshchina*!"

"*Oblomovshchina*!" the writer repeated in puzzlement. "What's that?"

"I'll tell you, but give me a moment to collect my thoughts and sort out my memories. And you write it down; who knows, it might be useful to someone sometime."

And the story he told was the one you have just read.

Translator's Note

Anyone venturesome enough to undertake the task of translating—and especially retranslating—a foreign language classic is confronted with a host of daunting policy decisions and judgment calls, any one of which may lay him open to "second guesses" from critics who would have made a choice that he did not. Part of the problem in the particular case of *Oblomov* is that its author wrote for a vastly more homogeneous and narrow readership than does a contemporary translator of his work—especially into English. Add to this the fact that the culture gap between his Russian readers in the 1860s and the English speaking readers of his work in translation, wide enough even at that time, has now been widened much further by the passage of time. Readers of *Oblomov* today are more than 150 years removed from the events and setting described by Goncharov.

The English into which a translator of the 1850s would have rendered the original has by now splintered into a score of different "Englishes" used in various parts of the world. Of these, the two major contenders are still the British and American versions.

Born, raised, and educated in Britain, but having made my career in the U.S., although I may not exactly bestride the Atlantic like a Colossus, I do have a foot on either side. This, like the two humps on a Bactrian camel, while supplying dual sources of nourishment for his stock of English, imposed on this translator an extra burden and responsibility, namely that of judging whether a given word, phrase or colloquialism would come across as too distinctively British for the American reader or, much less likely, too American for the British reader.

Once a version had been adopted, everything else, at least in the immediate vicinity, had to be consistent. At times, indeed, what were to me particularly felicitous solutions that were too identifiably American or British had to be sacrificed in favor of renderings which, while perhaps less striking, were less likely to raise eyebrows, "earbrows," or hackles on either side of the Atlantic.

One consideration which often tilted the balance in favor of U.S. usage is the fact that in the area of idiom and cultural exchange with the U.K., the U.S. is, by an overwhelming margin, a net exporter. As a result, British readers are far more familiar with and tolerant of American usage than vice versa.

With *Oblomov*, the problem hits you between the eyes in the very first paragraph; the translator has to decide whether Oblomov is lying down in his "apartment" or his "flat," thus setting an important precedent for subsequent choices. These familiar everyday divergences, usually involving nouns, are, of course, only the tip of the iceberg. Happily, Oblomov's dwelling was a "walk-up." This not only spared the translator the "lift/elevator" issue, but also undoubtedly reinforced its tenant's reluctance to leave it.

Dialogue, of course, poses different and more difficult problems of this kind. The further down the socio-educational scale one descends, the harder it is to strike a balance between keeping the language natural and colloquial and maintaining Anglo-American neutrality. Once you have mediated the competing claims of, for example,"guys," "fellows," "chaps," and "blokes," you have committed yourself to far-reaching problems of consistency.

Another important translation policy issue which had to be resolved is that of the "vintage" of the target language. There is a school of thought which believes that it should be of the same vintage as that of the original. In the case of *Oblomov*, published in the 1850s, the desirable English would have to be that of Charles Dickens or Mark Twain, with whom he was roughly contemporaneous. I believe that the case against this thesis is overwhelming. First and foremost is the author's intent.

Goncharov undoubtedly intended *Oblomov* to be read not only by those who shared his language and culture, but by his *contemporaries*. He certainly did not intend the language of his work to have the same archaic impact on his readers in the Russia of the 1850s that it must now have on Russian speaking readers of the early 21st century. Russian-speaking readers are themselves distanced from the original by the passage of time; if English-speaking readers, already distanced as they are from the original by the fact of translation, were confronted by an *Oblomov* translated into Dickensian English, an archaic vernacular no longer their own, they would be even further distanced by the gratuitous addition of this factor to the already formidable gulf of language and culture. No native English speaker of the present day is a native speaker, or writer, of Dickensian English.

Among the many judgment calls made by this translator was the decision, after much reflection, to render the original Russian обломовщина "oblomovshchina" as a transliteration, *oblomovshchina*, a clean break with hallowed tradition which clearly calls for some explanation.

This decision was arrived at by a process of elimination, backed by a solid body of precedent for the accommodation, and even adoption by English, of transliterations of words of foreign origin. Examples from Russian include; "droshky," "troika," "sputnik," "dacha," "izba," "samovar," and the hybrid "refusenik."

Traditionally, the Russian original has been translated as "Oblomovism" or "Oblomovitis." For whatever reason, neither of the other possibilities, "Oblomovhood" or "Oblomovness" seem to have been explored. "Oblomovness," although not very neat or slick, would, I believe, have been a closer approximation to the author's intent and would not have been open to the same objections as "Oblomovism" or "Oblomovitis." What are these objections?

First, one of the most frequent uses of the suffix "-ism" with proper names, as in the case of Marxism, Buddhism, and Darwinism, indicates adherence to a system of theory, belief, or practice, religious, political, philosophical, scientific, etc., founded or propounded by the individual to whose name the "-ism" is suffixed.

Second, in such cases as "Spoonerism" and "Malapropism" it is used to indicate a particular eccentricity or idiosyncrasy typified by the original bearer of the name. "Oblomov-ism" might come close to fitting this usage, were it not for one important difference; if "Oblomovism" means anything, it is not the single caricatured feature exemplified by Dr. Spooner or Mrs. Malaprop. If Oblomov had been depicted as this kind of one-dimensional caricature famous for nothing but lying down all day long, as indeed he has become for many outside Russia who know nothing about him except his name, "Oblomovism" might have "made the cut." However, *oblomovshchina* is, if anything, not just a single symptom, but a syndrome.

A third use embraces such clinically pathological conditions as Sadism, Masochism, and Daltonism. Thus, the use of "Oblomov-ism" to translate the Russian original would seem to be disqualified on all three counts.

The same applies to the suffix "-itis," which has a more clearly defined and narrower use. Classically, it has been used to form the names of diseases affecting different parts of the body. It is also sometimes used, by extension and often facetiously, to denote a state of mind or behavior akin to an obsession. An illustration of the difference comes easily to mind. Although the writer of these words might fairly be diagnosed as suffering from a bad case of Oblomovitis, no one who has actually completed a translation of *Oblomov* could possibly be charged with *oblomovshchina*. Thus, *oblomovshchina* as a rendering of its Russian original has the merit of not conveying inappropriate and misleading associations and overtones.

Oblomov contains numerous references to and descriptions of the feelings, emotions, attitudes, and moods of its characters. More often than not, these attributions and descriptions are voiced by the author himself. This area of language places the translator in a particularly acute dilemma, since it constitutes a special case of the generic conflict or tension between the "dated" language of the original and the "updated" language into which it should be cast in order to be faithful to the author's intent, while appearing perfectly natural to a contemporary readership.

Freud-derived and Freud-inspired words and concepts have trickled down via the psychoanalytical school into casual, everyday English and are used unselfconsciously by people with no thought of their ideological origins. Words such as "complex," "syndrome," "hang-up," and "inhibition," are now standard and spontaneous usage in English, and I felt it correct to use terms appropriate to our time and place to convey feelings and emotions expressed by the characters in Oblomov or attributed to them by its author, expressed in the terms appropriate to his time and place. For example, today in English we are very free with our use of the word "guilt" to describe our own feelings; in Goncharov's day, "guilt" was something that tended to be attributed to others by oneself or to oneself by others. The feeling no doubt existed, but was not described in that way. Thus, стыд "styd," literally "shame," appears at times and in context to be a feeling which we would more naturally describe as "guilt."

Other uses of such words, which the reader will find in context, include: "compulsion," "self-esteem," "repressed," "depressed," "psyche," "pressure," "impulse," "achievement," "agonize," "vegetate," "personality," "suppressed (feelings)," "frustrated," "sublimate," "fulfillment," and "self-conscious."

In comparison with almost all other European languages, English is the maverick or odd-man out when it comes to the second person pronoun. English alone makes do with the single word "you." Russian, with "ty" and "vy," like most of the other languages, makes use of a singular and a plural version. However, the uses to which these pronouns are put are by no means necessarily just grammatical. Russian also uses these two versions, "ty" (singular) and "vy"(plural), to convey distinctions of respect or deference due to superior status of age or rank. Broadly speaking "vy" is used when speaking to one's elders and betters and "ty" to one's juniors and inferiors. When two people of comparable station interact, the choice of "ty" or "vy" will often depend on the degree of familiarity.

This has a direct bearing on the problem of translating one of the most appealing comedic aspects of *Oblomov*, the master-servant exchanges between Oblomov and Zakhar.. Here the stumbling block of the British-American divide arises in a special way. There are two competing models for the dialogue between master and servant. On the one hand, there is the Britain of Dickens with its landed gentry and its servants—the "upstairs-downstairs" model—where the relations between the two classes, and hence the language of the exchanges between them, was clearly delineated, formal, and cold to the point of frigidity. On the other hand, there is the antebellum American plantation-owning gentry with their slaves.

The relations between slave and master in the U.S. and between serf and master in Russian in roughly the same part of the nineteenth century had much more in common with each other than either had with the British master-servant model of the same period. The former were marked by the same paradoxical mixture of familiarity, even intimacy, on the one hand, and brutality and even outright cruelty on the other.

The language of Zakhar's exchanges with his master could be impudent, even insolent to the very limits of insubordination, but it would have been unthinkable for him to have transgressed to the point of addressing him as "ty," or ever making him the subject of anything but a plural verb—another token of the proper deference to a superior. Equally unthinkable was the possibility of Oblomov ever addressing Zakhar as "Vy" or making him the subject of a verb in the plural. Thus, no matter how insubordinate the content, these lines were clearly drawn and never crossed. As so often when corresponding idiomatic devices are unavailable in the target language, the remedy lies in transferring the necessary semantic charge to another part of the sentence.

Having pled guilty to the charge of Oblomovitis, I should perhaps attempt to plead extenuating circumstances. *Oblomov* has been a favorite of mine for many years. When I first read it, I could not help being struck by the contrast between its status as a classic, and indeed a seminal masterpiece, in the literary pantheon of the Russian speaking world, and the relative ignorance and neglect of it in the English speaking world. There has not, to my knowledge, been a major new English translation of *Oblomov* for some fifty years.

Oblomov, among other things is a masterpiece of humor, but not always of a kind that hits you over the head or elbows you in the ribs. "Mildness" is for Goncharov one of Oblomov's besetting characteristics, and it is by humor of the same mildness that the author invites the reader to join in his gentle but unremitting deriding of his hero, although Oblomov, of course, is too complete, fully realized, rounded, and even tragic a figure just to be held up for our derision. It is this humor and irony, which peeps shyly out of both the narrative and the dialogue that, if it has not defeated, has certainly dampened and dented past attempts at translation by translators whose roots in the target language may not have been sufficiently deep and nuanced.

Through his creation of Oblomov and the world he inhabits, Goncharov has laid bare a quintessential, although sometimes latent element in the Russian national temperament which has touched a nerve in generation after generation of Russian readers—a quintessence to which Ilya Ilyich Oblomov has lent his name. It is not for nothing that this word, a syndrome to which one-word translations like "idleness" or "apathy" do scant justice, has become a byword, a legend lodged deep within the folklore, consciousness, and yes, even the collective unconscious of the Russian people—*oblomovshchina*.

Stephen Pearl
New York City, April 2006

Stephen Pearl was a simultaneous interpreter at the United Nations for more than thirty years and was Chief of English Interpretation there for fifteen years. A graduate of St. John's College, Oxford University, with an M.A. in Classics, Pearl first acquired his knowledge of Russian at the Department of Slavonic Studies, Cambridge University, in preparation for his duties with the Royal Air Force. He lives in New York City.

A NOTE ON THE TYPE

This book was set in 11 point Adobe Garamond with a leading of 12 points space. Garamond is related to the alphabet of Claude Garamond (1480–1561) as well as to the work of Jean Jannon (1580–1635), much of which was attributed to Garamond. This relatively new interpretation of Garamond, designed by Robert Slimbach, is based on the Original Garamond as a typical Old Face style.

The display font, Didot LH Roman, was designed by Firmin Didot in Paris in 1783. The Didot types defined the characteristics of the modern (or Didone) roman type style, with their substantial stems flowing into extremely thin hairlines; the serifs are straight across with virtually no bracketing. Designed by Adrian Frutiger for digital technology in 1992, Linotype Didot retains all of the features that make Didot types superior for book work and other text use.

Composed by Jean Carbain
New York, New York

Printed and bound in the U.S.A.